French Tales of
Mad Scientists
(Vol. 1)

FROM THE SAME PUBLISHER

French Tales of
Mad Scientists
(Vol. 1)

by
**André Caroff, Georges Espitallier,
Henri Falk, Arnould Galopin,
Gustave Le Rouge** and **Jules Verne**

Translated by
**Brian Stableford
Jean-Marc & Randy Lofficier**

A Black Coat Press Book

ISBN 978-1-64932-257-9. First Printing. October 2023. Published by Black Coat Press, an imprint of Hollywood Comics.com, LLC, P.O. Box 17270, Encino, CA 91416. All rights reserved. Except for review purposes, no part of this book may be reproduced or transmitted in any form or by any means, electronic or mechanical, including photocopying, recording, or by any information storage and retrieval system, without permission in writing from the publisher. The stories and characters depicted in this novel are entirely fictional. Printed in the United States of America.

TABLE OF CONTENTS

Introduction

The mad scientist is a stereotypical, archetype who is often a cliché, and commonplace in popular fiction. He can be absent-minded and harmless, or wicked and dangerous. French science fiction, in particular, features a remarkable number of novels and stories on this theme, enough to justify the three volumes that we intend to devote to this topic.

Science fiction's first mad scientist was probably Restif de la Bretonne's Victorin, the protagonist of *La Découverte Australe par un Homme Volant* [Discovery of the Austral Continent by a Flying Man],[1] published in 1781. Victorin is a young scientist who devises a set of artificial wings which enable him to reach speeds of over a hundred miles per hour. He uses his invention to abduct his beloved Christine, before setting her up on top of a mountain as queen of her own utopia. At that point, Victorin considers using air power to become master of the world, but eventually, embarks on the exploration of the Southern Hemisphere, where he visits several fantastic islands.

Goethe's *Doctor Faust* (1808), a character from German folk tales, is an alchemist endowed with occult powers, who despairs of acquiring universal knowledge. Driven to the limit by ambition, he makes a pact with the Devil, trading his soul in exchange for knowledge.

Mary Shelley's *Frankenstein* (1818), which tells the story of a young scientist who creates a sapient creature in an unorthodox scientific experiment, needs no introduction here.

These three pioneering texts encapsulate the basic archetypes of the mad scientist: he is obsessed with his research; he develops innovative technologies at the cutting edge of his era's knowledge, often out of sheer daring; he appears to be lacking in common sense; he likes to play God without realizing the consequences of his actions.

Jules Verne's Captain Nemo from, *Vingt Mille Lieues sous les Mers* [Twenty Thousand Leagues Under the Sea] (1870), and its sequel, *L'Île Mystérieuse* [Mysterious Island] (1875), introduced the character of Captain Nemo, one of the most interesting and complex eccentric scientists: science is his refuge, Nemo is a man so wronged that he is willing to commit unspeakable deeds in the name of revenge. He is the first modern anti-hero.

Verne's *Robur le Conquérant* [Robur the Conqueror] (1886), and its sequel, *Maître du Monde* [Master of the World] (1904), are variations on Nemo, except that, in this case, Robur is quite unlike the romantic Nemo. The steely, grim, megalomaniacal engineer is a dangerous madman who represents the dan-

---

[1] Black Coat Press, ISBN 978-1-61227-512-3.

gers of unfettered science. Robur is one of the first mad scientists in science fiction, and his plan to make himself "Master of the World" became one of the most notorious genre clichés of all times.

In 1886, Robert Louis Stevenson portrayed another breed of mad scientist in *The Curious Case of Dr. Jekyll and Mr. Hyde*, in which we discover that the two title characters are one and the same. The former is a respectable English scientist who has discovered a potion that allows him to bring out his evil side by transforming himself into a monstrous being, becoming the latter.

In 1888, Louis Boussenard, whose adventure novels were serialized in the *Journal des Voyages*, penned *Les Secrets de Monsieur Synthèse* [The Secrets of Mr. Synthesis] (1888) in which the eponymous mad scientist seeks to control the evolution of Man and change the orbit of the Earth.

In *Face au Drapeau* [Facing the Flag] (1896), Verne's Thomas Roch designs a rocket-powered missile intended to be launched from a submarine—the first time such a weapon was imagined. That same year, H. G. Wells published *The Island of Dr. Moreau* (1896), the protagonist of which had no qualms about playing with nature, which he altered in terrible ways thanks to his skill as a surgeon. *The Invisible Man* (1897) featured the brilliant Dr. Griffin, who perfects a method to render himself invisible. His status as an outcast, and his newfound power gradually tip him over the edge into megalomaniacal madness.

Around the same time, French MD André Couvreur created the mad Dr. Caresco who, in *Caresco, Surhomme* [Caresco, Superman] (1904),[2] rules over the body-shaped island of Eucrasia whose inhabitants have been transformed—he'd say, improved—by advanced surgical techniques. The natives are addicted to sensual pleasures, subservient to Caresco's will. In 1909, Couvreur went on to invent another, even more eccentric mad scientist, Professor Tornada, in *Une Invasion de Macrobes* [An Invasion of Macrobes].[3] (To be included in Volume 2 of this series.)

Maurice Renard created his own mad doctor in *Le Docteur Lerne* [Doctor Lerne] (1908),[4] which was dedicated to Wells. In it, a scientist transplants organs not just from animals to men, but also from plants, and even machines.

The Nyctalope made his first appearance in *Le Mystère des XV* [The Mystery of the XV] (1911),[5] in which a mad scientist named Oxus tries to conquer Mars; but the series really began with *L'Homme Qui Peut Vivre dans l'Eau* [The Man Who Could Live Underwater] (1908) in which the same Oxus grafts a shark's gills onto a man, christened the Hyctaner, and tries to conquer the world. Ultimately, he is foiled by the Nyctalope's father.

---

[2] Black Coat Press, ISBN 978-1-61227-254-2.
[3] In *The Exploits of Professor Tornada* (Volume 1), Black Coat Press, ISBN 978-1-61227-279-5.
[4] Black Coat Press, ISBN 978-1-935558-15-6.
[5] *The Nyctalope on Mars*, Black Coat Press, ISBN 978-1-934543-46-7.

The Nyctalope returned in *Lucifer* (1920).[6] In it, another megalomaniacal scientist, Glo von Warteck, tries to take over the world by using his "Omega Rays" and "teledyname".

In *Le Meurtrier du Globe* [The Murderer of the World] (1910),[7] Gaston de Wailly imagined that the Earth is a living being whose surface we inhabit as parasites. Moved by revenge against that "evil beast", which destroyed his family in an earthquake, a mad scientist schemes to literally murder the world by striking at its vital organs. (To be included in Volume 3 of this series.)

Gustave Le Rouge's archetypal mad scientist saga, *Le Mystérieux Dr. Cornélius* [The Mysterious Dr. Cornelius], was serialized in 1912-13.[8] One of its chapters is included in this volume. Dr. Cornelius Kramm and his brother, Fritz, rule an international criminal empire called the Red Hand. Cornelius is a brilliant surgeon, nicknamed the "Sculptor of Human Flesh" because of his diabolical ability to alter people's likenesses through the science of "carnoplasty".

Les Voleurs de Cerveaux [The Brain Stealers] (1920) by Jean de Quirielle featured a mad scientist who coupled human brains together to create a giant power battery.

In Cyril-Berger's *L'Expérience du Dr. Lorde* [The Experiment of Dr. Lorde] (1922), the eponymous mad scienrist discovered the scientific reality of the soul, which he calls the "odic fluid", and for revenge, transfers that of a murderer into another man.

In 1928, Guy d'Armen penned the classic *La Cité de l'Or et de la Lèpre* [The City of Gold and Leprosy] (1928)[9] which featured a secret Tibetan city ruled by an immortal mad scientist named Natas (Satan spelled backwards). Anyone who escaped immediately died of leprosy. Natas was eventually defeated by the heroic Doctor Francis Ardan. In *Les Géants du Lac Noir* [The Giants of Black Lake] (1931),[10] Ardan goes on to fight mad scientist Khyzil Kaya who rules a secret city under the Gobi Desert with the help of giant spiders and other mutants.

In José Moselli's *L'Empereur du Pacifique* [The Emperor of the Pacific] (1932-35), mad scientist Ambrose Vollmer turns a Pacific atoll into a nightmarish *Doctor Moreau*-like kingdom of radio-controlled zombies and human experiments.

From Mary Shelley to H. G. Wells, 19th century authors were privileged witnesses to prodigious scientific advances that were at the root of profound social transformation.

---

[6] *The Nyctalope vs Lucifer*, Black Coat Press, ISBN 978-1-932983-98-2.

[7] Black Coat Press, ISBN 978-1-61227-408-9.

[8] Three volumes, Black Coat Press, ISBNs 978-1-61227-243-6, 978-1-61227-244-3 and 978-1-61227-245-0.

[9] Black Coat Press, ISBN 978-1-932983-03-6

[10] Black Coat Press, ISBN 978-1-61227-483-6.

The fears aroused by some of these, particularly in biology and chemistry, combined with the stubborn positivism of seeing science as the ultimate solution to all ills, crystallized into the literary archetype of the mad scientist, inspired by the myths of Prometheus and Faust. After World War II, this figure underwent major transformations. The Nazi experiments and the development of the nuclear bomb had a lasting impact on our imaginations, as well as on our conception of scientific ethics, and the archetype changed forever. The mad scientist no longer worked in isolation, but rather at the heart of an organization, like André Caroff's Madame Atomos from the last story presented in this volume.

Welcome to French Tales of Mad Scientists, Volume 1!

Jean-Marc & Randy Lofficier

Jules Verne: *Doctor Ox's Experiment*

Une Fantaisie du Docteur Ox *is a humorous short story by Jules Verne, dating from 1874. It was first published in a collection entitled simply* Le Docteur Ox; *the other short stories in that volume were from much earlier in Verne's career, some dating back to its very beginning. The ztory itself was first read in January 1872 at the Hôtel de Ville d'Amiens, then appeared for the first time in March 1872 in the magazine* Le Musée des familles.

A year later, Verne republished the story in the Journal d'Amiens. *If he was so keen to have it published in his adopted town, it was not out of vanity, but out of mockery, for the fictional town of Quiquendone was, at least in his opinion, a quiet, polite town, just like Amiens.*

A comparison of the original, little-known version published in the Musée des familles *with the text published two years later by Hetzel in* Le Docteur Ox *reveals important and significant differences. All the piquancy, irony, satire and even eroticism of the original text had been erased. We do not know if this was Hetzel's work, or Verne's self-censoring hand.*

The character of Doctor Ox would reappear, in an even more disturbing context, ten years later, as the main protagonist and embodiment of Evil in Verne's play Voyage à travers l'Impossible *(1882).*

J.-M.L.

1. How it is Useless to Seek, Even on the Best Maps, for the Small Town of Quiquendone.

If you try to find, on any map of Flanders, ancient or modern, the small town of Quiquendone, probably you will not succeed. Is Quiquendone, then, one of those towns which have disappeared? No. A town of the future? By no means. It exists in spite of geographies, and has done so for some eight or nine hundred years. It even numbers two thousand three hundred and ninety-three souls, allowing one soul to each inhabitant. It is situated thirteen and a half mile north-west of Oudenarde, and fifteen and a quarter mile south-east of Bruges, in the heart of Flanders. The Vaar, a small tributary of the Scheldt, passes beneath its three bridges, which are still covered with a quaint medieval roof, like that at Tournay. An old château is to be seen there, the first stone of which was laid so long ago as 1197, by Count Baldwin, afterwards Emperor of Constantinople; and there is a Town Hall, with Gothic windows, crowned by a chaplet of battlements, and surrounded by a turreted belfry, which rises three hundred and fifty-seven feet above the soil. Every hour you may hear there a chime of five octaves, a veritable aerial piano, the renown of which surpasses that of the famous chimes of Bruges. Strangers—if any ever come to Quiquendone—do not quit the curious old town until they have visited its Stadtholder's Hall, adorned by a full-length portrait of William of Nassau, by Brandon; the loft of the Church of Saint Magloire, a masterpiece of sixteenth century architecture; the cast-iron well in the spacious Place Saint Ernuph, the admirable ornamentation of which is attributed to the artist-blacksmith, Quentin Metsys; the tomb formerly erected to Mary of Burgundy, daughter of Charles the Bold, who now reposes in the Church of Notre Dame at Bruges; and so on. The principal industry of Quiquendone is the manufacture of whipped creams and barley-sugar on a large scale. It has been governed by the Van Tricasses, from father to son, for several centuries. And yet Quiquendone is not on the map of Flanders! Have the geographers forgotten it, or is it an intentional omission? That I cannot tell; but Quiquendone really exists; with its narrow streets, its fortified walls, its Spanish-looking houses, its market, and its burgomaster—so much so, that it has recently been the theater of some surprising phenomena, as extraordinary and incredible as they are true, which are to be recounted in the present narration.

Surely there is nothing to be said or thought against the Flemings of Western Flanders. They are a well-to-do folk, wise, prudent, sociable, with even tempers, hospitable, perhaps a little heavy in conversation as in mind; but this does not explain why one of the most interesting towns of their district has yet to appear on modern maps.

This omission is certainly to be regretted. If only history, or in default of history the chronicles, or in default of chronicles the traditions of the country, made mention of Quiquendone! But no; neither atlases, guides, nor itineraries speak of it. M. Joanne himself, that energetic hunter after small towns, says not a word of it. It might be readily conceived that this silence would injure the commerce, the industries, of the town. But let us hasten to add that Quiquendone has neither industry nor commerce, and that it does very well without them. Its barley-sugar and whipped cream are consumed on the spot; none is exported. In short, the Quiquendonians have no need of anybody. Their desires are limited, their existence is a modest one; they are calm, moderate, phlegmatic—in a word, they are Flemings, such as are still to be met with sometimes between the Scheldt and the North Sea.

2. In Which Burgomaster Van Tricasse and Counselor Niklausse Consult About the Affairs of the Town.

"You think so?" asked the Burgomaster.

"I do," replied the Counselor, after some minutes of silence.

"You see, we must not act hastily," resumed the Burgomaster.

"We have been talking over this grave matter for ten years," replied Counselor Niklausse, "and I confess to you, my worthy Van Tricasse, that I cannot yet take it upon myself to come to a decision."

"I quite understand your hesitation," said the Burgomaster, who did not speak until after a good quarter of an hour of reflection, "I quite understand it, and I fully share it. We shall do wisely to decide upon nothing without a more careful examination of the question."

"It is certain," replied Niklausse, "that this post of Commissioner is useless in so peaceful a town as Quiquendone."

"Our predecessor," said Van Tricasse gravely, "our predecessor never said, never would have dared to say, that anything is certain. Every affirmation is subject to awkward qualifications."

The Counselor nodded his head slowly in token of assent; then he remained silent for nearly half an hour. After this lapse of time, during which neither the Counselor nor the Burgomaster moved so much as a finger, Niklausse asked Van Tricasse whether his predecessor—of some twenty years before—and not thought of suppressing this office of Commissioner, which each year cost the town of Quiquendone the sum of thirteen hundred and seventy-five francs and some centimes.

"I believe he did," replied the Burgomaster, carrying his hand with majestic deliberation to his ample brow; "but the worthy man died without having dared to make up his mind, either as to this or any other administrative measure. He was a sage. Why should I not do as he did?"

Counselor Niklausse was incapable of originating any objection to the burgomaster's opinion.

"The man who dies," added Van Tricasse solemnly, "without ever having decided upon anything during his life, has very nearly attained to perfection."

This said, the Burgomaster pressed a bell with the end of his little finger, which gave forth a muffled sound, which seemed less a sound than a sigh. Presently some light steps glided softly across the tile floor. A mouse would not have made less noise, running over a thick carpet. The door of the room opened, turning on its well-oiled hinges. A young girl, with long blonde tresses, made her appearance. It was Suzel Van Tricasse, the Burgomaster's only daughter. She handed her father a pipe, filled to the brim, and a small copper brazier, spoke not a word, and disappeared at once, making no more noise at her exit than at her entrance.

She handed her father a pipe

The worthy Burgomaster lit his pipe, and was soon hidden in a cloud of bluish smoke, leaving Counselor Niklausse plunged in the most absorbing thought.

The room in which these two notable personages, charged with the government of Quiquendone, were talking, was a parlor richly adorned with carvings in dark wood. A lofty fireplace, in which an oak might have been burned or

13

an ox roasted, occupied the whole of one of the sides of the room; opposite to it was a trellised window, the painted glass of which toned down the brightness of the sunbeams. In an antique frame above the chimney-piece appeared the portrait of some worthy man, attributed to Memling, which no doubt represented an ancestor of the Van Tricasses, whose authentic genealogy dates back to the fourteenth century, the period when the Flemings and Guy de Dampierre were engaged in wars with the Emperor Rudolph of Hapsburg.

This parlor was the principal apartment of the Burgomaster's house, which was one of the pleasantest in Quiquendone. Built in the Flemish style, with all the abruptness, quaintness, and picturesqueness of Pointed architecture, it was considered one of the most curious monuments of the town. A Carthusian convent, or a deaf and dumb asylum, was not more silent than this mansion. Noise had no existence there; people did not walk, but glided about in it; they did not speak, they murmured. There was not, however, any lack of women in the house, which, in addition to Burgomaster Van Tricasse himself, sheltered his wife, Madame Brigitte Van Tricasse, his daughter, Suzel Van Tricasse, and his domestic, Lotchè Janshéu. We may also mention the Burgomaster's sister, Aunt Hermance, an elderly maiden who still bore the nickname of Tatanémance, which her niece Suzel had given her when a child. But in spite of all these elements of discord and noise, the Burgomaster's house was as calm as a desert.

The Burgomaster was some fifty years-old, neither fat nor lean, neither short nor tall, neither rubicund nor pale, neither gay nor sad, neither contented nor discontented, neither energetic nor dull, neither proud nor humble, neither good nor bad, neither generous nor miserly, neither courageous nor cowardly, neither too much nor too little of anything—a man notably moderate in all respects, whose invariable slowness of motion, slightly hanging lower jaw, prominent eyebrows, massive forehead, smooth as a copper plate and without a wrinkle, would at once have betrayed to a physiognomist that Burgomaster Van Tricasse was phlegm personified. Never, either from anger or passion, had any emotion whatever hastened the beating of this man's heart, or flushed his face; never had his pupils contracted under the influence of any irritation, however ephemeral. He invariably wore good clothes, neither too large nor too small, which he never seemed to wear out. He was shod with large square shoes with triple soles and silver buckles, which lasted so long that his shoemaker was in despair. Upon his head he wore a large hat which dated from the period when Flanders was separated from Holland, so that this venerable masterpiece was at least forty years old. But what would you have? It is the passions which wear out body as well as soul, the clothes as well as the body; and our worthy burgomaster, apathetic, indolent, indifferent, was passionate in nothing. He wore nothing out, not even himself, and he considered himself the very man to administer the affairs of Quiquendone and its tranquil population.

The town, indeed, was not less calm than the Van Tricasse mansion. It was in this peaceful dwelling that the Burgomaster reckoned on attaining the utmost limit of human existence, after having, however, seen the good Madame Brigitte Van Tricasse, his wife, precede him to the tomb, where, surely, she would not find a more profound repose than that she had enjoyed on earth for sixty years.

This demands an explanation.

The Van Tricasse family might well call itself the "Jeannot family." This is why:

Everyone knows that the knife of this typical personage is as celebrated as its proprietor, and not less incapable of wearing out, thanks to the double operation, incessantly repeated, of replacing the handle when it is worn out, and the blade when it becomes worthless. A precisely similar operation had been going on from time immemorial in the Van Tricasse family, to which Nature had lent herself with more than usual complacency. From 1340 it had invariably happened that a Van Tricasse, when left a widower, had remarried a Van Tricasse younger than himself; who, becoming in turn a widow, had married again a Van Tricasse younger than herself; and so on, without a break in the continuity, from generation to generation. Each died in his or her turn with mechanical regularity. Thus the worthy Madame Brigitte Van Tricasse had now her second husband; and, unless she violated her every duty, would precede her spouse—he being ten years younger than herself—to the other world, to make room for a new Madame Van Tricasse. Upon this the Burgomaster calmly counted, that the family tradition might not be broken. Such was this mansion, peaceful and silent, of which the doors never creaked, the windows never rattled, the floors never groaned, the chimneys never roared, the weathercocks never grated, the furniture never squeaked, the locks never clanked, and the occupants never made more noise than their shadows. The god Harpocrates would certainly have chosen it for the Temple of Silence.

3. In Which Commissioner Passauf Enters as Noisily as Unexpectedly.

When the interesting conversation which has been narrated began, it was a quarter before three in the afternoon. It was at a quarter before four that Van Tricasse lit his enormous pipe, which could hold a quart of tobacco, and it was at thirty-five minutes past five that he finished smoking it.

All this time the two comrades did not exchange a single word.

About six o'clock the Counselor, who had a habit of speaking in a very summary manner, resumed in these words:

"So we decide…"

"To decide nothing," replied the Burgomaster.

"I think, on the whole, that you are right, Van Tricasse."

"I think so too, Niklausse. We will take steps with reference to the Commissioner when we have more light on the subject later on. There is no need for a month yet."

15

"Nor even for a year," replied Niklausse, unfolding his pocket-handkerchief and calmly applying it to his nose.

There was another silence of nearly a quarter of an hour. Nothing disturbed this repeated pause in the conversation; not even the appearance of the house-dog Lento, who, not less phlegmatic than his master, came to pay his respects in the parlor. Noble dog! A model for his race. Had he been made of pasteboard, with wheels on his paws, he would not have made less noise during his stay.

Towards eight o'clock, after Lotchè had brought the antique lamp of polished glass, the Burgomaster said to the Counselor:

"We have no other urgent matter to consider?"

"No, Van Tricasse; none that I know of."

"Have I not been told, though," asked the Burgomaster, "that the tower of the Oudenarde gate is likely to tumble down?"

"Ah!" replied the Counselor; "really, I should not be astonished if it fell on some passer-by any day."

"Oh! before such a misfortune happens, I hope we shall have come to a decision on the subject of this tower."

"I hope so, Van Tricasse."

"There are more pressing matters to decide."

"No doubt; the question of the leather-market, for instance."

"What, is it still burning?"

"Still burning, and has been for the last three weeks."

"Have we not decided in council to let it burn?"

"Yes, Van Tricasse—on your motion."

"Was not that the surest and simplest way to deal with it?"

"Without doubt."

"Well, let us wait. Is that all?"

"All," replied the Counselor, scratching his head, as if to assure himself that he had not forgotten anything important.

"Ah!" exclaimed the Burgomaster, "haven't you also heard something of an escape of water which threatens to inundate the low quarter of Saint Jacques?"

"I have. It is indeed unfortunate that this escape of water did not happen above the leather-market! It would naturally have checked the fire, and would thus have saved us a good deal of discussion."

"What can you expect, Niklausse? There is nothing so illogical as accidents. They are bound by no rules, and we cannot profit by one, as we might wish, to remedy another."

It took Van Tricasse's companion some time to digest this fine observation.

"Well, but," resumed the Counselor Niklausse, after the lapse of some moments, "we have not spoken of our great affair!"

"What great affair? Have we, then, a great affair?" asked the Burgomaster.

"No doubt. About lighting the town."

"Ah, yes. If my memory serves me, you are referring to the lighting plan of Doctor Ox?"

"Precisely."

"It is going on, Niklausse," replied the Burgomaster. "They are already laying the pipes, and the works are entirely completed."

"Perhaps we have hurried a little in this matter," said the Counselor, shaking his head.

"Perhaps. But our excuse is, that Doctor Ox bears the whole expense of his experiment. It will not cost us a *sou*."

"That, true enough, is our excuse. Moreover, we must advance with the age. If the experiment succeeds, Quiquendone will be the first town in Flanders to be lit with the oxy... What is the gas called?"

"Oxyhydric gas."

"Well, oxyhydric gas, then."

At this moment the door opened, and Lotchè came in to tell the Burgomaster that his supper was ready.

Counselor Niklausse rose to take leave of Van Tricasse, whose appetite had been stimulated by so many affairs discussed and decisions taken; and it was agreed that the council of notables should be convened after a reasonably long delay, to determine whether a decision should be provisionally arrived at with reference to the really urgent matter of the Oudenarde gate.

The two worthy administrators then directed their steps towards the street-door, the one conducting the other. The Counselor, having reached the last step, lit a little lantern to guide him through the obscure streets of Quiquendone, which Doctor Ox had not yet lit. It was a dark October night, and a light fog overshadowed the town.

Niklausse's preparations for departure consumed at least a quarter of an hour; for, after having lit his lantern, he had to put on his big cow-skin socks and his sheep-skin gloves; then he put up the furred collar of his overcoat, turned the brim of his felt hat down over his eyes, grasped his heavy crow-beaked umbrella, and got ready to start.

When Lotchè, however, who was lighting her master, was about to draw the bars of the door, an unexpected noise arose outside.

Yes! Strange as the thing seems, a noise—a real noise, such as the town had certainly not heard since the taking of the donjon by the Spaniards in 1513—terrible noise, awoke the long-dormant echoes of the venerable Van Tricasse mansion.

Someone knocked heavily upon this door, hitherto virgin to brutal touch! Redoubled knocks were given with some blunt implement, probably a knotty stick, wielded by a vigorous arm. With the strokes were mingled cries and calls. These words were distinctly heard:—

"Monsieur Van Tricasse! Monsieur the Burgomaster! Open, open quickly!"

The Burgomaster and the Counselor, absolutely astounded, looked at each other speechless.

This passed their comprehension. If the old culverin of the château, which had not been used since 1385, had been let off in the parlor, the dwellers in the Van Tricasse mansion would not have been more dumfoundered.

Meanwhile, the blows and cries were redoubled. Lotchè, recovering her coolness, had plucked up courage to speak.

"Who is there?"

"It is I! I! I!"

"Who are you?"

"Commissioner Passauf!"

Commissioner Passauf! The very man whose office it had been contemplated to suppress for ten years. What had happened, then? Could the Burgundians have invaded Quiquendone, as they did in the fourteenth century? No event of less importance could have so moved Commissioner Passauf, who in no degree yielded the palm to the burgomaster himself for calmness and phlegm.

On a sign from Van Tricasse—for the worthy man could not have articulated a syllable—the bar was pushed back and the door opened.

Commissioner Passauf flung himself into the antechamber. One would have thought there was a hurricane.

"What's the matter, Monsieur le Commissaire?" asked Lotchè, a brave woman, who did not lose her head under the most trying circumstances.

"What's the matter!" replied Passauf, whose big round eyes expressed a genuine agitation. "The matter is that I have just come from Doctor Ox's, who has been holding a reception, and that there..."

"There?"

"There I have witnessed such an altercation as... Monsieur the Burgomaster, they have been talking politics!"

"Politics!" repeated Van Tricasse, running his fingers through his wig.

"Politics!" resumed Commissioner Passauf, "which has not been done for perhaps a hundred years at Quiquendone. Then the discussion got warm, and the Advocate, André Schut, and the Doctor, Dominique Custos, became so violent that it may be they will call each other out."

"Call each other out!" cried the Counselor. "A duel! A duel at Quiquendone! And what did Advocate Schut and Doctor Gustos say?"

"Just this: 'Monsieur Advocate,' said the Doctor to his adversary, 'you go too far, it seems to me, and you do not take sufficient care to control your words!'"

Burgomaster Van Tricasse clasped his hands; the counselor turned pale and let his lantern fall; the Commissioner shook his head. That a phrase so evidently irritating should be pronounced by two of the principal men in the country!

"This Doctor Custos," muttered Van Tricasse, "is decidedly a dangerous man—a hare-brained fellow! Come, gentlemen!"

On this, Counselor Niklausse and the Commissioner accompanied the Burgomaster into the parlor.

4. In Which Doctor Ox Reveals Himself as a Physiologist of the First Rank, and as an Audacious Experimentalist.

Who, then, was this personage, known by the singular name of Doctor Ox?

An original character for certain, but at the same time a bold savant, a physiologist, whose works were known and highly estimated throughout learned Europe, a happy rival of the Davys, the Daltons, the Bostocks, the Menzies, the Godwins, the Vierordts—of all those noble minds who have placed physiology among the highest of modern sciences.

Doctor Ox was a man of medium size and height, aged—but we cannot state his age, any more than his nationality. Besides, it matters little; let it suffice that he was a strange personage, impetuous and hot-blooded, a regular oddity out of one of Hoffmann's volumes, and one who contrasted amusingly enough with the good people of Quiquendone. He had an imperturbable confidence both in himself and in his doctrines. Always smiling, walking with head erect and shoulders thrown back in a free and unconstrained manner, with a steady gaze, large open nostrils, a vast mouth which inhaled the air in liberal draughts, his appearance was far from unpleasing. He was full of animation, well-proportioned in all parts of his bodily mechanism, with quicksilver in his veins, and a most elastic step. He could never stop still in one place, and relieved himself with impetuous words and a superabundance of gesticulations.

Was Doctor Ox rich, then, that he should undertake to light a whole town at his expense? Probably, as he permitted himself to indulge in such extravagance—and this is the only answer we can give to this indiscreet question.

Doctor Ox had arrived at Quiquendone five months before, accompanied by his assistant, who answered to the name of Gédéon Ygène; a tall, dried-up, thin man, haughty, but not less vivacious than his master.

And next, why had Doctor Ox made the proposition to light the town at his own expense? Why had he, of all the Flemings, selected the peaceable Quiquendonians, to endow their town with the benefits of an unheard-of system of lighting? Did he not, under this pretext, design to make some great physiological experiment by operating *in anima vili*? In short, what was this original personage about to attempt? We know not, as Doctor Ox had no confidant except his assistant Ygène, who, moreover, obeyed him blindly.

In appearance, at least, Doctor Ox had agreed to light the town, which had much need of it, "especially at night," as Commissioner Passauf wittily said. Works for producing a lighting gas had accordingly been established; the gasometers were ready for use, and the main pipes, running beneath the street pavements, would soon appear in the form of burners in the public edifices and the private houses of certain friends of progress. Van Tricasse and Niklausse, in their official capacity, and some other worthies, thought they ought to allow this modern light to be introduced into their dwellings.

If the reader has not forgotten, it was said, during the long conversation of the counselor and the burgomaster, that the lighting of the town was to be achieved, not by the combustion of common carbureted hydrogen, produced by distilling coal, but by the use of a more modern and twenty-fold more brilliant gas, oxyhydric gas, produced by mixing hydrogen and oxygen.

The Doctor, who was an able chemist as well as an ingenious physiologist, knew how to obtain this gas in great quantity and of good quality, not by using manganate of soda, according to the method of M. Tessié du Motay, but by the direct decomposition of slightly acidulated water, by means of a battery made of new elements, invented by himself. Thus there were no costly materials, no platinum, no retorts, no combustibles, no delicate machinery to produce the two gases separately. An electric current was sent through large basins full of water, and the liquid was decomposed into its two constituent parts, oxygen and hydrogen. The oxygen passed off at one end; the hydrogen, of double the volume of its late associate, at the other. As a necessary precaution, they were collected in separate reservoirs, for their mixture would have produced a frightful explosion if it had become ignited. Thence the pipes were to convey them separately to the various burners, which would be so placed as to prevent all chance of explosion. Thus a remarkably brilliant flame would be obtained, whose light would rival the electric light, which, as everybody knows, is, according to Cassellmann's experiments, equal to that of eleven hundred and seventy-one wax candles—not one more, nor one less.

It was certain that the town of Quiquendone would, by this liberal contrivance, gain a splendid lighting; but Doctor Ox and his assistant took little account of this, as will be seen in the sequel.

The day after that on which Commissioner Passauf had made his noisy entrance into the Burgomaster's parlor, Gédéon Ygène and Doctor Ox were talking in the laboratory which both occupied in common, on the ground-floor of the principal building of the gas-works.

"Well, Ygène, well," cried the Doctor, rubbing his hands. "You saw, at my reception yesterday, the cool-bloodedness of these worthy Quiquendonians. For animation they are midway between sponges and coral! You saw them disputing and irritating each other by voice and gesture? They are already metamorphosed, morally and physically! And this is only the beginning. Wait till we treat them to a full dose!"

"Indeed, master," replied Ygène, scratching his sharp nose with the end of his forefinger, "the experiment begins well, and if I had not prudently closed the supply-tap, I know not what would have happened."

"You heard Schut, the Advocate, and Custos, the Doctor?" resumed Doctor Ox. "The phrase was by no means ill-natured in itself, but, in the mouth of a Quiquendonian, it is worth all the insults which the Homeric heroes hurled at each other before drawing their swords, Ah, these Flemings! You'll see what we shall do some day!"

"We shall make them ungrateful," replied Ygène, in the tone of a man who esteems the human race at its just worth.

"Bah!" said the Doctor; "what matters it whether they think well or ill of us, so long as our experiment succeeds?"

"Besides," returned the assistant, smiling with a malicious expression, "is it not to be feared that, in producing such an excitement in their respiratory organs, we shall somewhat injure the lungs of these good people of Quiquendone?"

"So much the worse for them! It is in the interests of science. What would you say if the dogs or frogs refused to lend themselves to the experiments of vivisection?"

It is probable that if the frogs and dogs were consulted, they would offer some objection; but Doctor Ox imagined that he had stated an unanswerable argument, for he heaved a great sigh of satisfaction.

"After all, master, you are right," replied Ygène, as if quite convinced. "We could not have hit upon better subjects than these people of Quiquendone for our experiment."

"We—could—not," said the Doctor, slowly articulating each word.

"Have you felt the pulse of any of them?"

"Some hundreds."

"And what is the average pulsation you found?"

"Not fifty per minute. See, this is a town where there has not been the shadow of a discussion for a century, where the carmen don't swear, where the coachmen don't insult each other, where horses don't run away, where the dogs don't bite, where the cats don't scratch; a town where the police-court has nothing to do from one year's end to another; a town where people do not grow enthusiastic about anything, either about art or business; a town where the gendarmes are a sort of myth, and in which an indictment has not been drawn up for a hundred years; a town, in short, where for three centuries nobody has struck a blow with his fist or so much as exchanged a slap in the face! You see, Ygène, that this cannot last, and that we must change it all."

"Perfectly! perfectly!" cried the enthusiastic assistant; "and have you analyzed the air of this town, master?"

"I have not failed to do so. Seventy-nine parts of azote and twenty-one of oxygen, carbonic acid and steam in a variable quantity. These are the ordinary proportions."

"Good, Doctor, good!" replied Ygène. "The experiment will be made on a large scale, and will be decisive."

"And if it is decisive," added Doctor Ox triumphantly, "we shall reform the world!"

5. In Which the Burgomaster and the Counselor Pay a Visit to Doctor Ox, and what Follows.

Counselor Niklausse and Burgomaster Van Tricasse at last knew what it was to have an agitated night. The grave event which had taken place at Doctor Ox's house actually kept them awake. What consequences was this affair destined to bring about? They could not imagine. Would it be necessary for them to come to a decision? Would the municipal authority, whom they represented, be compelled to interfere? Would they be obliged to order arrests to be made, that so great a scandal should not be repeated? All these doubts could not but trouble these soft natures; and on that evening, before separating, the two notables had "decided" to see each other the next day.

On the next morning, then, before dinner, Burgomaster Van Tricasse proceeded in person to Counselor Niklausse's house. He found his friend calmer. He himself had recovered his equanimity.

"Nothing new?" asked Van Tricasse.

"Nothing new since yesterday," replied Niklausse.

"And the doctor, Dominique Custos?"

"I have not heard anything, either of him or of the Advocate, André Schut."

After an hour's conversation, which consisted of three remarks which it is needless to repeat, the Counselor and the Burgomaster had resolved to pay a visit to Doctor Ox, so as to draw from him, without seeming to do so, some details of the affair.

Contrary to all their habits, after coming to this decision the two notables set about putting it into execution forthwith. They left the house and directed their steps towards Doctor Ox's laboratory, which was situated outside the town, near the Oudenarde gate—the gate whose tower threatened to fall in ruins.

They did not take each other's arms, but walked side by side, with a slow and solemn step, which took them forward but thirteen inches per second. This was, indeed, the ordinary gait of the Quiquendonians, who had never, within the memory of man, seen any one run across the streets of their town.

From time to time the two notables would stop at some calm and tranquil crossway, or at the end of a quiet street, to salute the passers-by.

"Good morning, Monsieur the Burgomaster," said one.

"Good morning, my friend," responded Van Tricasse.

"Anything new, Monsieur the Counselor?" asked another.

"Nothing new," answered Niklausse.

But by certain agitated motions and questioning looks, it was evident that the altercation of the evening before was known throughout the town. Observing the direction taken by Van Tricasse, the most obtuse Quiquendonians guessed that the Burgomaster was on his way to take some important step. The Custos and Schut affair was talked of everywhere, but the people had not yet come to the point of taking the part of one or the other. Advocate Schut, having never had occasion to plead in a town where attorneys and bailiffs only existed in tradition, had, consequently, never lost a suit. As for Doctor Custos, he was an honorable practitioner, who, after the example of his fellow-doctors, cured all the illnesses of his patients, except those of which they died—a habit unhappily acquired by all the members of all the faculties in whatever country they may practice.

On reaching the Oudenarde gate, the Counselor and the Burgomaster prudently made a short detour, so as not to pass within reach of the tower, in case it should fall; then they turned and looked at it attentively.

"I think that it will fall," said Van Tricasse.

"I think so too," replied Niklausse.

"Unless it is propped up," added Van Tricasse. "But must it be propped up? That is the question."

"That is, in fact, the question."

Some moments after, they reached the door of the gasworks.

"Can we see Doctor Ox?" they asked.

Doctor Ox could always be seen by the first authorities of the town, and they were at once introduced into the celebrated physiologist's study.

Perhaps the two notables waited for the Doctor at least an hour; at least it is reasonable to suppose so, as the Burgomaster—a thing that had never before happened in his life—betrayed a certain amount of impatience, from which his companion was not exempt.

Doctor Ox came in at last, and began to excuse himself for having kept them waiting; but he had to approve a plan for the gasometer, rectify some of the machinery, but everything was going well! The pipes intended for the oxygen were already laid. In a few months the town would be splendidly lit. The two notables might even now see the orifices of the pipes which were laid on in the laboratory.

Then the Doctor begged to know to what he was indebted for the honor of this visit.

"Only to see you, Doctor, to see you," replied Van Tricasse. "It is long since we have had the pleasure. We go abroad but little in our good town of Quiquendone. We count our steps and measure our walks. We are happy when nothing disturbs the uniformity of our habits."

Niklausse looked at his friend. He had never said so much at once; at least, without taking time, and giving long intervals between his sentences. It seemed to him that Van Tricasse expressed himself with a certain volubility, which was by no means common with him. Niklausse himself experienced a kind of irresistible desire to talk.

As for Doctor Ox, he looked at the Burgomaster with sly attention.

Van Tricasse, who never argued until he had snugly ensconced himself in a spacious armchair, had risen to his feet. I know not what nervous excitement, quite foreign to his temperament, had taken possession of him. He did not gesticulate as yet, but this could not be far off. As for the Counselor, he rubbed his legs and breathed with slow and long gasps. His look became animated little by little, and he had "decided" to support at all hazards, if need be, his trusty friend the Burgomaster.

Van Tricasse got up and took several steps; then he came back, and stood facing the doctor.

"And in how many months," he asked in a somewhat emphatic tome, "do you say that your work will be finished?"

"In three or four months, Monsieur the Burgomaster," replied Doctor Ox.

"Three or four months—it's a very long time!" said Van Tricasse.

"Altogether too long!" added Niklausse, who, not being able to keep his seat, rose also.

"This lapse of time is necessary to complete our work," returned Doctor Ox. "The workmen, whom we have had to choose in Quiquendone, are not very expeditious."

"How not expeditious?" cried the Burgomaster, who seemed to take the remark as personally offensive.

"No, Monsieur Van Tricasse," replied Doctor Ox obstinately. "A French workman would do in a day what it takes ten of your workmen to do; you know, they are ordinary Flemings!"

"Flemings!" cried the Counselor, whose fingers closed together. "In what sense, sir, do you use that word?"

"Why, in the amiable sense in which everybody uses it," replied Doctor Ox, smiling.

"Ah, but, Doctor," said the Burgomaster, pacing up and down the room, "I don't like these insinuations. The workmen of Quiquendone are as efficient as those of any other town in the world, you must know; and we shall go neither to Paris nor London for our models! As for your project, I beg you to hasten its execution. Our streets have been unpaved for the putting down of your conduit-pipes, and it is a hindrance to traffic. Our trade will begin to suffer, and I, being the responsible authority, do not propose to incur reproaches which will be but too just."

Worthy Burgomaster! He spoke of trade, of traffic, and the wonder was that those words, to which he was quite unaccustomed, did not scorch his lips. What could be passing in his mind?

"Besides," added Niklausse, "the town cannot be deprived of light much longer."

"But," urged Doctor Ox, "a town which has been unlit for eight or nine hundred years…"

"All the more necessary is it, then," replied the Burgomaster, emphasizing his words. "Times alter, manners alter! The world advances, and we do not wish to remain behind. We desire our streets to be lit within a month, or you must pay a large indemnity for each day of delay; and what would happen if, amid the darkness, some affray should take place?"

"No doubt," cried Niklausse. "It requires but a spark to inflame a Fleming! Fleming! Flame!"

"Apropos of this," said the Burgomaster, interrupting his friend, "Commissioner Passauf, our chief of police, reports to us that a discussion took place in your drawing-room last evening, Doctor Ox. Was he wrong in declaring that it was a political discussion?"

"By no means, Monsieur the Burgomaster," replied Doctor Ox, who with difficulty repressed a sigh of satisfaction.

"So an altercation did take place between Dominique Gustos and André Schut?"

"Yes, Counselor; but the words which passed were not of grave import."

"Not of grave import!" cried the Burgomaster. "Not of grave import, when one man tells another that he does not measure the effect of his words! But of what stuff are you made, Doctor? Do you not know that in Quiquendone nothing more is needed to bring about extremely disastrous results? What, if you, or anyone else, presumed to speak thus to me…"

"Or to me," added Niklausse.

As they pronounced these words with a menacing air, the two notables, with folded arms and bristling air, confronted Doctor Ox, ready to do him some violence, if by a gesture, or even the expression of his eye, he manifested any intention of contradicting them.

But the Doctor did not budge.

"At all events, Doctor," resumed the Burgomaster, "I propose to hold you responsible for what passes in your house. I am bound to insure the tranquility of this town, and I do not wish it to be disturbed. The events of last evening must not be repeated, or I shall do my duty, sir! Do you hear? Then reply, sir."

The Burgomaster, as he spoke, under the influence of extraordinary excitement, elevated his voice to the pitch of anger. He was furious, the worthy Van Tricasse, and might certainly be heard outside. At last, beside himself, and seeing that Doctor Ox did not reply to his challenge,

"Come, Niklausse," said he.

And, slamming the door with a violence which shook the house, the Burgomaster drew his friend after him.

Little by little, when they had taken twenty steps on their road, the worthy notables grew calmer. Their pace slackened; their gait became less feverish. The flush on their faces faded away; from being crimson, they became rosy. A quarter of an hour after quitting the gasworks, Van Tricasse said softly to Niklausse, "An amiable man, Doctor Ox! It is always a pleasure to see him!"

25

6. In Which Franz Niklausse and Suzel Van Tricasse Form Certain Projects for the Future.

Our readers know that the Burgomaster had a daughter, Suzel But, shrewd as they may be, they cannot have divined that Counselor Niklausse had a son, Franz; and had they divined this, nothing could have led them to imagine that Franz was the betrothed lover of Suzel. We will add that these young people were made for each other, and that they loved each other, as folks did love at Quiquendone.

It must not be thought that young hearts did not beat in this exceptional place; only they beat with a certain deliberation. There were marriages there, as in every other town in the world; but they took time about it. Betrothed couples, before engaging in these terrible bonds, wished to study each other; and these studies lasted at least ten years, as at college. It was rare that any one was "accepted" before this lapse of time.

Yes, ten years! The courtships last ten years! And is it, after all, too long, when the being bound for life is in consideration? One studies ten years to become an engineer or physician, an advocate or attorney, and should less time be spent in acquiring the knowledge to make a good husband? Is it not reasonable? and, whether due to temperament or reason with them, the Quiquendonians seem to us to be in the right in thus prolonging their courtship. When marriages in other more lively and excitable cities are seen taking place within a few months, we must shrug our shoulders, and hasten to send our boys to the schools and our daughters to the pensions of Quiquendone.

For half a century but a single marriage was known to have taken place after the lapse of two years only of courtship, and that turned out badly!

Franz Niklausse, then, loved Suzel Van Tricasse, but quietly, as a man would love when he has ten years before him in which to obtain the beloved object. Once every week, at an hour agreed upon, Franz went to fetch Suzel, and took a walk with her along the banks of the Vaar. He took good care to carry his fishing-tackle, and Suzel never forgot her canvas, on which her pretty hands embroidered the most unlikely flowers.

Franz was a young man of twenty-two, whose cheeks betrayed a soft, peachy down, and whose voice had scarcely a compass of one octave.

As for Suzel, she was blonde and rosy. She was seventeen, and did not dislike fishing. A singular occupation this, however, which forces you to struggle craftily with a barbel. But Franz loved it; the pastime was congenial to his temperament. As patient as possible, content to follow with his rather dreamy eye the cork which bobbed on the top of the water, he knew how to wait; and when, after sitting for six hours, a modest barbel, taking pity on him, consented at last to be caught, he was happy, but he knew how to control his emotion.

On this day the two lovers—one might say, the two betrothed—were seated upon the verdant bank. The limpid Vaar murmured a few feet below them. Suzel quietly drew her needle across the canvas. Franz automatically carried his line from left to right, then permitted it to descend the current from right to left. The fish made capricious rings in the water, which crossed each other around the cork, while the hook hung useless near the bottom.

From time to time, Franz would say, without raising his eyes:

"I think I have a bite, Suzel."

"Do you think so, Franz?" replied Suzel, who, abandoning her work for an instant, followed her lover's line with earnest eye.

"N-no," resumed Franz; "I thought I felt a little twitch; I was mistaken."

"You will have a bite, Franz," replied Suzel, in her pure, soft voice. "But do not forget to strike at the right moment. You are always a few seconds too late, and the barbel takes advantage to escape."

"Would you like to take my line, Suzel?"

"Willingly, Franz."

"Then give me your canvas. We shall see whether I am more adroit with the needle than with the hook."

And the young girl took the line with trembling hand, while her swain plied the needle across the stitches of the embroidery. For hours together they thus exchanged soft words, and their hearts palpitated when the cork bobbed on the water. Ah, could they ever forget those charming hours, during which, seated side by side, they listened to the murmurs of the river?

The sun was fast approaching the western horizon, and despite the combined skill of Suzel and Franz, there had not been a bite. The barbels had not shown themselves complacent, and seemed to scoff at the two young people, who were too just to bear them malice.

"We shall be luckier another time, Franz," said Suzel, as the young angler put up his still virgin hook.

"Let us hope so," replied Franz.

Then walking side by side, they turned their steps towards the house, without exchanging a word, as mute as their shadows which stretched out before them. Suzel became very, very tall under the oblique rays of the setting sun. Franz appeared very, very thin, like the long rod which he held in his hand.

They reached the Burgomaster's house. Green tufts of grass bordered the shining pavement, and no one would have thought of tearing them away, for they deadened the noise made by the passers-by.

As they were about to open the door, Franz thought it his duty to say to Suzel:

"You know, Suzel, the great day is approaching?"

"It is indeed, Franz," replied the young girl, with downcast eyes.

"Yes," said Franz, "in five or six years…"

"Good-bye, Franz," said Suzel.

"Good-bye, Suzel," replied Franz.

And, after the door had been closed, the young man resumed the way to his father's house with a calm and equal pace.

7. In Which the Andantes Become Allegros, and the Allegros Vivaces.

The agitation caused by the Schut and Custos affair had subsided. The affair led to no serious consequences. It appeared likely that Quiquendone would return to its habitual apathy, which that unexpected event had for a moment disturbed.

Meanwhile, the laying of the pipes destined to conduct the oxyhydric gas into the principal edifices of the town was proceeding rapidly. The main pipes and branches gradually crept beneath the pavements. But the burners were still wanting; for, as it required delicate skill to make them, it was necessary that they should be fabricated abroad. Doctor Ox was here, there, and everywhere; neither he nor Ygène, his assistant, lost a moment, but they urged on the workmen, completed the delicate mechanism of the gasometer, fed day and night the immense piles which decomposed the water under the influence of a powerful electric current. Yes, the doctor was already making his gas, though the pipe-laying was not yet done; a fact which, between us, might have seemed a little singular. But before long—at least there was reason to hope so—before long Doctor Ox would inaugurate the splendors of his invention in the theater of the town.

For Quiquendone possessed a theater—a really fine edifice, in truth—the interior and exterior arrangement of which combined every style of architecture. It was at once Byzantine, Roman, Gothic, Renaissance, with semicircular doors, Pointed windows, Flamboyant rose-windows, fantastic bell-turrets—in a word, a specimen of all sorts, half a Parthenon, half a Parisian Grand Café. Nor was this surprising, the theater having been commenced under Burgomaster Ludwig Van Tricasse, in 1175, and only finished in 1837, under Burgomaster Natalis Van Tricasse. It had required seven hundred years to build it, and it had, been successively adapted to the architectural style in vogue in each period. But for all that it was an imposing structure; the Roman pillars and Byzantine arches of which would appear to advantage lit up by the oxyhydric gas.

Pretty well everything was acted at the theater of Quiquendone; but the opera and the opera comique were especially patronized. It must, however, be added that the composers would never have recognized their own works, so entirely changed were the "movements" of the music.

In short, as nothing was done in a hurry at Quiquendone, the dramatic pieces had to be performed in harmony with the peculiar temperament of the Quiquendonians. Though the doors of the theater were regularly thrown open at four o'clock and closed again at ten, it had never been known that more than two acts were played during the six intervening hours. "Robert le Diable," "Les Huguenots," or "Guillaume Tell" usually took up three evenings, so slow was the execution of these masterpieces. The vivaces, at the theater of Quiquendone, lagged like real adagios. The allegros were "long-drawn out" indeed. The demi-semiquavers were scarcely equal to the ordinary semibreves of other countries. The most rapid runs, performed according to Quiquendonian taste, had the solemn march of a chant. The gayest shakes were languishing and measured, that they might not shock the ears of the dilettanti. To give an example, the rapid air sung by Figaro, on his entrance in the first act of "Le Barbier de Séville," lasted fifty-eight minutes—when the actor was particularly enthusiastic.

Artists from abroad, as might be supposed, were forced to conform themselves to Quiquendonian fashions; but as they were well paid, they did not complain, and willingly obeyed the leader's baton, which never beat more than eight measures to the minute in the allegros.

But what applause greeted these artists, who enchanted without ever wearying the audiences of Quiquendone! All hands clapped one after another at tolerably long intervals, which the papers characterized as "frantic applause;" and sometimes nothing but the lavish prodigality with which mortar and stone had been used in the twelfth century saved the roof of the hall from falling in.

Besides, the theater had only one performance a week, that these enthusiastic Flemish folk might not be too much excited; and this enabled the actors to study their parts more thoroughly, and the spectators to digest more at leisure the beauties of the masterpieces brought out.

Such had long been the drama at Quiquendone. Foreign artists were in the habit of making engagements with the director of the town, when they wanted to rest after their exertions in other scenes; and it seemed as if nothing could ever change these inveterate customs, when, a fortnight after the Schut–Custos affair, an unlooked-for incident occurred to throw the population into fresh agitation.

It was on a Saturday, an opera day. It was not yet intended, as may well be supposed, to inaugurate the new illumination. No; the pipes had reached the hall, but, for reasons indicated above, the burners had not yet been placed, and the wax-candles still shed their soft light upon the numerous spectators who filled the theater. The doors had been opened to the public at one o'clock, and by three the hall was half full. A queue had at one time been formed, which extended as far as the end of the Place Saint Ernuph, in front of the shop of Josse Lietrinck the apothecary. This eagerness was significant of an unusually attractive performance.

"Are you going to the theater this evening?" inquired the Counselor the same morning of the Burgomaster.

"I shall not fail to do so," returned Van Tricasse, "and I shall take Madame Van Tricasse, as well as our daughter Suzel and our dear Tatanémance, who all dote on good music."

"Mademoiselle Suzel is going then?"

"Certainly, Niklausse."

"Then my son Franz will be one of the first to arrive," said Niklausse.

29

"A spirited boy, Niklausse," replied the Burgomaster sententiously; "but hot-headed! He will require watching!"

"He is in love, Van Tricasse. He loves your charming Suzel."

"Well, Niklausse, he shall marry her. Now that we have agreed on this marriage, what more can he desire?"

"He desires nothing, Van Tricasse, the dear boy! But, in short—we'll say no more about it—he will not be the last to get his ticket at the box-office."

"Ah, vivacious and ardent youth!" replied the Burgomaster, recalling his own past. "We have also been thus, my worthy Counselor! We have loved—we too! We have danced attendance in our day! Till to-night, then, till to-night! By-the-bye, do you know this Fiovaranti is a great artist? And what a welcome he has received among us! It will be long before he will forget the applause of Quiquendone!"

The tenor Fiovaranti was, indeed, going to sing; Fiovaranti, who, by his talents as a virtuoso, his perfect method, his melodious voice, provoked a real enthusiasm among the lovers of music in the town.

For three weeks Fiovaranti had been achieving a brilliant success in "Les Huguenots." The first act, interpreted according to the taste of the Quiquendonians, had occupied an entire evening of the first week of the month. Another evening in the second week, prolonged by infinite andantes, had elicited for the celebrated singer a real ovation. His success had been still more marked in the third act of Meyerbeer's masterpiece. But now Fiovaranti was to appear in the fourth act, which was to be performed on this evening before an impatient public. Ah, the duet between Raoul and Valentine, that pathetic love-song for two voices, that strain so full of crescendos, stringendos, and piu crescendos—all this, sung slowly, compendiously, interminably! Ah, how delightful!

Fiovaranti had been achieving a brilliant success in "Les Huguenots."

At four o'clock the hall was full. The boxes, the orchestra, the pit, were overflowing. In the front stalls sat Burgomaster Van Tricasse, Mademoiselle Van Tricasse, Madame Van Tricasse, and the amiable Tatanémance in a green bonnet; not far off were Counselor Niklausse and his family, not forgetting the amorous Franz. The families of Doctor Custos, Advocate Schut, of Chief Magistrate Honoré Syntax, of Norbert Sontman the insurance agent, of the banker Collaert, gone mad on German music, and himself somewhat of an amateur, and the teacher Rupp, and the master of the academy, Jerome Resh, and the Commissioner, and so many other notabilities of the town that they could not be enumerated here without wearying the reader's patience, were visible in different parts of the hall.

It was customary for the Quiquendonians, while awaiting the rise of the curtain, to sit silent, some reading the paper, others whispering low to each other, some making their way to their seats slowly and noiselessly, others casting timid looks towards the bewitching beauties in the galleries.

But on this evening a looker-on might have observed that, even before the curtain rose, there was unusual animation among the audience. People were restless who were never known to be restless before. The ladies' fans fluttered with abnormal rapidity. All appeared to be inhaling air of exceptional stimulating power. Everyone breathed more freely. The eyes of some became unwontedly bright, and seemed to give forth a light equal to that of the candles, which themselves certainly threw a more brilliant light over the hall. It was evident that people saw more clearly, though the number of candles had not been increased. Ah, if Doctor Ox's experiment were being tried! But it was not being tried, as yet.

The musicians of the orchestra at last took their places. The first violin had gone to the stand to give a modest la to his colleagues. The stringed instruments, the wind instruments, the drums and cymbals, were in accord. The conductor only waited the sound of the bell to beat the first bar.

The bell sounds. The fourth act begins. The allegro appassionato of the inter-act is played as usual, with a majestic deliberation which would have made Meyerbeer frantic, and all the majesty of which was appreciated by the Quiquendonian dilettanti.

But soon the leader perceived that he was no longer master of his musicians. He found it difficult to restrain them, though usually so obedient and calm. The wind instruments betrayed a tendency to hasten the movements, and it was necessary to hold them back with a firm hand, for they would otherwise outstrip the stringed instruments; which, from a musical point of view, would have been disastrous. The bassoon himself, the son of Josse Lietrinck the apothecary, a well-bred young man, seemed to lose his self-control.

Meanwhile Valentine has begun her recitative, "I am alone," etc.; but she hurries it.

The leader and all his musicians, perhaps unconsciously, follow her in her cantabile, which should be taken deliberately, like a 12/8 as it is. When Raoul appears at the door at the bottom of the stage, between the moment when Valentine goes to him and that when she conceals herself in the chamber at the side, a quarter of an hour does not elapse; while formerly, according to the traditions of the Quiquendone theater, this recitative of thirty-seven bars was wont to last just thirty-seven minutes.

Saint Bris, Nevers, Cavannes, and the Catholic nobles have appeared, somewhat prematurely, perhaps, upon the scene. The composer has marked allergo pomposo on the score. The orchestra and the lords proceed allegro indeed, but not at all pomposo, and at the chorus, in the famous scene of the "benediction of the poniards," they no longer keep to the enjoined allegro. Singers and musicians broke away impetuously. The leader does not even attempt to restrain them. Nor do the public protest; on the contrary, the people find themselves carried away, and see that they are involved in the movement, and that the movement responds to the impulses of their souls.

"Will you, with me, deliver the land,
From troubles increasing, an impious band?"

They promise, they swear. Nevers has scarcely time to protest, and to sing that *"among his ancestors were many soldiers, but never an assassin."* He is arrested. The police and the aldermen rush forward and rapidly swear "to strike all at once." Saint Bris shouts the recitative which summons the Catholics to vengeance. The three monks, with white scarfs, hasten in by the door at the back of Nevers's room, without making any account of the stage directions, which enjoin on them to advance slowly. Already all the artists have drawn sword or poniard, which the three monks bless in a trice. The soprani tenors, bassos, attack the allegro furioso with cries of rage, and of a dramatic 6/8 time they make it 6/8 quadrille time. Then they rush out, bellowing:

"At midnight, Noiselessly, God wills it,
Yes, At midnight."

At this moment the audience start to their feet. Everybody is agitated, in the boxes, the pit, the galleries. It seems as if the spectators are about to rush upon the stage, Burgomaster Van Tricasse at their head, to join with the conspirators and annihilate the Huguenots, whose religious opinions, however, they share. They applaud, call before the curtain, make loud acclamations! Tatanémance grasps her bonnet with feverish hand. The candles throw out a lurid glow of light.

Raoul, instead of slowly raising the curtain, tears it apart with a superb gesture and finds himself confronting Valentine.

At last! It is the grand duet, and it starts off allegro vivace. Raoul does not wait for Valentine's pleading, and Valentine does not wait for Raoul's responses.

The fine passage beginning, *"Danger is passing, time is flying,"* becomes one of those rapid airs which have made Offenbach famous, when he composes a dance for conspirators. The andante amoroso, *"Thou hast said it, aye, thou lovest me,"* becomes a real vivace furioso, and the violoncello ceases to imitate the inflections of the singer's voice, as indicated in the composer's score. In vain Raoul cries, *"Speak on, and prolong the ineffable slumber of my soul."* Valentine cannot "prolong." It is evident that an unaccustomed fire devours her. Her b's and her c's above the stave were dreadfully shrill. He struggles, he gesticulates, he is all in a glow.

The alarum is heard; the bell resounds; but what a panting bell! The bellringer has evidently lost his self-control. It is a frightful tocsin, which violently struggles against the fury of the orchestra.

Finally the air which ends this magnificent act, beginning, *"No more love, no more intoxication, O the remorse that oppresses me!"* which the composer marks allegro con moto, becomes a wild prestissimo. You would say an express-train was whirling by. The alarum resounds again. Valentine falls fainting. Raoul precipitates himself from the window.

32

It was high time. The orchestra, really intoxicated, could not have gone on. The leader's baton is no longer anything but a broken stick on the prompter's box. The violin strings are broken, and their necks twisted. In his fury the drummer has burst his drum. The counter-bassist has perched on the top of his musical monster. The first clarinet has swallowed the reed of his instrument, and the second hautboy is chewing his reed keys. The groove of the trombone is strained, and finally the unhappy cornist cannot withdraw his hand from the bell of his horn, into which he had thrust it too far.

And the audience! The audience, panting, all in a heat, gesticulates and howls. All the faces are as red as if a fire were burning within their bodies. They crowd each other, hustle each other to get out—the men without hats, the women without mantles! They elbow each other in the corridors, crush between the doors, quarrel, fight! There are no longer any officials, any burgomaster. All are equal amid this infernal frenzy!

They hustle each other to get out

Some moments after, when all have reached the street, each one resumes his habitual tranquility, and peaceably enters his house, with a confused remembrance of what he has just experienced.

The fourth act of the "Huguenots," which formerly lasted six hours, began, on this evening at half-past four, and ended at twelve minutes before five.

It had only lasted eighteen minutes!

8. In Which the Ancient and Solemn German Waltz
Becomes a Whirlwind.

But if the spectators, on leaving the theater, resumed their customary calm, if they quietly regained their homes, preserving only a sort of passing stupefaction, they had none the less undergone a remarkable exaltation, and overcome and weary as if they had committed some excess of dissipation, they fell heavily upon their beds.

The next day each Quiquendonian had a kind of recollection of what had occurred the evening before. One missed his hat, lost in the hubbub; another a coat-flap, torn in the brawl; one her delicately fashioned shoe, another her best mantle. Memory returned to these worthy people, and with it a certain shame for their unjustifiable agitation. It seemed to them an orgy in which they were the unconscious heroes and heroines. They did not speak of it; they did not wish to think of it. But the most astounded personage in the town was Burgomaster Van Tricasse.

The next morning, on waking, he could not find his wig. Lotchè looked everywhere for it, but in vain. The wig had remained on the field of battle. As for having it publicly claimed by Jean Mistrol, the town-crier—no, it would not do. It were better to lose the wig than to advertise himself thus, as he had the honor to be the first magistrate of Quiquendone.

The worthy Van Tricasse was reflecting upon this, extended beneath his sheets, with bruised body, heavy head, furred tongue, and burning breast. He felt no desire to get up; on the contrary; and his brain worked more during this morning than it had probably worked before for forty years. The worthy magistrate recalled to his mind all the incidents of the incomprehensible performance. He connected them with the events which had taken place shortly before at Doctor Ox's reception. He tried to discover the causes of the singular excitability which, on two occasions, had betrayed itself in the best citizens of the town.

"What can be going on?" he asked himself. "What giddy spirit has taken possession of my peaceable town of Quiquendone? Are we about to go mad, and must we make the town one vast asylum? For yesterday we were all there, notables, counselors, judges, advocates, physicians, schoolmasters; and ail, if my memory serves me—all of us were assailed by this excess of furious folly! But what was there in that infernal music? It is inexplicable! Yet I certainly ate or drank nothing which could put me into such a state. No; yesterday I had for dinner a slice of overdone veal, several spoonfuls of spinach with sugar, eggs, and a little beer and water—that couldn't get into my head! No! There is something that I cannot explain, and as, after all, I am responsible for the conduct of the citizens, I will have an investigation."

But the investigation, though decided upon by the municipal council, produced no result. If the facts were clear, the causes escaped the sagacity of the magistrates. Besides, tranquility had been restored in the public mind, and with tranquility, forgetfulness of the strange scenes of the theater. The newspapers avoided speaking of them, and the account of the performance which appeared in the *Quiquendone Memorial*, made no allusion to this intoxication of the entire audience.

Meanwhile, though the town resumed its habitual phlegm, and became apparently Flemish as before, it was observable that, at bottom, the character and temperament of the people changed little by little. One might have truly said, with Dominique Custos, the doctor, that "their nerves were affected."

Let us explain. This undoubted change only took place under certain conditions. When the Quiquendonians passed through the streets of the town, walked in the squares or along the Vaar, they were always the cold and methodical people of former days. So, too, when they remained at home, some working with their hands and others with their heads—these doing nothing, those thinking nothing—their private life was silent, inert, vegetating as before. No quarrels, no household squabbles, no acceleration in the beating of the heart, no excitement of the brain. The mean of their pulsations remained as it was of old, from fifty to fifty-two per minute.

But, strange and inexplicable phenomenon though it was, which would have defied the sagacity of the most ingenious physiologists of the day, if the inhabitants of Quiquendone did not change in their home life, they were visibly changed in their civil life and in their relations between man and man, to which it leads.

If they met together in some public edifice, it did not "work well," as Commissioner Passauf expressed it. At the town-hall, in the amphitheater of the academy, at the sessions of the council, as well as at the reunions of the savants, a strange excitement seized the assembled citizens. Their relations with each other became embarrassing before they had been together an hour. In two hours the discussion degenerated into an angry dispute. Heads became heated, and personalities were used. Even at church, during the sermon, the faithful could not listen to Van Stabel, the minister, in patience, and he threw himself about in the pulpit and lectured his flock with far more than his usual severity. At last this state of things brought about altercations more serious, alas! than that between Gustos and Schut, and if they did not require the interference of the authorities, it was because the antagonists, after returning home, found there, with its calm, forgetfulness of the offences offered and received.

This peculiarity could not be observed by these minds, which were absolutely incapable of recognizing what was passing in them. One person only in the town, he whose office the council had thought of suppressing for thirty years, Commissioner Michael Passauf, had remarked that this excitement, which was absent from private houses, quickly revealed itself in public edifices; and he asked himself, not without a certain anxiety, what would happen if this infection should ever develop itself in the family mansions, and if the epidemic—this was the word he used—should extend through the streets of the town. Then there would be no more forgetfulness of insults, no more tranquility, no intermission in the delirium; but a permanent inflammation, which would inevitably bring the Quiquendonians into collision with each other.

"What would happen then?" Commissioner Passauf asked himself in terror. "How could these furious savages be arrested? How check these goaded temperaments? My office would be no longer a sinecure, and the council would be obliged to double my salary—unless it should arrest me myself, for disturbing the public peace!"

These very reasonable fears began to be realized. The infection spread from 'change, the theater, the church, the town-hall, the academy, the market, into private houses, and that in less than a fortnight after the terrible performance of the "Huguenots."

Its first symptoms appeared in the house of the banker Collaert.

That wealthy personage gave a ball, or at least a dancing-party, to the notabilities of the town. He had issued, some months before, a loan of thirty thousand francs, three quarters of which had been subscribed; and to celebrate this financial success, he had opened his drawing-rooms, and given a party to his fellow-citizens.

Everybody knows that Flemish parties are innocent and tranquil enough, the principal expense of which is usually in beer and syrups. Some conversation on the weather, the appearance of the crops, the fine condition of the gardens, the care of flowers, and especially of tulips; a slow and measured dance, from time to time, perhaps a minuet; sometimes a waltz, but one of those German waltzes which achieve a turn and a half per minute, and during which the dancers hold each other as far apart as their arms will permit—such is the usual fashion of the balls attended by the aristocratic society of Quiquendone. The polka, after being altered to four time, had tried to become accustomed to it; but the dancers always lagged behind the orchestra, no matter how slow the measure, and it had to be abandoned.

These peaceable reunions, in which the youths and maidens enjoyed an honest and moderate pleasure, had never been attended by any outburst of ill-nature. Why, then, on this evening at Collaert's, did the syrups seem to be transformed into heady wines, into sparkling champagne, into heating punches? Why, towards the middle of the evening, did a sort of mysterious intoxication take possession of the guests? Why did the minuet become a jig? Why did the orchestra hurry with its harmonies? Why did the candles, just as at the theater, burn with unwonted refulgence? What electric current invaded the banker's drawing-rooms? How happened it that the couples held each other so closely, and clasped each other's hands so convulsively, that the "cavaliers seuls" made themselves conspicuous by certain extraordinary steps in that figure usually so grave, so solemn, so majestic, so very proper?

Alas! what Oedipus could have answered these unsolvable questions? Commissioner Passauf, who was present at the party, saw the storm coming distinctly, but he could not control it or fly from it, and he felt a kind of intoxication entering his own brain. All his physical and emotional faculties increased in intensity. He was seen, several times, to throw himself upon the confectionery and devour the dishes, as if he had just broken a long fast.

The animation of the ball was increasing all this while. A long murmur, like a dull buzzing, escaped from all breasts. They danced—really danced. The feet were agitated by increasing frenzy. The faces became as purple as those of Silenus. The eyes shone like carbuncles. The general fermentation rose to the highest pitch.

And when the orchestra thundered out the waltz in "Der Freyschütz," when this waltz, so German, and with a movement so slow, was attacked with wild arms by the musicians—ah! it was no longer a waltz, but an insensate whirlwind, a giddy rotation, a gyration worthy of being led by some Mephistopheles, beating the measure with a firebrand! Then a galop, an infernal galop, which lasted an hour without any one being able to stop it, whirled off, in its windings, across the halls, the drawing-rooms, the antechambers, by the staircases, from the cellar to the garret of the opulent mansion, the young men and young girls, the fathers and mothers, people of every age, of every weight, of both sexes; Collaert, the fat banker, and Madame Collaert, and the counselors, and the magistrates, and the Chief Magistrate, and Niklausse, and Madame Van Tricasse, and Burgomaster Van Tricasse, and Commissioner Passauf himself, who never could recall afterwards who had been his partner on that terrible evening.

But she did not forget! And ever since that day she has seen in her dreams the fiery Commissioner, enfolding her in an impassioned embrace! And "she"— was the amiable Tatanémance!

9. In Which Doctor Ox and Ygène, His Assistant, Say a Few Words.

"Well, Ygène?"

"Well, master, all is ready. The laying of the pipes is finished."

"At last! Now, then, we are going to operate on a large scale, on the masses!"

10. In Which it Will Be Seen that the Epidemic Invades the Entire Town, and what Effect it Produces.

During the following months the evil, in place of subsiding, became more extended. From private houses the epidemic spread into the streets. The town of Quiquendone was no longer to be recognized.

A phenomenon yet stranger than those which had already happened, now appeared; not only the animal kingdom, but the vegetable kingdom itself, became subject to the mysterious influence.

According to the ordinary course of things, epidemics are special in their operation. Those which attack humanity spare the animals, and those which attack the animals spare the vegetables. A horse was never inflicted with small-pox, nor a man with the cattle-plague, nor do sheep suffer from the potato-rot. But here all the laws of nature seemed to be overturned. Not only were the character, temperament, and ideas of the townsfolk changed, but the domestic animals—dogs and cats, horses and cows, asses and goats—suffered from this epidemic influence, as if their habitual equilibrium had been changed. The plants themselves were infected by a similar strange metamorphosis.

In the gardens and vegetable patches and orchards very curious symptoms manifested themselves. Climbing plants climbed more audaciously. Tufted plants became more tufted than ever. Shrubs became trees. Cereals, scarcely sown, showed their little green heads, and gained, in the same length of time, as much in inches as formerly, under the most favorable circumstances, they had gained in fractions. Asparagus attained the height of several feet; the artichokes swelled to the size of melons, the melons to the size of pumpkins, the pumpkins to the size of gourds, the gourds to the size of the belfry bell, which measured, in truth, nine feet in diameter. The cabbages were bushes, and the mushrooms umbrellas.

The fruits did not lag behind the vegetables. It required two persons to eat a strawberry, and four to consume a pear. The grapes also attained the enormous proportions of those so well depicted by Poussin in his "Return of the Envoys to the Promised Land."

It required two persons to eat a strawberry

It was the same with the flowers: immense violets spread the most penetrating perfumes through the air; exaggerated roses shone with the brightest colors; lilies formed, in a few days, impenetrable copses; geraniums, daisies, camelias, rhododendrons, invaded the garden walks, and stifled each other. And the tulips—those dear liliaceous plants so dear to the Flemish heart, what emotion they must have caused to their zealous cultivators! The worthy Van Bistrom nearly fell over backwards, one day, on seeing in his garden an enormous "Tulipa gesneriana," a gigantic monster, whose cup afforded space to a nest for a whole family of robins!

The entire town flocked to see this floral phenomenon, and renamed it the "Tulipa quiquendonia".

But alas! if these plants, these fruits, these flowers, grew visibly to the naked eye, if all the vegetables insisted on assuming colossal proportions, if the brilliancy of their colors and perfume intoxicated the smell and the sight, they quickly withered. The air which they absorbed rapidly exhausted them, and they soon died, faded, and dried up.

Such was the fate of the famous tulip, which, after several days of splendor, became emaciated, and fell lifeless.

It was soon the same with the domestic animals, from the house-dog to the stable pig, from the canary in its cage to the turkey of the back-court. It must be said that in ordinary times these animals were not less phlegmatic than their masters. The dogs and cats vegetated rather than lived. They never betrayed a wag of pleasure nor a snarl of wrath. Their tails moved no more than if they had been made of bronze. Such a thing as a bite or scratch from any of them had not been known from time immemorial. As for mad dogs, they were looked upon as imaginary beasts, like the griffins and the rest in the menagerie of the apocalypse.

But what a change had taken place in a few months, the smallest incidents of which we are trying to reproduce! Dogs and cats began to show teeth and claws. Several executions had taken place after reiterated offences. A horse was seen, for the first time, to take his bit in his teeth and rush through the streets of Quiquendone; an ox was observed to precipitate itself, with lowered horns, upon one of his herd; an ass was seen to turn himself ever, with his legs in the air, in the Place Saint Ernuph, and bray as ass never brayed before; a sheep, actually a sheep, defended valiantly the cutlets within him from the butcher's knife.

Burgomaster Van Tricasse was forced to make police regulations concerning the domestic animals, as, seized with lunacy, they rendered the streets of Quiquendone unsafe.

But alas! if the animals were mad, the men were scarcely less so. No age was spared by the scourge. Babies soon became quite insupportable, though till now so easy to bring up; and for the first time Honoré Syntax, the schoolmaster, was obliged to apply the rod to his youthful offspring.

There was a kind of insurrection at the high school, and the dictionaries became formidable missiles in the classes. The scholars would not submit to be shut in, and, besides, the infection took the teachers themselves, who overwhelmed the boys and girls with extravagant tasks and punishments.

Another strange phenomenon occurred. All these Quiquendonians, so sober before, whose chief food had been whipped creams, committed wild excesses in their eating and drinking. Their usual regimen no longer sufficed. Each stomach was transformed into a gulf, and it became necessary to fill this gulf by the most energetic means. The consumption of the town was trebled. Instead of two repasts they had six. Many cases of indigestion were reported. Counselor Niklausse could not satisfy his hunger. Burgomaster Van Tricasse found it impossible to assuage his thirst, and remained in a state of rabid semi-intoxication.

In short, the most alarming symptoms manifested themselves and increased from day to day. Drunken people staggered in the streets, and these were often citizens of high position.

Doctor Custos had plenty to do with the heartburns, inflammations, and nervous affections, which proved to what a strange degree the nerves of the people had been irritated.

There were daily quarrels and altercations in the once deserted but now crowded streets of Quiquendone; for nobody could any longer stay at home. It was necessary to establish a new police force to control the disturbers of the public peace. A prison-cage was established in the Town Hall, and speedily became full, night and day, of refractory offenders. Commissioner Passauf was in despair.

A marriage was concluded in less than two months—such a thing had never been seen before. Yes, the son of Rupp, a teacher, wedded the daughter of Augustine de Rovere, and that fifty-seven days only after he had petitioned for her hand and heart!

Other marriages were decided upon, which, in old times, would have remained in doubt and discussion for years. The Burgomaster perceived that his own daughter, the charming Suzel, was escaping from his hands.

As for dear Tatanémance, she had dared to sound Commissioner Passauf on the subject of a union, which seemed to her to combine every element of happiness, fortune, honor, youth!

At last—to reach the depths of abomination—a duel took place! Yes, a duel with pistols—horse-pistols—at seventy-five paces, with ball-cartridges. And between whom? Our readers will never believe!

Between Franz Niklausse, the gentle angler, and young Simon Collaert, the wealthy banker's son.

And the cause of this duel was the Burgomaster's daughter, for whom Simon discovered himself to be fired with passion, and whom he refused to yield to the claims of an audacious rival!

11. In Which the Quiquendonians Adopt a Heroic Resolution.

We have seen to what a deplorable condition the people of Quiquendone were reduced. Their heads were in a ferment. They no longer knew or recognized themselves. The most peaceable citizens had become quarrelsome. If you looked at them askance, they would speedily send you a challenge. Some let their moustaches grow, and several—the most belligerent—curled them up at the ends.

This being their condition, the administration of the town and the maintenance of order in the streets became difficult tasks, for the government had not been organized for such a state of things. The Burgomaster—that worthy Van Tricasse whom we have seen so placid, so dull, so incapable of coming to any decision—the Burgomaster became intractable. His house resounded with the sharpness of his voice. He made twenty decisions a day, scolding his officials, and himself enforcing the regulations of his administration.

Ah, what a change! The amiable and tranquil mansion of the burgomaster, that good Flemish home—where was its former calm? What changes had taken place in your household economy! Madame Van Tricasse had become acrid, whimsical, harsh. Her husband sometimes succeeded in drowning her voice by talking louder than she, but could not silence her. The petulant humor of this worthy dame was excited by everything. Nothing went right. The servants offended her every moment. Tatanémance, her sister-in-law, who was not less irritable, replied sharply to her. M. Van Tricasse naturally supported Lotchè, his servant, as is the case in all good households; and this permanently exasperated Madame, who constantly disputed, discussed, and made scenes with her husband.

"What on earth is the matter with us?" cried the unhappy Burgomaster. "What is this fire that is devouring us? Are we possessed with the Devil? Ah, Madame Van Tricasse, Madame Van Tricasse, you will end by making me die before you, and thus violate all the traditions of the family!"

The reader will not have forgotten the strange custom by which M. Van Tricasse would become a widower and marry again, so as not to break the chain of descent.

Meanwhile, this disposition of all minds produced other curious effects worthy of note. This excitement, the cause of which has so far escaped us, brought about unexpected physiological changes. Talents, hitherto unrecognized, betrayed themselves. Aptitudes were suddenly revealed. Artists, before common-place, displayed new ability. Politicians and authors arose. Orators proved themselves equal to the most arduous debates, and on every question in-

40

flamed audiences which were quite ready to be inflamed. From the sessions of the council, this movement spread to the public political meetings, and a club was formed at Quiquendone; whilst twenty newspapers, the *Quiquendone Signal*, the *Quiquendone Impartial*, the *Quiquendone Radical*, and so on, written in an inflammatory style, raised the most important questions.

But what about? you will ask. Apropos of everything, and of nothing; apropos of the Oudenarde tower, which was falling, and which some wished to pull down, and others to prop up; apropos of the police regulations issued by the council, which some obstinate citizens threatened to resist; apropos of the sweeping of the gutters, repairing the sewers, and so on. Nor did the enraged orators confine themselves to the internal administration of the town. Carried on by the current they went further, and essayed to plunge their fellow-citizens into the hazards of war.

Quiquendone had had for eight or nine hundred years a *casus belli* of the best quality; but she had preciously laid it up like a relic, and there had seemed some probability that it would become effete, and no longer serviceable.

This was what had given rise to the *casus belli*.

It is not generally known that Quiquendone, in this cozy corner of Flanders, lies next to the little town of Virgamen. The territories of the two communities are contiguous.

Well, in 1185, some time before Count Baldwin's departure to the Crusades, a Virgamen cow—not a cow belonging to a citizen, but a cow which was common property, let it be observed—audaciously ventured to pasture on the territory of Quiquendone. This unfortunate beast had scarcely eaten three mouthfuls; but the offence, the abuse, the crime—whatever you will—was committed and duly indicted, for the magistrates, at that time, had already begun to know how to write.

"We will take revenge at the proper moment," said simply Natalis Van Tricasse, the thirty-second predecessor of the Burgomaster of this story, "and the Virgamenians will lose nothing by waiting."

The Virgamenians were forewarned. They waited thinking, without doubt, that the remembrance of the offence would fade away with the lapse of time; and really, for several centuries, they lived on good terms with their neighbors of Quiquendone.

But they counted without their hosts, or rather without this strange epidemic, which, radically changing the character of the Quiquendonians, aroused their dormant vengeance.

It was at the club of the Rue Monstrelet that the truculent orator Schut, abruptly introducing the subject to his hearers, inflamed them with the expressions and metaphors used on such occasions. He recalled the offence, the injury which had been done to Quiquendone, and which a nation "jealous of its rights" could not admit as a precedent; he showed the insult to be still existing, the wound still bleeding: he spoke of certain special head-shakings on the part of the people of

Virgamen, which indicated in what degree of contempt they regarded the people of Quiquendone; he appealed to his fellow-citizens, who, unconsciously perhaps, had supported this mortal insult for long centuries; he adjured the "children of the ancient town" to have no other purpose than to obtain a substantial reparation. And, lastly, he made an appeal to "all the living energies of the nation!"

With what enthusiasm these words, so new to Quiquendonian ears, were greeted, may be surmised, but cannot be told. All the auditors rose, and with extended arms demanded war with loud cries. Never had Advocate Schut achieved such a success, and it must be avowed that his triumphs were not few.

The Burgomaster, the Counselor, all the notabilities present at this memorable meeting, would have vainly attempted to resist the popular outburst. Besides, they had no desire to do so, and cried as loud, if not louder, than the rest:

"To the frontier! To the frontier!"

As the frontier was but three kilometers from the walls of Quiquendone, it is certain that the Virgamenians ran a real danger, for they might easily be invaded without having had time to look about them.

Meanwhile, Josse Liefrinck, the worthy chemist, who alone had preserved his senses on this grave occasion, tried to make his fellow-citizens comprehend that guns, cannon, and generals were equally wanting to their design.

They replied to him, not without many impatient gestures, that these generals, cannons, and guns would be improvised; that the right and love of country sufficed, and rendered a people irresistible.

Hereupon the Burgomaster himself came forward, and in a sublime harangue made short work of those pusillanimous people who disguise their fear under a veil of prudence, which veil he tore off with a patriotic hand.

At this sally it seemed as if the hall would fall in under the applause.

The vote was eagerly demanded, and was taken amid acclamations.

The cries of "To Virgamen! to Virgamen!" redoubled.

The Burgomaster then took it upon himself to put the armies in motion, and in the name of the town he promised the honors of a triumph, such as was given in the times of the Romans to that one of its generals who should return victorious.

Meanwhile, Josse Liefrinck, who was an obstinate fellow, and did not regard himself as beaten, though he really had been, insisted on making another observation. He wished to remark that the triumph was only accorded at Rome to those victorious generals who had killed five thousand of the enemy.

"Well, well!" cried the meeting deliriously.

"And as the population of the town of Virgamen consists of but three thousand five hundred and seventy-five inhabitants, it would be difficult, unless the same person was killed several times…"

But they did not let the luckless logician finish, and he was turned out, hustled and bruised.

"Citizens," said Pulmacher the grocer, who usually sold groceries by retail, "whatever this cowardly apothecary may have said, I engage by myself to kill five thousand Virgamenians, if you will accept my services!"

"Five thousand five hundred!" cried a yet more resolute patriot.

"Six thousand six hundred!" retorted the grocer.

"Seven thousand!" cried Jean Orbideck, the confectioner of the Rue Hemling, who was on the road to a fortune by making whipped creams.

"Adjudged!" exclaimed Burgomaster Van Tricasse, on finding that no one else rose on the bid.

And this was how Jean Orbideck the confectioner became general-in-chief of the forces of Quiquendone.

12. In Which Ygène, the Assistant, Gives a Reasonable Piece of Advice, Which is Eagerly Rejected by Doctor Ox.

"Well, master," said Ygène next day, as he poured the pails of sulphuric acid into the troughs of the great battery.

"Well," resumed Doctor Ox, "was I not right? See to what not only the physical developments of a whole nation, but its morality, its dignity, its talents, its political sense, have come! It is only a question of molecules."

"No doubt; but..."

"But?"

"Do you not think that matters have gone far enough, and that these poor devils should not be excited beyond measure?"

"No, no!" cried the Doctor. "No! I will go on to the end!"

"As you will, master; the experiment, however, seems to me conclusive, and I think it time to..."

"To?"

"To close the valve."

"Never!" cried Doctor Ox. "If you attempt it, I'll throttle you!"

13. In Which it is Once More Proved that by Taking High Ground All Human Littlenesses May Be Overlooked.

"You say?" asked Burgomaster Van Tricasse of Counselor Niklausse.

"I say that this war is necessary," replied Niklausse, firmly, "and that the time has come to avenge this insult."

"Well, I repeat to you," replied the Burgomaster, tartly, "that if the people of Quiquendone do not profit by this occasion to vindicate their rights, they will be unworthy of their name."

"And as for me, I maintain that we ought, without delay, to collect our forces and lead them to the front."

"Really, monsieur, really!" replied Van Tricasse. "And do you speak thus to me?"

"To yourself, monsieur the Burgomaster; and you shall hear the truth, unwelcome as it may be."

"And you shall hear it yourself, Counselor," returned Van Tricasse in a passion, "for it will come better from my mouth than from yours! Yes, monsieur, yes, any delay would be dishonorable. The town of Quiquendone has waited nine hundred years for the moment to take its revenge, and whatever you may say, whether it pleases you or not, we shall march upon the enemy."

"Ah, you take it thus!" replied Niklausse harshly. "Very well, monsieur, we will march without you, if it does not please you to go."

"A Burgomaster's place is in the front rank, monsieur!"

"And that of a Counselor also, monsieur."

"You insult me by thwarting all my wishes," cried the Burgomaster, whose fists seemed likely to hit out before long.

"And you insult me equally by doubting my patriotism," cried Niklausse, who was equally ready for a tussle.

"I tell you, monsieur, that the army of Quiquendone shall be put in motion within two days!"

"And I repeat to you, monsieur, that forty-eight hours shall not pass before we shall have marched upon the enemy!"

It is easy to see, from this fragment of conversation, that the two speakers supported exactly the same idea. Both wished for hostilities; but as their excitement disposed them to altercation, Niklausse would not listen to Van Tricasse, nor Van Tricasse to Niklausse. Had they been of contrary opinions on this grave question, had the Burgomaster favored war and the Counselor insisted on peace, the quarrel would not have been more violent. These two old friends gazed fiercely at each other. By the quickened beating of their hearts, their red faces, their contracted pupils, the trembling of their muscles, their harsh voices, it might be conjectured that they were ready to come to blows.

But the striking of a large clock happily checked the adversaries at the moment when they seemed on the point of assaulting each other.

"At last the hour has come!" cried the Burgomaster.

"What hour?" asked the Counselor.

"The hour to go to the belfry tower."

"It is true, and whether it pleases you or not, I shall go, monsieur."

"And I too."

"Let us go!"

"Let us go!"

It might have been supposed from these last words that a collision had occurred, and that the adversaries were proceeding to a duel; but it was not so. It had been agreed that the Burgomaster and the Counselor, as the two principal dignitaries of the town, should repair to the Town Hall, and there show themselves on the high tower which overlooked Quiquendone; that they should examine the surrounding country, so as to make the best strategic plan for the advance of their troops.

Though they were in accord on this subject, they did not cease to quarrel bitterly as they went. Their loud voices were heard resounding in the streets; but all the passers-by were now accustomed to this; the exasperation of the dignitaries seemed quite natural, and no one took notice of it. Under the circumstances, a calm man would have been regarded as a monster.

The Burgomaster and the counselor, having reached the porch of the belfry, were in a paroxysm of fury. They were no longer red, but pale. This terrible discussion, though they had the same idea, had produced internal spasms, and everyone knows that paleness shows that anger has reached its last limits.

At the foot of the narrow tower staircase there was a real explosion. Who should go up first? Who should first creep up the winding steps? Truth compels us to say that there was a tussle, and that Counselor Niklausse, forgetful of all that he owed to his superior, to the supreme magistrate of the town, pushed Van Tricasse violently back, and dashed up the staircase first.

Both ascended, denouncing and raging at each other at every step. It was to be feared that a terrible climax would occur on the summit of the tower, which rose three hundred and fifty-seven feet above the pavement.

The two enemies soon got out of breath, however, and in a little while, at the eightieth step, they began to move up heavily, breathing loud and short.

Then—was it because of their being out of breath?—their wrath subsided, or at least only betrayed itself by a succession of unseemly epithets. They became silent, and, strange to say, it seemed as if their excitement diminished as they ascended higher above the town. A sort of lull took place in their minds. Their brains became cooler, and simmered down like a coffee-pot when taken away from the fire. Why?

We cannot answer this "why;" but the truth is that, having reached a certain landing, two hundred and sixty-six feet above ground, the two adversaries sat down and, really more calm, looked at each other without any anger in their faces.

"How high it is!" said the Burgomaster, passing his handkerchief over his rubicund face.

"Very high!" returned the Counselor. "Do you know that we have gone fourteen feet higher than the Church of Saint Michael at Hamburg?"

"I know it," replied the Burgomaster, in a tone of vanity very pardonable in the chief magistrate of Quiquendone.

The two notabilities soon resumed their ascent, casting curious glances through the loopholes pierced in the tower walls. The Burgomaster had taken the head of the procession, without any remark on the part of the Counselor. It even happened that at about the three hundred and fourth step, Van Tricasse being completely tired out, Niklausse kindly pushed him from behind. The Burgomaster offered no resistance to this, and, when he reached the platform of the tower, said graciously:

"Thanks, Niklausse; I will do the same for you one day."

A little while before it had been two wild beasts, ready to tear each other to pieces, who had presented themselves at the foot of the tower; it was now two friends who reached its summit.

The weather was superb. It was the month of May. The sun had absorbed all the vapors. What a pure and limpid atmosphere! The most minute objects over a broad space might be discerned. The walls of Virgamen, glistening in their whiteness—its red, pointed roofs, its belfries shining in the sunlight— appeared a few miles off. And this was the town that was foredoomed to all the horrors of fire and pillage!

The Burgomaster and the Counselor sat down beside each other on a small stone bench, like two worthy people whose souls were in close sympathy. As they recovered breath, they looked around; then, after a brief silence:

"How fine this is!" cried the Burgomaster.

"Yes, it is admirable!" replied the Counselor. "Does it not seem to you, my good Van Tricasse, that humanity is destined to dwell rather at such heights, than to crawl about on the surface of our globe?"

"I agree with you, honest Niklausse," returned the Burgomaster, "I agree with you. You seize sentiment better when you get clear of nature. You breathe it in every sense! It is at such heights that philosophers should be formed, and that sages should live, above the miseries of this world!"

"Shall we go around the platform?" asked the Counselor.

"Let us go around the platform," replied the Burgomaster.

And the two friends, arm in arm, and putting, as formerly, long pauses between their questions and answers, examined every point of the horizon.

The two friends, arm in arm

"It is at least seventeen years since I have ascended the belfry tower," said Van Tricasse.

"I do not think I ever came up before," replied Niklausse, "and I regret it, for the view from this height is sublime! Do you see, my friend, the pretty stream of the Vaar, as it winds among the trees?"

"And, beyond, the heights of Saint Hermandad! How gracefully they shut in the horizon! Observe that border of green trees, which Nature has so picturesquely arranged! Ah, Nature, Nature, Niklausse! Could the hand of man ever hope to rival her?"

"It is enchanting, my excellent friend," replied the Counselor. "See the flocks and herds lying in the verdant pastures—the oxen, the cows, the sheep!"

"And the laborers going to the fields! You would say they were Arcadian shepherds; they only want a bagpipe!"

"And over all this fertile country the beautiful blue sky, which no vapor dims! Ah, Niklausse, one might become a poet here! I do not understand why Saint Simeon Stylites was not one of the greatest poets of the world."

"It was because, perhaps, his column was not high enough," replied the Counselor, with a gentle smile.

At this moment the chimes of Quiquendone rang out. The clear bells played one of their most melodious airs. The two friends listened in ecstasy.

Then in his calm voice, Van Tricasse said:

"But what, friend Niklausse, did we come to the top of this tower to do?"

"In fact," replied the Counselor, "we have permitted ourselves to be carried away by our reveries…"

"What did we come here to do?" repeated the Burgomaster.

"We came," said Niklausse, "to breathe this pure air, which human weaknesses have not corrupted."

"Well, shall we descend, friend Niklausse?"

"Let us descend, friend Van Tricasse."

They gave a parting glance at the splendid panorama which was spread before their eyes; then the Burgomaster passed down first, and began to descend with a slow and measured pace. The Counselor followed a few steps behind. They reached the landing-stage at which they had stopped on ascending. Already their cheeks began to redden. They tarried a moment, then resumed their descent.

In a few moments Van Tricasse begged Niklausse to go more slowly, as he felt him on his heels, and it "worried him." It even did more than worry him; for twenty steps lower down he ordered the Counselor to stop, that he might get on some distance ahead.

The Counselor replied that he did not wish to remain with his leg in the air to await the good pleasure of the Burgomaster, and kept on.

Van Tricasse retorted with a rude expression.

The Counselor responded by an insulting allusion to the Burgomaster's age, destined as he was, by his family traditions, to marry a second time.

The Burgomaster went down twenty steps more, and warned Niklausse that this should not pass thus.

Niklausse replied that, at all events, he would pass down first; and, the space being very narrow, the two dignitaries came into collision, and found themselves in utter darkness. The words "blockhead" and "booby" were the mildest which they now applied to each other.

"We shall see, stupid beast!" cried the Burgomaster, "we shall see what figure you will make in this war, and in what rank you will march!"

"In the rank that precedes yours, you silly old fool!" replied Niklausse.

Then there were other cries, and it seemed as if bodies were rolling over each other. What was going on? Why were these dispositions so quickly changed? Why were the gentle sheep of the tower's summit metamorphosed into tigers two hundred feet below it?

However this might be, the guardian of the tower, hearing the noise, opened the door, just at the moment when the two adversaries, bruised, and with protruding eyes, were in the act of tearing each other's hair—fortunately they wore wigs.

"You shall give me satisfaction for this!" cried the Burgomaster, shaking his fist under his adversary's nose.

"Whenever you please!" growled Counselor Niklausse, attempting to respond with a vigorous kick.

The guardian, who was himself in a passion—I cannot say why—thought the scene a very natural one. I know not what excitement urged him to take part in it, but he controlled himself, and went off to announce throughout the neighborhood that a hostile meeting was about to take place between Burgomaster Van Tricasse and Counselor Niklausse.

14. In Which Matters Go So Far that the Inhabitants of Quiquendone, the Reader, and Even the Author, Demand an Immediate Dénouement.

The last incident proves to what a pitch of excitement the Quiquendonians had been wrought. The two oldest friends in the town, and the most gentle before the advent of the epidemic, to reach this degree of violence! And that, too, only a few minutes after their old mutual sympathy, their amiable instincts, their contemplative habit, had been restored at the summit of the tower!

On learning what was going on, Doctor Ox could not contain his joy. He resisted the arguments which Ygène, who saw what a serious turn affairs were taking, addressed to him. Besides, both of them were infected by the general fury. They were not less excited than the rest of the population, and they ended by quarrelling as violently as the burgomaster and the counselor.

Besides, one question eclipsed all others, and the intended duels were postponed to the issue of the Virgamenian difficulty. No man had the right to shed his blood uselessly, when it belonged, to the last drop, to his country in danger. The affair was, in short, a grave one, and there was no withdrawing from it.

Burgomaster Van Tricasse, despite the warlike ardor with which he was filled, had not thought it best to throw himself upon the enemy without warning him. He had, therefore, through the medium of the rural policeman, Hottering, sent to demand reparation of the Virgamenians for the offence committed, in 1195, on the Quiquendonian territory.

The authorities of Virgamen could not at first imagine of what the envoy spoke, and the latter, despite his official character, was conducted back to the frontier very cavalierly.

Van Tricasse then sent one of the aides-de-camp of the confectioner-general, citizen Hildevert Shuman, a manufacturer of barley-sugar, a very firm and energetic man, who carried to the authorities of Virgamen the original minute of the indictment drawn up in 1195 by order of Burgomaster Natalís Van Tricasse.

The authorities of Virgamen burst out laughing, and served the aide-de-camp in the same manner as the rural policeman.

The Burgomaster then assembled the dignitaries of the town.

A letter, remarkably and vigorously drawn up, was written as an ultimatum; the cause of quarrel was plainly stated, and a delay of twenty-four hours was accorded to the guilty city in which to repair the outrage done to Quiquendone.

The letter was sent off, and returned a few hours afterwards, torn to bits, which made so many fresh insults. The Virgamenians knew of old the forbearance and equanimity of the Quiquendonians, and made sport of them and their demand, of their *casus belli* and their ultimatum.

There was only one thing left to do—to have recourse to arms, to invoke the God of battles, and, after the Prussian fashion, to hurl themselves upon the Virgamenians before the latter could be prepared.

This decision was made by the council in solemn conclave, in which cries, objurgations, and menacing gestures were mingled with unexampled violence. An assembly of idiots, a congress of madmen, a club of maniacs, would not have been more tumultuous.

As soon as the declaration of war was known, General Jean Orbideck assembled his troops, perhaps two thousand three hundred and ninety-three combatants from a population of two thousand three hundred and ninety-three souls. The women, the children, the old men, were joined with the able-bodied males. The guns of the town had been put under requisition. Five had been found, two of which were without cocks, and these had been distributed to the advance-guard. The artillery was composed of the old culverin of the château, taken in 1339 at the attack on Quesnoy, one of the first occasions of the use of cannon in history, and which had not been fired off for five centuries. Happily for those who were appointed to take it in charge there were no projectiles with which to load it; but such as it was, this engine might well impose on the enemy. As for side-arms, they had been taken from the museum of antiquities—flint hatchets, helmets, Frankish battle-axes, javelins, halberds, rapiers, and so on; and also in those domestic arsenals commonly known as "cupboards" and "kitchens." But courage, the right, hatred of the foreigner, the yearning for vengeance, were to take the place of more perfect engines, and to replace—at least it was hoped so—the modern mitrailleuses and breech-loaders.

The troops were passed in review. Not a citizen failed at the roll-call. General Orbideck, whose seat on horseback was far from firm, and whose steed was a vicious beast, was thrown three times in front of the army; but he got up again without injury, and this was regarded as a favorable omen. The Burgomaster, the Counselor, the Commissioner, the Chief Magistrate, the Schoolmaster, the Banker, the Rector—in short, all the notabilities of the town—marched at the head. There were no tears shed, either by mothers, sisters, or daughters. They urged on their husbands, fathers, brothers, to the combat, and even followed them and formed the rear-guard, under the orders of the courageous Madame Van Tricasse.

The town crier, Jean Mistrol, blew his trumpet; the army moved off, and directed itself, with ferocious cries, towards the Oudenarde gate.

At the moment when the head of the column was about to pass the walls of the town, a man threw himself before it.

"Stop! stop! Fools that you are!" he cried. "Suspend your blows! Let me shut the valve! You are not changed in nature! You are good citizens, quiet and peaceable! If you are so excited, it is my master, Doctor Ox's, fault! It is an experiment! Under the pretext of lighting your streets with oxyhydric gas, he has saturated…"

The assistant was beside himself; but he could not finish. At the instant that the Doctor's secret was about to escape his lips, Doctor Ox himself pounced upon the unhappy Ygène in an indescribable rage, and shut his mouth by blows with his fist.

It was a battle. The Burgomaster, the Counselor, the dignitaries, who had stopped short on Ygène's sudden appearance, carried away in turn by their exasperation, rushed upon the two strangers, without waiting to hear either the one or the other.

Doctor Ox and his assistant, beaten and lashed, were about to be dragged, by order of Van Tricasse, to the round-house, when…

15. In Which the Dénouement Takes Place.

…When a formidable explosion resounded. All the atmosphere which enveloped Quiquendone seemed on fire. A flame of an intensity and vividness quite unwonted shot up into the Heavens like a meteor. Had it been night, this flame would have been visible for ten leagues around.

The whole army of Quiquendone fell to the earth, like an army of monks. Happily there were no victims; a few scratches and slight hurts were the only result. The confectioner, who, as chance would have it, had not fallen from his horse this time, had his plume singed, and escaped without any further injury.

The whole army of Quiquendone fell to the earth

What had happened?

Something very simple, as was soon learned; the gasworks had just blown up. During the absence of the Doctor and his assistant, some careless mistake had no doubt been made. It is not known how or why a communication had been established between the reservoir which contained the oxygen and that which

50

enclosed the hydrogen. An explosive mixture had resulted from the union of these two gases, to which fire had accidentally been applied.

This changed everything; but when the army got upon its feet again, Doctor Ox and his assistant Ygène had disappeared.

16. In Which the Intelligent Reader Sees that he has Guessed Correctly, Despite All the Author's Precautions.

After the explosion, Quiquendone immediately became the peaceable, phlegmatic, and Flemish town it formerly was.

After the explosion, which indeed did not cause a very lively sensation, each one, without knowing why, mechanically took his way home, the Burgomaster leaning on the Counselor's arm, Advocate Schut going arm in arm with Doctor Custos, Franz Niklausse walking with equal familiarity with Simon Collaert, each going tranquilly, noiselessly, without even being conscious of what had happened, and having already forgotten Virgamen and their revenge. The general returned to his confections, and his aide-decamp to the barley-sugar.

Thus everything had become calm again; the old existence had been resumed by men and beasts, beasts and plants; even by the tower of Oudenarde gate, which the explosion—these explosions are sometimes astonishing—had set upright again!

And from that time never a word was spoken more loudly than another, never a discussion took place in the town of Quiquendone. There were no more politics, no more clubs, no more trials, no more policemen! The post of Commissioner Passauf became once more a sinecure, and if his salary was not reduced, it was because the Burgomaster and the Counselor could not make up their minds to decide upon it.

From time to time, indeed, Passauf flitted, without anyone suspecting it, through the dreams of the inconsolable Tatanémance.

As for Franz's rival, he generously abandoned the charming Suzel to her lover, who hastened to wed her five or six years after these events.

And as for Madame Van Tricasse, she died ten years later, at the proper time, and the Burgomaster married Mademoiselle Pélagie Van Tricasse, his cousin, under excellent conditions—for the happy mortal who should succeed him.

17. In Which Doctor Ox's Theory is Explained.

What, then, had this mysterious Doctor Ox done? Tried a fantastic experiment—nothing more.

After having laid down his gas-pipes, he had saturated, first the public buildings, then the private dwellings, finally the streets of Quiquendone, with pure oxygen, without letting in the least atom of hydrogen.

This gas, tasteless and odorless, spread in generous quantity through the atmosphere, causes, when it is breathed, serious agitation to the human organism. One who lives in an air saturated with oxygen grows excited, frantic, burns!

You scarcely return to the ordinary atmosphere before you return to your usual state. For instance, the counselor and the burgomaster at the top of the belfry were themselves again, as the oxygen is kept, by its weight, in the lower strata of the air.

But one who lives under such conditions, breathing this gas which transforms the body physiologically as well as the soul, dies speedily, like a madman.

It was fortunate, then, for the Quiquendonians, that a providential explosion put an end to this dangerous experiment, and abolished Doctor Ox's gasworks.

To conclude: Are virtue, courage, talent, wit, imagination—are all these qualities or faculties only a question of oxygen?

Such is Doctor Ox's theory; but we are not bound to accept it, and for ourselves we utterly reject it, in spite of the curious experiment of which the worthy old town of Quiquendone was the theater.

Georges Espitallier: *The Nickel Man*

L'Homme en nickel *is an item of popular pulp fiction, initially published as a feuilleton serial in* La Science Française *in 1897 and reprinted in book form the same year. It was the work of one of the most prolific contributors to the periodical in question, and it appeared there under the pseudonym "Georges Bethuys," one of several signatures employed by the military historian and journalist Georges-Frédéric Espitallier (1849-1923) (who also used the pseudonym of "Pierre Ferréol"). Like most of the fiction published in the popular science magazines of the day, it attempts to place scientific notions in the context of a plot that reproduces many of the standard features of the feuilleton fiction of the day, in this case borrowing abundantly from the nascent genre of detective fiction. One suspects that the puzzle with which* L'Homme en nickel *confronts the detective who functions as its main protagonist would not have confused Sherlock Holmes for more than a few minutes, and the fact that the reader knows the answer from the very beginning only serves to make the policeman's deductive powers seem even weaker, but the story tries as hard as it can to make up for that rickety logic with zest and fast-paced movement, in a manner that was to become familiar in pulpish speculative fiction; in consequence, deserves some credit as a pioneering exercise in a hybrid genre that was to become far more sophisticated as it became much more prolific during the 20th century.*

B.S.

1. A Singular Scientist

Pilesèche was a man devoid of ambition.

His present situation was sufficient for him, even though it was humble; he was a mere laboratory assistant to a physiologist who enjoyed both renown and a very bad character—in consequence of which the poor laboratory assistant was more accustomed to being shoved around than kind words.

Népomucène Grillard—for, after all, it is appropriate to provide a portrait of the master before setting out that of the servant—belonged to the category of scientists who are surly and disagreeable to their fellow men. Born a peasant, his boorish behavior had conserved the rustic imprint of his origin. He had isolated himself, struggling against a life that was not easy at the outset, and developed an innate combative instinct. His obstinacy had triumphed over obstacles, but he had not tried to rid himself of his native rudeness, and, as his scientific notoriety had increased, that lack of amenity had seemed to grow, because he did not feel any need to repress it.

His first impulse—the best, it is said—was always to receive anyone who approached him with an initial attack. The burlesque odyssey of his academic visits, when he had thought of trying to obtain a chair in the Institut, was legendary in the vicinity of the Sorbonne. By dint of effort he had then succeeded in putting on an almost smiling face when he passed the threshold of the scientist whose vote he was trying to win in the great struggle, but after five minutes of conversation, the animal inside him found itself unleashed, and, trampling the flower-bed of his future colleague, gradually increasing the pitch of his dry falsetto voice, he would take a stand opposed to his interlocutor's theories, pouring out irony by the bucketful and arguments by the mouthful, and the conversation would end in a dispute, with a loud noise of slammed doors that left him, the last man standing, alone on the academician's landing.

He cut his visits short before arriving at the contest, and renounced forever the hope of ever putting on the coat with green palms.

If he was aggressive with his colleagues, it is easy to deduce what his relationship was like with the students who aspired to learn science in his shadow. His laboratory was an inferno; gradually, a void had formed around the scientist, to whom only the timid Pilesèche remained faithful.

The latter would perhaps have preferred an easier master, but he was a creature of habit, and in any case, he had never had sufficient energy to detach himself from bonds to which he gradually became accustomed. He was a kind of eccentric, a great timid child devoid of will-power, whose only passion was for study, with a certain nonchalance in the fashion in which he devoted himself to it.

The physiology on which he worked possessed him entirely, but when he had poured out his contingent of ideas in the common endeavor, it never entered his head that he had anything to do with the result; never, even in the depths of his soul, did he make any kind of claim to their paternity. Népomucène Grillard appeared to him to be a divinity looking down from on high upon feeble humanity, and one does not collaborate with the gods; one serves them.

In any case, having no needs and satisfied with very little, Pilesèche went through life full of an insouciance that was painted all over his person. He had long, unkempt hair; its gray color might have been natural, but was more probably due to an abundant dust generously spread all the way to the dirty collar of the worn and discolored frock-coat that enveloped, without really dressing, his long bony body. The rest of his costume was in keeping.

Along with his athletic appearance, the man had a timid, adolescent expression; his gestures were gauche and maladroit. For anyone who considered him at a glance, he might have passed for a scholar or a Bohemian; he was both at the same time.

There are bilious individuals who live for a long time, to the misfortune of their contemporaries, but it is nevertheless necessary to recognize that exaggerated movements of bile are not favorably to the principles of sound hygiene. For that reason and many others, Népomucène Grillard, when he reached the age of sixty-five, felt himself declining—physically declining, that is; his mentality was not afflicted, nor his energy, nor, most of all, his character. And yet, the aged scientist had embarked on a whole series of experiments that he would not have wanted to leave incomplete.

As time was pressing, he had the imprudent temerity to test some of his physiological discoveries on himself, which was the surest fashion of hastening his end, for the human body is not an experimental field in which the infinitely small can deliver battle without causing damage to the substratum of that microcosm.

The scientist had also launched himself into the new sciences that claim to approach the problems of hypnosis and life after death, and which solicit so many people nowadays. All that overwork had ended up ruining his constitution, to the point that one day, it was necessary to take to his bed.

With his bulldog manners, Monsieur Grillard had never managed to keep a domestic servant for more than a week, and when he fell ill, he could not abide any other care than that of his laboratory assistant, to which he was accustomed. It was necessary then for the latter to comply with all the old man's caprices and not impose his presence on him more than was necessary.

Occasionally, he risked an observation, such as: "It's imprudent to remain alone at night, my dear master; allow me to stay with you..."

"Leave me alone," the other replied.

"You have to eat; make a little effort, or you'll die of starvation."

"What are you doing? Besides, starvation or something else, what does it matter? I feel that I'm at the end of my tether."

"Oh, my dear master, you're not there yet. You're going to get your strength back—but it's necessary to look after yourself."

"Go away. Stop harping on and leave me in peace. You can't tell me anything, damn it! I know better than you are how I am..."

Sometimes, Pilesèche exerted himself on another subject, perhaps even more scabrous.

"You have a nephew, Monsieur; you need to think about asking him to come..."

"A fine fellow, who makes music!"

"Pardon me, but I'm told that he's given up music for sculpture. I imagine he thought that the change might give you pleasure."

"Ha ha! Music or sculpture, it's all one: I don't like the arts. What is there in them that's positive? Can one find theorems that regulate those strings of sensations? And those statues, fixed and frozen—are they worth as much as a mor-

55

sel of flesh palpitating under my scalpel? Get away—you can talk to me about all that when the arts are sciences."

Thus rejected, his efforts wasted, the poor assistant, undiscouraged, brought up the subject of an orphan niece, with whom the scientist scarcely occupied himself except for paying her boarding-school fees, even doing good in an egotistical fashion.

"She's in a convent, isn't she?" Grillard interrupted. "Let her stay there!"

Pilesèche was, therefore, quite astonished when the old man, one day, softening his voice, summoned him to his bedside and made him party to his intentions.

"I sense that I don't have much longer to go, and, before dying, I want to see my nephew Népomucène. He's an animal, but he's my nephew, and I want to give him my instructions. Go look for him tomorrow evening and bring him here. If you don't find him, search—I don't want to see you without him, you hear me?"

"What if I were to bring him tomorrow morning?"

"How painful it is never to be understood! Not before tomorrow evening, I tell you. I'm not in the habit of repeating myself!"

A few moments later, the scientist called out: "Pilesèche, prepare me an electric bath!"

An electric bath!

The assistant did not believe in the efficacy of that medical treatment, which Monsieur Grillard had improved for his own usage, but how could he oppose his master's will?

"Are you going to contradict me incessantly?" the old man growled.

In order not to excite his bile any further, Pilesèche heated up the water and, uncovering a long vat that was normally used for galvanoplasty, he poured in the liquid, slightly sharpened with a little acid to increase its electrical conductivity.

While taking his bath, Grillard had the custom of lying down on a rattan trellis placed in the bottom of the vat and serving as an insulator. He gripped the cylinders in both hands. The electric current thus ran through his body, while on slight electrolytic reactions occurred on the surface of his skin. He felt a frisson running over his sickly limbs. It felt like ants swarming throughout his being, which at least procured him a temporary relief.

That evening, he made a new demand. He took it into his head to increase the conductivity of his body by having it coated in plumbago. Pilesèche tried in vain to resist, but it was finally necessary for him to grip the heavy brush steeped in a pot where the black lead was thinned down, and to start daubing the maniac, who had stripped off his last garment.

Grillard stood on the floor, trembling, his hands leaning on the bed, and there was no more lugubrious sight than that skeleton, scarcely covered by parchment-like skin, gradually coated with a layer of black, as shiny as wax.

When the grotesque operation was terminated, Grillard signified to his assistant that he was to go away and leave him alone.

"But what about your bath?" said the latter.

"I can take it perfectly well on my own."

And as Pilesèche was accustomed by habit to passive obedience, he left, while the old man, his back bent, supporting himself on the walls, headed toward the half-full vat.

As he went past the slate-topped table mounted in sliding grooves, however, he stopped, listened to make sure that the door of the apartment had closed behind Pilesèche, and, seizing a piece of chalk with one hand and some pieces of paper lying on the table with the other, he began rapidly transcribing a previously-prepared inscription, the letters of which followed one another in complete incoherence.

Having done that, the ambulant black phantom finally reached the galvanoplastic vat. He poured into it the contents of a bottle full of a glittering crystalline salt, lit a reflector lamp placed nearby, and lay down in the bath, after having opened the tap of a small reservoir, whose water began to flow into the vast in a thin trickle, with a monotonous murmur.

The old man had placed himself in the vat in his usual position. Thus extended, with his knees brought back toward is meager breast, only his face, tilted backward, emerged from the water. He searched with his gaze for a brilliant point that the lamp picked out on a silver ball suspended in front of him. Motionless, his eyes jaundiced by icterus and immeasurably wide open in fakiristic contemplation, he waited...

Silence had fallen, lugubriously. Nothing could be heard but the purr of the stove and the susurrus of the trickle of water that was solely causing the level in the vat to rise. Gradually, the water covered the scientist's closed mouth. Only the nostrils, eyes and forehead appeared above the liquid surface. Already, however, all consciousness had disappeared from the inert and rigid body. Népomucène Grillard had put himself into complete catalepsy by staring fixedly at the luminous dot trembling on the polished surface of the silvery ball.

The water was still rising, its meniscus climbing to assault the projections of the emaciated face.

And the electricity did its work on the molecules of that exsanguinated flesh, gently and slyly depositing solid particles appropriated from the decomposing salts: an impalpable dust of nickel, which clung on to the layer of plumbago and gradually covered it...

2. A Sinister Discovery

On the 31 December 1890, St. Sylvester's Day, at eight o'clock in the morning, the Rue de la Montagne-Sainte-Geneviève was crowded, in spite of the glacial fog, with businessmen and housewives who were running in quest of breakfast, their heads swathed in wool, clutching the traditional milk-jug in their numb fingers.

Two eccentrics, rather incongruous in their appearance and costume, were striding over the damp and sticky paving stones; they did not seem excessively out of place, however, in the midst of the other passers-by, the stiff slope in question not normally being the rendezvous of the flower of the aristocracy.

One of the two, his figure clasped in a black velvet jacket, had a simple scarf wound around his neck; it was the only concession he made to the rigor of the temperature, for he was holding his hat in his hand in spite of the season, proudly throwing back his long black hair, lustrous a well-groomed, with a leonine gesture.

The other, by contrast, was very negligently clad, with no attention to detail; that was Népomucène Grillard's laboratory assistant, and the succinct portrait previously painted dispenses us with describing the costume he was wearing.

"So, my dear Pilesèche," said the man in the velvet jacket, continuing the conversation, "my uncle has suddenly felt his familial fibers vibrating?"

"He has, at least testified the desire to see you," the other replied, not without a certain reticence.

"I'm still amazed, not being accustomed to such tenderness on his part."

"The sentiments are modified, Monsieur Bémolisant, and soften at the approach of death."

"And you think that the old man is there?"

"I believe that it would be very difficult for him to get better. I think he's worn out. He's developed an extreme nervous sensitivity, and I've been able to observe profound disturbances in his organism of late. However, he might live for a few weeks yet; yesterday evening, when I left him, Monsieur Grillard was not exactly worse; he merely manifested the desire to be alone, and dismissed me rather abruptly, I have to say..."

"In order not to misrepresent his amiable character. You're an angel of forbearance, Monsieur Pilesèche, and in your place, I would have broken his retorts over his head a long time ago."

"Are you astonished, then, that he has quarreled with you?"

"What do the doctors say?" asked the other, after a brief pause.

"The doctors? You can hardly doubt that he's refuse their intervention, and you know how determined he is..."

"How stubborn, you mean. Yes, yes, I know my dear uncle, although he banished me from his presence a long time ago. I know that one can't easily get him to give in. He's doubtless a great scientist, but what an insupportable fellow!"

Pilesèche pursed his lips with an indulgent gesture. "Everyone has his little faults; I'm used to his and I'm no less affected for that by the sad state to which I see him reduced. Oh, since a month ago the laboratory no longer exists. Even before being bed-ridden, the poor man had no heart for anything. Experiments begun were left incomplete. There was only his most recent research...you know, his research on the occlusion of living beings?"

"The occlusion of...," said the other, nonplussed. "He was working on the occlusion of living beings. What on earth can that be?"

"You don't keep up with the reports of the scientific societies?"

"Eminently unhealthy nourishment, Monsieur Pilesèche—no, I don't read them. The occlusion...ha ha! My dear uncle definitely had a very accentuated crack in the brain. At his age, it's pardonable."

"You can laugh, but I assure you...the results are precise and I myself..."

"What you too? Well, you're a bit touched yourself, my friend. Anyway, it's not astonishing. The great man's laboratory assistant...and it's contagious. But come on, explain it to me: what is this occlusion, of which I've never heard?"

"Artist as you are, you must have heard mention of some recent very singular discoveries. In the course of digging in perfectly virgin ground, incontestably undisturbed for several centuries, it sometimes happens—rarely, I admit—that is breaking blocks of stone, one sees emerging from one of them a toad, which yawns and stretches: a living toad, awakening after a centuries-long sleep..."

"And you've seen that yourself?" said Bémolisant, incredulously.

"No, I haven't seen it myself," the laboratory assistant replied, mildly, "but our experiments prove the possibility of the phenomenon. We've reproduced it artificially; we've hermetically sealed up toads, frogs, even cats..."

"For centuries?" the artist interrupted, holding his ribs.

"For a few days—but that's sufficient to demonstrate the conditions in which a living being can remain like that, without dying."

"You're amazing!"

"No, no, it's quite simple. It's quite evident that it you content yourself with enclosing your subject brutally, whatever it might be, it will die quickly, asphyxiated. But in the multitudinous phases of hypnotic sleep, there's one, still little known, that resembles death but isn't. It isn't catalepsy, properly speaking, in which the subject doesn't cease to breathe and the blood still circulates; it's like a paralysis of the entire organism, a complete suspension of life..."

"And the animal can live without air, without light?"

"It lives...if one can call the complete arrest of all the vital functions living."

"And what do you do to enclose it in its pebble?"

"The prison doesn't matter, so long as it's hermetic; the one that Monsieur Grillard normally employs is a metallic envelope deposited by galvanoplasty."

"It's only scientists that have such ludicrous ideas!"

"Pooh! Have you forgotten your theories about music, then? Do you think that the six-thousand-note scale with which you once wanted to endow us wasn't at least as singular?"

"So I wasn't understood by the men of my time, and in order not to lower my art by vile concessions to the level of my contemporaries devoid of ears, I renounced music..."

"You see..."

"Now I do sculpture...decadent sculpture...you'll see! A revolution, my dear, a revolution! The primitives were nothing, the Byzantines nothing more; the art has never been understood like this..."

"You were talking about cracked brains a little while ago, Monsieur Bémolisant. I have reason to believe that, by virtue of atavism, you..."

"Oh! I'm misunderstood before I've even spoken!"

They arrived at the coaching entrance of an old house of rather sordid appearance, and, after darting a distracted glance at the lodge, deserted for the moment, they climbed the somber staircase whose sticky handrail adhered to the fingers.

The fourth floor landing, to which insipid and nauseating odors rose up from the rest of the house, was illuminated by wan daylight falling vertically through a glazed skylight open in the roof.

Pilesèche took a large key from his pocket and introduced it into the lock of a door painted in yellow ocher.

"My uncle lodges a long way up," said the artist, out of breath after his climb.

"That's because of the laboratory; one can't find appropriate premises to let everywhere."

"And then, admit it, landlords don't like having such a constantly grumpy tenant..."

They went into a gloomy vestibule, which gave access on one side to a small kitchen, and on the other to a room decorated with the name of the drawing room and furnished with four rickety armchairs. At the back was the door to the laboratory, the biggest room in the apartment: the only one in which Népomucène Grillard lived, and which was really useful to him.

The two newcomers were walking on tiptoe, as is appropriate in the apartment of an invalid. Pilesèche gently lifted the latch of the laboratory and pushed the door. The vestibule was suddenly invaded by a violent flood of light and empyreumatic odors.

The laboratory was illuminated from above, like a painter's studio. The raw daylight fell upon tables overloaded with an inextricable tangle of glassware: flasks of various shapes, test-tubes and reagents of all colors in recipients of every form. There was a microscope, and countless items of bizarre apparatus, in chaotic disorder. An enormous chimney-hood, on which iron-clad furnaces, earthenware crucibles and pot-bellied retorts were strewn, completed the encumbrance of the fin-de-siècle alchemist's lair, while various guinea-pigs, cats, frogs and toads were scratching in their cages or beneath bell-jars scattered here, there and everywhere.

The scientist's laboratory also served as his bedroom, but the iron-framed bed, on which a meager mattress was thrown, attested that Népomucène Grillard was no sybarite.

The newcomers approached it with muffled footsteps, in order not to trouble his slumber. Wasted effort! They were astonished—on might almost say frightened—to find the bed empty.

Pilesèche opened his eyes wide in bewilderment, but no exclamation could escape his gaping mouth, so tightly was his throat constricted by that unexpected spectacle.

"Come on, let's pull ourselves together," said Bémolisant, the first to recover the power of speech, passing his hand over his forehead. "If he's not here, he must have gone out, improbable as the supposition might seem. The concierge will have seen him go past. I'll go and question her."

The artist ran downstairs and presented himself at the lodge, where the concierge was in the process of warming up her milk, with his back turned.

"Has Monsieur Grillard gone out?" asked Bémolisant, out of breath.

"Out! Oh, the poor old man. He's not in any state to go for a walk. He's in bed. It's a month, now that he hasn't been down and I haven't seen him. Monsieur Pilesèche gives me news of him every say, for you can imagine that, with his everlasting bad mood, I don't risk going upstairs to offer him my services."

The good woman had turned round, hands on hips. "You can go up confidently. He's at home, in bed…unless Monsieur Pilesèche is putting one over on me," she added, laughing thickly.

Bémolisant had no desire to persist. While going back up as hastily as he had come down, it occurred to him that the sudden disappearance was going to seem singular to many people, to say the least.

Pilesèche was waiting for him at the door, his expression utterly distressed, pale and worn out, his arms dangling. "I've found him, alas," he moaned, in a cavernous voice.

"He's hanged himself, perhaps?" the other queried, anxiously.

"No, worse than that."

"Well, what? You're killing me with your reticence…"

"Come…"

Taking hold of his jacket, the laboratory assistant led him to a corner of the laboratory, where Bunsen piles and galvanoplasty vats were scattered. One of them had unusual dimensions; it was full of a green-tinted liquid in the middle of which one could make out the black form of a human body.

"There he is," murmured Pilesèche, strangled by emotion.

"He's drowned himself!"

"No…he's *metalized* himself."

61

"What do you mean?"

"Like the toad, Monsieur Bémolisant, like the toad!" He shook his arm.

"But he's dead, at any rate?" said the nephew.

"Oh, it's probable. The human species doesn't have a long life, alas."

They both stood there, immobile and mute before the strange spectacle.

Suddenly, Bémolisant, moved by a sudden inspiration, uttered a stifled exclamation. "But my friend, there's something you haven't thought of..."

"What's that?"

"We're going to be accused of having killed him."

"Oh my God! But that's absurd!"

"It's less absurd than supposing a sick man capable of steeping himself in a galvanic bath all on his own. Think about it! No one has seen him for a month; he's been sequestrated. He's found in that state; there's been a violent death. We're the only ones who've been in here; it's us that will be accused. You and me—both of us."

The other was stunned. "You're right," he moaned, wiping his forehead. "What are we going to do, then?"

"I don't know. Perhaps he's left a note, a piece of paper announcing his fatal resolution. That will suffice to get us off the hook..."

"Alas, he's capable of not having done anything, in order to play one last trick on us."

"Let's look anyway."

Their eyes troubled by anguish, they looked everywhere, on the tables and in the drawers.

Nothing.

Suddenly, however, their eyes fell upon the blackboard, which bore the following singular inscription:

READ CAREFULLY:
bfoomgtqkl ovyesqnuesrsngbnljuefrplfyesqn
ugnxglpretkynqitcpsgstknptfzpftifpcfyesk fj
gpbutigoskeneruteexrbpdbvetvangnugtjpsutu
dvipps.

"It's a cryptogram! To mock us one last time for our ignorance. Can you decipher it, at least?" demanded the laboratory assistant.

"Oh, as to that, no."

"Then we're back with the sword of Damocles hanging over our heads."

After a moment of silent meditation, in which their minds were heavy with pitiful thoughts, Bémolisant said, with a somber expression: "Pilesèche, the moment has come for grave decisions."

At that remonstration, the other straightened up, ready for anything.

"It's necessary for the corpse to disappear," the artist concluded, his voice whistling.

"Ah!"

It will disappear; we'll take it away. And later..." His voice attained the extreme limit of tragic falsetto; one might have thought that it was escaping his brain through his cranium. "...Later," he continued, in the stifled tone of a traitor in a melodrama, "well, we'll be able to explain the disappearance. The most urgent thing is to get rid of the evidence."

The two men leaned over the vat. The laboratory assistant opened the tap.

The liquid ran out slowly, and its soft, musical susurrus contrasted strangely with the sinister situation. Gradually, the contours of the body emerged in their black envelope; one might have thought it a statue emerging from the mold, still covered with a layer of powdered oxide.

Unconsciously, as if he were still in the middle of one of his habitual experiments, the laboratory assistant rubbed the cheeks with the palm of his hand, where the metal whitened, polished without difficulty.

"It's nickel," he said, finally.

The body, clad in its metallic pellicle, was holding two nickel cylinders in its hands, attached to the negative pole of the pile.

"He's heavy," murmured Bémolisant, trying to lift him up.

"How are we going to get him out?" asked Pilesèche.

"How, above all, are we going to get him past the concierge without arousing suspicion?"

"Oh, my head's splitting. I'm not made for conspiracies!" He let himself fall on to a chair, his head bowed—but Bémolisant shook him rudely

"Come on, a little nerve, damn it! Are we little girls?"

"You talk about it so casually...I've never been accused of any crime until now."

3. In which the Peregrinations of the Nickel Man begin

An hour later, a cab stopped outside the door of the house and Pilesèche got out, while Bémolisant went through the arch with three day-laborers he had recruited in the Place Maubert.

The concierge was on the threshold of her lodge.

The laboratory assistant made violent efforts to give his face a smiling expression, the muscles taut, and he saluted her. In spite of his determination not to allow his emotion to show, he was frightfully pale, more gauche than ever, his movements feverish and disordered.

"Bonjour, Madame Paponot," he succeeded in saying, in a strangled voice.

"Bonjour, Monsieur Pilesèche," the stout lady replied. "And your M'sieur, how is he?"

"Uh, he's still nearly... you know... it comes and goes."

Bémolisant started up the stairs; the concierge pointed at him, laughing. "That *artiss* in velvet, all hot under the collar, asked me a little while ago whether your invalid had gone out! Poor fellow! It's not the time!"

"Oh no, Madame Paponot, it's really not the time." He added, by way of correction: "The gentleman is a scrap metal merchant."

"Oh—not an *artiss?*"

"No, no, he's a scrap dealer. One can't turn around up there, it's so cluttered—so I said to Monsieur Grillard, what if we were to get rid of all our superfluities?"

"Good God, what are those? You scientists, you have these words..."

"It means our scrap metal, our old stuff—you know."

"Oh, yes...and the poor man agreed? That must be the first time in his life he's ever agreed with someone."

"When one's ill, you know, one becomes more human. But I'm chatting, and my men are already upstairs. *Au revoir*, Madame Paponot, *au revoir*."

Quickly, he ran up the rickety steps in order to catch up with Bémolisant and the porters, whom he let into the laboratory.

Then, showing them the vat, over which he had nailed a lid of planks, he said: "This is it."

One of the men took hold of the long box by one of its corners and tested its weight.

"Damn," he said, letting it fall back. "It's no featherweight."

"Of course not," Bémolisant replied, as tranquilly as he could. "Scrap metal is heavy."

Everyone lent a hand to the task, and the box was finally taken down, with a great deal of difficulty, to the coaching entrance.

Pilesèche had no desire to chat; he went past the lodge rapidly, in a hurried manner—but that did not suit Madame Paponot, who stopped him.

"Hey, M'sieur Pilesèche!" she shouted after him. "A bit of advice—today's Saint Sylvester, as you know. It seems to me that I can't decently avoid going up tomorrow to wish the poor m'sieur a happy new year, like my other tenants..."

No, no!" exclaimed the laboratory assistant, precipitately. "He can't see anyone. That might put him in a bad temper...and strokes can arrive so quickly, you know. Don't worry, I'll give you your present, and you won't have to put yourself out."

The box was loaded; the porters were dismissed.

The coachman leaned over toward his clients, already installed in the vehicle.

"Where are we going, bourgeois?" he asked.

That was a question that Pilesèche had not anticipated. Was it necessary to shout out loud he place that they had chosen as a refuge? They might as well put the police on the track immediately.

64

Fortunately, the artist had anticipated the eventuality, and, putting his head through the window, he shouted an address at the coachman chosen at random. When they reached the Rue des Écoles, however, while the horse continued its rapid trot, he lowered the glass again and, sticking out half his body in order to get closer to the driver, he said to him, without being heard by the passers-by: "I've changed my mind, Coachman—we'll go directly to Avenue Clichy, number..." He pronounced the number so quietly that the coachman could hardly hear it.

When Bémolisant sat down again, he turned to his companion, who was mopping cold sweat from his brow. "The flight is consummated," he said, in a dramatic tone.

The other started. "Are we being pursued?" he said, bewildered.

"Pursued! I certainly hope that nothing will be discovered. It will be as well, moreover, in order that no suspicion arises, if you go back there as usual."

"Oh, I'd never dare! Just think! I'd have to answer the concierge's incessant questions, give her news of the pretended patient, recommence what I did just now, lying impudently. It's beyond my strength."

"Do you want to ruin us, wretch? If you're not seen again, people will become anxious; they'll break down the door; they'll discover everything. It's absolutely necessary to go back...at least until we've found a solution to this inextricable situation. Furthermore, now I think about it, you've forgotten to erase the inscription that will attract all eyes to the blackboard. We've even omitted to copy it."

"What's the point, since we can't decipher it?"

"We're going to dry, damn it! I'm not going to admit defeat. A little energy, Pilesèche."

"I will, I will...I'll go to the laboratory...not today, but tomorrow, when I've recovered somewhat from all this emotion," said Pilesèche, in a tone that contained more resignation than resolution.

After meditating for a while, the artist resumed speaking. "It's no good," he said. "I've thought hard, but everything I've just seen seems strange, and I can't understand how the fellow came to bury himself in that vat. Tell me a little about the premises of the affair, as an examining magistrate might put it."

"Don't talk about examining magistrates! You'll give me the shakes. Anyway, what can I tell you that you don't know? Your uncle had a few manias, but nothing that allowed such a design to be foreseen. He was bad-tempered, not insane. I can only explain his final action by supposing that he wanted to carry out one last experiment on himself. He didn't say anything about it to me. Ill, crippled by pain, he certainly felt that he was on the way out, and it was then that he manifested the desire to see you. You were his nephew and his godson— that's only natural. How could I know that he's planned everything to make you a witness to that sad spectacle?"

"I ought to have mistrusted that abrupt return to good sentiments."

"What else can I tell you? Yesterday, I found him in a bad mood, as usual. I brought him eggs, hoping to make him eat, but he sent me packing, along with my eggs."

"He was obviously not an easy patient."

"He asked me for an electric bath..."

"My God, what's that?"

"It's the bath in which we found him, but instead of a metallic salt susceptible of yielding a galvanoplastic deposit, we normally put in pure water, simply sharpened with a little acid to increase its electrical conductivity."

"Oh, very good! The traitor was preparing the execution of his sinister project."

"Evidently. I'd hardly closed the door, no doubt, than he wrote the cryptogram that intrigued us so much and plunged himself into the bath, after having added nickel sulfate and ammonia."

There's one thing that I can't explain. So long as he was conscious, he wouldn't have been able to plunge completely under the water, where he would have choked—and yet we found him submerged, which would have been indispensable in any case for the deposit to form evenly over his entire body."

"Oh, the explanation is quite simple. Didn't you notice a small reservoir placed above the vat, the liquid from which was discharged through a rubber tube. Your uncle lay down first in such a way that his nostrils were above the surface of the water, and the flow coming from that small reservoir finished covering his face gradually. He would have had to be in the state of special catalepsy that I've mentioned to you by then, but he could put himself into it and he would have prepared himself for a long time by means of his experiments in hypnotism. It was sufficient for him to say to himself: at such a time, *I'll fall into catalepsy*, for phenomenon to be realized by autosuggestion."

"I see now how things must have happened, but that doesn't change our situation. Try telling that to the police commissioner, and he'd laugh in your face. Listen, it's necessary to work out what we're going to do. We'll take the cada...." He stopped and resumed: "...the parcel directly to my studio, but if you run into my wife, don't say anything to her about this adventure. Above all, don't say anything to my mother-in-law. You know how talkative women are; they're easily led by the nose, so that if the police were to interrogate them, I don't know how we'd get out of it."

It was necessary to recruit a few more porters to take the box upstairs.

"It's a bronze statue," Bémolisant told them.

"It doesn't astonish me anymore that it's so heavy," one of them replied.

The studio was situated on the floor above the apartment in which the artist's family lived, so neither Madame Bémolisant nor her mother, Madame Legris, was able to see what was happening in the house.

66

When the two accomplices were alone in the large room in the middle of which the funereal package lay, they let their arms fall alongside their bodies with an enormous sigh of relief.

"Finally," said Bémolisant, "We can breathe."

"It's only a respite, alas. It won't be possible for us to hide Monsieur Grillard's disappearance forever."

"But thanks to our stratagem, at least we have time to think about it."

"Shouldn't we remove his metal envelope?" hazarded the laboratory assistant, "For after all, if he isn't dead..."

"Get away! Now you're believing in this nonsense. It's one thing for toads to wall themselves up without coming to any harm...no, no, don't worry; my uncle is well and truly defunct, and his cadaver is much less troublesome inside its nickel box than otherwise. If we don't succeed in concealing him from all eyes, well, so far as everyone else in concerned, he's a statue, nothing more."

With these reflections, the nickel-plated man was removed from his vat and placed in a corner, lying down in his natural attitude. While Bémolisant searched for a serge curtain in order to hide him to the extent that it was possible, Pilesèche started rubbing the surface of the metal in order to polish it and complete the appearance of a piece of sculpture.

He had only just finished that task when someone knocked on the studio door.

"Perhaps it's the police," one of them whispered, fearfully.

"What if we don't answer?" added the other, equally anxious.

"They'll break down the door. It's better to be bold."

That boldness did not go as far as to calm their nerves, and they were both wearing singular expressions when Bémolisant went to open the door.

4. In which an Influential Critic Intervenes in the Affair

Two men were waiting on the threshold, but the newcomers did not seem to justify so many apprehensions. They were perfect gentlemen, art lovers who had come to visit the studio.

"Baron d'Estrèchini!" exclaimed the artist, recognizing one of them.

"In person. You promised me, my dear, to show me some decadent sculpture. I've come to ask you to keep your promise, and I've brought Antoine Leroux, the influential critic, whom you'll have to suborn...if he'll allow himself to be."

"Ah! Delighted," said Bémolisant, still holding the door ajar. "Positively enchanted, but I don't know if I can let you in. I..."

"What! Perhaps you have a model here at present?"

"Yes, precisely."

"That doesn't matter. All the models know us; we no longer intimidate them." And without paying any further attention to the artist's hesitation, he added: "Go in, Leroux."

"After you, Baron."

"Come, come—no ceremony on the threshold of the sanctuary."

Pilesèche, who had taken off his coat in order to take the nails out of the box, had just picked up a feather duster. He was dusting everything within reach feverishly and indistinctly, without daring to turn round, for fear that his distraught features might betray his emotion.

"It's for this amiable fellow that you were going to turn us away?" queried the Baron, perceiving him.

"Not badly built for a model," added the influential critic, looking him up and down with the eye of a connoisseur. "I haven't seen him around. Good muscles…a little gauche, perhaps, but it's up to the sculptor to rectify the pose.

"Let's see these sculptures—show us!" said the Baron, pivoting on his heel and looking around.

The studio was cluttered with mounts and mock-ups. The two strangers started casually lifting up the damp cloths that were preventing the clay from drying out, but the sight of the masterpieces underneath failed to inspire any enthusiasm in the critic, who pursed his lips in a disapproving grimace that did not augur anything good.

Bémolisant had taken possession of the Baron, and was seeking to impregnate him with the extravagant principles of decadent sculpture.

"The goal of art, Monsieur," he said, "is not merely to give a more or less faithful representation of our fragile terrestrial envelope. If it were, the animal painters, who are obsessed with realism of representation, would be the foremost among us. But art ought to aim higher, and, disengaging the human from that which is animal, ought to seek the soul in its hidden folds, to render it visible, tangible…"

"And sensible," finished the influential critic, in a bantering tone, continuing to ferret around while the sculptor continued his discourse.

Terrified, Pilesèche saw Monsieur Leroux coming closer and closer to the nickel-plated man, over which he had hastily thrown a serge curtain. He would dearly have liked to draw his attention in another direction, but how?

Not without a similar anguish, Bémolisant had seen the critic progressing toward the terrible statue, and although he carried on talking, he had absolutely no idea what he was saying, being uniquely preoccupied with those movements. The Baron lent a sustained attention in vain to the nonsense in question; he could not extract any meaning from the string of words.

Suddenly, the critic, perceiving indistinct forms on the floor, enveloped by a serge curtain, lifted up a corner of the cloth.

Bémolisant could not suppress an exclamation. Pilesèche dropped an old plate, which smashed on the floor.

Antoine Leroux uttered an expressive: "Ah!" and took a step back, raising his lorgnon to his eyes. After a brief contemplation, he came, at a measured pace, to take the artist by the arm, and, smiling enthusiastically, said: "Oh, my dear, that's not good of you...no, it's not good to amuse us with bagatelles and these frightful mock-ups when you're hiding a masterpiece in a corner. But it's quite simply admirable! It's marvelous! Better than that: it's a revolution! Oh, if that's decadent sculpture, I accept it; I acclaim it, and you can count one adept more."

Emotionally, he took hold of both the artist's hands and shook them vigorously. "Come," he said to the Baron, finally. "Come and see this marvel." And, dragging him toward the statue, which was gleaming under its white patina, he said: "Look at that! What vigor! And what simultaneous morbidity! How downcast that man is in his suffering! Nature could never have translated it with that precision of genius. It's hollowed out by an energetic thumb, without weakness." He turned to the poor artist. "It's for a tomb, no doubt?"

"Yes, yes," the latter hastened to reply. "It's for a tomb."

"And you've titled it...?"

"I haven't titled it yet."

"Oh! Don't forget that a good title is halfway to success."

"But I don't have any intention of exhibiting it."

"Yes, I understand: a tomb is an intimate work. But an artist has a duty to himself and his century. A masterpiece is part of the patrimony of humankind. Oh, but you will exhibit it; moreover, I shall begin a campaign in my newspapers, and I promise you a prodigious, colossal, unprecedented success..."

"But I beg you...I'm frightened by the thought of the public paying attention to my humble person."

"Damn! That's the first time I've encountered such modesty combined with such talent. No, no, I shall force your hand. I'll run to book the hall in the Rue de Sèze, and tomorrow morning you'll hear my first beat of the tom-tom..."

A few minutes later, the visitors took their leave, and the influential critic was heard exclaiming, as they went downstairs: "A revolution, my dear, a veritable revolution in art!"

That scene had completely overwhelmed the two accomplices. They no longer knew where they were, if they were dreaming or awake. Events were dragging them away in a desperate whirlwind, and before they had been able to formulate a plan, or even measure the depth of the abyss open before their feet, they had slid into it invincibly, driven by blind fatality.

Who can tell? But for the arrival of those importunate visitors, they might perhaps have collected their scattered wits and found some means of announcing the entirely natural death of the poor uncle. Yes, that was what it had been necessary to do—but there was no more time.

And, on thinking that, everything that they had just done finally appeared to them as the height of absurdity.

It was while they were still in the laboratory that the solution was simple and easy. What they should have done was strip the cadaver of its metallic envelope by carefully dissolving the nickel; then they should have laid the body suitably washed, in the bed. Who, then, would have been astonished to learn of the death of an old man who had been at the end of his resources for a month?

Could the doctor called to issue the death certificate have found any disquieting particularities, even if he had done a complete autopsy? It hardly seemed probable.

So, the two men had been perfect imbeciles. They finally perceived that, too late to repair the damage.

And they looked at one another, desolate.

"My dear Pilesèche!"

"Monsieur Bémolisant!"

"We have to flee."

"Do you think so?"

"I can't, however, allow that man, that cadaver, to be exhibited in public..."

"Eh! How can you do otherwise? If we run away, people will wonder why. Let's not attract investigation in our direction. You see, it's me who's being reasonable now. I can feel my courage coming back; I feel that I'm capable of the boldest designs, and if it's necessary to be bold..."

He was abruptly interrupted; several raps sounded on the door, and in spite of his brilliant attestation of energy, Pilesèche went pale, anxiously seizing his feather duster, while Bémolisant went to open the door, fearfully.

The artist found himself face to face with his wife, who was anxious because he had not come down at the usual time for lunch.

"That's true!" he replied. "I haven't eaten!" He turned to the laboratory assistant. "Are you hungry, Pilesèche?" he added, in a desolate tone.

"I hadn't noticed it."

"Me neither—but it doesn't matter. Would you like to have lunch with us, Pilesèche."

"Ah! If you like." He seemed to be saying: *Are we not indissolubly linked to one another by this complicity in a crime...that we didn't commit? Can one of us act without the other?*

I am not even certain that, in the confusion of his ideas, he had not managed to convince himself that perhaps they were, in fact, guilty, albeit with attenuating circumstances, so great was the obsession pursuing them.

They went down to the floor below, where the Bémolisant studio was situated: a very modest apartment, redolent with the restricted means of its tenants.

Still preceded by Hélène, they went into the dining room, where Madame Legris, the mother-in-law, was already sitting at the laden table, feeding a baby sitting in a high chair.

"Finally, there you are!" she said, through pinched lips, peering at her son-in-law through her spectacles.

That simple sentence was pregnant with storms. Bémolisant bowed his head. It was necessary to reply, though. "Mother-in-law, I can explain..."

"I know that you always have excellent reasons, my son-in-law."

"What do you expect? It's necessary not to treat artists like other men. Art has its demands, to which its high priests must yield..."

"Oh, I've certainly perceived that, since I've had the honor of being the mother-in-law of a high priest of art."

Hélène wanted to cut short a discussion that was threatening to turn bitter, and while Pilesèche hid himself as best he could behind his host, she said: "Maman, Népomucène has an excellent excuse today. You know that he's been to see his poor Uncle Grillard, who is also his godfather."

"Aha! The reconciliation scene! You can tell us all about it..."

Tell them all about it! The two men were in torment.

"How is your uncle?" the pitiless woman continued.

That was certainly a very indiscreet question, to which Bémolisant was not tempted to reply immediately. He went blank. He remembered, just in time, that he had not introduced his companion, and stood aside in order to allow him to appear.

"This is his assistant, Monsieur Pilesèche, whom I introduce to you, and who will be having lunch with us."

"A guest! Oh, Monsieur, excuse us; my son-in-law never has others. He brings us guests without warning—that isn't done! We have the greatest pleasure in receiving you, and we would have been glad to do so in a dignified fashion. You must take account of the unexpectedness..."

She stood up swiftly and ran to the kitchen, where Hélène was already cooking a supplementary omelet.

Pilesèche was confused. He stammered a few excuses, and would have liked to hide in a hole—but Bémolisant forced him to sit down, and a few minutes sufficed to restore good order.

When everyone was at table and had soothed the pangs of a hunger that could wait no longer, Madame Legris returned to the charge.

"Now, give us news of your uncle."

Madame Legris was a plump individual, quite replete, whose moist lips sketched an eternal smile, the expression of which adapted nevertheless to circumstances. When it was a matter of an illness or some other sad subject, that smile became appropriately tearful, and for the moment, it was with an expression of lugubrious compassion that she asked after the health of the uncle—the dear uncle—who, after having treated his nephew rigorously, had suddenly appeared on the horizon with the physiognomy of a good uncle with a legacy to leave.

It seemed, however, that her question was not addressed to anyone. Bémolisant eluded it; Pilesèche was busy cutting up bits of food for the baby.

It was, however, impossible to escape that redoubtable interrogation for long. The good woman took the latter directly to task in his turn.

"You who live in his intimacy, Monsieur Pilesèche, tell us what you're thinking."

"Oh, he's very ill, very ill," replied the laboratory assistant, shaking his head.

"Ah! You fear a fatal outcome, then?"

"I fear so…I certainly fear so," repeated the poor man, at a loss

"To be sure, you see us all deeply affected. Come on, Népomucène, tell Monsieur how affected we are, for after all, he's your uncle. One doesn't lose an uncle without emotion. This one wasn't always good to us, but we practice the forgetfulness of insults."

The good lady paused momentarily on order to let that profession of faith produce its full effect. Then she resumed, in a low voice: "He's rich, isn't he?"

"I believe that he enjoys…that he enjoys a modest ease."

"It's only just that it should remain in the family, and my son-in-law is his only nephew."

"Forgive me, Madame, but there's a niece, at a convent in Fontenay-sous-Bois."

"Oh, that's right! Poor, dear child, now she's alone in the world!" groaned Madame Legris.

"Oh, her uncle wasn't a great resource for her, for he paid very little attention to her."

"We'll go to collect her, pamper her…Népomucène, do you know your cousin?"

"I've only seen her when she was very small, Mother-in-Law."

"Hélène, we're going to go to Fontenay-sous-Bois, aren't we? It's necessary that the child witnesses her uncle's last moments."

"No, no, Mother-in-Law. Let's not get carried away, if you please. My godfather doesn't like anyone forcing his hand, and doesn't want to see anyone he hasn't summoned personally."

"So, Hélène, your wife…"

"My wife, like everyone else, will be obliged to leave him tranquil. I don't suppose, in any case, that that will cause Hélène any mortal chagrin, since she doesn't know him."

"Very well, very well," riposted Madame Legris, slightly piqued. "But if it's not permitted to us to testify our sympathy to the dying man, it's not forbidden for us to take an interest in our cousin, our co-inheritor. She must be bored to death in her convent; we'll go in search of her. She'll live with us, and the regulation of the succession can only be facilitated by good relationships between the heirs."

"But Mother-in-Law, I really don't know why you want to regulate prematurely a succession that isn't open and might well escape us. How do you know what my uncle's testamentary dispositions are?"

"That's right! Come straight out and say that he's disinherited you! So you argued with him? For after all, if he summoned you, is doubtless wasn't with the intention of telling you that he was disinheriting you!"

"I haven't said anything of the sort."

"...On the contrary, it was to be reconciled with you. Come on, have you or have you not been reconciled with your uncle?"

Bémolisant was undergoing torture. That woman, unconsciously, was twisting the knife in the wound. He did not know what to say, and answered obliquely.

"Yes, of course...but does one ever know? Can one ever say? I'm not at odds with my uncle, but..."

"Well, then," Madame Legris concluded, "let's be tranquil. We'll act as we please. You have no understanding of sentimental matters."

In response to that apothegm, to which there was no answer, Bémolisant thought it best to lower the flag, and he finished lunch with his nose in his plate.

5. A Revolution in Art

All Paris invaded the gallery in the Rue de Sèze, where the Hungarian painter Shaparazzy was exhibiting his works. But it was not exclusively the paintings of the celebrated artist that attracted the elegant and select crowd of première patrons.

Everyone was rushing, in fact, to see—finally—the statue whose praises the entire press was singing, with a great reinforcement of hyperbole, and a great clash of cymbals.

Only one discordant note had been struck within the concert, by the journal *Art classique*—but the tendencies of that specialist periodical being well-known, that very criticism was a certificate of modernity that had to add further advantage to the magisterial work, exhibited thanks to the care of the valiant critic Antoine Leroux.

The latter had set his heart on assuring its success, and, while one scarcely caught a glimpse of the sculptor—this Bémolisant whose name had been unknown yesterday—the journalist multiplied his efforts as if it were a matter of personal importance. It is true that he drew a profit from it that was no less effective for being indirect, for his name was, on this occasion, pronounced at least as often as that of the artist.

The newspapers waxed lyrical in his regard. One read comments such as: "The savant critic whose marvelous flair has been able to discover a modern Praxiteles..." or "We owe to the illustrious critic the opportunity finally to admire, etc..." or "With an abnegation and a disinterest that does him honor, the eminent Antoine Leroux had sworn to reveal this neglected talent to the artistic world; he has kept his word..."

In brief, there was around his name an honest acclaim to which he was not at all averse.

On the day when the Exhibition opened, he never quit the room where the nickel statue had been placed, lying on a pedestal covered in red velvet, in the middle of the principal gallery.

And it was, in fact, a strange and magisterial work, that metal statue representing a man who was tensed as if in the final coma of his agony: the features emaciated by suffering, the skeleton jutting forth beneath the skin, the breast hollowed out by a spasm, the hands clutching two short metal cylinders of which, to be sure, no one could quite explain the significance, and the eyes, finally, wide open to the horrors of surging death.

The lovers of prettiness in art had no need to go to that exhibition, but those in search of eternal verity, those whose souls were open to all pity, shivered as they approached that moribund, and felt their hearts squeezed by a dolorous grip.

Antoine Leroux went from group to group, explaining, provoking enthusiasm that never seemed sufficiently spontaneous.

It was a triumph, a stunning triumph. For a week, the newspapers resounded with the name of Népomucène Bémolisant. People were astonished that they had not heard mention of him before, and a few critics occasionally hinted that the artist in question resembled many others who had found a work in a stroke of luck and had emptied themselves in that single effort—one work, and one alone—with no yesterday and no tomorrow. For Bémolisant, who suddenly appeared like a meteor, had produced nothing until then; it was quite possible that his fortune would be exhausted in that flash of genius.

Those prophets of ill-omen, however, were clamoring in the desert—or, to put it more accurately, their voices were drowned out by the concert of enthusiasm and admiration.

Even the government seemed excited, as if by the advent of a Messiah. What! A master had been born, and did not bear the official stamp! What use, then, was the École? What was the point of the Grand Prix? They did not go so far, however, as to hold it against him that he had no attachment, and the director of the Beaux-Arts was already skillfully feeling out the critic and the sculptor, in order to acquire the work for the State.

Monsieur Bémolisant, at the first mention of that, seemed to jump out of his skin. It was as if someone had made a monstrous suggestion. The statue was not for sake; it was destined to ornament a tomb—the tomb of Monsieur X, as the label said.

Who could that Monsieur X be, whose family had commissioned a statue stark naked and in such a state of morbid emaciation?

We are usually pleased to ornament our deceased, to idealize them, to drape them in ample folds in a noble attitude; and the public found the nudity of the dying man a trifle bizarre for the coronation of his tomb. It was admirable as a work of art, but it was absurd when one thought of its destination.

From there to making up stories about that mysterious and eccentric family it was only a short step, and that served to defray the curiosity of the public, as well as filling the columns of newspapers.

The artist's studio was besieged by reporters, to whom he replied as best he could—which is to say, with the first thing that came into his head. By dint of explaining to them his conception of art and the secret thoughts that had led him to conceive that superb work, he ended up taking himself seriously in his role as a reformer, and perhaps ended up believing that he really was the author of the statue—but a cold shower brought him abruptly back to a sense of reality

That irresistible and chilly disillusionment was inflicted upon him by a journalist at bay, Jean Saure, well known for the elegant fashion he had of being indiscreet.

The reporter had forced his door, notebook in one hand, pencil in the other, and without wasting any time, interrogated him. Between the questions and in the course of the interview he let the latest gossip escape.

"Oh, by the way, dear Master," he put in, "in spite of the mystery you've tried to suspend over your statue, we've now finally identified the original that it represents/"

"What! How?"

"Yesterday, in a group of people who had come to see the work and were discussing its anatomical perfection, Doctor Delcourtil suddenly cried out, on seeing it: 'But if I'm not mistaken, it's the image of Népomucène Grillard!'"

"Ah!" groaned Bémolisant, who felt faint.

"Monsieur Grillard might have lived as a misanthrope and hardly ever shown himself, but he's sufficiently well known in the scientific world; a few academicians were summoned, who recognized him immediately. This evening's newspapers will be very well documented on the subject. But everyone is crying; 'But the man isn't dead yet; how has Monsieur Bémolisant dared to exhibit his statue...a statue that represents him struggling in his death throes?'"

"That's precisely where the mystery, the enigma begins," Bémolisant stammered, for the sake of saying something.

"That enigma you're going to help me clarify. I promise you a leading article in my paper. You'll never have had such acclaim, such a magnificent success."

"No, no...I beg you...no publicity; I'm the enemy of fame. It offends my most intimate family sentiments. Look, I'll buy your silence with a confidence..."

"Ah! Now you're talking!"

"But swear to me that you'll keep what I'm going to tell you to yourself."

"Word of a reporter!" said Jean Saure, with an enigmatic smile.

"Well, know then that Monsieur Grillard is my uncle. He's very ill...perhaps he's dead at this moment. I wanted to retain his features such as they appeared to me in that supreme illness, to erect a monument worthy of him, to make him, in his final hour, the supreme homage of my talent."

"That's a whole novel in outline. I understand everything: your reluctance to exhibit, your hesitations, which Antoine Leroux only vanquished by trickery, your persistent silence regarding the original of the statue. Perfect, perfect... I'll run along...I don't want to know any more. I'm expected at the paper. It's necessary that the public know your great soul, and finally appreciate you..."

"No, no, I implore you. You swore to me to keep silent..."

"And you reminded me of my oath: thank you!" said the reporter, making his escape before the artist was able to stop him.

Bémolisant was furious. He sensed a vague danger suspended over his head. Without knowing in what form the danger would fall upon him, he was invaded by an extreme anxiety.

No matter; it was the day that his exhibition closed; he was about to regain possession of his work and finally remove it from indiscreet curiosity. It was about to change domicile and be lost to sight. He hoped that, as one fad follows another, Paris would soon forget him in favor of some new attraction at the zoological gardens or the winter circus.

When evening came, therefore, he went to the Rue de Sèze in order to reclaim his statue and regulate his account. The entrance fees had produced a considerable sum, and his share of that celestial manna was rather tidy.

He stuffed the bills and gold coins into his pockets, pinching himself in order to convince himself of the reality of the windfall.

The statue had been carefully packed. In front of the gallery it was hoisted on to a fiacre that was waiting at the door. Bémolisant was about to climb into the cab himself and leave when a man hurtled toward him, shoved him into the fiacre, leapt in after him, closed the door and, leaning out of the lowered window, shouted at the coachman urgently: "To the Gare de Lyon!"

That man was Pilesèche.

Pilesèche, pale and wan, his features distressed, trembling with fear.

Seizing the artist by the arm, sticking his lips to his ear, he whispered, in a voice so distraught that the other started, gripped by the contagion of that fear: "The police are on our heels."

"Wretch! What's happened, then?" he demanded.

"Oh, let me pull myself together first."

He made use of his moustache to fan himself, although it was a cold January day, as breathless as if he had run all the way across Paris.

Finally, reassembling his courage and his idea, he said: "I've just been to the house."

"On the Montagne Sainte-Geneviève?"

"Yes. It's on fire. It's a furnace. There were firemen blocking the street. The steam-pumps were launching torrents of water, but to no avail. The flames were spurting out of the windows, crackling, with black and acrid smoke. It was horrible. And in the middle of it I saw a police commissioner wearing his sash and giving out orders. Madame Paponot came out to talk to him, and raised her arms toward the skies. I wondered if I ought to go up, but quickly reckoned that it was better to keep quiet. That suits my character better—and besides, the fire might have helped us, in sum, by permitting it to be supposed that my poor employer had perished in the flames."

"You're right," opined the artist, "and it's all for the best."

"What, all for the best! But listen—that's not all...unfortunately. I found myself in the midst of people of the neighborhood, who were too occupied watching the fire to recognize me. They were talking about the cause of the disaster. One said that it had begun in the distiller's cellar, the other that it had started under the eaves. 'In any case,' he added, as soon as Madame Paponot perceived it, she immediately thought about the gentleman who's ill that nobody ever sees him. Perhaps it's him, she said, who started the fire. A sick person, you see—that can happen...especially if there's no one looking after him'

"At that moment Madame Paponot was with the commissioner, gesticulating as if she were demanding something of him. Then the commissioner turns to the firemen. 'Hey,' he said, in a loud voice, there's a man in the mansards who's ill and disabled. Is anyone willing to go up and find him?'

"Two or three firemen run forward shouting: 'Me! Me!' They set up the telescopic ladder, which goes up all the way to the fourth. A fireman jumps on to it and goes up it like a cat; he staves in the window-frame of the laboratory, whose panes have already exploded, and disappears into the furnace. The crowd utter a cry of admiration and terror...he finally reappears, alone..."

"Naturally!"

"Then there's an immense cry of disappointment. 'He hasn't got him!' But he, to reassure them, shouts in his turn from the top of the ladder: 'There's no one there!' He comes back down, rapidly. The commissioner is waiting, and questions him. The fireman reports that he's explored the apartment and couldn't find the old man.

"The commissioner shakes his head and is thinking about it, without saying anything, when I hear murmurs in the crowd: 'It's odd, all the same, a man on his death-bed taking off like that on the very day of the fire. There's a mystery in this, for sure... a mystery such as Richebourg[11] never invented, and the police will stick their noses in, have no fear...'

"Those words, you see, Monsieur Bémolisant, are engraved in my brain. I saw everything spinning; I nearly fainted, and I ran away as fast as my legs

---

[11] The enormously popular but now forgotten *feuilletoniste* Émile Richebourg (1833-1898)

could carry me. How did I get here? I don't know, for I was running without a goal. Instinctively, I looked for you, and I'm more tranquil now that I've found you."

"But what do you expect us to do?" groaned the artist.

"We have to flee..."

"Flee where? They'd catch us at the frontier. Why take me to the Gare de Lyon?

"To go to Switzerland."

"Fool—we'd be arrested there and extradited without further ado."

"Damn! Let's go to the station anyway; we'll leave the cab there, to put the police off the track. Oh, I'm becoming artful! On the way, we'll think of a means of getting away."

The vehicle was still moving. Finally, it piled up outside the station. The coachman hailed porters, who unloaded the heavy package and put it on a station trolley, not without commenting on the considerable weight of the oddly-shaped box.

The travelers seemed very hesitant about the destination to which they wanted it to go. In the end, they decided to deposit it in the left luggage office; it was a temporary solution, which had no other advantage than giving them time to sort things out—but it was all very well to step back from the edge of the ditch; eventually, they would have to jump it.

Presumably, inspiration came to them, for, half an hour later, Bémolisant came back on his own, drawing a little handcart that he had hired, leaving a ten-franc deposit as guarantee. He took the statue out of the left luggage office and after having it loaded on to his vehicle, he set off in the direction of the Seine.

On the Boulevard Diderot, Pilesèche rejoined him, darting anxious glances to the left and right, and the two of them were swallowed up by the crowd...

6. *A* Fin-de-Siècle *Detective*

Monsieur Rosamour was smoking a cigar by the fireside. Sunk in a softly-padded armchair, his feet crossed in the American fashion on the marble mantelpiece, Rosamour abandoned himself to the pleasure of daydreaming. He liked that quiet idleness in a cozy apartment, where his artistic temperament had assembled a few paintings and costly trinkets. His gaze wandered from one to another, and life appeared to him in its brightest colors.

Rosamour did not, however, spend all his time doing nothing. He had a métier, or, let us rather say, a profession. He was a detective: a *fin-de-siècle* detective who had broken the mold of the police of old. He was an accomplished gentleman, correctly dressed, clean shaven, perfectly polished and susceptible of cutting a brilliant figure in any society.

His colleagues at the Rue de Jérusalem[12] regarded him with a disdain pierced with a certain jealousy, because, without having the air of being up to much, he had had a few successful cases at the outset of his career, and had treated them with means so unexpected that they wondered whether the young puppy was not about to turn the old methods upside-down—which caused the hairs of the old conservatives of the Sûreté stand on end.

He claimed to be inaugurating the new type of the scientific detective.

"Modern science," he said, when he let himself go in telling the story of his vocation, "has put within our range resources still unutilized, in which it is sufficient to draw with full hands. Unfortunately, the ordinary run of policemen, ingenious and adroit as they are presumed to be, are notoriously insufficient in their education. Personally, I'm a Doctor of Science and a laureate of the Institute. When I reached the age to choose a profession, I said to myself: *What scientific career is as yet unexploited?* And I perceived a lacuna in the police: that was my opportunity.

"Certainly, my honorable colleagues have been able to take advantage of the most obvious conquests of science—railways, the telegraph and the telephone—but science intervenes in many other aspects of our lives every day, and for someone who knows it thoroughly, it is a torch, a sure guide, which it is necessary not to abandon for a single instant. In a general manner, and above all, what I want to introduce into my police research, is the scientific method, and to that end I've worked hard; the study of the masters has permitted me to glimpse the rules of what I might call the great strategy of the art.

"Those rules, which were instinctive to them and which they applied, so to speak, without being aware of it, I claim to have classified in my mind, and I march almost with a sure step along the way, leaning on the experience of the ancients, served by modern scientific methods. No more empiricism: experimental logic! According to the case, I can apply the methods of any of my illustrious predecessors...at least to the extent that our physical means permit me to. Before acting, I always ask myself: what would Vidocq, Lecoq, Macé or Goron have done? And then: what should I, Rosamour, do?"

Was not the young *fin-de-siècle* detective still a trifle lacking in the manner explaining his sound principles?

He even claimed not to limit the scope of his method to classical science, and was not reluctant to seek help from the occult sciences, or those reputed as such—I mean hypnotism and induced sleep, whether he utilized the clairvoyance of extra-lucid mediums or sought to hypnotize suspects himself.

In vino veritas, says the adage, and some people are not far from admitting that it is just as easy to get the truth out of a somnambulist as a drunkard.

One could argue about that endlessly, and sustain that the aforesaid subject is not as unconscious as one would like to believe; that he takes a malign pleas-

---

[12] The then-headquarters of the French Sûreté.

ure in parading his medium and his audience through a heap of extravagant stories, and that in the end, especially when his interests are at stake, he will resist suggestions and indiscreet questions with all his might. To that Rosamour replied that nothing is absolute, but, even supposing that hypnotized subject does not always tell the whole truth, it is incontestable that he is not in entire possession of himself, and betrays himself all the more easily by his reticences or his contradictions.

What does a policeman require? A presumption, a clue, a guiding thread, a word let slip that puts him on the track, ready to check the indications given severely and subsequently find their material verification.

A judgment based on revelations acquired in that state, either from the guilty person or a third party, would doubtless be iniquitous, but is it still bad when one only seeks within the revelations a means of investigation?

For our part, we cannot say and almost dare say that the method will only ever prove its worth by the manner of its application.

As for Monsieur Rosamour, he was convinced that he applied it with the greatest prudence, and we have no reason to contest the high opinion that he had of himself.

These delicate problems, where the very essence of our psychic nature—to use the language of initiates—is at stake, without science having succeeded in grasping the link that attaches it to the corporeal world, are attractive by virtue of the marvelous that surrounds them and the element of the unknown that is inseparable from them.

So, Rosamour was in the meditative attitude appropriate to an individual haunted by such grave thoughts. He was smoking his cigar and could, by reaching out his hand, pick up a little book from a table, in which his paper-knife marked the page that he had begun.

It was not a work by just anyone; the book treated the subject of the divining rod and was signed Chevreuil.[13] Such a name guaranteed the value of the contents.

And Rosamour was thinking about what he had just read.

As everyone knows, a divining rod is a forked stick, a simple hazel rod, which water-diviners—which is to say, those who make a particular specialty of detecting subterranean watercourses—hold out in front of them. At the moment when they are directly over the spring, the rod becomes active and bends, twisting the hand, thus indicating the precise spot in which it is necessary to dig.

---

[13] The well-known painter and occultist Léon Chevreuil (1852-1939) had not yet built a reputation as a popularizer of occult science in 1890, when this scene is set, and the subsequent reference to "his day" suggests that the intended reference might be to the perfumer Étienne Chevreuil, who had a strong interest in spiritism and associated subjects, but does not appear to have published any books on the subject.

If the explanation is difficult, the fact is undeniable, and attested by people worthy of trust. The majority of scientists no longer refuse to admit it nowadays, while surrounding it with reticences and circumlocutions tending to protect the infallibility of science.

But if the divining rod is capable of indicating springs, might it not be applicable to other searches? That is what one is tempted to ask. Examples abound of people who have sought to discover, by that means, hidden metals, buried treasures, even criminals...

Ah! That was what interested our policeman most keenly, and a medium enjoying a certain reputation had been pestering him for some time with offers of service, assuring him that he enjoyed that precious faculty. Rosamour was seeking to enlighten his religion by rereading Chevreuil's treatise.

In truth, there were fors and againsts in the book, which dated from a era when it had appeared revolutionary to discuss such "nonsense," as people said, and although the illustrious scientist seemed to admit the results obtained with the rod in the search for springs, he was evidently a great deal more skeptical with regard to treasures and criminals found by that means. The repeated failure of a large number of experiments was bound to give him reason for doubt.

In brief, the conclusion of the work was, firstly, that in no case was there any direct action of the object sought on the rod; if the latter moved, it was because of an unconscious action on the part of the men; and secondly, that the rod turned, most frequently, when the operator believed that it ought to turn—which is to say, at the moment when, for one reason or another, the operator was convinced that he was above the object sought.

Right, Rosamour said to himself. *I can admit that the rod is only the tangible sign of the phenomenon, but that it's the man himself, without being aware of it, on whom the presence of the water, when it's a matter of a spring, exerts its action. Which Chevreuil had difficulty understanding, because, in his day, the study of the psychic phenomena that are approached so boldly today, and seem less extraordinary, had not been carried out in depth. When one sees the hyperexcitability of the senses that can be obtained in certain subjects in the various phases of the second life, can one not admit that, by autosuggestion, one can succeed in acquiring a kind of flair, a particular and exceptional lucidity?*

The skeptics cry: "What are you telling us, with your rod? That the instrument that discovers water today by undergoing disorderly movements above a spring will, if you ask it for old tomorrow, cease turning when it passes over a subterranean aqueduct in order to agitate over a treasure? That's too obliging."

But that's the confirmation of the theory, Rosamour continued, *for that flair, suddenly awakened, goes toward the object of the autosuggestion, not toward others. Why, then, should one not succeed in also following, using the same means, the tracks of criminals/ Not everyone will be up to it, but it's sufficient for it to be possible, and that there are special constitutions capable of acquiring the necessary flair.*

And Rosamour picked up the book again in order to reread the instructive and quasi-marvelous story of the water-diviner Jacques Aymard, who had pursued murderers by that means in Lyon, and had put his hand on the real guilty parties.[14]

As if to provide a counterweight to that story, so clear, it had to be admitted that subsequent attempts made by the same operator had been completely fruitless, but it was necessary to take account of the fact that the circumstances were not the same. It had been suddenly announced to him that a crime had been committed in the street, and, full of confidence in his power, the diviner, who had not reasoned as we have just done, proclaimed loudly that he would find the guilty parties, but it seemed that he lacked a point of departure; he wandered at random, and ended up in places where the murderer could not be.

Rosamour smiled; those results did not appear to him as contradictory as people said, and he thought he could explain them simply.

"To follow a trail," he said, "one needs to be holding one of the ends. Can a dog find an object that is unfamiliar, without having got the scent in advance? In the case of the murder in Lyon, which gave him his success, Jacques Aymard had gone down into the cellar where the crime had been committed. In that circumscribed space he had been put, so to speak, virtually in the presence of the murderers, who had left something of themselves there—their spoor, if you like. He had the trail.

"On the contrary, a crime is committed in a street, at an indeterminate spot; he murder has merely passed by; what permits his trail to be distinguished from those of other passers-by. In those circumstances, Aymard could not find the murderer, because he had absolutely no idea who he was pursuing, and was not impregnated, so to speak, by the personality of that particular individual."

And the policeman drew from all that the conviction the water-diviners— to leave them that name—are capable of discovering any object or person, but that it is necessary to put them in preliminary contact with the object or person in question.

He was, therefore, in no doubt that the practice in question, so singular at first glance, might render great service in certain criminal cases, and he promised himself that he would use that precious means of investigation advantageously when the opportunity presented itself, with a set of favorable circumstances.

He was at that point in his reflections when a whistle-blast summoned him to the telephone that he had taken care to install above his work-table.

The head of the Sûreté ordered him to put himself without delay at the disposal of the police commissioner at the Panthéon.

---

[14] The anecdote about Jacques Aymard's attempt to transfer his supposed water-diving skills to the detection of a murder in Lyon, at the end of the 17th century, is reported in numerous 19th century texts.

As soon as he had changed clothes, our man was on his way.

As you will have guessed, the mystery whose discovery the fire in the Rue de la Montagne had permitted was not unconnected with the abrupt summons that had torn Monsieur Rosamour away from his studies in cerebral physiology, to plunge him into the midst of the positive operations of his profession.

7. On Induction in Criminal Matters

Madame Paponot, the concierge of the burned building, had been singularly disturbed on hearing the cry of "Fire!" resounding in the stairwell.

She was dozing lightly, plunged in her big armchair, wrapped up next to the purring stove.

Suddenly, at that cry, she had found herself on her feet, eyes open, prey to a tremor that she had, however, succeeded in quelling very rapidly, in order to go and see where the fire was.

Already, all the way up the staircase, there was a frightful racket of doors opening and people running down, uttering screams of fear, interjections, appeals for help and lamentations.

A neighbor, possessed of a clearer head, ran to the nearest fire alarm, while someone else closed the gas taps and the tenants began throwing their furniture and bedding out of the windows.

The firemen arrived quickly, moreover; the steam-pumps were set up and launched their sprays at the blaze. The flames had already invaded the stairwell, however; it was necessary to let the fire go and preserve the neighboring houses.

The tenants had been able to get out in time, but the disaster had been so rapid that most of them had been able to save very little by way of possessions.

It was necessary to consider it fortunate that there was no personal injury to deplore—for, all things considered, the disappearance of Monsieur Grillard definitely seemed to be anterior to the conflagration.

That disappearance was nonetheless singularly intriguing to the police commissioner who was conducting the investigation into the cause of the fire. What could have become of the bizarre tenant whom all the witnesses declared to be incapable of quitting his bed? That was what the magistrate asked himself, and which he tried to clarify by means of a confused interrogation, to which Madame Paponot brought her customary volubility.

The excellent woman explained to him with expressive gestures and an infinity of details that she had not seen her tenant with her own eyes for six weeks. She had been told that he was ill, but she could not affirm herself that he was not in any fit state to leave his room. She had been told, however, that he never left his bed, and that same morning..."

"Who told you that?" the commissioner put in, impatiently.

"Monsieur Pilesèche, of course. His helper...what do you call it? His laboratory assistant."

"And where is this laboratory assistant?"

"At home, no doubt. He only comes twice a day to see his boss, give him what he needs and do a little housework. Hold on, though," the doorkeeper remarked, as if struck by a flash of enlightenment, "in fact, I haven't seen him since the day before yesterday."

"Aha!" said the commissioner, and with pressing the point any further, added: "Which physician visited your tenant?"

"He detested them all equally and didn't want to see any of them."

"So there was no one but this Pilesèche who went into his room?"

"I believe so. Monsieur Grillard is something of a boor, and it wasn't a good idea to knock on his door. I, who am speaking to you, Monsieur le Commissaire, even though I'm the concierge of the house, I said: *That's no reason to let someone die like that without help*, but every time I said to Monsieur Pilesèche: *I'll go see to your boss now and again, and take him some soup*—and I'm famous for that, you know, I'm praised for it—Monsieur Pilesèche replied to me: 'Oh, Madame Paponot, you know Monsieur Grillard; how can you think of going to disturb him? It'll put him in a terrible temper, and you'll be the cause of him having a fit.' You understand, me, I'm a good woman at heart, although a trifle abrupt at first sight, and I wouldn't have wanted any harm to come to that poor man, so I stayed on my stairs, without daring to knock at the door."

"And that never seemed singular to you?"

"In truth, now that you mention it, it does seem slightly shady, but what do you expect. I'm a concierge, I'm not here to spy on the tenants."

The commissioner allowed her to launch into a long speech on the duties of her estate; he reflected, and searched among those elements of information for the conductive thread, which escaped him.

The first hypothesis that he examined was that the invalid, seeing himself suddenly threatened by the fire, had made a supreme effort and had succeeded in reaching the staircase, where he had been suddenly enveloped by the flames. Although it was important not to neglect that supposition, however, it nevertheless ran into implausibility at several points.

On the other hand, was it not necessary to see a singular coincidence between the disappearance of the old man and the fire breaking out suddenly with extreme violence?

Could he have started the fire himself in a fit of delirium, and escaped via the rooftops? That was impossible, in his condition, and by dint of reflection, the commissioner found a combination of facts that suggested something quite different.

No one had seen the scientist for six weeks; his laboratory assistant took care to ward off any unwelcome visit. And what was that laboratory assistant? A menial employee, come down in the world, who, after completing his studies, had never found the energy necessary to get out of his rut and quit the bohemian life into which he had lapsed.

84

Was it impossible, given those data, to reconstruct the drama? First there had been a sequestration. The shameless bohemian had doubtless wanted to obtain from his ailing master that he should become his heir, or something analogous—there was no shortage of motives; that was for the examining magistrate to determine in a more precise fashion. The other had resisted. In a final scene of quarrel and struggle, the exasperated assistant had seen red and killed him. Suddenly, faced with his crime, he had been seized by a sudden terror; what should he do now? How could he avoid indiscreet questions?

He had hidden the body, and had started the fire in order to destroy the all the traces of the crime.

Was that not a logical deduction of the entire sequence of events? Was it not a succinct summary of a criminal history such as one encounters every day—a banal history, in truth, for the criminal had not any particularly ingenious imagination in deflecting suspicion.

But was the story, in fact, so banal?

Were there not, in those various facts, disconcerting circumstances, mysterious points well worthy of intelligent research by a policeman devoted to his métier?

That was the road followed by the commissioner's thoughts; he smiled at the hope that such an investigation, well-handled and expertly deduced, would do him honor.

To be sure, he did not want to bring the Sûreté into the affair, wanting all the merit for himself, but he did not have any agent on his staff clever enough and capable of carrying out the delicate research that it would be necessary to undertake. It was therefore necessary to resign himself to telephoning the Prefecture of Police in order that a sleuth could be put at his disposal. That was what he did.

Then, after taking time out to regulate another affair and give his orders, the magistrate picked up his hat and got ready to go out for lunch.

On the threshold of his office, he found himself face to face with a very correctly-dressed young man who greeted him ingenuously.

The newcomer might have been thirty; he was a fairly handsome fellow, with a pink and youthful face ornamented by a blond moustache over the full red lips of an amiable philosopher. Beneath semicircular eyebrows, with gave him a slightly naïve expression, gray eyes devoid of any gleam hid behind the shiny lenses of a myopic's lorgnon. Nothing about him attracted attention—not even his costume, which was no less banal for being correct. He was a dull or neutral individual.

He bowed, with an unpretentious smile; then, in a bland and colorless voice, he said: "I've come to place myself under your orders, Commissioner."

The magistrate considered him briefly, trying to put a name to the inoffensive face.

"Why, of course," he said, finally. "It's Monsieur Rosamour. I confess that I didn't recognize you."

"Which proves," said the young man, with an imperceptible hint of satisfaction, "that it's not necessary, in order to put on a disguise, to employ make-up outrageously, as some of my colleagues do. You know my principles: disguises are never very difficult to penetrate; a cunning malefactor who knows that he's being watched never lets himself be taken in. False beard, false wig: there's always a point at which the artifice can be pierced."

"I know that; it's not for nothing that they call you the scientific detective."

"And I'm proud of meriting that appellation."

"Well then, we're going to understand one another perfectly. Come with me, and I'll explain what it's about on the way."

Like a man who can manage his effects, the commissioner recounted the story of the previous day's fire, the mysterious disappearance of the aged tenant, and the sequestration of which he had evidently been the object. He set out, piece by piece, the scaffolding of his hypotheses, and deduced with great logical force the charges that weighed upon the scientist's laboratory assistant."

"And you've mounted a search for this laboratory assistant?" Rosamour put in, toying negligently with his cane.

"Immediately," the magistrate relied, "And if my agents can put their hands on him, they'll bring him to me and put him under lock and key without further ado."

"I advise you not to do that."

"Why not?" replied the other, nonplussed.

"It's obvious. He can be questioned, and will be, but it would be premature to arrest him or make him aware of the suspicions that are weighing upon him. Thus far, for what can he be reproached? Have you seen the *corpus delicti*—the cadaver? Where is the man who has disappeared? Perhaps his disappearance can be explained quite naturally. The laboratory assistant will reply to you, like Cain: 'Am I his keeper? I left him yesterday, as usual; he was in bed. If he's disappeared, it's without my knowledge. You want to hold me responsible, but have you any proof that I had anything to do with it? First, find the fellow, dead or alive.'"

"You believe he's innocent, then?"

"Me? Not at all. I don't believe anything. I examine the situation; I feel out the terrain, and I say to you: remember the Gouffé affair.[15] A man and a woman kill a bailiff and get rid of the body. Heavy charges are laid against them; people are sure—morally certain—of their guilt, but the investigation is absolutely par-

---

[15] The trial of Michel Eyraud and Gabrielle Bompard for the murder of Toussaint Gouffé in February 1891 was one of the great *causes célèbres* of the period, and the memory would have been very fresh when this scene is supposedly set.

alyzed because there isn't a cadaver. The trunk in which the victim was enclosed turns up, and things change their aspect completely. Are we not in the presence of a similar case? What we need to discover is the man who has disappeared."

"I agree with you, but my conviction is that we'll only find him by following the trail of his laboratory assistant. Monsieur Grillard, you see, wasn't…"

"Monsieur Grillard?" the policeman interjected. "Did you say Monsieur Grillard?" He pulled a newspaper out of his pocket. "Perfect: here's an item of information concerning him."

Unfolding a copy of *Le Petit Journal*, he pointed out an article to the commissioner.

Finally, we have been able to penetrate a part of the mystery enveloping Monsieur Népomucène's masterpiece. The magnificent statue that All Paris has been admiring in Georges Petit's gallery is destined for the tomb of Monsieur Grillard, the uncle and godfather of the eminent artist, who wanted to render him the filial homage of his talent. His idea was perhaps a trifle bizarre, and not everyone will understand how it was possible to represent the image of a man still alive—although very ill, it seems—in the last spasms of mortal agony. Although it is always legitimate for genius to seize nature in the raw, there is in this circumstance a lack of good taste on which it is not appropriate for us to dwell.

"There, it seems to me," observed the commissioner, rubbing his hands, "is an incident that might help us in our research. It's necessary to find this sculptor, and I have no doubt that we shall obtain precious information through that channel."

"I'm convinced of it, as if you care to give me *carte blanche*, I believe I shall be able to bring you an abundant harvest of information in a matter of hours."

They had just reached the commissioner's domicile when a secretary, running after him, announced that Pilesèche had not been found at his habitual lodging and that it had been impossible to discover what had become of him.

Monsieur Rosamour took some notes, wrote down a few names and addresses, and, hot on the trail, set forth at a rapid pace.

It did not take him long to collect the information that seemed to him to be the most urgent, and a few hours later, getting down from a carriage at the commissioner's door, he hastened to the policeman's study.

"Am I on time?" he asked.

"You're punctuality itself," the other replied. "We'll see if you're equally precise in person. Sit down and tell me the result of your investigations."

"First of all, no *person*, if you please."

"Aha! The scientific method!"

87

"Exactly. Pilesèche, thirty-three years old, a pauper, unsuccessful, whose timidity and gaucherie have always prevented him from mounting to anything. Not in need."

"Eh? Appetite coming and going, one isn't astonished to discover one day, in hidden recesses, needs that one didn't suspect."

"I understand; we'll see about that later. Second individual: Bémolisant, something of crackpot, started out making music; quarreled with his uncle, who didn't like the arts and didn't encourage them. Our artist wanted to renew the methods of music, cursed his contemporaries for not understanding him, and, shaking the dust of old Europe off his boots, went to Tonkin to look for more naïve enthusiasts among primitive peoples. In the midst of hair-raising adventures—if they're true—made the acquaintance a widow named Legris, whose daughter he married. Music continuing not to pay, the handsome Népomucène—for he's a good-looking chap—set up as a vermouth merchant in Haiphong. Returned to France as soon as he'd amassed some small savings, and, returning to the arts, took up sculpture. Suddenly revealed himself by the statue representing his dying uncle.

"In that regard, I don't know for sure as yet whether he was reconciled with Monsieur Grillard, but doesn't that seem to you to be quite probable? That statue isn't a work that one makes up; it's evidently made from nature. He's seen his model; it's even necessary to admit that he's seen him often, which contradicts the concierge's declaration that no one went up to see the old scientist. That's one of the points I have to investigate, and perhaps I'll succeed in elucidating it. As for the artist, unfortunately, I did see him, because..."

The commissioner pursed his lips and said to himself, privately, that it was hardly worth the trouble of posing as a champion of new methods in order to bring in such a poor harvest. This was lyricism, not information; anybody could have done it better. He thought, however, that he ought to encourage the young policeman.

"Well," he said, "you haven't been wasting our time, but we still have a lot to do."

"Wait a moment—I haven't finished."

"Ah! Let's have it..."

"Such was the fashion in which my characters were described to me, and by way of conclusion, they don't seem cut from the cloth of great criminals. They aren't equipped to hurt a fly."

"Beware of angry sheep."

"I understand that, and I'll be wary of taking any premature consequence from such vague premises. We're in the presence of individuals in whom there is no predisposition to crime, and it we were able to examine their heads we doubtless wouldn't find the superb atrophies that are the evident marks of criminal instincts. Nevertheless, one circumstance is sufficient to lead even the mildest of men to crime: poverty, anger, momentary madness. If the investigation of an affair weren't made up of a thousand contradictory elements, police work would be banal. To arrive at the motives that have enraged our sheep, however, it's nevertheless necessary to know their primitive character precisely: that's done."

"Yes, my friend, but we're no further forward now than before.

"Wait! Let me tell you one item of news—a very important item..."

"Ah! Finally."

"Do you know why I can't put my hand on Monsieur Bémolisant

"I beg you not to spare your efforts; don't leave me in suspense..."

"Because he's disappeared."

"Ah! Everybody in this affair has disappeared, then! But that corroborates my suspicions—admit it! There's a link between all these events, no doubt about it, and our artist is mixed up in the affair somehow."

"I'm not denying it. Yesterday evening, when he went to the Rue de Sèze to collect his statue, a man—it must have been Pilesèche; he fits the description—arrived like a hurricane, shoved him into the cab that was waiting for him and got into it after him, shouting "Gare de Lyon!" to the coachman. The cab was number 10,406. I questioned the driver; I have his statement and his description of the bizarre box containing the statue."

"We have to telegraph the frontier."

"What the point? For one thing, it would be too late, as they've had all night to flee. Secondly, it's unnecessary, since our fugitives didn't leave by train. They simply deposited the heavy crate in the left luggage office, which they took out again not long afterwards. Then they went along the Boulevard Diderot, where I lost track of them."

"Good. They wanted to put us off the track and went to the Gare d'Orléans. That's elementary."

"Not at all. No one saw them either at the Gare d'Orléans or the Gare Montparnasse."

"Damn! In Paris, nothing is lost; we need to find them."

"Oh, don't worry; I'm not overly bothered about that, sure that well find them when we need to do so. The scientific method, you see. I don't play the Indian and sniff the traces of moccasins on the asphalt when I have better things to do. For the moment, and before anything else, I have to find my scientist, dead or alive. So I'll leave, after having calmed your legitimate impatience—at least, I hope so. I'll set out on the hunt again."

The commissioner seemed more resigned than convinced. "Go on, then," he said. "And don't waste any time, for if our men are still running, we'll have difficulty catching up with them."

"What do you expect? In any case, they had twenty-four hours start. If they wanted to reach the frontier, they'll have done so. Wherever they are, though, we'll collect them just as easily, when the time comes. Let's allow them to run and not give them any warning before having assembled a formidable body of evidence against them."

When he had gone, the commissioner stood up in a bad mood, and strode back and forth in his office, muttering. He was disturbed by Rosamour's methods. The old game seemed to him to be preferable to all those subtle theories. He could not understand why, having picked up the trail of the two fugitives, the agent had not tracked them until he caught them.

He could easily have imposed his way of seeing on Rosamour, but he would be shouldering a heavy responsibility in case of failure by preventing him from acting as he wished, and he decided to wait for the result of the preliminary investigations.

In any case, it was quite certain, as the policeman had said that the two fugitives would, indeed, be easy to find while they were dragging a hundred-and-fifty kilo parcel around with them.

8. How Rosamour Became Increasingly Perplexed

Madame Paponot had sensed that her importance was singularly inflated by being mixed up in this mysterious affair. She gladly told all her neighbors about the police interrogation to which she had been subjected. She even embellished it, adding to her own role, attributing replies to herself by which the magistrate's intelligence had evidently been enlightened.

In brief, without her, the mystery would have passed unperceived. She had just saved society, and, satisfied with her busy day, perhaps slightly fatigued by the incessant talk, she was returning majestically to her lodge, which was almost the only part of the building still intact, when she found herself confronted by well-dressed man with a pince-nez shielding his eyes, who bowed gracefully and said to her, without the slightest hesitation: "Bonjour, Madame Paponot."

"What, you know me?" said the concierge, straightening up in surprise.

"Do I know you! But certainly I know you. I've come to ask you for some information about the fire."

"Aha! You're a *journaliss*..."

"You've guessed it! Well, I wouldn't have hidden it from you any longer."

"You've arrived very late, you know. I've already seen five or six."

"Oh, that's nothing; there's plenty more to recount. I'm the one who put it in the paper that throughout the blaze, the concierge, Madame Paponot, displayed superb courage and energy."

"You put that, my lad? Well, that's kind; you're a nice young man. It's true, all the same, that I wouldn't have believed myself to be so courageous. I came and went-it was all the same to me!"

Rosamour—for it was him—had a bundle of newspapers under his arm. He searched it. "Look," he said. "You can see the article...oh, damn, I can't find it; I must have dropped it. I'll send it to you; I'd like you to read it." At the same time he unfolded some illustrated papers, and stopped, as if by chance, at the portrait of the hero of the day, the sculptor Bémolisant.

"A fine head," said Madame Paponot, looking at it. She leaned over the engraving, and added: "But if I'm not mistaken, I know that face. A funny idea, putting a scrap-dealer in the paper."

"A scrap-dealer!"

"As sure as my name's Madame Paponot."

"There's 'sculptor' written under the picture."

"Perhaps he is a sculptor, but he's a scrap-dealer for sure. I even said to Monsieur Pilesèche: 'Who's that *artiss*,' and he said: 'He's not an *artiss*, he's a dealer come to collect our old scrap metal.'"

"Perhaps it's not the same man. Have you seen him several times?"

"In truth, no. He only came that once on the thirty-first of December. You can see that I remember the date, and then, a face like that, one can't be mistaken."

"Monsieur Pilesèche was making fun of you."

"Monsieur Pilesèche never makes fun of me," said Madame Paponot, stiffening herself, scandalized by such a suggestion. "He'd have a job."

"That's true. And what did the two of them do, that day?"

"They had porters with them, who brought down a big crate full of scrap metal."

"So you saw what was inside?"

"In truth, no, but they said it was—not to mention that it was heavy. The men were sweating."

"And it was big, this crate?"

"Long, mostly—six feet at least. One might have thought it was a coffin."

"Ah! And they loaded the crate on to a carriage."

"Of course. They were going to the Quai des Augustines, from what they said to the coachman."

"I'd be very curious to see how your eccentric tenant was installed, if it's not too badly burned up there."

"One corner's still there, but you'll understand that I can't risk myself on the stairway. I'm a little heavy, and it might collapse. But if you want to, don't hesitate. Go gladly. You'll be all alone."

Rosamour did not need the invitation issued in that picturesque form to be repeated, and set about scaling the shaky charred steps, cluttered with rubbish of every sort.

On the upper floors, the firemen had set up a ladder to replace the demolished staircase, and he reached the landing on which the smoking remains of the floorboards remained, thanks to a few joists that were still intact.

The panels of the apartment door were three-quarters burned, but the lock was still attached to its slot and the policeman observed that it had been locked with a key. It was, therefore, inadmissible that Monsieur Grillard had tried to get out during the blaze, for he certainly would not have taken the trouble to lock the door again.

Administering a thrust of his shoulder to the remaining woodwork, Rosamour passed over the threshold of the apartment and walked with precaution over the beams. The first two rooms had been completely obliterated by the flames. Beyond them, thanks no doubt to the presence of a partition wall, the laboratory still existed in part, encumbered by the mass of rubble that the roof had accumulated there in collapsing.

At the back wall, a cracked section of what had been the chimney-hood still remained. The slate-topped table, which a counterweight permitted to be raised and lowers at will, was intact. In one of the corners was the scientist's iron-framed bed, and nearby, heaped up pell-mell, cages containing the asphyxiated cadavers of animals and broken or twisted apparatus.

The disorder was indescribable. Rosamour took it all in at a glance, and advanced further into the middle of the slates and debris, clouds of black soot escaping therefrom under his feet.

He went to the bed and, methodically clearing away the clutter heaped upon it, examined it carefully. It had not been remade since the scientist had slept in it for the last time. There was no visible trace of blood beneath the stains inflicted by the fire, but the agent was surprised, on lifting the covers, to find a crumpled nightshirt and a cotton bonnet thrown carelessly on to the bed.

Two hypotheses presented themselves to the detective's brain. Either the scientist was dressed when he left the apartment, or, if there had been a crime, the murders had stripped their victim naked in order to make him disappear more easily. In any case, it could not be admitted that Monsieur Grillard had been surprised by the fire in his bed.

Rosamour left it until later to have those pieces of evidence taken away in order that he could examine them more closely. Without concerning himself with hem any further, he continued his inspection.

On the top of the stove, in the midst of broken retorts, he noticed objects of bizarre form, and, on approaching, found that there was a collection of motionless small animals, especially frogs. When he reached out to touch one, he observed that the brown color covering it was due to a thick layer of dust and soot. Underneath, the polish of metal appeared. The strange fauna was nickel-plated.

At first, the policeman only looked at all that out of simple curiosity. What connection could the objects have with his own research? But a sudden reflection stopped him.

Had not these metal animals, nickel-plated like the sculptor's statue, been sculpted by the same hand? In that case, they attested that Bémolisant, the sculptor, and his uncle were not such strangers to one another as they appeared to be.

In any case, it was curious to observe works in the home of one of them that had evidently come from that of the other.

Let's put one of these paperweights in my pocket, Rosamour said to himself, continuing his investigations.

In spite of his attention, though, he did not find a single object that put him on a new track, and he was about to leave when his gaze fell upon the slate blackboard. He noticed the outline of letters there, or, rather, the vague traces left by chalk after a rapid and summary erasure.

A man who knew the importance of the smallest details, the policeman approached again, trying to read the inscription. The string of letters was inconsequential, and made no sense.

It was scarcely probable that a scientist like Monsieur Grillard had wasted time on a handwriting exercise, and as the letters were not reminiscent of chemical formulae or mathematical calculations, our man, very intrigued, resolved to clarify the matter.

He searched for a bit of sponge, which he moistened lightly in the bottom of a dish, and dabbed the inscription, without rubbing it, in such a manner as not to erase is any further.

Immediately, thanks to the greater contrast between black and white, the characters stood out with sufficient distinction. There were gaps, unfortunately, but after a rapid examination, Rosamour remained convinced that he was in the presence of a cryptogam.

The most urgent thing was to collect it, at all costs.

Calmly, the policeman took out his cigar-case, to which, in the place where it is often customary to embed a small watch, there was an orifice closed with a lens several centimeters wide. He aimed that eye at the slate board, pressed a small button next to the catch, and, having completed that simple operation, replaced the case in his pocket. He had just photographed the inscription.

That done, and quite tranquilly, he retraced his steps and went back down to the ground floor.

Madame Paponot was waiting for him on the threshold of her lodge.

"Come in and I'll give you a lick with the brush," she said. "You're a little untidy. Well, did you see anything good in the attic?"

"In truth, nothing worth the trouble of going up there," Rosamour replied, in a disenchanted fashion. "Anyway, I'm wasting my time. All this isn't my business; I'm just a journalist. Well, *bonsoir*, Madame Paponot."

"You'll send me the paper in which there's mention of me, won't you?"

"You can count on it..."

Rosamour took away several precious items of information from the theater of the blaze. None, however, was of a nature to extract him from his perplexity. The cryptogram was so truncated that it would certainly not be easily deciphered.

By way of recapitulation, he went over the facts that appeared to him to be established.

First of all, Bémolisant had come to see his uncle. How many times? The concierge affirmed that he could not have made more than one visit; at any rate, he could not have gone past the lodge often without being seen. During his visit on December the thirty-first—the only one clearly established—with the connivance of Pilesèche, he had concealed his identity and the two of them had taken away a heavy box of unusual form.

What could the box have contained? That was perhaps the nub of the problem.

If the laboratory assistant and the nephew had murdered the old man, was it probable that they had enclosed the cadaver in such a box? No; they would have chosen a recipient attracting less attention by virtue of its length. The concierge had said that one might have taken it for a coffin. One does not choose a coffin to transport a body that one wishes to make disappear. One puts it in a trunk of usual appearance, by folding it up. If the box was long, it was because it contained something long and rigid. Furthermore, the weight of a body was insufficient on its own to make it as heavy as it was said to be.

Was it the statue?

But how had it got into the scientist's abode? A statue of that size does not arrive at someone's home without being noticed. It would have been seen on arrival, as on departure…unless the method used to produce it only permitted it to be contrived in the laboratory…

And Rosamour remembered that nickel lent itself to galvanoplastic deposit.

"Bah!" he said. "Bémolisant would have had to come back often for that operation, as well as to establish a mock-up, and until there's proof to the contrary, it's necessary to admit that his visits were rare."

He slapped his forehead.

"Of course!" he added, continuing his monologue. "One session would suffice for a molding from life; perhaps it was a plaster mold that was transported thus. The fellow does; he's molded; and then his cadaver is made to disappear, one way or another. Perhaps it was burned in the laboratory furnace…

"Yes, but a mold cut up into pieces doesn't occupy such a great length. I'd rather believe that it was the statue itself, obtained by galvanoplasty, that the two men took away. When I've visited the artist's studio and observed that he hasn't installed any equipment for galvanoplasty, I'll believe that my deduction is the only logical one. And the proof is the toad that I have in my pocket, and which was obtained by the same procedure…

"Come on, let's not get carried away prematurely in hypotheses, and let's not abandon the scientific method for an instant."

The agent took out his watch.

"Good," he murmured. "I still have time to go see Madame Bémolisant and get her to talk."

9. What Happened at the Artist's House

The artist's domicile had been in a singular disarray since the disappearance of its master.

Bémolisant had announced as he went out that he was going to fetch his statue and collect the fee for its exhibition.

That operation should not have taken long and could not have retained him beyond dinner time. He had been patiently awaited, however, for he had not accustomed his family to overly meticulous punctuality. At eight o'clock, however, the child had been crying; they had fed him and put him to bed. At nine o'clock the women had decided to sit down at table in their turn, but without any great appetite.

"I wouldn't be anxious," Madame Legris said, "if he hadn't collected a considerable sum of money, but these days, you hear about people murdered in the boulevard, which isn't reassuring."

Weary of waiting, at about one o'clock in the morning, the ladies had resigned themselves to going to bed, but at the slightest noise, Madame Bémolisant, who was not asleep, shuddered, thinking that she could hear someone at the door.

Early the next morning, she went to the Rue de Sèze, where no one could tell her anything; all that anyone knew was that the artist had collected five thousand francs, had taken the statue and left in a fiacre with another man, who had joined him.

She went home and imparted that discovery to her mother, all of whose attention was immediately focused on the high figure of the receipts.

"Five thousand francs!" she said. "That would come in handy, for our capital is considerably eroded. I don't suppose your husband has thought of spending it all on his own..."

"Oh, Maman, you know Népomucène; he's incapable of such an action. He has his faults, I grant you, but he's honest and disinterested."

"Then it's necessary to go to the police and ask that they make the necessary investigation."

Hélène set forth and asked for directions to the local commissariat. When she went in, she approached an employee timidly, who was leaning back in his chair stretching his arms.

"What do you want?" he asked.

"Monsieur le Commissaire?"

"He's gone out. What do you have to say to him?"

"It's just that...I'd like to speak to him..."

"Since I've told you that he's gone out, if you don't want to say what brings you here, you can go away."

He picked up his newspaper "It's just that...it might be urgent."

"Well then, explain yourself."

"My husband didn't come home last night."

"Ha ha ha!" chuckled the clerk. "It happens."

"He'd just collected a large sum of money."

"What a rogue. Go on, make your declaration." He had reached out a hand to pick up a printed form, which he filled in as he interrogated the young woman and as she replied.

When he had finished, he said, by way of conclusion: "That's that. You can go home, little lady, and sleep tranquilly. Husbands don't get lost. They always turn up."

Hélène was no more reassured by that imbecile's comments than by the verbiage of her mother, who found every consolation.

"Listen," she said to her daughter when she came back come. "Népomucène isn't the husband you need. He's a crackpot, and I groan every day over the circumstances that forced me, in Tonkin, to give him to you as a husband. It wouldn't be any great loss, you see..."

"But with all his faults, he's my husband!"

"A colonial husband! The most unfortunate thing is that he's disappeared with the money, just at the moment when—I don't know how—he'd created a certain celebrity. Oh, perhaps it's a stroke of luck after all, for he wouldn't have been able to sustain his renown."

"But since he'd succeeded in making that statue..."

"There's something incomprehensible in that, you know. A statue doesn't sprout overnight like a mushroom. He can say that he wanted to give us a surprise, but we'd have seen him making the mock-up, coming and going, and the model...and the founder...what do I know? I repeat, I scent trickery."

"It doesn't matter. I'm very anxious."

"You're playing your role..."

The discussion was interrupted by the arrival of a visitor, who insinuated himself into the apartment as soon as the door was ajar, and said, as he handed over his card: "Is it to Madame Bémolisant that I have the honor of speaking?"

"Yes, Monsieur," Hélène replied, while she scanned the piece of cardboard with her eyes, and read: *Isidore Boissonnald, Enquiry Agent, Director of Family Security.*

"Madame," said the short man, taking a seat that no one had offered him, "my card indicates to you the kind of business in which I'm occupied: it's principally research in the interests of families. I can say without boasting that I've never taken charge of an affair without seeing it through to the end. My agents are all possessed of a skill that one doesn't encounter in the official police, for the simple reason that it's necessary to pay talent what it's worth. I'm not miserly with them, but, on the contrary, I'm extremely easy-going with families. We get paid by results, and except for a small fee to cover our expenses we don't receive any money until we have succeeded. Finally, you can be sure of our most complete discretion. My motto is *Hush!* and my blazon, a finger over lips..."

During this little speech, Hélène examined the singular visitor, whose broad face framed by slack cheeks was illuminated by a perpetual vague smile beneath a fleeting and uncertain gaze.

"Monsieur," she said finally, "I don't quite understand what you want with me..."

The other took on an expression of afflicted and discreet condolence.

"Oh, my God, Madame, it's quite simple! My agency has learned, at an early hour, of the disappearance...the cruel disappearance"—he emphasized the addition—"of the eminent artist whose wife you are, and I have come to offer you my services to find him."

"I don't believe I should hide it from you that I've already approached the commissariat. Perhaps it's necessary to wait for the result."

"Oh, Madame, don't be under any illusion. The Prefecture won't do anything. Act yourself, don't waste any time, for searches are much more difficult when they're belated."

At the same time the officious individual inspected the furniture which was not of a kind to give a high idea of the resources of the family and the remuneration that might be expected therefrom.

"But in sum, Monsieur," said the young woman, "what do you think of this disappearance?"

"I must confess that we avoid all hazardous and premature hypotheses; we only occupy ourselves with affairs with which we are charged. If you would like to pay us a modest sum of a hundred and fifty francs for our initial research, I will be able to tell you shortly what it is necessary to think of this occurrence. Then, depending on the difficulty of the ulterior research, according to whether there has been a murder, a sequestration or a flight, and, finally, whether it is necessary to operate in France or abroad, I shall quote you a simple, categorical and definitive fee."

"Permit me to consult my mother, for, in truth, I'm very embarrassed," Hélène relied, after a moment's hesitation.

But Madame Legris, as soon as she was brought up to date, hastened to declare that she saw no opportunity for that expense.

"Think about it," said the enquiry agent. "Perhaps you'll reproach yourself later for having neglected such a justified step. The sum for which I'm asking scarcely covers my initial expenses. Anyway, you have my address, and I shall come again tomorrow to obtain our definitive reply.

He stood up and headed for the door, slowly, like a man who still hopes that there might be a change of mind, but he was allowed to depart, and as he went out backwards, he collided with a man who was just reaching out for the electric bell-push.

Isidore Boissonnald turned around and darted an oblique glance at the newcomer, a man correctly dressed, who stood side to let him pass.

Madame Bémolisant could not hide. She allowed the new visitor to come in, slightly annoyed by all these disturbances.

"I shall not employ any subterfuge or artifice with you, Madame," said the newcomer, without any preamble. "My name is Rosamour, but that will tell you nothing. I have come to collect some information from you regarding your husband's disappearance."

"I'm desolate, Monsieur, but the agent who his just left has already proposed to make a similar search..."

She held out the card that she was still holding to Rosamour. Without taking it, the policeman darted a negligent glance at it.

"...And I refused his proposal," Hélène continued, before having had a response from the Prefecture of Police, to which I made my declaration."

"Good! Precisely—I've been charged by the Prefecture to ask you various questions that will aid us in the research that you have requested."

"That's different. Please sit down, Monsieur."

"First of all, what indications do you have regarding the present whereabouts of your husband?"

"None, Monsieur, and as he had just collected some money, I can only suppose one thing, alas, which is that he has been drawn into some trap."

Rosamour was perhaps not absolutely of the same opinion, but he did not let anything show and contented himself with asking a few questions about the employment of the sculptor's day.

"I'm obliged," he added, "also to obtain information about your family situation. You must excuse me, Madame, but our task is delicate and seemingly insignificant indications are sometimes flashes of enlightenment for us. You live with Madame your mother and a child. I have no need to ask you whether Monsieur Bémolisant was a model husband?"

"He never went out."

"Good. Does he have relatives?"

"An old uncle that he never sees, because they'd quarreled."

"Monsieur Grillard."

"That's right. Do you know him?"

Rosamour made an equivocal gesture that might have passed for a negation. "But I'm told that the uncle and nephew had been reconciled, to such an extent that Monsieur Bémolisant had made a statue of his uncle. It must, therefore, have been necessary for him to visit him quite often?"

"I don't know; so far as I know, he only saw Monsieur Grillard once."

"On December the thirty-first, no?"

"Precisely. It's an easy date to remember. I even recall that Népomucène came back late and went up to his studio with Monsieur Pilesèche, his uncle's laboratory assistant, so that, when they didn't come down for lunch, I went up to knock on his door. It was one o'clock and he hadn't thought of going to table."

"Did the Messieurs seem a trifle emotional, overexcited?"

"Your question reminds me that they did, in fact, have a slightly singular air. Monsieur Pilesèche had even taken off his coat and dusted it, which seemed bizarre to me. But it's not astonishing that they were a little overexcited, for that was the day when Monsieur Leroux had convinced my husband to exhibit his work."

"Ah! His statue was finished?"

"Yes, it had just been brought."

"Monsieur Bémolisant had been occupied with the statue for a long time?"

"I can tell you that I'd never heard mention of it before."

"That's odd."

"All the odder because my husband likes to talk about the artistic ideas that are on his mind."

Good, thought Rosamour. *There's a statue that no one has mentioned the day before, and whose arrival coincides with the visit to the uncle. That's what was in the box; that much is evident. But it doesn't help us to discover what has become of the original.*

After that aside he resumed: "And you've doubtless informed Monsieur Grillard of his nephew's disappearance?"

"No, Monsieur. I confess that the idea never occurred to me. I don't know him at all, personally, and he doesn't seem to be desirous of making my acquaintance."

"And since then you've had no news of him?"

"No, Monsieur. When the laboratory assistant came here in recent days I asked about him, because the worthy Monsieur Pilesèche never talks about him otherwise. The poor man is very ill, he told me."

"Well, Madame," the policeman said then, in his most solemn tone, emphasizing his words, "I can be more explicit. The house in which your uncle lived burned down yesterday, and Monsieur Grillard has disappeared."

"In the flames?" asked Madame Bémolisant, whom Rosamour was observing from the corner of his eye, but whose face expressed nothing but the sharpest surprise and the most sincere horror.

"I don't believe so."

"But what is it necessary to suppose, then? Monsieur Grillard was ill and couldn't leave his room. Someone must have removed him!"

"All suppositions are admissible; it's all a matter of finding the right one. Who are Monsieur Grillard's heirs?"

"My husband and his cousin Sophie, who is at the convent of Fontenay-sous-Bois," Madame Bémolisant replied, without hesitation. "You believe that a thief...?"

"I don't believe anything, Madame. Until now, I haven't settled on any hypothesis. But I can't hide from you any longer that this disappearance, coinciding with that of your husband and Monsieur Pilesèche, who was with him, permits the gravest suspicions.

"Oh! Monsieur, you're frightening me. You've taken a solemn tone. Good God, what is it? What are these suppositions?"

It was evident that the young woman was sincere and knew nothing; it would not have been possible to play a learned role so perfectly.

"Can one not suppose," the policeman added, measuring the effect of his words, "that the laboratory assistant and your husband have something to do with the old man's disappearance?"

"I don't understand," Hélène replied, with a naivety that was not feigned.

"Monsieur Bémolisant saw Monsieur Grillard on the thirty-first of December. Admit for a moment that the latter received his nephew with some sarcasm; a dispute might have followed. Your husband is quick-tempered, impatient— you recognize that yourself. He might have been carried away, and in a moment of anger..."

"Enough, Monsieur, enough! Your supposition wounds me, and I can't tolerate the formation of such an accusation in my presence."

She had risen to her feet, cold and dignified, her hand extended in an energetic gesture. But Rosamour, without quitting his chair and without departing from his calmness, continued in the same tone of voice.

"You're wrong to get so excited so soon," he said. "One doesn't respond to an explicit accusation with a disdainful silence. I'm pointing out a danger to you; it's necessary to confront it and tackle the enemy hand-to hand."

"My husband, a murderer!"

"Unintentionally."

"No, Monsieur, it's not possible. You're lying..."

"It's not me that it's necessary to accuse, for the hypothesis isn't mine. Furthermore, I will say that I'm seeking the truth without any prejudice. But it's up to you, Madame, since you're sure of your husband's innocence, to help me bring it to light. I've told you the hypothesis that will seem the most plausible to many people; do you have another to put in its place?"

"What do you want me to say? I'm overwhelmed by that frightful accusation. It's a hammer-blow that has stunned me, and I can only cry loudly in the ardor of my conviction that he's innocent!"

"That is unfortunately insufficient to counter the charges against him. But you can see the frankness with which I'm acting toward you; return the favor. Trust me. Be sure that nothing would give me greater joy than demonstrating Monsieur Bémolisant's innocence, if he is innocent. Think, then! Everything accuses him, and I have to destroy that scaffolding. It's a task worthy of me. I'm speaking to you as an artist, after having spoken to you as a man, for I have a heart, you see; I'm accessible to pity, to generous sentiments, and when I see a weak individual in tears, a woman devoid of support, I'm always tempted to spring to her defense...

"It's agreed, then; henceforth, we're allies. You'll help me as much as you can to discover the truth. But it's understood that you'll speak without any afterthought, that you won't hide anything from me under the pretext that it might be unfavorable to your thesis. I'm a confessor; it's necessary to tell me everything."

Finally, resignedly, she said: "Question me, Monsieur. I'll answer."

The conversation was a long one. In spite of the excellent memory on which he pried himself, Rosamour took notes.

When he parted from Madame Bémolisant, he addressed a few words of encouragement to her. "Have confidence," he said, "and whatever happens, don't worry. I don't know whether I'll be able to come back to see you soon; I might be forced to depart on a journey sooner than I would wish—but even if you don't hear mention of me, have no fear; I'll be watching and working."

He headed for the door. "Oh," he said, turning round. "If the gentleman who was leaving as I arrived comes back, send him away—and above all, don't tell him anything. He's one of those swindlers who only seeks to fish in troubled waters."

When Rosamour was back in the street, he lit a cigar philosophically and hummed a tune from an operetta. *It wouldn't take much*, he thought, *for that poor woman's conviction to persuade me. Instinctively, moreover, it seems to me that they're two imbeciles who are running away naively, without having killed anyone. At any rate, Madame Bémolisant is a precious auxiliary in finding them. But where's the body?*

He went into a small restaurant, where he ate a hasty meal, and prepared to make a tour of the editorial offices of the principal newspapers. His principle was that the press ought, for anyone who knew how to play the game, to be the best auxiliary of the examining magistrate and the policemen—but it was necessary, for that, not to let it spread indiscreet information as it liked. The best way to make sure of that was to inform it himself.

He recounted the story in his own fashion, enlivening the details that it suited him to publish and not neglecting to say, in accordance with the well-known fallacious formula, that the police were on the track of the mysteriously vanished individuals.

After which, Rosamour hastened to go to bed. He had nothing better to do. Were the reporters not taking charge of the task now?

The following day, in fact, the principal newspapers published long sensational articles under the headline *The Mystery of the Panthéon*, which imparted to the public the marvelous discoveries of their reporters. It was demonstrated, by peremptory reasoning, that the celebrated artist Bémolisant had not been murdered, but had fled with the laboratory assistant of the eminent physiologist Grillard. What means of locomotion had the fugitives employed? In what direction was it necessary to look for them? As many questions calculated to deflect less skillful individuals.

We have, said one of the articles, *discovered the merchant who rented his handcart, and, furnished with an exact description and the number of the vehicle, it was not difficult to assure ourselves that no cart fitting that description has been abandoned in Paris, or even in the suburbs. On the other hand, the package that the artist was carrying is too singular and recognizable for it to have gone unnoticed at a railway station; in reality, the two men have not taken a train. They must have passed through the fortifications on foot, which seems to be confirmed by the declaration of a customs officer at the Porte de Bercy. We shall know before long where the fugitives are. Our reporters and cyclists are departing in all directions.*

Rosamour rubbed his hands.

The next day, a benevolent reader notified a newspaper that he had encountered two travelers answering the description, in a state of complete dilapidation, at Voves, on the Vendôme line, a hundred kilometers from Paris.

"Where the devil are they going?" Rosamour asked himself—and answered himself almost immediately: "To Saint-Nazaire, no doubt. They're counting on embarking there for America. At the rate they're going, I have a week in hand."

He went to give an account of his initial results to the examining magistrate, Monsieur Fischer, who had been taken the mysterious affair in hand, substituting himself for the commissioner. Then he prepared to continue his search.

In order to obtain more precise information he sent a description of the fugitives everywhere, but without issuing any arrest warrant. He wanted to keep track of them and have them watched, but not arrested prematurely.

That description, which he communicated to the press, was a marvel of sagacity.

The Bureau of Anthropometric Measurements had succeeded in reconstituting Bémolisant's characteristic dimensions with the sole aid of a photograph and clothing found at his home. As for Pilesèche, it had been necessary to do without his photograph, none of which existed. From the size of the footwear left at his lodgings it had been concluded that he was about one meter seventy tall—above average. His garments had indicated his corpulence; the traces left by the friction of jutting bones at his elbows, knees and shoulders had furnished other measurements. That was the scientific method, applied in its fullest extent.

When Monsieur Boissonnald came to knock on Madame Bémolisant's door to find out whether the night had given her advice, the artist's wife contented herself with telling him that, on due reflection, she had renounced any further research.

The enquiry agent withdrew, slightly discomfited by the vanishing of a nice windfall; cases being scarce and time being short, it was important not to miss any opportunities that cropped up, but he was particularly vexed to see the ground being cut from under his feet by the Prefecture of Police—for he was not duped by that defeat, having recognized Rosamour, and not doubting for an instant the part the latter had played in his disappointment. If the Prefecture was going to snatch the bread out of his mouth, his métier was going to become impossible.

Enveloping Rosamour in his resentment, he thought, angrily: *I'll pay you back for this. If I can do you a bad turn, in my fashion, you'll be disenchanted before long.*

10. The Result of a Session of Hypnotism

There was a veritable snowstorm that evening, and the wind was shaking the windows of the Cheval Boiteux inn—said to be the best in the village of Briseval, at the end of the bridge over the Loir—rudely.

The frightful weather was not at all to the liking of a fairground performer whose bright leotard could be seen beneath a threadbare overcoat, and who was counting on putting on a little display of his various skills in the main room, where the local bigwigs ordinarily gathered, with the precious assistance of Miss Adda, his acolyte, who was to submit with a good grace to the most curious, amusing and simultaneously instructive experiments in hypnotic suggestion.

The showman put of the commencement of the session as long as possible, for the audience only consisted of two big fellows playing billiards and a few peasants drinking their mazagrans and chatting around a table in the midst of a cloud of smoke.

Miss Adda was sitting next to the stove, from which a damp mist was rising. She was short and thin, with pale, fatigued features, a sad and pensive expression, hiding her pink stockings and short spangled skirt under a grimy tartan deprived for the fringes that had once ornamented it.

The showman, who called himself Professor Joël, was, by contrast, a solid fellow, all muscles; his black hair was plastered over his narrow forehead by pomade. His sharp face was provided with a superb aquiline nose beneath which extended the long waxed tips of a shiny moustache. He was striding back and forth impatiently in front of the stove, slowly sipping a glass of eau-de-vie.

An old woman was knitting at the counter, indifferent to everything that was not a purchase.

Suddenly, the door opened under a gust of wind, which entered violently, chasing snow and cold into the overheated room, and with it came the two strangest individuals imaginable.

Imagine two tall bodies in long frock coats, their shoulders disappearing under the snow, collars turned up over the icy rivers of their beards, clutching unspeakable top hats. Their shoes were enveloped in muddy snowballs, while long yellow streaks climbed the legs of frayed, worn trousers that were crying mercy.

"The door! The door!" clamored the chorus of young peasants, who knew about city ways.

103

One of the newcomers, blinded by the light and the warm vapor of the inn turned round awkwardly, grabbed the batten of the door, which was banging on the wall, and sealed the hole through which the wind was blowing.

Then both of them let themselves fall on to the nearest bench, a few paces away from Miss Adda, whom that abrupt interruption had snatched from her reverie and was staring at them with an extinct gaze. They seemed half-dead of cold and fatigue. The shorter one nevertheless stood up and went toward the innkeeper.

"Madame," he said, his jaw numbed by cold and scarcely capable of articulating the words, "be good enough to give us some good hot soup, quickly, and a bottle of wine. After that, we'll see."

The worthy woman inspected their sorry state—but, given the frightful weather, who would have looked any better? She hastened to bring them what they wanted, and when she uncovered the fuming soup-tureen, the man said to the hostess, but not very loudly, as if in a confidential tone: "We have a crate on a handcart with us; we've put it in the shed. Please keep an eye on it."

"People hereabouts aren't in the habit of stealing," the old woman snapped.

"It wouldn't be easy to take away, I know—but still, it's necessary that you know that it's ours."

"All right. Are you staying here overnight?"

"Yes, let us have a small room."

Then they began eating like starvelings, without saying anything more. Miss Adda was staring at them obstinately, and involuntarily. As soon as they had come in, a magnetic force had imposed itself on her will, making her turn her head in their direction. Her gaze was drawn to one of them in particular, whose tall gangling body was bent over his plate.

The two travelers asked what else could be served to them, and in the blink of an eye had swallowed a bowl of mutton stew and a large chunk of cheese.

That substantial repast seemed to cheer them up. They sat back on the bench with a certain air of satisfaction, as hot coffee was brought to them.

"Oof! That's better," gasped the older one. "I was absolutely done in."

"We're not out of difficulty yet, my dear Pil...my dear friend," the other replied. "We're not halfway yet."

They were talking in low voices, leaning toward one another.

"In spite of everything, we ought to count ourselves lucky, the way things are going, and if it weren't for those damned newspapers talking about us and making me anxious. I could believe that we'd been forgotten."

"Yes, but you read that note in the *Figaro*."

"Bah! The papers want to seem well-informed. If they were on our track, we'd have been arrested already, damn it."

"I wish I could share your confidence."

At the same moment, two gendarmes came in, immediately followed by a traveler enveloped in an ample fur coat.

The arrival of those worthy representatives of the authority appeared to disturb the two travelers. They huddled over a newspaper, the reading of which suddenly seemed to absorb them completely. The gendarmes paid no heed to them, and went to sit down in a corner, with their usual solemn tread.

The young man who had come in after them began by darting a circular glance around the room, and, perceiving the readers, who did not succeed in hiding their faces completely, he came to sit down not far away from them, looking at them with a satisfied expression.

Well, thought the newcomer, *chance has favored me, and I'll telegraph my fortunate discovery to the paper.*

When he questioned the innkeeper, however, as she poured him a glass of hot punch, he learned with some disappointment that the Briseval telegraph office closed at seven o'clock in the evening, and would not open again until seven in the morning. It was necessary to resign himself, and, as reportage never loses its rights, he resolved at least to interview the people he seemed to be seeking or pursuing. He only needed some incident to give him the opportunity.

He had not overlooked the gendarmes, and laughed covertly as he lit a cigarette. *Those brave soldiers of the law, who are sipping quietly in their corner, have no suspicion that the two criminals who about whom all Paris is talking are four strides way from their kepis. It's not me who'll tell them—I'm a reporter, not a detective.*

As for the two individuals he was considering so lightly as criminals, they had seen the reporter come in, but he had been too well wrapped up in his furs for much of his face to be visible. Now that he was sitting down, by contrast, his overcoat was ajar. Bémolisant, who was watching him from the corner of his eye, could not suppress a gesture of bewilderment, and he leaned toward Pilesèche.

"We're no longer safe," he said. "There's someone who knows us."

"Are you sure?"

"I've seen that face before somewhere. Hang on...the memory's coming back. He's a journalist who came to interview me once."

"And you think he's recognized you?"

"I'd bet on it. Who can tell whether he might be here tracking us, in order to be the first to report our arrest?"

"You're frightening me. That journalist, those gendarmes...we're doomed, then!"

"Keep quiet—but let's try to slip away."

From that moment on, they maneuvered as adroitly as possible in order to leave the room without attracting attention, but to complete their misfortune, the showman, judging that no one else was likely to turn up at that late hour, had taken off his overcoat and was blocking the internal door by means of which the fugitives had planned to escape.

The performer commenced his patter.

"Mesdames et Messieurs," he said, "I have the honor of submitting to your competent attention a few curious experiments that have earned me the suffrage of highly placed people, and even crowned heads. I shall begin by doing a few card tricks and feats of strength, in order to get my hand in and develop my magnetic fluid. After that, I shall have the honor of introducing you to a remarkable subject whom Doctors Bernheim and Charcot[16] have tried to lure away from me with gold. I shall submit you thereafter to experiments in somnambulism, hypnotism, Mesmerism, suggestion and catalepsy; these experiments are absolutely unprecedented and new, astonishing and mysterious creations that have no relationship with those of certain charlatans who call themselves, alas, my colleagues, have been able to put before you. Everyone knows that Professor Joël is no charlatan. I could, like some people I could name, earn a great deal of money with trickery, but I have always preferred the art and the science."

After that brief introduction, the session commenced.

The first part, in which only Professor Joël was in play, offered nothing of particular interest, except for the extraordinary dexterity of the experimenter, who juggled with his cards and made them do whatever he wanted.

When he had finished, he announced that Miss Adda was going to prepare for her appearance, while he made a tour of the amiable society, which would want to recompense the skill of his performance and encourage him for the sequel.

The two travelers who had been first to arrive, in whom the reader will have had no difficulty recognizing Bémolisant and Pilesèche, did not have to be begged to put their obol in the bowl; that generous gesture reassured the landlady, who was watching them from the corner of her eyes, that they were definitely not penniless vagabonds, as she had briefly feared.

In the meantime, the young woman had risen to her feet and thrown her tartan over a chair. Her eyes, atonal a little while before, were now shining with a feverish light. She braced herself in her satin corsage, which creaked, and beneath the body of a sickly child, a kind of innate distinction was definable, which the abjection of her métier had not succeeded in obliterating entirely.

She advanced at a languid pace, swaying on her hips with the customary gait of a ballerina. The showman tightened the hem of her skirt with a leather strap.

"We're going to begin," he said, finally, "with a few experiments in catalepsy. Catalepsy, Mesdames et Messieurs, is one of the phases of hypnotic sleep. Similar to death, it gives the body a cadaverous rigidity. The muscles tense with

---

[16] The neurologists Hippolyte Bernheim (1840-1919) and Jean-Martin Charcot (1825-1893). The former developed the theory of suggestibility in attempting to account for the phenomena of hypnotism, while the latter made extensive use of hypnotism in his famous investigations of "hysteria" at the Salpêtrière.

a superhuman force. You're going to see each of this frail creature's limbs become as stiff as a steel bar.

He had grasped her by the wrists, and, looking into her eyes twenty centimeters from her face, he concentrated all the force of his being in the fixed gaze.

The most complete silence reigned in the inn, where all the audience members were waiting, leaning forward, hypnotized themselves, reluctantly intrigued, and holding their breath.

Half a minute was sufficient. Suddenly, Miss Adda fell into the arms of the strong man. The latter made a sign to Pilesèche, who happened to be closest to him.

"Come and help me, Monsieur, I beg you."

At that appeal, the laboratory assistant felt very ill-at-ease, not wanting to put himself so much in evidence, but his companion shoved him—would not a refusal have attracted more attention?

"Come, come," insisted Joël. "You're not going to leave me alone with this charming burden in my arms?"

Pilesèche stood up and advanced toward them.

"Bring up a chair, please. Lift Miss Adda up by the feet and place them on the edge of the chair, while I place her head on a second support.

And the young woman, completely rigid, was suspended like a bridge, only supported by her heels and the back of her neck.

An "Ah!" of astonishment ran round the room.

"Oh, don't exclaim yet. This is nothing—and to give you a better idea of the strength of the tensed muscles, the Monsieur who is helping me will prove to you that a frail woman can carry him without buckling." He had placed a napkin over the subject's body. "Climb up, Monsieur," he added. "Climb up without fear."

The other did not want to.

"Climb up, since he says so," clamored the impatient peasants.

He made his decision, and stood up on the rigid body.

"Weigh upon her as heavily as you like," said the showman. "Are you scared of falling?"

Miss Adda did not budge under the burden, and more than a wooden beam.

"Well, Messieurs, you can see that the subject supports eighty kilos without flinching. What do say to that? But look, solely by the force of my gaze, I shall now return flexibility to her muscles. Don't move, Monsieur..."

He gazed fixedly at certain tensor muscles, which gradually gave way. The body sank down gradually, as of the bridge were breaking in the middle—but when the operator ceased gazing, the immobility became complete again.

"Now we'll return her to her original position—and all, Messieurs, by the power of my gaze alone."

And the body straightened, obedient to the imperious will that commanded it, lifting the laboratory assistant up again.

"Take note that the insensibility is complete," the operator continued. "Approach, Messieurs; you can prick or pinch the subject; she won't feel a thing... Now, if you're completely convinced, we're going to wake Miss Adda up and pass on to recreative experiments in somnambulism and suggestion.

Pilesèche had got down.

Joël blew on the closed eyes of the young woman, and spread out his hands, as if to draw away the fluid. Miss Adda uttered a sigh, and Joël supported her at the moment when, waking up, she was about to collapse on the floor.

The audience cried "Bravo!" and started clapping, but the professor stopped them with a gesture.

"Some of my colleagues, to deceive their audience, make passes and grimaces, roll up their sleeves and assume diabolical attitudes, but Messieurs, nothing is simpler than hypnosis; I'll show you how true savants operate. Pay attention!"

At the same time, he clicked his fingers in front of Miss Adda's eyes. She, suddenly gripped by the gaze, started following the fingers everywhere they went, in abrupt zigzags, twisting her body in order not to lose sight of the digits that had hypnotized her, leaning over backwards in atrocious equilibria, her eyes wide open.

That went on for a few minutes.

After that fatiguing activity, Miss Adda was woken up again, and set forth on a little quest of her own. Professor Joël announced that he was about to go from strength to strength—"as chez Nicolet"—and, in accordance with suggestions with which the audience would collaborate, he would show his gratitude for the flattering attention that was being lent to him by making some experiments in second sight,

That alluring program proceeded with increasing interest, and Pilesèche, gradually forgetting his present situation, recovered his old enthusiasm for science. He had an increasing desire to substitute himself for the charlatan, crying to him: "Friend, what you're doing is merely the infancy of the art. I've known many other things for a long time, Let me take your place, and you'll see!"

Without having to be begged now, as soon as the magnetizer asked for assistance, he presented himself, and as he guessed in advance what the other desired, his actions came to a nominated point neatly and precisely, so that Joël could no longer reckon him a simple curiosity-seeker.

Thus, during a brief pause, the impressed operator whispered in his ear; "You're in the game, eh, my dear chap?"

"Not exactly, but I have a few tricks up my sleeve."

"Messieurs!" cried the professor, no longer worrying about his assent, and turning to his audience, "I'd like to introduce a little diversity into the session, and this Monsieur will show you a few experiments of his own. You'll be able to see that there's no trickery involved, and that Miss Adda is a truly remarkable subject."

"He's an accomplice!" someone shouted.

"Get away!" shouted the others.

And Pilesèche, enfevered, no longer thinking about anything but science, set about realizing the most difficult and marvelous experiments. In his hands, the young woman was an instrument of extreme sensitivity. She shivered as soon as he looked at her, and it only required a simple imposition of his hands to make her pass through all the phases of the strange state, still so little known, in which the human organism seems, step by step, to live distinct lives successively, progressing further and further toward an acuity of perception so keen that it extends across time and space. Miss Adda seemed to be under his complete dependency, drawn to him by an irresistible force, never taking her eyes off him, even during her periods of lucidity.

"The two of us could do great things," said Professor Joël, his eyes widening in their turn.

"More, more!" cried the members of the audience, stamping their feet in enthusiasm.

The gendarmes had risen to their feet, open-mouthed in surprise at all that sorcery. The reporter brought his hands together in his pockets, with the curious instinct of his métier. Only Bémolisant did not abandon himself to the general fever, thinking that it would have been more prudent to slip away.

The young woman, sitting on a chair with her eyes closed, with Pilesèche behind her, drawn up to his full height, his hair thrown back, his eyes bright and his left hand on the subject's had

"Can you see?" he asked.

"Yes, said the other, softly, with some effort. "I can see a little, but take me further."

Pilesèche pressed down harder on her hair.

"Ah!" Miss Adda continued, as if a veil had been torn away. "I can see! I can see!"

The laboratory assistant extended his right hand. The audience was mute, held in suspense. But suddenly, in a lower voice, in the midst of the silence, and with a gesture of fear, she said: "Oh! Poor man, poor man, save yourself! You're being pursued. Be careful—they know who you are and where you are."

The laboratory assistant shivered. His face went pale, and his entire body was shaken by a nervous tremor.

Everyone's eyes were fixed on him now.

Some were laughing, not knowing what was happening. But the gendarmes were also looking at the singular operator. They looked at one another and started talking in whispers—and one of them, taking a piece of paper from his pocket, seemed to be comparing the individual with a description.

"It's him," he said, in a low voice, to his companion. "There's no arrest warrant, but we can't let the opportunity pass."

And, heading toward the traveler slowly, like a man going about his business who is not about to let his target escape, he said in a loud voice: "Monsieur Pilesèche, I arrest you."

Bémolisant stood up abruptly, He looked for a way out, but the second gendarme, turning toward him, spread out his arms.

"Don't try to leave, I beg you," he said, in his turn.

"What is all this?" cried the audience members, absolutely astounded.

The gendarmes were glad to display their sagacity. "They're the murderers of the Panthéon quarter," they said, simply.

"Oh!"

At that reproving cry, everyone stood back, leaving the two accomplices in the hands of the authority.

"My word!" murmured the reporter. "I had nothing to do with it—but what a fine telegram in the morning!"

"Damn it, gendarmes" cried the professor, gripped by a fit of philanthropy and gratitude toward the man who had lent him his assistance. "Let me at least post bail for the criminals!"

"Thank you very much," replied Bémolisant, in a dignified tone, "but we're not criminals, and we don't accept charity." The artist, who had been so afraid of being caught a little while before, had recovered his courage now that he was a prisoner.

"Brigadier," said the reporter, presenting his card to the gendarme. "I'm Jean Saure, a journalist well known even in this remote region. Will you allow me to ask these Messieurs a few questions?"

"Are you mocking the public force? A journalist? What does that matter to me? Address yourself to the public prosecutor."

"Very well, grim soldier; I shall fall back in good order."

The gendarmes had carefully bound the prisoners' wrists.

"And now, right turn, and march!" said the brigadier. "To prison!"

11. In which the birds are flushed out

Briseval's prison was the vulgar lock-up that ornaments the Mairie of any self-respecting village: a small, dark, narrow cell wedged under the staircase, designed to hold incorrigible drunkards rather than hardened criminals. It was not used often, not because people were any more virtuous in Briseval than elsewhere, but because there was an indulgent sympathy there for the joyful lovers of the local drinking den.

The principal usage of the cell was to serve as a store-room for the instruments of the town's brass band.

The corners of the cell were furnished with spiders' webs, with their tenants, and water was dripping down the walls of the low and poorly-ventilated room. It was scarcely possible open the door, let alone close it again.

When the two prisoners found themselves anyone in that obscurity, they let themselves fall on to the dusty planks that served as a camp bed and remained silent for a moment, overwhelmed by the horror of their situation.

The wind was blowing through the ill-fitted planks of the door, and the poor fellows were numb with cold.

"A bad night is soon passed," said Pilesèche, finally, "and we'll be taken before an examining magistrate tomorrow. I'd as soon get it over with as drag out my sad existence along the highways. What do you expect? I'm not made for adventures."

"And as you can't demonstrate your innocence, you'll rot in a cell until they drag you to the assizes, where an idiot jury will convict you, and you'll take your head to the scaffold, for a crime you haven't committed!"

"Brrr! You're sending cold chills down my spine. But what the hell! Since we're caught, let's be fatalistic, and let our destiny work itself out..."

"You can say that if you like—me, I'd prefer to save myself if there's a means."

"It's only in novels that one digs tunnels under the walls to escape from prison."

"But this badly-closed room isn't a prison; there must be a way of getting out of it."

Pilesèche shook the door. "It's solid, at any rate," he said, "And the lock's enormous."

"Come on, my friend, my good Pilesèche, we don't have time to waste, and those damned gendarmes are bound to be back first thing in the morning. Think hard. Do you need tools? Here's my knife, for they forgot to search us."

"Listen—I'll give it a try. I noticed that this cell is under the staircase. If the steps aren't made of stone, it might be possible to attack them."

Groping with his fingertips, he approached the declivity formed by the ceiling of the cell. The point of the knife succeeded in chipping away a few flakes of plaster and laid bare a simple lattice, easy to destroy. Behind it there was nothing but a wooden step—but the oak boards were solid and well-fitted; the knife was chipped and there was a risk that it might break.

Picking up a bench, Pilesèche made use of it as a lever, leaning it on a second bench placed at right angles. The step, retained by notch-boards, bent in the middle, and Bémolisant took advantage of that opportunity give a vigorous blow to the vertical plank that served as a counter-step, and which, being less thick, gave way easily enough.

All that made a lot of noise, but people are accustomed to paying no attention to the racket made by a caged prisoner; people in a lock-up do not behave like angels.

The prisoner listened briefly to see of anything abnormal succeed the noise, and then, squeezing through the opening they had contrived, they found themselves in the vestibule of the Mairie. Their captors had thought they had done enough by locking the doors, and, by virtue of habit, had left the keys to the interior doors in the locks. Everything was going smoothly.

The fugitives hesitated as to the direction to take, and finally decided to go out via the gardens, after having locked the door and thrown the key into a field.

The squall had calmed down, chasing away the clouds, and the moon's silvery rays were reflecting from the snow.

As soon as they had escaped the enclosures and were in open country, Pilesèche signaled to his companion that he could not leave the body of his former employer at the mercy of the local people.

"Just think," he said. "What if, by chance, he were still alive!"

"Oh, again...!"

"It doesn't matter—it's a scruple you ought to share. Follow the road, walking slowly, while I go back to the inn. Don't worry—no one will see me. I'll get the cart and catch up with you in a few minutes. If I'm caught, too bad— save yourself, without worrying about me, and...good luck."

Bémolisant hesitated over letting his companion take the risk alone, but the other would find it easier to get himself out of trouble that way, so, all things having been considered, they split up.

Pilesèche started running, sticking close to the walls. The snow stifled the sound of his footfalls.

He had no difficulty reaching the courtyard of the inn and slipped into the shed—but the place where he had left the cart a few hours before was now empty.

Assuming that the gendarmes had taken possession of that piece of evidence, he retraced his steps rapidly, and as soon as he had caught up with his companion they both moved behind the hedge bordering the road, so that they could walk while sheltered from view.

They made haste, to the extent that the fresh snow, in which they sank ankle-deep, permitted.

Suddenly, they perceived by means of the moonlight a vehicle stopped on the road a hundred paces ahead of them. They moved closer with caution.

There, its wheels caught in the snow, was one of those large fairground caravans, whose vast flanks can accommodate an entire family, with the accessories of their trade.

Between its shafts, a single meager horse was striving to drag the heavy machine, and its panting breath, condensed by the cold, was forming a cloud of vapor around its head. A man was encouraging it with a forceful reinforcement of oaths and whiplashes, while a woman was trying to push one of the wheels.

The two fugitives moved closer, and were not a little surprised to see, attached behind the vehicle, a little handcart which bore a strong resemblance to their own, and recognized, in the charioteer and his acolyte, the performers of the previous evening.

They told themselves that there might be some advantage to be gained from the situation, and that in any case, they were not running any great risk in revealing themselves to a man who, by virtue of his profession, must be more often at odds with the police than with malefactors.

Quitting the shelter provided by the hedge, therefore, they leapt out on to the road and marched resolutely toward the performers.

Professor Joël saw them, and recognized them immediately. He was evidently wondering what disposition the two dangerous criminals might have toward him, but he was vigorous and scarcely accessible to fear. At any rate, he remained prudently in position, ready to receive them in case of aggression.

The two men did not seem to be paying any attention to the handcart that had been stolen from them, however, and Joël was the first to speak, in a good-humored tone.

"Well, well, Messeigneurs—so we've given the gentlemen of the constabulary the slip!"

"Monsieur," said Bémolisant, "you don't know us, but we swear to you that we're honest men. There's been a mistake. Help us to get out of it, and give us shelter in our vehicle."

"We're no longer as proud as we were yesterday evening. Personally, I don't see anything in your difficulties with the police, but to offer you the hospitality of my house would be a little risky. The gendarmes are after you, and I don't want them on my back."

Miss Adda gazed at her Master with an imploring expression, without daring to say a word but gripped by a supreme pity.

"It would be so easy for you to hide us in the back of your vehicle," hazarded Pilesèche.

Bémolisant joined in with more solid arguments.

"We're not without money," he said, "and we'd be grateful for your hospitality. Combining actions with words, he took a five-hundred-franc bill out of his wallet.

Five hundred francs!

Joël's eyes gleamed with covetousness. Five hundred francs! These people, so poorly dressed, must be very great criminals to have five hundred francs in their possession. Where the devil had they stolen that money? After all, that wasn't his business. His fingers stretched out toward the blue piece of paper, which disappeared immediately into some pocket or other.

"Come on," he said, "let's not waste time here. Give me a hand to get my wheels out of this accursed snow, and perhaps we can come to some arrangement."

The two men applied themselves to the wheels, while Joël whipped the horse, which, having recovered its breath, put sudden pressure on its collar and succeeded in getting under way again.

"Now let's chat," said the mountebank. "I'd like to get you out of difficulty, but one good turn deserves another. You doubtless still have a few notes in your pocket. Hire my outfit and you can remain my associates, and least as far as Nantes. I'm dreaming of spectacular shows and phenomenal receipts." He addressed Pilesèche. "You play the hypnotist like no one." He turned back to Bémolisant and added: "And you must have some hidden talent?"

"I play all kinds of musical instruments pleasantly," the artist replied, modestly.

"That's perfect." In a detached tone, he added: "I won't hide it from you that I thought to render you a real service by getting rid of the cart and the crate that you neglected to take to prison; all that might have fallen into the hands of the gendarmerie. It's no trouble. I've even committed the indiscretion of looking to see what's in the box. As an anatomical specimen it's not bad. We'll exhibit it and I'll take change of the patter. Now it's time to hide; dawn's about to break. Climb inside with Miss Adda.

They did not need to have the suggestion repeated.

In the depths of the vehicle there was an immense wicker basket. Joël explained to them that it was the nacelle of a balloon that he used for ascensions in large towns where there as a chance of suitable receipts. The two fugitives climbed into the nacelle, over a clutter of objects of every sort. Adda carefully arranged the rigging of the balloon, which succeeded in hiding them from view without inconveniencing them.

"You'll be in clover there," said the showman, laughing broadly. "At the slightest alert, burrow down under that mass of fabric—they won't find you under all that."

The side road that the caravan had been following had joined the highway again, where the snow was not as deep and required less effort from the emaciated horse that was pulling the mobile house. The showman climbed on to the driving seat, with Miss Adda by his side, still silent, but emotional without showing it, turning round from time to time to check that the others were well hidden.

It had been daylight for some time already and they had occasionally crossed paths with carts whose drivers, well wrapped up, cracked their whips to warm themselves up, when they suddenly heard two horses trotting behind them. Joël craned his neck to see who the early morning riders were.

"Look out! This is the critical moment," he said, ducking back into the vehicle hurried. Don't move and leave it to me."

It was the two gendarmes.

The noise of the cavalcade drew nearer, and the representatives of the public force, drawing level with the vehicle, fell into step with it.

"Bonjour," said the brigadier. "Have you seen anything unusual this morning?"

"My word, no. Not many people about because of the cold, and if I didn't have to get to Courtalain in good time, I'd have slept in late at the inn—but what can you do? One has to make a living."

The brigadier darted a suspicious glance into the depths of the carriage.

Without paying any heed to that, Joël continued: "By the way, Brigadier, if you have a yen to take the numbness out of your limbs and have a drop, I've got a nice bottle of rum in the bottom of the basket. Let me offer you two fingers. My beast can get his breath back in the meantime."

He did, in fact, bring his horse to a halt. "Adda, get that bottle and glasses," he went on. And so saying, he leapt to the ground, stamped his feet and stretched his legs.

In her turn, Adda briskly leapt down from the footstep and presented glasses to the two gendarmes. They hesitated, still suspicious, but the fairground performers seemed so innocently confident.

The brigadier placed his horse sideways, in order to get a better view of the inside of the vehicle. It was crammed with boxes and baskets; there was no space wasted and even less disposable.

"Well, what about your amiable crooks yesterday evening?" said Joël, in the most natural fashion in the world.

"In truth," said the brigadier, laughing sardonically, "I was wondering whether you were taking then away in your wagon?"

"No jokes, Brigadier; I don't carry vermin with me. But what do you mean? Has someone stolen them?"

"They've decamped. They're clever fellows, but they can't get very far on foot, and we'll show them that one can't make fools of us twice. I hoped that you might have run into them."

"Haven't seen anything of them. They've more likely cut across the fields."

"Too bad, too bad..."

The gendarmes clicked their tongues, raised their fingers to their kepis as a sign of gratitude, and resumed their trot.

12. On the Track

Rosamour, a stubborn man, persisted in occupying himself uniquely with finding Grillard, dead or alive.

That was the *corpus delicti*; in its disappearance lay the whole of the mystery that the police had to decipher. Thus, the policeman, without wasting his time running after the fugitives, was collecting the slightest indication, in order to reconstitute, piece by piece, the kind of life that the scientist ordinarily led.

In truth, Monsieur Grillard's relations were restricted and very intermittent. Among the people who might be able to shed some light on the habits of Népomucène Grillard, Rosamour suddenly thought about his notary, Maître Durand, a shrewd fellow who had known him for a long time, having been at the École de Droit when the future scientist was frequenting the laboratories of the Sorbonne, and who, not being afraid to stand up to him, had always remained on good enough terms with him—which is to say in a permanent dispute that never went as far as falling out.

When Rosamour sought to obtain some enlightenment, however, Maître Durand contented himself with smiling and shaking his head, and his mocking eyes sparkled behind his spectacles. He knew nothing more than the public, but "that old devil Grillard was so extraordinary in every way that he was bound to finish in an extraordinary fashion." As for him, all he could say was that he was the depository of his testament.

"Aha!" exclaimed Rosamour. "I hoped so; that document might perhaps tell us something..."

"Not so fast," the notary interrupted. You'll only have access to that information in six months' time, at the earliest."

"How's that?"

"I'm only to open it six months after his actual or presumed death."

"Very well—but to inform the police..."

"The police and the notariat are two different things. Professional secrecy, Monsieur—what about that?"

Rosamour had a strong desire to by-pass the lawyer's professional secrecy and obtain a formal warrant from an examining magistrate to search the office that had the pretention of being a tomb of secrets—but that was a major step that would certainly have put him at odds with the entire chamber of notaries, and he went home pensive, cursing the fatality that blocked all his best schemes.

It was in that state of mind that a message from Monsieur Fischer, the examining magistrate reached him, summoning him to the Palais urgently.

Only taking the time to grab an overcoat, our policeman hurtled into the street.

The magistrate as waiting for him, striding back and forth in his office impatiently.

"They've been arrested!" he cried, as soon as he saw him, showing him the yellow slip of a telegram open on the desk.

"Who?" said Rosamour, still thinking about nothing but his cadaver in his distress.

"Eh? Bémolisant and his acolyte, of course. What do you expect me to be thinking about, if not this accursed Panthéon affair—my nightmare?"

"Damn it!" the agent could not help saying. "That upsets my plans. What impetuosity people have, arresting people before it's time! Have you any means of confounding them and getting them to confess?"

"Bah! The worthy gendarmes might have been a little hasty, but it's done now. It's a matter of making the best of it. Perhaps it's a fortunate diversion, anyway, since your research hasn't turned up anything."

"Patience! One can't expect to fall on the right track at the first step—but I persist in believing that old Grillard's corpse is the key to the mystery, and that it's necessary, above all, to find it. Anyway, since the two fugitives have been arrested, I'll go..."

"Yes, by talking to them cleverly, you'll certainly be able to tie them in knots, and end up finding the truth—although, to tell the truth, those two fellows appear to me to be much less naïve than they seemed at first. Mistrust, Monsieur Rosamour, mistrust—they're sly ones; they're very clever."

"Oh, very clever," replied Rosamour, with absolute skepticism. "Anyway, I'll go, and we'll see..."

At that moment, someone knocked on the door. An office boy handed another telegram to the examining magistrate, who opened it. On reading it, however, his expression suddenly changed, in spite of the mask of impassivity that was habitual to him. It was with pinched lips, without saying a word, that he handed the piece of paper to the policeman.

The latter read it attentively in his turn, shook his head and sketched a vague smile.

"I see," he said, "that if the gendarmes of Briseval arrest people inappropriately, they let them escape in the same fashion. That doesn't change my plans, if you don't mind. I'll set out anyway, and I won't take long to find our fugitives, be sure of that."

"I suppose, in fact, that they're continuing to make for Nantes and Saint-Nazaire, by a more-or-less roundabout route, still having the intention of taking to the sea."

"I'll follow them step by step."

"Don't let them slip through your fingers at the last moment and embark."

"They won't embark without me."

"Try to succeed—public opinion is beginning to get impatient. The press, which never loses an opportunity to criticize the police, is already shouting from the rooftops that it's another file to be closed and that we can only arrest criminals if they turn themselves in."

"I'd like to see the reporters doing our job!"

Rosamour was particularly piqued by the examining magistrate's slightly sarcastic remarks, but he was forced to recognize their justice. In spite of all his skill and all his steps, the case was no further forward than on the day it had been assigned to him. He had collected an ample dossier of information. He knew every detail now of the lives of Bémolisant and Pilesèche. He had been able to reconstruct their comings and goings throughout the week that had preceded Grillard's mysterious disappearance and the one that had followed it. Only one thing escaped him—and that was the only important one.

What had become of the estimable scientist?

Of him, there was no trace.

He had come to believe that it was definitely his body that had been taken away in the box. But what had become of it thereafter, and where had the statue come from? The sole hypothesis that did not come to his mind was to identify the body with the effigy.

The nature of the metal and the opinion of competent people suggested that galvanoplastic methods must have been used to fabricate that statue, which no founder has cast; that was a conclusion acquired—but no galvanoplastic workshop in Paris or the surrounding area had ever been commissioned to carry out such work.

Learning that Monsieur Grillard's last endeavors had necessitated the employment of those processes of metallization, and that the scientist must, in consequence, have had the necessary equipment in his laboratory, Rosamour, moving from one deduction to another, was inclined to believe that the statue must have been finished there; it must, therefore have been the statue that was in the box, which was more in accordance with the excessive weight than the policeman's first hypothesis.

But in that case, once again, what had become of the scientist?

There was no way out of the dilemma: the box contained either the body or the statue, and in either case, the mystery, for being different, was no less indecipherable—as well as the famous cryptogram on which he had counted momentarily to supply the key to the enigma.

Decidedly, the examining magistrate was right. It was to the presumed guilty parties that it was necessary to go to seek the solution to the problem.

The agent ate a hasty meal and took the train at twenty minutes past midday with a ticket to Gault Saint-Denis, the nearest station to Briseval. There he took a cab, which deposited him at the door of the gendarmerie of the latter village.

The brigadier had just returned, rather discomfited by his fruitless pursuit.

Rosamour showed him his warrants and, without wasting time criticizing him for his inopportune intervention, he submitted him to a routine interrogation. Then he had himself taken to the prison, silently examined the location, gave orders for a locksmith to come and open the door giving access to the gardens, and had no difficulty finding the tracks of the fugitives. The snow had preserved them, and it was easy enough to follow hem step by step.

The two men must have separated outside the enclosing wall of the Mairie. The footprints of one of them were lost on a path leading back to the village, confused with those of other pedestrians, but the other had gone across the fields, going round the houses in order to reach the westbound road to Courtalain.

He had waited there for a few minutes, as testified by the trampling of the snow in that location, but he had eventually been rejoined by his companion, and both of them had continued on their way, following the hedge instead of the road.

All of that was written in a clear and precise fashion on the great white page. There was no mistaking it. Suddenly, however, the tracks stopped again. A further trampling indicated a new halt, and then the two fugitives had leapt on to the road. The imprints of their heels could be seen deeply embedded in the snow by the roadside. From then on, it was difficult to follow them because of the other tracks with which they were confused.

Escorted by two gendarmes, Rosamour continued his investigations as far as a place where there was a muddy dip in the road. The snow was no longer intact there, except between two profound ruts, on either side if which it had been crushed, mixed with earth and water to form a horrible sludge.

A vehicle had stopped there. The white area indicated the place protected by the body of the vehicle. In front of it, the horse had stamped its feet for some time, trying to gain purchase for its hooves, and then had pulled away. The carters, by exciting it or pushing the wheels, had got it moving.

Rosamour examined everything, leaning over the ground, without making the two gendarmes party to his reflections. They were wondering what could possibly there to interest the clever fellow from the Sûreté.

When he had finished his examination, the agent turned to the brigadier and asked him, in an indifferent one: "Since you traveled along this road shortly after the escape, you can tell me what vehicles you encountered."

"Oh, indeed. They weren't very numerous, in any case, given the weather. The first one was saw was that of a conjuror who gave a performance yesterday evening at the Cheval Boiteux. As I told you, it was during that performance that the arrest was made..."

"Ah! Give me a few details. Where was this vehicle when you encountered it?"

"About three kilometers from here."

"Did you look inside?"

"Ah!" said the other, swelling up with pride. "One knows one's métier. I stopped the vehicle, without making any fuss, and I could see all the way to the back. There was no one hiding there."

"You didn't go inside?"

"I didn't think it was worth the trouble."

"Well, my good man, you were mistaken; your two birds were there."

"You're joking," said the brigadier, who was strongly tempted to hold his sides.

"Where was your conjuror going?"

"To Courtalain, where he's giving a performance this evening."

Rosamour looked at his watch. It was too late to think of catching up with the fugitives that day. In any case, there was no urgency since he now knew where to find them. He therefore went tranquilly back to Briseval, telegraphed the examining magistrate to reassure him, installed himself at a small table in the Cheval Boiteux, near the stove—the same one at which the artist and the laboratory assistant had dined—and ordered a comfortable repast, which consoled him for his fatigues.

13. An Unexpected Ascension

The entire quarter of Nantes surrounding the gas factory was on holiday. It was the day of the fair, and in the little square the fairground booths were set up, ranging from the humble tents where waffles were spreading the odor of frying to the ample theater whose façade disappeared behind painted canvases.

When dusk came, everything was illuminated, as brightly as by day. Big drums of every caliber began to thunder, with the strident accompaniment of cymbals. The French horns, bugles, trombones and ophicleides all sang their favorite songs. The mechanical orchestras, their hundred flags blowing in the wind, bellowed furiously in the midst of wooden houses gleaming with gilt and facets of mirrors.

And the crowds went by, in a perpetual jostle of elbows, with an indescribable riot of cries, catcalls, exclamations of joy, growls and yelps. Everyone was at the fête, all having a good time!

Among the establishments that the inexhaustible parade passed there was one, in particular, that arrested the members of the public as if it had seized them by the collar. That was a pavilion of restricted dimensions, decorated with paintings in which a superb woman clad in a low-cut dress could be seen, in all the attitudes that somnambulistic sleep can produce. A gentleman in a black suit, wand in hand, evidently represented the skillful operator who realized the marvels in question.

And on the trestles, that same gentleman in a black suit—but in the flesh and bone—with a beautiful smile and beautiful words on his lips, was inviting the crowd to come into the tent with noble gestures.

A rather thin young woman was leaning on one of the tent-poles and occasionally adding something to the proprietor's patter.

"Come in, Mesdames et Messieurs; it only costs ten centimes—two sous! You'll see the most astonishing things. Hypnotism demonstrated! Extra-lucid somnambulistic sight! Come in, Mesdames et Messieurs.

To one side of the platform, a clown with a white face and a village bridegroom with a red nose were making deadening music. The former was banging a bass drum and cymbals with formidable wrist-power, the later blowing into an enormous trombone, with clicks and clacks every time the long slide went in or out to its full extent. The sounds that sprang from the brass instrument, along with the vibrations of the shrill rattle, tore the most hardened eardrums. It was a *danse macabre* of triple crotchets, a hectic jig of delirious triolets, cascading over the broken rungs of a fantastic scale of incoherence.

And the grotesque artiste who was inflating his cheeks to blow into that tube has such an expression of unalloyed satisfaction that the public guffawed, stamped their feet, howled with joy and shouted for more at the top of their voices, with an exhilarating enthusiasm.

But the man in the black suit rang the big bell, and the music fell silent.

It was just in time; the artiste was on the point of collapse. His entire face was swollen and as red as his vermilion nose. He sponged his temples, and while the patter ran its course he leaned toward the clown

"Finally," he said, "I've found an audience that understands my music! I've been all over France, America and Asia. I've given concerts to high society and savages, but no one ever applauded like this crowd."

"This crowd had an instinct for decadent music, my dear Bém..."

"Call me Arthur, I beg you."

The clown also had his share in the success. It was not that he was particularly amusing, or that his sallies were marked with the English humor, reminiscent of an epileptic undertaker, that one loves to encounter nowadays in artistes of that genre. He was absolutely deadpan, sulky and sad, and it was his sadness that was funny. In the bouffant trousers that dressed his legs, with the sun on his belly and a half-moon on his back., he was so gauchely maladroit, so blissfully taciturn and stiff, that one could not look at that white face with its two eyebrows like grave accents without laughing until one cried.

"Come on, Monsieur Clown, say something amiable to the honorable society!"

It was the black suit that pronounced those engaging words, and, taking Monsieur Clown by the arm, he made him do a pirouette, while that unexpected shock caused the marionette to stagger and beat the air with his long arms.

People writhe with laughter, and when the invitation to "Enterrrrr!" resounded again, there as a veritable stampede that threatened to overturn the trestles, stave in the planks and bring down the whole tent.

Inside, the spectators arranged themselves on the benches, poorly covered with red fabric, which was coming away in tatters.

At the back, a platform represented the stage. At the foot of the stage was a red velvet pedestal, over which a muslin veil was thrown, vaguely outlining the forms of a recumbent body.

The young woman who has just appeared at the door was sitting on the stage, with a weary and disenchanted expression. The clown was astride a bench. Finally, when the village bridegroom and his trombone had taken their places in a corner, the man in the black suit advanced toward the audience and bowed, one hand on his heart, like a vulgar comic-opera tenor.

"Mesdames et Messieurs, you must have heard mention of Professor Joël. I can say without boasting that renown precedes me wherever I go. The Académie itself has taken an interest in my work, and I defy anyone, in that honorable society, to carry out experiments more curious than those you are about to witness. But enough preamble! You're impatient—strike up the band!"

The trombone launched a series of furious notes. When the chromatic scale was extinguished, Professor Joël bowed again.

"Before putting on display before you all that hypnotic science has of the mysteriously sublime, let me give you a few necessary explanations regarding the anatomical constitution of the human body.

While pronouncing that emphatic exordium, he lifted the veil that was covering the red pedestal, on which a recumbent body appeared, painted in a cadaveric hue, with greenish tints of advanced decay.

"You have before you, Mesdames et Messieurs," the professor continued, "the reproduction of a masterpiece of statuary, in which the anatomy of the human body is, so to speak, sculpted in the quick."

And to think, thought the melancholy village bridegroom, *that it's me who painted my uncle in those lugubrious colors!*

With the tip of his wand, Joël gave his physiological demonstration, accompanying it with big words and grand gestures, but his audience was primarily griped by the eyes. Everyone stood up on the benches and jostled one another in order to see "the masterpiece of statuary" and that strange thin and pale man whose bones were jutting out through his green-tinted flesh.

That was, however, only a curtain-raiser, and the real performance was yet to commence—but before then, the professor had a recommendation to make to the public.

"Don't forget, Mesdames et Messieurs, that tomorrow, at two o'clock in the afternoon, in the square in front of this establishment, the inflation and ascension will take place of a monstrous balloon. I shall have the honor of performing, on a trapeze suspended below the nacelle a thousand feet up in the air, the most perilous acrobatic feats that you have ever seen. And now, I shall begin..."

We shall not describe that session of hypnosis, in which the clown played the major role, Professor Joël contenting himself with commenting and making speeches, explaining the experiments that his auxiliary was carrying out on the entranced young woman.

Among the spectators there was one young man who had placed himself beside the village bridegroom, and who, while the latter was not blowing into his trombone, did not disdain to chat to the instrumentalist.

At first there were exclamations and expressions of admiration. The experiments impassioned and enthused him. He was a traveling salesman, he said, and had seen all sorts of things, but he had never seen anything as impressive. Then he came back to the anatomical statue.

"Is it made of wax?" he asked, naively.

The artiste shuddered. "I don't know," he replied.

"It's astonishing how much it resembled a drawing I've seen in the illustrated papers. It was a sculpture by Bémolisant—you know, the artist who disappeared.

The other shifted in his chair, with an evident malaise.

"It's said that he murdered his uncle," the spectator continued, in a tranquil and detached manner.

"That's absurd, idiotic...what do you want?" exclaimed the other, immediately biting his lip.

"Me? I don't want anything at all. I'm just saying what there is in the newspapers.—but perhaps you know better than I do, if you know him..."

"If I know him, if I know him...why do you think I know him?"

"Well, no, I don't say that. How do I know? It doesn't alter the fact that the old man can't be found. And yet, if he hasn't been murdered, he could reappear, and then the slander would shut up, wouldn't it?"

"Well, it's easy for you to talk. It's always easy to settle questions. I'd do this, I'd do that—but when one finds oneself in a tight corner, one finds that it isn't so easy to get out of it. In fact, I don't know him, this sculptor; I'm just talking..."

"To make conversation, that's all—understood."

"But I have a sympathy for him. One ought to have, between artistes. And I say to myself: who knows? Perhaps he's in a situation that's too implausible, and, if he tried to make people believe it, everyone would laugh in his face. They'd cry: 'Tell it to the marines, old man! You can't take us in with tales like that!' And all the evidence is against him, everything demonstrates that he's guilty...it's just a supposition, you understand, a simple supposition..."

"Oh, that's how I take it."

"He says to himself then: I've been very stupid to fall into the wolf-trap. I could swear my innocence till the cows come home, but they'd convict me anyway, and I want to keep my skin.' What do you think of that reasoning, eh?"

"That it's sane enough. Unless he's guilty, in which case I'd understand even better why he's running away."

"You wrong to believe that. Anyway, I'm not trying to convince you."

"All the more so as it's not me that it's necessary to convince, but the police."

That observation had the power to make the artiste shudder. In a low voice, he repeated: "The police, the police...yes, it's the police."

When the performance finished, the audience got up to leave, with a frightful hubbub.

The pretended commercial traveler politely took his leave of the trombonist. Scarcely had he turned his back when a head leaned toward the artiste's ear and murmured: "Don't trust the man who was just talking to you—he's a policeman."

The unfortunate village bridegroom started trembling in every limb.

At that moment, the man in question turned round and, perceiving the man who had just spoken to the musician, said to himself: *Why, what can that serpent*

Boissonnald be doing here? That's not obvious. He'd better not put a spoke in my wheel or, word of a Rosamour, he'll regret it.

The following day, which was Sunday, the fair was in full swing.

The preparations for the launch of the balloon were being made solemnly, as is befitting when it is a matter of interesting a crowd and extracting good money from its pockets.

Ropes had been extended to form a large circle; within that area several rows of chairs had been set out, in which the most curious or the most fortunate spectators had taken their places.

In the middle of the circle, one of the openings of the gas main had been uncovered.

The envelope of varnished calico forming the balloon was lying on the ground like a huge fishing net, the valve in the center. A broad tube, similarly made of varnished calico, was fitted to the gas conduit, the other end extending underneath the aerostat to the orifice that have it access.

Professor Joël had abandoned his black suit; he appeared in the spangled leotard of a simple acrobat, ready to perform gymnastics underneath the nacelle that could be seen a few paces away, rigged out and ready to be attached to the balloon's net as soon as the inflation was complete.

Pilesèche, in his clown costume, and Bémolisant, the trombone-playing village bridegroom, were there again, along with Miss Adda, who was circulating among the spectators, selling them oranges and barley-sugar.

It was a bright, sunny day with a dry cold that that had not kept anyone away. The audience was numerous and its members well disposed to take pleasure in the spectacle they had been promised, the preparations for which Joël was explaining to them in a stentorian voice.

Two or three employees of the gas factory, in braided caps, were lending their collaboration to the inflation. The gas was gradually introduced into the envelope, which swelled up awkwardly, like the spontaneous generation of an enormous mushroom.

The cords of the net were attached to sacks of ballast, which held the fragile machine in place, preventing it from rising too quickly. The men had to bring the bags closer together, attaching them lower down, as the gigantic ball rose up, forming a gilded dome inside the mesh of the net.

The equator of the thousand-cubic-meter sphere is already visible; it is filling up rapidly now. The pear-shaped neck appears. The time has come to fit the nacelle; it is attached.

With scrupulous care, Joël verifies all the junctions, makes sure that no cleat is faulty, that no mooring-rope will break in mid-air, imperiling the human lives that are about to confide themselves to the frail craft. The material is a little old, but with precautions the ascension will be accomplished without a hitch. The passengers announced in the program are Joël, Miss Adda and a volunteer.

While Joël does his perilous exercises on the trapeze, Miss Adda will guide the aerostat. As for the benevolent passenger, he has paid a rather large sum to procure the emotions of a voyager in space.

The aides attach a French flag to the suspension cords; the anchor is hanging over one of the sides of the nacelle, and to maintain equilibrium, the other side is fitted with the guide-tope rolled up into a ball.

Everything is ready.

Joël was in the nacelle, methodically arranging the instruments and sacks of ballast.

Miss Adda was selling the last oranges, and the novice passenger was saying interminable adieux to his family; one might have thought that he was about to embark on a long voyage.

In the meantime, Pilesèche and Bémolisant, in their eccentric costumes, were making furious music—but the artiste did not have the same verve as the previous evening. The immutable principles of absolute music were no longer speaking to his heart. He had many other preoccupations, and it seemed to him that he could still hear the mocking cry: "Look out! It's the police!"

And all of a sudden, his eyes, scanning the circle of spectators surrounding the aerostat, his eyes encountered the enigmatic visage of the so-called traveling salesman who had been denounced to him.

The man's words and gestures came back to his mind. He interpreted and explained them in the worst possible light, while, with inflated cheeks, he blew unconscious notes nevertheless into the mouthpiece of his trombone.

That man had talked about Uncle Grillard!

Was that not enough? Had he not given, himself, and without being solicited, all the reasons that condemned the laboratory assistant and the artist?

Then, leaning toward his companion—his accomplice—between two brazen squawks that split the ears of an indulgent public, Bémolisant spoke in a low voice, confiding his anxieties to him. He showed him the danger that was surging forth like the head of Medusa.

And the spectacle unfolds. The preparations are complete. Joël gives the order to remove the final sacks of ballast hanging from the net, which are keeping the balloon nailed to the ground. Several men put their weight on the nacelle to prevent the aerostat from flying away into the atmosphere, but their number is insufficient. Joël calls for a few volunteers. Oh, there's no lack of them! They emerge from the ranks of the audience and launch themselves into the circle reserved for the maneuver.

Several brush past the two musicians.

At the same time, a voice whispers in their ears: "He's the police!"

And when their haggard eyes go once again to the commercial traveler, the subject of so much anguish, the voice continues, bringing their fear to a peak: "He's going to arrest you at the end of the performance. Save yourselves."

Arrest them! They go pale and tremble in their tight and grotesque costumes. As if moved by a spring however, they have both stood up, dropping the trombone and the big drum. They are face to face, consulting one another with their gaze, in the midst of the crowd, whose members are also on their feet to watch the departure, all gazes fixed on the balloon—for the solemn moment has arrived. Impatiently, Joël calls out to his passenger, who is stretching out his adieux with kisses and compliments.

Miss Adda, with one hand on the edge of the wicker cage, her head turned toward the unhurried traveler, is ready to climb into the nacelle.

But suddenly, abruptly, in the midst of a confusion of aides jostling one another, two large bodies fray a passage through the men still retaining the balloon. Those two bizarre phantoms leap into the nacelle. As if they have agreed to act and speak in unison, they utter a cry in unison: a single, vibrant, resounding cry:

"Let go!"

At that powerful, unexpected cry, the surprised aides instinctively lift the hands that are retaining the aerostat, and the latter, suddenly free, bounds like a thoroughbred whose bridle has been released.

An enthusiastic hurrah rises with it.

The spectators have only seen in that unexpected turn of events a comic effect prepared in advance. They applaud.

The passenger, abandoned on the ground, stares open-mouthed at his vehicle in flight, and Miss Adda, brushed by the nacelle as it escaped, remains motionless in stupor.

In the audience, however, one man had straightened up, surprised and also anxious, while beside him, another man who has approached murmurs ironically in is ear: "You're stumped, Monsieur Rosamour."

"Stumped!" the agent replied. "Not yet. There's the telegraph for worthy men—but you'll pay for this, Monsieur Boissonnald."

Balloons launched from fairgrounds do not, as a rule, come down far away. Rosamour had no doubt that by telegraphing the authorities in the region toward which the balloon was heading, he would have news of it that same evening.

Now, the balloon had been carried away by a north-easterly wind. It was heading toward the sea, which might force the aeronauts to come down sooner than they would have wished.

In spite of the favorable circumstances, the night did not bring any news.

The following day also passed without anything being heard of the aerial voyagers. They had flown away into the sky, and they had not come down again.

Boissonnald was right. Rosamour was stumped.

He did not want to admit defeat, however, and he went back to the tent, where Miss Adda was awaiting, silently and fatalistically, the denouement of the singular affair.

She did not understand as yet exactly what had happened, and had no doubt that the aerial voyagers might return at any moment. Time was passing, however, and her confidence was ebbing away. A dull anxiety had been born within her, and a kind of obsession. It was not the image of Joël that passed through her mind—Joël was always harsh, with never a kind word—but that of the unfortunate Pilesèche, so sympathetic to the young woman's miseries, even though he scarcely talked to her. It seemed that his magnetic power had not only exerted a temporary influence over her, but had installed itself as sovereign throughout her being. When he spoke, she listened, lost in a dream, as if his voice were singing. When he approached, she felt his proximity instinctively, and turned her head. And now that he was no longer there, it was like a great void in the middle of which she was completely disorientated. A part of her had departed with her magnetizer, without her being able to render account of what had disequilibrated her, and that exteriorization, as it were, of her faculties.

When Rosamour came to question her, he found her anxious and agitated. She looked at him suspiciously, without replying. Instead of threatening her, the agent was gentle and insinuating; he was only looking for the truth, the proof of innocence.

At Pilesèche's name she had shuddered, and Rosamour pulled that string, saying that it was in the interests of the young man that he gather all the information that might facilitate his recover.

Then Adda, quite simply and without any evasion, told him the story of the association from the day that Joël had met the two supposed criminals.

Criminals! Who could possibly believe that they were? She had seen them at close range, had lived with them, and she swore that they were not.

She became excited as she said that, and then her speech fell back into calm monotony, as if wearied by the effort.

Certainly, she had told him all that she knew—he had no doubt about that—but what she knew scarcely cast any light on the problem. Rosamour left, discouraged by the conversation; he made a minute inventory, without finding anything in the midst of the gaudy trash cluttering the tent and the vehicle that might aid him in his task. He kept a few papers for examination at leisure, although even they appeared at first glance to be insignificant.

As he did not want to return to Paris empty-handed, however, he invited Miss Adda to accompany him—she was still a witness—and registered as baggage the famous nickel statue, stripped of the layer of paint with which it had been daubed, shining beneath its white patina.

14. The Wreck of a Balloon

The idea of attempting the aerial route to escape the pursuit of the gendarmes does not involve any more danger than that implicit in tranquilly buying a railway ticket for a distant location, but it is less practical.

Murderers and other large-scale malefactors do not always have a ready-inflated aerostat to hand, fiacres generally being more common in our streets. The balloon, moreover, is a costly means of locomotion that does not lend itself easily to mystery.

Joël had been utterly astounded on seeing those two fantastic beings leap into the nacelle: a clown and a village bridegroom, two estimable murderers—for it must be said that he if had once listened, with a benevolent smile, to their fantastic explanations regarding their imaginary crime, he had not been duped for a single instant. It was not him, Joël, who could be taken in by such tales; he had seen far too much of the world to be credulous.

"What's got into you?" he shouted, with a formidable oath, when, after that abrupt irruption, the balloon, escaping from the grip of its guardians, flew away into the air.

The wicker nacelle, poorly attached to the encircling net and violently jolted, oscillated like a salad-shaker, and the aeronauts were forced, in order not to be slammed into one another, to cling on to the rigging.

They had made a sudden bound five hundred meters into the air before the acrobat had recovered from his surprise. It was truly a little late to give the crowd, amazed by that unexpected departure, the spectacle of pirouettes executed on the bar of the trapeze that the balloon had lifted up with it and which was swinging furiously. In any case, the incident had been so unexpected and comical that the members of the public, believing it to be a farce cleverly planned to tease their appetite for novel fare, were clapping their hands fervently and crying "Bravo!" with all the force of their combined lungs.

The clamors rose up in discordant gusts all the way to the narrow receptacle in which were crouched the three most singular passengers imaginable: an acrobat, an improbable clown and the most horribly grease-painted of village bridegrooms, with his flowery waistcoat, his gigantic collar shapelessly turned down, his Bluebeard suit with large brass buttons and his beribboned bouquet.

Joël was furious, and he had no lack of reasons to be. Was he not about to lose his reputation, by virtue of not having completed his program?

"But since they're applauding...!" the former laboratory assistant objected, timidly.

"You're nothing but an idiot!" the other interrupted, violently. "What about the passenger I was supposed to bring—is he applauding too? He's been left on the ground...and carrying away his money. Is that the way to do things, eh? I wouldn't care about that, if it weren't necessary to go back to Nantes for the rest of the kit, but we're going to have to do that...and we'll be lucky if the police don't get mixed up in it..."

Bémolisant and Pilesèche lowered their heads and received the downpour without saying anything. From time to time, the artiste tried to get a word in. "Listen...," he said, timidly—but immediately, the insults rained down even harder, and the orator had considerable reinforcements of oaths in his throat.

128

Everything comes to an end, however, even the great fits of anger of acrobats and professors of magnetism. Joël finally fell silent, breathless, and Bémolisant was able to make his speech.

He explained the cause of their panic. He related the mysterious advice uttered twice over, and the head of Medusa suddenly appearing in the form of an agent of the Sûreté with a mocking expression.

It makes no difference whether one is innocent, there are things one cannot help and, in truth, without reflection, they had both had the same idea, of taking off for the clouds. Perhaps it was stupid, but after all, one could hardly blame them.

"Well, it's very clever, what you've just done," Joël muttered. "As if the telegraph has been created for nothing! You'll be picked up when you disembark from the balloon, and thanks to you, I'll be caught in the net. But if that happens, damn it, you'd better get ready to pay me back!"

During this altercation, rapid as it was, as the insults had followed one another like javelins in some Homeric combat, no one was keeping watch on the progress of the balloon, which had continued rising until it reached an altitude of a thousand meters and then had started flying rapidly south-westwards.

An immense plain of hilly cloud extended beneath the nacelle, pierced here and there by somber holes, shafts of a sort, at the bottom of which patches of brown earth could be perceived.

Above them gilding the yellow cambric dome of the balloon, the sun was shining in the transparent and rarefied atmosphere. In spite of the clouds floating higher in the sky, which obscured it at intervals, its rays warmed the aerial globe somewhat, and it resumed its ascendant trajectory as it dilated in that heat.

Gradually, however, as it continued its course, the aerostat penetrated into a glacial mist in which the iridescent light was scattered by the turbulence of microscopic crystals of nascent snow.

For the aeronauts, all indication of movement had disappeared. The aerostat seemed to be motionless in space, in the middle of a block of unpolished glass, drowned in a diffuse light.

No more earth, no more sky! No noise was rising up from the ground to the nacelle. It was a grim solitude; oblivion in the midst of the golden darts of radiant light.

Bémolisant was shivering with fever and cold, while Pilesèche, his head in his hands, forgot his observer's temperament, unconscious of the marvelous spectacle that was offered to him without his having to seek it out.

The acrobat Joël was certainly not sacrificing himself to the ideal, and his poetic tastes did not solicit him to prolong the voyage for the vain pleasure of contemplating the aerial scenery. A fairground ascension is not exactly an amusement for the man who carries it out; he considers that he has done enough for is audience when he has made a prestigious departure, and as soon as he has disappeared into the clouds he has nothing more pressing to do that return to earth as rapidly as possible, in order to avoid excessively considerable expense in returning by railway. It had required the surprise and the heat of the dispute to cause him to forget those principles of sage economy, in order for him not to have yet determined the descent by a vigorous tug on the valve.

On the other hand, the perspective of the tricorn hats and sashes that he was expecting to appear on landing rendered him rather perplexed and irresolute. Was it necessary to stop, or to gain ground, in order to return to earth in some remote spot where it would be easier to get away?

The atmospheric circumstances took responsibility themselves for answering the question.

The balloon was weighed down by a multitude of spangles and needles of ice. Under that burden, and as the gas contracted by virtue of cooling, the aerostat began to descend. There were no reference points, but in order to be certain of the fall it was sufficient to look at the flaccid fabric, which was hollowing out beneath the huge sphere maintained in the broad mesh of the net.

Joël threw a few pieces of cigarette paper out of the nacelle, which seemed to rise up rapidly toward the sky, simply because the aerostat was descending much more rapidly than they were.

The aeronauts felt a vertical wind strike their faces. Finally—the last indication—the flag suspended from the rigging was lifted up, fluttering under the resistant action of the air.

It seemed that they were heading for the ground at a speed that was already vertiginous. The acrobat judged it prudent to slow that hectic progress by emptying a sack of ballast.

The fog did not permit the ground beneath the nacelle to be distinguished, but a dull murmur could be heard, like the distant rumble of trains in the vicinity of a large train. The noise was rather bizarre in its continuity, and grew in volume as the altitude diminished.

In order better to perceive and analyze it, Joël leaned over the fragile wicker of the nacelle.

The fog seemed to become less dense. The iridescent crystals, charged with electricity, were attracting one another, hastening together and aggregating into snowflakes. That snow was falling on to the balloon, already bristling with needles of frost—a white coat whose layer was thickening and making the aerial vehicle heavier. The danger was imminent, for its speed was accelerating rapidly.

"Damn!" cried Joël. "Ballast, quickly! We're falling!"

It was, indeed, a rapid fall that was now precipitating the balloon toward the earth, and already, through the snow, daylight was visible.

Obstinately leaning halfway out of the nacelle, the acrobat tried to catch a glimpse of the murmurous ground, and suddenly shouted: "Damnation! It's the sea!"

The sea! It was the sea that was producing that strange murmur. It was the sea, rolling wave after wave, breaking on rocks.

The shore was close by, but the balloon had already passed over it, and, while falling, it was continuing its course out to sea!

"We're doomed!" howled Joël, his hands clenched in his hair.

"We need to find a contrary current," hazard Pilesèche.

"Imbecile! A contrary current! Empty ballast, animal! That's all that you can do..."

And, setting an example, the two men nervously threw sacks of ballast into the sea, without even untying them, abruptly and hastily, each time delivering a shock to the aerostat.

And when the ballast ran out, it was all the instruments there were in the nacelle, and anything that was loose, heavy or light, including the anchor, whose rope was rapidly cut by a stroke of a knife.

As if it had understood the danger, the aerostat, thus unburdened, slowed its velocity, and finally paused two or three hundred meters above the swell that was oaring beneath it. But it did not rise up again, and there was nothing left to lighten it any further.

It was still heading westwards, and toward the west there was nothing but water, as far as the eye could see, and on the water, only a few distant sails that were disappearing over the horizon, without having seen the airship in distress.

His anger passed, Joël, in the face of danger, had recovered all his composure. It was not the first time that he had confronted peril in his adventurous life, and he thought about the best means of prolonging their suspension at a moderate height until a ship, passing close by, perceived the balloon and came to its aid.

But time was passing and the balloon, after a brief respite, resumed its downward movement. he guide-rope hanging from the nacelle suddenly touched the surface, and, gradually plunging into it, lightened the aerostat slightly...but not enough, alas, to interrupt the descent, which continued irremediably.

The aeronauts had nothing more to throw out. Then discouragement gripped them: what was the point of delaying the fatal outcome? No ship appeared that could pick up the unfortunates, and now they were waiting, instinctively clinging to the rigging...

Abruptly, an impact!

The wicker nacelle dipped into the sea, which submerged it momentarily, soaking the unfortunates to the skin.

Joël, with his knowledge of the métier, had climbed into the circle of the net, but, pushed by the wind, the balloon lay down on the sea, leaving its rigging trailing in the waves, and the acrobat with it.

Under the deballasting effect of the nacelle dipping into the water, however, the gas recovered a little force and lifted the entire rig, which, with a new surge rose up fifty meters—only to fall again immediately.

And those lugubrious somersaults, the last bounds of an exhausted horse, were repeated until the balloon, having used up all its energy, flaccid and convulsed, stood up by the wind like a huge body without a soul, resumed skimming the waves, only slowed down by the heavy burden that it was still dragging, half-submerged, hollowing out a long wave behind it.

That envelope of cotton fabric, bloated and undulating, in which gusts of wind hollowed out pockets with sinister flopping sounds, resembled, in the light of the setting sun, a monstrous octopus sustaining in its tentacles three condemned men, just sufficiently to prolong their agony.

Every shock that plunged them under water gave them a vision of the anguish of death.

Pilesèche and his companion had tried to escape the waves by climbing up to the net as well. With their feet on the edge of the nacelle, they hoisted themselves up as far as they could—but their position was even more atrocious there; they were rolled in all directions, only hanging on to the ropes by their stiffened hands, battered by the waves, blinded by the icy mist...

And, letting go, they fell, devoid of strength and courage, into the bottom of the nacelle, losing consciousness and perception of their surroundings.

Were they not already in the strange slumber that resembles the vestibule of death? How many minutes separated them now from eternity?

15. An Agents' Square-Dance

As he boarded the train that was to take him back to Paris Monsieur Boissonnald found himself torn between two contrary sentiments, and, according to whether he turned his ideas heads up or tails up, he found a face that was cheerful or sad, like the double image of Heraclitus and Democritus.

In him, Democritus was weeping for the lamentable outcome of the particular affair that had brought him to Nantes—for, in truth, it was only a fortunate combination of circumstances that had allowed him to stumble by chance on to the tracks of the fugitives.

Heraclitus was laughing in thinking about the nice trick he had just played on his colleague Rosamour, whose somewhat arrogant manner had the gift of making his hair curl.

He counted, moreover, on not leaving it there, and working to discredit the "scientific detective" by all the means at his disposal.

Who could tell? Perhaps there was a place to take there, and the private enterprise that he had undertaken had not been sufficiently successful that he would disdain an opportunity to return to the administrative bosom, if some striking coup could open the door to him.

That is why Master Boissonnald, as soon as he arrived in Paris, thought that he ought to present himself in the office of Monsieur Fischer, the examining magistrate in charge of the Panthéon affair.

Boissonnald had assumed his most hypocritical expression and his most enigmatic smile. He found the magistrate in a state of nervous overexcitement, easy o understand, for he had just received a telegram from Rosamour announcing the aerial flight of the two criminals. Did that fact not corroborate all his suspicions? A further telegram informed him, moreover, of the negative result of all the agent's attempts to discover where the balloon had landed. Finally, Rosamour announced his imminent return, and more ample verbal explanations.

Boissonnald therefore arrived in time to be the first to furnish details of the incident. In doing so, he took a malign pleasure in charging his colleague with all possible stupidities, so effectively that the magistrate, who drank in his words and was already quite prepared to depreciate the conduct of an unsuccessful agent, was convinced that he was dealing with a complete idiot.

In the meantime, Rosamour was on his way to render an account of his lack of success. That is never a situation full of attractions, and we would be lying if he said that he was not crestfallen.

As for the welcome that waited him, he was under no illusions in that regard. The method that he had thought it best to employ in the affair had never pleased the examining magistrate. One success could legitimate his initiative. He had failed; it only remained for him to pay for the breakages.

Such were the reflections that were agitating him on the cushions of the express between Nantes and Paris, but as, all things considered, he was not lacking in a certain dose of philosophy, our policeman ended up going to sleep and dreaming that he had stolen Icarus' wings and was improbably giving chase to the fugitives through the skies.

On arrival in Paris, the time had not get come to go to the Prefecture of Police. He therefore occupied himself with lodging Miss Adda in a nearby hotel, in order to have his witness near to hand when needed. As for the nickel statue, as well as the other items that he had thought he ought to retain from the acrobat's frippery, he had them transported to his own apartment. The rest had been left under seal in Nantes.

When Rosamour decided to go to the Prefecture he was not surprised to be received coldly by the head of the Sûreté, who nevertheless held him in particular esteem.

"My good friend," the latter said, "the scientific method has not held up. What do you expect? You've made too much noise with your operations. Of someone else one would be content to say that he'd been unfortunate; of you, they'll say that you've been maladroit. That's what comes of wanting to reform humanity. Now, I advise you not to go to see Fischer for the moment. He's furious with you. It's necessary to say that you've demolished yourself throughout this affair—a child of fifteen wouldn't have had your naivety."

"But nothing is lost," Rosamour protested. "Our fugitives have escaped into death, for it's obvious that they've fallen into the sea; otherwise I'd have picked up traces of them. The affair is therefore liquidated in that respect. There now remains the other aspect of the problem to resolve, the victim to recover. Let me disentangle that—I'll take responsibility for penetrating the mystery. We'll see then whether or not I'm maladroit..."

"Ta ta ta...if I were alone, free in my movements, I wouldn't say no, and you'd be able to get your revenge, but anything I can do would be futile. Someone else has been found for that task."

That declaration fell upon the agent like a cold shower. "Ah!" he said, finally. "And may one know to whom the affair has been entrusted?"

"Yes, indeed...all the more so as Monsieur Fischer felt obliged to go over my head in order to go in search of that idiot Boissonnald."

"Well, well...so it's Boissonnald!"

Rosamour was perhaps about to say more, but he stopped, prudently, thinking that the moment for confidences had not yet come.

"As for you, my dear," the head of the Sûreté added, "my advice is that it's time to disappear and wait in solitude for things to pick up again." With the skepticism of a man accustomed to the perversity of things down here, he added; "Your time will come."

"To put it another way, I've got the boot."

"Sorry...you understand. Such a resounding failure—the court requires a scapegoat."

"Fair enough. I know how to occupy my leisure."

"Then all's for the best. No hard feelings and, when the time comes, when all the noise has died down, count on me open the door."

"Much obliged."

As Rosamour as leaving, he turned round. "There's no point, then, in going myself to report..."

"Absolutely. Boissonnald has rendered you the service of sparing you that trouble by reporting your actions in detail—he happened to be there at the moment of the escape."

"Oh, I know, and I'm far from sure that he didn't have anything to do with it."

"Aha! He's a sly one..."

Rosamour stuck his hat on and left the Prefecture of Police in a state of complete exasperation. With his hands in his pockets and his teeth clenched, he strode along the quais at a rapid pace, with no objective in mind, trying to reassemble his ideas and settle on a line of conduct.

What could he do?

Rancor is a poor adviser, and for the moment he was all rancor, only seeking the best means of putting one over on the examining magistrate and the successor who had got him so briskly sacked.

Someone was about to poach on his preserves! And if that individual found the key to the mystery, he, Rosamour, would pass for a naïve fool!

All was not said and done yet, of course, and he was not about to let go. There were two players in the game, if you please; it remained to be seen who would reach the goal more rapidly, and in the meantime, he would use all cunning of a Mohican to put Boissonnald off the rack, mystify Fischer, and roll over the police and the court alike, to snatch their prey from them if the aeronauts ever reappeared on the horizon and especially—above all!—to prevent them from finding the old scientist, the pivot of the entire affair.

To start with, he did not feel any urgency to hand over to the clerk the few pieces of evidence that he possessed and to make known the only interesting witness that had been involved in recent events. Miss Adda was in a safe place; he had taken great care not to mention her to a living soul; no one would know who had caused her to disappear, and Boissonnald might search for her for a long time. It was more probable, however, that the latter would be much more interested in the two fugitives, unless he had accepted once and for all that the unfortunates had perished in the waves.

As if to corroborate the hypothesis, the newspapers announced that the wreckage of a balloon, deprived of its nacelle, had been found in the sea, and that the balloon could not be any other than the one from the Nantes fair. And indeed, as soon as that news reached the court, the file on the affair was hastily closed, there being no point in further pursuit since the guilty parties—who could doubt now that they were guilty?—were indubitably dead. It was, in any case, an honorable fashion to finish with an annoying investigation on which no one had succeeded in casting any light. There would always be time to take it up again of new circumstances required it.

Even Boissonnald was not overly keen to follow such an obscure trail, which did not augur anything good. He had got the job and was quite comfortable there, what point was there in risking committing some stupidity in a complicated affair that had sunk his predecessor?

Everyone was, therefore, satisfied—even public opinion, which, not doubting the culpability of the two fugitives, finally had the denouement of the drama—a picturesque denouement in which the crime had been punished by ineluctable fatality, as was appropriate.

Rosamour was the only one not to be content, doubtless because he was too difficult to satisfy: the only one not to bury the affair, because he judged that his self-respect demanded that he provide a different denouement, his goal having always been before all, to find the old scientist and explain his disappearance.

While those in official regions were occupying themselves with other matters, Rosamour, in the shadows, was setting up new batteries.

Only one thing worried him one cannot make war without funds, and funds were lacking now that he was no longer drawing a salary from the Prefecture. But it is not with a mind as inventive as the former detectives that one allows oneself to be stopped by such details. He had already glimpsed the means of procuring the necessary resources. Had he not brought back the nickel statue that everyone thought admirable? Would it not be possible to sell that uncontested masterpiece?

He thought, in addition, that there was a certain Madame Bémolisant in a corner of Paris to whom he had promised news of her husband. The moment had come. He had a definite sympathy for the poor woman, and judged that it was time to put her in the picture regarding the artist's fate.

Privately, Rosamour thought that, if the latter had found death as a way out of his adventure, it was no great loss, estimating that, as a husband, Bémolisant had always been more of an encumbrance than an asset—which was perhaps a reckless judgment. The agent wanted to convince himself, at least, that the widow would only be according him the just tribute of regret that convention demands in our society, steeped in conventions of evident absurdity.

He promised himself, at any rate, to console her as best he could, not wanting a pretty woman to weep for too long.

At the house in the Avenue de Clichy he found the two poor women desolate, firstly because they had had no news of the vanished artist, and secondly because they were running short of money. For one of them, at least—I mean Madame Legris—the second reason even surpassed the first, the grief of losing a son-in-law being unable to compare with a financial wound.

"Oh, I was right!" cried Madame Bémolisant's mother, the respectable Madame Legris, the very model of mothers-in-law. "Could one find the least confidence on that artist's brain? There he is, running around the world, leaving his wife and child behind without a care."

"But mother," the young woman pleaded, mildly, "why accuse him when he's doubtless the victim of an inexorable fatality?"

"Ta ta ta. I know what I think: he's a simple imbecile."

He two women hardly ever read the papers. They were therefore unaware of the latest events, and Rosamour, with a hypocritically saddened expression, was obliged to pick up his story at an early point.

What Madame Bémolisant wanted to know first of all was whether, if her husband had not fallen into a trap, he was still alive,

"Alas, Madame," said Rosamour, avoiding the question, "there is still some uncertainty as to his fate, but I saw him not long ago..."

"You've seen him! He's alive, Monsieur?" she interrupted, leaning toward him anxiously.

"He was, at least, alive a few days ago—but let me tell you about my journey."

Briefly, he passed in review the various incidents in the flight of the two men whom no one, to begin with, was pursuing; their unfortunate arrest in Briseval; how they had escaped from prison, and how they had associated themselves for a few days with Professor Joël.

Perhaps he insisted more than was necessary on the moral decadence of the two unfortunates who had not hesitated to deliver themselves, as grotesque marionettes, to the mockery of the public. Was he hoping to kill affection and regret in the heart of the wife by means of the ridicule of the situation?

Finally, he recounted the final episode of the odyssey: the flight in the balloon.

"But after all, why were they running away?" Madame Legris objected, yet again, not daring to add: *if they aren't guilty?*

"I don't know," Hélène replied, mildly, in her stubborn fashion, "but what I do know is that my husband is incapable of a bad action, much less a crime."

The policeman took pity on that superb confidence. "You're right," he said, "but one can kill without being a born criminal. One can also run away without being guilty, for fear of being accused. If one sees an entire body of evidence loom up against one, and cannot perceive, on the other hand, any way of proving one's innocence, that's enough to make a man lose his head, unless he has an exceptionally strong mind. One runs away then, like a hare, without thinking that the flight itself furnishes a further argument to the case for the prosecution."

Madame Bémolisant followed his argument avidly, which responded so well to her own thoughts. As Rosamour spoke, it seemed to her that the evidence was shining bright. She acquiesced with a gesture; her eyes lit up with hope; tears were scintillating in the lashes.

"Yes, Monsieur, yes," she said, finally. "That's definitely it; he was afraid, and he fled. It's not necessary to seek elsewhere for the explanation of his conduct. And Monsieur Pilesèche went with him. Weren't they both timid and fearful individuals, as naïve as children, and knowing so little of life!"

"They might have made one another afraid," Rosamour continued. "One coward is nothing, but two cowards are capable of going to the ends of the earth by pushing one another. They were faced with a *fait accompli*—an inexplicable death. They suddenly saw the accusation looming up before them, inevitable and irrefutable. In the impossibility of responding to it, they thought to escape by flight..."

"That's evident. I'll go tell that magistrate. I'll tell him..."

"Don't take the trouble. It's too simple to appear plausible. In magistrates' offices, they look for more subtle motives, and you'd be wasting your time. Then again, there's no urgency now; the unfortunates might have found supreme deliverance in the waves to which their balloon transported them..."

"Do you think so, Monsieur"

"Who can say? In any case, if some ship has picked them up they're doubtless safe now, out of reach of the law, which has abandoned the chase. Let's allow all the noise to die down, then."

"But Monsieur, the rehabilitation—it's for me that it's necessary, and for my fighter, who bears his name..."

"You shall have it...you shall have it in full. I want to prove the innocence of our two scatterbrains—but give me a free hand; it's by finding the old uncle that I'll succeed in that. Don't worry; the honor of your name isn't indifferent to me. The more I get to know you, the more I feel borne toward you by the respectful sympathy that first made me your ally."

And gradually, he consoled her, like a child that one soothes with kind words; that music rose from his heart to his lips, and even intoxicated him.

He showed her the future open before her, full of radiant sunlight, succeeding the morose past. Could one despair, at her age? Her heart would awake on day, of its own accord, to the joy of living, in the midst of those who loved her, when time had done its work. She had had the strength to suffer, would she not have the patience to wait for the new spring in which everything within her would be reborn?

Was she listening to him, her eyes fixed and her cheeks pale and sad? Or were her thoughts wandering in the distance, over the waves where the treacherous nacelle had sunk?

16. In Search of the Cadaver

"A *labadens*![17] Rosamour, my friend!"

"Jean Saure! Is that you, old comrade?"

"The king of reportage in person. Ah! The recognition scene always make a sensitive heart beat faster."

"It's been such a long time since we ran into one another. And then, like this, unexpectedly, on a street corner..."

"To be frank, my dear friend, the encounter isn't absolutely fortuitous; if I'm in these parts it's partly to look for you. I need you."

"Aha!" said the other, without blinking, but bracing himself to withstand the rude assault of a man wanting to borrow money.

He was mistaken, though; the comrade did not have designs on his wallet, and all anxiety vanished as soon as he spoke again.

"Aren't you in charge of the investigation of the Grillard-Bémolisant affair?" the journalist continued.

"Um," said Rosamour, with compromising himself.

"I'm on the hunt for news; I need you to give me some. Go on, talk: my paper is waiting."

"Well, whatever it costs me, I'll make you a confession..."

"A confession free of all artifice..."

"Absolutely free of all artifice..."

"Make your confession, then—but you know, I don't trust myself; it's not in my métier to let myself by taken in."

---

[17] A *labadens*, in Parisian argot, is an old friend from school or university.

"All men, in all métiers, have the same pretention…and they get taken in all the same. No matter…it's quite clear that I have an idea at the back of my mind, and I'll tell you what it is…"

"Without beating around the bush?"

"Without beating around the bush. I'm a policeman; you need me. You're a journalist; I need you. Let's join forces, and all will be for the best."

Jean Saure linked arms with the detective. "Golden words," he said. "Come and have a beer. There's nothing better to aid confidences."

The two men stopped under the awning of a café, and Rosamour was finally able to formulate the confession promised with a mysterious expression.

"You know, my dear Jean, since the papers have said so, that my two fugitives slipped through my fingers and took off like sparrows. That small misfortune would be nothing, but for the wrath of the court, which has got me the boot. Now, you know that I'm rancorous, vindictive and not patient; you can therefore conclude that I'm not taking my disgrace as benevolently as people would like to believe. For want of being able to do official police work, I shall launch myself into opposition. I have my plan; I'll let you in on it. The two of us will undertake the counter-investigation. The magistracy is searching for the murderer; we're searching for the victim. I need Père Grillard, dead or alive. We'll demonstrate the perfect innocence of Bémolisant and his acolyte…"

"What! You think they're innocent!"

"Until there's proof to the contrary. I'll tell you my reasons. We demonstrate that the examining magistrate is a blockhead, that Boissonnald is a murky individual, that Rosamour is a great man, the rival of the great policemen of the past…"

"Who were decorated!"

"I'll be content with a simple statue."

"You shall have one."

"It's a veritable campaign that I'm undertaking against the Sûreté and the Court; I shan't be content until I've ground my enemy into the dust."

"Go, Redskin!"

"But for that I need a newspaper—a newspaper that will take the lead and won't be afraid—and that's where our role begins."

"Oh, my friend, I'll introduce you to my editor, who likes nothing better than slinging mud at the administration. You can make your pitch; your natural eloquence will seduce and persuade him. All the reporters on the paper are ready to launch themselves on the various tracks you indicate. As for me, I'll take charge of putting the boot into your examining magistrate. I'll be mocking, I'll be mordant, I'll prick him and harass him. It's a task, at least, and not banal."

"Is your editor capable of putting funds into the enterprise?"

"Don't worry about that—to get one up on the police, he won't back off."

And as ideas come in the course of conversation, the two friends quickly fell into agreement regarding the first operations of the campaign.

First of all, it was necessary to interest public opinion, to prepare for a turnabout in favor of the suspects. Now, great humanitarian sentiments do well in newspapers headlines and columns; a subscription in favor of Madame Bémolisant could not fail to have a prodigious effect. Given a little push, the public, in its turn, would feel sorry for the undeserved fate of the unfortunate woman and the innocent baby struck so cruelly by the unjust accusation leveled against her husband.

"Yes, unjust. Hasn't the investigation been marked by the most evident prejudice. Where's the evidence of culpability?"

And all the usual speeches about judiciary errors...

There was an entire war machine on which the two friends counted of making use like a catapult to batter the defenses of the Sûreté that had so ludicrously sacked the most scientific of its detectives.

And what a racket there would be around the subscription, to come to the aid of the pitiable victims of an unmerited insult!

And finally, the statue! Did they not have the statue? That statue was a flag, as Joseph Prudhomme would have said. They were going to exhibit once again the marvelous work of the sculptor whose disappearance in such mysterious circumstances attracted so much attention.

The dispatch-room of the paper seemed entirely indicated for that manifestation, which would take on the color of a charitable intervention in favor of a tearful family. Was it not in that dispatch room that once could see, every day, the flower of current affairs, to which the paper, raising the trumpet to its lips, never failed to give a noisy publicity?

Tombolas, charity sales, pictures to hang on the wainscoting, autographs by the man of the hour, with his photograph in his latest cravat: to that kaleidoscope, the public willingly applied its eye.

In truth, that was the drumbeat that the two conspirators needed.

And in the meantime, Rosamour went to establish his batteries solidly, before unmasking them and battering a breach in the theory so briskly erected by the examining magistrate

What he had not said was that he counted on inaugurating, in order finally to discover what had been the fate of the unfortunate Monsieur Grillard, a method as bold as it was unusual.

The story of Jacques Aymard, the "sorcerer" of Lyon and his divinatory wand was running through his mind. Was this not the case on which to try out the singular means that had succeeded so well in that circumstance?

Rosamour also thought that Miss Adda might be useful to him in realizing that project.

She was, to begin with, the "sensitive individual" described by the Baron von Reichenbach,[18] for whom the nature has manifestations unknown to common mortals. The policeman had witnessed experiments that left no doubt as to the sensibility of her nerves.

Without even being plunged into a provoked trance, she perceived the odic effluvia that escape from the asperities of various bodies, but which are only detectable by a few individuals. If someone raised a hand in a dimly-lit room she saw a kind of slight flame springing from the fingertips, and that flame differed in color according to whether it was emanated by the left or the right hand.

It was sufficient for her to hold a glass in her left hand for a few minutes for the water it contained to take on, for her, an insipid and disagreeable taste and make her feel nauseated, whereas water appeared pure and agreeable to her when she held it in her right hand.

One would never finish if it were necessary to identify all the bizarre and unhealthy sensations that the young woman experienced, which made her a remarkable subject for study.

Rosamour judged that all these precious faculties might finally find their application. It was only necessary for him to be able to put Miss Adda on the track of the old scientist. With that end in mind, the policeman assembled a few clothes that had belonged to Monsieur Grillard and, making a package of them, went to the cheap hotel where he had lodged the young woman, having given her instructions to show herself as little as possible.

The instruction has been almost superfluous; after the overworked existence that she had dragged out on the road, the former ballerina was avid for repose and tranquility. She lived in her little fifth-floor room, only descending occasionally to buy a cornet of fries or the few sous' worth of cooked meat that constituted the bulk of her nourishment.

She stayed there, often in bed or sprawled in an old armchair with wornout springs, doing nothing, motionless, her gaze lost in a dream…and her dream went into the distance, all the way to the sea, where she thought she saw a balloon floating, disaster-stricken. And among the passengers in the frail nacelle, she only saw one: the one who had so much empire over her; the unfortunate clown, Pilesèche.

Her imagination concentrated then on that singular spectacle; her vision darkened; her entire being became numb, as if, even at a distance, she could feel the effluvia of her former magnetizer passing through her.

Was that not because he was still alive?

---

[18] Carl von Reichenbach (1788-1869) was a scientific researcher who made several notable discoveries in chemistry and was a significant pioneer in research into the relationship between electricity and magnetism, which he attempted to associate with a universal field of energy he called "odic force." He also supposed the latter to be responsible for the phenomena of hypnotism.

That conviction invaded her entirely, and when, with a violent start, she woke up again, agitated, excited by fever and nervous overexcitement, she conserved that belief that the aeronauts had not perished. She tried to make Rosamour share it, but he shook his head. No, no, the sea did not return its victims; anyway, they would have heard mention of it.

And what was the point in paying any more attention to the unfortunate shipwreck-victims? The key to the problem was the vanished cadaver; and it was the cadaver that it was necessary to find, at any price.

Putting her into contact, therefore, with all the objects that had belonged to the scientist, he questioned her, pushing her lucidity toward that sole question: where was the old man's body?

She did not reply.

Large beads of sweat testified nevertheless to the efforts she was making to see with the eyes of her soul and the grasp a trail that was incessantly hidden.

He decided to make one last attempt, and took her to the former dwelling of the mysterious victim.

The rubble had been partly cleared; the walls had been shored up, but the repair work had not progressed beyond the first floor. He was nevertheless able to hoist the young woman up to the former laboratory, which remained in almost exactly the same state as on the day after the fire, except that the charred beams had been supported by stays, and planks had been thrown laterally to make an almost continuous and accessible floor.

Silently, Adda went along the walls, feeling, sniffing, her eyes staring beneath half-closed lids, folded into herself, and sometimes shivering.

Suddenly, she stopped, her neck taut, her nostrils dilated, as if she had perceived the distant odor of the object for which she was searching. Her hand extended forwards, pointing at an invisible phantom that was fleeing before her, zigzagging like a pursued hair; then she started walking.

Adda went down the ladders that she had had so much difficulty climbing without any assistance, marched through the streets, without hesitation, without stopping…marching continuously, until, at the top of the Avenue Clichy, she stopped for a few seconds outside Madame Bémolisant's door; then, as if picking up a fresh trail, she resumed her curse, going back down toward the great boulevards; hesitated again at the intersection of the Rue de Sèze; set off again more urgently in order to steer toward the house where Rosamour lived, after detours and backtrackings that had taken her all the way to the Gare Montparnasse…

Rosamour, who was following her, was exhausted.

Miss Adda did not seem to feel the fatigue of that hectic course, and her feet skimmed the ground, hardly touching it. Her pace accelerated, while unfortunate detective ran out of breath following her and it was with a flagellating stride that he climbed the stairs leading to his apartment.

In front of the closed door she stopped, breathless, and banged on it violently with her fist until the policeman had opened it.

Adda went in like a hurricane, with an "Ah!" of relief and triumph—but, immediately vanquished, her entire being relaxed, as it were, abruptly, and she fell, inert, outside the cupboard in which the nickel statue lay...

Oh, poor Rosamour scarcely spared a thought for that statue, as he let himself fall in his turn into an armchair, his face convulsed and streaming after that hectic steeplechase.

For a moment, he had been hopeful: the somnambulist had such an inspired expression. She was walking with such a sure and rapid pace toward her invisible goal! But on seeing her climb the stairway of his own house...

Good! thought the disappointed policeman, laughing humorlessly. *You're going to see that the cadaver is hidden in my apartment! I'm hiding Père Grillard, or giving shelter to his murderer! Too bad—my subject isn't as brilliant as I hoped, and I'm back to square one....*

Regathering his wits, he went on: *I only have one hope left: the indecipherable cryptogram contains the key to the enigma; it's up to me to bring it out.*

He was tired out by such a gallop, however, and incapable for the moment of stringing two ideas together. He was still mopping his brow and panting when Adda woke up and rubbed her eyes, also exhausted, her limbs aching, incapable of moving them without crying out, and utterly unconscious of what had happened.

Rosamour was still under the impact of his failure when his friend Jean Saure came to find him. The news that he was bringing was not made to comfort the poor detective.

To be sure, the press campaign was going well; public opinion was already showing a benevolence toward their cause, while the court was under vigorous attack. But time was passing and the need for money was making itself felt. Madame Bémolisant had confessed, blushing, that her resources were almost totally exhausted, and the war could only be continued with the aid of new subsidies.

It was necessary to sell the statue.

An Englishman, a kind of Barnum, had made an enticing offer. They might be able to do even better by organizing a public auction.

The agent acquiesced to all his friends' proposals, leaving him complete liberty to act, without the strength to think and devoid of courage.

He only had one idea left: to harness himself like a Benedictine to the deciphering of the cryptogram. That was where salvation lay. The rest scarcely mattered...

17. Saved from the Waters

On the deck of the little steamer *Francine* two streaming bodies lay, clad in grotesque costumes, which the waves had lacerated in a bizarre fashion.

The drowned men were lividly pale, insensible to any stimulation. They scarcely had a pulse-beat, and no breath was emerging from their breasts.

Sailors and passengers surrounded them with muffled exclamations, while two or three crouching men strove to reanimate them, massaging them in order to restore some warmth to their icy extremities, imposing rhythmic tractions on their tongues in order to reestablish the automatic movement of human respiration, which maintains the hearth of life.

A physician, without saying much apart from issuing brief commands, was presiding over that work, and listening at intervals to see whether the hearts had begun to beat under the violent stimulation of napkins soaked in boiling water and abruptly applied to the epigastrum.

Standing up, his legs apart, with his hands in his pockets, a short broad-shouldered man, solid and thickset, was smoking his pipe. He was the commandant of the vessel, Captain Carbagnac, a southerner of good vintage, who had no need to proclaim the fact; his accent did that for him.

"Stand aside, the lot of you!" he cried, in a stentorian voice, to the sailors whose circle was getting tighter, intercepting the daylight and the respirable air. "Nevertheless," he said, addressing the doctor, "We interrupted their bath at a good time."

The doctor, very busy, only replied with a grunt—but the other had no need of an interlocutor; his loquacity could do without replies.

"Look—one of them moved... It's not so bad... With good fur gloves and vigorous rubbing, you can wake the dead... Poor fellow, they don't look so good, all the same... Well, it would be a great pity, old man, if Captain Carbagnac was deflected from his route for corpses... I have confidence, me... I said to myself: Doctor Caudelot is no fool, he'll get these fellows out of it... What desolates me, damn it, is not to have saved the balloon. I'd gladly made a captive ascent...a don't worry old man, a *captive* ascent...Captain Carbagnac owes it to his crew, his passengers, and his family...but nevertheless, imagine how delighted these worthy fellows will be with our rival. Go sound a fanfare! Trying to disengage the nacelle, the damned balloon found a means of flying away with the remains of the net, and that buckle of gas flew away as if it were neither more or less than a soap-bubble..."

One of the drowned me opened haggard eyes and his lips moved, murmuring softly: "Where am I?"

And that question, escaping like a breath, they divined without hearing it.

The other came back with a spasm. "The police! The police!" he repeated, pursued all the way to the coma of asphyxia by an obsessive anguish.

And they both fell back into their unconscious immobility—but their hearts were finally beating; their breasts were rising, aspiring the oxygen of life, and falling back in irregular somersaults.

The doctor stood up and readjusted the sleeves that he had rolled up. "Now I'll answer for them," he said, finally.

"So much the better, thank God," exclaimed the captain, in a voice that he had doubtless borrowed from the thunder of his homeland. "Hey!" he continued, "You four lads, here! Lift these fellows up for me and stick them in hammocks with good blankets. We'll chat later."

Although a trifle abrupt, Captain Carbagnac was a good man. If he did not present a tender appearance and sacrificed nothing to sensitivity, he was none-theless humane in his fashion. While continuing his pacing, therefore, hands be-hind his back and the wind in his face, he smiled, content with the fortunate re-sult of the rescue, the smile broadening within the superb collar of beard that framed his broad full-moon face.

And, resuming his customary preoccupations, he went back to his daily in-spection, like a man who knows the importance of detail, barking orders to port and starboard, darting a glance through the open hatchways all the way down to the engine room, not disdaining to check the propriety of the *houteilles*—which is the name by which the place designated with the initials W.C. is known on the deck of a steamship.

Finally, having given a cabin boy who got under his feet a clip round the ear, he went down to the lower deck.

There, side by side in two hammocks, the two drowned men were trying to recover their thoughts, and the same words came back to their unconscious lips incessantly.

"Where am I?" said one.

And the other, agitated, as if he were trying to escape an obsession, repeat-ed: "The police! The police...!"

The first was parading bewildered eyes around him while his hammock swayed in the swell "Bémolisant!" he murmured, on perceiving his companion. And, after searching his memory for something that gradually came back to him, he added: "Where's the other one?"

"The other one, the other one?" the captain repeated, between his teeth. "It appears that there was another one...well, my friend, he's gone to the bottom. I haven't seen him."

He turned toward the doctor. "The brave fellows seem to me to have come through it; we'll be able to submit them to a little interrogation. I'm curious, at least, to know their stories, these actors..."

Did one of the shipwreck-victims understand those words. Perhaps—he turned over in his hammock as if to escape the announced interrogation, while the other muttered more loudly: "The statue...! The statue...!"

145

That excitation was followed by the most complete prostration; the unfortunates remained unconscious for twenty-four hours.

They emerged from it at the same time. When Pilesèche opened his eye and learned toward his neighbor he encountered the other's atonal gaze.

"Are we alone?" he murmured.

"Yes," replied the other, nodding his head.

And in fact, that part of the deck was deserted, everyone being busy with his duties.

"Where's the ship going?"

"I don't know."

"Are we discovered?"

"Alas!" said Bémolisant, without answering the question. "Pilesèche, what have they done with my uncle?"

"What must he be thinking, if he's still alive inside his nickel envelope, in being himself submitted to such ordeals?"

"We need to find him and free him," Bémolisant added, with a start. "But how do we get out of here?"

"How do we get back to France...in spite of the gendarmes and the police?"

"As long as they haven't signaled our capture by semaphore..."

"What if we were to throw ourselves in the water?"

"What would have been the point of making so much effort to save ourselves?"

"I can't live like this..."

There was a momentary silence then, and Pilesèche, propping himself up on his elbow, without saying anything, swung his long thin legs out of the hammock.

His poor empty head could scarcely hold itself upright, and slumped from one shoulder to the other. Everything around him was spinning, while the pitching and rolling of the vessel swung the hammock back and forth above the floor, which seemed to be fleeing. But his eyes fixed persistently on a pile of neatly-folded clothes, doubtless destined to replace the rags that had survived their shipwreck. He gazed at the small objects that had been removed from their pockets: their knives, their purses, and finally the wallet in which the poor laboratory assistant and opportunist clown had stuck a few papers, among which he had so carefully folded up the copy of the famous cryptogram taken from the scientist's laboratory.

He had never had time to try to decipher that cryptogram, and had ended up forgetting that it was in his wallet—but an obsession, brought on by illness, drew him back to it now. Who could tell whether the key to salvation might be contained therein?

All kinds of methods came to mind by which it might be easily deciphered. Finally, it seemed to him that he only had it before his eyes, reading it would be straightforward.

Moved by that obsession, stiffening himself against the numbness that was invading him, he leaned out of the hammock and stretched out his arm in order to reach the wallet with his fleshless hand. Just as he grasped it avidly, however, a pitch of the vessel caused him to lose his equilibrium.

Pilesèche tumbled on to the floor, where he remained unconscious until a sailor, passing by, came to lift him up like a feather and replace him in is hammock, without perceiving that the invalid was clutching the precious wallet in his clenched fist, and pressing it against his heart.

As soon as he thought he was alone Pilesèche took out the piece of paper, soaked by sea-water, and absorbed himself in the contemplation of the half-effaced hieroglyphs...

The two castaways were well cared for. They were administered cordials and soups that formed a delicious diet after the wretched fare of their life as fairground performers. Only one anxiety clawed at them, and that was wondering whether their identities had been unmasked and the news of their capture had reached France.

When Captain Carbagnac came by, they usually pretended to be asleep, as much to listen and try to overhear some indication as to avoid questions. They only risked opening their eyes when they judged that their incognito had definitely not been penetrated.

"Well, my sleepers who've woken up," said the captain rubbing his hands. "That was a nice snooze! And now, my little sinners, it's time to tell me whether you want to go all the way to the Congo or whether you want me to drop you off in cow country.

"Are we on the coast of France?" hazarded Pilesèche.

"Oh, as to that, no, and if Captain Carbagnac hadn't had bad weather and the wind in his face, the *Francine* would have passed Madeira by now, at least. All that I can do for you, if you want to leave us, is deposit you preciously on the coast of Portugal. A little far from Paris, it's true, if that's your destination. All the same, it's still Europe, and by addressing yourself to the French consul, you could be repatriated gratis, with all the honors due to you."

Address themselves to the French consul? That did not seem to them to be advice to follow. But bah! Once ashore they would be able to get out of trouble. They still had enough money in pocket, which simplified things.

The two unfortunates therefore accepted the captain's offer, and while the Francine set a course for the little port of Vila Nova de Milfontes, Pilesèche and Bémolisant got ready to leave the ship, dressing in costumes that were half-naval and half-civilian, which they owed to the munificence of their rescuers, the passengers and he captain.

One morning, the ship dropped anchor in the harbor, and the two castaways immediately took their places—not without having thanked Captain Carbagnac and the doctor warmly—in a launch that was going to take advantage of the unscheduled port of call to renew the provisions of fresh food.

It was a good opportunity to take a stroll on *terra firma*. The worthy captain of the *Francine* spruced himself up a little and, in company with Dr. Caudelot, had himself taken ashore; they were both glad to stretch their limbs and to have news of what had been happening in the world since their departure.

After an hour spent chatting with the French consul, the two friends went to install themselves on the veranda of the best local hotel, for a little siesta and to catch up with their correspondence.

Facing large glasses full of iced cocktails, while the captain wrote a letter, Caudelot started reading newspapers in various languages. Before the rest, however, he scanned the French papers that the consul had lent them, following them in chronological order, devouring the detail of news items, important and petty, that had captivated public attention for an hour while they were at sea.

Suddenly, the excellent doctor uttered an exclamation that made Carbagnac jump in his rattan armchair.

"Damn it, my dear," exclaimed the commandant of the *Francine*, "you must have encountered something phenomenal!"

"Phenomenal—you said it!"

"Make me party to this sensational news, then."

"Do you know who we saved from the waters?"

"Two fairground performers, I suspect..."

"I'll give you a hundred guesses."

"No idea, my dear doctor—don't leave me in suspense."

"We've saved Père Grillard's murderers!"

"Good God! I don't believe it."

"Just read the story of their escape in a balloon..."

"In truth, it's a strange case. But it's not my job to tip off the police about the villains they've let slip through their fingers. Anyway, they can't be far away, and if the consul's got his wits about him, he won't have any difficulty recognizing the famous Panthéon murderers in the heroes of the story we've told him. It's his business, not mine. All the same, though, I'll tell the story to my brother while I'm writing to him—they'll have a good laugh on the Canebière when they hear what specimens Captain Carbagnac took the trouble to save."

18. In Which We Encounter Arrieros and Smugglers

Meanwhile, the fugitives had judged it prudent not to stay too long in the town.

They had regularized their presence, thanks to declarations and statements signed by Captain Carbagnac, who had explained their situation. One cannot require shipwreck-victims to be carrying on their person all the necessary documents establishing their identity, and by avoiding certain indiscreet questions by people who were devoid of suspicion, they were soon able to continue on their way.

In order to conserve their resources, while thinking that they might occasionally be able to use diligences and railways, they departed on foot, all their luggage tied up in a handkerchief on the end of a stick.

They walked without saying anything, doubtless mulling over the same thoughts in their heads.

In front of them stretched a dusty road bordered by stunted trees, curved toward the east by the sea breeze.

The sunlight was sparkling on the reddish dust that was kicked up by the hooves of mules, and the road extended like a long ribbon, plunging into the depths of ravines and scaling hills. It seemed to them that they could already perceive, in the distance, on the blue mountains, the vague silhouettes of French customs officers...

Without looking back they marched, drawn toward their native soil by an unconscious force, in spite of the menacing storm that they sensed before them.

Could they hope to pass unperceived through the mesh of the net extended along the frontiers, where the hundred eyes of Argus inspected new arrivals, no matter how insignificant they seemed?

And if they succeeded in crossing the dangerous line, would they still be sheltered from all danger as they approached Paris, to which they would be fatally drawn back?

But their present security, after the moments of terrible anguish that they had passed through, produced a physical relaxation in them that they had not previously known. When they had passed a restful night in a rather smelly inn, in the midst of innumerable insects that constituted a disagreeable permanent garrison in the straw extended for sleeping, they found themselves back on the road to France, refreshed and replenished, no longer thinking about anything, under the ardent sun, which was making the cicadas sing in the long grass.

Pilesèche was still depressed, in consequence of which he did not say much; he has less resilience and a less supple imagination than his companion, and a brief encounter with a picturesque gypsy camp was insufficient to distract him from his preoccupations.

By contrast, the new impressions chased away the impressions of sad past ordeals in the artist. He was dreaming about fandangos glimpsed in the evening by the tremulous light of the moon and the stars, and the old popular songs, mocking or sentimental, were singing within him to the accompaniment of guitar and castanets.

Where were the nebulous principles of decadent music, then, and the famous scale of six thousand notes whose apostle he had been? Was Bémolisant about to convert to the musical religion of the old race that sang to coming into the world? Or was that old race about to bring Bémolisant back to a taste for its

149

naïve melodies? An arduous problem, no doubt, about which one could argue for a long time, for the time was lacking for a conclusive experiment—but it is worth noting that the artiste bought castanets and a guitar, and started to sing, during the pauses in the voyage, the old *romanceros* that have never been written down and are transmitted from mouth to mouth, with the warm accents of old heroic dialects.

Unfortunately, music and the fandango had no purchase on the scientific mind of the former laboratory assistant. Physiology had no truck with such nonsense, and he had been nourished on the xs and ys of vivisection. While his companion scraped the taut strings and pinched arpeggios or sad diminished sevenths, resolving ironically into broken cadences in order not to conclude in banal perfect chords, Pilesèche labored on the translation of his cryptogram or stirred in his head the alternatives contained in the question: "Is Monsieur Grillard still alive in his nickel envelope?"

Let us confess that he dared not make a definitive response, and remained in a dolorous perplexity.

They went by, however, and the voyagers crossed, one by one, the sierras that constitute the skeleton of ancient Iberia, reaching the foothills of the Pyrenees.

As they got closer to the frontier, they felt increasingly invaded by heavy apprehensions. The stages of their journey shortened, under the most various pretexts, and the voyagers scarcely dared advance, invincibly retained by the dread of the vague peril that they were about to confront.

On coming out of a village, they encountered a small band of men following the same route, driving mules laden with rather voluminous bales. Those *arrieros*, cigarettes in their lips beneath their vast sombreros, darted suspicious glances at them, hardly inclined to encourage conversation.

The two fugitives, however, experienced such a keen need to ask questions and find out which was the best road and the surest means of deceiving the surveillance at the frontier that they approached the muleteers and tried to strike up a conversation with some banality regarding the heart and the oppressive sun— an eminently insinuating exordium familiar in all countries.

The man who appeared to be the leader of the band and who was marching proudly, with his hand stuck in the leather buckle of his hazel-wood *maquilla*, only replied in monosyllables, with a sullen expression which would have put off his interlocutors if they had not long since double their dose of philosophy.

Bémolisant was well aware that he did not inspire confidence in the Spaniards, but necessity has no law; he needed the aid of local people; these looked somewhat like smugglers, which was not injurious to his program, and it was necessary to take advantage of the fact, at all costs.

Taking the bull by the horns, therefore, he told them that he did not know the country, and asked if he might join them to follow the road—to which the leader replied, summarily: "*A su disposicion de Usted!*"

To the *Usted*, it was a matter of bowing graciously as a sign of mute gratitude, his repertoire of the Castilian language not being very rich in appropriate formulae. Above all, he was careful not to appear to perceive the decidedly mediocre pleasure that the offer of his company seemed to cause the descendant of El Cid Campeador;[19] and, as the other did not unclench his teeth, he began a monologue aloud, asking questions and supplying replied.

They stopped to eat in the hollow of a valley where the fresh water of a stream was cascading, and each of them took his provisions from his sack. Bémolisant ever amiable, emitted a few coarse pleasantries in a whimsical Spanish that had the privilege of bringing a smile—was it a smile?—to the Olympian face of his mute companion.

The latter deigned to open his mouth and interrogate the Frenchmen as to their civil estate—after which, without allowing the impression left by that suspicious interrogation to be divined, he stretched out on the grass, turned his back on the honorable company, and dozed off for the siesta.

There was nothing to do but follow his example, but Pilesèche did not have Bémolisant's superb confidence. He dared not close an eye, thinking that the brave men of Navarre, with their ferocious eyes as sharp as the daggers stuck in their red belts, looked more like bandits than honest transporters of merchandise.

Gently, he nudged his companion's elbow to recommend prudence, but the insouciant artist was asleep.

When the sun was in decline again, the entire caravan, upright in response to a guttural summons, set forth again. The leader seemed to have lost his mistrust; Bémolisant, judging the moment favorable, told himself that he was not risking anything, after all, and started tell him his story—or, at least, a romance sufficiently adapted to the circumstances.

What the other understood from it, quite clearly, was that the two young men had come a long way—their papers said so, at least—and that they wanted to get back into France, with some reason for not wanting to attract attention there; and that, in sum, they wanted his help to cross the frontier incognito.

The Spaniard gradually relaxed. He explained to them exactly what métier he was following, with his band. He took confidence so far as to tell them his name, which was Juan Calcadores, a native of a little posada near Sos. All that was of no fundamental importance, but what interested the fugitives most keenly was that they were about to reach a small hamlet populated by people who made a habit of traversing the frontier for the requirements of their commerce. In spite of the euphemisms it was easy to understand that it was more a matter of smugglers than globe-trotters—but Calcadores reckoned them to be resourceful men, and that was sufficient.

---

[19] The 11th century hero Rodrigo Diaz de Vivar was known both as El Cid (the Lord) and El Campeador (the Champion).

Furthermore, they were approaching their goal. The path climbed up with abrupt bends, suspended on the flank of a mountain overhanging a deep and sheer ravine. Dusk had arrived and the moon was at the zenith, over the narrow fissure that some Roland's sword had carved into the mountain. The men were marching behind their mules, slowly but at a steady pace, without breathing more rapidly.

Unlike them, Bémolisant did not have legs hardened to that kind of exercise; he rubbed his thighs and sponged his forehead, looking forward to the blessed threshold where he would finally be able to get a little well-earned rest.

It was the furious barking of half a dozen dogs that first signaled the strange little hamlet, composed of a few small huts wedged in the hollow of an overhanging rock. Through narrow and smoky windows a few rays of light filtered, which were abruptly extinguished in response to the noise, and in the darkness a voice shouted: "Who goes there?" in a tone more menacing than amicable.

Calcadores responded in his turn with a few sonorous interjections that resembled a password, and the little troop continued to advance. While the *arrieros* disappeared with their mules beneath the somber arch of a portal, however, Juan told the Frenchmen to stay where they were for a minute and allow him to warn the person who was to be their host about their presence.

Fortunately, the negotiations did not take long, and following a little old man, bent with age, who appeared to be the master of the place, Bémolisant and Pilesèche penetrated into a room of moderate size, into which people of all sorts were already crowded, some eating and drinking around a massive table, others lying down along the walls, wrapped in rags that had been cloaks, with the hoods pulled down over their eyes.

Pilesèche advanced hesitantly, his eyes blinded by the light that suddenly struck them. The sordid room gave him the impression of a brigands' cave, from which he had little chance of emerging alive. Meanwhile, as all eyes—and what eyes!—peered at the newcomers, the master, sitting them down at the table, pushed toward them a large loaf of black bread, already considerably eroded, and a bowl of milk full of *migus*—pieces of bread fried in unpurified oil—which emitted a nauseating odor of rotten olives.

It would probably not have been a good idea to venture into that place with the air of cosseted nabobs, but our two companions did not have the look of fortunate aristocrats in quest of the unexpected, who might be robbed profitably.

When they had attempted to appease their hunger with a few unspeakable concessions to Spanish cuisine, the two Frenchmen were taken to a corner by their aged host, who made them a speech with all the nobility of which he was capable

"Señor Juan tells me that you desire a guide to traverse the frontier by night, and that you are counting on our help—but that is a perilous enterprise for us; how much will you pay?"

152

"We still have a little money, and you can be tranquil, worthy Caballero; your recompense will be as if you had saved King Don Sancho, your august ancestor."[20] Bémolisant judged that romantic language was appropriate, and that one does not speak to a man of Navarre, however scant a hidalgo, as one speaks to a Marseille street-porter or an Auvergnat water-carrier.

The old man allowed himself to be flattered and discussed the price of his small service. They soon fell into accord, however, and when the bargain was concluded the artist asked whether there was some shelter in which one might sleep—but the house only had that one room, and the travelers had no other recourse than to lie down in the darkest corner on the *esteras*—the coarse mats covering the bare ground.

They were beginning to get drowsy, in spite of the numerous insects that took their bodies for pasture, when the sound of a guitar that was being strummed caused the artist to open his eyes.

The spectacle was worth the trouble. Fuliginous and reeking lamps had been set on the ground which illuminated from below a tall young woman whose black hair was decked with a rose and twisted in a kiss-curl over her forehead. She adjusted her castanets and caused her satin corset to crack over her hip, as if to test the elasticity over her back.

Along the wall, men and women were ranged, cigarettes in their lips, while a flautist played a prelude of scales on a three-holed *chirola*, and another musician plucked the strings of his guitar.

Bémolisant raised his head. The mañola, hamstrings taut, launched into a *zoreico*, a primitive dance without attitudes, but rapid and brisk, to the accompanying rattle of the enraged castanets.

Ah, what rhythm!

For the moment, Bémolisant was all rhythm; he had learned rhythm on Spanish soil, where everything ends up in a bolero, and, willingly seizing a Basque drum or drawing *fin-de-siècle* chords from a guitar with the flight of his five thin fingers, he hammered out the victorious rhythm.

Under the oblique glimmer of the vacillating lamps, the great shadow of the dancer elongated, capricious and fantastic, over the poorly roughcast and blackened walls. Abandoning the old rhythms, she sometimes swayed on her hips, provocative and never weary, down to the ground, her throat extended for a kiss, the suddenly reared up as if to flee, with a laugh that displayed her white teeth, and exclamations that the musicians and the audience repeated.

The dances only ended with the exhaustion of the dancer and when the lamps went out for want of oil, but Bémolisant was already asleep again, snoring conscientiously, accompanying the last arpeggios of the guitar with a regular rhythmic purr.

---

[20] Sancho I was king of Portugal from 1185 to 1212.

He was sleeping profoundly when a vigorous hand came to shake him by the shoulder. It was necessary to get up and set forth on the march, silently, in the dark, along narrow paths on which the feet could hardly place themselves.

The smugglers took the lead, each one with a bale on his shoulder and a blunderbuss in his hand. The two Frenchmen brought up the rear, somewhat breathless and barely able to distinguish, under the tremulous light of the moon, the girl that the old smuggler had given them to serve as a guide, and who was marching in front of them with all the grace of her sixteen years, at a brisk pace, unhampered by her short skirt. Peppa turned round from time to time to check that they were following and to encourage them with a familiar appeal, and then she fell silent.

Dawn paled the high summits; the path plunged down into gorges. Undoubtedly, they were on the French slopes, and it was a matter of keeping out of sight of the customs officers.

By virtue of what mischance did the band run into an ambush just as it emerged on to a small plateau on the saddle of a pass?

In the blink on an eye the alarm was given, but it was too late to change course; they were numerous, however, and the smugglers fell upon the enemy, daggers drawn, while two of them took cover behind a rock and leveled their blunderbusses.

Peppa, with a resolution that denoted a certain habitude to such adventures, had grabbed Bémolisant by the arm and dragged him into a clump of tall fir trees, while Pilesèche tried to follow them, bumping into branches, his footing ill-assured on the slippers' needles

The customs men were too busy fending off the Spaniards to pursue the fugitives, who hurried along, clinging on to rocks and branches.

The sound of gunshots gradually faded away in the distance, and they finally reached a muleteer's trail that led directly to the next village.

Peppa, anxious about the outcome of the battle in which her people were engaged, wanted to go back, and, after giving the Frenchmen her final instructions bade them adieu and wished them a successful end to their journey.

They were now in France, and in spite of their fatigue, hastening their pace, they resumed their route.

19. The End of an Auction

Elbows leaning on his worktable and his head plunged into his open hands, Rosamour was trying to decipher a puzzle.

He had a photographic print in front of him in which all the letters were reproduced, one after another, without any apparent connection.

The letters, which stood out in white against the black background of the print, were, unfortunately, partly effaced, with lacunae where characters disappeared, scarcely leaving a nebulous trace, while the sponge that had passed over the inscription had striped it with broad milky streaks, endearing it illegible.

The photographic paper was curling at the edges, and in order to keep it flat, Rosamour has placed the paperweight he had picked up in Monsieur Grillard's laboratory, a nickel toad, on one edge, while a heavy ivory paper-knife maintained the opposite edge.

The agent concentrated all his attention on the characters, which, although belonging to a familiar alphabet, were nevertheless as many hieroglyphs.

By dint of patience, however, he had succeeded in transcribing the letters that seemed indubitable and replacing by crosses those that were effaces, and had obtained the following inscription:

bfoomgtqklu++++esqnuo
+++agtb+++++ef++fy
esqnugnx++++et kgn+etc+
+gst+np+++pftofpcfyesk+
+++++ihoskenc++tec x+
++dbvetvaugn ugtjpsutu++
++++

His eyes fatigued by that difficult decipherment, and without allowing himself to be put off by the numerous lacunae in his transcription, the agent set about considering the physiognomy of that sequence of letters, while reflecting that the invalid must not have searched very hard for his cryptographic system and must have used the simplest.

Following a familiar method, it was necessary to look to see whether any group of letters was reproduced several times. In fact, each of the ternaries *esq*, *qnu* and *yes* was reproduced twice. After that, it was necessary to test whether the cryptogram might have been composed simply by means of a key of three letters or numbers. Rosamour thus began to separate the letters into groups of three, taking account as much as possible of the effaced characters.

If his hypothesis was correct, each of those groups of characters ought to correspond to the key—which is to say that all the first letters of the various groups came from the same alphabet; in the same way, all the second letters had been formed by a second alphabet, and similarly for the third.

Having separated out the list of first letters he looked to see which one was repeated most frequently; it was *e*. Now, in French—as in the majority of European languages, in fact—it is *e* that is most frequently repeated letter; it followed that the first letters of the groups had not been subject to any alteration.

It was different for the other two series of letters; in the second, the f was most frequently repeated, and in the third it was *g*, which indicated that the *e* of the natural language was indicated in one case by *f* and in the other by *g*. Now, *e* *f* and *g* follow one another in the ordinary alphabet, so the key to the ternary might be 123, indicating that the second letter was displaced by one rank and the third by two.

Nothing was simpler. The clever fellow shrugged his shoulders before such ingenuity, and reproached himself for not having searched sooner for what the document might contain, which he swiftly transcribed as follows:

Bemoletpilt...erontco...meta... ee..evrnotev... esixm.. sa.. ess. mor... perience-veri...... heoriem... redu... datestamentetinstru......

Alas, alas! The puzzle was still as puzzling as it had been before the decipherment.

A few words were easy to recognize; firstly there was a question of *Bemol...* and *Pil...*; the word *mort*—death—was recognizable, and testament. *Experience*—experiment—was also definable, but what experiment? And did the letters *veri*, which followed it, mean that the experiment verified the *(t)heorie*: the theory?

"Good," said the agent. "Monsieur Grillard carried out an experiment that might lead to his death. He mentions his testament and his instructions. But all that doesn't say a great deal, and certainly isn't sufficiently explicit..."

After reflection and with a significant grimace, he added: "It doesn't explain anything at all. As many question marks as before! I really can't present myself armed with this incomplete and incoherent cryptogram."

Again he plunged his head into his hands, his eyes obstinately fixed on those shreds of phrases, whose image was dancing in his congested brain, his nerves taut to the point of exasperation, while his temples were throbbing.

The truncated words filed past before his eyes, and he completed them with the most bizarre assemblages. He read in them whatever he wished, instantly demolishing what he had painstakingly edified, without, alas, the help of logic. He adapted new syllables to them, trying the most unusual combinations, but it was all devoid of meaning, and his overheated imagination, drawing away from the immediate goal, went back to the beginning of the most mysterious and bizarre affair that he had ever encountered.

He saw himself before the magistrate again; he saw himself, presumptuous and sure of is method, the scientific method. "The fugitives," he had said, "I have at the end of a telegraphic wire...the key item of evidence, the cadaver—doubtless a cadaver—I shall envelop with my tightest deductions: it can't escape me..."

But the fugitives were at the bottom of the sea!

And the cadaver was still undiscoverable!

Finally, he saw himself in the home of the young widow, whose dolor had moved him from the start, and whose gentle face haunted him more than was reasonable now.

Abruptly his thought found a bifurcation there, and set off along the flowery paths of idyll. The career that he had embraced had brought him nothing but disappointments; lassitude took hold of him; he dreamed of a tranquil life in perfumed fields. A farm by the seaside, with a discreet and tender housewife, children playing barefoot in the grass...

His dream came back to the young woman whose sad eyes had troubled him so much. Was she not the good farmer's wife he needed?

And why not?

The satisfactions that the poor woman had found with her first husband would not leave her eternal regrets, and since Bémolisant was dead—oh, quite dead, since the sea does not yield its prey—it was quite permissible to dream of a new union in which they would both be perfectly happy...

Eyes half-closed, Rosamour let his domestic fantasy run down that slope, and smiled, as of the odorous breeze was already rustling the foliage in his orchard, in the midst of which the image of Hélène floated.

And it went on...and on...when his gaze, staring, encountered the piece of paper again—the infernal piece of paper that retained the indecipherable mystery.

Suddenly plunged back into reality, he felt a surge of irresistible anger rising within him. Oh, the idyll was a long way off. The professional gripped him again...

What! There was an obstacle that he could not overcome! A grain of sand, a mere nothing, was stopping him!

He stood up, furiously, pushing back his armchair, and started pacing pack and forth. The carpet stifled the noise of his footfalls, which hit the floor violently, but he talked aloud, hurling insults at people and things, insulting himself, showing his fist to the four walls...

It was, in brief, one of those sudden fits of anger that serve as a safety-valve for our irascible machine, and which rise, and rise, with an increasing din, until the final explosion...

It did not help him to decipher the cryptogram. But it relieved all his slowly-accumulated frustrations.

The objects that came to hand flew across the room, and, finally seizing the little nickel toad that was holding down the photographic print, he hurled it at the floor in its turn, violently...

But what the...?

It seemed that the impact had animated the metal!

The stunned toad hopped, awkwardly throwing itself between Rosamour's legs—who, opening his eyes wide, moved his feet out of the way to avoid the contact of the disgusting creature.

What a singular dream! Was he going mad?

And abruptly, he brought his heel down on the gray back of the toad, which he crushed with a curt sound. But immediately, recovering possession of himself, passing his hand over his forehead to drive away the last residues of anger, he leaned over his victim and examined it,

The animal had shiny metal scales on its back, and on the carpet lay a thin envelope of nickel. The paperweight had merely been an animal imprisoned within a frail pellicle of metal.

Suddenly, light dawned in his brain, illuminating an entire sheaf of facts incomprehensible until then. The statue! Why should the statue not also be the chrysalis of a living being?

Was not the experiment to which the cryptogram referred the metallization of a human being? And had not the two supposed criminals fled, frightened by the horrible operation in which they had doubtless collaborated?

But is not the most urgent thing to go and rid the man who was buried alive of the rigid envelope that enclosed his body? A cadaver, evidently…for a human being does not have the strength of resistance of a vulgar toad. The crucial piece of evidence is there; it will be revealed at the propitious moment, and will display the flair and science of the detective.

Damnation! The statue is about to be sold at auction, with the aid of a great reinforcement of advertising that does honor to the ingenuity of Jean Saure, the *fin-de-siècle* journalist. Imagine the face of the buyer!

And Rosamour arranges in his imagination an entire spectacular *coup de théâtre*, for the public exhibition, in the midst of which he will cry: "Stop! You're buying a statue and you're being given a man. A man can't be sold— there's an error in the merchandise! Rosamour is a great detective!"

Content with that discovery, the agent picket up his cane and his hat, and went out to go see Madame Bémolisant, whom it was necessary to tranquillize.

The young woman was accustomed to seeing in him an amiable savior, and had conceived a grateful sympathy for him. When he appeared, it was like a ray of sunshine that suddenly illuminated her sad interior. She often invited him to dinner; he was so cheerful, so full of delicate attentions for Madame Legris, who was quite delighted by them, and even for the baby, which he dandled on his knees—with the consequence that he had gradually introduced himself into the life of the widow, and his presence was desired when it was anticipated.

That day, Hélène welcomed him with a smile, glad to see her friend at a moment when a certain discouragement had overtaken her. And he set about consoling her, talking to her about the future that would open the doors of a new life to her. He made discreet allusions to the dreams he had glimpsed of a communal existence.

Blushing, she closed his mouth with a word; but he told himself that she was gradually getting used to the idea, and, without insisting on his premature projects, he told her about his discovery.

"You see!" she exclaimed. "My husband couldn't be a murderer!"

"Eh? He's as good as if he'd participated in the operation."

"He wouldn't only have been yielding to his uncle's demands."

"Does one obey a madman when he says: *kill me?*"

Hélène was about to reply, but, summoned by the doorbell, she ran to open the door of the apartment.

The door was scarcely ajar when two tall, thin bodies, clad in an incongruous fashion, slipped through the narrow gap, with a backward glance to make sure that they were not pursued.

The young woman had uttered an exclamation, and she stared at them, trembling, without daring to speak, nailed to the spot by stupor.

Those bizarre individuals with hirsute beards and dusty, stained garments, were Pilesèche and Bémolisant—or perhaps their ghosts—emerged from the waves that had engulfed them, suddenly surging forth to come and reproach her for her forgetfulness.

"It's me," said the artist. "It's really me. You thought you'd never see me again, didn't you? But anything can happen..."

The first shock having passed, she threw herself into his arms.

"Oh, Népomucène, what joy! What surprise! You...you, alive!"

The other kissed her, and let himself fall into a chair, exhausted. "Don't speak so loudly. What if someone were to hear?" And as he perceived Rosamour, who emerged from the next room and came forward, Bémolisant suddenly sat up straight, galvanized. "The police!" he cried, his voice whistling in distress.

And Rosamour, in his turn, furious at that untimely appearance, which wrecked all his plans, exclaimed: "You! What are you doing here? Why aren't you dead? Was it necessary to come back to dishonor your wife?"

Hélène looked at him, astonished and anxious. What? Hadn't he said just now that they weren't guilty?

"Not guilty!" replied the agent, with bitter scorn. "Not guilty of having lent their collaboration to a mortal experiment! Certainly, the law will want to arrest such accomplices! Tell the examining magistrate about scientific experiments! Come on—they have only to run away, and since no one is worrying about them any longer, since they're believed to be dead, they can live in some obscure corner where they'll be forgotten, these resuscitated dead men..."

But Pilesèche spoke in his turn. "What do you mean, collaborating in a mortal experiment? Monsieur Grillard left proof that we had nothing to do with it; before disappearing, he wrote a cryptographic declaration on the laboratory blackboard..."

"I know that," the agent interrupted, impatiently.

"Well, if you know that, you know the terms of the declaration?"

"Yes, certainly, but..."

"Me, I have the translation..." He took out his wallet.

Professional instinct gripped Rosamour again; his expression cleared; he was curious to know how Pilesèche had deciphered the inscription, and was already no longer thinking about the annoyance cause to him by the reappearance of the two phantoms.

"Come on, let's see," he said. "Aha! It's complete—no lacunae."

"I copied the inscription before passing the sponge over it."

Rosamour read:

Bémol et Pil trouveront cops métallisé. Enlèveront enveloppe six mois après. Si mort, experience vérifie pas théorie. Maître Durand a testament et instructions.

"Which is to say: Bémol and Pil will find body metalized. Remove envelope after six months. If dead, experiment does not verify theory. Maître Durand has testament and instructions."

"Perfect," said the agent. "But who will persuade the examining magistrate that this isn't a document made up for the needs of the case?"

"You, Monsieur Rosamour," said Hélène, intervening very judiciously, "since you photographed the half-effaced inscription. It will be easy for you to clarify the matter. And you know, I no longer understand you; you've given me enough signs of devotion for me nor to doubt you any longer, and yet, since the arrival of these unfortunates, you haven't ceased to attack them. When they weren't here you wanted to search for them everywhere; they appear and it's almost with threats that you greet them. Come on, find our cordial sympathy again, and help us to get out of this cruel situation."

Rosamour was not a bad fellow, and was not a man who, for having seen the equilibrium of barely-sketched dream shattered, would abandon himself for long to an initial burst of spite. Thus, he immediately promised his most active collaboration, already sketching out a plan of campaign that would get him back into the Sûreté with the honors of war. Had he not untangled all the threads of the mysterious affair and put his hands on the actors in the drama, at the same time as the victim?

In truth, hazard had played a greater role in that than science.

Pilesèche wanted to go immediately and rid his former employer of his hermetic envelope. "He's alive," he never ceased repeating. "He's still alive, and we have to get him out as soon as possible."

Bémolisant could scarcely believe it, but he was shaken by the laboratory assistant's superb confidence. As for Rosamour, he was content to shrug his shoulders at the idea. Nevertheless, whatever condition the fellow was to be found in, it was time to hasten the solution.

Just then, Jean Saure arrived with news. The time was approaching when the statue would be put up for auction in the newspaper's dispatch room, which was already full of people—the All Paris of the premières. He had been astonished not to see his friend Rosamour arrive.

The latter brought him up to date with the situation and instructed him to run and inform the head of the Sûreté that, if he would care to be present at the

160

sale on the stroke of three o'clock, he would take responsibility for showing him the so-called criminals for which Boissonnald had sought so ineffectively, and also the so-called victim.

In the meantime, the dispatch room presented the most animated appearance.

The statue had been placed well in view, on a pedestal covered in red velvet, in front of a small platform where the auctioneer as chatting with a few collectors while awaiting the time of the sale.

On chairs scattered throughout the room, ladies in beautiful dresses, lorgnettes raised, were chatting and laughing. There was an indescribable hubbub of pearly laughter, subtle compliments and society gossip, all overlapping.

The head of the Sûreté had not hesitated to accompany the journalist. On arrival at the threshold of the dispatch room, he found himself face to face with Rosamour, who said to him, smiling: "This is my revenge, Monsieur." At the same time, he stood aside to reveal two individuals dressed in costumes that were half-Spanish and half-naval—for they had not had time to change out of the borrowed clothes that had permitted them to make their journey. "These are the famous criminals that you believed to be dead. I have brought them to you as a gesture of good will; I'm handing them over to you."

The head of the Sûreté glanced behind him to make sure that he had two agents there ready to take possession of the two bandits. Rosamour noticed the movement.

"Oh," he said, "do me the favor of leaving them at liberty for the moment; I'll answer for them, and you'll doubtless be inviting them to return home tranquilly in a little while."

Accompanied by the magistrate they had all gone through the vestibule and through the door-curtain on hearing the voice of the auctioneer repeating bids and warming up the auction.

"Come on, Messieurs, this statue in a masterpiece by an artist now dead, who will make no more. We're at eighteen thousand francs; who'll make it nineteen…?"

"And now," said Rosamour, "would you like me to show you Monsieur Grillard? Come with me."

Two or three collectors had been disputing the statue, but the battle had slowed and the auctioneer, his hammer raised, was about to confirm the sale.

"No one else? At twenty thousand! That's all? Sold!"

At the same time, the hammer fell on the nickel breast, which rendered a dull sound, and, as if the impact, feeble though it was, had reawakened a dormant life in the statue, the metal began to quiver under increasing vibrations. The limbs stirred, as if to break their rigid articulations. The torso rose up in a supreme effort.

There was a confused rumor in the room. Everyone had risen to their feet, terrified by such a prodigy.

Suddenly, like a suit of armor opening and falling away, the pellicle of nickel cracked everywhere; a specter sat up, frightful to behold, the eyes bulging from their orbits, blackened skin appearing under the metallic scales, which fell away like dead skin from a leper.

He projected his arms forward, uttered a loud cry and fell back upon the red velvet.

This time, the man was really dead.

The ladies fled, screaming, jostling one another at the door in an indescribable tumult, while Pilesèche tried to fray a passage toward his former master. He was torn between the horror of the spectacle and scientific curiosity.

The experiment had succeeded!

Conclusion

The author could have closed this story with the last lines of the preceding chapter, for the abrupt discovery that put an end to the mystery of the nickel statue was the conclusion of the whole dramatic adventure, and the reader will easily divine that Rosamour had no difficult in exonerating the two unfortunates he had taken under his aegis from the suspicions that had so cruelly weighed upon them.

He handled things so skillfully, moreover, that his own role in the affair took on the most brilliant appearance. He was the one who had contrived everything and discovered everything; he was the authentic *deus ex machina*; the Sûreté had no more to do than make their apologies to him for having treated him so badly, and reintegrate him into the ranks, with a promotion.

Privately, Rosamour was perhaps less proud. He confessed that after having taken to much pride in his personal science, he had owed his eventual success to chance alone. A little modesty is never unbefitting; he promised himself that if future. He will undoubtedly have important cases to work on in future, for his has conquered the complete confidence of his superiors and the officers of the court, who no longer swear by anyone but him.

Bémolisant has renounced decadent sculpture and, for the love of rhythm that the Spaniards had awoken in him, he has returned to music. The heritage of Uncle Népomucène, in any case, permits him that new fantasy, and even Madame Legris, to whom that windfall has brought serenity, forgives his flights into blue skies inaccessible to vulgar souls.

As for Pilesèche, he is continuing his experiments in physiology and hypnotism; he has devoted a veritable cult to the venerable scientist who proved, by his autovivisection, that the occlusion of living beings of the primate class is as facile as realizing that of a mere toad.[21]

Nevertheless, if the author of this story dared to offer any advice to his readers, it would be to engage them not to try it at home.

---

[21] But was he reunited with poor Miss Adda, who probably received no apology from Rosamour for his stupidity in not realizing that she had, in fact, found the missing scientist for him? Surely we are entitled to be told, and perhaps entitled to take it for granted that she did, in fact, marry Pilesèche and live happily ever after.

Il se fit enduire de plombagine. (Page 10.)

Original illustration from *The Nickel Man*

Arnould Galopin: *The Man With the Blue Face*

L'Homme à la figure bleue *must have been written as a follow-up to Arnould Galopin's first speculative novel,* Le Docteur Oméga *(1906)*[22] *and was intended to be published as such, but did not actually get into print at the time, although the author appears to have deposited a sample of the text with the Bibliothèque Nationale, perhaps as a means of registering evidence of its existence for copyright purposes. He subsequently included that title in the lists of his works included in the prefatory material of his later books, and continued to do so even after it had actually been published, in 1928, as* Le Bacille.

The latter edition contained a note explaining that the story was set in the past and that the monstrous crime it describes would no longer be practicable, thus suggesting the possibility that the reason why the novel was not published in 1907 was that the potential publisher feared that someone might actually attempt to carry out the act of terrorism featured in the story's climax. The non-appearance of the book might help to explain why Galopin's subsequent works—almost all aimed at younger readers rather than the adult audience of the present text—stuck much more closely in their speculative inventions to conventional Vernian devices.

The novel had lost some its shock value by 1928, and also some of its plausibility, because the science of bacteriology, especially in relation to pathology, had made considerable progress in the previous twenty years. Considered as a 1907 text, however, it is notable for its attempts to extrapolate a science then in its infancy, and also as an addition to the long tradition of stories attempting to focus on the unusual psychology of scientists. The book carried a dedication to the author's father, Augustin Galopin, "Professor of Physiology, pupil of Claude Bernard," which explained both its inspiration and its relative sophistication. Like almost all stories in which scientists unleash disaster, it is routinely dismissed by historians and critics as a "mad scientist story," but it illustrates very clearly, albeit in rather garish fashion, that most stories of that kind are actually accounts of inordinately sane men who are driven to breaking point and beyond by the woeful incomprehension, willful stupidity, and coarse brutality of their "normal" neighbors. If they do eventually go mad, it is because their highly-refined minds fail to resist, in the end, the brutal insanity of the society that does not deserve them.

B.S.

---

[22] tr. as *Doctor Omega*, Black Coat Press, ISBN 978-1-0-9740711-1-4

He went staggering, like a lugubrious child,
Like a madman. The crowd opened in front of him...
Léon Dierx[23]

I

He appeared abruptly at the corner of the street and advanced, seemingly wearily, his chin on his chest and his face hidden by a huge black silk bandana.

A woman who nearly bumped into him uttered a piercing scream and fled, fearfully.

Almost at the same moment, confused exclamations rose up on all sides:

"Him!"

"Him again...!"

"Oh, the horror!"

"The monster!"

There was a long murmur, a moment of recoil, and, instinctively, all the faces turned away.

For a few seconds he remained motionless, fixing on those who surrounded him two yellow eyes, moist and shiny; then he uttered a long sigh and resumed walking, slowly, under the jeers.

As he went past an outbuilding in the process of demolition, someone threw a lump of plaster after him, which shattered at his heels in a cloud of white dust, and a bold street-urchin went to far as to tug on his overcoat.

The man turned round and looked at the child, who remained nailed to the spot, terrified, his mouth open and his fingers splayed.

A crowd had gathered, overexcited and tumultuous.

"If we hadn't arrived, he would surely have hit him," said one woman, with a threatening gesture.

"Certainly," said another. "Only the day before yesterday, you know, he ran after my little boy. Even when we got home, the poor kid was shaking. His blood had 'turned.' As they say."

"But why isn't he locked up? They locked up that beggar in the Rue d'Orléans, you know—the one whose face was burned and had two red holes instead of eyes."

"That's true...and he wasn't as ugly as this one, and never moved from the one place...he was always outside the door of the orphanage. Those who didn't want to see him only had to pass by on the other side of the street...while one encounters this individual everywhere."

"Doubtless he lives in the neighborhood?" someone asked.

---

[23] The lines are from Léon Dierx's poem "Lazare" [Lazarus] (1867).

166

"Yes, quite near here, next door to the fodder-merchant, in the little house at the corner of the Passage Tenaille."

"We need to get rid of him," growled an old gentlemen afflicted by a tic, punctuating the sentence with a swish of his cane and a wink.

"The Commissaire says that he can't do anything,"

"Oh, we'll see about that! Yes, we'll see. After all, it's scandalous. Truly, it can't go on."

The man was already some way off. His tall, curbed silhouette gradually dissolves into the pale luminosity of the dusk, and for a long time after he had disappeared, the crowd remained grouped on the sidewalk, cursing the unknown man whose brief appearance had disturbed them so strangely.

For the month or so that the man they called "the Horror" had been living in Montrouge, he had been going out regularly at nightfall, like the bats. He went along deserted streets, timidly sticking close to the houses, seeking as far as was possible to hide in the shadows. The first time he had been seen he had provoked a sentiment of anxious curiosity, a kind of indefinable malaise, as if people experienced something strange and abnormal at the sight of him, which frightened and disconcerted them. Then, at length, fear had given way to aversion and aversion to disgust. They were afraid of the man, and they detested him at the same time, because he troubled the quietude of peaceful folk and was obstinate in living as other people did, when he seemed condemned by nature to lead the existence of ancient lepers. For two pins, they would have demanded that he cover his head with a veil and advertise his presence with a rattle.

He had become a kind of public enemy; a dull rage seethed at his approach, and but for the policemen, he might have been lynched, so forceful was the hatred again the man, who could not, however, be reproached for anything but his ugliness. There are physiological miseries that overexcite the nerves and which, after having caused a frisson, end up making hair stand on end. They become an obsession, and at the sight of them, instead of an exclamation of pity, it is a cry of fury that escapes, for modern altruism adapts poorly to certain complications and does not like to be subjected to too rude a proof. It is understood that everyone loves his neighbor, and is sometimes disposed to help him and console him, but only on condition of not forcing hearts to overly heroic devotions.

Darkness had fallen completely when "the Horror" arrived back at his home, a small two-story building with a cracked façade and disjointed shutters, situated almost on the edge of the Avenue de Maine.

The building, which was protected against collapse to the left by worm-eaten beams, backed on to an outbuilding on the right, in which bales of hay and straw were visible, symmetrically stacked. An interior courtyard connected the outbuilding to the meager house, but now that the latter was inhabited, a kind of partition had been hastily erected, formed of disparate and half-rotten planks, linked together at the top by a crosspiece of new fir-wood. Two windows overlooking the courtyard had been blocked by means of brackets, and the black marks of shutters could still be seen on the wall.

The hovel belonged to a neighboring fodder-merchant; it had been abandoned for some time and its owner had decided to demolish it when a man of about fifty, who said he was a physician, had asked to rent it one day, and had signed a three-year lease. "It's for one of my friends," he had said. "A scientist who desires to be tranquil..." The name of Martial Procas had been entered on the receipt for a year's rent paid in advance, and the man had gone away.

Two days later, a large removal van stopped in front of the building, and the movers had not taken long to clutter the sidewalk with broken furniture, packages, bales and a large quantity of bizarre instruments and objects like those seen in laboratories: retorts with curved stems or convoluted rims, bell-jars tapering at the base, spherical or ovoid flasks with narrow necks, pear-shaped aludels made of clay, stacked inside one another. Then there was a profusion of test-tubes—straight, bent and U-shaped—cupels, crucibles, bottles, filter-funnels, eudiometers and siphons.

Passers-by stopped, intrigued by such a mass of mysterious things, and gazed with suspicious eyes at the invasion of glassware.

Finally, the movers took two cupper furnaces out of the vehicle, a small iron bedstead, a Norman dresser, a faded red velvet divan, a few chairs, a large oak table that resembled a work-bench...and that was all.

The men waited for someone to come and tell them where to put it all, and when the tenant did not show himself, they went to install themselves in a wine-shop, after having asked a small boy to come and tell them "as soon as the parishioner arrived."

It was necessary to believe, however, that the "parishioner," as they called him, was in no hurry to occupy his new dwelling, for he did not make his appearance until the moment when the street-lamps were beginning to light up.

Although it was May and quite warm, he arrived in a closed cab—one of those archaic fiacres that one encounters by night in the courtyards of railway stations, driven by rubicund and unkempt sexagenarians. After paying the coachman, he pulled a black felt hat down over his eyes, put a hand over his face and plunged rapidly into the vestibule of the house. One might have thought, on seeing him, that he had suddenly been struck, and, stunned by the blow, was fleeing in order to escape an invisible enemy.

The movers, having been alerted, appeared, grumbling, their tread heavy and unsteady.

"Oh, it's not right," said one.

"The fellow's decidedly making fun of us," said another. "Just wait—we'll sort out his glassware, and properly. If there are breakages, too bad—it won't be our fault, since it's dark."

A dry, slightly nasal voice emerged from the vestibule.

"Don't break anything, my friends, I beg you. There'll be a good tip."

The movers looked at one another, and started laughing stupidly, nudging one another with their elbows.

The chief of the crew, a tall fellow with tattooed arms coiffed in a red bonnet, replied in a drawling faubourgian accent: "Don't worry, Bourgeois, we'll take care of your vessels. As long as there's a good tip, it's okay. Come on, lads! Let's begin with the furniture. We'll see to the glassware later."

And with gestures with which they strove to alleviate their bad manners, the men loaded their shoulders with the meager furniture that was heaped pell-mell in the street.

That took scarcely a quarter or an hour, and then they "attacked" the glassware, getting down to work with a meticulous care that they exaggerated in a ridiculous manner.

Meanwhile, the tenant had not yet shown himself. Hidden in a room on the first floor, he rapidly interrogated every time he heard the stairs creak: "What are you bringing up?"

"The bed."

"Good…on the first…the room to the left."

A few moments later, he asked again; "What are you bringing now?"

"Glass trinkets."

"The room to the right downstairs, on the ground floor."

Sometimes his voice sounded very nearby, sometimes it was slightly muffled, coming from the depths of a room or a corridor, but the movers were never able to see who was speaking to them. When they draw nearer to the place where the singular individual was, they heard a rapid rustle, and saw a shadow that brushed the walls and disappeared behind a door. One of them, who was wearing espadrilles, succeeded in unearthing the "parishioner," but the latter, taken by surprise, abruptly turned his back and stayed in a corner, bending down slightly, as if he were arranging something.

When everything was brought in, set down and fixed, the man asked again: "Where are my microscopes? I can't see them."

"What's he talking about?" asked one of the movers.

"I don't know," his comrade replied. "I think he's asking for his my-roscopes."

"They're in a black wooden box," said the invisible man, without emerging from the corner where he was lurking.

"Oh yes! I know what you mean," said the chief of the movers. "We'll bring it up, Bourgeois. The box is downstairs in the hallway. Beg pardon! Sorry—we forgot it."

Coins were then heard clinking, and the tenant announced: "I'm putting your money on the mantelpiece of the room on the right."

The movers came forward rapidly, but when they arrived the man had disappeared.

The chief counted the money, clicked his tongue in satisfaction, and then bowed ironically and said: "It's all there…and generous. Thanks a lot, Boss, and *au revoir*! No, I can't say that, since I haven't seen you…but that's okay, you're very good all the same. Let's go! Until next time!"

There was a sound of hob-nailed boots on the stairs, sonorous stumblings, and then the door slammed shut.

The man listened for a few moments, standing still at the top of the stairs. When he was quite sure that the movers had gone, he came down very rapidly, shot the bolt of the main door, and lit a candle. Then he threw himself down on the old red divan that lay in the midst of a frightful mess, put his head in his hands, and started sobbing.

II

Who was that dolorous individual? Where did he come from? Why did people abruptly turn away when he approached? There must, in consequence, be something terrifying and horrifying about him?

Yes. He was ugly: atrociously ugly, with an ugliness that surpassed anything imaginable. Not that his face was ravaged by some kind of lupus, labored by a repulsive tumor, or covered in nasty wounds; he was not subject to any deformity; no accident had contorted his features. What rendered him ignoble and monstrous was simply his color.

It was blue…entirely blue. Not an apoplectic blue extracted from violet dregs of wine, but a raw, violent, almost bright blue, intermediate between Prussian blue and ultramarine.

I have lived in hospitals for a long time. I have seen all the deformities and all the monstrosities that nature is sometimes pleased to heap on poor humanity, but I have never encountered a monster more repulsive than the one whose heart-rending narrative I have undertaken to relate.

Nothing was as impressive at that face, which seemed to be that of a decomposing cadaver, but which, however, was illuminated by two yellow eyes in which the dolor of life gleamed, and the exasperation of no longer being counted among the living. Only the pen of an Edgar Poe could render such a frightful vision. It caused a frisson and a fascination at one and the same time.

And yet, the man had once been handsome! His long curly hair, with tawny reflections and his profound velvety eyes had caused more than one woman's head to turn when he was lecturing at the Sorbonne on the arid subject of bacteriology—for some of them had acquired the habit of going to his lectures as they might go to a five o'clock tea party, and on the tiers of the amphitheater there was a striking contrast between those socialites in sparkling outfits and the hardworking students, paled by late nights, buttoned up in their miserable frockcoats.

Embarrassed by that feminine invasion, Martial Procas' students had ended up grouping together at the back of the auditorium, where they indulged from time to time in indecent practical jokes, the most anodyne of which involved crushing ampoules of sulfur or blowing iodoform powder over the hats and corsages of the beautiful auditors.

Those petty annoyances did not deter Procas' admirers. They were perfectly well aware of being out of place in that intellectual environment, but they came anyway, in ever-increasing numbers, elbowing one another like fish-wives in order to get as close as possible to the young master's podium. A few took notes, for the sake of appearances, and their slender fingers laden with rings could be seen running rapidly over cloth-bound notebooks; others, franker and a trifle cynical, contented themselves with gazing at the professor with eyes like sleepy doves, and swooning extravagantly after some demonstration that would have required preliminary scientific studies to be comprehensible.

Those lectures, mortal for the profane, seemed to delight the young women in the audience—"the tangents," as the student maliciously labeled them, because they had the habit, when the lecture was over, of approaching Procas and brushing him slightly. Nothing put off those "bacteriomaniacs." Procas could have been talking Hebrew or Hindustani, and they would still have been numerous in their presence on his course.

Soon it became a frenzy, and in the evenings, at the salons, no one was talking about anything but the young professor.

"What, my dear, you weren't at Monsieur Procas' last lecture? Oh, what an admirable session you missed! He spoke to us for an hour about pathogenic microthingies. It was delightful! I'd never have thought that one could be interested in microbes in that fashion."

And among those enthusiastic socialites there was soon no topic of conversation but bacilli; some of them even set up little laboratories at home, and bought test-tubes, microscopes and jars—but refrained, of course, from any study. They only talked a great deal about bacteriology, as the young women of our day waxed ecstatic about Nietzsche and found him "exquisite" without ever having read him. They became "microphiles" as they had once become Nietzscheans, without knowing why, out of snobbery.

Nevertheless, something other than snobbery infiltrated the admiration that those women professed with regard to Procas. Unlike the author of *Zarathustra*, he was not a distant figure "burning with the fire of his own thought," someone impassioned with individualistic ethics, a superman intensively cultivating vital energy and striving to find a morality of the will. He was a visible, palpable individual, who would not even have needed to be a scientist to trouble hearts. And women were all the crazier about him because he seemed indifferent to the advances they made to him.

His latest volume on *Phagocyte Cells*—seven hundred pages in Jesus octavo, with colored plates—had the success of a novel of adventure. The first edition sold out in a fortnight and it was necessary to reprint it, to the great amazement of the publisher, who had never seen a scientific work take off like that. It then became a matter of good taste to have *Phagocyte Cells* on one's drawing room table, and a portrait of the author on the piano.

If Martial Procas had not been a timid individual, he would have been able to possess the most audacious of his admirers—those who came to find him to ask for a dedication—one after another, because those visits were always preceded by a little letter mauve or lily-pink letter, which left no doubt as to the intentions of the signatory; but Procas, brought up in modest circumstances, the son of a petty optician in the Faubourg Saint-Denis, felt ill-at-ease in the presence of a worldly woman, and always affected a coldness under which, nevertheless, a great intimate emotion was palpitating.

"I must pass for an imbecile in women's eyes," he often said, "but what do you expect? It's stronger than I am. I've ventured into society a little, but I'm still a savage..."

As much as he felt himself a master at the Sorbonne, with a Petri dish in his hand, triumphant and superior, he was hesitant and gauche in his apartment in the Rue Soufflot. He only had to offer his lips to accumulate kisses, but he scarcely dared to offer his hand, and did not even seem to perceive the brutal pressure that slender trembling fingers imprinted thereon.

That timidity, which was mistaken for disdain, did not fail to give rise to critical gossip. Soon, his listeners were all convinced that they had a rival.

If, in the course of his lectures, Procas turned his head more frequently toward one brunette, or smiled as he looked at a blonde, eyes charged with hatred immediately flashed thunderously at the privileged individual, and the quivering bacteriomaniacs murmured "It's her!" between their pretty teeth.

Then, they took stock of the one they believed to be the elect, with ironic smiles wandering over their lips, and when the lecture ended there were whispered conversations in the corridors, punctuated by busts of insolent laughter, expressions of disgust and little fits of significant coughing.

After a few months, all of Procas' listeners had fallen out mortally; each of them believed that they saw in another a preferred rival; but the most enraged of all were the women in decline, those who could not believe in the outrage of the years, who were striving in vain to hide annoying nasty crows'-feet beneath skillful make-up. They were truly intrepid, and abandoned all their occupations—if they had any—in order to play detective.

Unfortunately, as they were unaware of the savant deductive method of Allan Dickson,[24] they could not discover the slightest "flagrante delicto" and were

---

[24] Allan Dickson was a detective invented by Galopin, who appeared in a number of short stories published in the first decade of the century, some of which were subsequently integrated into the portmanteau novels *La Ténébreuse Affaire de Green-Park* (1910) and *L'Homme au complet gris* (1912), the latter of which

reduced to spying on one another—which gave rise to singular misunderstandings and led to a few minor scandals about which two or three families blushed.

And while this feminine surveillance was exercised around him, Procas calmly continued his research into pathogenic bacilli. Perhaps he would have lived impregnably in his ivory tower if he had not accepted a few invitations.

He went to two or three salons—always the same ones, for nothing weighed upon him so much as a first welcome. Intimacies did not take long to become established; he found some of his admirers there; the flirtations began. Procas was on the fatal slope. From flirtation to love there is only one step to take, and that heart, which had thus far beaten for science alone, finally knew the torment of amour.

The woman who was able to capture that savage was an American named Margaret, who was familiarly nicknamed Lovely Meg. We shall dispense with painting her portrait by employing, in order to depict her, the precious and scholarly terms that always make a heroine the sweetest, most captivating and most ideal of creatures. We shall simply say that Margaret was beautiful. Furthermore, she was knowledgeable, having undertaken challenging studies at the University of Baltimore, and she was certainly the only one of Procas' listeners capable of understanding the professor's scientific explanations.

She really was the woman of whom he had always dreamed, the companion who might be a collaborator as well as a lover, with whom one could still talk when one has finished laughing. It did not take him long to fall madly in love and, for fear that someone else might take her, he married her. Poor innocent, who thought that a "yes" might be sufficient to enchain a woman's heart!

For a month, there was a triumph of love, a folly of caresses, an intoxication. Procas no longer lived except for Meg, and his passion was all the keener for having been so long contained. Like all true lovers, he was ferociously jealous. He made a luxurious nest for her, in which he intended to keep her for himself alone, far from the tumult of society and the gazes of the crowd.

At first, Meg accepted that role of captive goddess, which flattered her romantic temperament. A skeptic by atavism, like all American women, she did not imagine that there really could be men as tender as the heroes of fiction. It seemed amusing to be pampered and coddled like a little girl, but at length she wearied of that claustral life and of the poor lover who was always kneeling before her. She even reached the point of finding him perfectly ridiculous, and made him understand one fine morning that she would like to replace the honeymoon with a little sunlight.

Procas resigned himself to it, with death in his soul. He was obliged to go out, to show himself in society again. Then his wife demanded that he resume

---

included an episode that introduced him to his obvious model, Sherlock Holmes, and is available as *The Man in Grey*, Black Cat Press, ISBN 978-1-61227-484-3.

his bacteriological research, doubtless to put an end to an intimacy that was becoming troublesome.

We shall not undertake to recount here how Meg, who had an incessant need for money and for whom her husband's resources were no longer sufficient, went about augmenting her luxury. The woman is only due to play an episodic role in our story; she is no more, in sum, than a shadow, a figure who passes by and must soon fade into darkness.

One day, Procas, who was still very smitten and whose mind had never even been brushed by suspicion, learned abruptly of Meg's infamy. The proofs were there, cynical and overwhelming. The woman who was his entire life, to whom he had sacrificed his ambitions as a scientist, his dearest dreams, had deceived him odiously. Letters forgotten in a writing-desk whose drawer had been left ajar had told him of the atrocity, the frightful truth.

A dull rage rose within him.

Suddenly, he became motionless, his pupils dilated, his gaze fixed. His lips moved, but nothing came out except a vague whimper, inarticulate sounds that resembled the wailing of a tiny baby. He put his hands to his breast; his breath was short and staccato; his face, pale at first, colored abruptly; it became red, almost purple; the whites of her eyes were bloodshot; one might have thought that the blood impelled toward the face by a violent pressure was about to spring forth of all the pores in its skin. Pink foam trickled from his mouth. Then, vacillating like a tree shaken by the wind and felled, he suffered one last shudder and collapsed backwards, his gaze anguished, uttering a sinister cry that resembled the gurgle of a man whose throat has been cut.

III

At the noise he had made when he fell, a domestic came running. He lifted Procas up and carried him to his bed.

Soon, the whole house was in turmoil, and a physician, alerted by telephone, arrived in a matter of minutes. He was a blond young man, very myopic, newly established in the neighborhood. He approached Procas and examined him rapidly. The unfortunate was still unconscious, and his violet-tinted face was a horrible dark stain upon the whiteness of the pillow.

Assisted by the valet, the doctor lifted the patient up slightly and removed his clothing. Procas' body appeared in all its nudity, with large blue patches on the skin. Cavernous laughter escaped from his throat.

That's singular! the young practitioner reflected. *Cyanide poisoning? Asphyxia by lighting gas? No, it's impossible. In the former case he'd have been dead for a long time, in the latter, there'd be an odor in the air that would leave no doubt. It's more likely an attack of apoplexy, although...in sum, I believe I ought to bleed him...*

And, approaching the domestic, who was looking at him with frightened eyes, he said: "Quickly! A strap and a basin."

When he had what he had requested he washed Procas' arm carefully. The patient hiccupped, and then vomited.

"How cold he is!" said the domestic.

"Yes," murmured the physician, "and that's strange…for in these sorts of attacks, the temperature always goes up, not down."

"Perhaps he's going to die?"

The doctor continued washing the sick man's arm. When the skin seemed sufficiently clean, he coiled the strap around it, above the elbow, in order to make the veins of the forearm stand out. They seemed enormous, intensely blue. Then he passed his lancet through a flame and was preparing to plunge it into the flesh when someone put a hand on his shoulder.

He turned round, and found himself face to face with a tall old man with a cool, calm gaze.

"Professor Viardot!"

"Yes…I was passing. Someone told me what had happened to my poor friend, and I came up. With your permission?"

And the illustrious master approached the invalid.

"It's an attack of apoplexy, isn't it?" asked the physician.

"You think so?"

"Indeed!"

"You're in error, my friend…and you can put your lancet away. Have you noticed these blue patches?"

"Yes…and I confess that they surprised me."

"Were they as large as they are now when you arrived?"

"No…at the most, they had the diameter of a five-centimes coin, and were fairly scarce."

"Ah! Look, now they're less spaced out; they're getting larger and closer together; they're even showing a tendency to join up and fuse…within an hour, they'll have invaded the entire cutaneous surface, and the poor fellow's body will be uniformly tinted with a very characteristic blue coloration. Now let's check the mucous membranes…"

Viardot asked for a spoon, and opened Procas' lips and teeth. The patient was still inert.

"Look," said Viardot to his colleague.

"The interior of the mouth is an intense blue."

"As well as the tongue and the pharynx! The eyelids are also becoming colored. Do you have your thermometer?"

"Here it is."

"Good. Take his temperature."

There was a long silence, during which the two men did not take their eyes off the invalid for an instant. Then, at a sign from Viardot, the young physician looked at his thermometer.

"Thirty point four degrees," he said.

"I was sure of it. When Procas recovers consciousness, his temperature will probably go back up to thirty-five or thirty-six degrees, but never to thirty-seven. Poor fellow! If he escapes, he'll only be a shadow of his former self. He might still hang on for a year or two, perhaps three, but he'll remain hideously repulsive, and he'll often be in pain. At the slightest abrupt movement or the slightest effort, the choking sensation will take hold of him again. The slightest exercise will give him vertigo. He won't be able to run or walk rapidly without experiencing a frightful oppression, accompanied by palpitations and anguish."

"Yes...yes, I'm beginning to understand."

"Look at the lips now. They're deep blue, as are the nostrils and the ear-lobes. Examine the hands; notice that deformity of the fingertips. Is it sufficiently evident? The last phalanx is swollen, rounded, as if displayed; the nails are thick, broad and curved back."

"Indeed. Why didn't I notice all that sooner?"

"These cases of cyanosis are extremely rare, my friend, and young practitioners can be excused for not recognizing one. In general, it's a matter of congenital affliction, and the individuals afflicted usually die very young. Very few reach thirty. On the other hand, if the contraction of the pulmonary artery in acquired—which is to say, as a consequence of an adult malady, as in his case—the illness can reveal itself at any age in life. I've had occasion to treat Procas for acute rheumatism; in that era, his heart was affected; an endarteritis of the pulmonary artery had contracted the opening of the vessel. I often said to him: 'Be very careful, my friend, or your heart will do you a bad turn.' Unfortunately, I wasn't mistaken. Since then, the contraction has only got worse. All these symptoms: the blue coloration, the dyspnea, the apathy and the cooling that we now observe in him, are explained by the fact that from now on, he'll have too much venous blood and not enough arterial blood; too much carbon dioxide and not enough oxygen. It will be an eternal asphyxia."

"But how have these accidents been provoked today?"

"Undoubtedly, they could have burst forth yesterday, or not until tomorrow. It's surely some emotion that brought on this crisis...a very violent emotion."

And Professor Viardot, who was doubtless up to date with certain details of Procas' life, slowly shook his head as he looked down at the invalid, with a sad expression.

Then, as he got ready to leave, the young physician said: "What must I do, Master?"

"Nothing. Wait until he recovers consciousness. Then, on my behalf, recommend that he rest: absolute tranquility of the body and the mind. Let's go! *Au revoir*...I'll be back soon."

Procas finally came round. He did not remember anything, however. He knew that something had happened to him—but what?

He looked at the physician with a bewildered expression, raked the sheets with his fingernails, and then, suddenly, his bloodshot eyes fell upon Meg, whom a chambermaid, fully informed about her mistress' life, had gone by auto to fetch from the depths of Passy. A long sigh escaped his breast; he shuddered, and tried to get up, but fell back heavily, grinding his teeth.

Meg, who had leaned over him, straightened up almost immediately, chilled by fright. Procas' eyes were fixed upon her, but in such a strange fashion; there was such a surge of hatred in that gaze, at the same time as a profound distress, that she divined immediately what had happened. Her husband knew everything!

Then, slowly, as if hypnotized, she retreated to the door, opened it abruptly, and fled like a madwoman from the bedroom into which she had once brought love, and where she now left behind nothing behind but despair and shame.

For a week, the physicians were unable to pronounce judgment on Procas' fate, for his malady followed a strange, disconcerting route. Sometimes the invalid seemed to be on the mend; sometimes he fell back into a disquieting immobility akin to coma. Finally, his condition seemed to ameliorate, but the frightful blue tint, instead of diminishing, became, on the contrary, deeper and deeper. It finished up reaching the entire body, but it was the face that was the worst afflicted. Frequently, he felt an intense internal cold and his body temperature immediately dropped in an alarming fashion. He also had frequent hemorrhages and sometimes vomited blood. Then he experienced atrocious palpitations, which almost always terminated in generalized convulsions with a considerable analogy to veritable epileptic crises.

Professor Viardot, who came to see him twice a day, strove in vain to make him feel better, but Procas, increasingly obsessed by the memory of Meg as soon as he could collect his ideas, remained deaf to any exhortation. He was, moreover, convinced that he was going to die, and was even anticipating with a kind of impatience the fatal moment when his eyes would close forever, and when his incessantly laboring thought would finally fade away into gentle nothingness.

Poor Procas! It is necessary to believe that he had not yet suffered enough and that his dolorous existence would not stop there. His ordeal, alas, was only just beginning.

One evening, when he could hear the regular snoring of the domestic charged with watching over him, coming from the next room, he slipped quietly out of bed and groped his way to Meg's room. Once inside, he turned the commutator, and headed toward the little writing-desk where he had found the accursed letters.

They had disappeared.

Procas stood there, bewildered, wondering whether he had not had a frightful dream, and whether his poor, sick imagination might have created that lamentable history of treason in its entirety.

But no...he was certain that he had held them, those letters. He could still see one of them, among others, which began with the words: *Sweet Meg, darling of my heart*... He remembered that it had been a trifle crumpled, and that it bore a figure in relief in one corner, with interlaced initials. There had also been a telegram with an address in the Avenue Friedland, where there was mention of a missed rendezvous, and another love-letter signed *Robert*, in a ridiculous and pretentious style.

He had wanted to find those letters again, in order to screw them up, tear them apart, trample them underfoot and, in sum, take out on them all the rage that was biting his flesh.

He started searching all the items of furniture, emptying out the contents of drawers pell-mell on the carpet, furiously breaking open boxes and caskets.

Woken up, the domestic immediately came running. Perceiving him, Procas uttered a howl like a wild beast, and gestured at him to go away. And in his gesture there was something so menacing that the servant fled, prey to a mad terror, absolutely convinced that his master had lost his reason.

Soon, the news spread like a burning fuse: *Monsieur is mad...furiously mad...he's certainly going to do something terrible...*

In a trice, the house was deserted; those domestics who had not fled locked themselves in their rooms and barricaded the doors.

When Procas could no longer hear any sound, he started pacing back and forth, sometimes stumbling over the debris strewn over the floor, holding on to the furniture as soon as his legs buckled under him.

Suddenly, he stopped. A portrait of Meg hanging on the wall was gazing at him with wide, astonished eyes. He contemplated it for a few moments, and then slowly kissed the head, compressing with his two hands the disorderly beating of his heart. Now that his fury had calmed, and his hatred had given way to a great depression, he felt that he was becoming weak, and if Meg had come back at that moment, he would probably have thrown himself at her feet like a guilty man.

He looked at the portrait again, his breast shaken by little convulsive sobs, and then went into the drawing room, which lit up as soon as he opened the door. The piano was still open, and still displayed on the lectern was a lullaby by Grieg that he loved to hear and often played with Meg, because he found a sweet and melancholy charm in the melody, by which his lover's heart was strangely troubled.

On a sideboard, in a crystal vase, flowers were finishing dying. He took one and raised it to his lips.

At that moment, the clock on the mantelpiece suddenly stopped ticking. One might have thought that a heart had suddenly ceased beating, and a lugubrious silence filed the room.

Procas shivered.

His gaze fell upon the mirror in which two electric bulbs were reflected. He approached it mechanically, clutching the poor crumpled flower in his trembling hand, but stopped, terrified, like a man who perceives a phantom before him.

It was the first time he had seen himself since the terrible crisis had struck him, and he thought he was the victim of a nightmare. It seemed impossible that it could be him, that blue monster, ridiculous and sinister, more hideous than a Japanese mask. He closed his eyes, and then reopened them after a few seconds. The frightful head was still before him, grimacing and malevolent.

He pinched himself violently in order to assure himself that he was really awake, and pronounced a few inconsequential words. The mirror sent back the movements of his arm and his lips.

Then he was afraid.

With a hesitant gesture, he pressed an electric button and waited, anguished, no longer daring to look into the mirror.

No one responded.

He opened a door and called. His dry, hoarse voice was lost in the darkness. Nevertheless, he repeated his appeal, even striking the floor with a chair. Nothing stirred within the house.

"My God!" he stammered, trembling. "My God!"

And he crouched down in a corner, folding himself up and gripping his head with both hands.

Now he took account of everything. Words pronounced at his bedside came back to mind: "Blue coloration…he'll remain frightful…terrifying... Poor fellow!"

Yes, people had said that. Everything was now precise in his bruised brain. He guessed why the domestics had not responded to his appeal.

"I frighten them," he murmured. "They too have abandoned me!"

He understood then that he was no longer anything but a human wreck, a horrible and repulsive thing. And in the heavy atmosphere of the silent room, he dreamed dolorously, his gaze bleak and vague.

IV

The next day, when Professor Viardot came to visit Procas, the concierge brought him up to date. "Monsieur went mad yesterday. He tried to kill his people."

"That's impossible!"

"I assure you..."

"Do you have the keys to the apartment?"

"Here they are...but be careful, Monsieur. It might be better to call the police."

"There's no need."

"Oh, Monsieur! Be careful...it seems that he's in a state of terrible excitement. He was heard knocking over furniture all night."

Professor Viardot went upstairs on his own, and went into the apartment. At first, he could not find his patient, but he eventually discovered him. He was crouching in a corner and seemed to be asleep. At regular intervals his shoulders rose and fell convulsively, and his teeth could be heard chattering.

The doctor touched him lightly.

Procas started like a surprised animal, uttered a groan and looked up. On recognizing his old friend he tried to get up, and braced himself with his hands on the floor—but he was so weak that he fell back, whimpering.

The physician picked him up and carried him back to his room, and then put him to bed, as he would have done for a small child.

Procas looked at him with wide, troubled eyes.

"It's madness, my friend. Were you trying to kill yourself?"

The invalid did not reply. He clutched the doctor's hand and burst into sobs.

"Come on! Courage!"

But Procas could no longer hear him. His poor head was reeling, his mind adrift, and he pronounced incoherent words.

"Meg...Meg! She will always be thus...there...close to me...even closer...always closer... Meg! Meg! Oh, how cold your little hands are! Look at me! Answer! It's me...you know full well.... Meg! My lovely Meg! The sun...how beautiful it is...flowers! Flowers, Meg! I want them...why are you hiding them? No...no...I don't want them any longer...I no longer want...oh, that portrait! Those letters...your lying eyes...they lie...they always lie...is it you that I see in that mirror? Meg! Meg! Are you dead? Speak to me...I want to hear your voice...oh, I'm afraid! I'm afraid!"

He tried to get out of bed, but the doctor was holding him solidly.

Exhausted by the effort, Procas remained immobile, his lips quivering. Then the divagations continued, confused and oppressive.

"My queen...my little queen...look at me...smile again...don't run away. Why are you leaving me, Meg? Oh, those letters again! And there, in the mirror...that frightful man! Get rid of him, Meg! Get rid of him! Play...quickly, play our pretty lullaby...always play...oh, that's it...keep playing...tra la la la, la la la...tra la la...la la...la...la...!"

That song, which resembled a death-rattle, died slowly on his lips. Then he became drowsy, his frightful blue face swaying to the right and the left.

Professor Viardot was sitting beside the bed, holding his friend's hand in his own. At times, Procas shivered; his lips parted and little shrill groans escaped, which resembled the whimpering of a puppy.

That drowsiness was of short duration, however. The sick man did not take long to open his eyes, and seemed quite astonished to find someone beside him.

"Are you feeling better?" the physician asked.

"Yes. Why, it's you! Thank you—you're very kind."

"Do you want anything?"

Procas made a vague gesture. What could he want?

"You can't stay here on your own."

"That's true...I remember...I'm alone. They've all gone...they're afraid of me."

"I'm going to take you away."

"Ah! Take me away?"

"Yes, to a house where I have friends. They'll look after you."

"I'll scare them too. I scare everyone, even myself!"

"Come on, calm down. Will you promise me not to budge from your bed while I'm away?"

Procas nodded his head. "I promise."

"Good. Try not to think about anything. Try to sleep. Only sleep can calm you down, heal you."

"Heal! What's the point?"

"Oh, now you're starting again!"

"No, no. I'll listen to you. I'll try to sleep."

The doctor went to fetch a little water in a glass, and let a few drops fall into it from a little bottle that he took from his pocket.

"Drink," he said. "It will calm you down."

Procas drank meekly, grimaced a smile, and then closed his eyes, allowing his head to fall back. A few minutes later, he was asleep.

Then Professor Viardot went out silently, closed the door and went rapidly back downstairs. Once in the street, he looked at his watch.

It was half past eleven. He had missed his lecture. It was the first time that had ever happened to him.

At midday a motorized ambulance took the patient to the Rue Oudinot, to a sanitarium where the doctor had reserved a room.

I shall not describe Procas' convalescence. It was long, dolorous and interrupted by frequent relapses, which often gave rise to fears of an abrupt denouement.

Procas recovered his strength, however, and one morning. Dr. Viardot came to tell him that he could go out.

In that poor empty head, the fire of which had finally been eased by rest, there was then a complete reversal. The past seemed entirely obscure, the intellect that had vacillated momentarily became once again what it had been before "the event." The man who could no longer live among humans had renounced dying.

He set forth, his heart somewhat settled once again, his head full of projects—but the tide did not take long to send the wreck back, and Procas, more discouraged than ever, ran aground in his old friend's house, threw himself into his arms and murmured, in a broken voice:

"Oh, you'd have done better to let me die! Death is a hundred times preferable to the atrocious existence I'm leading. I'm an object of disgust. People pursue me in the street like a malevolent beast. I've had enough; I want to put an end to it."

Professor Viardot took his hands. "My poor Procas, I know how you must be suffering and what tortures you must be undergoing every day. To someone else, perhaps I'd advise suicide, but I order you to live. You must." And as Procas made a gesture of protest, the doctor continued in a vibrant voice: "Yes, I order you to live, you understand, because, in the midst of your distress you have one friend that will never abandon you, which will be sustain you by itself—and that friend is Science. You have already endowed your country with precious discoveries; you have, in large measure, augmented humanity. A man like you cannot disappear; he owes it to his country. Live in isolation, but live within your mind. Work enables one to forget life. Install a laboratory for yourself in some remote corner, far from the indiscreet gaze of the crowd; search, investigate—become, in a word, what you were a few months ago.

"Tomorrow, I'll go find you a little house where you can live quietly. I'll have all your apparatus and glassware transported there, and you'll see that you won't take long to be reclaimed by your former mistress, the one who never betrays us. I'll come to see you from time to time, and you can tell me about your research. I'll renew your courage, restimulate your energy, and I'm certain that, before long, you won't regret having followed my advice.

"One doesn't disappear like this, damn it, when one can do great things, when one senses in one's heart that sacred spark that can turn worlds upside down by hastening the march of progress. As long as one has a task to fulfill down here, one doesn't desert one's post—that would be cowardice!

"Listen to me carefully, Procas, you know that I love you like a son, that I was at one time the only one to support you against certain colleagues who were criticizing your methods. If I've broken lances for you, if I've been attracted to terrible intimacies, it's because I divined in you a man capable of taking a giant step forward in science. Well, today, in memory of our old struggles, I'm begging you…imploring you…to go back to work and continue to march forward.

"Instead of marching in bright sunlight, you'll be advancing in the shadows, but what does it matter, since it's only the result for which we're searching? Life is nothing in itself, my poor friend; it's a phase that it almost always dolorous, but it's necessary to know how to employ it usefully, to extract from it

182

all that it can yield to us, and it's on that condition alone that it's worth the trouble of being lived. Do you think that I place much value on my own life? No—not in the least, but I try to prolong it as much as possible, because I believe that I'm useful, and might become even more so."

As he spoke, Professor Viardot embraced Procas with the affection of an older sibling sending his younger brother into combat.

V

Procas had taken refuge in the little house in the Avenue de Maine. He spent his days behind the windows, gazing out. Although he strove to react, to master himself, he felt a great sadness invading him. The past—the entire past—came back to his mind.

Can one accustom oneself to forgetting between one day and the next? A long time after a stone has fallen into a lake, it leaves traces of its fall. A life that has collapsed is like that stone. It was more than three weeks before Procas was able to resume his work.

Finally, one day, he reinstalled his laboratory as best he could. He took his microscope out of its box: an excellent instrument with a revolving objective-carrier capable of enlarging to two thousand diameters, and installed it before a window, which, thanks to a white wall situated directly opposite, received an intense and very even light. For his nocturnal labors—if he ever had the courage to work by night, as he had before—he made use of a Ranvier albo-carbon lamp.[25]

He also set up a Chamberland autoclave[26] with a small cylindrical heater, which could produce a temperature between a hundred and twenty and a hundred and twenty-five degrees. In order to be able to maintain his cultures at a desired temperature favorable to their development, he prepared an incubator. It was a metallic box protected against external variations in temperature by an envelope of felt and warmed by a burner.

Then he arranged a quantity of test-tubes on the worktop, large Erlenmeyer flasks, Pasteur matrasses, a few scalpels, pairs of scissors, forceps, separators

---

[25] Louis-Antoine Ranvier (1835-1922) was a pathologist and histologist. He had nothing to do with the invention of the intense albo-carbon lamp patented by James Livesey, but he did recommend its use in microscopy in the journal he co-founded with Edouard Balbiani, *Archives d'anatomie microscopique*.

[26] The high-pressure steam autoclave for sterilizing surgical and experimental equipment was invented by Louis Pasteur's collaborator Charles Chamberland (1851-1908) in 1879.

and Roux syringes—in brief, all the apparatus necessary to prepare culture media.[27]

After that, he had Professor Viardot send him a provision of peptones, gelatin and tubes of the gelose known as agar-agar—the exotic product that, as everyone knows, comes from an alga from the Indian Ocean.

However, he no longer had the sacred fire. What had once enthused him left him almost cold today. He went back and forth in the room indecisively, hesitating to light his autoclave. A few lines discovered in a German work occupied him for a week, because it was a matter of a rather curious discovery, but he soon fell back into his habitual apathy. He became more and more absorbed in reverie. He thought about the woman who had caused his misfortune, and wondered whether he might have been guilty in her regard.

He even reached the point of imagining that he had been a detestable husband, since he had not been able to retain the woman he had wanted for his companion. Gradually, that idea took form in his mind with ever-greater precision...and he accused himself of having neglected Meg too much. If he had been able to understand her, perhaps the catastrophe would not have occurred and he would have continued to live happily with her. But he had not known! And that was why that chapter of his life had come to an end, abruptly, without consequence, without anything!

He sensed that he was now a poor, impotent, pitiful individual, and at times he was haunted by the idea of suicide. On the mantelpiece of his laboratory he had a small bottle of potassium cyanide, and he often looked at it. Once, he picked it up and took out the stopper, but the memory of his former master came back to mind. He had promised to work, and he could not break his word. He put the bottle back and masked it with another, in order not to have it constantly in view any longer—but he often thought about it, especially at night, when he could not sleep and felt the pain of living exasperating, with the agony of a wound that no balm could soothe.

There were weeks when he spent entire days lying on his divan, his eyes half-closed, listening to the noises in the street and the mechanical chiming of the hours. When darkness fell, he put on his overcoat, turning up the collar in order to hide his face, and a felt hat with the brim pulled down, and went out to buy his dinner, for he no longer dared go into a restaurant, since the day when he

---

[27] Conical flat-bottomed flasks were named after Emil Erlenmeyer (1825-1909), who popularized the design in the 1860s. A matrass is a round-bottomed flask with a long, narrow neck; Louis Pasteur used them to seal in culture media to prevent airborne contamination. A Roux syringe is a large injector used for repeated dosing; modern versions are semi-automatic, but the primitive model developed by Émile Roux (1853-1933) of the Pasteur Institute simply had an internal scale for measuring doses and was easily dismantled so that the parts could be conveniently sterilized.

had been refused service in a frightful cheap eatery in the Rue des Plantes. He had gone in timidly and sat down, but when the owner had turned up the gaslight and perceived him, he had gestured to him to get out, without a word. And Procas had gone, chased away like a mangy dog.

Now, therefore, he waited until it was dark in order to slip out, hugging the walls as far as the corner of the Rue Gassendi. There was a little shop there where an old woman that everyone called Maman Mélie sold fried potatoes, sausages and fish, all cooked in the same fat. The first time she had seen Procas, in the dim light, she had mistaken him for a negro. "There you are, my old Sidi—that's fifteen sous." And squinting, she had tipped hot sausages into a yellow paper cornet. Procas had paid without saying a word, and since then he had gone back every night in search of his meager pittance.

Maman Mélie, who was a good woman, had taken pity on him, and always served him copiously. Nevertheless, she confessed to her clients that the "Sidi" frightened her, and that she dared not look at him. "I've never seen such a monster," she said. "A face like that surely isn't natural. It would be better to be dead!"

And everyone shared her opinion. Yes, the man was truly too repulsive.

Soon, curiosity-seekers were drawn to Procas, and the scenes that he had taken so much trouble to avoid recommenced. They lay in wait for him, and when he made his appearance there were gibes and insults. Often, the poor man was obliged to go home without bringing back his meager meal.

One evening, he tried to talk to the crowd, to implore its pity. His words were greeted with bursts of laughter and he was obliged to flee, ashamed and discouraged.

Having returned home, he sat down at his table and burst into tears. He understood that he would never be able to turn back the tide, and that his life would be a perpetual dolor. Perhaps, among those who jeered at him, there might have been a few who were accessible to a generous impulse, but they allowed themselves to be dominated by the others. Crowds are easily influenced; one man is sufficient to draw them toward good or evil.

One evening, however, more irritated than ever, Procas tried to stand up to the malevolent people, and was nearly lynched. After that, he passed for a furious madman, and timorous citizens demanded his internment.

He had hopes that things around him might ease off eventually, but he realized then that his enemies would not lay down their arms any time soon.

From time to time he received a visit from Professor Viardot, who interrogated him about his work, suggested ideas to him and kept him up to date with recent communications made to the Académie de Médecine.

Those conversations comforted poor Procas somewhat. He emerged from his lethargy, and promised to get back to work, but when he found himself alone again in his cold house, discouragement took hold of him, and he felt more disillusioned than ever.

If he had still had someone with him, a living being that he could have heard coming and going, to whom he could address a few words, perhaps he would have recovered a taste for living, but thus far, no one had consented to enter his service. A housekeeper sent by Maman Mélie had come for a week, but then she had collected her wages and never come back. To those who interrogated her she invariably replied: "Perhaps he's not a bad man, but he frightens me. Just the sight of his yellow eyes made my shiver."

Then he had remembered a laboratory assistant he had once employed, and had written to him. Aristide—that was the assistant's name—had presented himself one morning and had consented to remain with Procas, but Aristide was an inveterate alcoholic. When he was drunk, he upset everything in the house, breaking retorts and flasks and insulting his master. Procas had to sack him. There was a fuss; a policeman was obliged to intervene, and the rumor ran round the neighborhood that the man with the blue face had tried to kill his domestic.

Procas was reduced once again to living alone. Then a veritable apathy, a gradual exhaustion of his person, and frequent crises overwhelmed him, and he went into a visible decline.

Professor Viardot tried, however, to revive his courage.

"Come on, Procas, get back to work..."

"What's the point?"

"You must...I want you to...I want it, you understand?"

In response to that imperious tone, the invalid seemed reanimated; he promised, and swore that he would relight his autoclave—but as soon as the professor had left, he fell back into bleak depression.

Nothing interested him. An indifference to everything concerning matters of life was definitely anchored within him. The external world no longer existed; he now experienced a profound disgust for humankind, and only desired one thing: the moment of supreme serenity.

In the neighborhood, meanwhile, at length, people no longer paid attention to him. People almost got used to seeing him, and two or three people even began speaking to him. In the evening, he was able to go out in search of nourishment without being abused as before.

The appeasement was taking place. Doubtless people had understood how cruel it was to persecute a poor inoffensive individual. Crowds have their mood-changes, and sometimes feel sorry for their victims.

At first, Procas was surprised. He was momentarily bewildered, like a man who, after having lived in darkness for a long time, suddenly returns to the light. Then he gradually recovered his confidence.

A visit from Professor Viardot completed the restoration; the fog in the midst of which he had been living for months finally dissipated; he saw things more clearly again, put his laboratory in order again, re-examined his test-tubes, cleaned the lenses of his microscopes, and prepared his incubator.

The bacteriologist was reborn...and when his former master came to see him again, he found him poring over gelatine plaques.

VI

Procas had returned to work. He had almost forgotten that he was a poor man condemned to live alone, like a leper, and in the little room where an odor of gas and collodion floated, he "sowed" his bacilli.

The days that had once seemed interminable now flowed so rapidly that he sometimes forgot to go to the Rue Gassendi. He contented himself then with chewing a crust of bread and installing himself again in front of his work-table.

Riffling through an old manuscript that contained an account of one of his voyages to India, he had found a study of the plague bacillus, and had resumed his interrupted work ardently.

Professor Viardot, astonished to see him so active after a long period of depression, aided him with his advice, and now came almost every day. Then they entered into long discussions; Procas became as animated as he once had been at the Sorbonne, sustaining some theory or other, citing texts—and his former master listened to him, delighted to have rediscovered the man he had known before.

While Procas recovered his appetite for work, however, events were in preparation that were once again about to turn his life upside down. It is often at the moment when one begins to hope again that catastrophes occur.

One morning, he received a visit from the Commissioner of Police, accompanied by his secretary. The officer had a severe expression, and seemed embarrassed. He looked at Procas, cast a glance around the room, and said: "Monsieur, complaints have been received from several sources..."

"Complaints?"

"Yes...and my duty is to conduct an investigation."

"What is it about, Monsieur? I'm wondering what reproach anyone can make to me." Procas pointed to the door of his laboratory, where his autoclave was humming. "As you can see," he said, "I devote myself to research. I'm occupied with bacteriology. Being unable to frequent society any longer, because of my illness...I try to forget...by working..."

"You once taught at the Sorbonne?"

"Yes."

"You never receive visitors?"

"I only see Professor Viardot, my master. I was discouraged, and thought about escaping existence. He has helped me to recover, gave me new energy, and, as you can see, I've resumed work."

The Commissioner looked in all directions. His eyes paused on the autoclave, the incubator and the large work-table crowded with small items of glassware.

187

"You never go out?"

"Never, Monsieur…except to go and buy a few provisions in the vicinity. But I never go very far…"

While Procas was speaking, the Commissioner's secretary had opened a cupboard and inspected its shelves. He also opened a large wooden chest in which the scientist kept his manuscripts.

"Come on, Monsieur," Procas murmured. "Of what am I accused?"

The Commissioner did not answer the question. He contented himself with asking: "You have several rooms?"

"Yes, four. The one I use as a study, the kitchen that I've converted into a laboratory, and two bedrooms on the first floor."

"Good. Let's go upstairs."

"It's a search, then?"

"Yes, Monsieur, and I'm acting in accordance with a warrant from the public prosecutor."

"Inspect everything, Monsieur," said Procas, whose voice was tremulous, "but I confess that your visit surprises me. For what can I be reproached? My life is simple. If someone had made a complaint against me, it can only have come from enemies, for I have enemies. I'm an object of horror, and perhaps someone in the neighborhood wants to get rid of me—but I do not harm to anyone: I'm an unfortunate man disfigured by a frightful malady. Instead of feeling pity for me they hate me, because I scare children. But I've already told you that I only go out at night and I hide my face as much as I can."

That had been said in such a sad tone that the Commissioner felt sorry for the man with the dolorous mask, lamentable in the old black suit that had become too large for his meager frame.

"If I need a character witness," Procas continued, "you can interrogate Professor Viardot, 12 Rue de Sèvres. He'll tell you who I am, because he knows me. He knows what my life has been, since the day when I was obliged to isolate myself in this house. I have an entirely honorable past behind me, Monsieur. My former colleagues can testify to that, if necessary…"

"I'm convinced," said the Commissioner. "Excuse me, but I was obliged to carry out the step I've just taken. Believe me, I shall address a report to my superiors in which I shall demonstrate the inanity of the accusation made against you."

"But may one know what that accusation might be, Monsieur?"

"In these sorts of cases, there's always a great deal of exaggeration, and we're accustomed only to attach a mediocre importance to the denunciations that reach us every day. Most of the time we ignore them, but there are instances in which we're obliged to follow them up, if only to give satisfaction to public opinion. Don't worry; it will stop here and you'll be left in peace. Continue your research. I understand that only work can make you forget everything, and I apologize for having come to disturb you—but we sometimes have to carry out painful missions."

And so saying, the compassionate officer shook Procas' hand. It was the first time in a long while that anyone had shaken the hand in question—a stranger, that is—and he experienced a singular emotion at that contact. He thought that it was a return to normal life, and forgot his dolor momentarily. He escorted the Commissioner and his secretary to the door, and such was his disturbance that he neglected to ask the question that was still burning his lips for a third time.

When his visitors had gone, he stood motionless at the window, wondering what it was of which he could have been accused. He could see people in the street engaged in animated discussion, who were turning to look in the direction of his house from time to time.

He let the curtain that he had lifted fall back, and went into his laboratory.

Although the Commissaire's words had reassured him momentarily, now that he was alone, left to his own thoughts, he felt invaded by a strange anxiety. The accusation must, after all, have been serious, since they had come to search his house, like the house of a malefactor. Had his enemies not laid down their arms, then? He had thought he was s tranquil now...

Perhaps I've been accused of being a forger? he thought. And a pale smile brushed his lips.

In the afternoon, he waited in vain for Professor Viardot, who had been coming almost every day for a week to follow the progress of his work. In the evening, he received a telegram informing him that his former master was ill. Briefly, he thought about going to the Rue de Sèvres, but he decided to wait. Perhaps it was only a slight indisposition. Then again, to tell the truth, he dared not present himself at the house where he had once been received, when he had been a man like any other. He understood that now, whatever happened, he could no longer quit his lair.

There are unfortunate individuals who, at length, end up forgetting their infirmities, but Procas was well aware of his condition. His life had to end there, in that wretched building, far from society, far from everything that had once been dear to him. Once, however, he had had a nostalgic desire to see one again the quarters where he had lived happily, full of dreams and illusions, and he had taken a taxi at nightfall and had gone to the Rue des Écoles, opposite the Collège de France, and then the Rue Soufflot, in front of his former dwelling. The second-floor apartment that he had once occupied was let now. The four windows overlooking the street were illuminated. Shadows were moving back and forth behind the tulle curtains. Then, all the past rose up within him, and he dissolved in tears.

He spent a frightful night, and took a long time to recover from the emotion he had experienced.

There are memories that it is necessary not to retain within oneself, for, like a wound that is beginning to scar over, they become more painful if the bandage of forgetfulness that covers them is removed.

VII

He still did not know why the Police Commissioner had come to his house. While working, he thought about that visit, and reproached himself for not having demanded an explanation.

The poor fellow had no suspicion that just when he thought that peace had finally returned, a dull rumor had rumbled in the neighborhood. Groups formed here and there; discussions had been held on doorsteps; and there was a concert of maledictions against the man that they called "the monster."

For about a month, people had stopped paying attention to him when he went out to go to Maman Mélie's shop in the Rue Gassendi. People had even become accustomed to rubbing shoulders with the repulsive being who emerged at dusk like some horrible phantom, timidly shirting the houses in search of shadowy corners, quickening his pace when he passed under the light of a street-lamp. The sentiment of horror and disgust that he had inspired at first had gradually attenuated, and he sometimes overheard a few words of pity as he passed by.

People were beginning to feel sorry for him when something happened that suddenly disturbed minds. The son of a haberdasher in the Rue Liancourt, a ten-year-old boy, had suddenly disappeared. A week later, in spite of assiduous searching, he remained undiscoverable. It was thought at first that he had run away, the child having a vagabond humor, but with the aid of gossips, the word "murder" had been pronounced. The last time the child had been seen, he was playing at dusk at the corner of the Passage Tenaille and the Avenue du Maine, just outside the house of the "monster."

Suspicions were immediately directed at Procas. People playing detective had posted themselves outside his windows in the evenings, listening to what was happening inside. Through the crack in a shutter a strange apparatus had been perceived, like some sort of boiler, from which a muted hum could be heard. A sinister blue flame flickered beneath that boiler, over which the meager silhouette of Procas sometimes leaned.

What mysterious work was he doing? What purpose could that receptacle resembling a percolator serve?

The curious also distinguished a large wooden table on which bizarre implements were arranged, gleaming like knives. Someone even affirmed that they had seen blood on the floor.

That was more than was necessary to overexcite the imagination of simple folk, and the rumor spread with the rapidity of a gunpowder fuse that "the monster" had abducted the child, butchered him and then burned him in his boiler.

190

Denunciations flowed into the Police Station in the Rue Sarrette, and people came to give evidence under oath, with the exaggeration that people addressing themselves to the law always put into their testimony. It was then that the Commissioner, in order to give satisfaction to public opinion, had obtained a search warrant from the Court.

While he was in Procas' house, the crowd gathered on the sidewalk had waited anxiously for the result of the search. They were convinced that "the monster" was going to be arrested, so they were disappointed when the magistrate and his secretary reappeared alone. Some risked interrogating them before they got back into their vehicle, but only obtained vague responses, which they immediately interpreted in favor of their thesis.

What was surprising, however, was to see that no official surveillance was established in the vicinity of the house in the Passage Tenaille. Neighbors promised to spy on the monster, and did not fail to do so. When he went out, he was followed by the butcher's son, a thickset brute, drunk most of the time, who was nicknamed "Bat d'Af"[28] by the local cobbler. He repeated to all-comers: "Have no fear; if he tries it again, I'll be down on his neck, and how!"

Procas wondered, anxiously, why those people, who had ended up no longer paying attention to him, were now looking at him with the eyes of wild beasts. He would have liked to talk to them, but fear held him back. Besides which, what would he have said to them? Then again, having lived for so long in solitude, he had lost the habit of speech. Furthermore, with his illness, his voice had become weak and toneless; when he spoke, he ran out of breath, and was obliged to start over twice to finish a sentence he had begun. Under the empire of emotion, he choked and had coughing fits, sometimes followed by epileptiform crises. He sometimes lay prostrate on his divan for hours, breathless, almost suffocating, laid low by dyspnea.

He did not hide it from himself that one of those crises would eventually kill him, but that did not frighten him, for he had got used to the idea of death. There were, however, days when he wanted to live for a few more months in order to complete a study on the saprophytic microbes on which he had been working before the misfortune that had turned his life upside down, and which he had resumed on the advice of his friend, Professor Viardot.

A Danish scientist had recently published a paper of saprophytes, but the work was incomplete, the conclusions too uncertain, and Procas intended to demonstrate that his foreign colleague had only taken up again, while amplify-

---

[28] A conventional contraction of "Bataillons d'Infanterie Légère d'Afrique" [African Light Infantry Batallions], which were penal units formed from convicts who had not yet done their military service, and soldiers subjected to disciplinary punishment.

ing them, the theories of Schlumberger falsified by Dujardin-Beaumetz.[29] He, Procas, was on the road to a discovery: a discovery to which he would bequeath his name, and from which science would profit. It was not vanity that guided him, but only the desire to do useful work. Every day, he put inseminated test-tubes in his incubator, inseminated them again and gradually obtained different results.

He had wanted to bring his former master up to date with his research, but Professor Viardot was still ill. Procas had received two letters from him, and then nothing more. He had wanted to telephone, but at the Post Office where he had presented himself he had been greeted in such a fashion that he had been obliged to withdraw.

Then, one evening, he took a taxi and went to the Rue de Sèvres. Not daring to go into the concierge's lodge, he sent the driver to ask for news.

A few minutes later, the man came back. "The Professor died four days ago. He was buried yesterday."

Procas gave his address in a tremulous voice, and dissolved in tears. When he got home, he let himself fall on to the divan, overwhelmed by grief. So, now he was alone in the world, with no friend to whom he could confide his pain. Solitude; cold solitude! What reason to live did he have now?

For two days and two nights he was, so to speak, no longer conscious of what was happening around him.

Finally, the animal got the upper hand again, and he perceived that he was hungry. It was dark. He went out.

People were assembled outside his door. When he appeared, he was greeted with cries of hatred; a great murmur rose up.

Procas looked around

"Come on, my friends," he said. "What have I done?"

"Murderer!" shouted a woman, advancing toward him, brandishing her fist.

"Wretch!" growled a man. "Oh, you're asking what you've done?"

"He's got a nerve!" said another.

The crowd swelled.

Understanding that it was impossible to make the furious mob listen to reason, Procas shrugged his shoulders and started walking, hastening his steps. Threats and maledictions rained upon him from behind. It was the women who were the most excited.

---

[29] The first reference might be to the marine engineer Charles Schlumberger, who published a number of studies of miscoscopic species in the 1890s, although I cannot locate one on any kind of bacteria. Édouard Dujardin-Beaumetz (1868-1947) studied the plague bacillus at the Pasteur Institute throughout the first four decades of the 20th century. The use of the term "saprophyte" in this paragraph and elsewhere is, however, puzzling, as it refers to species that live on dead or decomposing matter.

Procas continued on his way, sticking close to the walls. When he had bought his modest meal, he returned precipitately, but at the corner of the Rue Liancourt, people threw themselves upon him.

In spite of his malady, Procas had remained fairly vigorous; he struggled furiously, succeeded in freeing himself, and fled, pursued by a howling mob. Having arrived at his door he took out his key, and tried to insert it in the lock, groping.

Just as he was about to open it, two eyes were fixed upon him—two eyes in which there was astonishment, and goodwill. It was a dog: a poor dog, filthy, pitiful and shivering, which seemed to be saying to him, like Baudelaire's dog: "Take me with you, and of our two miseries, we might perhaps make a kind of happiness."[30]

Procas was moved by that gaze, which was doubtless the reflection of an inferior soul, but a gentle and benevolent soul, ignorant of human hypocrisies. He let the animal in. Numb with cold and shivering, it licked his hand, and went to lie down in the laboratory, in front of the autoclave, which was filling the room with a gentle warmth.

Outside, the cries redoubled. Stones began to hit the shutters. Procas was wondering, anxiously, whether they might be about to break down the door and invade the house, when a loud voice, the authoritarian voice of a policeman, launched a resounding "Move on!" There were protestations, and an argument began, but then the noise died away in the distance.

Then, after making sure that the windows were firmly shut, Procas went to sit at a little table, set out his modest dinner, and then whistled to the dog, which came to lie down, quivering, at his feet.

VIII

Sometimes, in life, there are encounters that encourage and reanimate. One dog now replaced, for Procas, the entire human race. The soul of a man and that of a beast fused in a reciprocal affection. That man, pursued by the hated of the crowd, needed friendship; hazard had sent him a dog.

Procas remembered then that he had once been a grim vivisectionist, who had killed a number of dogs in order to try to obtain the mysteries of life from their poor quivering bodies, in order to combat his neighbor's ills. He saw once again, as if he had only quit it the day before, the large room with white walls, in which the poor animals sent by the pound had agonized, tied to boards or easels, skinned, bloody, uttering plaintive little yaps or howls of pain. That rent his heart. It seemed to him impossible that he had been able, coldly, to cut up living animals, which were incapable of feeling, according to Malebranche.

---

[30] The quotation is the last line of the prose-poem "Les Bons chiens" (1869).

His mind went back, reluctantly, to one poor little dog that he had tortured or nearly a fortnight. He saw once again the supplicant gaze of the animal, which death did not want, and from which he had removed scraps of flesh, muscles and tendons on a daily basis, with a cold impassivity. He had also removed an eye, which had left the poor animal with a big red hole in its head, through which bone was visible.

He also remembered another dog, which he had kept pinned to a table, its paws splayed, after having made a large incision in its side, in which he had placed a silver tap. He had been a torturer of animals, an executioner, almost without necessity, a little by habit, and because he believed that vivisection was a convenient means of investigating certain physiological phenomena, refuting some argument or other, or proving some item of knowledge that no one contested.

For the so-called good of humanity, he had sacrificed poor creatures, and that humanity, which he had then loved more than anything else, was the same one that now threatened to put him to death, slowly but surely, while the animal, a sibling of those he had once sacrificed, was consoling him in his solitude for the injustice of men.

After having dissected the dead, he had dissected the living, in order to lay bare and observe the functioning of the hidden parts of the poor organisms. Without vivisection, he had accustomed himself to repeating—perhaps to excuse himself—no physiology, no scientific medicine, would be possible, and he considered, in the words of Claude Bernard, that it was "necessary to see a large number of animals die because the mechanisms of life could only be unveiled and proven, by means of a knowledge of the mechanisms of death."

And he killed without keeping count, convinced that one could extrapolate from the animal to the human, even though, in a number of cases—as has been demonstrated—the effects of certain poisons of a psychic order, such as morphine, cocaine and atropine did not produce the same effects on animals as on human beings.

And it was all of that that he thought about now, in looking into the benevolent eyes of the animal he had taken in. The intelligence of animals had not preoccupied him much before; he had considered them primarily as animate machines, automata with well-regulated movements but only able to take vague account of their actions. Now he recognized his error and even became indignant about the cruelty of Malebranche.

What? he said to himself, *that philosopher was able to claim that animals don't feel? Is an animal not organized in the same way as a human being? Does it not have the same senses, the same nervous system? Does it not give the same signs of receiving impressions? Why should the cry of an animal not express pain in the same way as the cry of a child? When humans are not perverted by habit and by cruelty, they cannot see animals suffering without suffering them-*

selves; is that not manifest proof that there is something in common between them and us? For sympathy is always an effect of similarity.

Procas was ashamed of what he had once been. And he stroked the dog, lavished affectionate words upon it, as if he wanted it to forgive him for his laboratory crimes.

The animal that he had made his companion belonged to the race of barbets. Its grey pelt had the dull coloration of animals that are not well cared for. One of its forepaws, the right, was deformed, slightly twisted inwards. A long scar was visible on its back, the result of some recent blow with a stick.

It had once had a collar, for the fur on its neck had retained the trace of it, but it had doubtless been removed in order that no charitable passer-by would be able to return it to its owner. And the poor animal had been obliged to wander the streets for a long time, to judge by the mud with which its belly and paws were stained. Chased, harassed, stoned, it must have traveled straight ahead for a long time, avoiding human beings, its torturers, only finding a little tranquility when dusk fell, and moving on again as soon as the street-sweepers came to remove the rubbish in which it sought its life.

What instinct had guided it to Procas? How had that dog, rendered half-feral by the malevolence of humans, been bold enough to implore the aid of a stranger who, like everyone else, might have greeted it with kicks, accompanied by the utterance that it had heard so many times: "Get away, filthy beast!" Whence came the confidence of the abandoned animal in a human being as unfortunate as itself? Is there a mysterious affinity between creatures that are suffering?

Procas, who had stopped speaking months ago, spoke now to his dog, as if he were confronted by a confidant capable of understanding him. He had given him a name; he called him Mami—a simple diminutive of "*mon ami*"—and it really was a friend that he now had beside him.

Gradually, Mami was transformed; his fur, which had once hung down in long dirty hanks, became neat and shiny. In his great sad eyes, truly human eyes, a little flame now gleamed. At the sound of Procas' voice, he rolled over on to its back and yapped softly. In the early days, however, he remained a little apprehensive; every caress surprised him; but gradually, he became accustomed to his new master.

Procas had made him a bed with old blankets, in a corner near the incubator. It was warm there, and Mami lay there blissfully while the poor scientist worked, bent over his table, where large volumes were piled up and glass slides were protected by wooden boxes.

The worthy dog undoubtedly dreamed, because he was agitated occasionally by an abrupt start, raised his head and let it fall back again with a little growl of satisfaction. Perhaps he was reliving, while asleep, the dolorous hours of his existence as a stray, when he fled with its tail between his legs, peppered by stones thrown by children, in search of a place where he could licks his wounds, far from his enemies, in the protective shadow of night.

He only closed one eye when he slept, though. As soon as Procas made a movement, he looked at him, and only dropped off again when he saw him poring over his books.

Procas was now absorbed by a new discovery, and often forgot meal-times. Thanks to the sobriety acquired in the course of long days of wandering and starvation, Mami did not eat much. A crust of bread, a bone to gnaw and a few meager scraps of nourishment, and he was satisfied. In any case, what more could he want? He had a name, and he belonged to a master who did not beat him. Was that not sufficient for the happiness of a dog?

He would have liked to remain perpetually huddled in his corner, in the mild warmth of the incubator, so when Procas got ready to go out he became anxious. The street frightened him. Once outside, he walked apprehensively at Procas' heels, his ears lowered, his muzzle at ground level, darting fearful glances to either side, as if he expected his old enemies to surge forth at any moment. Children, especially, frightened him, and if he perceived one, he stuck close to his master. He was never happier than when they resumed the homeward route. As soon as Procas had opened the door, he plunged into the vestibule rapidly and started jumping and yapping, as if to say: *Now I'm tranquil; the evil people who made me suffer so much can't get to me here.*

For Mami, every passer-by was an enemy. If he heard a noise in the street he growled dully until Procas had reassured him. Then he licked his hand, shivered and went to lie down near the incubator, his muzzle on its paws, his eyes half-closed, attentive to the slightest movement of his great friend, who talked to him from time to time in a soft voice, as one speaks to a little child.

IX

The poor scientist had found a little tranquility again. He was beginning to get reaccustomed to life. While working, he held long conversations with his dog.

He no longer felt so alone; a living being was coming and going around him, animating the house. When he had inseminated his culture broths and disposed them in his incubator, he sat down on his divan and read.

He received scientific journals regularly, which he never failed to scan. In general they were not very interesting; he only found banal communications therein or embryonic studies of subjects that were often a trifle fantastic. Now and again, however, his attention was retained by the announcement of a discovery or a laboratory experiment carried out by a foreign scientist, who only gave incomplete details of his work, exempt from formulae and precisions.

One day, while reading one of those communications, he felt a surge of anger. In a long article, an English bacteriologist attributed to himself all the merit of a discovery regarding *Proteus vulgaris*.[31] Now, it was Procas who had first demonstrated the harmful potential of that bacillus, which he had cultivated successfully two years earlier. It had even been the object of one of his lectures at the Sorbonne, and Dr. Roux had congratulated him warmly at the time. The plagiarism was flagrant, and Procas, under the spur of indignation, immediately set about writing a protest, in which he took the man who had had the impudence to appropriate his work violently to task. He covered ten large sheets of paper with his compact handwriting, but, as he was about to send his protest off, he said to himself: *What's the point?*

Would it be useful, then, to call attention to himself, to reveal the jealousies of his colleagues that were still smoldering under the ashes? He recalled the words of his former master, Professor Viardot: "Work in the shadows, without caring about the external world. Our lives, as scientists, do not belong to us but to humanity."

Procas' excitement faded away abruptly. He smiled in disenchantment, and threw his letter in the fire. Nevertheless, although he had renounced the glory that he could no longer accumulate while alive, he experienced a bitter sadness at the thought that someone else might benefit from his own work. Oh, if he had been as he once was, if he had been able to show himself, to speak in public, with what joy he would have sent that unscrupulous English scientist, that shameless bandit who pillaged modest workers, to the pillory!

To discharge his bile, he spoke, while pacing back and forth, his face turned toward an invisible audience, sowing his futile words in the void, becoming excited, raising his voice—to the great alarm of poor Mami, who doubtless imagined that the imprecations were addressed to him; he looked at Procas with wide frightened eyes, not daring to budge, perhaps expecting to be expelled from the house where he was so comfortable, after so many days of misery. He was only completely reassured when his master leaned over to stroke him.

There was calm thereafter. Procas resumed work—but it was written that the unfortunate fellow was not to live in peace in his hermitage. The hatred of his neighbors, still brooding since the mysterious affair of the child's disappearance, was suddenly reawakened, more forcefully.

After the Commissaire's visit, people had kept quiet for a few days, but in the shops and workshops, the commentaries continued. Everyone was convinced that little Maurice, the haberdasher's son, had been kidnapped by the monster, and that the latter, having slaked some bestial passion on the poor child, had cut him into little pieces and burned them in his "cooker." As always happens in such cases, the number of his accusers increased by the day. Some claimed to have seen little Maurice, shortly before his disappearance, playing outside Procas' door. Others affirmed that the following day they had smelled an odor of

---

[31] A rod-shaped bacterium that inhabits the intestines of animals and humans, sometimes infecting wounds. It was first described in 1885 by Gustav Hauser.

roasted flesh emerging from the house in the Passage Tenaille. Imaginations became heated. Some people were already talking about breaking into the monster's home and "setting his account."

One morning, fat Nestor,[32] the son of the butcher whose house was next door to Procas', went to see the Police Commissioner in the company of two shopkeepers who were reputed to be sober individuals and who belonged to the electoral committee of Monsieur Jacassot, the local député. Immediately received by the officer, they sat down gravely in his office, and Barouillet, one of the shopkeepers, in his capacity and an orator at public meetings, took the floor.

"My name is doubtless known to you, Monsieur le Commissaire, and you must know that I have the reputation of being a serious man."

The Commissioner nodded his head indulgently.

"If I have decided to come to you with these gentlemen, it is because I thought it my duty as a citizen to make you aware of certain facts that are causing a disturbance in our neighborhood. Now, you know as well as I do that the first concern of the law is to maintain surveillance of the actions of suspect individuals."

"Get to the point, please," said the Commissioner, irritated by that preamble.

"I'm getting there, Monsieur, I'm getting there. A child has disappeared, little Maurice Pinchon, and in spite of all research, he had so far remained undiscoverable."

"Yes, I understand. Is it the man in the Passage Tenaille that you're accusing again?"

"Because everything is against him. He's some sort of madman, a maniac capable of anything, on whose account one has the worst information..."

"What is this information?"

"First of all, he took up residence in the Passage Tenaille, so to speak, clandestinely. One evening, individuals of villainous appearance brought a heap of bizarre objects, among which was a kind of stove, or oven, of an unusual form. Then again, he has implements that are not seen anywhere else: all kinds of pincers and curved knives—I brief, devices that are not Catholic. Once installed, the man shut himself up and only came out at nightfall, like a malefactor in fear of being recognized. Do you find that natural, Monsieur le Commissaire? Come on, is there no reason to suspect that individual? He's more than suspicious, and if the police don't decide to take action, I fear that the people who have risen up against him might do something drastic..."

---

[32] The butcher's son is invariably named as "gros Nestor," which implies coarseness and brutality as well as a mere excess of weight, but there is no English adjective covering the full range of implication that would be applied as a commonplace epithet in the same way.

"The man is an unfortunate fellow disfigured by a frightful malady. That explains why he shows himself in public as little as possible."

"He's a madman, a maniac, and you know as well as I do, Monsieur le Commissaire, of what those sick individuals are capable. There are inoffensive madmen, but this one is dangerous."

""Reassure yourselves; if he were dangerous, I would not have hesitated to have him imprisoned. I've searched his house. I've interrogated him at length, and I've been able to convince myself that he's harmless. He's a scientist, a bacteriologist, whose name was once celebrated."

Fat Nestor thought that he could risk a remark. "Scientists, when they become criminals, are more dangerous than the others."

"Certainly," Barouillet approved. "We've often had the proof of it. And look, Monsieur le Commissaire, if you'll be good enough to listen to me for a moment longer, I'll tell you something that might make you reflect. Do you recall the date when the 'man' took up residence in the Passage Tenaille?"

"In truth, no. I believe it was about six months ago..."

"Five months and fourteen days exactly. It was the evening of the twenty-third of May."

"The date hardly matters."

"I beg your pardon; on the contrary, it's very important. If I say that it's because I too have carried out an investigation with Parizot, the paint merchant in the Avenue du Maine, and we've made a discovery that you shouldn't neglect."

"I'm not in the habit of neglecting anything," replied the Commissioner, dryly, "when it's a matter of enlightening the law."

"Oh, I know, I know! You misunderstood me. I simply wanted to inform you of a fact that might be of interest. Notice that I'm affirming nothing. No, far from it; I'm only pointing out a coincidence to you. Yes, that's the word: a coincidence...which struck Parizot and me. Exactly eleven days after the installation in the Passage Tenaille of the man you call a scientist, the cadaver of a little girl was discovered underneath the projectionist's booth at the Carillo Cinema—the little Soubiroux, whom the murderer had cut into pieces. You remember the affair. The arms, the legs and the trunk of the poor little girl had been stacked up carefully on top of one another, and the head placed on top of the bloody assemblage. Only a madman could have committed such a crime—a sadistic madman—for the physician certified that the little girl had been raped with an unusual brutality..."

"I know all that, but I don't see what it has to do with..."

"Of course, Monsieur le Commissaire, but the most serious thing is that our individual was seen in the vicinity of the Carillo Cinema on the evening of the crime."

"By whom?"

"Oh, several people."

"Give me their names and I'll summon them to my office."

"Their names I don't know. One hears something said, you understand, but one doesn't think of asking people what their names are. All that is certain is that I've heard more than ten people affirm the same thing. It's rather troubling, isn't it? Juxtapose that with the disappearance of little Maurice, and you'll admit that there's god reason to be disturbed. Two crimes, almost blow for blow—and what crimes! It makes one think. And then, you said yourself that the man in the Passage Tenaille is a scientist, a bacteriologist—one might as well say a physician...and only a physician can cut up a body so skillfully..."

"Or a butcher."

Fat Nestor protested, indignantly. "Oh, I know," he said, "whenever a murderer cuts up a body properly, people immediately say that it's a butcher who did it—but that's stupid, yes, utterly stupid. Just because one knows how to cut up a sheep or a calf, that's no reason why one should be capable of butchering a human being. Butchers have broad backs, of course, but you tell me whether anyone thinks that they're more criminal than anyone else. Me, I confess that I'd be very embarrassed if I had to slice, section and carve the flesh of a Christian. That's the business of medical students. Everyone to his trade."

The Commissioner, who wanted to get rid of those visitors, as prolix as all people are when they enter into the details of some story, as quickly as possible, promised to mount a narrow surveillance on the little house in the Passage Tenaille.

"That's right," said Barouillet. "Keep an eye on the individual, and you'll see that you'll learn something new before long. For our part, Nestor and I are going to keep watch. No matter how clever he is, we'll succeed in catching him in the act. When he thinks he's quite safe, he'll doubtless attempt something else, but we'll be there, and I guarantee that we won't hesitate to grab him and bring him here."

"No imprudence," advised the Commissioner. "Warn me before doing anything whatsoever, because an error could cost you dear, you know."

X

For several days, Procas had not been feeling well. He usually had atrocious crises at night, which left him so exhausted that it was impossible to get up in the morning. It began with a sudden frisson and a sharp pain below the ribs. The heat of the skin, the rapidity of the pulse, anorexia, thirst and an intense cephalgia always presaged the crisis. His respiration was short, anxious and frequent. Soon, he had a little dry cough, felt a salty taste on his tongue, and was then obliged to get up, for he knew that those symptoms always led to hemophthisis. At that moment he experienced the need to breathe deeply, and went into the little courtyard situated behind his house. It did not take long for his blood to return, and the suffering that he experienced then caused him to utter stifled groans.

He feared those crises, of which he always had warning, and these days made arrangements so as not to have to go outside. He remained confined in his laboratory, his legs swathed in a woolen blanket, reduced to almost complete immobility. His poor dog, who did not understand any of it, came from time to time to lick his hand, and Procas spoke to him gently, in a toneless voice—a voice that seemed to emerge from a box filled with cotton wool. In order to warm up again, he sat by his autoclave, and got up from time to time, supporting himself on his table, to look at the glass slides that he had placed in a small shelf-unit. For he continued to work, although he was under no illusion regarding the ultimate outcome of his malady.

He knew full well that one of those crises would kill him one day, that it would be abrupt and devastating. His heart would stop dead, and he would drop as if he had been shot. Death did not frighten him; he had been prepared for it for a long time. A few weeks before, he had even wanted it, but today he was haunted by an anxiety.

What would become of poor Mami when he was no longer there? At that thought, a great sadness took hold of him, and he almost regretted having taken the animal in.

Then he remembered a lady named Romieu, a fervent antivivisectonist who had waited at the door of his laboratory one day and had broken her umbrella on his back, calling him: "murderer!" Who could be more interested in a poor dog commended to her than that furious friend of animals?

Procas knew that Madame Romieu was the president of the League Against Vivisection, and he remembered the address of the League, whose members had so often expressed their views in newspapers and journals. He therefore wrote a long letter to that former enemy, which could not fail to move her, but he dared not give his real name; he altered it slightly and signed himself Procas.

At the same time he wrote to a notary with whom he still had some funds deposited, asking him to be kind enough to call on him.

It was nearly two years since the two men had seen one another. When they found themselves in one another's presence in the little house in the Passage Tenaille, they shook hands, but the notary's grip was rather soft. Procas evidently inspired an invincible repugnance in him. Perhaps he also feared that the disease might be contagious, for he only remained with his client for a few minutes.

In any case, Procas had very little to say to him. He enquired briefly about the sum he had on deposit at the office—a sum that served his interests, providing for his living expenses—and handed the notary a sealed envelope, saying: "When you learn of my death, you should immediately inform the person whose name you'll find in this letter, whom I institute as my sole heir."

"That will be done."

"Good—but it's necessary to hasten to warn her, because I charge her in my testament with…in sum, a grave and urgent responsibility."

"You can count on me. But let's hope that I occupy myself with that affair as late as possible."

Procas made a vague gesture, and the notary, who had refused to sit down, went away rapidly, like a man who fears being contaminated.

When he had gone, Procas shrugged his shoulders.

"You see, my poor Mami," he said. "People flee from me like the plague. For them, I'm an object of horror. There's only you, my good dog, who has any amity for me."

Mami came to lick his master's hand.

"Yes, you're good, you…and perhaps you understand that I'm unhappy; but it will soon be necessary for us to part, Mami. I sense that I don't have much longer, that the end is nigh. The days I'm living at this moment are days of grace; every hour that goes by warns me that I'm heading for the tomb. Oh, life! She was very beautiful, though, and I fell in love with her. I was too happy; I thought it would last forever! How stupid it is to have such ideas!"

A fit of coughing cut off his speech, and a trickle of blood stained his lips. He got up, took a few steps across the room, and let himself fall on to the old divan that now served him as a bed, because he no longer had the strength to go upstairs to the bedroom on the first floor. The slightest effort left him breathless and anguished. Asphyxia was lying in wait for him, and he was well aware of it, for he had studied his malady now. Among the studies made of cyanosis he had procured those of Doctors Debove and Vaquez, Constantin Paul and Variot.[33] He even experienced a scientific curiosity in following the progress of his own illness.

However, the crises began to become rarer; his heart resumed functioning in an almost normal fashion, and he was finally able to obtain a little rest.

Like an invalid entering into convalescence, he recovered a taste for life, and resumed is interrupted work. Soon, bent over his work-table, with his dog at his feet, he was inseminating his cultures. Science had him in its grip again. Someone could have knocked on his door and introduced themselves into his

---

[33] The pathologist Georges Maurice Debove (1845-1920) collaborated with numerous other workers, including the cardiologist H. Vaquez, whose explanatory description of the symptoms of cyanosis, as quoted in Debove's *Manuel de diagnostic medical* (1900), apparently forms the basis of Viardot's (somewhat exaggerated) description of Procas' condition. The physician Constantin Paul had described numerous relatively mild cases, going back to the 1870s, and was routinely cited in all the reference books of the period. Jean Variot also recorded cases in the same way, and offered hypotheses to account for the phenomenon similar to those of Vaquez.

house then, without him hearing anything—but he sometimes fell back into his habitual apathy and spent days lying on his divan, his mind lost in a vague reverie.

At those times, the entire past flowed back into his mind. He saw the great hall of the Sorbonne again, where the women crowded to hear his lectures; he remembered the slightest details of his debut as a lecturer; and then his idyll with Meg, the first words they had exchanged, the confession that he had dared to make one day, came back to his memory.

He experienced a kind of dolorous pleasure in evoking those too-brief moments, in ruminating his defunct happiness, like those old men who revive in memory the happy days of their youth. Sometimes, he wondered what had become of Meg. He had kept her portrait, and looked at it often; he forgot the harm that the woman had done him, and wanted to see her again—but without her seeing him, for he understood fully that he could no longer show himself to her. A tenderness gripped him, in which he lingered for long hours—and then, abruptly, he put the portrait back in a cupboard and strove no longer to think about the vanished woman. But a first love cannot be uprooted from a heart so easily.

A fortunate man can laugh at the women who have occupied his life, but Procas had only loved once, and his entire being still vibrated when he remembered the happy hours, too brief, that he had lived with Meg. He was a sentimental rather than a sensual person, and it is well known how unfortunate men are who love primarily by heart...

One day, he had the idea of writing to Meg. He did not know her address, but was sure that if he sent the letter to Mrs. Reading, her confidante, it would be handed on to her. He had no hope of attracting his former wife to his home, but it would have been pleasant to confide his distress to her, to obtain a response and to correspond with her as if with an invisible friend who shares your troubles and consoles you with kind words, which are perhaps nothing but literature, but whose softness is a delightful balm for a suffering soul.

He drafted a long letter, in which he carefully refrained from making any allusion to the past. He simply spoke about his misfortune, and gave an account of his life and his work since the malady had forced him to isolate himself from society.

He reflected, however, Meg, yielding to an impulse of pity, was quite capable of seeking information, discovering his address—and then she might come, might see him.

No, no, that was not possible.

He tore up the letter and went back to work. He wanted to take advantage of the respite that the malady was giving him to bring to a conclusion the research that, in spite of everything, impassioned him and made him forget his suffering for a time.

He had noticed that certain bacilli that had previously been thought to be inoffensive were, in fact, very dangerous when isolated. They developed rapidly then and did not take long to produce thousands of colonies. He was able to combat them by causing them to be absorbed by other saprophytic microbes much better adapted to their nutritive environment.

The assiduous work to which he devoted himself, however, fatigued him greatly, and from time to time he experienced the need to get some air. He waited for nightfall, and left the house, accompanied by Mami. He went along the Avenue de Maine, the Rue Gassendi and then the Rue Froidevaux, which runs alongside Montparnasse cemetery and is almost always deserted at night. Then he went back home, after having obtained a few provisions from the vendors where he still bought food, but who had been displaying an increasing hostility toward him for some days. Instead of serving him quickly, as before, they left him standing in the shop, and were no longer embarrassed by treating him harshly. Although he paid very dearly, they only gave him the worst gods, and one day, when he hazarded a timid observation, he was rudely rebuked.

More recently, he had begun obtaining his provisions from a small shopkeeper in the Rue de Lunain who had consented to come to his domicile; he brought provisions for a week on Monday and deposited the parcel in the antechamber.

"How much?" Procas asked.

The delivery man passed his bill under the door, and Procas paid, without showing himself, by expending his arm through a narrow gap. He always gave a generous tip.

One day, however, the delivery man no longer came.

He went to make inquiries, and the proprietor informed him that he did not want to serve "people like him."

XI

Procas had thought that he would eventually be forgotten, but now, suddenly, he sensed hatred growling once again around his dwelling.

In the evening, if he opened a window, he saw people stationed outside his door. If he went out, he perceived shadows gliding along behind him, keeping close to the houses. He heard bizarre noises in the courtyard behind his laboratory, and one night, he thought he saw a man climbing over the wooden fence separating it from the Passage. Truly, that life was no longer tenable, and the poor man, always apprehensive, wondered continually whether his house was about to be attacked. He thought about moving, of going to live elsewhere, in some remote corner of the suburbs, but who would want him? All doors closed as soon as he was perceived. Then again, even if he found a residence, would he be able to install his autoclave, there, his incubator, and all the apparatus garnishing his laboratory?

For the first time, a sentiment of revolt took possession of him. The intense meditation of that gentle and resigned soul was succeeded by a muted anger against those people he did not know, and who were taking a ferocious joy in torturing him.

To think, he said to himself, *that no one will have pity on me! If they only knew how I'm suffering!*

One night, when sleep fled him, he had opened the window overlooking the avenue, for one of his crises of choking had taken hold of him. Leaning on the sill, he allowed his gaze to wander over the glistening roadway, where automobiles were gliding by rapidly, projecting long conical beams in front of them. A few belated passers-by were hurrying home. A drunkard sitting on a bench was talking to himself. The twelve strokes of midnight took flight from the church of Saint-Pierre de Montrouge, and Procas was just about to close his window again when a man loomed up on the sidewalk lit by a gas-lamp and advanced, his fist clenched, shouting: "Murderer! Murderer!"

Procas thought at first that it was the drunkard coming toward him, but it did not take him long to recognize his neighbor, the butcher's son.

"Yes, murderer! If the police protect you, we'll do justice ourselves!"

"Come on, my friend," said Procas. "Is it really me that...?"

"Yes, yes, it's really you, blackguard. Oh, I don't know what's stopping me from bashing your vile face in!"

And so saying, fat Nestor tried to reach the window-sill.

Procas, understanding that there was no reasoning with the fanatic, swiftly closed the shutters and engaged the latch.

The butcher, who had been drinking, did not cease vociferating, but someone must have taken him away, for there was a brief discussion, and Procas heard no more. He went to bed, but took a long time going to sleep.

The fellow was drunk, he said to himself, *but he called me murderer—me!*

He was anxious. The scene had disturbed him. He remembered the visit that the Police Commissioner had made, the search of his house that had been carried out, and a host of thoughts assailed him. He still did not know about the disappearance of the haberdasher's child; otherwise, he would have understood. He stopped at the idea that his ugliness alone was the cause of everything, and wondered, momentarily, whether they might be trying to frighten him in order to rid the neighborhood of his presence.

He would have liked nothing better, but where could he go?

"Bah!" he murmured. "They'll end up calming down. Anyway, they see so little of me; I'll go out as little as possible."

The next day, when he woke up, he heard people talking outside his door.

"There's evidence now," said a voice he recognized as that of the young butcher. "Yes, there's evidence. They'll soon see that we're not mistaken."

Procas quietly opened the door slightly, but the group had drawn away, and he only caught a few scraps of phrases, which signified nothing to him.

Poor Procas—if he had been able to hear what they were saying, he would have been terrified!

In fact since their visit to the Police Commissioner, fat Nestor and Barouillet, assisted by a former inquiry agent who undertook amateur police work, had been spying covertly on Procas. Every evening, the three men met in a little café situated at the corner of the Rue Liancourt and the Avenue du Maine, and exchanged the information that each of them had been able to gather.

Bezombes, as the agent was named, brought to that collaboration the acquisition of twenty years of private police work and was well able to apprehend "criminals" because, he said, he had undertaken many difficult investigations. In reality, Bezombes was a poseur, a man of limited intellect who had read a lot of crime fiction and fancied that he had the talents of a detective.

One evening, when Nestor and Barouillet displayed a certain skepticism about the results of his investigations, he told them, in a confident tone: "there'll be something new tomorrow."

And, indeed, the next day, he went to find them at the café.

"We wanted proof," he said to them. "Well, I have it. You can trust an old sleuth like me to follow a trail. Following a trail is the infancy of the art, but it's necessary never to let go of it. Often, it doesn't lead anywhere; it's then that what is commonly called flair, and what I call deduction, intervenes. One starts on a road, one thinks it's good, and suddenly, one reaches a crossroads where there are several roads. Which to choose? It's often necessary to review the whole investigation, to proceed, so to speak, mathematically, to extract the unknown, and their likes the difficulty. Ordinary policemen, when they come to arrest a malefactor, are mostly assisted by benevolent informers, but me, I scorn those often-interested denunciations, which often have no other result than confusing everything. I go straight to the point, armed solely with information that I've collected, and I almost always obtain a clue. Perhaps you're going to say that it's a matter of luck? No—luck is a word devoid of meaning. For me, it's the logical consequence of a long meditation and a series of deductions."

At this point, Bezombes interrupted himself in order to sip his aperitif. Fat Nestor and Barouillet looked at him, surprised. They did not know yet what he was going to reveal to them, but they were anticipating a *coup de théâtre*.

"From deduction to deduction," Bezombes continued, stroking his graying beard, "I've arrived at the conclusion—which is to say, the proof. Until now we've only had presumptions—grave, it's true, but insufficient to motivate the arrest of the guilty party. Today, I have certainty."

"Ah! Finally!" said fat Nestor. "So we can prove to the Commissioner that we're not imbeciles."

"Thanks to me," said Bezombes, modestly.

"Oh, certainly, thanks to you."

"And this certainty?" asked Barouillet, slightly vexed by no longer being able the principal role in the investigation.

"I can let you put your finger on it," Bezombes replied emphatically, "if you wish."

"Go on, then!" cried Nestor, without asking how it is possible to put one's finger on a certainty.

"Well, come with me!"

"Where to? Is it far?"

"You'll see."

All three of them got up, and Nestor paid the bill. It was always him who paid, but he did not regret his money, so glad was he to be mixed up in a sensational affair.

The owner of the café stopped Bezombes on the doorstep. He had not dared to join in the three men's conversation, but while lending an ear to it, he had heard a few words that had intrigued him.

He winked interrogatively at the enquiry agent.

"All right," replied Bezombes. "Very well, in fact."

"You've got him?"

"Of course."

"It's not too soon. Ah! Good for Monsieur Bezombes! Murderers have to watch out for him."

"Bah! It's just a matter of having been in the business for twenty years."

"Oh, that's not a reason. There are men who's been in the police as long as that and never pinched a criminal. Our Commissioner, Monsieur Morisseau, for example."

"We'll give Commissioner Morisseau a surprise!" said Nestor.

They went out. Bezombes marched on ahead, as befits a leader, but Nestor and Barouillet soon fell into step to either side of him, in order to reestablish equality.

A few moments later they went into the yard of the forage-merchant whose house was next door to Procas'.

The merchant, a stout Auvergnat who was known in the neighborhood as "Grinchu," was in the little shed that served as his office. On recognizing Bezombes he could not suppress a surge of ill-humor.

"You again!" he said.

"Yes, Monsieur, me again. I regret disturbing you, but in the interests of justice..."

"All right, all right—what do you want? Do you want to get into my neighbor's yard again? Leave the poor devil alone—he's unhappy enough as it is."

"You don't know what your tenant is, Monsieur, and if you did..."

"I know that he's a poor fellow, that's all, and that it's necessary to have no heart to harass an offensive individual this way."

"Inoffensive? You believe that?"

"Of course I believe it."

"You won't think so for long—and when he's arrested, when the newspapers reveal what he's done, you won't use the same language."

"Don't you know what he's accused of?" hazarded Barouillet.

"It's always easy to make accusations."

"Today, we'll have proof."

The forage-merchant shrugged his shoulders. "Ah, leave me alone with your stories. Have you been sent by the Commissaire de Police? No, you haven't. Well then, get out."

"But, Monsieur…!" said Bezombes.

"Don't Monsieur me."

"You're refusing to let us go into your tenant's yard?"

"What do you want to do there? You saw it yesterday, didn't you? Well, that's enough."

"I want to show these Messieurs."

"These Messieurs aren't the police, I suppose?"

"No, but they have an interest, as I have, in discovering and catching a murderer."

"A murderer! Don't make me laugh. I think you're all mad. Go home—that's better than…"

"You're refusing, then?"

"Yes."

"You don't have the right, when it's a matter…"

"No right? No right? What are you telling me? Am I the master in my own home or not?"

"Yesterday, though, you consented to let me…"

"Possibly, but today I don't want to. Is that understood? It'll turn into a procession in the end."

"Monsieur," said Barouillet, in a nobly paternal tone, "the superior interests of justice, security…"

"You, go bray at your public meetings and leave me in peace."

There was nothing to be done. Père Grinchu was one of those stubborn and bad-tempered old men who have no fear, if need be, of throwing a punch—and the Auvergnat was solidly built. He was beginning to lose patience, and turning as purple as an aubergine. Bezombes and his two friends thought it prudent to beat a retreat.

"What a brute!" said Barouillet, when they were in the street.

"I wanted to lay him out," growled Nestor, who was always talking about beating people up but was, fundamentally, as cowardly as a hare.

XII

The most vexed of the three was certainly Bezombes, who had not expected such a reception. He had thought that he was going to astonish his

208

friends, and had received a slap in the face. How could he have suspected that that animal Grinchu, who had been almost amiable the previous evening, would behave so boorishly the next day?

They went back to the little café in the Avenue du Maine, and held a conference there. Nestor and Barouillet still did not know what Bezombes had discovered in Procas' yard, for the enquiry agent had not yet said anything that might clarify the mystery. Bezombes, like all pretentious and hollow individuals, liked to hold back his effects before pressing the spring that caused the jack-in-the-box to spring forth.

"What are we going to do now?" asked Nestor.

Bezombes, his elbows on the table, and frowning, seemed to be plunged in laborious meditation. He only emerged from his reverie to raise the Lemon St. Raphael that Nestor had ordered to his lips. He drained his glass in a single draught, wiped his lips with the back of his hand and finally consented to reply.

"What are we going to do? Well, obviously, we're going to ask the Commissioner to accompany us to Grinchu's."

"Oh, the Commissioner!" said Barouillet. "We can hardly count on him. He'll tell us once again that he'll investigate, and that will be all. He'll let the affair drop. What we can tell him won't convince him. His mind is made up. I saw that when I went to see him with Nestor. He made us welcome, I admit, but he didn't seem to take what we were saying seriously. Those people don't like ordinary citizens to interfere with the police. They always have a tendency to believe that witnesses are lying or exaggerating."

"When one brings them evidence, however...," said Bezombes.

"Yes, I don't deny it—but have you really got any?"

Bezombes gave a slight shrug, and took his time before replying: "I have it."

Nestor and Barouillet looked at him. Fundamentally, they were unconvinced, even though they trusted their friend.

"I have it," Bezombes repeated, gazing with an astonished expression at his empty glass. "I wanted to show it to you on the spot, but since that boor Grinchu didn't want to let us into the yard, I'll tell you everything. Listen to me, and you'll see whether I'm not supported by seeming proofs. I'm not one of those fantastic detectives like Sherlock Holmes, who build suppositions on suppositions and emit hypotheses, one of which must fatally lead to the discovery of the murderer. Me, I'm a precise, methodical man. I only believe what I see. Now, I've seen."

At that point Bezombes stopped, in order to enjoy the effect that his affirmation produced. His two listeners, conquered by his assurance, waited anxiously, leaving toward him, eager to catch the words that were about to fall from his lips.

"Yes, I've seen, that which there is to be seen. First, you need to know what I did to arrive at my conclusion. The affair was delicate. A child had disappeared, suspicions fell on the man in the Passage Tenaille, but that was all. There was no proof that the poor kid had been murdered. Some vagabond might have taken him away. According to what I've heard, the child wasn't very intelligent; his mother says herself that he was naïve and trusting, very easy to influence. The last time he was seen he was playing on his own at the corner of the Avenue du Maine, almost directly opposite our man's house. All that was very vague, and nothing had come along to focus my suspicions, when Barouillet reminded me about the murder of little Soubiroux, which happened a few days after the monster moved into the neighborhood. On the other hand, the information I'd collected soon shored up my conviction. Twice, the ignoble individual from the Passage Tenaille had been seen following children in the Rue Gassendi."

"That's true, said Nestor. "Last week, little Cheiret, the son of the concierge at number 44, came home frightened, saying that a man had followed him all the way to the corner of the Rue Liancourt."

"So you see," said Bezombes, "my information is correct. You understand that, before accusing the recluse of the Passage Tenaille, it was necessary to obtain information about him. When I had sufficient, I started following him, and I noticed that he did indeed look at children with a strange expression, especially the little girls coming out of the school at dusk. He stood in a doorway in a bizarre fashion. To be brief, I'll pass over certain details. Our individual must be a satyr, and he was doubtless in search of some new victim. From there, I followed this reasoning: Since the haberdasher's child disappeared when he was opposite the house in the Passage Tenaille, he must have been attracted into the house, and as he hasn't reappeared, he must have been murdered. You see how everything fits together marvelously."

"Indeed," conceded Barouillet. "But you'll see that our imbecile of a Commissaire won't allow himself to be convinced."

"Wait—all that's just the *hors-d'oeuvre*. I'm arriving at the main course. Since little Maurice had gone into the recluse's house and hadn't come out again, his body must be somewhere. Now, the testimony of serious people had told me that, the day after the disappearance, smoke had been seen coming out of our individual's chimney. Why, in that rather mild weather, had he lit a fire, if not to incinerate his victim? Several passers-by also smelled an odor of burned rubber that day, such as is emitted by human bodies when they're roasted over a fire."

"Exactly," said Nestor. "I smelled that odor myself, and I even said to my father: 'What's burning? It's jolly sharp.'"

"That, it seems to me," Bezombes continued, raising his voice—for he had noticed that the customers were listening—"is a commencement of proof. An ordinary detective would be content with that, but it wasn't sufficient for me. I needed visible proof, something that confirmed my conviction and would permit me to say to the law: 'You're looking for the guilty party, well, I, whom am neither a Commissioner nor an Inspector, have found him.' So, I pursued my investigation. A murderer, no matter how skillful he is, can't cut a body into pieces without that dire operation leaving traces. Twice, by climbing over the fence, I got into the little yard that you know, and, equipped with a hooded lantern, I carefully examined the wall, the door and the flagstones lining the ground. And it was on the flagstones that I found what I can call 'the crucial piece of evidence.'"

All the listeners were breathless, looking at Bezombes admiringly.

"It's that crucial piece of evidence that I wanted to show you, and which you would have seen, like me, in the satyr's yard, if that idiot Grinchu hadn't refused to let us into his house."

"But what was that crucial piece of evidence?" someone asked, timidly.

"Those pieces, I should have said," Bezombes went on, "for there were several—yes, several. Large bloodstains, still quite visible, as big as hundred-sou pieces, and even bigger. Doubt is no longer possible. It's definitely in that yard that the wretch cut up his victim."

The customers had gradually drawn nearer in order to listen to Bezombes, who had gradually raised his voice as he saw his audience growing. They were all unanimous in recognizing that the enquiry agent had the soul of a great policeman.

While savoring those eulogies, Bezombes replied in a modest fashion to those who congratulated him: "No, no, you're exaggerating. It was sufficient, to bring the investigation to a conclusion, to have a little judgment; the rest is a matter of routine. With the elements I had in hand, I had to succeed. It was all a matter of not letting go for an instant of the thread that I held, and above all of not allowing myself to be influenced by anyone's opinion. Straight to the goal—that's my method. I hesitate at first; I throw out probes here and there, and then, when I sense that the ground beneath my feet is firm enough, I advance boldly."

Nestor never ceased repeating, while widening his great bovine eyes: "That's marvelous! Marvelous!"

Barouillet, a little put out by not having discovered anything, was more reserved, contenting himself with slowly nodding his head s a sign of approval. The most enthusiastic of all, however, was a local rentier, Père Corbineau, a man with a nutcracker chin and eyes like a white rabbit, who howled in a thin, broken voice: "Three cheers for Bezombes! Three cheers for Bezombes!" They had all the difficulty in the world making him understand that it was not a matter of a celebration but a matter that, until further notice, must be kept absolutely secret.

Everyone promised not to say anything, but an hour later, from the Lion de Belfort to the Rue de la Gaîté, no one was any longer greeting anyone except with the words: "Well, there it is, eh? It seems that he's pinched!"

XIII

The next day, early in the morning, Nestor and Barouillet rang Bezombes' doorbell. He lived in a modest ground floor apartment in the Rue Boulard, at the back of a courtyard. On a glazed door, a placard could be seen bearing the boldly-traced words: *Marius Bezombes, Legal Adviser, Defender in the Magistrate's Court. Divorce Enquiries, Family Research, etc.*

Bezombes was waiting for them. He was sitting at a little table cluttered with dusty files. On the black marble mantelpiece, between an alarm clock and a carafe, a plaster bust representing Justice was enthroned, one of whose scales was broken. There was a mahogany chest of drawers in a corner, which had been transformed into a filing-cabinet.

"Oh, there you are," said Bezombes. "Give me a minute. Sit down. Just time to sign a few documents, and I'm all yours."

Barouillet let himself fall into an old armchair upholstered in red rep, from which a cloud of dust emerged. As for fat Nestor, he brought forward a chair, the only one in the room, but, realizing that if he sat down on it, it would collapse under his eight, he remained standing, leaning against the wall, admiring himself from afar in the mirror above the mantelpiece.

"Ah!" said Bezombes, finally, taking off his large celluloid spectacles. "I've finished. Let's talk about out affair." And, pivoting in his seat, which yielded a dull grating sound, he turned to face his visitors. "Today," he said, "We enter into the period of action, the decisive period. It's necessary that this evening, tomorrow at the latest, our individual is behind bars."

"It's a pity we can't arrest him ourselves," growled Nestor. "I'd have had great pleasure getting me hands on that villain."

"That's the business of the police," said Bezombes. "Our role is limited to delivering the murderer."

"Will it at least be known that it's us—pardon me you—who have discovered him?"

"Perhaps. But it's necessary not to count on it too much, for the police have a habit of always claiming the credit for themselves. The moment one isn't in the club, one doesn't count. You'll see that the Commissioner won't even congratulate us."

"The Commissioner," said Barouillet, shrugging his shoulders, "is capable of not taking our visit seriously. When Nestor and I went to see him, he scarcely listened to us. In your place, Bezombes, it isn't the Commissioner to whom I'd address myself."

"The head of the Sûreté, then?"

"Perhaps—but there's something even better."

"Oh? What's that?"

"That would be to go to a newspaper. If the press gets involved in the affair..."

"My word, perhaps you're right. That way, the police wouldn't be able to attribute all the merit for the investigation to themselves, and there'd be some mention of us. It's not that I want the renown…no, I'm a modest man, and if I'd wanted to carry on like some people…well, in sum, your idea isn't bad. Do you know someone at a newspaper?"

"Yes, a reporter for the *Égalité*, who has come to our meetings several times during electoral campaigns. He's also a friend of Monsieur Jacassot, our député."

"Well, let's go see him. We'll explain the affair to him, and if he's an intelligent fellow, he'll be able to make a sensational article out of our information. I can already see the headline: *The Satyr of Montrouge… Horrible details.* It'll be one in the eye for the Commissioner."

"Oh, steady on, Bezombes. Don't imagine that journalists move as fast as that. And the legal investigation—you're not thinking about that."

"That's true, but there's no need for an examining magistrate here. Haven't we got proof?"

"Obviously…nevertheless, it's better to act prudently. Let's go visit my friend and see what he says. Journalists are clever, and they often find means of saying a lot without saying anything at all."

As Bezombes did not appear to understand, he explained: "Yes, when one can't put forward a fact, for fear of compromising oneself, one proceeds by insinuations, by implication. You'll see. Oscar Phinot understands those sorts of articles. It's by means of insinuations and implications that he demolished Taupin, our député's opponent."

"Oh! Your journalist is called Phinot? I've seen that name before somewhere."

"Possibly. He writes a great deal, and is beginning to acquire a certain reputation. Let's go find him. If the affair doesn't interest him, we'll fall back on the Head of the Sûreté."

"When can we see him?"

"In the afternoon, generally. In any case, I'll telephone him to announce our visit."

"That's good. To do well, it will be necessary for the article to appear tomorrow morning. I'll jot down a few notes on paper, which might be useful to him. I'll wait for you here—come and pick me up as soon as you've obtained a meeting. But wait, I've just thought of something. It's necessary not to let our man slip away, isn't it? What if, when they come to arrest him, the house is empty?"

"No danger," the butcher's apprentice replied. "I'll keep an eye on him."

Nestor and Barouillet shook hands with Bezombes, and withdrew.

To the people they met and who interrogated them with a little movement of the head, they replied, with an enigmatic smile. "There'll be some news before long."

Groups were already beginning to form outside the little house in the Passage Tenaille, and Barouillet was annoyed.

"Do you want to ruin everything?" he said. "If you stand there planted like pickets, he'll suspect something, and slip through our hands. Go home and wait. We'll be rid of that individual within twenty-four hours."

"Yes...people have been saying that for a long time," murmured a little man afflicted with a red birthmark on his right cheek, "but he's still there!"

It was at that moment that Procas had lifted the curtain at his window.

"Look, you can see that he's listening to us," said Barouillet. "You're definitely going to compromise everything. It'll have been well worth the trouble of going to such lengths."

The curiosity-seekers dispersed slowly, while Procas wondered, anxiously: "But what's the matter with them? What do they want? I don't understand what's happening at all."

XIV

When the crowd is in league against a man, the man must necessarily succumb, unless he can impose himself upon it by audacity and violence. Now, poor Procas did not have what was necessary to stand up to the unchained mob that was growing by the day. While he sought in vain for the reasons for the muted war that had been declared upon him, the leaders were collecting evidence against him—or seeming evidence—that was having a snowball effect and was being deformed by imagination with the customary exaggeration of the common people.

Bezombes continued to draw up what he called his "plan of campaign," and everyone in the neighborhood, with was now in ferment, was waiting for a *coup de théâtre*.

Accompanied by fat Nestor and the solemn Barouillet, he had gone to the offices of the *Égalité* in the Boulevard Montmartre. Received by Phinot, whom Barouillet had alerted by telephone, he had, with his Southern verve, explained to the reporter the "reasons" on which he supported his accusation of Procas. Those reasons seemed plausible, and Phinot, who was searching for a subject for a sensational article in order to get back into the good graces of his editor, who had reproached him for certain "duds," had welcomed Bezombes' revelations enthusiastically. Nevertheless, rendered prudent by a recent gaffe, which had earned the director of the *Égalité* a rather stiff fine and two months in prison, he did not launch himself wholeheartedly into the affair. He contented himself with testing the waters. In a front page article only transparent to initiates, he skillfully primed the pump of scandal.

The next day, people were snatching copies of the *Égalité* all over Montrouge. The fire had taken hold. Those who still doubted the culpability of the "man of the Passage Tenaille" considered him from then on as a frightful

214

criminal, and were astonished that the police had not yet arrested him. Bezombes, flanked by Nestor and Barouillet, stopped off in numerous cafés, where he held forth untiringly, explaining for the hundredth time how he had been able to discover the guilty party.

That evening, when Procas went out at dusk in search of his dinner, he was followed by a dozen individuals, whose number was gradually augmented, and when he returned home, a sinister, menacing clamor went up: "Death! Death!"

Frightened, he plunged into the vestibule with his dog, slammed the door shut and started listening behind a shutter, wondering whether the fanatics were not about to break in. He still did not understand what had unleashed their anger, but he realized now that life was no longer tenable, and that he would probably be obliged to flee the neighborhood where his appearance provoked such hatred.

He perceived a few fragmentary phrases, which only augmented his anxiety, without enlightening him as to the motive for the abrupt change of mood. He finally realized that his ugliness could not be its sole cause, and that there must be something else, but the poor fellow was far from suspecting the terrible accusation that was weighing upon him.

For a moment, he had the idea of writing to the Commissioner and asking for police protection, but he renounced the idea, hoping that the fury of the crowd would eventually die down, as it had died down a few months earlier.

The mob, harangued by Bezombes, who had become the man of the moment, abstained from any manifestation for a week.

"It's up to the law to take action," Bezombes never ceased repeating. "Let's wait; it's impossible that the wretch can enjoy impunity for much longer. An investigation has been opened, I know. We'll soon see the murderer arrested."

Bezombes was mistaken. An investigation had, indeed, been opened, but had the result of having him summoned to see the Commissioner, who had demanded, in rather hot terms what he was playing at. Bezombes had tried to get the upper hand, but he was reminded of an affair of loans taken out on bonds, which had never been fully clarified, and it which he had played a role that was more than shady. He was even advised, in his own interest, to keep quiet in future, and not to trespass on the prerogatives of the police.

Bezombes went out utterly crestfallen. That evening, he met Nestor and Barouillet at the café, but carefully refrained from telling them how he had been received by the Commissioner.

"It's always dangerous to get mixed up in these affairs, you see," he told them. "The police don't like people saying that they've made a mess of things. They'd rather let a guilty man escape than frankly admit their incompetence. Me, I've seen it; I've done all that I can do, in the interests of our neighborhood. I tried to unmask an evil-doer, and it seems to me that I've succeeded, but the police take a dim view of all that. Soon, if this goes on, it'll be the accusers who are the guilty parties. I renounce any further part in the affair. Others can replace me, but personally, I'm sick of it."

Nestor protested. "What, Monsieur Bezombes, you're talking like a coward? No, you mustn't do that."

"I have spoken," said Bezombes, in a peremptory tone.

Barouillet intervened. "Come, come, you're not going to throw the towel in just like that. Ought we to worry about the police? Duty commands us to remain in the breach. Is it at the moment when we hold all the trumps that we're going to abandon the game? What will people think of us? Since our Commissioner is incapable, it's up to us the take action. I'm going to go find Phinot, and he'll show the Commissaire something."

"No, no," protested Bezombes. "Let's not get into a fight with the Commissioner. We wouldn't win. It would be the earthenware pot fighting the iron pot. These policemen are diabolically vindictive, and capable of all kinds of rascality."

"What do we have to fear?" Barouillet retorted. "Our conscience has nothing for which to reproach us has it? One can search our lives. Me, I don't give a f about the Commissaire, and if he persists in turns a deaf ear and protecting the murderer, well, I'll have him sacked...yes, sacked, you hear. I'm going to address myself, no later than tomorrow, to Monsieur Jacassot, our député. He'll go to the Prefect of Police if he has to, and you'll see that he'll make your Commissioner dance. He'll have to take action, or explain himself."

Bezombes did not feel tranquil, because of the old affair of the loans that threatened to surface again. This, he showed himself opposed to "direct action." He could not, however, renounce everything without appearing to be a coward. He got out of it rather cleverly.

"Unfortunately," he said, "I don't have enough connections to go to war against people who dispose of secret influences and belong to the police freemasonry, which is as powerful as the Jesuits. But you, Barouillet, who are on the best of terms with our député, Monsieur Jacassot, and have friends at the *Égalité*, can achieve a result. Me, I've carried out an investigation; that ended with the discovery of the murderer, but the police refuse to act. It's necessary to force them, and you alone can do that."

Barouillet was deeply touched. He swelled up with pride, frowned, struck a pose as if he needed to be begged, and then, very gravely, uttered these words:

"Since it's necessary, I'll take action, even though I don't like to put myself forward."

"Remember that you're working in the interests of everyone, and the mothers of families will be grateful to you for having rid them of an individual who is an object of horror and dread for them, who has become a public danger."

"But you'll continue to assist me with your advice, Bezombes, I suppose?"

"Can you doubt it?"

Barouillet brought a round of drinks, and fat Nestor another; then they parted, arranging to meet again the next day.

Now Bezombes was almost tranquil; the affair was following its course, but he was no longer involved. It would be the excessive Barouillet who would shoulder all the responsibility, in company with fat Nestor.

If Bezombes remained in the shadows, however, he continued nevertheless to lead a clandestine campaign.

Barouillet, glad to be no longer under the tutelage of the inquiry agent, talked loudly, telling anyone who cared to listen that he would "soon force the hand of the police." When he passed by, the shopkeepers called out to him, bombarding him with questions, and his response was always the same: "I've made a round of the newspapers. You'll see what a fine scandal is going to burst out."

People listened delightedly, and drank in his words; he was congratulated.

Meanwhile, the man of the Passage Tenaille—the "satyr," as people called him—continued to come and go at nightfall, followed by a mob who abused him in a cowardly fashion and accompanied him as far as his door. Fat Nestor was always part of that mob, because, in accord with Barouillet, he had instituted the "surveillance" of Procas, whose abrupt disappearance was feared. Street urchins joined in with the cortege, and one of them, having wanted to get too close to the "satyr" one evening, was forced to beat a prompt retreat by the menacing fangs of Mami, whom the shouts of the children rendered furious.

"That filthy cur," said fat Nestor. "I'll have its blood it before long, you'll see. While we're waiting to get rid of the man, I can always take away the pooch's appetite for bread."

XV

Everyone in Montrouge was expecting the famous *coup de théâtre* any day, but it was a long time coming. A fortnight had passed since Bezombes had "passed the baton" to Barouillet—a fortnight during which increasingly overexcited minds had gradually arrived at such a state of exasperation that anything was to be feared.

Prudently, Barouillet, who had not succeeded in his measures, remained shut up at home, prey to an illness that was probably simulated. As for Bezombes, he no longer showed himself in the little café in the Rue Liancourt. Only fat Nestor, with his brutal tenacity, continued to spy on Procas, and whenever the poor fellow went out, he abandoned his stall and followed the "satyr." Idlers and people out of work, as well as a few harpies, joined him in dogging the steps of the poor man.

To escape the enemies who were massing behind him, Procas sometimes turned a street-corner swiftly and huddled in some doorway, but he was always denounced by Mami's growling. Then the crowd surrounded him, menacingly, and he fled, shaving the walls. As soon as he went into a shop to buy bread or a little meat, a gang formed outside the door and irritated voices peppered him with a strong of insults. Some shopkeepers refused to serve him, and he was soon obliged to go beyond the Rue de la Tombe-Issoire to procure a few meager provisions.

One evening, near the Reservoir Montsouris, at the corner of the Avenue Reille, he was set upon by a group that included fat Nestor. They took hold of him brutally, tore off his clothes, and would probably have lynched him if the police had not arrived.

Half-mad, Procas ran home, but when he reached his door, he could not see Mami. He whistled and called, but the dog did not appear. Procas called again, and, seized by a sinister presentiment, he started searching.

He retraced the route that he had already followed, still whistling, fearing disaster. The dog remained undiscoverable. Procas thought that the animal, maddened by the scene that had occurred, or pursued by stones thrown by the children, might have fled in the direction of Montsouris. All night long he searched the neighborhood, returning ten times over to his door in the hope that Mami might have come back.

In the morning, at daybreak, he was sadly going home, still conserving a faint hope of finding his dear companion, when, at the corner of the Rue Saint-Yves, he saw a large grey mass in the gutter. He approached it, bent down, and recognized his dog, his poor Mami, his head crushed, in a pool of blood.

Procas uttered a heart-rending cry, his fist extended into the air in a threatening gesture. Then he picked up the animal and carried him away in his arms. Those who saw that horrible man with the cadaver of the dog that he was carrying like a child stood there astonished, and a few permitted themselves to laugh, but Procas looked at them with such a terrible expression that they recoiled, paralyzed by the yellow eyes, which seemed to be those of a demon.

Having returned home, Procas deposited Mami's cadaver on the table in his laboratory, and burst into tears.

So, he was now alone, completely alone. He had only had one friend any longer, and they had killed him.

Why?

Was he responsible, the poor animal? Was he also the enemy of those brutes? He did not bother anyone, though. He was a poor dog, very gentle, very fearful, and if he sometimes showed his teeth, it was to defend himself rather than to attack. The street-urchins had often teased him and harassed him, and he had never bitten any of them. He seemed, like his master, resigned to suffer. He only asked for a little pity, that was all. And they had killed him, without any motive…except, perhaps, because he was his dog, the accursed Procas' dog. Why had they not attacked the man, instead of killing an inoffensive animal?

And Procas sobbed, holding poor Mami's cold paw in his hand.

For a long time he remained beside that blood-spattered cadaver, whose sad eyes, veiled by death, still conserved an infinite tenderness, and in which there was an almost-human expression.

Suddenly, there was a sound of voices outside that made him shiver. Returned to a sentiment of reality, he raised his head, looked toward the window, and distinguished moving shows between the poorly-drawn curtains, which were magnified immeasurably by the light of a street-lamp. Inertia and torpor were abruptly succeeded in Procas by a dull wrath. He went to the window, opened it, and shouted in a terrible voice: "Go away! Go away, wretches!"

A volley of insults greeted him, but he stood up to the storm. He was no longer the poor, retiring, fearful individual who ought to pass unperceived in the street. He was now a resolute man, ready to attack, a man crazed by despair and wrath, rendered capable of anything. Under the raw light of the gas-lamp, which struck him full in the face, there was something so terrifying about him that the voices insulting him fell silent.

"Wretches! Wretches!" he howled, showing them his fist.

But an oppression seized him, and blood rose into his throat. He scarcely had the strength to close the window, and he collapsed, breathless and suffocating, struck down by a fainting fit.

When he came round, the sunlight was illuminating his room, where a fine golden dust was dancing in a conical sunbeam, like a swarm of minuscule insects. Still lying on the floor, he experienced a sharp sensation of cold. He was shivering, his teeth chattering. He looked around, astonished, but the idea of getting up did not even come into his mind. He remained recumbent, still shivering, his throat dry and his limbs so weary that he did not feel the courage to make any movement. The noises from the street reached him, attenuated, scarcely perceptible, there was such a buzz in his ears. Everything in his mind was vague.

He thought for a moment that during his crisis he had had a frightful nightmare, as often happened, but a frightful doubt gripped him. He forced himself up painfully, bracing himself on his elbows and knees. The first thing he saw was the table on which his dog was lying, and then he remembered everything. He moved closer, staggering like a drunken man, and passed his hand over the dull coat of the animal.

He stood there motionless, his forehead furrowed, his eyes staring. He appeared very calm; it was discernible that he was pursuing an idea that was gradually taking form in his mind. Suddenly, his face lit up; he turned toward the window with a defiant expression, as if to threaten invisible beings, and then uttered these words:

"Poor Mami, they've killed you, but you'll be avenged before long...and it's you that will serve for my vengeance."

XVI

The following day, in the little café in the Rue Liancourt, fat Nestor and Barouillet were talking in low voices. Something had happened that they could not help finding slightly troubling.

Bezombes had disappeared, without warning.

"It's decidedly incomprehensible," said Barouillet. "Bezombes would have told us if he had to go away. I've noticed that he seemed very preoccupied, but I didn't expect that he'd just disappear."

"Perhaps he's gone to the provinces on business," Nestor suggested.

"No, it must be something else."

"What?"

"That's the question!"

"What if he's been murdered? The man of the Passage Tenaille might have found out that Bezombes had unmasked him. How can we know? That horrible individual is capable of anything. He never showed himself before, but now he's opening his window, looking at people, letting himself be seen, and continually insulting them verbally. The other evening, he called us wretches and showed us his fist. I can guarantee that if he's been able to get hold of one of us, he'd have spent a bad quarter of an hour. He's like a furious madman."

"It's the death of his dog that's put him into that state."

"He'll see many others, then, for as long as they don't arrest him, we're going to give him an escort every time he goes out. Come on, Monsieur Barouillet, why isn't the fellow locked up?"

"I don't understand it."

"You've taken a grip on the affair, though, with influential individuals?"

"Yes, our député has been to see the Commissioner, but he got the same response as us. According to him, the man of the Passage Tenaille isn't dangerous."

"But what about the evidence Bezombes collected?"

"The Commissaire says it's childishness."

"Oh, of course! What does he need, then?"

"Me, I'm giving up on the affair. I'm wasting my time on it, and not getting anywhere."

"What about the newspapers?"

"The editor of the *Égalité* now says the same as the Commissioner."

"That's too much! Well, I'm not abandoning the game, and we'll see whether they don't decide to arrest the satyr soon. It's all very well to say that he isn't dangerous, but in the meantime, the haberdasher's kid hasn't turned up, and they haven't found the murderer of the girl in the cinema. Now, to complicate things, Monsieur Bezombes had disappeared too. You can say what you like, but all that isn't natural. Oh, if I could just get inside the house in the Passage Tenaille for five minutes, I can guarantee you..."

And fat Nestor nodded his head in a significant manner.

Barouillet sipped his vermouth-cassis pensively. He did not understand any of it either. He had launched himself full tilt into the wretched affair, but he now took account of the fact that the influence he enjoyed in the neighborhood, in his capacity as electoral agent, did not match that of the Commissioner. Where Jacassot had failed, he could not help but fail too. It was better to abandon the game, but discreetly, skillfully, for he feared becoming suspect to those he had drawn in his wake.

Nestor, more combative, was, as he delighted in repeating, determined to "get to the bottom of it." His conviction was firm. The police were protecting a murderer, but he would be able to disentangle the truth.

"Another round, Monsieur Barouillet?"

"No thanks—another time."

"It's all right, you know. Go on, another little apero—it can't do any harm."

Barouillet allowed his arm to be twisted.

"Fill them up, Père Chevassu," ordered Nestor, pointing to the empty glasses.

The proprietor, a fat, pale bald man with an ebony black moustache, immediately arrived with two bottles. While pouring, he smiled. It was obvious that a question was burning his lips.

Finally, he asked: "And Monsieur Bezombes? We don't see him any more..."

"He's disappeared," Nestor replied.

"You doubtless mean that he's traveling?"

"Disappeared, I tell you. No one knows what's become of him. Mysterious things have been happening in this neighborhood for some time."

Père Chevassu became thoughtful. "Truly, he said, no one knows what's become of him?"

"How many times do I have to repeat it?"

"Damn! Damn! That's annoying. Yes, very annoying...it's just that...it's not my business...not at all...I trusted him, you see, and..."

"Does he owe you money?"

"Exactly."

"A lot?"

"I think so...fifteen hundred bullets."

"Impossible!"

"It's the truth."

"And he borrowed it all in one go?"

"No...in three lots...it as for business, you understand, and...I didn't think I could refuse him, inasmuch as he was recommended by you."

"Oh, that's too much!!" exclaimed Barouillet. "He never said a word to us about that."

"He came to see me several times...he seemed very agitated...the affair was preoccupying him greatly, and he was, it seems, obliged to make certain payments in order to obtain information. In brief, I let him have fifteen hundred francs. If he doesn't come back, I'm cooked."

"Bah! He'll come back. Bezombes is, I believe, an honest man..."

"But if he were an honest man, he wouldn't have said that he was recommended by you. That's a lesson. I won't be taken in again..."

And Père Chevassu, whose wife had just called him, headed back to his counter.

"That's shady, that story," said Nestor.

"Yes, rather," murmured Barouillet.

There was a silence.

"Do you want to know what I think?" said the apprentice butcher, eventually. "Well, I was always suspicious of Bezombes. What does he live on, anyway? No one ever comes to his office. And when he was occupied with our affair, he was always in the café. He talked, that's all. Anyway, whether he comes back or not, that doesn't prevent us from continuing what we've begun, does it?"

"Oh, I've already told you that I'm giving up on it."

"Seriously?"

"Seriously."

"Oh, that's not good, what you're doing there, Monsieur Barouillet. Leaving your friends like that, no, it's not good. What will people think in the neighborhood? We'll look like clowns."

"But what do you want me to do, my friend? You can see that we've run into insurmountable difficulties. We have the police against us; they don't want it to be said that we were cleverer than them...and you know, when one attacks the police, no good comes of it."

"Bah! You and I have nothing to fear, do we? They won't lock us up because we want to get rid of a dangerous individual. I'd like to see the Commissioner say something to me—I'd give him a fine welcome. I'm an honest man, me; I have nothing to reproach myself for, so I'm tranquil. Since everybody's quitting me, I'll work alone, and I'll give my head to be cut off if I haven't succeeded in getting the individual from the Passage Tenaille pinched within a fortnight. Besides, it's quite simple...if they don't arrest him, the local people will kill him, one evening, just as we killed his dog. They've had too much of him, and I know lads who won't hesitate to do him in."

"Oh, not that, eh?" said Barouillet. "That would be serious, and might cost you dear."

Fat Nestor shrugged his shoulders. "There are things that sort themselves out. Everyone has it in for that man, and sooner or later, he'll end up copping it."

XVII

Procas kept the corpse of his dog for twenty-four hours, during which he removed several morsels of flesh; we shall see why in due course. Then, one evening, he buried him under the bank of the fortifications.

From that day on, he was no longer the same man. He surrendered himself, reluctantly, to criminal meditations. In vain he tried to chase away the atrocious thoughts that assailed him, but he could not succeed in doing so. The idea of vengeance ended up crystallizing in his brain.

Ordinarily, under the influence of a violent anger, a man dreams of a thousand projects of vengeance, and then gradually resumes possession of himself. A thunderbolt has turned his entire being upside down, but once the commotion dies down, he recovers his calm of mind.

In Procas, a sequence of commotions—for he had to face the fury of the crowd every day—gradually led to a subjective, almost hypnotic psychic depression destructive of all morality. He was not yet mad, since he was acting deliberately, but his brain was no longer that of a sane man. Under the effect of grief, his self was transformed, and he arrived at the most monstrous conceptions. A kind of momentum drew him into crime without him making any attempt to restrain himself.

That state of mind might appear explicable in a primitive individual, but in an intellectual like Procas it seems a monstrosity. In order to be enlightened as to the psychology of the unfortunate, to descend into the darkness of his soul, it is necessary to go back to the genesis of the evil. Procas is a neuropath with overstimulated meninges; he has anatomical lesions. His sensations are now reaching the paroxysm of violence. Their intensity has ended up stifling the voice of conscience. He is no longer rational. His actions are prey to an obsession. All his mental forces are concentrated on a single objective: vengeance. He no longer sees anything but that, and in his solitude, he ruminates the most terrible things.

Such an individual requires calm, but the hostile crowd that he sensed around him, and the cries of hatred that reached him every day, through the walls, all exasperated him more and more.

He reinstalled himself in his laboratory and went back to work—but this time, it was no longer to endow humankind with a discovery; it was to sow death among his fellows.

And it would be the tissue that he had removed from his dog that the poison would be hidden. He remember that, in the course of his previous endeavors, he had carried out a number of experiments culturing microbes in milieux containing substances extracted from the spinal cord and the brain-tissue of dogs. He had even extracted a material that he called "medullose," which, added in minimal doses to nutritive milieux, had the property of augmenting considerably the virulence of pathogenic microbes. But it was necessary for him to select, among the latter, the one that could cause death most readily. He remembered then all the infectious maladies that he had once studied, and consulted reference-books on bacteriology, but did not find what he wanted.

For reasons that will soon be understood, it was via water that he wanted to propagate the microbe. The virus of bubonic plague, which he considered momentarily, is undeniably one of the most active, but have not recent experiments shown that water only plays a secondary role in its propagation?[34] In order to provoke an epidemic, it was necessary to find a new, redoubtable poison. Where could he find the unknown germ, the tiny invisible creature that would slyly penetrate the entrails and kill more surely than a revolver bullet?

Procas was prey to a dull rage. He would never be able to avenge himself on those who had made him suffer so much, and continued to torture him every day.

While riffling through an old manuscript, however, he was struck by the notes he had made in India regarding a certain epizoon of rats. He had noticed that thousands of those rodents perished in twenty-four hours, and that at the same time, the inhabitants of a small village near Madura were afflicted by a hitherto-unknown disease.

He had devoted himself to scrupulous research, had isolated and cultivated an extremely tenuous bacillus, difficult to stain, and which, inoculated into rats and mice, brought about the same ravages as those produced by the mysterious epizoon. For a long time, after his return to France, he had studied that question, and had written a detailed report of his discovery, but had never determined to publish the work, to which he had given the title "Researches on *Bacillus murinus*."

Later, in Marseilles, where he had been sent by the Minister of the Interior in order to study the prophylactic measures to be taken against the plague, which had claimed a few victims, he had, while dissecting a cadaver, collected and isolated the same *Bacillus murinus* that he had discovered in India.

Now that he remembered all the details, he had a sudden idea. He searched his collection of microbes and found a test-tube containing a culture of the bacillus in question, but it was almost dried out. Its virulence—which is to say, its aptitude to develop in an animal body and secrete bacterial poisons there—must now be ineffective. It was therefore necessary to rediscover the bacillus, isolate it, and cultivate it again.

From that day on, he could be seen every night removing a plank from the palisade that separated his dwelling from the forage shed. With a little lantern in his hand, he set out traps, and then searched the ground, in the hope of discover-

---

[34] The reference is to the experiments carried out by Kitastao and Yersin in Hong Kong in 1894, which apparently confirmed the suspicion that rats played a significant role in the plague, although they did not reveal the vital role of fleas.

ing a dead rat. There were a great many rats in the hangar, and he did not despair of finding what he was looking for.

In a week, he captured a dozen rodents, but one night he found two that were dad. He immediately proceeded with their autopsy, and took blood from the heart, after having first burned the surface of the viscera in question, in order to avoid any possible contagion. Then he distributed the blood in nutritive milieux prepared in advance, and after twenty-four hours, obtained different cultures.

In the majority of those cultures he found the well-known Danysz bacillus,[35] which produces a disease in rats very similar to human typhoid fever. A few days passed in feverish work. With minute patience, Procas dissected the cadavers of rats one by one, injecting test tubes with a quantity of their blood, but the *Bacillus murinus* still did not appear.

One night, however, he found more dead rats than usual in the forage store. He collected five.

There was no doubt about it; an epizoon had manifested itself—and what confirmed it was that the traps he set every night were now empty. It is well-known that when an epidemic breaks out, the rats, which are no less intelligent than other animals, flee from the nucleus of infection and emigrate to other locations.

Procas was overjoyed when he recognized lesions on the dead rats he had just found exactly similar to those he had observed in India. He removed various blood samples from the animals, and, twenty-four hours later, he was able to observe a white streak on the gelose with characteristic lateral ramifications.

No doubt was any longer possible; he finally had his *Bacillus murinus*.

Then he took a glass slide, deposited a drop of the culture on it, spread it out with the tip of a pipette, stained the preparation with a compound he had made, and then examined it under the microscope. In the field of the apparatus he observed the presence of short, slender bacilli.

It really was the bacillus he sought; he recognized it perfectly. It only remained for him to carry out what is known as the "Koch triad," which consists of inoculating receptive animals with the microbe.[36] He injected the virus under

---

[35] Jean Danysz (1860-1928), a Polish microbiologist specializing in the development of methods for the destruction of agricultural parasites and pests, joined the Pasteur Institute in 1893, bringing with him a bacillus, *Salmonella enteritidis*, which became known as the "Danysz virus" when he promoted it enthusiastically as a possible means of killing rodents. At that time, the term "virus" did not have the specific meaning that it later acquired, but was simply a generalized term for a virulent agent.

[36] The pioneering bacteriologist Robert Koch (1843-1910) identified the agents responsible for tuberculosis, cholera and anthrax, and standardized a methodol-

the skin of three living animals; he introduced it into the intestines of three others in the form of food pellets.

The first three succumbed in twenty-six hours; the other three only died after four days. The virus already seemed sufficiently violent, but it was weak, of it were compared with the one found in the rats of the Indian village. Procas was not discouraged, however. He knew that, thanks to the procedures of modern bacteriology, one can increase the virulence of microbial pathogens considerably and transform a microbe that is almost inoffensive for a particular species into a virus mortal for that species.

In this case, his dog, his poor Mami, would render him one last service. The medullose would enter into play and collaborate with the augmentation of the toxicity of *Bacillus murinus*.

From then on, he employed a very effective method invented by Metchnikoff, Roux and Salimbent during their scientific research on the cholera toxin.[37] He introduced little capsules of collodion filled with culture broth and medullose inseminated with *Bacillus murinus* into the peritoneum of rats.

He operated with all aseptic precautions in order to avoid infection of the peritoneum, which might have distorted the results of the experiment. Two or three days later, he sacrificed the animal and removed the capsule in order to inseminate the culture in a new collodion capsule and then introduce it into the peritoneum of another rat. When the virus had passed alternately through the organisms of several rodents it became much more active.

Soon, he succeeded in killing rats in three or four hours. Finally, by multiplying the passage of cultures through several rats, Procas obtained an exceedingly toxic virus.

XVIII

He was at that point in his research when another crisis laid him low. One evening, when he had worked very late, he was suddenly dazzled; a red light passed before his eyes and he collapsed on the table in his laboratory.

When he recovered his awareness of things it was broad daylight. So far as he could tell, it must be nearly midday. The circulation on the sidewalks was more active, and in the restaurant situated not far from his dwelling he could hear the sound of plates and glasses clinking.

---

ogy for such detective work, based on the logical extrapolation of "Koch's postulates." The "triads" to which the text refers are an aspect of that methodology,
[37] The Russian biologist Élie [Ilya] Metchnikoff (1845-1916) became one of the leading lights of the Pasteur Institute and received the Nobel Prize for Medicine in 1908 for his work on phagocytosis. Dr. Dalimbent, another employee of the Institute, most commonly cited with reference to his work on malaria, remained far more obscure

He tried to go as far as the window in order to pull the curtains and block a ray of sunlight that was blinding him, but he was incapable of taking a step. He fell to his knees, and it required all his strength to drag himself as far as the divan, on which he stretched himself out, with great difficulty.

It was impossible for him to remain lying down, however, and he had to sit up. His heart seemed to be about to stop at any moment, and Procas compressed his chest with his cold hands. His head was empty of thought; he was conscious of nothing except his illness, the phases of which he followed with anguish.

He remained doubled up for a long time, his gaze fixed, like a man fearful of a catastrophe; then he experienced a strange sensation. His vision became obscured, his ideas became imprecise; it seemed to him that he had suddenly been transported into an unreal world, far from conscious life. He had the impression that his spiritual being had deserted his body, that he was floating in space, and he wondered if this might be death—but no, for when he touched one of his limbs, which he pinched, he was conscious of the pain.

He was still there some time later, nailed to his divan, motionless, and as cold as a man of wax. When he thought he was a little better, he formed the project of going to the window and opening it in order to breathe in a draught of fresh air, but he was apprehensive of the moment when he stood up, because he was well aware that the slightest effort might provoke a further crisis. If only he had, at least, been able to sleep!

At the price of dolorous efforts he had succeeded in leaning backwards and supporting his head against the wall. At first, he experienced some relief, and closed his eyes. A relative wellbeing followed, which did not last long, for the new position he had adopted put too much strain on his thoracic muscles and compressed his respiration. He was obliged to lean forward again, with his elbows on his knees, and to stay like that, without making a movement.

An ardent thirst was burning his throat. He was shivering, his teeth were chattering and he felt the cold overtaking his extremities, running along his arms and legs, and rising toward has breast.

Is this the end? he thought.

That prospect did not frighten him. On the contrary, he envisaged it with serenity, astonished still to be alive. The noises of the street reached him, mutedly, and he almost wished that he could no longer hear anything, that he could flee forever the world where he had encountered no pity, the people whose footsteps he could hear on the sidewalk, the hoarse voices, and the bursts of laughter, which were all tortures for him.

After a further crisis, less violent than the others, which held him prostrate on his divan, he recovered a little physical tranquility and was able to take a few steps across the room. He drank a large glass of water, but as his legs were buckling, he was obliged to sit down. It was three days since he had eaten anything, but, still prey to fever, he was not hungry…a little water was sufficient.

The shock that he had experienced had brought a certain relaxation to his mind. He was no longer thinking about anything, but as life took hold of him again, the memory returned of everything that had happened. An insurmountable agitation gradually penetrated him, and even if he had wanted to forget, it would have been impossible for him to do so.

When he was finally able to go out to get his provisions, he found the same hostile crowd in front of him, and the desire for vengeance that was slumbering in his heart was reawakened, more violently than ever.

Fat Nestor, who had not laid down his arms, was more determined than ever. He had taken on more importance since the defection of Bezombes and Barouillet, and it was now him that was "leading the dance."

He had turned improvised detective. In the evening, he stationed himself at a small window overlooking the house in the Passage Tenaille and the fodder-shed. With a patience that never weakened, he lay in wait for the man he called "the satyr" for hours on end. He imagined that the latter was preparing to flee.

What maintained that idea in him was that he had not failed to remark Procas' comings and goings with his little hooded lantern, while hunting rats. Nestor had concluded that he had packed his trunks and was looking for wood with which to make crates in which to lodge all his equipment.

He had even thought that it was his duty to warn the proprietor, Père Grinchu, who had shrugged his shoulders and shut the door in his face. Furious, Nestor had begun spreading calumnies on the fodder-merchant's account the following day, accusing him of being "in cahoots" with "the murderer."

The affair was visibly taking on new proportions, and the crowd, so easy to convince, was now in tow to fat Nestor, who, the produce of the role of administrator or justice that he believed he was playing, stoked up the hatred on his partisans every day. He made speeches in the street, and people listened to him complaisantly, for what he said corresponded exactly with what a number of local people thought.

It is well-known that common people have an unfortunate tendency to see mystery everywhere, and to imagine that certain privileged people have a special grace. They have an iron conviction that the law is pitiless for the humble, while it reserves all its indulgence for those who belong to a certain social category.

The whisper had gone around that "the man of the Passage Tenaille" must once have played a political role that had made him party to certain secrets, and that it was for that reason that the police were protecting him.

"If he was a poor devil like us," Nestor never ceased repeating, "he'd have been locked up long ago."

Every day, in the workshops, on the doorsteps and in the shops there were mysterious conversations; everyone wanted to seem well-informed; some old gossips, who did not lack imagination, competed in embroidering the rumors, and some of them had turned the head of mother of the missing child that the poor woman, convinced that Procas had murdered her son, was among the demonstrators every evening when "the satyr" emerged furtively from his dwelling.

Where would it all end?

Nestor was convinced that the police, faced with that popular movement, which was becoming more important every day, would eventually take action.

But Procas' hatred grew along with that of the fanatics, and one evening, when, pursued by a howling band, he had once again been insulted, molested and struck, he reached home in such a state of exasperation that the idea of vengeance brooding within him, but which had perhaps been attenuated, was revived more fervently than ever.

"They'll have brought it on themselves!" he cried, in a hoarse voice.

And the following day, he resumed his frightful task.

XIX

He was not yet sure that the virus he had discovered would be able to act as effectively on a human being, but he had an intuition of it. The experiments he had carried out seemed conclusive. He was not at the end of his project, however. Although he had succeeded in isolating an exceedingly violent infectious agent, which ought to produce terrible effects, it was necessary that the virus would be able to propagate in water, in order that the toxic germs could multiply therein. That was an essential condition to obtain an epidemic that would not be limited to a few isolated cases.

There, a difficulty emerged.

Water, as everyone knows, is not ordinarily sterile. It always contains a fairly considerable quantity of bacteria, which do not develop in living organisms but develop at the expense of dead matter—which is to say, saprophytic bacteria. And that quantity depends on the very variable conditions of climate and proximity to some source of contamination.

Have not 415,000 microbes been found in a cubic centimeter of water from the Seine? And as many as 6,680 in the water that aliments Paris? It follows that the purest water conceals a microbial fauna, and enough organic material to nourish thousands of bacteria for a certain length of time.

In sterilized water microbes propagate even more. Water massively invaded by bacteria does not permit the facile development of the bacilli that live in it, and in the same way, does not permit the evolution of a new microbe, unless it is much more robust than the first inhabitants of the element. It is the eternal law of the struggle for existence that governs relations between those invisible beings, as it governs the relations of humans: the strong eat the weak.

Based on that fact, some scientists have put forward the opinion that the purest water, from the bacteriological point of view, is often the most dangerous, when it is impossible to protect it against contamination by some local nucleus of infection.

We beg pardon for these few scientific details, but they are necessary to the comprehension of what will follow, and serve to explain the terrible drama that is about to be played out.

Most pathogenic microbes develop quite easily in sterilized water, but when put in the presence of other saprophytic microbes that are much better adapted to that nutritive environment, it is necessary for them to sustain a fierce struggle for existence, and most of the time, they end up being vanquished.

The life of pathogenic microbes in the liquid element depends on numerous factors. First of all, there is the chemical composition of the water, principally its richness in organic matter; in addition, there is the elevation or depression of temperature, the presence or absence of light and movement. Finally, there are other conditions that depend on the microbes themselves: their vitality and resistance in the battle with their enemies.

When the pathogenic microbe begins to get the upper hand in that struggle for existence, and the others perish, there is than an increase in the nutritive matter in the water, at the expense of the cadavers, and the victorious microbe can develop much more abundantly.

Procas had taken water from the city supply and submitted it to the Koch method. After heating tubes containing gelatin impregnated with meat broth to a temperature of forty degrees, he added a certain quantity of water. The dissolved gelatin was then poured into glass vessels known as Petri dishes.

Ordinarily, the colonies of microbes appear after twenty-four or thirty-six hours in the form of little white dots, and the numeration of those colonies gives the total number of microbes in the quantity of water used for the insemination.

The city water analyzed by Procas was not rich in microbes; their number did not exceed eighteen hundred per cubic centimeter. It was evident that the water in question could offer a favorable environment to *Bacillus murinus*; the struggle for existence would not be very difficult. To verify that fact, Procas inseminated a cubic centimeter of *Bacillus murinus* in a five-liter flask filed with city water. Every six hours, he spread specimens of that water on the gelatin and counted the number of colonies that appeared after twenty-four hours in the incubator.

The second experiment revealed a notable diminution of colonies of the bacillus and in thirty hours they had almost completely disappeared. The rat bacillus, which was so potent and so tenacious in the animal organism, was vanquished by the invisible creatures.

But Procas was not discouraged. On the contrary, the difficulty stimulated him. He knew full well that one can habituate any bacterium to new conditions of life by changing those conditions gradually. He inseminated his *Bacillus murinus* in a flask containing less meat and more sterilized water, and produced a series of cultures, gradually diminishing the quantity of organic material, However, the bacilli introduced into unsterilized water disappeared after a time.

On the other hand, the inoculation of that culture into rats demonstrated that its virulence was noticeably attenuated, and eventually lost its potency altogether.

This time, Procas was utterly discouraged, and might perhaps have renounced continuing his experiments if the hostile cries he heard from outside had not stimulated his energy and maintained his idea of vengeance.

He continued his research, and began to wonder whether, in consequence of a cooperation between two or more microbial species, he might be able to achieve a kind of bacillary union.

Science furnishes several examples of that "symbiosis," an association of microbes that appears to be useful, and even necessary, to the life of a determined type. Has not Metchnikoff observed that the combination of the cholera vibrion with a few other species, such as, for example, *Sarcina*, an inoffensive parasite of the human intestine, is one of the most virulent?

It was necessary to find a microbial type that was able to increase the resistance of the *Bacillus murinus*.

He carried out a number of trials, but the results were always the same. The bacillus was attenuated in the water and its virulence disappeared there almost completely.

Would he, then, be forced to renounce his vengeance? Would science be impotent to procure him the poison that would annihilate hundreds of human lives?

Every day he became angrier; he became more deeply absorbed in his idea of vengeance; eventually, he thought about nothing else. He was exasperated, half-mad.

When the shouts and insults of the people massed outside his door reached his ears, instead of frightening him, as before, he laughed in a sinister fashion, gently lifted his curtain, stared at all the individuals who were insulting him and thought that if he succeeded in isolating and multiplying the bacillus for which he was searching, the specter would soon reappear of the Black Death that had traveled through the valleys of Europe centuries before, sowing terror and ruination in its path...

He rejoiced in that thought that, for all those individuals who were making him suffer, there would soon be the darkness of the tomb. No regret or pity found a place in his soul.

Coldly, he envisaged the consequences of his action, and awaited with impatience the day when he would be able to suppress his enemies with a simple gesture.

In his laboratory, by the light of a flickering gas-lamp, long into the night, he carried out his deadly work with the fever of a scientist working solely for the sake of science.

XX

Thus far, none of his trials had succeeded; he always ran into the same difficulties, and the microbes he disseminated lost their virulence once they were plunged into the water.

One day, he had the idea of drawing water from an old, very deep well that was in his yard. He was not expecting anything good from the new experiment when, to his great surprise, he discovered that the *Bacillus murinus* developed very abundantly in that unsterilized water.

After twenty-four hours, the number of microbes contained in the liquid diminished, while his bacillus developed increasingly. There was no doubt about it; the initial cause of that augmentation of virulence was due to one of the microbes inhabiting the well, and the same results could be obtained with the pure culture of those microbes in sterilized water. He isolated them, cultivated them separately, and then developed them with the *murinus* adapted to life in the well water and the city water.

The problem was solved! Procas was finally holding his vengeance: two microbes, which, cooperating with one another, became extremely virulent. He carefully prepared a culture of the two bacilli in a two-liter flask, and then let himself fall upon his divan, uttering a profound sigh.

It only remained to accomplish the decisive act: the one that he has been ruminating for such a long time.

Everything was ready—and yet, he hesitated. For long hours he remained motionless, his head in his hands.

Come on, he said to himself internally, *it's necessary to decide. Have they had any pity on me?*

He stood up, approached the vessel, put it under his arm as if he were ready to take it away, and took a few steps across the room. A frightful struggle began within him. He put the flask down again, went to sit down, and became pensive again...

He recalled all his days of misery, the tortures that the savage crowd, which never gave him a moment's respite, had forced him to endure. He started pacing again, suddenly opened the window, and took a deep breath, plunging his gaze into the darkness.

The hour sounded at Saint-Pierre-de-Montrouge, grave and tremulous. It was raining. Clouds were racing across the sky with large wan patches in places. He shook his fist at the street.

Swiftly, he put on his overcoat and hat, and, hiding the flask under his left arm, he opened his door and went out.

In the houses, his enemies were asleep, tranquil and confidant.

Procas went up the Avenue du Maine as far as the church of Montrouge, took the Rue d'Alésia, turned right into the Rue Tombe-Issoire and reached the

Rue Saint-Yves. Having arrived at the place where he had discovered the cadaver of his poor Mami a few weeks earlier, he stopped, out of breath, because he had been walking rapidly and was sweating copiously. Recalling the tragic evening when they had tried to lynch him, he saw his dog once again, huddling against him and growling. Then everything was effaced in his mind; he no longer retained anything but the memory of the anguish that he had experienced thereafter, when he had run around searching for Mami, and had found him, at daybreak, lying in the gutter.

"The wretches! The wretches!" he never ceased repeating, prey to a dull anger that was gradually accentuating. At that moment, everything in him was exasperated. He was no longer reasoning, and was only thinking about one thing: vengeance.

He started walking again, advancing furtively, like a malefactor who senses that he is being watched. He was almost certain that no one had seen him, but he was trembling, and sought convulsively to make himself small.

The rain was still falling with a weary noise. The lights of Paris formed a great vacillating mist in the distance, above the houses.

Having reached the corner of the Avenue Reille and the Rue Saint-Yves, he got his bearings. In front of him, the reservoir of Montsouris had the appearance of an enormous tumulus covered with a thick lawn, like one of those gigantic sepulchers that one sees in some Asian cities. On one of its side, little glazed edicules rose up, and in the north-west corner, there was a stone construction surmounted by a metallic kiosk, which was reminiscent of the bridge of a steamship.

He remembered having come here a few years before, with a delegation of municipal councilors and chemists, to examine that were known as the "arrival tanks" into which the siphons of the Vanne, the Lunain and the Loing discharged. It had been a matter of a Hygiene Committee investigation. In his capacity as a bacteriologist, Procas had been appointed to study on location the dangers of the contamination of the water by the dust that the wind might blow into the adduction vessels, and he had been struck by the ease with which someone could penetrate into the reservoir at that time, which was now protected by solid barriers.

He went along the Avenue Reille and then the Rue de la Tombe-Issoire and the Rue Saint-Yves, which framed the two sides of the great grassy tumulus, and understood that he would never succeed in scaling the walls.

He tried to open a little door framed in the stone, but could not do it. It would have been necessary to force the lock. Procas would not have hesitated to do that, but all that he had on him was a little knife, the blade of which would have snapped at the slightest effort.

While he was reflecting in a shadowy corner, the silhouette of a policeman appeared, moving along the neighboring houses. He waited until the silhouette had disappeared, and then made a second tour of the reservoir. It was as well-defended as a fortress.

With rage in his heart, he took the road back to his dwelling.

The rain had stopped, and a brisk wind was causing the glass of the street-lamps to rattle. Large clouds, like cotton wool peppered with soot, were filing across the sky, illuminated from time to time by a ray of moonlight.

Procas was so troubled that he went astray. Instead of turning left to rejoin the Rue d'Alésia via the Avenue Parc-de-Monsouris, he turned right and found himself in the Rue de la Glacière.

After a long hesitation, he finally recognized his route, but he was so exhausted that he had to sit down on a bench. He was invaded by a torpor, and would probably have let himself fall asleep if a policeman had not called to him rudely: "Don't you have a home to go to?"

"Yes, Monsieur," Procas replied, startled, like a man emerging from a dream.

"Go to bed, then. One doesn't sleep on benches."

Procas stood up. He drew away, his tread heavy, under the suspicious gaze of the policeman.

When he got home, he saw a piece of paper stuck to his door. He tried to read it but, not being able to do so, detached it. He went into his laboratory, switched on the light, and words traced in large letters by a maladroit hand appeared in the lamplight.

Villain! Murderer! Since the police won't arrest you, we'll settle your hash before long.

Procas did not even become indignant. He shrugged his shoulders, crumpled up the piece of paper and threw it into a corner.

He knew full well, of course, that he had nothing good to expect from that overexcited populace whose hatred was growling around him. Threats scarcely moved him.

His flask, placed in front of him on the table, scintillated in the light. *It's me who'll settle your hash, you wretches*, he thought, *and you'll have brought it on yourselves.*

He undressed slowly and lay down on his divan, which he had now converted into a bed—a bed without sheets, with two coarse military blankets. He had left the lamp lit, because for some time, darkness had frightened him. Outside, the rain had started falling again. Procas was drowsy, exhausted by fatigue, and ended up falling asleep.

When he woke up, it was broad daylight. His lamp was burning low, spreading a wisp of black smoke through the room, but he did not have the strength to get up. The prospect of having to live another day sickened him. His failure of the previous evening had discouraged him, but he had not renounced his project of vengeance. The idea was anchored in his mind with such force that he regarded it as something necessary, a kind of obligation that he could not avoid.

He let himself slide out of bed, put on his clothes, which were still damp, and headed for the kitchen, where he had installed his autoclave.

There, he opened the drawer of an old table, rummaged among the objects within, and pulled out a metal stem terminated at its extremity by a double hook, It was the implement he used to withdraw red-hot tubes from the fire that he had heated in order to sterilize them. He searched for a file, which he eventually discovered on a shelf, and, returning to his laboratory, started filing the piece of metal carefully.

That work took him nearly three hours, and when he had finished, Procas threw himself down on his divan again.

He seemed quite tranquil, and at times, a smile creased his hideous face.

XXI

That morning, fat Nestor, contrary to his habit, neglected to knock on Procas' door proffering threats. He had received a visit from Barouillet, who had given him some serious news.

Bezombes had been arrested and taken to the Commissariat in the Rue Sarrette.

"It's the police taking their revenge," growled Nestor.

"Perhaps," said Barouillet, but what's certain is that Bezombes has been accused of fraud."

"Père Chevassu has lodged a complaint?"

"Oh, there are several complaints, it's said. That Bezombes isn't worth much..."

"Possibly, but even so, he rendered us a valuable service."

Barouillet made a vague gesture.

"Yes, all the same, he furnished us with the proofs that we lacked."

"Who can tell?"

"What, you doubt it?"

"Bezombes exaggerated everything. He's a narcissist who only seeks to make himself look good. In any case, whether he exaggerated or not, what's certain is that he's a dishonest man, and he took advantage of the affair to cheat several of the local merchants, and it's very regrettable that we associated with him, because, after all, we were his friends. They only saw him with us...if they were to suppose..."

"Come on, Monsieur Barouillet, everyone in Montrouge knows us. We have businesses, status. We don't owe anyone anything. When the bank employees come to see us, they never leave pieces of paper..."

"I don't deny it—but people are so malevolent..."

"Bah! It's nothing to do with us. Let Bezombes get himself out of it."

"We'll probably be summoned as witnesses."

"Well, we'll tell them what we know. They can't lock us up just because we've been in the company of a crook. These things happen. One makes the acquaintance of a man; one thinks he's honest; if one finds out later that he's a rogue, one isn't compromised for that. Bezombes deceived us, that's all, but that doesn't stop me thinking that he was sincere when he was on the trail of the satyr..."

"How did it get us any further forward?"

"Oh, Monsieur Barouillet, with all due respect, you abandoned us, and you were wrong..."

"No, my friend, I wasn't wrong. I understood that there was nothing more to be done. Our man, for reasons I don't know, undoubtedly disposes of great protection, since, in spite of all the evidence accumulated against him, he's still at liberty. My opinion—have I any need to say it?—hasn't varied. I think he's guilty of a crime, perhaps several, but so long as he isn't caught in the act..."

"To catch him in the act, it's necessary to keep him under surveillance, to spy on him…and that's what I do, every day…or rather, every evening. Ordinarily, he only goes out to fetch his dinner, and once he comes back, he doesn't set foot outside again. Well, last night, he went out at about midnight. I heard him open his door. I went to the window and I saw him heading in the direction of Montrouge church. But when I got downstairs, he was already far away..."

"You're sure you saw him go out?"

"As sure as I am that you're standing in front of me. I've been watching him…because I have patience, and when I occupy myself with an affair, I see it through to the end. Yes, I watched for him and I saw him come back. It might have been about two o'clock in the morning. Do you think it's natural, going out like that? One of these days, we're going to hear that someone's been murdered, and no more will be said about it. Oh, damn it! I'll pinch the satyr or may I lose my name. From tonight onwards, I'll be on sentry duty again."

"But you can't stay up every night..."

"I'll sleep during the day. My father will take my place on the stall—but it's necessary that I finish it."

"I admire your energy, and most of all your persistence, but I think you'll be wasting your time."

"We'll see, Monsieur Barouillet, we'll see. Until now we didn't know that the satyr went out at night. Now we'll try to find out what he does with his time. Nothing honest, that's for sure..."

"I wish you luck. In any case, don't forget that you can always count on me."

Nestor burst out laughing. "Ah," he said, clapping Barouillet on the shoulder in a familiar fashion, "you've changed your mind…we can arrange to share the work, then. We'll take turns to follow the individual."

""I'd do it with pleasure, but the municipal elections are coming up, and all my evenings are taken, you understand. I'm campaigning for Malavaux, and..."

"What? I thought you supported the sitting councilor?"

"No, Bellerive hasn't kept his promises. He's taken things too easily with the electors. We need a man who'll occupy himself actively with the neighborhood. Oh, if it had been any other time, I'd have been glad to help you, but it's impossible, you see..."

"I'll work alone, then, and do my best to succeed. It will happen, perhaps sooner than you think...and I'll be able to say that I, too, have acted in the interests of the neighborhood."

"People will be grateful to you."

The two men shook hands and parted. Nestor emerged on to his doorstep, where he stood motionless, imposing and superb. To those who passed by, he nodded his head slightly or saluted them with a gesture of his hand.

The role that he had assumed placed him in the Avenue du Maine, and like Bezombes, he assumed a mysterious expression when anyone spoke to him about "the affair."

Everyone was convinced that he knew something but did not want to say anything yet. At aperitif time, however, in the little café in the Rue Liancourt, he imparted a few confidences to two or three friends, who hastened to repeat everywhere that Nestor was about to astonish everyone, and those who has thus far considered him to be an utter imbecile would begin to take him seriously.

It was him, in sum, who was maintaining the hatred of everyone in the neighborhood against Procas—a hatred that would probably have attenuated otherwise, and then died down, as every popular fury tends to do. People continued to spy on the unfortunate scientist, and to "escort" him when he went in search of a few meager provisions, which he did not lays obtain, because the majority of the shopkeepers had made an alliance with the crowd. He was often obliged to go as far as the Rue de la Gaîté and the Rue d'Odessa, where he inevitably found new enemies, who joined in chorus with the others.

It is only just to recognize that, for several days, Procas, who was sure of avenging himself on everyone, had adopted a provocative attitude. Once, he had fled like a poor beast, pursued by thrown stones, but now he stood up to the howling band that escorted him. Often, he stopped, folded his arms and stared at the mob. It is certain that that would end badly one day; he was repeatedly attacked, because he was becoming increasingly odious.

The day before, a piece of paper had been nailed to his door; that evening he found another, on which a guillotine had been drawn, with the words: *Deibler is waiting for you.*[38]

---

[38] Anatole Deibler was the Republic's chief executioner from 1899 until he dropped dead in a Metro station in 1939.

He smiled and went in. He seemed quite calm. He ate a crust of bread and a little roasted meat, and threw himself down on the divan filly dressed, after having set his alarm clock for midnight.

When the little bell began to vibrate, Procas got up. He took a few steps across the room, toward the window, and listened. Then, putting on his coat, he stood still for a few moments. Finally, he put his hat on, pulling down the brim, picked up his flask, and went out quietly, after having extinguished his lamp.

Scarcely was he outside than he heard footsteps behind him. He turned round and saw a shadow, hugging the walls. By the light of a street-lamp he recognized his enemy and started thinking about ways to put him off the track.

Instead of following the Avenue du Maine he went into the Passage de la Tour-de-Vanves, where the darkness was almost complete, turned rapidly into the Rue Asseline, and hid in a doorway.

Fat Nestor stopped, indecisively, and then, not seeing anyone, continued along the entire length of the street. He went past Procas without perceiving him, came back into the Passage and went all the way back to the Avenue—but Procas had already reached the Rue d'Alésia via the Rue Didot, and then followed the Avenue d'Orléans and the Rue Beaunier, which opened opposite the main entrance of the Montsouris reservoir.

He immediately turned into the Avenue Reille, and stopped outside a little iron door framed in the wall.

The night was dark and slightly foggy. The glow of the street-lamps seemed to be shimmering in troubled water. Putting his flask on the ground, Procas, by means of the hook that he had fashioned the previous evening, started foraging gently in the lock. He finally heard a little click, and the door opened soundlessly.

He was inside.

A frightening tranquility reigned all around. He went up a few steps and reached the large grassy platform that covered the reservoir. Kneeling down on the damp grass, he listened momentarily, then got up again and, bending down, slid toward the glazed edicule that he could perceive vaguely in front of him.

He was trembling in every limb, and felt his heart beating precipitately in his breast. The horrible resolution that he had made was weakening by the minute, and he might have been on the point of turning round when the distant barking of a dog caused him to shiver.

That was the fashion in which poor Mami had barked when he sensed the hostile crowd behind him in pursuit of his master. That barking had something plaintive about it, and it rose into the night at regular intervals.

Procas shuddered. In a matter of seconds, his memories succeeded one another. He saw once again the howling mob of his enemies, their savage faces, their threatening gestures. He thought he could feel the brutal hand of the butcher boy on his shoulder, and hear Mami growling at his side—Mami, whose bloody remains he would soon find lying in the gutter...

And that stifled his dream of forgiveness. At a furtive pace, he continued to advance, hugging his flask to his chest

Why should I have pity on them? he thought.

He had arrived at the kiosk where the double siphons of the Vanne and the Loing opened. He only had to pick the lock of a glass door, which yielded easily. Having reached an iron ramp, he saw a black hole into which the water poured, seething.

His hands, which were holding the flask, had become chilled, and, as he was about to accomplish the fatal gesture that would sow death, his legs vacillated. He pulled himself together, though, stretched out his arm, hesitated again—and then, with an abrupt gesture, poured out the poison.

There was a slight noise. Something like a slight rustle of foliage...and that was all.

Procas was avenged. The irreparable deed had been done.

A frisson of dolor and voluptuousness ran through his entire body, and he fled, prey to a mad terror, thinking that he could see people all around him with fleshless arms, pitiful and supplicant.

He had difficulty finding the little door through which he had entered, but closed it silently, and launched himself into the dark streets, walking with an uneven, heavy tread. He had kept the flask. He threw it on to a patch of waste ground, where it shattered.

All night long he wandered like a lost dog, and only got home at dawn. As he put his key into the lock, a man suddenly surged forth.

"Ah! We'll have your hide, scoundrel!"

Procas turned round and recognized the apprentice butcher. He stared at him, smiled ironically, and closed his door.

XXII

The neighborhood woke up. Procas, who had no desire to sleep, in spite of his weariness, was sitting on his divan, his head in his hands. Now that a little clarity had returned to his mind, he was thinking.

What he had done was horrible, he realized. Tomorrow or the day after tomorrow at the latest, the urban ambulances would be speeding through the streets; the hospitals would be filling up with the dying; all the people who were now going cheerfully to work would soon be struck down by a strange illness, the cause of which would be sought in vain. Death would surprise men, women and children...

Children!

At that thought, Procas felt a constriction in his heart. In order to avenge himself, he would kill innocents, poor little creatures who did not know and did not yet understand anything of human suffering. And yet, had they not tortured him too? Had they not uttered cries of hatred as he passed by, and wild clamors? Were they not part of the barbaric multitude that harassed him every day? Had any one of them ever made the slightest gesture or uttered a single word of pity for him?

Procas, it is evident, by dint of meditating his vengeance, of satisfying it, had arrived at finding it just, almost natural. It is true that the suffering, and the persecution of which he had been the object, had, as we have explained, gradually disturbed his conscience. He was no longer a normal individual.

For the moment, he could only see one thing: he was about to read in faces, in his turn, dolor and anguish. When he sensed a sentiment of pity invading him, he immediately recalled everything that had been done to him, and the anger concentrated in his heart began boiling once again. He maintained around himself an ambience of memories, and avoided interrogating himself, for fear that he might condemn himself.

When dusk fell, he went out. As usual, the same unchained, mocking and evil mob gathered around him. He seemed insensible to the insults; he was no longer an irritable and furious man, as before, but an unconscious individual, as if in a state of hypnosis, for whom the external world no longer existed.

"He's jolly good this evening!" shouted one woman, who was following the crowd leading her child by the hand.

"Oh, you'd better watch out," said another. "Don't get too close. Beware!"

The new attitude of the man with the blue face astonished them, however, and they wondered whether that calmness was natural. Some of them wanted to see him baulk, and aggravated him, even jostling him, like animal-tamers whipping a wild beast to make it roar.

Procas was still impassive.

What's the point? he said to himself. *Tomorrow, they'll no longer be occupied with me...because they'll have another enemy, far more redoubtable.*

And with that thought, a malevolent gleam came into his eyes.

He was able to buy a few provisions that evening. When he went home, he noticed that his escort was still as numerous. He locked himself in, ate slowly, by the light of his little oil lamp, and then, as he sensed clearly that he would not be able to sleep, he picked up a book on bacteriology, and absorbed himself in reading a chapter selected at random.

From time to time, the rumble of a vehicle, the sound of hurried footsteps or a murmur of voices made him shiver. He listened momentarily, and then plunged back into his book, muttering: "No, not yet...it's too soon."

He calculated that the water in the reservoir would not yet have spread into the supply-pipes; it would take at least forty-eight hours for the contamination to be complete. And he followed in his imagination the development of his bacilli, whose colonies must be multiplying infinitely. He represented them as if he were looking at them through a microscope, swarming on a slide.

Suddenly, his head slumped forwards; he was asleep. Then his mind, transformed, denatured and amplified by the dream, showed him the bacilli enormously magnified, with gigantic antennae, the tentacles of octopodes and scintillating eyes. All of them were moving, twisting in slow convulsions, and he sensed the sticky monsters sliding over his body, gradually tightening around him, compressing his chest, choking him...

He uttered a cry and woke up.

He went to open the window. A man was standing outside his door. It was fat Nestor, lying in wait for him. Procas recognized him and, instead of closing the window again, stayed here, leaning on the sill. The apprentice butcher moved off, and went to hide some distance away. Perhaps he thought that his enemy was about to emerge, and was casting an eye over the street before leaving the house.

If there's any justice, Procas thought, *he'll be the first one to be struck down.*

He started pacing back and forth, because he was afraid of going to sleep and having another frightful nightmare.

Fatigue, however, ended up wearing him out, and he collapsed on his divan, where a brutal slumber was not long delayed in taking possession of him.

In the morning he woke up with a frightful headache; he bathed his forehead over a basin, and as the water trickled down his face he wiped it away carefully, fearing that it might already be contaminated. Now he no longer dared drink. Was it not necessary that he enjoy his triumph, and see those who had driven him to do what he had done suffering?

Ordinarily, he never went out in the morning, but today he went to buy the newspapers. A gang of street-urchins assailed him as soon as he set foot in the street, and the housewives chatting on the doorsteps heaped insults upon him, but Procas walked straight ahead, his head tilted forward, his eyes half-closed, like a man in a dream. That persistent calm, contrasting with his habitual state of fury, did not fail to cause surprise. People concluded that his conscience was not tranquil, and that he was doubtless expecting to be arrested soon. While they observed him slyly, he came back, reading a newspaper, which seemed singular.

What could he be looking for in the papers?

Those who had not yet had time to cast an eye over the morning papers hastened to the nearest newsstand and immediately started scanning the columns of the first, second and third pages, hoping to discover a clue there, but it was a waste of effort. However, one decorated old rentier who was mingling with the crowd called their attention to a news item that had not struck the minds of the curiosity-seekers. The item concerned a woman who had been strangled the previous evening in a sleazy hotel in the Rue de la Tombe-Issoire. She had come in at about midnight in the company of an individual who tried to hide his face, and who had disappeared before dawn.

Then, for the people gathered around the newsstand, it was as if a veil had been torn away from their eyes.

"Of course!" said someone. "That's what he was looking for in the paper!"

"For sure," said another. "It's him, and no mistake. For several days he's been going out at night. Where did he go?"

"You'll see," said the old rentier, proud of having given proof of his sagacity. "You'll see that this crime will go unpunished, like the others. Oh, he's clever, that fellow. He's not on his trial run..."

All day long, the murder in the Rue de la Tombe-Issoire was the object of conversations. Fat Nestor was fuming with rage.

"I lost him last night," he said. "I followed him, but he gave me the slip. If I'd been able to stay on his heels, that would have been it—I'd have had him. It must he him who did it!"

No one doubted it, until the evening papers cast light on the affair. The murderer had been arrested. It was someone named Mohamed Ben Agha, a manual worker in a factory on the Boulevard de la Gare. His victim's bracelet-watch had been found on him, and he had confessed.

There was general consternation, but everyone remained convinced nevertheless that "the satyr" was no better than that Mohammed, and that one day or other he would end up being caught *in flagrante delicto*.

XXIII

Procas was still waiting. He no longer cared about the crowd that growled as he passé by. One idea obsessed him: might the bacillus on which he had counted, whose toxicity had appeared evident to him, have lost its properties when it came into contact with an immense expanse of water? The reservoir, he knew, contained about two hundred thousand cubic meters. Might that mass have contained an element that he had not foreseen? No, though—his bacillus ought to annihilate all the others, for the experiments he had carried out on five or six liters of water had sufficiently proved the virulence and combativeness of his colonies. They must be in the process of developing, but had not yet reached the supply-pipes.

Sometimes, remorse took hold of him and he almost wanted to see his attempt fail, but when he found himself confronted by the hate-filled gazes of his enemies, and heard their imprecations and their insults, he felt his compassion evaporate.

Certainly, he did not intend to enjoy his triumph for long, because life was weighing upon him like a burden. Once his vengeance was accomplished, he would disappear.

In the afternoon, he went out. He noticed that people were looking at him, but without anger, and he thought that he even read a sort of compassion on some faces.

On the Avenue du Maine, at the corner of the Passage de la Tour-de-Vannes, people were conversing with an air of mystery. When he went by they did not greet him with the habitual clamors that had once rendered him madly furious. He would have liked someone to insult him, though, or even to hit him, because that would have maintained the anger in his heart, which he sensed gradually dying down.

He went home, opened his window and looked out at the avenue.

Usually, as soon as he appeared, there were savage cries and threatening gestures, but today, there was nothing.

Silence.

All day long he remained prostrate at his work table, play to a black depression. Thus, at the very moment when he had condemned it to death, the crowd was humanizing. And he sought in vain for the cause of that appeasement.

He ended up persuading himself that the calm was only apparent, and that they were plotting against him again. That had happened before; he had often thought that he was recovering a measure of tranquility, but the next day he had been assailed by a furious mob once again.

Night had fallen, but he remained at his table, without even thinking of lighting his lamp. Someone knocked on the door, and he shivered. Who could be coming to his home? He hesitated momentarily, and then lit the lamp.

Someone was calling now: "Monsieur! Monsieur!"

He decided to go and open the door, and fund himself face to face with two men—but recoiled on recognizing one of them as the apprentice butcher who had been his torturer, his executioner.

"What do you want with me?" he cried. "What do you want?"

"Monsieur," fat Nestor replied, "We'd like to talk to you."

"Talk to me? What do you have to say to me? You've probably come to murder me, wretch!"

"Calm down," said the second visitor, who was none other than Barouillet. "We've come to clear up a misunderstanding."

The phrase was perhaps poorly chosen, but Barouillet's head was stuffed with electoral clichés, lavishly employed in public meetings.

"Yes," he went on. "A misunderstanding...a regrettable misunderstanding."

Procas had stepped back. "Come in," he said, understanding that he might not have to fight the two men. He went into his laboratory. They followed him.

"Monsieur," said Barouillet, "we owe you an apology."

"Yes...exactly...apologies," agreed Nestor, bowing awkwardly. "Anyone can make a mistake, can't they?"

"And we've been mistaken, grossly mistaken," added Barouillet. "All this is the fault of an individual who is now in trouble with the law. He claimed to know...he convinced us, so to speak...we believed, for what he said was so precise and so concordant with the fact that it was impossible not to accuse you..."

Procas still did not understand. He was close to believing that it was a trick, and gazed anxiously at the two men, one of whom was his mortal enemy, who had unleashed the wrath of the crowd upon him many a time.

"Explain yourselves," he said. "What facts are you talking about?"

"You know very well," replied Barouillet.

"All I know is that I'm an object of horror, and that instead of feeling sorry for me you have all persecuted me. You've insulted me and attacked me. I only had one friend left in the world, a dog, a poor lame animal, and you killed him. Why? What have I done to you?"

"You've done all kinds of wrong to you. I recognize that. But your way of living, your mysterious nocturnal labors...all that seemed suspicious to us, and when little Maurice disappeared, we thought..."

"What did you think?"

"That you'd killed him."

"But that's horrible! So you were able to think me guilty of murder?"

Fat Nestor and Barouillet bowed their heads without replying. They were now conscious of the infamy of their conduct, and could not find anything more to say.

"Come on," said Procas, "talk. Why have you come today to offer your apologies to me, whom you perhaps still consider to be a murderer?"

"No," stammered Barouillet. "We know now that you're not guilty. The child has reappeared. He was abducted at the Fête du Lion de Belfort by gypsies, but he succeeded in getting away from them, and yesterday, the police brought him home. You can understand now why we're here. We're honest men and we recognize our mistakes. Someone put it into our heads, and then everyone accused you. Someone found traces of blood in your back yard. The child was playing outside your door shortly before he disappeared. Put yourself in our place—what would you have thought?"

Procas had sat down, his head in his hands; he was sobbing.

So they had thought he was a murderer, and he had had no suspicion of it. He had thought that it was his ugliness alone that had aroused the mob against him. If he had known! Why had no one said anything to him? Oh, he understood everything now: the visit of the Commissaire, the search, the howls of rage that went up at his approach, the fury of the people who believed him to be guilty.

"Monsieur," said fat Nestor, patting him gently on the shoulder, "don't torment yourself. It's all over now, we know that you're a worthy man. You no longer have any enemies, I assure you. Everyone in the neighborhood is informed now...and they feel sorry for you."

Procas dared not raise his head to look at the man who was speaking, the enemy who he was previously execrated, and who was now apologizing...who was finally pronouncing the words of pity for which he had waited in vain and which might have encouraged him to live.

At the moment that I no longer have any enemies, he thought, *when those who were persecuting me have come to offer me their hand, the poison is on the march, circulating in the supply-pipes, perhaps already claiming victims.*

He stood up abruptly, looked the two men in the face, and exclaimed, in a hoarse voice: "No! No...if you knew...I've suffered too much...I've suffered too much!"

And he fled, at a run.

"Poor fellow," murmured fat Nestor. "He's mad. Not astonishing, after such emotions. Oh, he's seen people harsh, and they nearly had his skin. It's stupid, all the same. And it's all the fault of that swine Bezombes. Why did we listen to him? Père Grinchu was right...he was the only one who saw clearly in all this."

Barouillet made no reply. He took the apprentice butcher by the arm and led him outside.

Newsvendors were running through the streets, stopping, distributing a few sheets that were still moist, and setting off again, howling: "Mysterious disease! Full details! The day's deaths!"

Vengeance sometimes wields a scythe that mows down innocents. This is what had happened...

Procas had wanted to avenge himself on those who had made him so unhappy, but the fatality that had always pursued him seemed to have attached itself to him. His bacillus was now claiming victims, the hospitals were filling up with the sick, but it was not in the Montrouge district that the terrible epidemic had burst forth.

Procas had assumed, like many Parisians, that the Montsouris reservoir distributed the water of the Vanne and the Loing to the inhabitants of the fourteenth arrondissement, and that they would be the center attained, but it was the first, the second, the third and the fourth that had received the poisoned water, and were already counting many cases of affliction.

On the terraces of cafes, in the restaurants and in the houses, men, women and children were falling down and writhing as if seized by vertigo. The urban ambulances were going back and forth before the terrified eyes of the population.

The disease commenced abruptly with violent shivering and vomiting. The temperature rose very rapidly and reached forty-one or even forty-two degrees within two or three hours. The pulse increased to a hundred and fifty beats per minute. Neural phenomena were also very marked; many victims were seized by convulsions; the skin was covered with a viscous sweat; blisters appeared on the face and the limbs, filed with turbulent liquid.

And the people who had escaped the scourge thus far awaited their turn, anguished and trembling. The inhabitants of ancient Pompeii, seeing the descending lava that was about to swallow them up, could not have been more terrified than the citizens of Paris during those tragic hours.

Procas was now wandering the streets, crazily. The visit of fat Nestor and Barouillet had devastated him. Remorse had broken his heart. Could he allow people to die who had ceased to be enemies, who had recognized the wrongs they had done to him, and were only asking to be forgiven? He would go to tell the whole story, reveal everything, to the Commissaire, to have the water in the supply-pipes stopped. Perhaps there was still time?

Yes, but once he had confessed his crime, it was necessary that he disappear. His resolution was quickly made. He would return home and take the little bottle of potassium cyanide, which he had often thought of raising to his lips, from the shelf....

He would confess his crime...and immediately put an end to his life...

The cries of the newsvendors suddenly attracted his attention. A tremor took hold of him. He bought a newspaper, read it by the light of a street-lamp, and felt his legs give way beneath him.

So this was how it had ended! Killing innocents! People he had never seen, who did not know him!

A long sob rose to his lips. He wanted to run all the way to his laboratory, but this time the shock had been too strong for a man whose life was now only hanging by a thread.

A choking crisis gripped him; his heart abruptly ceased beating, and he collapsed like a mass, thunderstruck.

Meanwhile, the physicians had finally recognized that it was the water that was carrying death through Paris, and the epidemic had been halted. No one knew, as yet, that a man, in order to avenge himself, had poisoned the Montsouris reservoir, and there were long discussions regarding the causes of the contagion.

Procas, picked up on the roadside, was transported to the Passage Tenaille, and the following day, all of Montrouge followed the meager coffin that took him to his final dwelling.

The murderer had become a victim, and the crowd, *which did not know*, threw flowers into his grave.

Pity had finally awakened—too late.

Note

The story you have just read is a retrospective one. It is now utterly impossible to poison a reservoir, the water of which is analyzed every day with the greatest care by the city's chemists. May the citizens of Paris be reassured!

A.G.

246

Gustave Le Rouge: *The Sculptor of Human Flesh*

The Sculptor of Human Flesh *is Episode 4 of* Le Mystérieux Docteur Cornélius *by Gustave Le Rouge (1867-1938), a serialized novel originally published in eighteen weekly parts by the Maison du Livre Moderne in 1912-13. It proved to be the author's most successful work, even inspiring a cycle of poems adapted from his work by the author's friend and first enthusiastic champion, the* avant-garde *poet and novelist Blaise Cendrars.*

By 1912, Le Rouge was already a highly experienced writer of popular works in the long tradition of French feuilleton fiction—having begun his career in that field, after a period of near-starvation as a Latin Quarter poet and publishing an assortment of short stories and items of non-fiction—by working in collaboration with Gustave Guitton on a series of sprawling endeavors, begun with what was intended to be a four-volume novel (it was actually split into eight by its publisher) collectively entitled La Conspiration des Milliardaires *[The Billionaires' Conspiracy] (1899-1900)[39]. Guitton and Le Rouge wrote three more long novels before going their separate ways, after which Le Rouge became far more successful than his former friend, whose solo career faded away and whose eventual fate—and, indeed, his entire life—remains mysterious.*

Le Mystérieux docteur Cornélius *is a deliberate return on Le Rouge's part to the milieu and genre of La Conspiration des Milliardaires, with the exception that American billionaires are here the victim of a vast conspiracy rather than the makers of one. Whereas the earlier series had a band of American plutocrats hiring a scientific genius to provide them with the weapons necessary to conquer Europe and hence obtain economic world domination, in* Le Mystérieux Docteur Cornélius, *the partners in a Trust monopolizing American production of corn and cotton become the targets of the insidious criminal association of the Red Hand, whose three mysterious Lords are the scientific genius Cornelius Kramm, his brother Fritz. and the renegade son of one of the billionaires.*

The sympathy accorded by the overarching plot of Le Mystérieux Docteur Cornélius to billionaires in general is an ironic reflection of literary convention. Le Rouge's own political sympathies were on the far left of radical socialism, but in his fiction, he was consciously following in the footsteps of numerous French anarchists who had turned to popular fiction as a means of making a

---

[39] Translated in four volumes as *The Dominion of the World*, Black Coat Press: *1. The Plutocratic Plot*, ISBN 978-1-61227-095-1; *2. The Transatlantic Threat*, ISBN 978-1-61227-096-8; *3. The Psychic Spies*, ISBN 978-1-61227-097-5; and *4. The Victims Victorious*, ISBN 978-1-61227-098-2

living—the most conspicuous examples being Jules Lermina and Michel Zevaco—and who embraced its conventional prejudices with an apparent wholeheartedness while retaining their tongues in their cheeks.

The notion of "organized crime" has now become so commonplace that it is not easy for modern readers to appreciate, without an imaginative leap, how unusual that concept was in 1912. It was not original, of course, and Le Mystérieux Docteur Cornélius *has a much more remote but even more obvious model than* La Conspiration des Milliardaires *in Paul Féval's pioneering series of seven romans feuilletons featuring* Les Habits Noirs *(1863-74)[40], but Le Rouge's updating of the notion was considerably more adventurous and spectacular than any of the other revisitations of the idea produced before the Great War.*

Cornelius Kramm is, in essence, an equivalent figure to Féval's Colonel Bozzo-Corona, and several other characters in the Le Rouge series also have near-equivalents either in the Colonel's coterie, or in the extensive cast of his victims and adversaries. The fact that Cornelius is an experimental scientist rather than a mere bandit, however, has numerous logical ramifications, which transform the fundamental nature of his conspiracy and its procedures. Arguable, they do not transform it nearly enough, because the logical ramifications in question are not extrapolated to what would nowadays be considered an adequate extent, but that is the inevitable fate of many pioneering enterprises; the writers who are boldest in taking first steps are often found wanting when it comes to developing more disciplined and far-ranging explorations. In spite of its limitations, however, the particular criminal conspiracy featured in Le Mystérieux Docteur Cornélius *does have some intriguing precedent-setting features. The notion of a criminal scientist employing his genius in the service of a vast criminal enterprise was not entirely new, and it must have seemed only logical in 1912 that anyone who was actually to undertake a large scale twentieth-century enterprise in plunder, making virtual war on a technologically-progressive society, would need scientific expertise in order to secure the necessary melodramatic inflation of its enterprise. That logic was, however, conspicuously lacking in much of the crime fiction of the era, and remarkably tentative in many of the instances in which it was manifest. Le Rouge is tentative too, but was nevertheless in the forefront of the early-20th century evolution of what was eventually to become a major literary mythology, fated to undergo an extraordinary elaboration and sophistication in the course of the century.*

B.S.

---

[40] Translated in Black Coat Press editions as *The Blackcoats*: '*Salem Street*, ISBN 978-1-932983-46-3; *The Invisible Weapon*, ISBN 978-1-932983-80-7; *The Parisian Jungle*, ISBN 978-1-934543-03-0; *The Companions of the Treasure*, ISBN 978-1-934543-26-9; *Heart of Steel*, ISBN 978-1-935558-05-7; *The Cadet Gang*, ISBN 978-1-935558-45-3; *The Sword-Swallower*, ISBN 978-1-61227-024-1.

1. The Red Hand Strikes

Eight men with hirsute beards of criminal appearance were sprawled idly around a large fire of brushwood, silently smoking a short-stemmed blue clay pipe, while a sheep, spitted on a long pole balanced between two forked branches, finished roasting in the flames.

The place where they were sitting was in a rugged gorge in the Californian Sierra, surrounded on all sides by sheer accumulations of rock covered in meager vegetation. A thin trickle of fresh water emerged from a cavern, near which stone bottles full of wine and whisky were piled up pell-mell, along with rifles, swords, pick-axes, spades, ropes and various other objects.

It would have been difficult to tell, at first glance, whether one was in the presence of a camp of gold-prospectors or a lair of bandits.

The second hypothesis would have been correct. The Black Canyon—that was the name the ravine had been given because of the dark color of its basalt rocks—had served for a long time as a refuge for a band of the thieves known as "tramps."

The tramps are the vagabonds of the New World, wandering incessantly from State to State, working for a few weeks in mines or large-scale agricultural enterprises, to depart afterwards at hazard, following the whim of their caprice, In France such travelers are usually inoffensive, only indulging in insignificant thefts, but it is not the same in America, where the cities are often separated by enormous distances, and where immense tract of wilderness exist; the tramps frequently form bands of audacious highwaymen.

The central authorities are almost powerless against them. They stop trains, pillage and set fire to isolated farms, rob travelers, and in the immense deserts of the West they constitute a redoubtable peril. Sometimes, they even form perfectly organized associations that terrorize an entire region, holding it to ransom.

It was to one of these associations that the eight individuals presently gathered in the Black Canyon belonged.

They were all wearing similar costumes: broad-brimmed hats, loosely-fitting waistcoats and trousers of coarse cloth, and stout knee-length boots, not forgetting brightly-colored belts through which were passed large-caliber revolvers and long daggers known as Bowie knives.

They all seemed to be waiting impatiently for the roast to be ready.

"I believe we can sit down at table," declared one of the tramps, suddenly. He was a man of athletic build whose gray beard came down to his belt. "For myself, I'm diabolically hungry."

Setting an example, Slug—that was the name of the man with the long beard—took out his Bowie knife, carved a large slice of bloody mutton, which he spread on a piece of biscuit, and set about eating it heartily. The other imitated him, and the animal's corpse was soon no more than a carcass, almost as well-cleaned as if the great red-brown vultures that were circling overhead had taken charge of the task.

When everyone had sat down and a bottle of whisky had been passed from hand to hand, the pipes were lit, charged with the harsh wood-cutter's tobacco known as "log cabin" and they chatted.

"I believed," said Slug, studying the sky, where large coppery clouds were accumulating, "that there's going to be a heavy downpour before nightfall. That'll be a stroke of luck."

"Why's that?" asked a young red-haired tramp, who answered to the name of Jackson.

"Because heavy rain doubles our chances," Slug replied, sententiously. Even if it only rains for a couple of hours, the bog in the defile will become impracticable."

"So the big job is today?" asked another. "You've had orders?"

"Yes," said Slug, proudly taking a greasy piece of paper from his pocket, which was covered with hieroglyphic symbols. "This is a letter that a cowboy gave me this morning while I was taking a turn around the mountain. It's signed by the Red Hand, and it's from the boss."

There was a profound silence at these words, which combined respect and curiosity. The seven tramps had drawn nearer to Slug, impatient to know more.

"What does it say, exactly?" asked Jackson.

"Yesterday, or even this morning," Slug replied, swelled up with importance, "I wouldn't have been able to tell you; now, it's different. I'll give you all the details. A fortnight ago, you saw a carriage going past hitched to four horses and escorted by a dozen armed cowboys and mounted policemen."

"Yes," Jackson replied. "And we asked why we weren't allowed to attack it—for the carriage to be escorted like that, it must have contained something precious,"

"It didn't contain anything at all—but today, it'll go along the same route, through the defile at the foot of the Black Canyon, and today—listen to me carefully—it's loaded with gold!"

The bandits' eyes sparkled with avarice beneath their bushy eyebrows.

"Yes," Slug went on "It contains the farm rents of the three large estates on the far side of the sierra, which belong, as you know, to William Dorgan, who's a partner with Fred Jorgell in the Corn and Cotton Trusts. Oh, I'm well-informed. I even know that one of William Dorgan's sons is leading the escort."

"As for that..." said one of the bandits, miming taking aim with a rifle.

"Well, no—that's where you're mistaken," said Slug, swiftly. "It's necessary to make sure that Joe Dorgan doesn't receive the slightest wound. He has to be taken alive; it seems that his capture is the most important part of the expedition. It would be better to let the money and the policemen go than not to make sure of his person. Is that understood?"

The seven tramps nodded their heads by way of assent, but they remained thoughtful.

At that very moment, large drops of rain flew through the air, and a heavy rainstorm soon began to descend. The tramps had to seek refuge in the grotto that served them as a storehouse. There, the rifles and revolvers were carefully checked and loaded, and Slug made sure that each of his men had an adequate supply of cartridges.

The rain had become torrential. Nothing any longer remained of the fire but a few blackened twigs, which the cascades tumbling down the rocks carried away to the bottom of the valley.

Slug rubbed his hands. "All this water," he said, "will accumulate in the bog in the defile; the carriage won't get out of that."

Suddenly, dominating the racket of the squall, three rifle shots rang out, repeated for some time by the echoes of the mountain.

Slug had gone slightly pale. "The bosses' signal," he murmured. "I need to go."

"When will you be back?" asked Jackson, also slightly nervous.

"I don't know. Wait for me. Don't do anything before I come back."

In the blink of an eye, he had slung his rifle behind his back, thrown an ample Mexican serape over his shoulders and had pulled his hat down over his eyes. Then he slid through the gap in the basaltic rocks and disappeared.

Left alone and watching the rain fall, which was covering the desolate landscape with a misty veil, the tramps waited silently, prey to a vague anxiety. Each of them felt a need to talk, but none of them dared speak first.

Finally, an old tramp named Bishop said in a slow voice: "I knew a Dorgan some years ago, who was also the son of a billionaire, but he wasn't called Joe, he was called Harry."

"It's not the same one," said Jackson. "It's his brother. I happen to know that the billionaire William Dorgan has two sons, Harry and Joe."

"It's Harry that I knew—the engineer. He was running the electric power plant in Jorgell City at the time. He was a good guy. I wouldn't like it if anything bad were to happen to his brother."

"Since the orders are not to do him any harm at all, you can sleep easy."

The conversation lapsed there, and no one dared strike it up again. Darkness was beginning to fall and the rain had not stopped. The tramps wondered, with a strange unease, what had become of their leader, and their anxiety was increasing when Slug reappeared. He was streaming with rain from head to toe, but his face was radiant.

"Everything's okay," he said, "but we don't have any time to lose. We need to have a bite to eat—we might have a long time to wait. Open a tin, let's have a little corned beef and a shot of whisky, and we'll be on our way."

Slug was obeyed precisely. In no time at all the tramps had eaten and gathered up their equipment, ready to leave. The return of their leader and the good of which he was giving evidence had animated them with a new ardor, but no one had dared to ask him any questions.

In water that came up to their knees the eight bandits followed the rugged slopes of the Black Canyon, which the rain had turned into a torrent, for some distance. They climbed over a mass of bizarrely-tormented rocks and came out into a defile bordered to the right and the left by imposing basalt walls.

"There's no other road," Slug declared. "They'll have to come through the defile, and we'll take them there. Once they've set foot in the bog I defy them to take another step. That's the moment we have to wait for before attacking. Then you open fire. Shoot at the horses first."

"Okay," said Jackson, "but how are we going to recognize Joe Dorgan. It might be that, without intending to shoot at him…"

"Never!" aid Slug, embarrassed by the objection. "I'm not exactly sure what to do—we'll have to try to recognize him by his costume."

"It seems to me that the simplest thing to do would be to shoot the policemen first. There'll be no mistaking them because of their uniforms."

"Yes, that's right—oh, one more thing that I forgot. Two envoys of the Red Hand might perhaps be taking a hand in the affair—it's necessary not to shoot them either."

Slug repeated these carful instructions to each of his men individually, and then posted each of them in a crack in the rock, where, through the profound darkness, further augmented by the rain, it would be impossible to see them.

An hour went by, slowly. In the holes where they were lying in ambush, the tramps felt fatigue and numbness grip them. Slug was extremely nervous, and noticed angrily that the rain was no longer falling as heavily.

"That's bad luck," he muttered between his teeth. "If the convoy's much later, the moon will be shining and the water will have time to drain away."

Impatience was beginning to get the better of him when he suddenly made out the faint sound of trotting horses.

Another quarter of an hour went by; the sound got closer and a dark mass, flanked by two red gleams of lantern-light, was silhouetted in the mist.

The carriage was now clearly visible, along with the dozen mounted guards accompanying it. The leader, cursing and complaining about the impossible route, forced the horses to follow the trail, which the rain had rendered similar to a pond—but when the carriage reached the deepest point, its heavy wheels stuck in the mud, and it was impossible to make further progress.

"We won't get out of this!" moaned the leader. "We're stuck in the mud all the way to the axle."

As if that statement were a signal, eight gunshots burst forth simultaneously. Three policemen fell to the ground, their skulls traversed by bullets; others were wounded, more or less seriously.

"The tramps!"

"The Red Hand bandits!"

"Help!

"We're doomed!"

All those cries erupted confusedly, and there were a few moments of terrible chaos, further augmented by the whinnying of a mortally-wounded horse.

One vibrant voice rose above the tumult, however; it was that of a rider who had so far remained behind the carriage. "Courage, my friends!" he cried. "If we weaken, we'll be wiped out to the last man. Take cover behind the carriage and return fire vigorously."

The bandits fired a second volley, but the policemen, following the advice of the rider—who was none other than Joe Dorgan—had had time to take refuge behind the carriage, and none of them was hit this time.

The policemen fired in their turn in the direction from which the bandits' gunfire was coming. A cry of pain responded to the discharge of the rifles. It was old Bishop, who, struck full in the chest, had just fallen out of the gap in the rock where he was ensconced.

"One less!" said Joe Dorgan. "Hold on! We'll end up getting the upper hand—they aren't as many as us."

The battle continued furiously, but the tramps, who, following Slug's orders, still remained hidden, had a considerable advantage over their adversaries. They could take aim accurately, while the policemen could only fire approximately and dared not quit the protective rampart that the carriage had become.

The battle might, however, have lasted a long time if Slug had not decided on a new tactic.

One tramp—it was Slug himself—suddenly bounded out of the darkness and plunged his Bowie knife to the hilt in the throat of one of the policemen, and fired almost instantly, blasting out the brains of another. Then he threw himself backwards, crawling toward the rocks.

"My friends," Joe Dorgan shouted, "let's abandon the money and beat a retreat!"

The men of the escort would certainly have liked nothing better than to obey, but all their horses had been killed or wounded, and flight, in those conditions, was almost impossible.

Nevertheless, they made the attempt.

By this time, there were only five of them, including Joe Dorgan. As soon as the battle began the lanterns had been broken, and the scene of the drama was only illuminated by the livid and intermittent flash of rifle-shots. The fugitives hoped to escape by courtesy of the darkness.

Two of them, going on ahead, slipped outside the protective shelter of the carriage. They had not gone two yards when they fell to the ground, shot dead.

"Forward!" cried Slug. "There are only three left!"

At this injunction, the tramps emerged from their holes, a Bowie knife in one hand and a revolver in the other.

In the blink of an eye, the fugitives were surrounded. Two revolver shots rang out. Jackson had just blown out the brains of the two policeman.

Joe Dorgan was left alone.

Browning in hand, he fought like a lion. He killed one of the tramps who tried to grapple him around the waist, and wounded Jackson in the shoulder, but he was bound to succumb to the force of numbers. Ten robust hands grabbed his arms and immobilized him. His Browning was torn out of his hand and he was tied up.

"Miserable murderers!" he howled, struggling. "Kill me, then, if you dare!"

No one deigned to reply.

"The battle's won now!" Slug shouted. "Give the wounded a few good thrusts with a Bowie knife, to take away any desire they might have to testify against us."

"That's already done," muttered an old tramp with a gray beard whose hands were dripping blood. Now it's a matter of getting the dollars out of the box."

The bandits had already surrounded the carriage when two riders emerged abruptly into the defile. By the light of the moon—which, now that the rain had stopped, was shining through the clouds—the tramps saw that the two newcomers were wearing masks over their faces.

Respectfully, Slug had hastened to meet them, and took hold of the bridles of their horses.

"The Red Hand's orders have been carried out faithfully," he said, his tone full of humility.

"That's good," said one of the men. In a low voice, he gave a few orders to Slug, and handed him a rather voluminous package.

Slug unwrapped the parcel. It contained a square flask and a wad of cotton wool.

Slug carefully soaked the cotton wool in the liquid contained in the flask, then, approaching slyly, he put it over the prisoner's face. Joe Dorgan uttered a dull groan; the insipid odor of chloroform filled his nostrils. He lost consciousness.

Immediately, Slug and one of the masked men carried him away carefully, and tied him securely to a horse that the emissaries of the Red Hand had taken care to bring with them and had left some way behind.

All that was done with extraordinary rapidity, under the stupefied gaze of the tramps, so intimidated by the presence of the "big bosses" that they had forgotten the carriage and the dollars.

The two masked men were preparing to climb back into the saddle when Slug thought he ought to ask for instructions regarding the carriage.

"Stupid question!" said one of the unknown men, impatiently. "Share it out according to the usual rules. We'll collect the Red Hand's share at a time to be arranged. And above all, no errors in the counting. We know the exact figure."

The unknown men mounted up. Placing the horse to which Joe Dorgan's inert body was tied between them, they disappeared at a gallop through the northern extremity of the defile

After having ridden for three hours in succession in the most profound silence through the roads carved into the mountain, they finally reached a properly constructed highway equipped with odometric markers and indicative signposts. Their horses were white with foam when they dismounted in front of a wretched inn constructed with badly-squared tree-trunks A silent stable-hand took their horses away after helping them to transport Joe Dorgan's body to a stone bench near the door.

No light appeared in the hovel's windows. The two men, who had now taken off their masks, paced up and down in the courtyard, chatting in low voices.

An hour went by. The emissaries of the Red Hand were beginning to show signs of impatience when the sound of an automobile became audible in the silence of the night.

Ten minutes later, a superb hundred-horsepower vehicle with luxurious bodywork, fitted out for long journeys, stopped in front of the inn with all its headlights on.

Like the servant who had taken charge of the horses, the chauffeur did not say a word. Silently, the two bandits and their prisoner, still inanimate, were installed in the interior of the vehicle, which immediately sped away in fourth gear.

Three days later, the same mysterious automobile, now covered with a thick layer of mud and dust, came into New York a little after midnight, and, after having traveled along Tenth Avenue at low speed, stopped in front of a luxurious property surrounded by high walls and closed by a wrought-iron gate. To one of the columns supporting the gate a black marble plaque was fixed, with an inscription in golden letters: *Dr. Cornelius Kramm*.

The chauffeur gave three blasts of the horn, regularly spaced. Both battens of the gate immediately opened, and the automobile was engulfed by the interior of the property.

The following day, news of the drama of which the desert near the Black Canyon had been the theater burst like a thunderbolt in New York, where the billionaire William Dorgan and his two sons were held in particularly high esteem.

By way of documentation, we shall reproduce one of the numerous articles that the *New York Herald* published on that subject:

A frightful crime has just thrown the State of California into consternation and put the family of one of our honorable fellow citizens, William Dorgan, in mourning. His younger son, Joe, has disappeared in tragic circumstances, and everything indicates that he has fallen victim to the bandits of the Red Hand.

Joe Dorgan, who, although only twenty-six years of age, had already given proof of brilliant talents as an administrator and a financier, had been charged by his father with recovering considerable sums due from the farmers of the immense estates that the billionaire possesses in the province of California. That region still has entirely desert regions entirely deprived of roads and railways, where public services are only organized as yet in the most defective fashion.

Joe Dorgan, who had completely his tour successfully, was returning with his escort, comprised of twelve mounted policemen. The money he had collected was contained in one of those robust carriages that are the only ones able to travel the rocky roads of the sierra. It was while passing through a defile, which recent storms had rendered almost impracticable, that the convoy was attacked.

Cowboys returning from one of the regional fairs found the atrociously-mutilated bodies of the twelve policemen next to the staved-in carriage and the disemboweled horses. One horrible detail is that each cadaver bore on the cheek the imprint of a hand crudely drawn in blood. The bandits of the Red Hand had left their sinister signature.

In spite of extensive searches, the body of the unfortunate Joe Dorgan has not been recovered. One dare not hope that he has been taken prisoner; it is supposed that the tramps must have thrown his body into one of the gulfs of the sierra. A company of mounted police is presently scouring the desert region, but thus far, the searches have only resulted in the discovery, in a rugged ravine known as the Black Canyon, of one of the lairs of the evil band, where an abundance of weapons, munitions and provisions of every sort were found. The hunt for the bandits continues, directed with indefatigable activity by the engineer Harry Dorgan, the victim's brother, who immediately traveled to the area.

We shall take advantage of this opportunity to give a few details of the Red Hand, the vast association of malefactors who, for several years now, has been terrorizing the western and central States of the Union. The Red Hand, powerfully organized and possessing, we are assured, ramifications all over the world, bears little resemblance to the famous Italian organization with the same name. Those making it up are almost all of American, German or Irish nationality. It includes among its ranks allies belonging to all classes of society—even, it appears, bankers, businessmen, physicians, officers and senior policemen in our big cities. That is what explains the inconceivable impunity from which the majority of its members has thus far benefited.

All the efforts made to exterminate these wretches have failed pitifully, but the limit has been reached. The crime that we have just related, which surpasses all the others in audacity and horror, ought to open the eyes of the public authorities. We hope that a special law will be voted by the Senate in Washington and that extraordinary credit will be put at the disposal of the police in order to track down the Red Hand's lairs and affiliates.

2. In Living Flesh

Dr. Cornelius Kramm was one of the most fashionable physicians in New York, and his establishment was scarcely frequented by anyone but billionaires, or at least multimillionaires. His enigmatic and sardonic physiognomy was displayed on the front pages of specialist periodicals as well as large-circulation dailies. His pamphlets, *The Esthetic Rationale of the Human Body* and *Scientific Means of Prolonging Youth in Men and Women*, were ardently read and commented on by scientists and socialites alike, and were universally appreciated.

At any rate, Cornelius Kramm was no ordinary physician. He left the vulgar work of curing disease to his colleagues; he only occupied himself with healthy people who were afflicted by some physical imperfection. In that field of endeavor he was worked virtual miracles.

Among a hundred others, the case of the brave Colonel MacDolmar, wounded by shrapnel in the Philippine War and deprived of his nose and half his face, was often cited. Dr. Cornelius had restored that wrecked physiognomy so effectively that scarcely any trace of the frightful mutilation remained. Thus, Dr. Cornelius Kramm was routinely designated by such nicknames as "the rejuvenator" or "the sculptor of human flesh." It was affirmed, doubtless with some exaggeration, that he was able to make a blind, toothless, wrinkled and jaundiced old spinster into a fresh and rosy young woman; many people were convinced that his power was unlimited.

The doctor, who had lived for some time in a new city in the Far West, had settled permanently in New York, where he owned an Academy of Beauty—an "Esthetic Institute," as they say in America—equipped according to the latest gifts of science and the supreme refinements of modern comfort.

Cornelius Kramm lived alone; his only family was a brother a little younger than himself, Fritz Kramm, who was a large-scale art dealer.

For several weeks the doctor had had as a guest a young American of a taciturn and misanthropic bent, whose was not—apparently, at least—undergoing any treatment, for he was endowed with a robust constitution and was in excellent health. He occupied an isolated room on the second floor of one wing of the house, completely isolated and overlooking the gardens. He only came down in the evenings to smoke a cigar while taking a long walk in the shade of the gardens, almost as vast as a park. Sometimes, too, he went to join the doctor in one of his laboratories, and had long conversations with him.

The individual who led this almost eremitic existence appeared to be perfectly satisfied with his situation. When he was alone, he plunged himself with extraordinary ardor into the most recent treatises on chemistry and physiology;

that work possessed such an attraction for him that he was never bored for a moment, and only took as much exercise as was necessary for his health.

Another bizarre feature of that reclusive existence was that every morning, an old Italian named Leonello, who had been in the doctor's service for many years, came to the recluse's room and took one or several photograph of him; he had accumulated about a hundred of them, in all possible poses: full face, in profile, sitting or standing, naked or fully-dressed.

That formality was not to the taste of the man who was its object and he had sought in vain to know why his image was being thus multiplied in the most diverse aspects. To all his questions, Leonello replied with evasive statements. Once, the young man attempted to refuse to pose, but the old Italian had only had to say, very courteously, that it was the doctor's orders; the recalcitrant photographic model had not persisted and had posed with a good grace in front of the lens of a powerful apparatus that produced life-sized prints of a perfect clarity.

One evening, when the strange guest of the Academy of Beauty was walking slowly along the shady paths of the garden, contemplating the star-filled sky with a pensive gaze, he thought her heard footsteps behind him, but was reassured when he turned round to find himself face to face with Leonello.

"Are you taking a little walk, as I am?" he asked the old Italian.

"No," the other replied, with an obsequious smile. "I was looking for you."

"The doctor wants to see me?"

"Precisely."

"I'm delighted. I'll join him immediately. Tell me, is he in his study or the laboratory?"

"I'll take you. He is indeed in the laboratory, but not the one you know."

"Give me directions."

"There's no point; you wouldn't be able to find it without me, so it's preferable that I accompany you."

"All right, I'll follow you."

"Take note that the laboratory to which I'm taking you is rigorously proscribed to everyone, even the doctor's closest friends, who do not know of its existence as yet. It's a great favor that he's doing you in admitting you to it."

While he was speaking, Leonello and his companion had gone into the main building and into a long corridor with marble floor-tiles, which mercury vapor lamps illuminated with a soft blue-tinted light. They stopped at the cage of an elevator.

"The doctor's laboratory isn't on the ground floor, then?" said the unknown man, surprised.

"No," said the Italian, tranquilly. "It's a subterranean laboratory." And he pressed the control button.

The elevator set off, and stopped in a kind of vestibule with ceramic walls that were absolutely bare, into which thick doors lined with leather opened. A rhythmic sound of piston-rods testified that the basement must contain powerful machinery.

"We've arrived," said Leonello. Pushing one of the doors, he stood aside to allow his companion to go in first.

As he emerged from the semi-darkness of the vestibule, the doctor's guest was dazzled.

He found himself in a vast room with a dome-like vault, the walls of which were entirely covered in white porcelain. Under the blinding electric lights, a confused mass of strange apparatus extended as far as the eye could see. On pedestals there were barbarously colored life-size anatomical models devoid of skin; cages mounted on glass floors according to the Arsonval method,[41] which permits an invalid to be surrounded by beams of electric radiance; armchair equipped with jacks, by means of which limbs could be immobilized or distended; and in one display-case there was a group of wax automata, colored so artfully as to give the illusion of life. Finally, in one corner, on the marble floor-tiles, semi-dissected cadavers were lying, in a state of perfect conservation, doubtless due to powerful antiseptics.

The atmosphere of that fantastic laboratory was saturated with an extraordinary balsamic odor that seemed singularly vivifying, the absorption of which doubtless formed an integral part of the treatment to which invalids were submitted.

On perceiving the newcomer, Cornelius Kramm had set down a test-tube into which he was in the process of decanting the contents of a flask, and came forward, smiling as amiably as was possible, given his sinister physiognomy.

"Good evening, my dear Baruch," he said, indicating a seat. "I'm delighted to see you. I've permitted myself to disturb you this evening because I need to have a serious chat with you."

"You have a splendid laboratory here," murmured Baruch Jorgell, more emotional than he wanted to appear.

"Yes, isn't it?" the doctor replied, negligently. "It cost me a great deal, but in terms of its installation the laboratory has the advantage that I'm perfectly tranquil here. I could, if the whim took me, skin one of my clients alive here, and let him howl as much as he pleased; no one would hear a sound."

"That is, indeed, convenient," Baruch murmured, less and less reassured.

The doctor had perceived his interlocutor's disturbance; a mocking smile tucked up his thin lips; his rounded, lashless eyes, like those of a bird of prey, sparkled behind his gold-rimmed spectacles.

---

[41] Jacques-Arsène Arsonval (1851-1940) was the great pioneer of the field of electrophysiology: the study of the effects of electricity on living organisms. In 1892 he was appointed as the director of a new biophysics laboratory at the College de France.

"Don't worry," he sniggered. "I only indulge in experiments in vivisection very rarely, and even then, it's always in the interests of science."

"What do you want to talk to me about, then?"

"I'll get to that. Do you remember, my dear Baruch, the situation you were in when you arrived here?"

"I remember that I had good reasons for coming. I'm obliged to you, and I'll never forget it, but there's no use talking about the past."

"On the contrary, it's very useful. I understand that certain memories are painful to you, but it's indispensable hat there should be no species of misunderstanding between us."

"Go on," said Baruch, unable to help going pale.

"When you came to me asking for shelter, you were accused of having murdered a French chemist, Monsieur de Maubreuil, whom you had robbed of his diamonds; you were being hunted everywhere; your description had been posted, there was a price on your head and hundreds of detectives were at your heels."

"That's true," the murderer replied, having had time to recover his composure. "You saved me; I'm not seeking to deny it. You even mentioned at the time an association between us and your brother that might lead to 'grandiose results'—your word. Since then, however, you haven't said any more about it."

"Well, the moment has come to acquaint you with those plans, which, as I told you, are grandiose—I don't take back the word. I'll get to the point. Let's see: between the two of us, are you enthusiastic to conserve your present physiognomy?"

"My physiognomy?"

"Yes—by which I mean the color of your hair, the expression of your face, the color of your skin: in brief, everything that constitutes your physical personality."

"I don't care about it in the least. I suppose you want to dye my hair and put on make-up to render me unrecognizable."

Dr. Cornelius shrugged his shoulders. "Dye and make-up—what a joke!" And he added, in a grave tone: "It's not a matter of that. The changes that you will undergo will be so radical and profound that you'll be a veritably new man."

"Impossible!"

"It's very possible. The experiment is certainly bold, but it doesn't involve any serious danger. My brother Fritz explained to you the other day some of the means that I employ to achieve my objectives; you've been able to observe that they're very ingenious and extremely simple."

"But why a complete transformation?" Baruch murmured, his heart constricted by a vague anguish. "Wouldn't a little retouching be sufficient?"

"No, not retouching! I see that I'll have to spell it out. One evening—today, for example—you'll go to sleep in the skin of Baruch Jorgell, notorious

260

criminal, wanted by the police of the entire world; and when you wake up, you'll have become, thanks to the magic of Science, one of the most brilliant members of the aristocracy, of the Five Hundred, the fortunate son of a billionaire father."

Baruch thought for a moment that the doctor had gone mad. "It's a dream," he murmured. "Science can't and never will be able to effect such a metamorphosis."

"Ha ha!" sniggered Cornelius. "If you think that, you don't know the resources of *carnoplasty*—a science that I've created in all its aspects. It's not for nothing, believe me, that they call me the *sculptor of human flesh*!"

Baruch Jorgell trembled in every limb. He already believed that he was to be subjected to an atrocious experiment, dissected while alive.

"I'd rather stay as I am," he stammered, in a voice choked by fear.

The doctor had risen to his feet, his face radiant with pride. "I could proceed without your permission," he said, "but I'd rather employ reasoning to convince you. When I've explained, you'll understand where your true interests lie." Abruptly, he added: "You know Joe Dorgan, the billionaire's son?"

"Quite well," said Baruch, surprised. "We took some of the same classes at Boston. Since then I've lost sight of him; I'm more familiar with his brother Harry, the engineer. He ran the power plant at Jorgell City, as you know, and courted my sister Isidora—that one I detest mortally."

"It's not a matter of him," the doctor put in, dryly. "It's a matter of his brother Joe. Be aware of the fact that there's a certain resemblance between you and Joe Dorgan. You're almost the same height and build. It's that resemblance that I'll guarantee to render as complete as possible. After a few weeks of treatment, it will be definitive."

"Including the face?"

"Even the face."

"Then there'll be two Joe Dorgans?"

"Not at all—because, thanks to science, the real Joe Dorgan will have taken on the exact physical appearance of the excessively famous Baruch Jorgell. Do you understand now? You'll pass your somewhat spoiled personality, as one does a fake coin, on to an obliging neighbor, who will give you his in exchange. It's quite simple."

Baruch was literally astounded.

"It's frightful!" he said. "It would be wonderful if it were possible, but I can see a thousand difficulties—to start with, Joe Dorgan wouldn't want to wear my false personality. He'd put up a devil of a struggle! He'd demand an investigation. The truth would come out."

Cornelius sniggered briefly.

"That's an eventuality that will never materialize," he said. "I give you my word that Joe Dorgan won't raise the slightest protest, for the very god reason that he'll have completely lost his memory of past events."

"Even if that's the case," Baruch replied, energetically, "and even if I succeed in putting on the exact appearance of Joe Dorgan, I couldn't simulate his voice, his gestures, his opinions or his thinking."

"All that is possible," the doctor continued, enthusiastically. "I have simple means of giving you Joe's voice and gait, even his gestures; you'll know the slightest memories of his past and his most secret thoughts. You'll possess his soul, to the extent that such a thing is realizable."

Baruch Jorgell recoiled in fear, his teeth chattering in terror. He understood that Cornelius was not lying, and that what he had announced he was going to do, in spite of any resistance. "What kind of man are you, then?" he stammered, wildly.

"Oh, nothing but a simple scientist—a very modest scientist, I assure you. There's no sorcery in the procedures I employ. I've simply perfected certain formulae in current use. When I've published the book about carnoplasty that I'm writing, the prodigies I accomplish, which excite so much astonishment, will be within the range of all physicians."

In spite of all Cornelius' eloquence, Baruch remained hesitant. "Well, no," he said, abruptly. "I refuse."

"As you wish," sniggered the doctor. "You're perfectly free, after all, not to accept my offer. You understand, though, that since you're opposing one of my projects—and your own interests—I can no longer keep you here. You'll leave here today, and once outside, you know what awaits you: prison and the infamous electric chair."

Baruch ground his teeth like a wolf caught in a trap. "I'll do as you wish," he muttered, effortfully. "I'm at your disposal. Oh, I knew you'd make me pay dearly for the service you've rendered me."

"I'm delighted to see you become more reasonable, but I repeat, it's wrong for you to be alarmed. Your life isn't in danger and you won't experience any pain. When I've succeeded, you'll be the first to heap me with blessings."

"I doubt that very much, but since I have to serve as the subject of this frightful experiment, start as soon as possible. I've made my decision."

"I know that you're courageous; we'll begin this evening, then. I'm glad to observe that you're in a perfect state of health, for tonight will be employed in operations that will require a certain measure of endurance on your part."

"I'm ready," the murderer murmured, resignedly. "But where's the man whose place I have to take?"

Cornelius Kramm pressed a switch. A curtain slid along its rod, uncovering an extension of the laboratory where there was a bed surrounded by a network of electric wires. On the bed lay a young man of almost exactly the same height and build as Baruch, but whose physiognomy more no resemblance, even distant, to the latter's. He seemed to be sleeping peacefully; his eyelids were closed and there was a vague smile on his lips.

While asleep he was recounting things in a low voice that were doubtless very interesting, for a recording phonograph was placed next to his bed on a small table.

"I have the honor of introducing to you the honorable Joe Dorgan," said Cornelius, sarcastically. "As you can see, he's admirably disposed to submit to the experiment we're about to undertake."

"But how did he get here?" Baruch asked, with a secret thrill of fear.

"Don't worry about that," said Cornelius. "What is interesting for you to know is that for more than a week, Joe Dorgan has been plunged into a hypnotic trance. I've given his orders to recall all his childhood memories and recount them, with the most trivial details, and the most minute accuracy. All of that will be scrupulously noted, in order that you might profit from it whenever you wish.

As Cornelius Kramm initiated him into the practical means of realizing his audacious plan, Baruch Jorgell gradually overcame his terrors. "Will it be necessary, then," he asked, "for me also to expose details of my memories and my projects to you?"

"Not at all. That will be completely unnecessary. Haven't I just told you that Joe Dorgan will lose all memory of his past life? When plastic surgery has given him an exact external resemblance to you, he'll undergo a small operation to the larynx to give him your voice, then a slight prick in the brain to relieve him of his memory."

"Why not simply make him disappear?"

"Fritz asked me the same thing, but I don't want that. First of all, the existence of a false Baruch is a guarantee of safety for you. Then again, I have my self-respect as a scientist. It pleases me to toy with difficulty and succeed in achieving a double transformation that the whole world would regard as implausible, or even impossible."

"Perhaps you're right. When the pseudo-Baruch has been well and truly electrocuted as Monsieur de Maubreuil's murderer, no one will ever think to search for me in the skin of Joe Dorgan."

"Don't forget that, thanks to me, you'll become William Dorgan's heir. One might say that you were born under a lucky star. Rejected by Fred Jorgell, you've immediately found another father, no less a billionaire than the first, in the person of William Dorgan." Cornelius Kramm added, sarcastically: "From now on, my dear Baruch, you'll be able to show your gratitude to your friends in a regal fashion."

"And I won't fail, you can be sure of that."

"If you were to fail," the doctor went on, with a muted threat in his voice, "It would be most imprudent on your part. My brother and I are not men who can be mocked with impunity."

"I never had any such intention!" Baruch protested, vehemently.

"Come on, calm down. We have complete confidence in you—otherwise, as you can imagine, it would be easy enough for us to choose someone else.

We've wasted enough time in explanations. We need to get to work immediately."

"I'm at your orders," said Baruch, calmly—and after contemplating his own features, which he would never see again, for one last time, in the full-length mirror handing on the wall, he sat down intrepidly in the large metallic armchair that Cornelius indicated to him.

The latter took a bottle from a cupboard and brought it close to Baruch's nostrils. The latter immediately fell into a deep sleep.

3. Another Man's Skin

The long and delicate operations by means of which Dr. Cornelius Kramm intended to bring about the strange metamorphosis lasted for several days, and were undertaken methodically.

Firstly, with Leonello's aid, the doctor took molds of his two subjects, and the two molds, mounted on pedestals, were reclad, thanks to color photography, with exactly lifelike complexions. With the aid of injections of warm paraffin wax beneath the epidermis, he provided Baruch's slightly thin features with the roundness that Joe's face possessed; by means of a skilful resection of the cartilage, he rectified the form of the nose. The resemblance of the two physiognomies began to appear in a striking fashion.

With his skeletal arms bare to the elbows, Cornelius toiled with a feverish ardor. Reshaping the living substance itself, adding and subtracting according to need, he truly merited his nickname.

When he had completed the initial sketch, with the aid of the scalpel and injections by means of a hypodermic syringe, he armed himself with a microscope. By means of pink and pale brown pigments, he reproduced the slightest flaws in the epidermis. No artist had ever put so much care into perfecting his work.

The hair and beard demanded laborious work in themselves. Hairs, measured to the centimeter, were depilated electrically, one at a time, from areas where they were too thick. In the places where they were too thin, Leonello made use of a special needle to plant the required number, as hairdressers do in cases of incurable baldness.

As for the teeth, the operation presented little difficulty; imprints in wax were taken from both patients by Cornelius; with the aid of a few strokes with a file and a few implants, a perfect result was obtained. The exact shade of the hair was produced by an indelible dye. The doctor had made a special study of alkaloids that have the property of modifying the color of the eyes; he decided that, in order to endow Brauch with Joe's dark eyes, internal treatment was indispensable.

Once these tasks were complete, Cornelius stood for some time in contemplation before his work.

"The resemblance is perfect!" he proclaimed, proudly. "It's impossible to do better. Now the proof is complete; I possess the secret of molding the human face to my whim, my fingers modeling living flesh like clay!"

Leonello extracted him from that lyrical enthusiasm. "Master," he said, "the work might be regarded as almost complete with regard to Baruch, but he's still more corpulent than Joe."

"It's easy to remedy that imperfection. By submitting the subject to a high-tension electrical current, an abundant transpiration will be produced. Like certain jockeys on the eve of a race, Baruch will grow thinner instantaneously, so to speak, or at least in a matter of hours. You can take care of that."

The singular treatment indicated by Cornelius was a complete success.

When Baruch came to, he experienced a strange and dolorous sensation. It seemed to him that he had been asleep for years. He felt a dull ache throughout his body, and he was as weak as an infant.

He opened his eyes and recognized, with a kind of stupor, that he was in his room.

Gradually, he recovered consciousness of himself. He remembered his visit to the subterranean laboratory, the strange pact that he had concluded—and then a kind of mist clouded his memories.

He tried to move.

He could not budge; his entire body was imprisoned in powerful elastic bandages and molds that immobilized him. His face was covered by a steel mask that tugged dolorously at his eyelids and the corners of his mouth.

He made an effort to escape the vice-like grip that held all the parts of his body, but could not do it. He uttered a dolorous groan. It was then that he perceived, a short distance away, the obsequious face of the laboratory assistant Leonello.

"Don't move," said the Italian. "I'm happy to tell you that the experiment undertaken by my illustrious master, Dr. Cornelius Kramm, has succeeded brilliantly. In a few weeks you'll be completely healed and can return to the palace of your father, Mr. William Dorgan, who is inconsolable over your loss."

Baruch's head reeled, vertigo invading his anemic brain. So the sculptor of human flesh had carried out his frightful promise to the letter. He was gripped by an irresistible desire to see his face. He could not bring himself to believe that Leonello was telling the truth.

"A mirror!" he stammered. "I want a mirror..." But he fell silent abruptly, gripped by a mad terror. It was no longer his own voice that he could hear; he no longer recognized its intonations.

"Stay calm," said Leonello, swiftly. "The doctor has recommended that you don't talk, and that you remain completely still. He's even forbidden you to eat for some time yet. I'll nourish you myself with the aid of liquid aliments."

Baruch uttered a stifled groan, whose significance Leonello understood. "Don't worry," he said. "It won't last long and you'll be well looked after. I shan't leave your bedside. I'll be here night and day, ready to divine whatever you might need. I understand what you want. You want to see your new physiognomy—it's a perfectly legitimate desire, after all, and I'll satisfy it right away. I'll free you—but just for a moment."

With infinite precaution, Leonello loosened the fastenings of the mask, removed it, and brought a mirror close to the patient's face.

Baruch Jorgell uttered a cry of amazement.

The astonished and melancholy face that was looking at him from the depths of the mirror was no longer his own. He had before him the features of the young man he had seen asleep in the subterranean laboratory before his metamorphosis: the features of Joe Dorgan.

He could not bear to contemplate that physiognomy—which was, henceforth, his own physiognomy—for long.

He closed his eyes; it seemed to him that he had just seen a ghost.

"Have you seen enough?" asked the Italian, ironically. "I hope you're content with your new face. I'll put your mask on again now."

Baruch made no gesture of protest; he allowed it to be done meekly. He felt madness invading his skull. He tried to go to sleep in order to stop thinking. Doubtless thanks to the narcotic drugs that he had been obliged to absorb, he fell into a profound slumber.

When he woke up the next day, he experienced the same painful sensations as the previous day, albeit to a lesser extent. During the time he remained awake, however, he was prey to a mortal ennui. He received a visit from Dr. Cornelius that day, accompanied by Fritz Kramm, who was frankly ecstatic about the marvelous result.

"It's astonishing," he declared. "I would never have believed that one could achieve such perfection in resemblance. It's truly prodigious."

"Except," Cornelius Kramm sniggered, "that it's not very agreeable for the person who submits to such an operation—but that's perfectly understandable." And as a flash of hatred passed through the eyes of the convalescent, still reduced to silence and immobility, he added by way of palliation: "But what a triumph when the treatment is finished!"

"It would, indeed, require a very shrewd detective to unearth Baruch Jorgell from beneath the skin of Joe Dorgan, which his double has put on like a new suit..."

"And which suits him marvelously."

"He certainly looks younger."

"More elegant!"

"More distinguished!"

"One can never be too elegant and distinguished when one's the son of a billionaire."

Baruch, who was forbidden to open his mouth, was put to the torture by these ironic consolations.

Leonello, meanwhile, left no stone unturned in trying to soothe the convalescent's lack of patience. He explained the progress of the healing process every day, and gave him the most devoted attention.

The days went by. Baruch Jorgell was devoured by ennui and impatience.

Finally, little by little, the wounds closed, the flesh violently brought together knitted, and one item and a time, the apparatus was removed. Baruch was able to get up and to take solid food.

For the murderer, thus miraculously metamorphosed, it was a true joy when the doctor permitted him to go down into the garden, supported by Fritz and Leonello.

He was completely cured, no longer experiencing any extreme weakness, but he was assailed by strange sensations. He was out of place in his new physical envelope; his body, retouched, so to speak, and remolded by the sculptor of human flesh, felt uncomfortable, like a garment that was too tight. His limbs vacillated; his gestures were uncertain, hive voice hesitant. He felt throughout his person the strange numbness of someone emerging by virtue of a miracle from a coffin.

"You're not yet accustomed to your new envelope," said the doctor who observed him attentively. "You still retain a certain awkwardness, a certain heaviness in your gestures and attitudes, which will soon disappear. In any case, I'm in a hurry to complete your cure."

"Why is that?"

"It's necessary for you to go to work." As Baruch manifested a certain astonishment, he went on: "Don't you remember what I said to you? Obviously, it's already a great deal to possess a physical resemblance to Joe Dorgan, but that's not all. You already have his voice; you require his speech, his thoughts, his gestures, tics and manias—everything, in sum, that constitutes a personality."

"But how can I do that?" Baruch asked, who had not yet had time to think about that in his mental confusion.

"I've thought of everything. In my subterranean laboratory there are several thousand phonograph scrolls that Joe was kind enough to dictate himself, and which contain everything we need. It will require a complete abstraction of your old self, and to for you habituate yourself to certain words and phrases. Do you have a good memory?"

"Not bad."

"Then all will be well."

"Permit me one more question," said Baruch, marveling. "That's all very well for words and phrases—but what about mannerisms and gait?"

"Everything's been anticipated, nothing left to chance. I've taken care to film Joe Dorgan in all his attitudes, standing, walking, lying down, sitting, eating and reading. You'll only have to imagine for a while that you're an actor, studying your part conscientiously."

"I'm sure I'll succeed," said Baruch. "I'll put all the time that's necessary into it—I want the adaptation to be perfect."

As Cornelius had foreseen, within a few days Baruch had forgotten his suffering and his seclusion, and was proud of having emerged alive and victorious from such a fantastic experiment. He showed all the more enthusiasm because he had initially been so hesitant.

From the next day onwards, he went down to the subterranean laboratory early in the morning and stayed there until the evening, working with a kind of fury to engrave in his memory, in an indelible fashion, the victim's attitudes and his very thoughts. He resumed work the following day, untiringly.

While the calm voice of the phonograph repeated the phrases, cheerful or sad, joking or serious, extracted from Joe Dorgan under the influence of hypnotic power, Baruch repeated them word for word, trying hard to reproduce the exact intonation. At other times, facing a cinematographic apparatus supervised by Leonello, he studied and reproduced the habitual gestures and facial expressions of his involuntary double.

There was something terrible about that phonographic phantom capering on the white screen in monochrome, while Baruch, his face contorted, strove to reproduce all his attitudes exactly.

From time to time, the Kramm brothers subjected their accomplice to a kind of examination. The doctor rubbed his hands, more satisfied every day.

"You're doing well," he said. "It's almost perfect. A few more hours of conscientious work, and you'll be completely Dorganified."

Baruch Jorgell was a scoundrel devoid of any kind of scruple; he had never felt remorse and had consented without hesitation to commit a further crime, but as he penetrated more deeply, with the aid of the phonographic conversation that he was obliged to learn by heart, into the thought of his victim, he felt a kind of embarrassment, akin to the commencement of shame.

Joe Dorgan had had an exemplary youth. As soon as he had completed his college studies at Boston, like his brother, the engineer Harry Dorgan, who was two years younger, he had become a valuable collaborator for his father. Very charitable, very sober and very hard-working, Joe had no vices; he was a loyal and honest friend.

On observing all these qualities, which he was obliged to assimilate whether he liked it or not, the murderer was prey to a cold rage. "Why," he cried, angrily, "Am I obliged to play this terrible role? Cornelius is a wretch! One might think that he were seeking to amuse himself by making me play the hypocritical role of a petty saint. But patience! The time is approaching when I'll be able to recompense myself for this abominable constraint!"

Grating his teeth, forcing himself to ape the honest man, Baruch got back to work, and his exasperation increased by the day.

Soon, however, another phenomenon emerged.

Spending all day in the subterranean laboratory filled with strange machinery, grimacing manikins and half-dissected cadavers, the murderer fell prey to frightful nightmares. His sleep was populated with variegated masks. The atmosphere, saturated with electricity and charged with gases with penetrating odors, gradually infected his brain; he realized that if his sojourn in that accursed place were to be prolonged, he would go completely mad.

When, in the evening, the enervations of fatigue set in and he happened to glance at himself in a mirror, he recoiled in fright. "It's terrible," he stammered, shivering in his every limb. "I'm becoming the authentic phantom, the living specter of my victim!"

Sometimes, at dusk or in the morning twilight, it was no longer Joe's face that the mirror reflected back to him; it was a face that was grave and sad beneath the long gray hair that crowned it: the vengeful face of Monsieur de Maubreuil, the French chemist he had murdered in order to steal his diamonds.

"Back, phantom!" he cried, his teeth chattering.

And, white with fear, he hastened to cover the mirror, or turn it to face the wall.

4. A Revenant

A few months before Joe Dorgan's disappearance, the excellent Mrs. Griffon, who ran an honorably-stocked boarding house in New York, had experienced a bitter disappointment.

A traveling salesman of chemical products—that, at least, was how he represented himself—had succeeded, thanks to false promises, in obtaining credit for several weeks. Then, abruptly, one Saturday, on the very day that he was supposed to settle his bill, he had disappeared, and since then, no one had had any news of him.

For an entire week, Mrs. Griffon had filled the hotel parlor with her lamentations.

"What a crook!" she exclaimed, indignantly, in talking about her boarder. "It's shameful, to deceive my trust like that, unworthy of a true Yankee!" And she concluded, dolefully: "I've had a lesson there from which I'll profit: never again will I give credit to anyone; I've sworn a solemn oath."

Mrs. Griffon might perhaps have resigned herself to that misfortune if some of her clients had not put a malign insistence into reminding her that the bad payer who had taken flight had borne an undeniable resemblance to the famous Baruch Jorgell, the murder of a French chemist. And they displayed before her, as if taking pleasure in it, copies of newspapers and magazines reproducing the murderer's photograph.

"You see, Mistress," they repeated, "you missed a superb opportunity there to get your hands on a reward of several thousand dollars."

269

"Then, you think that that mild young man really was the murderer of Monsieur de Maubreuil and a diamond-thief?"

"We're perfectly sure of it," clamored the chorus of boarders. "Just look at his picture."

And, in fact, there was a perfect resemblance between the celebrated murderer and the indelicate debtor...

After long reflection, she decided to go to the police station and make a formal declaration. She expected to be complimented for her zeal. To her great surprise, she was given a rather poor welcome by the chief of detectives.

"You'd have done well not to disturb yourself, Madam," he cried, furiously. "It's not today that you should have come. What were you thinking? You have at your table, every day, a rogue whose head is worth its weight in gold; you even remark naively that he resembles the portrait published in all the papers, and you only have the idea to come and see me when the bird has flown? Truly, it's unforgivable."

"But I didn't know! Do you think, sir, that if I'd known...? I even gave him credit..."

"You were stupid. Naturally, he didn't pay you?"

"No, sir."

"You're too naïve. He did well—you only got what you deserved. Now the murderer in on his way to some foreign land, or has gone to ground in some remote spot. We'll never find him!" As he showed the manageress of the boarding house out, he added, with a very ungracious expression: "The trail's gone cold—very cold, by now—and it's your fault. A pleasure to see you, Madam!"

She was in a very bad mood when she got back to the hotel.

The step that Mrs. Griffon had taken was not entirely useless however. Her deposition was reproduced by several newspapers, which brought a host of reporters to the hotel, desirous of knowing the slightest details about the famous Baruch Jorgell: his habits, his favorite games and the brand of his favorite tobacco.

Avid for exact information, the newspapers published full-length portraits of Mrs. Griffon and photographs of her parlor and dining-room.

After the reporters and the amateur detectives came the curiosity-seekers. There was an uninterrupted procession of idlers, delighted to visit the famous criminal's room and sit down in the very place where he had taken his meals. The hotel was never empty.

Since success had come, the proprietress had taken on a new importance in her own eyes. In the parlor where she presided over the distractions of her guests every evening, she took her stance in her armchair beside the piano in the manner of a great lady; now, it was only after being begged for a long time that she consented to tell new guests the hundred-times-repeated story of the murderer Baruch Jorgell, who had doubtless come to kill her.

"In sum," she concluded, "I only escaped death thanks to the protection of Providence."

And the entire audience shivered as they thought about the peril she had run.

For her, the solemn moment of the day was the one she devoted to reading the newspapers, in which exciting accounts were rendered of crimes, suicides and lynchings, in which the rich imagination of the reporters did not spare improbabilities.

But it was destined that Mrs. Griffon would not be long delayed in playing a leading role herself in one of the police tragedies that exercised such a powerful attraction upon her.

One evening, Mrs. Griffin, enthroned in her usual place between the piano and the tea-table, had just finished reading a long article devoted to Joe Dorgan, whose cadaver had not yet been discovered, when the electric bell of the outside door resounded precipitately.

"Toby," Mrs. Griffon ordered the waiter who had just served the tea and stale cake, "see who's at the door. If the person is of respectable appearance, show them into the waiting-room."

"Very good, Madam."

"I don't know," she added, "who can be presenting themselves at this hour."

Toby went out. He came back almost immediately, his face pale and his entire body agitated by a tremor of horror.

"What's the matter?" demanded Mrs. Griffon, majestically.

"Madam...Madam...!" stammered the waiter, inarticulately.

"What's the matter?"

"Madam..." Toby repeated, fearfully. The poor devil was so terrified that nothing more could be extracted from him.

Mrs. Griffon was more deeply disturbed than she wanted to appear. "Something extraordinary has happened," she murmured. "I'll go see for myself what intruder can have given Toby such a fright."

Slowly, to show that she was fully in control of herself, she folded up her newspaper, adjusted her pince-nez, and marched to the door in a deliberate manner.

She did not have time to go into the next room. She was almost knocked over by an individual with a distraught expression, in dirty and creased clothes, who came into the parlor like a gust of wind. He darted a glance around full of supplication and horror.

The newcomer had raised his head and was stammering incomprehensible words. His bony, emaciated face appeared in the bright light.

Mrs. Griffon, along with all the other people present, emitted a cry of fright. One old lady fainted; others took refuge behind the piano. As for Toby, he had disappeared under the table.

"Baruch Jorgell!" someone shouted, in the midst of an indescribable din.

"It's him! How dare he come back here!"

"He's going to kill us all!"

"Help!"

"Murder!"

Mrs. Griffon had remained standing still momentarily, as if frozen by amazement, but in the general panic she was the one who regained her courage first and understood, with admirable self-composure the necessities of the situation.

"Ladies and gentleman!" she commanded, in a thunderous voice. "Shut the doors and prevent the murderer from doing any harm, before he has time to make use of his weapons!"

It must be said that Baruch Jorgell did not appear at all redoubtable. He continued looking around with a vague and unconscious gaze, as if he had suddenly fallen into the hotel parlor from the moon.

At the masculine and comforting voice of Mrs. Griffon, the most cowardly recovered their courage. In the blink of an eye, Baruch, who had not raised a hand to defend himself, was grabbed by ten vigorous arms. He was knocked to the ground, solidly tied up with the curtain-cords and deposited in an armchair, without ceasing to roll his bewildered and bleak gaze around him.

After that brilliant capture, the entire assembly uttered a triumphant hurrah.

Mrs. Griffon was radiant with joy and pride. "Now, Toby," she said, with an admirable simplicity, "will you please fetch two policemen."

I shall take my revenge valiantly, she thought. *When I went to give information, I was poorly received. We'll see what they have to say this time.*

Her gaze brooded upon the wretch extended in the armchair as if he were a treasure. His own eyes were now welling with tears.

"It's really him, though," she murmured. "I recognize him—but one would think that he's lost his mind; he has an idiotic expression. It's God's punishment; remorse has doubtless addled his brain."

The hotel's boarders now formed a large circle around the murderer, whom they contemplated with wide eyes. So this was the cunning bandit, the murderer covered with crimes who had defied the police of the two worlds! A profound silence reigned in the parlor.

In spite of the gravity of the circumstances, Mrs. Griffon could scarcely hide a smile of satisfaction. Like the milkmaid in the fable, she was already counting up all the profits and advantages that such an important capture were going to bring her.

First of all, the reward, which was about to drop a thick wad of banknotes into her coffers; then there was the increasing and naturally gratuitous advertising from which the boarding-house was about to benefit. And was not all of that very little by comparison with the value of the glory of having rid society of a criminal of that magnitude? She could already see her picture appearing in pride of place alongside that of Baruch Jorgell.

On reflection, she thought that, with a view to future interviews, it might be as well to proceed with an initial interrogation, before the reporters and detectives had deflowered such a sensational subject.

"Ladies and gentlemen," she said, with as much gravity as if she were presiding over a court of law, "Does it not seem to you to be indispensable to address a few questions to the murderer?"

"Yes, of course, it's absolutely necessary," cried all the boarders, with one voice.

Baruch Jorgell, whose lamentable face was bathed by a torrent of tears, darted the gaze of a hunted beast around him.

"Infamous rogue," she said, "is it to murder me—me, whom you cheated unworthily, by abusing my generosity—that you've returned to this honest house?"

"There's no doubt about it," said Toby, who had emerged from underneath the table, where he had taken refuge.

"Silence!" said Mrs. Griffon. "Let the accused answer."

Baruch Jorgell did not emerge from his stupid dejection, however. To the reiterated questions of the proprietress of the family hotel, he only replied with inconsequential words.

"Yes, yes...I don't know...no..." he stammered, like a man making an incredible effort to remember.

At first, that was all that could be got out of him. However, by dint of tormenting him with multiple and reiterated questions, Mrs. Griffon ended up understanding that unknown individuals—doubtless accomplices—had brought the murderer to the door of the boarding house and had fled after pressing the doorbell.

"Tramps!" he stammered. "The Red Hand...yes!"

"He's trying to make us understand," said Mrs. Griffon, "that he belongs to the bandits of the Red Hand. It's doubtless because of that that he escaped the searches for such a long time."

"There's nothing to understand," said one of the boarders. "One would think he'd become idiotic, completely idiotic."

"All murderers end up like that. They drink gin or ether to escape remorse and end up losing their minds." She continued, in a tone full of sagacity: "Shall I tell you what's happened? It isn't difficult to deduce. Hunted everywhere, he must have found shelter with the malefactors of the Red Hand, and they must have rewarded themselves for their hospitality by stealing his diamonds. Once they'd robbed him, they got rid of him by bringing him back here."

"Why here rather than somewhere else?" someone asked.

"Perhaps he still has the diamonds?" Toby hazarded.

"That's true," replied Mrs. Griffon. "We haven't searched him."

"Perhaps," observed one of the boarders, "we don't have the right to do that?"

"As if!" retorted another. "As long as the search is carried out in the presence of honorable witnesses, it's perfectly legal."

"As legal as can be!"

"Let's search him!"

"Right!"

This motion was adopted unanimously, and Mrs. Griffon ordered Toby to explore the captive's pockets.

The improvised detective set to work before the anxious gaze of the audience. He deposited his finds as he went along on the lid of the piano. A Bowie knife of respectable size, a Browning, a block of tobacco and various other objects were seized, one after another, and finally, a wallet was found that contained a few banknotes and papers in the name of Baruch Jorgell.

"You see!" cried Mrs. Griffon. "There's no possible doubt about it—it really is Monsieur de Maubreuil's murderer."

But the audience had not yet reached the end of its excitement. Toby suddenly extracted from the lining of the waistcoat several colorless and transparent stones.

"I can assure you," said one of the boarders, who was a professional broker of precious stones, "that those are the most beautiful uncut diamonds that I've ever seen."

These interesting investigations were doubtless about to continue when two policemen abruptly irrupted into the parlor. After brief explanations they put handcuffs on Baruch Jorgell and led him away, each supporting him with one arm, for he seemed to be incapable of standing up. All the people present were invited to come to the police station to make their statements.

On the way, a terrible argument broke out between Mrs. Griffon, who wanted to claim the whole of the reward, and her boarders, who contended that they all had a right to a share. The police chief, to whom the case was submitted, declared that Mrs. Griffon would first be compensated for the money that was owing to her, and that she would have, in addition, the largest share. That compromise arrangement was agreed by everyone.

Baruch Jorgell was locked up in a solidly-barred cell and, when all the statements had been taken, the guests all returned to the boarding house, where Mrs. Griffon, in honor of such a memorable occasion, offered a bow of punch to all her residents.

5. Perplexity

The arrest of Monsieur de Maubreuil's murderer generated considerable publicity in America and throughout the world. Again Baruch Jorgell's picture appeared in the dailies and the magazines, this time flanked by that of Mr. Griffon and her boarders.

The event produced such a sensation that the abduction of Joe Dorgan, which still remained enveloped an impenetrable mystery, was almost forgotten.

Baruch had now taken his place in the ranks of illustrious criminals, and his biography was sold in small booklets illustrated with crude drawings. For some time, he was fashionable; his portrait was seen mounted on brooches and bracelets displayed in jewelers' windows. The enthusiasm of the idlers changed into a veritable delirium, however, when it was perceived, after the initial interrogations, that Baruch was counterfeiting madness, or, at least, stupidity, in an admirable fashion.

The most skillful magistrates and the wiliest detectives could not succeed in getting more out of him than fragments of sentences, inconsequential phrases whose ensemble presented nothing intelligible.

"What a great actor!" cried the idlers, admiringly. "He's turned them over, the lawyers, eh? You'll see that it will be impossible to get any confession out of him, and that the jury will be obliged to acquit him. Needless to say, you have to come to America to find criminals with that kind of strength."

After wasting a lot of time, the district attorney in charge of the sensational case was obliged to recognize that the accused was not in possession of a sound mind. The most eminent specialists in the Union were summoned as expert consultants. After a summary examination, they declared unanimously that Baruch Jorgell, afflicted by grave cerebral lesions, was utterly irresponsible.

This conclusion caused profound public disappointment. It was widely rumored that the murderer's father, the billionaire Fred Jorgell, had paid the doctors to save the life of his worthless offspring. The prison was besieged by a crowd whose members were talking about nothing less than lynching the murderer; it required two detachments of mounted police to reestablish order.

In any case, it was absolutely false that Fred Jorgell had paid the doctors summoned as experts; the billionaire, as he had loudly declared, had not wanted to do anything to save his son from punishment. He was glad, however, because of his daughter Isidora, that Baruch had not been condemned to execution. Then again, he preferred to think that his son had acted under the influence of madness than to supposing him entirely conscious of the monstrous crimes he had committed.

American law is opposed to condemning an insane person to death. In the presence of the formal declarations of the doctors, the jury rendered a verdict of not guilty by reason of insanity, and the court decided that he would be committed to a lunatic asylum—which is what madhouses are called on the other side of the Atlantic.

It seemed thereafter that the world was in haste to let silence fall upon the affair, which remained shrouded in profound mystery. Baruch Jorgell who had been taken to Greenaway Lunatic Asylum, was soon completely forgotten—but not by everyone.

There was still one person who was interested in the wretched madman; that was his sister Isidora. Soon after the trial, the young woman had a quarter of the monthly allowance she received paid to the director of the asylum, in order that her brother could have a private room and would not be subjected to any privation.

Isidora, who had a personal fortune that she had inherited from her mother, of which she had personal control, had not told her father about her intention; she knew that the billionaire would never forgive Baruch, even on his deathbed, and that he had forbidden the name of his unworthy son to be spoken in his presence.

Isidora, in contrast to many young women of the society of the Five Hundred, solely concerned with sumptuous clothes and new jewels, devoted a great deal of her leisure time to serious reading. Fred Jorgell adored his daughter and had such confidence in her judgment that he would not undertake any important operation without having consulted her. There was no example of Isidora having advised her father to undertake a poor speculation.

At present, Fred Jorgell was engaged, albeit courteously, in a financial battle against William Dorgan. After having been partners for a long time in the Corn and Cotton Trusts, each of them wanted to become the sole master of the market. It was thanks to Isidora that the struggle between the two magnates had not taken on a harsher character.

Isidora had been engaged to the engineer Harry Dorgan. The departure of Baruch, driven away by his father after the mysterious crimes whose author had been discovered by the engineer, had caused the projected marriage to be postponed. The enormous publicity given to the murder of Monsieur de Maubreuil had caused the marriage to be put off again, indefinitely. In spite of Harry Dorgan's persistence, Isidora had not wanted to consent to it. When the children of billionaires marry in America, it is the rule to publish portraits of the young couple, and Isidora could already see, in her mind's eyes, on the front page of every large-circulation daily, the pictures of "the murderer" and "the murderer' sister."

"Let's wait," she had said to the engineer. Meekly, Harry Dorgan had yielded to her reasoning, and he was still waiting.

That semi-rupture would not have prevented the two young people, who could have met one another frequently in the drawing-rooms of the Five Hundred, from maintaining a keen and profound affection. After the noisy publicity given to the assassination of Monsieur de Maubreuil, however, Isidora had retreated into absolute solitude. She spent entire afternoons walking in silent meditation through the long pathways bordered with orange-trees in the paternal park. She liked to isolate herself in the shade of a grove of venerable cedars, where there was a moss-covered marble bench.

Isidora often fell into strange reveries. By dint of reflection, she had been struck by the obscurities and contradictions that surrounded the crime and the criminal. She scented a mystery therein; she thought that the law had been much too hasty. She was intimately convinced that the truth of the sinister drama was much more complex than the detectives and the reporters, in haste to find a plausible explanation, had imagined.

With a dolorous anxiety, the young woman had read the interrogations of the sheriffs, the reports of the alienists and the accounts given to interviewers; that reading had left her very perplexed.

Certainly, she knew, Baruch was devoid of any kind of scruple, and even of any moral sensibility, but his intellectual health had been very robust and powerfully energetic.

There's an inconceivable enigma in this, she thought. *If my wretched brother had completely lost his memory, he would never have remembered the way to the boarding-house. He wouldn't have remembered it at all. Why didn't he recognize Mrs. Griffon or give any evidence of the fact that he had ever known her? Another enigma: what had become of the diamonds? How is it that there has been no trace of them anywhere? Gems that are a little larger than ordinary size are well-known to jewelers. As soon as a diamond of unusual size comes on to the market, it's immediately identified by special publications edited in London and Paris. It's necessary, therefore, that these diamonds must be in someone's possession—in the hands of an accomplice, or several accomplices. If so, why aren't the police looking for those accomplices?*

That problem became, for her, a piercing obsession. It was necessary for her to know the truth, at any price. She took a desperate resolution. Accompanied by her Scottish governess, Mrs. MacBerlott, she went to the lunatic asylum situated in a suburb four miles from New York.

Like everything one encounters in America, the madhouse offered a striking contrast between luxurious comfort and savage negligence. One entire wing of the buildings was constructed in marble and polychromatic ceramics, with bay windows with dazzling glass. It was there that the administrators were installed, the doctors and a few rich clients—former speculators for the most part, whose brains had been unhinged by overexertion. The poor lunatics were exiled to badly-built wooden huts, from which howls and lamentations rose up all day long.

As she went through the solid gate with the gilded lances that served as an entrance to that pandemonium, the governess could not repress a vague apprehension, and the director scarcely reassured her with his warm welcome.

Dr. Johnson, a Yankee of funereal gravity, was not unaware that he was in the presence of Miss Isidora Jorgell, the billionaire's daughter, and he put himself entirely at her disposal.

6. *In the Lunatic Asylum*

The director of the asylum felt a certain pride at possessing in his establishment an individual as notorious as Baruch Jorgell, whose crimes had occupied the entire world.

"Mr. Jorgell," he declared, "is surrounded by the most devoted care here; he is visited by celebrated alienists, among whom I can cite Dr. Cornelius Kramm. He was here the day before yesterday."

"Does he think," asked Isidora, emotionally, "that any hope can be maintained, if not for a complete cure, at least for an amelioration of the patient's condition?"

"I want to be frank with you, Miss; the doctor does not hold out any hope. Baruch Jorgell is stricken by a complete amnesia, and the alienists are in accord in deeming that the amnesia in question must have been caused by a violent shock, which produced a lesion that will certainly be incurable...barring a miracle."

Isidora uttered a profound sigh and silently followed the doctor along a sandy path bordered with trees in pots.

"You'll be able to observe," the director went on, "that the accommodation works are proceeding with the most fervent activity. A few months from now we'll have to hand the very best of everything discovered for the cure of the mentally ill: large gardens for the treatments of fresh air and physical exercise, operating theaters, electrical baths, radium baths and solar baths, nor forgetting the refrigeration room, indispensable in the treatment of hypochondria and acute neurasthenia."

Perceiving that Isidora and the governess were only listening distractedly, he added, with a smile full of promises: "Perhaps you'd like to see some of our patients? It's a favor that I don't often grant, and we have some very interesting cases here!"

"No thank you, sir," the young woman replied, coldly.

"I can assure you that you're missing an opportunity," he replied, insistently. "We have the aviator Nelson here, for example, who believes that he has been changed into an airplane, and had to be carefully watched to make sure that he doesn't climb up to the roof in order to take off; the automobile man who goes around all day swaddled in pneumatic tires and has to be prevented, with great difficulty, from drinking gasoline; and the cat man, who refuses any other nourishment than cream and raw liver, who spends all his time mewling, purring and scraping his fingernails of a plank. We also have...."

"I don't doubt," the governess interjected, "that all these patients are very interesting, but Miss Isidora has no interest in seeing those unfortunates, the sight of whom would only sadden her profoundly. She has come purely to visit her brother, and for that alone."

"Very well," murmured the director, slightly vexed but the poor response to his offer. "I thought it would be agreeable to you, but since it isn't, let's say no more about it. I'm unfortunately obliged to leave you for an urgent meeting, but here's the chief warder, who will serve as your guide."

And Dr. Johnson, after a ceremonious bow, entrusted the two women to the care of an athletic individual dressed in a yellow uniform with metal buttons and coifed in a bizarre soft leather helmet. He was the chief warder.

Isidora asked a few questions about her brother's condition, but the warder had precise instructions as to how to reply to the relatives of rich clients.

"Mr. Jorgell," he said, in an obsequious tone, "is as well as can be expected. We have only to congratulate you on his behavior. As for the care with which he is surrounded, you know, Miss, that the motto of the establishment is *tenderness, humanity and comfort*."

The man in the yellow uniform was careful not to mention the straitjacket, the cold showers and the whip, which he had no scruples about using when the patients showed the slightest inclination to be turbulent.

They had arrived at a high wall in which there was a little iron door fitted with a judas-hole. The warder took a bunch of keys from his belt and introduced the visitors into an enclosure whose soil, covered with meager grass, nourished a few stunted trees. This was doubtless the "vast garden" propitious for fresh air cures and physical exercise that the director had mentioned, Isidora thought, with a constriction in her heart.

Some thirty paying patients were, some prey to a dismal depression, others walking with a jerky step with emphatic gesticulations, under the alternately fixed and roaming gaze of four warders: the special gaze of jailers always wary of being unexpectedly attacked.

It was with great difficulty that Isidora recognized her brother.

She contemplated fearfully that dull gaze devoid of warmth, that thin face ravaged by remorse and malady, and the discolored lips like those of an old man. A fearful, stooped individual devoid of any precise age, his limbs agitated by a perpetual tremor: that was all that remained of the robust and energetic Baruch.

"I can't get used to the idea that that's my brother," the young woman murmured, with poignant sadness.

"It's really him, though," said the governess. "But how depleted he is—no more than a shadow of himself!"

Isidora took the hand of the madman and sat down beside him. "It's me, your sister Isidora," she said, forcing herself to smile. "How are you?"

Baruch raised his eyes to direct a gaze at the young woman from which thought was absent, and withdrew his hand fearfully.

"Come on, Baruch," said Isidora, with obstinate tenderness, "make an effort. Look at me! Isidora—doesn't that name remind you of anything?"

279

"Nothing," he muttered, in a hoarse voice. He was now looking at the young woman with a gaze that was slightly less extinct, through which something akin to a fugitive flash of thought passed. Then he put his hand to his head in a lamentable gesture.

"I can't remember any more," he stammered. "I don't know any more. What do you want with me? I'm very unhappy! Oh, very unhappy!"

Isidora turned away to hide the tears that rose to her eyes. She was running out of courage. She made one supreme effort, however; she did not want to go away without taking a little hope with her.

"Tell me your name," she demanded.

"I don't know..."

He hid his head in his hands and it was impossible for Isidora to get anything else out of him.

During that heart-rending scene, the governess had remained silent. She was invincibly attracted by the grimaces of an old gentleman who was prowling in the vicinity, walking on all fours and arching his back. He was the man who imagined that he had been changed into a cat. Suddenly, he began mewling in such a lugubrious fashion that the good woman felt frightened in spite of the presence of the warders.

"Miss Isidora," she said, "I think it's best if we go. The haggard expressions of all these unfortunates make the blood run cold. Perhaps our presence is annoying them. Let's go."

"You're right," the young woman murmured, sadly.

"Let's go," the Scotswoman repeated, fearfully, drawing nearer to her mistress. "That gentleman's frightening me with his mewling." She pointed at the madman, who had stopped a few yards away from her.

"We're going," said Isidora. "Perhaps it's better, after all, that Baruch has lost all memory of the past..."

They both hastened to leave the sinister garden and get out of the house of pain. They got back into the automobile that was waiting for them, which transported them rapidly in the direction of New York.

Isidora took a long time to recover from the terrible emotion she had just experienced.

"It's strange," she murmured. "I can't imagine that it's my brother Baruch that I've just seen. It seems to me that it's him, but not him: that the unfortunate that we've just left is merely a grotesque and pitiful caricature of the Baruch of old."

"Certainly," said the governess, "the illness has changed him a great deal."

"But then, there are things I can never explain. At certain moments I wonder whether my brother is really capable of all the crimes of which he's been accused. One can't say that he's mad, and he's no longer idiotic, since he can take account of his situation and is suffering. This visit has broken my heart..."

Isidora returned sadly to her father's palace, but her melancholy and her preoccupation had increased. She shut herself away thereafter in a retreat more profound than ever.

Every month, courageously, she went to the Lunatic Asylum and observed with despair that Baruch's condition had not changed at all. His intelligence and his memory remained plunged in the darkness of oblivion.

7. The Fire on Thirtieth Avenue

Until the day when his son Joe had been abducted, and doubtless murdered, by the tramps of the Red Hand, William Dorgan would have been able to consider himself one of the luckiest billionaires in the entire United States. Very prudent, he had only ever bet on sure things in the great battle of dollars, and his fortune had grown from year to year, without upsets, with a wise slowness. It was sufficient for him to take an interest in an enterprise for its success to be assured.

He had been as fortunate from the viewpoint of family life as that of business. His two sons gave him full satisfaction. He was sure of leaving behind him heirs worthy of his fortune and his reputation for probity.

William Dorgan was English by birth, and, as such, he loved comfort and good food. He was not one of those billionaires who work sixteen or eighteen hours a day without granting themselves the slightest distraction, living more miserably than the humblest of their employees. He was hard-working, but in a reasonable fashion, and it would have required an extraordinary catastrophe to force him to delay his dinner time. His cook was famous and all those who had had the honor of sitting down at his table declared that William Dorgan was a *bon viveur*, a good companion and an excellent fellow.

Physically, the billionaire offered a merry expression, a broad rubicund face framed by curly white hair. His features radiated generosity and a perpetual smile played over his fleshy kips. Affection sparkled in his bright gray eyes, as bright and lively as those of a mischievous schoolboy. Very simple in his manners, very liberal and very cheerful, William Dorgan unfailingly attracted the sympathies of those who had dealings with him.

Joe's disappearance had been a bolt from the blue.

In a matter of days, William Dorgan had lost his appetite, and had grown thinner; he neglected his business; nothing interested him any longer. One hope remained to him however: that the engineer Harry might find his brother.

Harry, in fact, in spite of the fruitlessness of his searches, was not discouraged. At the head of an elite troop, he continued to search the defiles and caverns of the mountain, the usual refuges of the tramps. As he had explained to his father, it seemed inadmissible to him that bandits as intelligent and as pragmatic as the companions of the Red Hand would have stupidly murdered a man whose ransom value was colossal.

William Dorgan had ended up sharing the engineer's conviction; he had even published in all the newspapers his willingness to pay any sum at all provided that his son was returned to him. But those promises, like Harry's searches, had not yielded any result.

Time passed without anything new materializing. William Dorgan had fallen into a state of neurasthenia, or, in older parlance, overwhelming spleen. He no longer went out, and paced back and forth in his study all night long, like a wild beast in a cage.

The billionaire's residence, at number 299 Thirtieth Avenue, was a luxurious edifice pretentious in its architecture, based on that of certain castles in the south of England constructed in the reign of Elizabeth. There were turrets everywhere, bell-towers, and arcades florid with sculptures. The dwelling pleased its owner so much that he had never wanted to leave it, even though it was built in one of the less aristocratic districts. It was, in fact, surrounded on three sides by immense dockyards, some enclosing bales of cotton and others construction timber belonging to various Trusts.

During the night, these dockyards were under the surveillance of six guards who took turns to make hourly patrols. One evening—it was a Saturday, and the workers had gone home early—at about ten o'clock, two of the guards, whose turn it was to make the round, emerged from the hut that they occupied in the courtyard of the dock and went into the cotton warehouse, equipped with a shielded lantern and each armed with a Browning.

In the most profound silence, the two men advanced into the middle of the vast warehouse. All around them, the bales of cotton formed regular cubes, between which narrow passages were fitted.

"I think, Slug," said one of the men, suddenly, in a low voice, "that it'll be today."

"You think so?" said the other, with a bizarre smile.

"Yes. I have a presentiment. And then, certain clues..."

"Your presentiment isn't mistaken. Look." And he took from his pocket a piece of paper on which a few lines were scrawled in hieroglyphic characters, and which had for a signature a hand crudely drawn in red ink.

There were a few moments of silence.

"It's astonishing," murmured the first speaker, in an unsteady voice. "I'd rather be in the desert, in the Black Canyon, my rifle in my hand, with our friends the tramps, than doing this job."

"What do you expect? I share your opinion, but, after all, we have to do what the bosses say. Besides which, I've received precise instructions. We're not running any kind of risk."

"Are the drums here?"

"Yes, since yesterday. The Red Hand got them in without anyone knowing. I couldn't say how myself. Now, to work—ten minutes delay could compromise everything."

Slug—the leader of the tramps who had murdered Joe Dorgan's escort—had bent down. He moved aside several bales of cotton and exposed a dozen drums similar to those used to contain oil.

"You see," Slug said. "All that we have to do is pour the contents of these drums over the bale."

"Then set fire to it?"

"Not at all. It will catch fire all by itself."

"Impossible!"

"It was explained to me that it's a chemical compound that contains phosphorus. When the liquid has evaporated, everything goes up in flames."

"That's terrible. Let's hurry. It seems to me that we might be roasted alive."

Slug made no reply, but he began to sprinkle the liquid contents of the drums over the cotton bales, with a haste that proved that he shared his accomplice's anxieties.

In less than a quarter of an hour, the two bandits had finished their criminal work. Then they slipped precipitately out of the dockyard, traversed the courtyard breathlessly and went out into the street, not without having taken the precaution of closing the exterior door behind them.

"Oof!" said Slug, once they were outside. "I'm glad that's finished. I don't like these tricks. I'd rather do battle with mounted policemen than do what we've just done again."

"Where do we go?"

"Follow me—someone's waiting for us; we need to give an account of our expedition."

The two bandits, who seemed to be in a hurry to get away from the theater of their exploits, headed at a run toward the city center, and did not take long to lose themselves in the Saturday night crowds.

At the very moment when the tramps had finished emptying the last barrel of incendiary liquid over the cotton bales, William Dorgan was walking back and forth agitatedly in his bedroom, situated on the second floor of the house. He was holding a letter he had received an hour earlier, from his son Harry.

The young man informed his father that the investigation had made no progress, even though the enquiries of the mountain policemen had extended all the way to the Mexican border. No serious trace had been found, in spite of the gold that had been distributed prodigally. The tone of the letter expressed profound discouragement.

"I'm desperate," murmured the billionaire, dejectedly. "If even Harry is losing hope, there's no resource left. Poor Joe!"

The old man could not hold back a profound sob. The engineer's letter slipped out of his hand.

A domestic had come in on tiptoe and had deposited a heap of letters and telegrams on a side-table. William Dorgan had watched him do it with a distracted gaze, as if absent-mindedly.

"Is that the post from San Francisco?" he asked, anxiously.

"No sir. You had a letter from Mr. Harry in the last batch; there can't be another one today."

The billionaire dismissed the man with a vague gesture and plunged back into his melancholy meditations.

"Poor Joe, my poor boy," he stammered, his throat squeezed by anguish. The stifled sobs continued. He went to the window, opened it very wide, and breathed in the icy night air gratefully.

In front of him, New York extended beneath a sky inundated with harsh electric radiation, with its monstrous perspectives of giant bridges and skyscrapers thirty or forty stories high; a menacing rumor, like the distant growling of thousands of wild beasts, rose from the enormous city.

William Dorgan stood motionless, unable to help being distracted from his dolor by the spectacle of the immense panorama of all that human activity.

"What good is this monstrous material progress?" he sighed. "Will anyone ever find a means of preventing people from suffering…?"

But his sentence was interrupted by a cry of stupor and fear.

Abruptly, with the suddenness of an explosion, and immense sheet of livid flame had just spring forth, rising up to the clouds, illuminating with a violent light the entirety of a vast horizon of monuments and houses.

"There's a fire in the docks!" the billionaire shouted, terrified.

Almost at the same instant, however, a second column of flames, as high as the first, rose up toward the sky.

A second later, a third nucleus of conflagration burst forth with the same suddenness and the same inexplicable violence; there was now a veritable sea of fire, with reddish waves and surf of russet smoke, undulating mightily in the evening breeze, and the billionaire's house, surrounded, was like a reef lost in the middle of a blazing ocean. The Gothic turrets and sculpted balconies stood out sharply against an apocalyptic backcloth. It had taken less than a minute for the cataclysm to erupt. There were entire blocks of houses on fire; an entire district was burning.

William Dorgan had recoiled from the window, driven backwards by the ardent breath of the blaze; already the windows of the house were breaking with a dry crackle, their frames already ablaze.

Losing his head, obedient more to the instinct of a panicked animal than to reason, the billionaire ran out of the room. The stairway was already full of smoke and the cage of the elevator was like the ardent mouth of a furnace.

"Help!" he cried, in a voice that resembled a howl. "Help! Help!"

Acrid fumes gripped his throat; he had to take refuge in the room, where the paintings were cracking and curling under the effects of the heat, and the disjointed parquet was already emitting thin jets of steam. He was blinded by the light of the flames, half-suffocated by the burning atmosphere filling the room. He could not find a way out; he understood that he was doomed.

Meanwhile, an immense clamor of desolation went up from the great city, wrenched from its pleasures by the red horror of the blaze, which was visible ten miles out at sea. Fire engines raced in dozens to the theater of the disaster, finding a path with difficulty through the crowds that two battalions of mounted policemen could barely contain.

It was soon obvious, however, that all efforts to ward off the scourge that had been unleashed on such a vat scale would be futile. It would have been necessary to pour an entire river on the blaze, alimented by so much highly combustible material. Fifteen-story skyscrapers were burning, but the jets of the most powerful pumps were incapable of rising above the eighth story. The rescuers were only thinking of one thing: to limit the spread of the fire, sacrificing one district completely in order to preserve the others; even that task seemed to be bristling with insurmountable difficulties.

Soon, a sinister rumor began to circulate through the crowd.

"The Red Hand! It was the Red Hand that set the fire!"

"All of New York is going to burn!"

"Two banks have been pillaged."

"The police are in cahoots with the bandits. We're doomed!"

There was panic. Many people hastened to their homes and the residents of buildings organized themselves into groups armed with revolvers and clubs, ready to defend their domiciles against the fire-setters.

Here, there and everywhere, groups of courageous rescuers precipitated themselves into the flames to pull out women, children and the sick. The crowds encouraged them with resounding cheers. It was not until the following day that it was perceived that the houses visited by these intrepid citizens had been comprehensively plundered.

In other places the panic had produced terrible stampedes; onlookers, especially women, had been trampled underfoot. The numerous cadavers that were found the next day had all been stripped of their jewelry and valuables.

Idlers gathered opposite William Dorgan's palace; it was not a banal spectacle to see a billionaire roasted alive in his palace; everyone wanted to witness such an event.

Many of William Dorgan's friends had brought extendable ladders and other rescue equipment, but no one dared risk themselves in the furnace. In any case, no one could be sure that the billionaire was not dead already.

Suddenly, a group of men cut through the crowd; among them were Dr. Cornelius Kramm, his brother Fritz and a young man who seemed to be prey to a violent emotion. Those three individuals seemed to have a great authority over the multitude. In a matter of minutes, under their direction, a huge iron ladder was extended along the façade of the house, the windows of which were now vomiting torrents of smoke mingled with flames.

The young man was wringing his hands in despair.

"My God!" he repeated, "Work quickly! As long as it's not too late!" And he stimulate the zeal of all those around him with carelessly-distributed banknotes.

Rapidly, he put on an incombustible asbestos costume and one of the helmets equipped with mica goggles, of which the firemen in certain American cities make use. Then he shook the hands of the Kramm brothers and launched himself forth up the ladder. In a few strides he reached one of the balconies of the house and, breaking the window with his fist, penetrated into the furnace.

The crowd uttered a long cry of admiration and fear, and then fell silent. All hearts were beating with the same anguish.

A minute went by, as long as a century. The young man did not reappear.

"I fear," Fritz murmured in his brother's ear, "that we waited too long."

"No," the doctor replied. "All my precautions have been taken; I can guarantee success."

Once he had reached the balcony, the mysterious rescuer, who seemed perfectly familiar with William Dorgan's house, went straight to the bedroom.

He arrived there at the moment when the crazed billionaire, his hair on fire and half-asphyxiated, had just taken refuge in a fitted closet, which—by a chance that subsequently seemed providential—had been entirely lined with sheet metal because important papers were stored there. In there, it was as if William Dorgan were inside a vast safe. Henceforth, he was no longer running the risk of being burned alive, but he only had a minimal interval before he was completely stifled.

The man clad in asbestos opened the closet door, seized the old man by the arms and carried him to the balcony against which he had leaned the iron ladder.

There he paused for breath; the most difficult part of the task was complete.

"Who are you?" stammered the billionaire, in a feeble voice.

The unknown removed the asbestos mask that was covering his features.

"My son! My dear Joe!" stammered the billionaire.

After so much violent emotion, however, the shock had been too much. William Dorgan fainted in the arms of the son who had so miraculously emerged from his captivity to save his life.

The members of the crowd began to applaud loudly, quivering at the drama that had just been played out before their eyes in a matter of minutes.

In the meantime, Joe Dorgan had attached a solid rope under his father's arms, thanks to which the old man, still inanimate, was carefully lowered down to the street. He had scarcely reached the ground when the house collapsed into the flames, with a dull explosion.

When William Dorgan came round, he found himself in one of the most comfortable apartments of the Atlantic Hotel. Dr. Cornelius and Joe Dorgan were mopping his brow with a counter-irritant solution and making him breathe smelling-salts.

When he opened his eyes, his first glance met his son's eyes, and immediately his face lit up with a smile. Contentment is the most powerful of remedies. A moment later, he was able to speak.

"My Joe is found!" he exclaimed. "I don't care about all the rest. Come into my arms, my son, that I might clasp you to my heart."

"Father," murmured the young man, profoundly moved, "I'm glad to have arrived in time to snatch you from the jaws of death."

The father and son embraced tenderly.

"My poor boy," the billionaire repeated. "If you knew how we've wept! Your brother Harry has been admirable. At present, he's still searching the rugged gorges of the Mexican sierra."

"Dear Harry—how happy he'll be to see me returned, safe and sound."

"You'll tell us all your adventures—but perhaps we ought to take precautions to make sure that what remains of the house isn't pillaged."

"Don't worry about that. Fritz Kramm has taken charge of the necessary measures. By now, the ruins of the house ought to be surrounded by a cordon of policemen, who won't let anyone near it. To make sure of their vigilance, I had fifty dollars given to each man, and promised them a similar sum tomorrow."

"All is for the best, then," said the billionaire. "My most important files are in armored safes that won't have suffered any damage in the fire. My fortune is on deposit in the State bank. As for the loss of the house, I consider it insignificant. I'll build a more luxurious one. Let's not think any longer about anything but rejoicing in your return. Have a bottle of old port sent up, and while we're drinking it, you can tell us the story of your adventures—for the moment, that's what interests me the most."

Joe Dorgan—or, rather, Baruch Jorgell disguised with the features of Joe Dorgan—then began to tell a story whose slightest details had been concocted in association with his two accomplices.

"You remember, Father," he said, "that in making my annual tour of your properties in the state of California, I had to bring back a considerable sum of money—a particularly difficult transport in a country devoid of roads and police, since it consisted mostly of coins and silver ingots. Following your recommendation, I had myself escorted by a dozen mounted policemen."

"That wasn't sufficient," Dr. Cornelius Kramm put in.

"That's true," said the narrator, "but it was all that was available, and I was told that the region had been tranquil for a long time. During my tour I didn't see anything worrying; as I'd been told, the region appeared to be entirely safe. It wasn't until we were going through the sinister defile at the Black Canyon that I perceived, when it was too late to turn back, how dire my error was. In the middle of the night, in a terrible rainstorm, the carriage carrying the money became bogged down in a narrow passage hemmed in on both sides by walls of rock from whose heights a single man could have kept an entire army at bay.

"It was an ideal place for an ambush. The tramps, who must have been lying in wait for us there for days, killed all my men one by one with rifle shots. Soon, in spite of desperate resistance, I found myself alone. The bandits tied me up, and I suddenly smelled the insipid odor of chloroform. A cold pad was placed over my nostrils and I lost consciousness.

"When I came round, I found myself in a desolate ravine surrounded in all directions by precipices, which must have been the crater of an extinct volcano. I was given a little roasted meat to eat and whisky to drink; then I was tied to a horse again and we set off on the march..."

"How is it," William Dorgan asked, suddenly, "that your brother Harry's searches, which covered a vat region bush by bush, had no result? That's what I can't fathom!"

"It's easily explicable. My captors seemed to be admirably well-informed. While my brother Harry was limiting his searches to the region near the Black Canyon, the tramps, covering several hundred miles by means of forced marches, had traveled a long way northwards, skirting the Rocky Mountains, where they were always sure of finding shelter in case of an alarm. I was able to convince myself, in the course of that obligatory journey, of the power of the Red Hand. Everywhere, the tramps found food-supplies and guides; sometimes we even received hospitality at farms of perfectly honest appearance. Finally, we made a definitive halt in a wooded valley to which access was only gained via a narrow path that ended at a furious torrent, over which the trunk of a fir-tree had been thrown by way of a bridge."

William Dorgan was all ears as he listened to this fantastic tale. "But in the end," he asked, impatiently, "how were you able to escape?"

"I'll get to that. The leader of the tramps, an old bandit condemned to death several times over, had decided that I would write to you myself to demand that you pay a hundred thousand dollars for my ransom."

"You had to write."

"Never! The tramps would have doubled their demands and wouldn't have released me once the sum was handed over. Then again, it's not in my character to give in to threats, under any circumstances. Furious at that refusal, the tramps decided to tame my by means of hunger; they put me on a diet of dry biscuit and water, while alongside me the brazenly scoffed beef and mutton stolen from the 'squatters' of the prairie, which they washed down with large draughts of whisky, and even wine. Many a time, my nostrils tickled by the perfume of a roast, I was on the point of giving in."

"My dear Joe," the old man exclaimed, "you conducted yourself in an admirable fashion." Moved by that heroism, he seized the hands of the man he took to be his son and squeezed them affectionately.

"Meanwhile," Baruch continued, "the bandits fell out. Following the classic procedure, some of them wanted to cut off my ears to send them to you, instead of the letter, and thus hasten the payment of the funds; others wanted to wait a little longer. Many fights resulted, with revolvers and Bowie knives. It was in the course of one of those bloody brawls that I succeeded in cutting my bonds without being detected. When night came, I crossed the footbridge, not without taking the precaution of tipping it into the torrent thereafter. The bandits were unable to pursue me. I heard their cries of rage, and their rifle-bullets whistled overhead.

"Eventually, I reached the clearing where the gang's horses were pastured. I leapt on to the best after chasing the rest into the woods, and after riding for three days I reached a small railway station lost in the middle of the prairie. I jumped on to the first train heading for New York. There, two gentlemen who had seen my picture in the papers generously lent me money to pay for my ticket and get a little nourishment in the restaurant car. At a station where there was a sufficiently long halt, I sent you a telegram."

"I must have received it," murmured the billionaire, "but I was in such a state of chagrin and prostration that I hadn't had the courage to open the letters and dispatches that reached me shortly before the fire broke out."

"It doesn't matter, since I'm here. When I arrived in New York I jumped into a taxi and arrived just at the moment when the house was enveloped by a sheet of flame. You know the rest, but I ought to put it on record that I was only able to procure the necessary rescue equipment thanks to Fritz and Cornelius Kramm. I scarcely knew them, from having met them some time ago at Fred Jorgell's receptions, but they remembered me, and they put themselves at my disposal with real devotion."

The billionaire thanked the doctor warmly, assuring him that henceforth, he would have no other physician.

Baruch Jorgell was radiant with joy, and his admiration grew for Cornelius, whose docile instrument he had so far been. From now on, thanks to the skillful staging of the fire, it was impossible for William Dorgan not to be absolutely convinced that he had recovered his son Joe.

While the real Joe languished in a lunatic asylum, Monsieur de Maubreuil's murderer and his accomplices were going to be able to share William Dorgan's billions.

N° 3. CHAQUE RÉCIT EST COMPLET EN UN VOLUME 25 Cent.

GUSTAVE LE ROUGE

LE MYSTÉRIEUX DOCTEUR CORNÉLIUS

LE
Sculpteur de Chair Humaine

LA MAISON DU LIVRE 28 R. MONSIEUR LE PRINCE PARIS.

Henri Falk: *The Master of the Three States*

Le Maître des Trois États *might well have been written as an exercise in psychological self-medication, to give its author, Henri Falque (1881-1937), who signed almost all his published writings Henri Falk, something else to think about instead of the horrors and terrors of the war rather than as a commercial exercise, and it is a rather surprising piece to find in the pages of the* Mercure de France, *in spite of Alfred Vallette's apparent covert sympathy for "scientific marvel fiction." An official organ of the Symbolist movement in its early years, the* Mercure *had gradually become conscientiously staid and respectable, and was well into its maturity by 1917, but* Le Maître des Trois États *probably went down better with its readers than the other major piece of French scientific marvel fiction published in 1917, J.-H. Rosny Aîné's* L'Enigme de Givreuse [42] *would have done. It is much more coherent and faster-paced, as well as funnier. The fact that it is set in the weeks immediately preceding the war lends it a slightly nostalgic tint, but adds an unusually wry note to the hapless scientist's final speech anticipating potential future applications of his ironically-doomed invention.*

Little biographical information regarding Falk is recoverable from contemporary sources, save for the dates of his birth and death, and what little can be inferred from the record of his publications. He seems to have built up a thriving career as an author of one-act comedies, and had begun to dabble in full-length comedy by 1914, when said career was decisively interrupted by the World War I. He was almost certainly mobilized as soon as the war began, and probably remained in military service until its end. Publication opportunities for any kind of fiction, especially comedy, were thin on the ground for the first few years of the war, but they began to broaden out again in 1917, he published Le Maître des Trois États. *Although it is an archetypical example of what Maurice Renard had called "le roman merveilleux-scientifique" [scientific marvel fiction], it is more broadly comic than most stories of that sort, and has some affinities with the kind of darkly farcical intrusive fantasy popularized in Victorian England by F. Anstey [Thomas Anstey Guthrie] in such works as* Vice Versa *(1882) and* The Fallen Idol *(1886), a coarser version of which had been revived in England during the war by W. A. Darlington in the stories subsequently collected in* Alf's Button *(Passing Show 1917-18; book 1919), when the authorities*

---

[42] Translated in a Black Coat Press edition as *The Givreuse Enigma and Other Stories.*

belatedly came round to the view that a little laughter was not merely permissible in terrible times, but might actually be good for morale.

When the war ended, and Falk returned to civilian life, he went back to the theater and produced more comedies, as well as song-lyrics and librettos for operettas. The play that was eventually to prove his most popular and influential, the flirtatious romance Pouche, *was written in collaboration with René Peter, first produced in 1923, then published the following year. It owes its modern fame to an English translation by Avery Hopwood,* Naughty Cinderella *(produced 1925; published 1934), which was adapted into the film* This is the Night *(1932). Alongside his theatrical work, Falk produced numerous prose pieces such as* L'Age de Plomb.[43].

By 1922, scientific romance had fallen into extreme disfavor in the French literary marketplace, and it is not surprising that Falk, like almost everyone else who had dabbled in the genre, gave up on it. His subsequent novels are all naturalistic. In the years preceding his somewhat premature death, he did some scriptwriting work for French films, and some of his own works were used as the bases for film scripts, but he made no considerable impact in that or any other arena.

B.S.

When I recall this fantastic history, sprawling in a real armchair and smoking a veritable cigar, it seems like a dream. Nevertheless, it happened—and I found myself mixed up in it at a critical time in my life. And it was me who put an end to its vicissitudes, by virtue of a terrible irresponsibility for which I still feel remorse. I am, however, counting on the final confession that my story will comprise to liberate my conscience completely. Perhaps certain aspects of my actions will allow me to be more than absolved: that is for my sovereign judge, the reader, to decide.

1. Two Disconcerting Phenomena

My name is Mesmin Cabri. I am 26 years-old. In 1910, my parents, notable tradespeople who lived in a provincial town, sent me to study law in Paris. My mind did, indeed, possess juridical abilities, and I nurture the hope of succeeding my patron, the advocate Maître X*** in his responsibilities. Having been taken into his chambers in the position of clerk in 1911, I quickly attracted his attention, with the result that, in July 1913, at which time I obtained my qualification, he raised my monthly wage by 3.50 francs.

---

[43] Reprinted in *French Tales of Cataclysms*, Black Coat Press, ISBN ISBN-13: 978-1-64932-110-7.

My physique is agreeable; I have an abundance of light chestnut-colored hair, a rosy complexion, a blond moustache, even white teeth and nicely-spaced green eyes. Symmetrical in my medium build, I know how to wear clothes and sustain a conversation. My faults—for I am being frank—are a slight overfondness for good food and feet that are perhaps a trifle large; my good qualities are intelligence, generosity, a good memory and modesty. That is enough of an introduction, since my role in this story will be entirely in the background.

Well-equipped, all things considered, with a clerk who did him honor, my employer did not neglect to invite me to receptions frequented by the society of the Court and High Finance. One evening, he even took me to an almost-intimate dinner, since I only counted, apart from myself, a dozen guests, who made me welcome when I arrived.

Now, in the course of one soirée at his home, I met an adorable creature, Suzanne Bic, the daughter of Maître Bic, a bailiff. We chatted, we danced, each charmed by the other. Rivals emerged in the meantime—who, indeed, would not have been smitten at first glance with that exquisite redhead with the fine figure, an apricot complexion, mouse-grey eyes, symmetrical teeth, arranged between her lips like fresh almonds in a divided strawberry?—but I seduced her right away, and that is a fact. We discovered that we had the same tastes: in literature, heroic drama; in music, Italian opera; in cakes, rum baba; in architecture, Louis XV style. In brief, to complete the ecstasy, we promised ourselves to one another.

I knew how to ingratiate myself with Maître Bic, a corpulent and ruddy-faced but worthy individual with short-cropped hair and a gold-rimmed pince-nez, by talking to him about unpaid debts and forced sales, and with the tall and dark Madame Bic, by escorting her to the buffet seven times. Recommended to them by my patron as a young man full of promise, they authorized me to pay them a visit in their fifth-floor apartment in the Rue Dante—a permission of which I took advantage the following Sunday. Need I go on? Monsieur Bic resigned himself, saw my parents, and came back satisfied. A month later, Suzanne and I, shivering with excitement, exchanged the chaste rings of betrothal.

A future of blue skies! I dazzled my future family with my knowledge, my manners and my wit. I loved to sustain, not without a certain brio, original opinions that alarmed the Bics, especially Madame, who was credulous and limited; I experienced the delicate pleasure of simultaneously amusing and troubling my tender Suzanne, emotional angel that she was. At the pronunciation of a paradox, she would say to me, blushing: "You frighten me, Mesmin!" Her bosom palpitated, she breathed lightly, and I collected the kiss suspended from her lips.

Everything was smiling upon me, then—even the household dog, a little fox-terrier name Fredaine, which Suzanne adored and which I stuffed with sugar candy. I had not the slightest inkling of the setbacks that were lying in wait for our happy plans.

One evening, Bic said to me: "Mesmin, an ambition that my wife and I have been nurturing is about to be fulfilled. We're beginning to get old and are having difficulty climbing stairs. Now, I've been able to rent a little house in Auteuil at a very affordable price, to which we are moving right away. I'm losing a month's rent, but I want to take advantage of the opportunity."

Although the news was of scant importance to me, I congratulated Bic warmly. My tender Suzanne went on: "Since you're about to spend three weeks with your parents, you'll find us in residence when you return."

"And you can help us choose the wallpaper, as you're a man of taste," her mother added.

I replied wittily, and as I was leaving Paris that evening, I obtained official permission to kiss my fiancée on the cheeks—an operation that, it goes without saying, had been effected many times unofficially. I shook Bic's hand, kissed Madame's, stroked Fredaine and left.

How my heart was beating three weeks later, as I emerged from the Metro that had brought me from the Avenue des Ternes, where I lived, to Auteuil station! On descending from the train I had a quick snack, tidied myself up a little, bought a bouquet of white roses and hastened toward the new residence of Suzanne and her parents. Eight o'clock was chiming. Nightfall, already imminent, was attenuating the heat of an August day. The Rue La Fontaine was long. I finally drew near to my paradise, and even recognized it at a distance, from the memory of a drawing that Suzanne had made me of its silhouette.

Finally, here I am! The entrance door is open. I go in, surprised not to encounter anyone, passing into a dark and sinuous corridor. Suddenly, a voice becomes audible at the far end of the corridor, shrill and fearful. I can't tell whether it's the voice of a man or a woman.

"Who's there? Who's there? Close the door, Eusèbe!"

I understand that I've got the wrong house. I turn around hurriedly, without making any reply, and once outside I look at the house number by the light of the risen Moon: 68, instead of 98! To the Devil with these little houses that all look alike!

In the street, I hasten toward my true objective—but as I walk, I experience a bizarre visual sensation: I seem to see, flying through the clear night, vague large forms of birds, and bounding across the street the giant and vaporous apparitions of various animals!

I attributed this hallucination of sorts to the hypersensitivity of my nervous system, focused on my fiancée, and finally rang the bell at number 98, where the round face of the chambermaid, Sophie, who came to open to door to me, caused me to utter a faint cry of relived satisfaction.

"I'm really here this time!" I exclaimed, gaily. "Monsieur, Madame and Mademoiselle Bic are at home I hope?"

"Yes, Monsieur Cabri," Sophie replied, introducing me into the drawing-room.

My Suzanne and her parents gave me a friendly welcome, but as if they were inhibited by some anxiety. Caught up in the joy of seeing them again, I did not take account of it at first, and politely waxed lyrical about the beauty of the little house and the charm of the drawing-room, whose large bay window opened via a few steps into a garden. The warm night was perfumed; Suzanne seemed to me more delightful than ever. Sitting next to her, however, beneath a lamp, I saw that her beautiful eyes had been weeping.

"What grief has clouded your eyes?" I asked.

She sighed.

Madame Bic replied on her behalf. "You know Fredaine, our pretty little fox-terrier?"

"What about him?"

Suzanne went on, in tears: "Lost! Lost since yesterday! I love animals so much! Poor little dear!" And she burst into sobs.

I consoled her as best I could, somewhat vexed to discover that my presence did not compensate for the absence of an animal.

Maître Bic, however, declared: "You might well cry. You're being punished for your negligence."

"Negligence!" Suzanne protested. "Oh, Papa! He must have got out and got lost in an area that's new to him."

"Got lost! What about his sense of smell! He's been stolen," opined Madame Bic.

The discussion resumed, heatedly, even bitterly—and as Fredaine continued to play the principal role, while I and my bouquet of roses remained confine to subaltern parts, I assumed an air of cool dignity, which did not seem to be to Suzanne's taste, for she criticized me thus: "Oh, I know very well that you detested him!"

"Me, Suzanne!"

"Yes, you. You played practical jokes on him—you pinched his tail and struck his nose as if to kill him!"

"Oh!"

She moved away from me to a settee, to sulk in the shadows beside the pen bay-window. Her parents started a game of piquet under the lamp. Naturally, I went to join Suzanne and knelt at her feet. How divine she was in that half-light! I murmured passionate protests to her in a warm, low voice. She turned her head toward the wall, but her hand was already linked with mine. Weary of kneeling, I gradually raised myself up, in order to sit on a little footstool set next to the settee.

As I sat down, however, a disconcerting phenomenon was manifest beneath me; instead of feeling, on contact, a hard and shiny wooden surface, I seemed to penetrate a gelatinous mass. At the same time my posterior exhaled a kind of confused moan—a muffled plaint like the hoot of a distant owl.

I bounded to me feet, and I saw…

I saw the dog Fredaine, in person, but in an appearance such that I was left speechless, and Suzanne sat there open-mouthed, in a petrified pose.

Her fox terrier was stretched on his belly along the footstool where I had just at down, but, while conserving his color and his fur, seemed no longer to have any but a doughy consistency. His paws—veritable feet of marshmallow, if I might put it thus—were dangling from the footstool on to the carpet; from his head, which he did not have the strength to hold up, to the end of his docked tail, which hung down like a stout piece of vermicelli, he was stretched out lamentably.

In brief, the dog was utterly soft, with the most disastrous, as well as the most unexpected, effect. In addition, he was emitting that kind of plaintive ululation that I had believed, momentarily, to have issued from myself. For that semi-formless dog was alive—inexplicably alive!

Suddenly, the air was rent by piercing screams. Suzanne, prey to—or not far away from—a nervous crisis, was struggling in my arms, accusing me of being responsible: "My darling Fredaine! You've crushed him! You've sat on top of him, you wicked man!"

"Me, Suzanne!"

The Bics hurried over, looking at the abnormal fox-terrier with bleak bewilderment. I protested that, to all evidence, I had sat on the dog, but that, after all, I did not weigh enough to turn him, by virtue of that fact, into a mollusk; that if I had crushed the dog, he would have barked immediately on feeling me weigh upon him; and that, finally, I had had the impression of compressing a soft body rather than a solid one. These peremptory explanations were nevertheless unsuccessful; the family Bic, frozen in amazement, watched the animal get down, effortfully, from the footstool. Now he was crawling over the carpet, a sort of hairy cynocephalous jellyfish with the feet of an octopus. The vile beast!—but simultaneously so ridiculous, with his swaying muzzle, that in spite of the ambient mystery, I could not help smiling. It was a bad move.

"Look at him laughing, now!" cried Suzanne. "Making fun of the harm he's done!"

"You're abusing our hospitality, young man!" said Monsieur Bic, dryly.

"But Monsieur," I went on, impatiently, "must I demonstrate to you once again the innocence of my backside? A crushed dog, damn it, has never taken it into its head to live in a state of softness!"

"You're right," said Bic. "That is a surprising phenomenon..."

"Supernatural!" murmured Madame.

"Unless," her husband continued, looking at me severely, "it's one of those tricks that young clerks are accustomed to play. The clerks of the court have been known..."

"But, good God...!" I exclaimed, angrily.

I was not crying out too soon; a second, even more disconcerting, phenomenon had just become manifest. On the Bics' card-table, harshly lit by the lamp, a handsome white rabbit had just appeared—by what magic? It was pricking up its ears, very much alive!

"A rabbit!"

The same exclamation—imposed by the evidence of the fact—sprang from our lips, but our eyes, this time, were no longer projecting the same gaze. If mine only manifested surprise, those of the spouses Bic allied to astonishment a strong suspicion in my regard. In less than ten minutes, since my arrival, the family dog had been transformed into a kind of living pâté, and a rabbit, unseen until now, had established itself on a table, emerging from nowhere.

Monsieur Bic coughed, paused momentarily, and solemnly pronounced: "This new apparition has confirmed my suspicions. Monsieur Mesmin Cabri, would you be so good as to admit that we consider you to be some kind of trickster, a practical joker, without any regard for the young woman that you claim to love, and devoid of any respect for her parents. I have, in consequence, the honor of asking you to leave."

"But Monsieur Bic....!"

"Leave!" he repeated, inflexibly, his forefinger extended toward the door.

"Suzanne!"

This supplication awoke no echo. My fiancée, terrified, remained huddled against her mother, whose protective arms were wrapped around her.

"Oh, the horrid thing is leaving droppings on my card-table!"

In response to his wife's exclamation, Bic seized the rabbit by the ears,

"And take away your rodent!" he proffered, throwing it at my head.

I caught the symbolic animal in mid-air, and left, swearing to set to work immediately to recover the good graces of the angry parents and my bewildered fiancée.

2. The Outstretched Hand

Once outside, I wanted to persuade myself that I had been the victim of a dream, but the enigmatic rabbit attested the reality. I let the embarrassing herbivore drop on to the pavement; it fled in fear—and while heading toward the Metro, I thought hard. Should I go to the police? To some private detective? Would it not be better, in view of my intelligence, of which I was justly proud, to use my own perspicacity to solve the mystery?

One immediate difficult stopped me, however; the seat of the mystery was the Bic's house—"Castel Bic," according to the rather pretentious inscription decorating the threshold—and I had been expelled from Castel Bic. My self-respect prevented me from reappearing there in any other guise than a victorious Oedipus. Moreover, the rabbit impressed me less than the dog. The idea of an elastic fox-terrier persisted in confounding me, and I imagined with compassion the family's prolonged state of amazement in confrontation with that spectacle.

The memory of the nebulous forms that I had seen flying and bounding in the street further augmented my confusion. Had I really been the victim of an illusion? Involuntarily, I associated the incident with those at Castel Bic, without any plausible reason.

I got back to my room, therefore in an anxious perplexity, and I spent a restless night, sailed by dreams. I saw Monsieur Bic as a rich man, in the place of his respectable superior, with a ridiculous rabbit's head; mounted on a steam-roller, he crushed my tender Suzanne on the road before me; I found no more than a flattened fiancée, like a pancake, while her mother reproached me vehemently for climbing on to her card table.

In brief, after a series of discomfiting little naps, I got up in some distress, my mind painfully extended toward the Inexplicable, of which I was the victim. My Sunday being free, I headed for Auteuil as soon as I had drunk my milky coffee and my three croissants, as if propelled by a force.

As I emerged on to the Rue La Fontaine, I perceived groups of residents engaged in discussions outside the doors. In one compact assembly, I even distinguished a policeman. I drew nearer. He was writing down statements in a greasy notebook, whose tenor appeared to me to have a direct link with the previous evening's events. Several inhabitants of the quarter had seen the unexpected emergence, either in the open air or in their homes, of a cat, a guinea-pig or a rabbit. Some had seen birds. One had even seen a marmoset. As soon as it appeared, each of these animals, fully alive, had commenced the leaps, flutters or capers characteristic of its species.

The majority of the old crones were crying witchcraft. Silently, and with concentration, I lost myself in thought. Suddenly, an idea lit up in my brain, and I asked several people the following question, full of consequence in my judgment: "Was the window of the room in which the animal appeared open or closed?"

All of my interlocutors replied: "It was open."

From that reply I concluded, privately—with a swiftness of induction to which it pleases me to render homage—that these animals had come from outside.

I acquired, moreover, the certainty that all the apparitions had been produced between 9 and 10 p.m. the previous evening—consequently, at the same time as that of the Bic rabbit. They must, therefore, all have proceeded from an identical point of origin.

From then on, the whole of my perspicacity was devoted to the problem of finding the departure point of the invisible animals that became visible at the point of arrival. I am too intelligent to believe in the supernatural, and I persuaded myself, in consequence, that the problem must have a humanly acceptable solution. Although I spent the rest of the day in mediation and observation, in the street, the woods and in cafés, however, the formidable contention of my mind only ended up giving me a terrible headache.

I dined in the open air and took my drink neat, in a tavern in Auteuil, which attenuated my headache slightly. When dark fell, before going home, I wanted to see the Castle of Lost Love again as the sad Pedestrian Errant. For 20 minutes I stood, sighing, beneath the windows of Castel Bic; then, dragging myself away with some difficulty, I continued on my way. It was then—about 100 meters further on—that a new apparition exacerbated my bewildered faculties to the extreme.

The street was almost deserted; the walls extended whitely, bathed in moonlight. As I passed in front of a house I saw hand emerging from a partly-open window at the level of a low entresol, which flattened itself against the exterior wall: a hand that was normal size to begin with but which soon stretched out, becoming elongated, as if constituted of a fluid material, until it was nearly a meter long. Then a wrist and forearm appeared, creeping down the wall like a serpent.

I stood there, stupefied, my eyes glued to the Mystery. Then, slowly, the wrist withdrew; the hand, doubtless having arrived at the limit of its elongation, came back up the wall, and the fingers, like five immense slugs, disappeared through the gap in the window, shrinking as they went.

I looked at the house more attentively, and, by an effort of memory, recognized it. It was the one into which I had gone by mistake the night before!

Impelled by curiosity, and even more so by a presentiment, careless of the dangers suspended over my head, I headed swiftly for the entrance door, hoping to find it open once again. It was closed. I rang repeatedly: no response. I hesitated for some time as to whether I ought to alert the police, but my legal knowledge reminded me that the law prohibits the violation of the homes of citizens after sunset. In any case, I preferred to have the sole honor of solving the prodigious enigma. Weary of ringing the doorbell, I drew away, resolving nevertheless to find out, without delay, what was going on in the house.

The street, as I have said, was almost deserted. There were only a few porters sitting in front of their lodges smoking their pipes, at widely-spaced intervals—which reminded me of the beautiful verses of the poet: "As soon as the heat becomes a little strong/All the concierges are on their doorsteps." The cheerful plumpness of one of them seemed to me to be heavy with confidences. I accosted him with an ingenious remark about the propitiousness of the warm weather for growing vegetables, and collected the following details:

The tenant of the house in question was a Monsieur Pitoulet, a widower with a private income. He lived alone, rarely went out and had few visitors. A daily woman came in to do his housework and cooking. He must be occupied with "electrical matters" because he had been seen taking various machines and instruments into the house, but he was secretive about his work; no one, save for a young assistant, was allowed to go into a large building situated in the garden, whose key he kept on his person. The housekeeper was bad-tempered, but the assistant seemed communicative; many things might be found out from him, but he had disappeared the night before. At any rate, Monsieur Pitoulet was polite to everyone and paid his bills on time; he seemed rather eccentric.

I learned nothing more. I understood, however, why my repeated ringing had been in vain: Monsieur Pitoulet, alone by night, had been afraid to open his door. All in all, I could do no more than wait until the following day to resume my investigation. Convinced that I was on the right track, I went home content.

The following morning I asked in chambers for a day's leave in order to attend to urgent business. I reached Auteuil at 8:30 a.m., determined to shed some light, if not on other enigmas, at least on—if I might employ the style of popular fiction—"the mystery of the elastic hand."

3. *Monsieur Pitoulet*

I took care to ring the doorbell with polite discretion. I heard brief and muffled footsteps approaching. The sullen face of an old woman appeared at a little peep-hole.

"What do you want?" she demanded, peevishly.

I raised my straw boater and asked, politely: "Is Monsieur Pitoulet at home, Madame?"

"First, who are you?"

"I am Monsieur Mesmin Cabri—here's my card."

"Is Monsieur Pitoulet expecting you?"

"Yes," I replied.

"I'll go see."

She shut the peep-hole in my face. A few curious neighbors were watching me. I whistled, idly. The footsteps returned; the peep-hole reopened; the old women reappeared.

"Monsieur Pitoulet doesn't know you."

"Is that possible?"

"Get lost."

"I beg your pardon!" As usual, a fortunate inspiration occurred to me. "Would you please tell Monsieur Picoulet that I've come about *the elastic hand.*"

"The elastic hand?"

"The very same. Go tell him. You'll find that he'll see me."

A further wait—but this time, the door opened. "Follow me," said the old woman, in a milder tone.

We went along the sinuous corridor and she introduced me into a brightly-lit room furnished as a study. I had scarcely entered when I saw a short, pale and thin man appear from a neighboring room. He seemed well-to-do, with a suspicion of a paunch. He was wearing a dressing-gown and a skull-cap with a tassel. His grey hair, rather long and combed back, uncovered a large forehead with bushy eyebrows, beneath which shone keen little black eyes. Above a salt-and-pepper moustache with waxed points was a narrow ruddy nose, and his chin was hidden by a pointed beard. In brief, it was the head of a shriveled and old-fashioned musketeer.

I bowed profoundly. He replied courteously, raising his skull-cap, and, holding my card in the tips of his fingers in an anxious manner, said in a shrill voice: "You want to see me, Monsieur? What about?"

I understood immediately that it was necessary not to treat the little man brusquely, and I replied mildly: "I permitted myself to disturb you, Monsieur, in the hope of rendering you a service. Yesterday evening, in front of your house, I perceived a hand emerging from a window that I can point out to you: a strange hand…"

I paused. He frowned, but remained silent.

I went on: "The hand was a living hand, which stretched inordinately…"

Another pause on my part. He swallowed his saliva, leaned on the back of a chair, and declared, with forced emphasis: "I confess, Monsieur, that I don't see why this story should interest me."

I then understood immediately that it would be better to treat the little man brusquely, and I replied forcefully: "Perhaps it will interest you when you know that I associate it with the disconcerting phenomena that I witnessed the evening before yesterday in this very street."

I watched his nose pass from red to cream. In a tremulous voice, which he tried to render ironic, he said: "Are you, by chance, a policeman?"

I seized the argument that was offered, and in a fit of eloquence, said: "Me! A policeman! Can you believe that, Monsieur? I am an honest young man who comes to you with a pure heart. I will tell you everything, Monsieur, laying my soul bare, for a presentiment whispers to me that you can save my compromised happiness. I am the fiancé of the most ideal of creatures, Mademoiselle Suzanne Bic, the daughter of Maître Bic, the well-known bailiff, who lives further along your street. She has banished me from her sight for having allegedly flattened her fox-terrier and caused the appearance of a rabbit that I had never seen before. Since then, I have tried in vain to vindicate myself. Now, I have learned that you are a great scientist as well as a worthy man. You can undoubtedly furnish me with a few scientific explanations of the surprising phenomena that I have reported to you, which will return my love to me. Oh, Monsieur, save my life!"

And I threw myself at his knees.

I heard him murmur: "The fox-terrier! Ah! The fox-terrier! That's it!" And he added, in a compassionate tone: "You poor young man. Get up, and we'll talk."

It was him who interrogated me—in a rather skillful fashion, I must say—with cross-checks designed to prove my frankness. I felt that I had gained his confidence.

301

Satisfied, he exclaimed: "I, Pitoulet, who have devoted myself to the happiness of humankind, do not want to be the cause of your unhappiness. Depend on me, young Cabri; I will give you back your fiancée."

"You are a good man, Monsieur Pitoulet!" And I threw my arms around him. We embraced momentarily.

Suddenly, he shouted: "Gudule!"

The daily woman appeared. "Make lunch for two," he ordered. Then he turned to me. "I'm inviting you. Since destiny seems to have desired to bring us together, I also have plans for you. I am, at this moment, conducting certain experiments, for which I require a devoted and discreet assistant. Will you be that assistant?"

"But am I qualified? Little versed in the sciences..."

"That's exactly what I need: relative ignorance; absolute devotion."

"But my job...I'm an advocate's clerk..."

"You'll leave your chambers. Suzanne is worth more than that," he concluded, slyly.

How was I able to explain to my patron, without difficulty, that family affairs demanded that I ask for extended leave? How was I able to obtain that leave immediately? Either I must have been persuasive, or he had no pressing need of my services at that moment. Whatever the reason, I returned to the Rue La Fontaine liberated.

During my absence—I have no idea how—Pitoulet must have verified the story of my engagement, for he welcomed me as if I were his own son, and we sat down to lunch cheerfully. He drank his wine neat, like me, and we imparted further confidences. In brief, after dessert, finding himself in perfect sympathy with his guest, he waited until Gudule had placed the coffee, cigars and liqueurs on the table, and then, not without solemnity, he expressed himself in these terms:

"First, I must ask for your word of honor not to reveal anything about the spectacle that you will shortly witness."

I swore a solemn oath. He continued:

"Cabri, chance favored you initially, by showing you that hand stretching along the wall; afterwards, it was a perfectly correct—and childishly simple— association of ideas that led you to think that I was no stranger to the phenomena in question, but before I explain them to you, permit me to tell you something about myself.

"I confided to you, between the Port-Salut and the apricots, that I had an unhappy marriage. To be more precise, my wife deceived me prodigiously. I had married the exuberant daughter of a large wallpaper manufacturer. Obliged to earn my own living from an early age, I had entered into his business as a mere employee. However, having an inventive mind with a scientific bent, I discovered a method of coloring that earned him a great deal of money.

302

"As I was working on a new invention, he offered me his daughter in order to attach me to him. I accepted, and I had reason, as is often the case, to congratulate myself on that decision, and also to regret it in certain respects—to regret it because, after two months of marriage, my wife attached herself to a series of lovers, successive or simultaneous, to the exclusion of myself; to congratulate myself on it because, henceforth sheltered from need, I was able to continue my research. I abandoned, of course, anything to do with wallpaper— which exasperated my father-in-law.

"I was already deemed to be an eccentric; I was soon charge with insanity, especially when certain papers that I had presented to the Académie proved incapable of attracting the attention of my official colleagues. I was nothing in their eyes but an irregular, a guerrilla of science, poorly regarded in the regular army of black and green cocked hats. Then again, I was devoid of urbanity, and had such a luminous nose...

"To cut a long story short, I complained to my father-in-law one evening about his daughter's misconduct—I had not dared to tackle my wife about it; she would have beaten me—and he submerged me in a cascade of insults, accusing me of having 'put one over on him.' He offered me by way of final settlement an income, on condition that I let the divorce go through on the grounds of my own faults and injuries. I accepted, for the sake of science but, being practical for once in my life, demanded a capital sum instead of a pension. To my father-in-law's dictation I wrote a few peremptory missives to imaginary ladies, was condemned by the court and, without delay, dedicated the price of my liberty to the installation of a laboratory.

"Having no needs, save for an occasional glass of good wine; all my small income was devoted to my studies. I have undertaken research of a special nature. It has lasted ten years, young man—but patience is the true form of scientific enthusiasm. This research has just reached a conclusion. You shall know what it was, and what its result has been."

Monsieur Pitoulet had risen to his feet, with his forefinger in the air, as if inspired—and he said: "Follow me!"

4. The Great Transmutator

We left the room and went through the garden. In an open space behind a few tall trees, I discovered a sort of closed hangar, the door of which Pitoulet opened for me. I went into what seemed to be a vast machine-room. There were no windows, but the glazed roof let light in. There was a profusion of electric lamps hanging from wires or fixed to the walls. Insulated electrical cables ran along the white-enameled walls.

Almost in the center of the rectangular room, on a glass-paved platform, protected by a glass ramp, stood a black mass at least four meters high: a sort of giant cylinder, enveloped, so far as I could judge, with some sort of tarry coat-

303

ing. We made a tour of the room in which the black cylinder lay, turning left at the entrance door. The entire length of the left-hand wall was fitted with a little walkway, reached by means of three steps. On an immense white marble console bolted to the wall above the walkway at head-height, an array of switches and levers displayed a copper gleam. Pairs of thick black cables emerged from the console, criss-crossing above our heads like an enormous spider's web and disappearing into the central mass.

We headed for the back of the room, and I saw that the enormous cylinder terminated, at that end, in a shining cone that seemed to me to be made of copper. The braids of rings that encircled the cylinder in places similarly seemed to be copper. In front of the cone was an immense stool—or, more accurately, a platform—at least two meters square, composed of some black shiny material reminiscent of black lead. To the right of the platform, vertically placed at head height, a marble console analogous to the one fixed to the wall, but much smaller, supported a varied set of switches. Behind the black platform stood another strange apparatus, a kind of metallic grille, four meters high if not more, similar in form to a car radiator, maintained by brackets sunk into the floor.

We went around the grille, which was parallel to the wall, and came back toward the entrance on the other side of the room, where I noticed various objects, most notably an enormous glass bell-jar—destined for what nightmarish cheese?—a machine that seemed to me to be a rotatory pump, and a little cabin bearing the inscription: *Cloakroom.*

"That concludes the proprietor's tour," said Pitoulet, with a satisfied expression.

I made no reply, prey to a vertigo of utter incomprehension. I discerned, obviously, that it was an electrical installation of a special kind—but what? What was its purpose?

"You seem somewhat at a loss," Pitoulet remarked.

"Indeed!"

"Have you studied electricity?"

"Yes, at school."

"Poor boy! But it's a marvel, of a sort, since you don't understand it very well. I'll tell you enough to put you in the picture—the essential facts."

He went on:

"Know, therefore, Cabri, my friend, that one science has always been my passion: chemistry, the science of sciences, in sum; that which penetrates the depths of things in order to discover the principle, the essence. It is to all the natural sciences what metaphysics is to philosophy, with the difference, nevertheless, that metaphysics plays with dreams, while chemistry works upon the real. Ah! To decompose to the extremity of unity the bodies that compose nature, to finally discover the essential matter! But we are far from that goal, and who knows whether we shall ever achieve it? The essential matter draws away when one gets close to it, vanishes when one thinks one has grasped it, and there remains of it, in the ultimate analysis, no more than a word: Energy, imagined by scientists to lull their ignorance—a word that, you might well think, is not the proclamation of a victory but the confession of a defeat.

"Which will triumph in the end—man, who pursues, or nature, which hides? Man, I firmly believe, for man is nothing but conscious nature, determined to know itself. For my part, I have pushed my research into the constitution of matter as far as I can, but chemistry is an immense domain, one sole branch of which suffices for a man's career. I therefore devoted myself to the chemistry of organic bodies—but that branch still being too vast, I took one of its side-roads and devoted myself to biochemistry, the chemistry of living bodies. The constitution of living matter then became the object of my research.

"I resolved to begin, methodically, by studying the molecular structure of its component parts, and as the best means of getting to know the intimate structure of a body is the comparative study of its variant states, the ides occurred to me of submitting bodies to an influence capable of modifying them physically. It seemed to me that the influence in question might be obtained by means of an electrical force or, more precisely, that of a very powerful magnetic field. 'Very powerful' is an understatement; I resolved to create a magnetic field of unprecedented power and, not without difficulty and expense, I ordered the construction of the apparatus you see here, which is, as you have doubtless guessed…"

"No."

"Well, you're as ignorant as one could wish. Which is…an electromagnet."

"That enormous cylindrical mass?"

"Yes. That mass, covered with an insulating envelope, is simply the most powerful electromagnet in the world. I had it constructed in Pittsburgh, U.S.A. The wire coils contained in its spools contain several hundred tons of copper. By means of a process that I have discovered, which constitutes the greatest originality of the apparatus, no heating is produced in the metal, in spite of the immense quantity of electrical energy circulating within it. The recording devices installed at intervals testify to that absence of heat. I confess, however, that my cooling system necessitates the employment of liquid air. That large platform placed on insulators is made of graphite. It is set at the dead center of the magnetic field produced by the electromagnet. Finally, the enormous grille that you see standing behind it is linked to a series of metal pieces buried in the floor, in such a way that communication with the ground is perfect. Contrary to what might seem to be the case, the grille is not made of iron but of lead, a nonmagnetic metal. It concentrates and reinforces the electromagnet's field of action, by limiting it.

"Once I was ready to bring this torrential source of magnetic energy into play, I began by studying the molecular structure of carbon, the essential component of living matter. I therefore submitted a block of specially-purified carbon to the influence of the magnetic field. I placed it on the graphite platform and switched on the current, in order to provoke a particular process of disaggregation, which there is no need to explain to you. It was then that the incident occurred that fortuitously revealed the capital virtue of my apparatus.

"Seated facing the platform, with my hands on the switches located in the external face of that marble slab, I was gradually increasing the magnetic flux when a cat slipped into the room through a gap in one of the glass panes in the ceiling. I set about trying to chase it out, but the fleeing animal leapt on to the experimental block of carbon. Oh, my dear Cabri! I heard a *miaow* and...but you'd better see for yourself."

He went out, went to a hutch in a corner of the garden, and came back holding a guinea-pig in his arms.

"Wait here a moment," he said. "I'll go switch on the dynamos."

He handed the animal to me and went into a shed situated some ten paces away.

"Yes," he said, on coming back, "I definitely need a new assistant. I can't do it alone. Let's go back into the laboratory now; I'll reproduce in this guinea-pig the phenomena observed in the cat...for all animals, including all human beings, are equal before the Great Transmutator. That's the name of my apparatus. Now, the experiment!"

5. The Properties of a Colloid

Pitoulet placed the guinea-pig on the graphite platform, climbed up on to the walkway running along the left-hand wall and set himself in front of the big marble console. He operated switches and depressed levers. Then he went to the console set beside the platform and rotated commutators, saying: "20,000 volts. Don't lose sight of the animal."

The latter remained motionless. Suddenly, it uttered a little squeal and made a slight hop, but fell back as if stuck to the platform, and began to subside, collapse and flatten out. Then, its slender legs no longer being able to support it, it spread out like a poultice.

"Stop!" cried Pitoulet, halting the action of the electromagnet. "Do you understand, now, how the cat that paid me a visit became elastic, just like the Bic girl's fox-terrier."

"I understand how," I said, aptly, "but I don't understand why."

"You'll understand why shortly. Let's finish the experiment. From an elastic state, this interesting little animal will become vaporous, if you please. 30,000 volts!"

And he switched the current on again.

"I don't see any change occurring," I said, after a few seconds.

"Wait," he replied. "Although the transition from the solid to the fluid state takes place gradually, that from the fluid state to the vaporous state is instantaneous."

Indeed, a few minutes later, the guinea-pig-poultice swelled up and suddenly rose upwards, transforming itself into a guinea-pig-cloud, rather vague in form but nevertheless recognizable, like a slanting shadow: a form neither diaphanous nor opaque, but smoky, if one might put it like that, with darker internal streaks in which the design of the skeleton was vaguely discernible—and that form, about a meter long and half a meter tall, swayed like a heavy mist above the graphite platform.

"Blow hard, with me," Pitoulet said, stopping the current.

We blew in unison, and the guinea-pig-cloud, expelled from the platform, was thus steered toward the enormous glass bell-jar that I had noticed while walking round the room. Pitoulet attached a cord to the handle at the top, passed the cord over a pulley, raised the bell-jar over the guinea-pig by that means, and then brought it down again upon the animal, thus trapping it inside.

"There it is, caged."

"But is it still alive?"

"Still. You see these three holes pierced in the bell-jar—they let in the air necessary to life."

"But…"

"Patience, impetuous Cabri. Sit down on the walkway with me. For the present, listen."

Then he explained:

"I told you just now that the science that has always excited me most of all is biochemistry. My entire achievement resides in a fortunate application of the laws of electromagnetism to the discoveries of biochemistry. About my part in the invention of the Great Transmutator I have told you all that I can. The rest remains my secret—but it is permissible not to hide anything from you regarding the biochemical conditions of the experiment.

"Every human being, as you probably know, is essentially made up of cells. Now, all these cells, interior protoplasm and walls alike, all the membranes that partition the organism in every direction and all the liquids that bathe it—blood, lymph, chyle, cellular sugar—are constituted by substances that bear the name of colloids. What is a colloid? It is an assembly of ultra-microscopic particles suspended in a liquid medium, which separates and unites them. Organic colloids—in humans, for example—are composed of albuminoid particles about a ten-thousandth of a millimeter large…"

"Small, you mean?" I suggested.

"Large small, as you please. Ten-thousandths of a millimeter are fearfully large compared with millionths of a millimeter. These particles, as I was saying, bathe in a liquid medium, which one might describe, in order to simplify things for your usage, as a saline solution. The human body is nothing but an assemblage of organic colloids. Now, the action of the magnetic field created by the electromagnet has the effect of modifying the consistency of the interposed liquid. In its normal state, that consistency is viscous. The influence of the electromagnet renders it more fluid. To put it another way, the action of the magnetic field has the effect of diminishing the coefficient of viscosity of the interposed liquid. That's quite clear, I imagine.

"What happens in consequence? The particles suspended in the liquid have more freedom of movement, the composite aggregate of the colloid becomes looser, and the consistency of the organism, formerly solid, becomes elastic. Taking the experiment further, however, as I increase the intensity of the magnetic field, the coefficient of viscosity is reduced in proportion, and the primitive liquid, the fluid, becomes vaporous. In addition, the organic particles that originally carried various electric charges, suddenly all acquire the same charge. That's a fact. Now, as everyone knows, two bodies carrying the same electrical charge repel one another. The distance between the particles is therefore enormously increased at a stroke—which is to say that the colloid suddenly passes into a vaporous state, and would pass into the state of a true gas if I increased the intensity of the magnetic field further. The guinea-pig colloid that you see under the bell-jar is, therefore, presently in the state of an organic mist. It would be exactly the same for a human colloid. I think you've understood that.

"The new state lasts for three hours; then a return to the natural state inevitably takes place. I haven't yet succeeded in shortening or extending the duration of the transformation. Thus, for about three hours, the new colloidal state persists without any apparent modification. However, internal processes begin to take effect as soon as the organism is removed from the influence of the magnetic field, and three hours later it reverts to its original state. It is worth noting that the organism must pass through the elastic state in order to attain the vaporous state, but returns directly and abruptly from the vaporous state to the solid state.

"You can now explain, I hope, the phenomena that disconcerted you so much. I found your fiancée's fox-terrier outside my door and, mistaking it for a stray dog, I used it in an experiment. Then I had to go out briefly. On my return I saw, in the street, a series of escaped organic mists. I went back inside so hurriedly that I left my door open. You must have followed close behind me, and came in behind me. In the laboratory, I found my assistant Eusèbe, who was amusing himself by lifting up the bell-jar in which I had enclosed a collection of mist-animals, with all the windows open. The elastic dog had vanished—from what you have told me, the brave animal must have crawled all the way back to its masters.

"When my assistant saw me come in, he fled into the garden. First of all, I tried to catch as many animals as possible in this metallic net; at that moment, I heard footsteps in my house; I remembered that I had left the door open, and it was then that I called out, is alarm: 'Who's there? Close the door, Eusèbe!" On that, you ran away. I called my assistant back mildly, but my decision was irrevocable. His recent misdeed demanded that I get rid of him immediately. He was a very intelligent fellow, but excessively curious and indiscreet. So much the worse for him...."

"You sent him packing?" I asked.

"Yes, completely."

"And you're not afraid that he'll talk?"

"No. I'm perfectly tranquil. He won't talk anymore." On these words, he emitted a short burst of shrill laughter, rather unpleasant, which caused me to shiver slightly.

"You've guessed the rest," he concluded. "My mist-animals spread out in all directions, and, when the time came, resolidified, like the rabbit in your fiancée's home."

"I understand," I declared. "But how do you explain the persistence of life through these changes of state? How do they breathe, eat…and return to nature that which it has given to us?"

"The answer, Cabri, is that the phenomena of digestion are considerably slowed down. The organism experiences no needs of any sort. As for the respiratory functions necessary to life, they continue. Nothing prevents atmospheric gases from penetrating an elastic organism in the ordinary way; as for liquid blood, it circulates easily, the coefficient of viscosity of its constituent colloids is diminished to the same extent as that of all the other parts of the body. In the vaporous state, on the other hand, the circulatory phenomena are modified; circulation is replaced by a particular interaction of organic particles, which I have not yet studied in depth; as for respiration, it becomes a sort of osmosis."

"One more thing, Master. You've mentioned the human organism several times. Have you, therefore, in addition to animal experiments, carried out experiments on humans?"

"Haven't you begun to suspect that 'the elastic hand' was my own hand?"

"Then, at that moment, you were entirely…"

"Entirely elastic. Yes, Cabri. Late yesterday evening, alone in my house, rid of my assistant, I climbed up on to the graphite platform. Like any scientist worthy of the name, I proceeded to experiment on myself."

"And you haven't come to any harm?"

"So little that, for your benefit, I shall do it again."

6. The Master of the Three States

With that, he headed for the cabinet bearing the inscription *Cloakroom*. As I interrogated him with my gaze, he said: "Clothes don't impede the operation at all, but the magnetic current corrodes them, so it's as well to wear as little as possible. It's also better to take off any rings, watch and chain, etc., whose metal might be profoundly altered. Give me a minute."

He went into the cabinet and returned shortly afterwards. He stepped up on to the walkway and carried out the operations necessary to convey the current on the marble console attached to the wall. Then he climbed up on to the graphite platform.

"Perhaps you haven't noticed this," he said, and showed me a sort of indicator on the inner face of the marble plate next to the platform, on whose dial I saw a needle and two inscribed words: *elastic* and *mist*. "It's a simple electric clock. As the case may be, I place the needle facing the word *elastic* or the word *mist*. As soon as the required state is obtained, the current automatically cuts out. In fact, I won't have the strength any longer to operate the commutators, get down from the platform or maintain the power of the magnetic field. Elastic or mist?"

"If you're going to make a full demonstration, Master, I'll need to see elastic *and* mist."

"So be it. Let's go."

Pitoulet stood upright on the platform; he set the needle to the word *elastic*, manipulated the commutators, and shuddered. His hair stood up slightly; then he seemed to experience a brief nausea. A moment later, he spoke: "The experiment doesn't prevent conversation, except that my voice will become increasing faint and tenuous."

"Tell me what you're experiencing, then, Master."

"A vague, temporary, heartache; at present, I have the impression that something elementary is melting away from me, through all my pores, and that a kind of reduced density is extending through my entire being. It's a very curious sensation of simultaneous lightness and subsidence. Look, my legs are flexing involuntarily...giving way..."

He was obliged to kneel down; his thighs weakened in their turn and he took up a crouching position. I placed myself at his level.

"Everything in me is softening," he continued, "my brain along with everything else. My faculties remain, however; the brain must therefore involve something other than cerebral matter—an interesting contribution to the study of the relationship between body and mind. Can you still hear me well enough?"

"Your voice is getting weaker, Master."

He collapsed on to his belly and subsided further by degrees: a human mollusk.

Suddenly, a bell rang.

"The current has cut out," he told me. "Stand aside a little, please—I'm going to get down."

His arms slid along the platform, and his hands passed over the edge; then they stretched—flowing, as one might say, toward the floor. The arms followed, then the head, then the whole body. And, like the fox-terrier and the guinea-pig, the great scientist began actually to slither. Having covered two meters, he called "Cabri!"—and his voice resembled the bleat of a little lamb. He tried to raise the head that he was maintaining, effortlessly, a few centimeters from the floor. I got down on all fours and lent him an ear.

"You'll have to help me curl up in a corner," he said. "We can talk more easily then."

I understood then the full sense of the popular expression "to pick something up spoon-fashion." I picked up that soft mass—proportionately—like a patissier handling dough for a tart, and propped it up, taking care to dispose the hindquarters at the bottom and the head at the top. When the operation as complete, Pitoulet thanked me with a flat smile what seemed to me to be the last word in ridiculousness. It was like looking at a image reflected in an acutely convex mirror.

"Sit down next to me," he said. "You're going to help me in a few experiments that I can't carry out on my own. If you open a cupboard that you'll find in the cabinet, you'll find a funnel, a liter of milk and some eggs. Bring them here."

I obeyed, and, following his instructions, I experimented with the possibility of feeding an elastic organism by pouting milk and raw eggs into his mouth with the aid of the funnel.

"Excellent," he declared. "The aliments zigzag inside me in a most agreeable fashion. Place a newspaper in front of me."

I did so. He read with difficulty, his sight being impeded by excessively flaccid eyelids. His nose remained sensitive to odors. His hearing was ameliorated—by virtue of a fortunate influence of the elastic state, he thought, on the perilymph and the endolymph of the inner ear.

Then I laid him down and stretched out his body to a length of four meters forty. I compacted him again and compressed him into a ball about 50 centimeters in diameter without him experiencing the slightest pain, but he began to choke and I relaxed my grip. His hair remained as it was; his teeth and nails, being slightly harder than the rest of his body, had the texture of rubber.

I was able to exercise all imaginable torsions on his limbs, and plaited his arms together without causing him a moment's discomfort. The parts of the body sustained by the skeleton were a little less soft than the others, and I experienced a stronger resistance in digging my finger into the skull than driving it into the abdomen.

"So you'll stay like this for three hours?" I said.

"No, Cabri, my friend, since you're here. Yesterday I had to spend the night in an elastic state, not being able to stand up or reach the commutators with my arms. But you can put me back on the platform, position the needle on the dial on the word *mist*, and turn the commutators in the direction that I indicate to you—and you'll see me become vaporous."

"Understood, Master. Nevertheless, I wonder how you were able, yesterday, to travel in the elastic state from the laboratory to your bedroom."

"By crawling slowly. Once I had reached my bedroom I wanted to take account of the power of elongation of a part of my body under the effect of gravity. Not without difficulty, I put my hand out of the lowest window, which started flowing down the wall. It was then that you noticed it. It required the greatest effort to bring it back, but I obtained some help from the asperities in the stone, which formed points of support for slithering. After which, I slid into the hollow of a mattress set on the ground in advance, and went to sleep until it was time to become my normal self again. Would you please place me on the platform?"

"Here goes, Master."

Half tugging and half pushing, I hoisted him up on to the apparatus, set the needle to *mist* and restored the current, according to his indications. After a brief interval, I saw him become blurred; within an instant, his body became imprecise, translucent but not transparent, in the fashion of a dirty window-pane. At the same time he grew, until he reached the ceiling, a vast shadow. Then the bell rang.

He advanced toward me. I retreated. Then I heard his minuscule voice, like the mewling of a cat, asking me: "Are you scared? Stand still."

I stopped moving, and Pitoulet passed through me—or, rather, I passed through Pitoulet—without any difficulty; after which, I perceived that a light greasy coating was covering my hands and face. I heard a thin laugh and, cocking my ear toward the ceiling, I perceived the explanation.

"Lipids, otherwise called fats, don't pass completely into the vaporous state, so they leave a slight trace on bodies that pass through them, and your face has just passed through the fattest part of my body. It's an unimportant detail. Transpierce me with that walking-stick."

I passed a cane through his body and met the wall. Then he put his hands on my cheeks; it was like a warmth devoid of contact. He asked me to walk over him, but my feet encountered nothing but the floor. No matter what I did, he remained indivisible, because he was ungraspable.

"This time," he went on, "I'll stay like this for three hours. I don't want to keep you for all that time. You can leave whenever you wish. I don't need anything. The vaporous state is perfectly euphoric."

It was 2 p.m. I kept him company for a while longer, then went out for a walk, after having promised to come back for dinner.

At 8 p.m., I was there, and I found him resolidified and very cheerful.

"Let's eat!" he cried. "I have a ferocious appetite."

"And everything went smoothly?" I asked.

"Without any hitch. Half an hour before the solidification, one experiences a vague discomfort, both superficial and profound, a shrill vibration of the entire being. There's a sort of 'critical point', which coincides with the preliminaries of the return to a normal state. As the internal work of the tissues proceeds, the misty state persists; there's a sudden, instantaneous pain—and it's all over. One finds oneself hale and hearty, as solid as before. Now, it's a matter of impregnating the ensemble of our colloids with old wine. What do you think?"

"I think," I said, sitting down, "that it's an idea of genius, like all of yours, my dear Master, and I remain, facing your discovery, rapt with admiration."

"You're right," he said, not without pride. "I have, in sum, succeeded in provoking a series of changes in organic bodies corresponding to those that are effected on inorganic bodies. One causes inorganic matter to pass between the three states of solid, liquid and gas. I have caused organic matter to pass through its own three states: solid, elastic and vaporous."

"And by virtue of that fact," I proclaimed, raising a glass of Clos-Vougeot to my lips, "you deserve, like all the most illustrious scientists, a sparkling epithet or a glowing nickname, by which your memory will be illuminated throughout posterity: I drink to *the Master of the Three States*."

And we clinked glasses, our eyes moist with emotion.

7. Two Nebulous Citizens

Having drunk a toast to *the Master of the Three States*, we drank one to my fiancée, then to Paris, then to Anjou, my native province, then to Brittany, which was his, then to the gracious sovereigns presently visiting the Capital, then to the colloids, and then...with the result that, by the end of the meal, we were enveloped by an aura of beatitude. Pitoulet's nose was scarlet.

"Come on," said my friend, "let's get some fresh air in the garden."

"Get some fresh air." A derisory expression. The air was heavy, without a breath of wind. We breathed with difficulty.

"Do you know what would be delightful?" he said. "A few hours in the vaporous state. One feels light, blissful...no weight in the stomach. I shall offer myself that pleasure. Will you accompany me to the laboratory?"

"Certainly, my dear Master."

Once beside the platform he said to me, smiling: "Will you climb up with me?"

"My word," I replied. "I'm strongly tempted. I won't hide from you that the elastic state doesn't attract me; it renders a man rather grotesque—and when I imagine my Suzanne and I thus metamorphosed, I experience a slight nausea. But the vaporous state seems to me to be distinguished."

"Get undressed, then, and climb up on the platform. Uh oh! Cabri, you're scared!"

"Me, scared? Can a scientific apparatus...?"

"If you aren't scared, Cabri, be less eloquent and more prompt. Get dressed and climb up on the platform."

"I will!"

I went into the cloakroom with him. We came out again naked. "There!" I cried. "Now, *en route* for the land of shadows!"

"How excited the young man is!" said Pitoulet laughing. "there—I've set the needle; I'm starting the current. It's begun!"

Oh, the bizarre sensation! A powerful prickling sensation, profound and total, overwhelmed my body from head to toe. Then I felt as if I were melting, collapsing into myself like a softened block of starch. Pitoulet and I were passing together into the elastic state—but we only passed through it; suddenly we began to grow. It seemed to me that all my organs were swelling up and becoming lighter. My face turned to Pitoulet's, which reached the ceiling of the room; our enormous vaporous looked at one another with a certain emotion. And, as we were on the same level, we were easily able to converse.

"We'll get down," Pitoulet said, "as soon as we hear the bell—and there it is! After you, my dear Cabri. We have three hours before us in the state of human clouds."

We left the platform. He continued: "The door is open. I've got an idea: we'll take a turn around the garden and see how we stand with regard to things."

"Excellent idea," I replied.

We moved around for a little while without tiring of enjoying the most delicate sensations. We walked—or, more accurately, glided—along the pathways, half as tall as the trees whose branches passed through us without any harm being done to them or us. We came upon sleeping birds, and stroked them without waking them up. The intimate perfumes of the high foliage bathed us; we breathed it in, seemingly throughout our entire being, with a delightful facility. In brief, the vaporous state was accompanied by a general delight, doubtless due to our lightness—for, according to Pitoulet's calculations, we weighed scarcely twice as much as the volume of air we displaced.

Thus walking and chatting, we came to the end of the garden, and looked to see what was happening in the neighboring houses. Invisible in the darkness, we looked through the windows at many a spectacle that gave us pleasure.

"Another time," Picoulet said, "you can shut me up, while in a vaporous state, in a thin sealed container. You can compress me without effort to the volume of a large melon. Nothing's easier, if one wants to travel incognito, that to have oneself transported by a friend in the guise of a child's balloon."

"I imagine so!" I exclaimed. "If only I could steal my Suzanne away from her parents by means of that artifice. I could carry her in compressed form, in my bosom!"

"Don't worry about that," he replied. "I've thought about it, and I've found 19 ways of getting her back."

"Oh, Master—you're my savior!"

"Would you like to test out the first means that I think excellent?"

"Do you need to ask?"

"Well, here it is. The street is deserted. Not a breath of air. I'll go out and appear before the spouses Bic as the spirit of an ancestor, who commands them to give you their daughter."

"Genius! Madame Bic has an iron-hard belief in spiritualism—and, in the intimacy of their home, she dominates her husband. It's to her that you should appear."

"What's her grandfather's name?"

"Gédéon Mornebler, a dealer in birds from the Isles. But can't I go with you?"

"Yes indeed, Cabri; the two of us will knock them dead."

"Nevertheless, Master," I added, "I'd like the scene to take place in the absence of my dear Suzanne, She's as sensitive as the clematis of the fields, and I fear..."

"We'll wait for the old people to be alone."

Brave Pitoulet! He spoke of "old people," although he was old himself, with the soul of a young man.

After discussing all the possible contingencies, we climbed over the garden wall and fell down into the street again like scarves of gauze—gas, I would risk, if I did not have to refrain, along with the great Victor Hugo (who did not always deprive himself of the privilege) from "the droppings of an airborne spirit."[44]

And here we are on the sidewalk. Not a breath of wind. We advance, colossal shadows, slightly overlapping—and after a few meters we see a young couple coming toward us, tenderly enlaced. As Pitoulet has foreseen, we are confused with the evening mist. Moreover, the lovers are scarcely occupied with the external world. They pass right through us without suspecting it, their lips united. Nevertheless—our hearing being very sensitive—we hear the girl say to the boy: "Don't you think, Gustave, that our kiss had a funny taste? It seemed as if I had grease on my lips?"

"I had the same impression, Isabelle," he replies.

In fact, their two faces have passed through our bellies. Then we cross the path of three artillerymen who are marching as if in a dream. They do not perceive us. We have almost arrived when an old lady on the opposite sidewalk undoubtedly sees us silhouetted by the light of a gas-lamp, for she points at the street-light with a squeal of alarm. Already, though, we have leapt over the garden wall of Castel Bic.

---

[44] Unsurprisingly, the intricacy of the wordplay in the original of this passage does not translate easily into English, although the similarity between *gaze* [gauze] and *gaz* [gas] does not disappear entirely. In *Les Misérables* (1862)— which, as its title suggests, is not exactly a barrel of laughs—Victor Hugo passes aphoristic judgment on punning with the harsh judgment that "*le calembour est la fiente de l'esprit qui vole*" [puns are the faeces of soaring wit]. Cabri's appropriation takes some advantage of a double entendre within the aphorism, which permits *esprit* to be construed as "spirit" instead of "wit,",but the initial reference likening his descent from the garden wall to the dropping of a gauze scarf also implies a subtler pun with respect to Hugo's terminology; when a lady deliberately drops a scarf in order that a gentleman in whom she is interested might pick it up and return it, such an action qualifies as a *feinte* [ploy], a word that can be modified by a transposition of letters into *fiente*, which I have elected to translate in the text, with due delicacy, as "droppings."

It was important now to act boldly and prudently. The night was dark. By bending down we were able to look in through the open window of the dining room, which was illuminated. Monsieur Bic, his pipe between his lips, was reading a newspaper. Madame Bic was knitting. My Suzanne was leaning through a book, but her beautiful eyes often looked up at the ceiling, pensively. A little while later, she left the room. Was she going to return? We made a tour of the house and saw her bedroom light go on. She got undressed. There was a blue nightgown lying on a chair beside her. Oh, how I would have loved to satiate my gaze on the charming spectacle of that state of undress! Pitoulet reminded me of the situation.

"Let's not waste time—this is the moment."

I tore myself away from that enchanted place with difficulty, and we went back to the dining room. We heard the sounds of a mandolin; my Suzanne was giving voice to her harmonious melancholy—which did not prevent Bic from declaring: "Our daughter is playing false notes."

The Barbarian! The notes, false or not, added the attraction of an unexpected morbidity to the nostalgic ballad. But it was necessary to get to work. Simultaneously, Pitoulet and I went through the window into the room, and we crouched down, him in front of Madame and me in front of Monsieur.

In our faint, shrill voices, we gave orders: "Not a gesture. Not a sound. Your lives depend on it."

In the lamplight, our enormous vaporous faces were clearly distinguishable. The spouses Bic started in unison and swallowed the cries ready to emerge from their open mouths. Bic dropped his pipe. Madame Bic put her hands together fearfully.

Pitoulet started immediately. "Clothilde Bic, I am the Spirit of your grandfather Gédéon Mornebler. I have come back on this memorable evening to tell you that I am watching over you, and to communicate my wishes. I order you and your spouse to marry your daughter to Mesmin Cabri, whose astral double I have evoked."

"Present!" I said to Monsieur Bic.

"Returned briefly from the Empire of Souls, I foresee, spouses Bic, that if your daughter marries him, you will all live long and prosperous lives. If not, then misfortune and damnation will be upon you all—misfortune and damnation!"

Pitoulet prophesied with the assurance of a professional revenant. He added: "You shall write a letter to Mesmin this very evening, and you will marry him to Suzanne within the month." He addressed himself to me: "I give you warning of that, astral double!"

"Duly noted, Spirit of Mornebler!" I replied, respectfully.

"And now," he concluded, "swear to obey me, Bics!"

"I swear," stammered Madame, curled over in fright.

Bic remained silent, rolling his eyes anxiously...but we heard my Suzanne's footsteps; we disappeared through the open window, but remained on watch in the shadows.

"I think the effect was successful," Pitoulet whispered.

"Let's wait and see," I murmured, anxiously.

On seeing her dumbfounded parents, Suzanne said, anxiously: "Papa! Mama! What's the matter? Tell me! You're frightening me!"

Bic leapt to his feet and leaned out of the window. Naturally, he saw nothing. He went back, muttering: "Some illusion...I've drunk too much coffee."

"What about me?" said his wife. "Too much lime-tea, perhaps?"

"There's something behind this..."

"There's the will of my grandfather Mornebler behind it. Face it—you saw him as clearly as you see me!"

"Grandpapa Gédéon?" Suzanne queried. "What do you mean?"

"Don't be afraid, my child," her mother replied. "Your father and I will discuss it. Is Monsieur Mesmin still to your liking?"

Only a maternal heart has such delicacy. Suzanne lowered her head and murmured: "Oh, yes!"

If Pitoulet had not restrained me, she would have received a shadow's embrace.

"Very well," her mother replied, "You shall marry him when you..."

8. A Gala at the Opéra

We would have loved to know more, but a light breeze sprang up, which blew us away from the window.

"Oh!" said Pitoulet. "Wind's the last thing we need. And here's the Moon showing its face. Let's get back to the laboratory."

"Let's get back," I agreed.

Lifted up by the breeze, we passed over the wall at a slightly greater height than was necessary, and fell back into the street. There, a surprise awaited us; the wind, which had been blowing gently between the enclosing walls of the garden, strengthened more briskly in the corridor of the street, in a direction exactly opposite to the one we needed to take.

A few seconds sufficed for us to observe, anxiously, that instead of advancing we were retreating rather rapidly. Like swimmers exhausting themselves by struggling against a current bearing them away from the bank, we exhausted ourselves resisting the wind that was drawing us away from the haven. I was horribly anxious. We were forced, after a short time, to turn around, with our backs to the wind, in order not to continue retreating blindly. In less than three minutes, it pushed us all the way to the end of the street, on to the Quai de Passy, and into a coaching entrance. There, we were sheltered.

"Well," I said to Pitoulet, who was huddling under the archway like me, "here's a nice situation."

"Let's wait for a calm," he replied.

I gazed along the Seine, and observed that the Alexandre III bridge, and the Grand and Petit Palais, were all lit up. "Look," I said to Pitoulet.

"Why so many lights?" he said.

"Have you forgotten that Paris is entertaining royal visitors?"[45]

"Unimportant..."

We prick up our ears. Behind the glazed door that closed the archway on the side of the courtyard, footsteps and voices can be heard. Dreading that an abrupt current of air might tear us apart, we decide to go out, inasmuch as the wind seems to us to have weakened—but whoosh! The westerly wind, actually more violent, drags us away in its course. It is at the speed of a trotting horse that we go along the pier toward the Place de la Concorde, in an oppressive silence.

Level with the Pont de l'Alma, the groups of strollers become frequent and dense, and the pier is brightly lit. Thus, in spite of the rapidity of our passage, we are immediately noticed. I shall not undertake to record the greater number of the exclamations that are uttered: some people collapse in fear, others stand there stupefied, others follow our course, and the most courageous throw stones at us—which, without doing us the slightest harm, strike people in the vicinity. Others, alerted by the rumor and the screams, run to meet us, passing through us and colliding violently with our pursuers.

In brief, as we reach the Place de la Concorde, the tumult becomes so loud that a brigade of policemen, posted in the courtyard of the Bourbon Palace, think it a manifestation of unrest and start striking out with their fists—an intervention that gives rise to a perfect brawl.

Amid the curses of men, the groans of women and the weeping of children, we were flying on at high speed, tracked by the policemen and our fellow citizens, when an opportunity was offered to us: the gate of the Jardin des Tuileries was closed. We slipped between the bars; the howling mob crushed itself against them, and thus lost track of us.

Beneath the trees the wind calmed down, and our moderated velocity permitted us to exchange a few impressions.

"We're rather a long way from Auteuil," I observed.

---

[45] Falk appears to be taking liberties with chronology here. The reader might well have deduced (and subsequent data will support the implication) that a little more than a year has now elapsed since the date of Cabri's initial qualification in Law, and that it is the beginning of August 1914, on the eve of the formal outbreak of the Great War, but the reference to royal visitors in Paris is suggestive of that year's state visit of King George V and Queen Mary, which actually took place in April.

"Oh, my poor Cabri! Just as long as we don't fall into the Seine! And as long as it doesn't rain!"

"What would happen?"

"I don't know. Perhaps we'd be seriously dissociated, disaggregated by the rain..."

"You might have told me that sooner!"

But the wind gets up again; our speed increases. A flash of light: the Rue de Castiglione. Then there's the Place du Carrousel, scintillating with electric globes. There, a brisk and powerful gust of wind blasts us through the gates, so forcefully that in less than a minute, here we are in the Avenue de l'Opéra, resplendent with 1000 lights. Black clouds are galloping across the sky, and we are galloping as rapidly as they are, There too, the crowd is not slow to notice our passage, and the scenes of the Place de la Concorde are repeated, increased in violence. The police, doubtless thinking it some anarchist plot, precipitate themselves forward with sabers drawn, while the mounted policemen make their horses dance. Howls, insults, battles...and the pursuit of the two phantoms pushed by the wind toward the Opéra, entirely bathed in blue light, the balconies of which are decked with red velvet carpets fringed with gold—the Opéra, where a gala reception is being given for his sovereign friends by the President of the French Republic!

A hope is mingled with my fear, however, for the Opéra is an enclosed space: a refuge, perhaps salvation. The wind is driving us toward the doors. O joy! One of them is open! We pass through the cordon of guards standing in front of the steps—who, their eyes directed toward the movement of the crowd, hardly notice our entry.

Without taking time to observe the scene that must be unfolding behind us, we penetrate into the vestibule, where a few ushers take fright, and, now masters of our direction, we leap from floor to floor, while the noise of hurrying footsteps and harsh argumentative voices decreases in our ears. In less than a minute, we find ourselves huddled in a dark redoubt at the summit of the edifice.

After a moment of relieved silence, we consult one another:

"Where are we?" Pitoulet asks.

"I don't know."

"Did anyone see us come in?"

"It's possible."

"Do you know what time it is?"

"10:30 p.m. by the clock on the Boulevard."

"I suspected as much," he replied. "Can't you feel a sort of internal vibration, which involves intermittent stabbing sensations that are quite painful?"

"Yes indeed. So what?"

"So, in approximately half an hour we'll resolidify."

"Thank Heaven! Let it come, the moment of liberation! I've had enough of the vaporous state."

"Keep it down Cabri, I beg you."

At that moment, we were interrupted by the unleashed racket of the orchestra. Presumably the performance was starting up again, after an interval. We were apparently in a part of the theater close to the stage, since we could hear the music so clearly. But where? In that dark place, we listened to duets, mixed choirs and sometimes to polite—very slight—applause.

Suddenly, the little nook lit up, and we realized that we were in a costume-store. Intruders were undoubtedly about to arrive; soft footfalls were already hastening. The door at the rear was open; we went out and wandered, troubled phantoms, through a labyrinthine series of corridors, and eventually heard the orchestra launch into the ballet from *Faust*. At the same time, we arrived at a long iron gallery bordered by a guard-rail; at the far end of the gallery scene-shifters were at work. Our head were touching the ceiling of the theater.

I realized that the gallery was the central arch when I saw the stage down below—far below—where a company of dancers was twirling. But sandaled scene-shifters, arriving from the direction of the circle, set out along the gallery, moving toward us. Pitoulet and I leaned over to see whether there was any exit in the direction of the garden. Presumably we leaned over a little too far, for— the guard-rail having no existence for us—we fell off the arch and began to descend, slowly, from the ceiling to the stage below.

How can I describe what happened next? We landed, immense foggy bales, beneath the convergence of multicolored spotlights, smack in the middle of the waltz from *Faust*, initially unnoticed by the whirlwind of dancers, who were entirely focused on their entrechats. Our appearance caused a certain disturbance in the auditorium and the orchestra, though—as is, I assume, easily believable. A murmur emanated from the musicians and the public, as indefinable as the apparition itself: a murmur that was prevented by official convention from mounting as far as exclamation.

Soon, a few dancers perceived that bizarre clouds were interposing themselves between them. A malaise, pregnant with catastrophe, hung in the air—a brief malaise, for the catastrophe burst forth, even more horrible than might have been expected. All of a sudden, it was no longer two phantoms that were mingled with the frolics of the dancers but—time having moved on—two flesh-and-blood individuals: two lamentable individuals at the extreme of humiliation, indecency and ridicule, irredeemably naked!

The orchestra, after a discordant crash, fell silent. Howling dancers ran away. The hall reverberated with protests.

We had time to see the President rise to his feet and the curtain fall, and that was all. An avalanche of blows, delivered by fists, canes and boots, fell upon Pitoulet and me. In the blink of an eye, we found ourselves wrapped up in sheets and, trussed up like sausages, thrown in the back of a taxi.

Ten minutes later, we were introduced, under strong escort, into the Commissariat.

320

9. Trypax and Larigoule

The Police Commissioner was a man with a crimson complexion, thick close-cropped hair the color of a crow's wing, bushy eyebrows, a thick moustache, jet-black eyes and shiny pointed teeth. A thick red neck protruded from the flared collar of his shirt, and his clenched fists, posed on his desk, were menacing even at rest. Beside him, a thin, round-shouldered man, pale and blond, with a thin moustache and soft cheeks, was poised to start writing, by the light of an oil-lamp.

The Commissioner listened to the report of the brigadier, his eyebrows coming together on his furrowed brow in a terrible manner. At the same time, he drilled us with his gaze, as black as his heart. The report said, approximately, that: "two non-qualified fanatics, dressed only in the attributes of nature, had sprung forth, without any functional reason, within the *corps de ballet* of the Opéra, occasioning a great perturbation in the military and civil personnel at the performance; that the representatives of public authority hidden behind the scenery had leapt on to the stage preventatively and reduced the delinquents to helplessness and modesty, by wrapping them up in skillfully-improvised materials."

"Very well," articulated the Commissioner. Addressing his agents, he added: "Search them!"

We were stripped of our bonds and wrapping. How many hiding places the simple human body conceals, in the suspicions of the police! Unimaginable! Pitoulet could not believe his eyes.

"Hidden objects: total, none," declared the brigadier.

"That's good," pronounced the Commissioner. To us he said: "Get dressed!"

Get dressed! Irony! Eventually, we draped ourselves as best we could, me in a heliotrope mantle, probably part of Faust's costume, and Pitoulet in a red cape, doubtless belonging to Mephisto, which had appropriately constituted our packaging.

"You, the old one!" thundered the Commissioner. "Your name, forenames, profession, age and address. Ready, Beauléon?"

"Yes, Monsieur Trypax," the secretary replied.

"Pitoulet, Jules-César-Guy, rentier, 63 years old, resident of Auteuil, 68 Rue de La Fontaine.

"You, the young one!"

"Cabri, Mesmin-Justin, 25 years old, advocate's clerk, 97 Avenue des Ternes."

"Can you explain the facts? You first, Pitoulet?"

I would never have suspected that a scientist of such genius would reveal himself to be so devoid of imagination at such a moment—for I understood immediately that he wanted to hide the truth. He stood there for a moment, mute, scanning all of us with wild eyes, and then he stammered, somewhat ridiculously: "It was an unfortunate coincidence."

"Thunder!" swore the Commissioner, thumping his desk hard enough to crack a nut. "I need an answer, not a commentary. What were you doing, in a state of nudity, accompanied by your acolyte, in the Académie Nationale de la Musique?"

Pitoulet remained silent. I tried to speak.

"Shut up!" howled Trypax. "I'm talking to the old cretin."

At that moment, the door opened, giving passage to a gentleman in a suit and top hat. The furious Trypax immediately became gracious.

"Monsieur Larigoule! Come in, I beg you."

I thought I remembered that Larigoule was the name of an important official in the Sûreté.

The visitor replied, in an amiable tone: "Don't disturb yourself. Continue your interrogation." Then he leaned over the scribe's shoulder and added, smiling: "I see that it hasn't got very far."

"It's this old cretin, who's stubbornly..."

For a few seconds, I inclined all my mental powers toward the elaboration of an acceptable story. I suddenly stifled a joyful "Eureka!" Decorating my face with the most wining of smiles, I began: "Monsieur le Grand Inspecteur en Chef..."

I was not entirely clear about Larigoule's rank, so I conferred upon him a title that, if not real, was at least flattering.

"Shut up!" roared Trypax.

"If he wants to talk, let's listen, my dear chap," said Larigoule, softly. "Cabri, Mesmin, advocate's clerk?"

"Qualified in Law, Monsieur le Grand Inspecteur. That tells you that I'm not a vagabond, any more than my venerable friend is. You see in us the sorry victims of a rather unfortunate adventure, for which we should not bear, civilly or criminally, the responsibility."

Larigoule looked at me, smiling, and I understood that his affability was more dangerous than Trypax's brutality.

Draped in our capes, we bowed in a dignified manner.

At the same time, I perceived dread and supplication in Pitoulet's eyes. I continued without delay, in order to reassure him.

"This is what happened. During the heat wave, my old friend Pitoulet, who lives, so to speak, in the country, invited me to stay with him. Now, with all his virtues, he's afflicted with a constitutional vice that he strongly desires to keep secret, but which I'm forced to reveal to you. He is subject to fits of somnambulism. This evening, after going to bed at 9:30 p.m., as usual, he got up, prey to one of these fits. As I was lodged in the next room, I heard him go out of his room and I followed him, without waking him up, for, as you know, nothing is more dangerous than waking a sleep-walker—especially if he's an old man—at the risk of killing him on the spot. So, Pitoulet opened the door and set out into the street. I tried several times to make him turn round, but he was blindly and obstinately following a determined direction. I had to limit myself to guiding him, in order to prevent him being knocked down by cars. He went down to the river, went over the Pont d'Iéna through the Jardins du Trocadéro, along the Avenue du Trocadéro as far as the Etoile, along the Avenue de Friedland and the Boulevard Haussmann, and went to the Opéra, with me still following, through the stage door…"

Larigoule half-closed his eyelids. He said to me, in a slightly mocking tone: "And no one stopped you as you went in?"

"No one."

"One question, young man. Explain your absence of clothing."

"That's extremely simple. It was so hot, this evening, in Auteuil, that we had decided to sleep entirely nude. When Pitoulet went out, under the influence of his fit, I was obliged to follow him without getting dressed, for fear of losing track of him."

"Bizarre. Truly bizarre!"

"Implausible!" bellowed Trypax.

"The truth," I insinuated, delicately, "can sometimes…"

"Agreed," conceded Larigoule, "but what surprises me most of all is that, in the course of this excursion, you didn't run into anyone."

"We did run into people."

"And no one took any notice of you?"

"No one."

"Not even the police?"

Without replying, I sketched a gesture of ignorance that was, I confess, a trifle disingenuous.

"And in the theater itself, you circulated without crossing the path of seamstresses, employees, stage-hands, or any other personnel?"

"We crossed the paths of numerous personnel."

"But no one questioned you?"

"No one."

"How did you get on to the stage?"

"By passing through two doorways. I tried, in vain, to hold Pitoulet back—but I followed him to the end, fearing that he might fall into the orchestra-pit. Our sudden arrest woke him up. He was very surprised to find that he was not in his bed."

"Oh, yes!" Pitoulet agreed, doubtless even more surprised by my inventive genius.

Trypax bit his knuckles; Larigoule remained thoughtful. Then, addressing Pitoulet, he said: "And you, what have you to say?"

"Nothing," my friend stammered. "I was surprised…very surprised…"

Silence fell.

"There's a mystery here," Larigoule concluded. "You haven't told the whole story."

"I beg your pardon…"

"Or your story is false from start to finish. But the police were at fault, I admit, since, until the moment of your appearance, you had been ignored. We shall set out to clarify the affair. Whatever ensues, you have explained yourselves, and your statements will be put on record. You can go home, both of you. Trypax, you will have these gentlemen accompanied, in order to verify their addresses."

"Certainly, Monsieur Larigoule." He addressed himself to us. "Countersign your statements. Good. Don't forget that you both remain at my disposal."

Draped in our capes, we bowed in a dignified manner.

"Go with them, Brigadier Grandcoeur."

The brigadier showed us out and summoned a policeman, who hailed a cab. All four of us set out for the Rue La Fontaine, the policeman alongside the driver and the brigadier facing us. We maintained silence, but in the shadows I felt Pitoulet's hand squeeze mine.

With the aid of crude ploys, the brigadier tried to trip us up. Poor fellow! We smiled at him pityingly. Finally, we arrived. As we were about to get down he held us back "Wait a minute. Percot, proceed with your verbal inquiry."

The policeman rang the doorbell, but Pitoulet called out: "There's no one in!"

"Have you the key, then?" asked the brigadier.

I looked at Pitoulet anxiously. He simply replied: "No." I shivered. Doubtless desirous of producing his own little effect on me, however, he added: "No…but you'll find it by lifting up that stone next to the door."

The policeman bent down and lifted the stone. A key was lying there, which opened the door.

"Do I need to describe the interior of my house?" asked Pitoulet, haughtily.

The policemen looked at one another. "No need," declared the brigadier. "You're home, all right. *Au revoir*, Messieurs…if you'd like to pay the fare."

"What!" Our first movement was to search for our pockets. The policemen burst out laughing. "Since you're home," the brigadier suggested to Pitoulet, slyly, "go get some money."

"That's a bit much!"

Pitoulet went in, came back with some money, and paid the coachman majestically. The policemen, convinced, drew away and we finally went into the dear little house that we had thought we might never see again, full of emotion.

10. Castel Bic

When the door was duly closed again on the police, my worthy Master and I, seized by a sudden impulse, threw ourselves into one another's arms.

324

"Alone at last!" we exclaimed, at the same time.

"Ah, my dear Cabri," Pitoulet went on, with a joyful sigh, "we've had a lucky escape!"

"I'm terribly hungry, my worthy Master!"

We had a substantial cold snack, went to close up the laboratory, and went to bed. We soon fell into a peaceful and deep sleep.

The following morning, as soon as we found ourselves back in the dining room in front of two bowls of hot chocolate, Pitoulet came toward me with his hands extended.

"To think that I forgot to thank you, yesterday, and to congratulate you on your presence of mind! Your sleepwalking story worked wonders."

"Yes," I replied, modestly, "it wasn't bad. Don't be deceived, though—I don't think we're finished with the curiosity of the police."

"Oh, my God!"

"Fortunately," I said, laughing, "they're not only thinking about us…"

The doorbell rang loudly. Pitoulet, almost fainting, supported himself on the furniture, and I stopped laughing. Gudule came in.

"A telegram for Monsieur Cabri."

I had asked my concierge to forward my correspondence to Pitoulet's address. I opened the folded sheet, read it, and uttered a cry of joy. "Listen, my worthy Master!" And I read aloud:

Dear Monsieur Mesmin,

The manner in which we sent you away the other evening appears to us, on reflection, a trifle precipitate. Come to lunch tomorrow at Castel Bic. Our Suzanne instructs me to tell you that she will be happy to see you again. Cordially,

Pancrace Bic.

"O joy! O joy!" I cried. "There's the result of our nocturnal visit. It's my turn to thank you, with all my gratitude, great and worthy Master! You'll excuse me for not dining with you?"

"Only too happy to have repaired a misunderstanding of which I was the cause."

The housekeeper came in again, the newspapers in her hand. I unfolded one of them feverishly. On the first column of the second page, we read:

An incident momentarily disturbed the gala performance at which our august guests were in attendance. Two theater employees, under the influence of the excitement caused by the presence of the sovereigns, irrupted on to the stage in a state of undress to take part in the ballet from Faust. They were immediately expelled. The incident did not prevent Their Majesties from enjoying the rest of the performance, for which they did not spare their august applause; they called the Director of the Opéra into their box, congratulated him warmly, and award-

ed him the Order of Choreographical Merit. Afterwards they retired, accompanied by the Head of State, visibly delighted by their evening.

We opened other papers; they all contained the same article, evidently fed to them.

"You can see by this communiqué," I said to Pitoulet, "that the matter is settled. The affair has been covered up. This preposterous story of drunken scene-shifters demonstrates the difficulty the police have found in explaining the inexplicable."

"So much the better, thank God!" he sighed.

On turning more pages, however, we found a few articles related to the pursuit of the phantoms, these very various, demonstrating the extent to which the same event can be reported differently by its witnesses.

One journalist wrote:

Yesterday evening, at about 10 p.m., on the piers, the crowds of strollers were able to witness a curious meteorological phenomenon. Two clouds vaguely affecting human form ran along, skimming the ground, and dissipated shortly afterwards. A few accidents were caused by the jostling as everyone ran to see the phenomenon.

Another wrote:

A certain quantity of heavy vapor escaped from a factory in Billancourt, and rolled along the piers in spirals yesterday evening. A few people were inconvenienced, but rapidly-administered first aid was able to counter the onset of asphyxia.

Yet another:

The Avenue de l'Opéra was the theater of a brief scuffle yesterday evening. A few people having cried "Ghosts!" the entire crowd, prey to a collective hallucination, thought it could see ghosts in a layer of mist produced by the heat: a further example of the imitative spirit of crowds, which the great psychologist Alfred Tarde would certainly have recorded in his immortal work.[46]

And another:

---

[46] This reference is mistaken; it was actually Alfred Tarde's father, Gabriel Tarde, who introduced the notion that crowds might be considered as being possessed of a "collective mind," which was greatly elaborated by Gustave Le Bon.

A few practical jokers let off fireworks yesterday evening in the Avenue de l'Opéra, in spite of the official prohibition. A thick smoke was emitted, causing a slight panic. The authors of this stupid joke have been taken to the police cells.

"There we go," I said, putting down the papers. "You can sleep easy. The main thing is that no reporter thought of making a connection between the phantoms in the street and the theater grotesques. On that, permit me to take my leave..."

"When shall I see you again?"

"I shall come back to shake you by the hand later in the day."

And I went home swiftly, in order to put on a seductive outfit.

On coming back to the Rue La Fontaine at midday, I did not notice anything abnormal in the vicinity of Pitoulet's house, and, filled with radiant emotion, with a bouquet of white roses in my hand, I rang the doorbell at the threshold of paradise.

Bic offered me a rough friendly hand-shake; I kissed Madame Bic's hand as she contemplated me with a fearful expression, which I pretended not to notice. Suzanne appeared, accompanied by Fredaine. I gave her my bouquet and had the joy of depositing an ardent kiss on her forehead, while my hands gripped hers.

I exclaimed, gaily: "He's better then, the little fox-terrier! I've thought long and hard about the adventure and found the explanation of the phenomenon that brought your criticism down upon me. He was ill, the poor dear, and, although I had been sent away, I should have come back with a veterinarian."

"It was, at any rate, a strange malady," Suzanne replied. "But he got better all on his own. Shortly after your departure, he resumed his natural form."

"You see, my dear, that I had nothing to do with it."

"I beg your pardon..."

Our amorous gazes met.

"As for the rabbit," I went on, after a pleasant pause, "it simply came in through the window..."

The parents Bic were listening to me; from the corner of my eye, I saw the mother, behind her daughter, shake her head dubiously, with a sigh.

We sat down to lunch; in the course of the meal I showed sparkling wit and verve, and sensed that Suzanne adored me more than ever.

On the other hand, I understood that her parents were nursing questions that they dared not ask in front of her. I was, therefore, unsurprised to see them make an excuse send Suzanne away after lunch, and go to enormous lengths to bring the conversation round to the nocturnal occurrence, without appearing to do so.

"Did you sleep well last night?" Madame Bic asked me.

"Certainly," I replied. "Why?"

"It's just that we dreamed about you," said her husband. "We saw you in a dream."

"I'm very flattered."

"And we thought, perhaps," his wife went on, "that you might perhaps have dreamed about us, by virtue of telepathy."

"I confess that I did not," I riposted, "but if I had been able to do so, it would have been a pleasure."

"There are such bizarre circumstances," she continued, with a deep sigh, "of a telepathic order. One often sees friends, distant relative, even dead ones…"

"In dreams?" I said, ingenuously.

"In dreams, or even in a waking state."

"By evocation, then," I said, very seriously. "I have seen spirit apparitions provoked by mediums. If the question interests you, I can recommend some good authors: Boirac, Richet, Colonel de Rochas…"[47]

"Are there also spontaneous apparitions," Madame Bic asked.

"They have been cited."

"What about 'doubles'? What are 'doubles,' exactly?"

"I can see, dear Madame," I said, bowing, "that the vocabulary of spiritism has no secrets for you. 'Doubles' are the imperishable astral envelopes of mortal terrestrial beings. We each have our double. When we disappear, it survives us and becomes our 'spirit.' But this is a big subject, and I fear…"

"Oh, do continue!" begged Madame Bic, hanging on my every word.

Solemnly, I replied: "There are grave matters therein, about which it is not appropriate to talk without precaution." I lowered my voice, adopting an emotional and mock-fearful tone: "Then again, if it is necessary to tell you everything, some of my friends have already seen my 'double' and—between ourselves—I don't like to talk about it."

Zap! Bang on the nose! The two spouses shuddered, and exchanged a long glance. Madame Bic made a gesture, and apparent precursor of a confession—but she doubtless did not dare.

Suzanne reappeared. The conversation ended there. My fiancée and I returned to the pathways of the garden for a sentimental promenade.

When I left her, I swore to come to see her again the following day.

---

[47] Falk probably had not had an opportunity to read Emile Boirac's *L'Avenir des Sciences Psychiques* (1917) before writing "Le Maître des trois états," and remembered the name from the preface cited in the note attached to the previous story. Charles Richet (1850-1935) was a biologist who also worked in the field of psychic research.

11. An Escape of Gas

Alone in the street, I remembered that I had promised to visit Pitoulet. As I approached his house, I saw a little crowd gathered outside his door. I pressed my pace, but before going in, I lent an ear to what the idlers were saying

I heard:

"The police are in the house."

"The Commissioner is having it searched."

"They're going to arrest the old maniac."

"He's running an illicit still."

I pushed through the crowd and bumped into two policemen, who forbade me to enter.

"Is it Monsieur Trypax who's in charge?" I asked.

"Yes," they replied, astonished.

"Go tell your master that Monsieur Cabri is at the door. You'll see whether he'll have me let in immediately."

"I'm not saying anything different," said one of the policemen, suddenly respectful. "My colleague will take you to him."

Accompanied by the policeman, I went into the scientist's study, where I found Trypax and Pitoulet face to face, the former crimson and more thunderous than ever, the latter pale and bewildered. My old friend greeted me with the gaze of a shipwreck-victim perceiving a rock.

Trypax greeted me with: "You've arrived just in time!"

The policeman, satisfied, went away. The Commissioner went on: "I was just about to have you picked up at your home."

"A needless trouble," I said, with pursed lips. "You can see that I'm not in hiding."

"There's nothing to be got out of the old cretin—but you, you're going to give me some answers."

"Pardon!"

In the delight that an excellent lunch and the joy of seeing Suzanne again had plunged me, I felt my dialectical faculties multiplied tenfold, and to avoid replying, I asked: "Am I being charged with something, by any chance?"

"No, but…"

"Am I to be called as a witness?"

"Not that either, but…"

"In any case, I'm as anxious as you are to be informed immediately. My deposition would be inoperative, for I am Monsieur Pitoulet's legal adviser, having taken responsibility for his interests. So, you've come to carry out a search?"

"Exactly. I have a warrant from the Investigating Magistrate. I have in my possession, moreover, a very interesting legal statement that my local colleague has communicated to me. Either I'm much mistaken, or Monsieur Pitoulet is the perpetrator who has infested the buildings in the neighborhood with various birds and mammals. I'm beginning to see what's going on!" He laughed ferociously, and shouted: "Beauléon!"

The secretary approached.

"Go and inspect the furniture," Trypax said, "and prepare seals for anything that seems suspicious. You, Pitoulet, take me to your laboratory."

"My labobo…"

"Exactly. You'll see that I know how to conduct an investigation. You're pulling the strings of some apparatus or other in a vast laboratory. Let's go."

How could we resist? The priest of science guided the profaner to the threshold of his sanctuary. I followed them. We went in, and Pitoulet closed the door. We were in front of the Great Transmutator again.

"What do you do with all this?" Trypax demanded.

In the presence of his machine, the inventor, as if inflated by parental pride, recovered his voice. "*All this*," he replied, in an almost arrogant tone, "is used in my experiments."

"What experiments?"

He murmured "*Margaritas ante porcum*,"[48] and continued: "Experiments related to certain problems in chemistry and physics."

"What problems?"

Trypax's insistence was visibly exasperating him. "That's my secret," he replied.

"There are no secrets from the police. I demand that you say what the problems are."

Pitoulet's nose went white, which seemed to me to be a sign of impending fury. After a pause, during which he seemed to reflect, I heard him reply, to my great surprise: "The problem of seeing through opaque bodies. When one climbs on to that platform and I start the machine working, one can see through walls."

As curious as he was authoritarian, Trypax leapt on to the platform and ordered: "Switch the machine on."

"Willingly."

With a diabolical smile, Pitoulet turned his manual controls and levers.

"I can't see anything," Trypax complained.

"Wait—you'll see."

"Oh! What! Oh! What's happening to me? Stop! I want to get down."

"You'd do better to remain calm."

And Pitoulet, snatching my walking-stick, pushed Trypax back on to the platform with a thrust of the handle. An instant later, his softening legs refused the enemy any further service; his body subsided, his voice weakened; he uttered moaning cries of "Help!" imperceptible from outside, and looked at us with round, terrified eyes.

---

[48] Pearls before swine.

"The full current!" Pitoulet exclaimed.

The agglutinate of colloids that constituted a Commissioner flattened before our eyes. The corpulent Trypax, like a giant frog, tried to jump off the platform, exhaling in a hoarse purr: "Murderer! Bandit! Stop!"

"On the contrary! Full current!"

And with his cane, Pitoulet maintained him on the platform. Soon, Trypax collapsed completely, and suddenly passed from the elastic state into the vaporous state: he became the giant shadow that no longer has any secrets for the reader. I expected to see the experiment stop there. Not at all! Suddenly, that shadow was effaced; the mist vanished and nothing—absolutely nothing—any longer remained of Trypax on the platform of the machine.

"Pitoulet!" I cried, astounded. "What have you done?"

The scientist switched off the current, and picked up a few metal objects from the platform that had fallen on to it during the operation: a ring, a watch, a propelling pencil, some coins and cuff-links. He put them in his pocket, stowed away the clothing half-reduced to dust in the cloakroom, and looked at me phlegmatically.

"I've just volatilized the Commissioner."

"But, damn it...!

We heard footsteps in the garden and opened the door. The aforementioned Beauléon presented himself, papers in hand. He scrutinized the room with his gaze and asked, with an astonished expression: "Where's Monsieur le Commissaire?"

"I don't know, my friend," said Pitoulet, quite calmly.

"Isn't he here, then?"

"Certainly not. He just left, a moment ago."

Beauléon went away.

Alone with Pitoulet, I resumed, in a voice blank with emotion: "What about Trypax?"

"Vanished. Beyond a certain voltage, the vaporous state becomes the gaseous state. Then the molecules dissociate. *Pfft!* And that's all. It's not important. A simple escape of gas!"

"*Escape of gas!* My word, that's rich! You've just killed a man."

"Me? Not at all. He's the one who wanted to take part in an experiment. He's had his experiment—absolute and total. Anyway, he was annoying me, that Trypax. He'd caused me too much trouble. So, *pfft!*"

Pitoulet was manifesting an increasing excitement I suddenly understood how that indiscreet young assistant he had told me about has disappeared. Another *pfft!*—and the assistant, an escape of gas...

I couldn't help shivering.

Beauléon suddenly reappeared, accompanied by a policeman, and asked again, in an anxious tone: "Where's Monsieur le Commissaire? What have you done with Monsieur le Commissaire?"

Very annoyed at being mixed up in this business, I replied swiftly: "I don't know anything. I was in the garden, where I had to isolate myself, and I've just returned this instant."

"You, Monsieur Pitoulet—answer!"

"I repeat, Beauléon, that Monsieur le Commissaire disappeared without saying anything. Respectful of the police, I'm waiting for him."

The secretary and the policeman searched the laboratory. I trembled in case they opened the cloakroom. The idea never occurred to them. Then they explored the whole of the garden and the house, from top to bottom. Then they conferred, and departed rapidly, doubtless headed for the Commissariat.

Lifting up a curtain, we saw the little crowd of gossips dissipate, but we noticed that two policemen were continuing to guard the door.

XII. Anticipations

Now, of the two of us, it was Pitoulet who was displaying self-composure. Sitting in his study, he relaxed in a satisfied manner, with the aid of an open newspaper. I felt extremely ill-at-ease. When he started humming, I said to him: "You do realize that the affair might get worse?"

"Not for you, eh?" he said in a sarcastic tone. "You tried to save your own bacon. Don't worry: I won't drag you back into it."

I adopted a discontented and frosty expression. Then he threw himself into my arms, saying: "Forgive me, my dear Cabri. I know how devoted you are, how generous. You've given me more than enough proof. But I couldn't bear that Trypax. He was becoming impossible. Can you imagine that he had been martyrizing me for two hours before you arrived—that he had begun to ferret through my papers; that he was about to deliver into the public domain a series of secret and sublime formulae?"

"But in the final analysis, has he completely and definitively ceased to exist?"

"He has vanished into infinity, for all eternity."

"The police will come back. What will you tell them?"

"Still the same thing: that he left. It's the truth. The experiment hasn't left any trace. I'll throw what remains of his clothing in the fire, and melt the metallic objects I collected, in the electric furnace."

"Do you know, my dear Master, that you're terrifying?"

"Be philosophical, Cabri, my friend. Man is nothing but a shadow, the shadow of a shadow, as has just been demonstrated to you. I promise not to make that proof integrally. I'm placid—timid, even—but in front of the machine, the product of my genius. I recover my pride, my arrogance. When I saw Trypax on the platform, I thought I was seeing a scorpion on a page of Montaigne: I got rid of the matter that was soiling the mind. I made a man disappear; so be it. That doesn't prevent me from dedicating all my might to the happiness of humankind. I shall orient my discovery, which is replete with moral and practical applications, toward that sacred goal. I shall dedicate myself to finding a means of prolonging these temporary changes of state at will. I confess to you that the elastic state seems scarcely susceptible of useful applications—it's more a state of comical intermediacy—but the vaporous state, well disciplined, seems to offer the most beautiful promises, especially if it becomes possible to steer without difficulty in the opposite direction to an average wind.

"Firstly, what moral benefits! Knowing that it has become possible to penetrate everywhere, in the form of a shadow, to be observed without being aware of it, every one of us will elect to live, in his own home as well as in public, according to the rules of morality. All citizens will become sages, all inhabiting houses of glass.

"But most of all, what practical benefits! How easy and charming displacements and voyages will become! No fatigue in the course of the journey, no compression in carriages. A sensation of perpetual lightness. Then, on arrival, solidification. Anonymous societies will be founded, which will install transmutators at crossroads, in town squares and on the platforms of railway stations, much as one sees automatic vending-machines scattered around today.

"A complete transformation of means of communication will follow rapidly. I can easily imagine the vaporous traveler being introduced into a sort of pneumatic tube that will project him over the longest distances. I also foresee a revolution in therapeutics; it seems likely that the vaporous state will greatly facilitate the diagnosis and treatment of diseases; as for surgical interventions— child's play!

"It is nevertheless important, in my view, not to divulge the results of my discovery to anyone else, for the time being. Imagine how our information service and organization of combat would gain in marvelous flexibility, in matters of armed conflict. A vaporous officer would be able to cross enemy lines, spy on councils of war and bring back priceless information without difficulty. It would be possible, in matters of troop movement, to accumulate soldiers and horses within military trains in unlimited numbers. One would shrug one's shoulders on reading the old logistical advice—forty men, eight horses; forty thousand men, eight thousand horses—the latter would be easily accommodated, for they would be embarked in a vaporous state and solidified on disembarkation.

"If parallel experiments could eventually be realized in the vegetable and mineral kingdoms, there would then be an absolute upheaval in the conditions of terrestrial life: nebulous rocks, solid clouds, soft trees. Everything that exists on the globe would be at the mercy of the human will.

"Thus, little by little, climbing the steps of successive discoveries, Science penetrates Nature more fully, and a day will arrive when, finally lodged in the very bosom of Being, it will fuse with the Universe, will be the Universe's knowledge of itself, the Consciousness of the World!"

Swollen with pride and lyrical, Pitoulet prophesied—but while admiring him, I thought that it would be better for me not to be mixed up in his affairs from now on, and to go back to living in my lodgings in the Ternes. I cleverly took advantage of the pretext of my renewed engagement to plead that it was necessary for me to look after my appearance, and that all, because all my clothes and underwear were at home, I was obliged...

"You're not going to abandon me?" he asked, anxiously.

"How can you think so, my dear Master?" I protested, without being too sure whether I was sincere or not. "Too many bonds of friendship unite us—but I'm going to the theater this evening with the Bic family. I'll come back to see you tomorrow morning, and we'll have lunch together."

"Oh! Thank you"

I left him, not without relief, for I dreaded seeing the police arrive at any moment to arrest both of us. I foresaw grave complications, and had only one desire: to get out of there. Let those who have never been betrothed cast the first stone at me! How could I anticipate that the adventure was about to come apart in such a brutal and unexpected fashion?

13. Catastrophe and Marriage

At the door of the house I had to negotiate with the policemen on sentry duty, to whom I had to present my identity papers. When they were eventually satisfied that I was not Pitoulet and that I had a domicile, they let me go. I left calmly and unhurriedly, but when I turned the street corner I started running and jumping, happy to be free again, as if escaping from a nightmare.

I spent an exquisite evening at the Opéra-Comique, seated next to my Suzanne. *La Vie de Bohème* was playing.[49] My future parents-in-law, very moved by the sad fate of Mimi, accepted the celebration of our marriage in a fortnight's time. Intoxication!

"It appears, my boy," Bic said to me, "that you have left your chambers. Are you, then, renouncing a juridical career?"

"Not at all, my dear Monsieur," I replied, "but I've been working in the library for the last few days, in order to prepare my thesis."

"Really," said Bic, interestedly. "What is its subject, then?"

---

[49] *La Vie de Bohème* (1849) was the stage version of Henry Mürger's account of literary life in Paris prior to the 1848 Revoution, based on short stories written in 1846-49, which were expanded into an episodic novel in 1851 and became the basis for Puccini's opera *La Bohème* in 1896. The character of Mimi became the archetypal tragic *grisette*.

Ingeniously, I improvised. "Posthumous litigation in cases of emphyteusis."[50]

I promised myself firmly to return to the chambers the following morning, in order to distance myself completely from Pitoulet, who had become excessively compromising. Nevertheless, the following day, I judged it impossible that I should fail to keep my promise.

I went to the scientist's house. The door as still guarded. I reeled off my name and status, and obtained free access. I found the old inventor sitting in an armchair, with a doleful expression. He offered me a limp hand.

"What's up, my dear Master?"

"Alas, dear Cabri, what good did it do to yield to my impulse yesterday? For one Trypax lost, ten are found! Now it's that accursed Larigoule who's torturing me...who is even more terrible, in his own sly and insinuating fashion. I could resist Trypax with silence, but I sense that *to him*, I shall confess everything. Since your departure there has been nothing but juridical visits, investigations, supplementary and complementary enquiries...

"Then again, yesterday, I took care to burn the clothes, but I hid the little metal objects in a cupboard, counting on melting them down today. Now, seals have been put on that cupboard, and when it's opened again, they'll find Trypax's pencil, watch and cuff-links. I can't explain that! Advise me, please! What can I do? I'm tempted to open the cupboard..."

I persuaded Pitoulet not to break the seals, severely prohibited by law, which would have also constituted a serious presumption of guilt.

"Oh!" he moaned, "if I could only get away! Still free in principle, however, I am, in fact, under surveillance. Yesterday, I wanted to go out. A policeman followed me, five paces behind. I had to turn back. My reputation is ruined. The entire neighborhood is convinced—so Gudule tells me—that I've buried Trypax in the garden. Me, an old man, him, that colossus! Are men more stupid than wicked, or more wicked than stupid? An insoluble enigma, that one!"

"But, my dear Master," I cried—for a luminous idea had just occurred to me, as so frequently happens—"in the face of serious danger, why not take a lesser risk? Go into the vaporous state! You can easily escape. The weather is fine, with not the slightest wind."

"Old fool!" he exclaimed. "You weren't thinking. Thank you, my young savior! Once solidified, I'll remain hidden long enough for it all to be forgotten. It's the very thing! Let's hasten to the laboratory!"

I had a strong feeling that I ought to leave him, but desire, and my sympathy for the unfortunate old man, impelled me to witness the experiment one last

---

[50] Emphyteusis is a kind of contract by which a heritable right of possession and use of land is ceded for a long period, or in perpetuity, on condition that the land is maintained in cultivation, or at least free from depreciation, and that an annual rent is paid.

time. I followed him. He undressed, switched on the current, climbed up on to the platform, set the needle to "mist" and rotated the commutators.

The transformation began, and followed its course. As Pitoulet passed into the vaporous state, however I was astonished not to hear the usual bell. The electric clock must have broken down, for the current continued to flow.

I heard Pitoulet's voice: "Switch off the current, Cabri—switch it off!"

I shuddered as I realized that Pitoulet was at risk of Trypax's fate, and I bounded to the switches. In my haste, though—oh, when I think about it, I tear out my hair in remorse!—I must have made some kind of false move; one of the commutators stuck, and the current did not stop.

I saw Pitoulet's cloudy form become vaguer and vaguer. Panic-stricken, I ran to the console on the wall, found the necessary lever, and finally cut of the current.

Pitoulet had not completely dissipated, but what remained of him was less than a mist: a shadow of vapor which, having doubtless become lighter than air, suddenly rose upwards and flew away through an opening in the roof.

I ran into the garden, looking upwards—in vain. I could no longer see anything. What had become of him? Was he going to melt into the atmosphere, be diluted in the ether? Immediately or eventually? Temporarily or forever?

There was nothing more for me to do in the laboratory; I had, alas, already done too much. An idea crossed my mind and I smiled in spite of my grief. Perhaps, among the interstellar spaces, the imponderable residue of Pitoulet might meet up with the impalpable remains of Trypax. What extraordinary debates would unfold in infinity between those two dusty shadows! And I also thought that morality, so dear to Pitoulet, might, at the end of the day, find its settlement in that abrupt end: he had disappeared, a victim of the apparatus that had taken at least two human lives…

Almost consoled, I put on my hat and went out, proudly, already preparing my replies to the questions that the police were certainly going to ask me.

Indeed, the following day, the Commissioner of my district summoned me to his office and asked me to explain Pitoulet's disappearance. I could only tell him that I had talked to the old gentleman the day before, in the course of visiting him in my capacity as his legal advisor, that the policemen on sentry duty had seen me leave on my own, and that I knew no more. With regard to me, the affair ended there.

Pitoulet's mysterious disappearance was an event in the street, an incident in the quarter, and a banal news-item so far as public opinion was concerned. He left no heir. I feared momentarily that he might have made me his legatee, which would have attracted the undesirable attention of the police in my direction. The Great Transmutator, with its accessories, was sold off on behalf of the State and broken up for scrap, along with the rest of the deceased's possessions. The public was only represented by the usual auction crowd. Nevertheless, and elegant unknown came along to acquire a kind of dial on which two bizarre words were inscribed: *elastic* and *mist*.

The reader will have recognized my style in this delicate gesture. The dial is on my desk in Paris while I am writing these lines in X***, whose first edition I will dedicate to my tender Suzanne, now my wife. They will explain to her certain phenomena anterior to our union, whose interpretation I was unable to correct sooner, having been mobilized three days after my marriage.

Oh, if only Pitoulet's "Anticipations" had been realized, we would have known Victory much more rapidly! I also hope that my story will cure my delicate mother-in-law of her belief in spiritualism.

I understand as I finish, even better than when I started, how much incredulity this perfectly true story will encounter. I will permit myself to refer them to the official communiqués and related newspaper articles that situate the adventure, without any possible argument, within contemporary history.

For now, I have said all that I have to say, and I feel that my conscience is clear. It only remains for me to conclude with a solemn farewell to my admirable and ignored master, Jules-César-Guy Pitoulet, who, if he had not flown through the roof in the flower of his genius, would one day have revealed himself to the world as one of the Colonels of Science, one of the Caryatids of Humanity.

ANDRÉ CAROFF

LA SINISTRE MADAME ATOMOS

ANGOISSE

Editions "FLEUVE NOIR"

André Caroff: *The Sinister Madame Atomos*

André Caroff was the nom-de-plume of André Carpouzis, born February 28, 1924, who died on March 9, 2009. In 1945, he was wounded in a battle against the Germans. After the war, André worked at the Casino de Paris, then at the Theater Modano, and later at the Folies-Bergères. He also appeared as an extra in a number of films, then took a series of forgettable jobs, including selling encyclopedias door-to-door, but eventually preferred the freedom of being his own boss and became a taxi driver. That was when he began to write and publish short stories in the daily newspaper, Le Parisien Libéré.

In 1956, publisher Fleuve Noir, founded in 1949 by Armand de Caro and Guy Krill for the purpose of publishing a great variety of popular literature, moved its offices to Boulevard Saint-Marcel, across the street from where André lived. He began submitting novels to them and, after four years of effort, his first novel, Névrose, *was published in the* Angoisse *horror imprint of Fleuve Noir under the non-de-plume of André Caroff.*

Caroff quickly became one of Fleuve Noir's major authors, publishing novels in their Spécial-Police, Espionnage *and* Angoisse *imprints. He wrote seventeen* Angoisse *novels, of which the most famous were his series featuring the sinister Madame Atomos, which has since become a cult classic in France, and was recently reissued by Black Coat Press' sister imprint, Rivière Blanche. Prior to creating Madame Atomos, Caroff had penned the adventures of François Petit, a sociopath à la Hannibal Lecter, visibly inspired by the real-life French serial killer, Doctor Petiot. (Petit appeared in three novels.)*

When Fleuve Noir cancelled its Angoisse *imprint, in 1974, Caroff moved to* Anticipation *for which he penned 34 novels until 1989. His series included the adventures of a futuristic space trooper named Rod (four novels) and the series Abel 6666 (eight novels), which took place in a computerized future. For the Espionnage imprint, he wrote a series of spy thrillers featuring the character of secret agent Bonder; many of these often contained minor sci-fi or horror elements. Two of Caroff's novels for the* Spécial-Police *crime thrillers imprint were filmed, including one which starred Alain Delon. Caroff also wrote 18 made-for-television movies, 45 radio plays, and, with his second wife, over 500 romance novels under the pseudonyms of Daniel Aubry and Danièle Thomas. At the time of his death, André was again writing science fiction novels for Rivière Blanche, having embarked on a vast, post-cataclysmic saga.*

The saga of Madame Atomos is comprised of 17 volumes published between 1964 and 1970, with a final novel, which had remained unpublished at the time, eventually coming out in 1979.

André Caroff understood right from the start that, in order to be both credible and different, his mastermind villainess had to be different from Sax Rohmer's Doctor Fu Manchu or Ian Fleming's megalomaniacal Ernst Stavro Blofeld. He succeeded beyond his wildest hopes with Madame Atomos. Madame Atomos does not seek to conquer the world or assert the supremacy of Oriental values like an old "Yellow Peril" villain. Her goals are simple: she seeks revenge upon the United States for the nuclear holocausts of Hiroshima and Nagasaki which cost her the lives of her loved ones. The morality of dropping the two atom bombs to speed up the end of the war has always been more debated outside of America. The irony is that Madame Atomos is just as much a creation of America as Osama bin Laden, because she is the evil embodiment of the consequences of our mistakes. Her fanatical hatred of America and obsessive desire for bloody revenge make her the first fictional terrorist with whom there are no possibilities of dialogue or compromise. In that, she is truly a ground-breaking character, more relevant today than ever.

J.-M.L.

Chapter I

Tac, tap...tac, tap...tac, tap....

It was as regular as the beat of a Diesel motor, and the road-sweeper ended up turning round to see what it was. The rain had been falling all morning, and the deserted streets were infinitely dismal. Sweeping miles of tarmac all one's life is not exactly enjoyable, but when it is necessary to do it in solitude, without saying a word, it is truly intolerable—so the road-sweeper leaned on his broom and pivoted on his heel.

The man coming along the street was limping on his right leg. He was bare-headed, with no overcoat, but—in spite of his white hair and livid complexion, and the cold and the rain—he stood up straight as he moved forward. He did not look at the edge of the sidewalk he was following, the bare trees, the lamp-posts or the pools of water.

The road-sweeper blew on his hands and smiled amiably. "Lousy weather!" he remarked.

The old man passed within three feet, stiff and icy.

Tac, tap...tac, tap...tac, tap....

The man's heels were steel-tipped and the loose lace of his left shoe was wriggling like a worm. His hands hung down by his sides, curiously motionless, without the slight swing that walking provokes, and his feet only seemed to part company with the ground at the cost of a fantastic effort. He was making rapid progress, however, in a jerky but effective fashion, seemingly insensible to his water-soaked garments and keeping his gaze fixed directly ahead.

The road-sweeper watched him cross the street, then turned his head as he heard the soft purring of the black car that was moving slowly, following the sidewalk. It was an enormous old Chevrolet with rusty chrome work, driven by a small yellow man in a felt hat, the rim of which hid half his face.

Further on, the old man turned in the direction of the town center, and the road-sweeper lost sight of him. Shortly afterwards, the Chevrolet changed direction in its turn and disappeared, releasing a puff of grey smoke from the corroded orifice of its exhaust-pipe.

The road-sweeper gazed at the cloud momentarily as the wind drew it out into a thread, then lit his cigarette-end and stoically resumed sweeping the greasy surface.

It as ten o'clock in the morning; the month of January was ending and people who had no reason to go out were staying indoors, by the fireside. It was very cold in Chinook, Montana.

Tac, tap...tac. tap....

The cashier darted a glance at the little old man who had just come in, saw that he was carrying a large suitcase and that he was completely soaked, and thought that a man of that age ought to take better care of himself.

The bank was almost empty. Apart from the cashier, there were five employees, all hunched over their work, and Mr. Linding, the manager, who could be seen behind his desk in a room whose door was ajar.

Harold, the cashier, resumed counting the wad of notes that Mr. Belegs of Belegs, Hunter & Co. had just given him. His lips were moving silently.

"Eight hundred, eight fifty, nine hundred, nine fifty...."

"Come on, Charlie!" said Mr. Belegs, impatiently. "You know full well it's all there!" He was speaking softly, complaining out of habit, but the felt slightly intoxicated in the warmth of the gas central heating and was in no hurry to get back to the cold air of his office. He lit a cigar, and looked at the old man with the suitcase through the flame of his match. The latter was standing still, midway between the door and the counter, and a large pool of water was beginning to form around his bizarrely joined feet. He was staring at the wall, where there was a poster advising subscription to a share-issue, but Mr. Belegs was quite sure that he could not see it.

Suddenly, the old man turned slowly, and his dull eyes settled on Mr. Belegs, then slid to the cashier's skull and fixed again on the wad of notes.

Mr. Belegs got such a bad feeling that he removed his cigar from his mouth, clenched his fist and wedged himself firmly on his feet, exactly as if the old man represented an immediate threat—imprecise, but certain.

Suddenly, Harold stopped counting and lifted his head, at the same time as the other employees. Mr. Linding appeared on the threshold of his office and removed his spectacles.

No one had said anything. Nothing had happened. The little old man had not budged. It seemed, though, that the atmosphere had suddenly thickened, to the point that the smoke that had been rising from Mr. Belegs' cigar in eddying spirals a second before now seemed to be extended like a cotton thread between the cigar and the ceiling.

"Well?" said Mr. Linding. "What's up?" He had intended to say something more, but shut up when he realized that no one was listening. Then, suddenly, he no longer had any desire to speak or move.

Everyone was as motionless as the old man with the suitcase. Mr. Belegs noticed that a fly that had been buzzing around a moment before must have settled, since he could no longer hear it. Then he reminded himself that it was January, and that the buzz could not have come from a fly. Then he no longer thought anything. Along with the employees, Harold and Mr. Linding, he watched the little old man go behind the counter, limp up to the safe and open the door. There, the old man lifted the lid of the suitcase and calmly started filling it with wads of bills.

When the suitcase was full, the old man closed it carefully, went back around the counter, and left without a backward glance. The batten of the door swung back after he had passed through, but nothing moved in the silent room.

Thirty seconds passed. Then, suddenly, Mr. Linding uttered a howl. "It's a hold-up! The siren, quick!"

Each employee's right foot stamped on the alarm pedal, and the siren linked to the police station howled lugubriously while Mr. Linding and Mr. Belegs rushed outside.

"There he is!" shouted Mr. Belegs.

The old man was, indeed, lying in the gutter—but the suitcase stuffed with cash had disappeared.

The police car turned the corner at a crazy speed, and braked in front of the bank. Six armed policemen leapt out.

"It's a hold-up!" Mr. Linding repeated, feebly—and collapsed, at the same time as Mr. Belegs, who was still beside him.

The policemen tried to reanimate them, but quickly discovered that they were dead. Then they went into the bank, and discovered the corpses of the five employees and Charlie Harold, the cashier. They were still warm.

"What's your name?"
"Harry Diamond."
"Occupation?"
"Road-sweeper."

The inspector let himself down into his armchair. "Well, Mr. Diamond," he said, wearily, "you claim to know this man?"

The road-sweeper leaned forward and looked at the picture of the old man with white hair. "It's definitely him," he said, "but I never said I knew him. I was just in the middle of sweeping when he passed by...."

"What time was this?" the inspector interjected.

"Ten o'clock in the morning."

"This morning?"

"Of course. It had been raining since first light, and this guy comes strolling through the flood without as much as a hat...."

"Where were you when you saw him?"

"Roosevelt Avenue."

"Where did he come from and which way was he going?"

"He was coming from the train station, heading for the town center."

"Had you ever seen him before?"

"No—nor the rust bucket that was following him."

The inspector started. "Are you certain of that?"

"And how! It was an old Chevy, driven by a little yellow chap with a felt hat pulled down over his mug."

"Yellow? Chinese? Japanese?"

"One of those. They all look the same to me. Then again, I say that, but maybe he was just suntanned."

The inspector made a sweeping gesture. "Let's get back to the Chevrolet, Mr. Diamond. What did it look like?"

"Black, with rusty hub-caps and a moth-eaten exhaust-pipe. I mean, it had done it's time! It was pumping smoke like all the devils in hell. It must have dated back to the War of Secession."

"You didn't notice its license plate?"

"No."

The inspector looked at the group of motionless detectives, and then returned his attention to the road-sweeper. "This man," he said, pointing to the picture the newspapers had published. "Did anything in particular strike you about him?"

Harry twisted his cap in his large hands. "Well, he said, "I thought it was peculiar...."

"What?"

"To begin with, he had a limp in his right leg; then again, when I spoke to him, he didn't even look at me."

"What did you say to him?"

"Oh, nothing special. It was raining, so I said 'Lousy weather', or something like that. There was no one about and I was bored. There's nothing odd...."

"So," the inspector cut in, "he didn't look at you and didn't answer you. Apart from that, Mr. Diamond?"

"Well, apart from that, he was as white as a sheet and as stiff as a broom-handle." He laughed briefly, rubbed his hands and added: "And I know my broom-handles!"

The inspector contrived a tight smile, and lit a cigarette. "That's fine, Mr. Diamond—I don't need you anymore."

The road-sweeper got up and left the room, feeling a certain sense of relief. The office had seemed a trifle airless.

As soon as the door had closed behind him, the inspector made a gesture. "Sit down, gentlemen."

The four men obeyed, the feet of chairs scraping the floor.

"Sullivan?" said the inspector.

The man consulted his notebook. "Black Chevrolet," he said, "1939 model, Ohio license-plate. We found it on Route 2 between Zurich and Harlem. The driver's seat had traces of mud and the back seat had the impression of an object that was probably metallic, about one foot by two, definitely heavy. No finger-prints." He closed his notebook and sat back, stretching out his legs.

"Detrick?" the inspector prompted.

The man removed a cigarette-end from his lips. "Nothing," he said. "No one saw the man. He wasn't carrying any identification and the labels had been removed from his clothes."

"How did he die?"

"I'm waiting for the medical examiner's report. I only know that he did have a limp—right leg. His prints have been sent to the FBI."

The inspector shook the ash from his cigarette and turned slightly to face the third detective. "Your turn, Lowey."

"I don't know the exact count," Lowey replied. "Only Linding and the cashier knew how much was in circulation at the critical moment. Belegs had brought $1500, and I think we can assume a total of something like $80,000. The tills hadn't been touched; they were content to take what was in the safe. There was no fuss; it all went off smoothly, and the people in the agency above the bank didn't hear a thing until the alarm went off. Only one young woman, who was coming back from college having felt ill, said that she noticed a black car. She wasn't able to say what make it was, but she remembered having seen it pull away from the sidewalk shortly before the alarm went off. In the meantime, she'd gone into the hallway of her building, and when she came out again after the alarm sounded the little old man was lying in the gutter, and Belegs and Linding were leaning over him. Then our car arrived. That's all."

The inspector stubbed out his cigarette in the ash-tray, violently. "Nine people dead for $80,000!" he roared. "It's beyond belief! Good God! Twain, do you at least know how they were killed?"

The fourth detective spread his hands in a gesture of helplessness. "Not yet, Chief. The medical examiner's reserving his judgment—he's asking the advice of two of his colleagues. Between two doors I vaguely heard talk of fulgurant coagulation of the blood, but that's hardly precise, is it? We'll have to wait for the medical examiner's report."

The inspector put his elbows on his desk, looked at his men, and said, unenthusiastically: "It's the first time in a long time that we've started an investigation without having the shadow of a lead! Sullivan, can't you get *anything* out of that Chevrolet?"

The detective shrugged his shoulders. "Tomorrow," he said, bleakly, "I'll know the name of its owner and the date when it was stolen—but that won't get us any further forward...."

The door opened violently, and the medical examiner came into the smoky room in a rush. He was red-faced, terribly overexcited. "I've got your report!" he snapped. "Hold on to your seats!"

A dull silence answered him. He took a step forward, into the light, and unfolded a sheet of manuscript with a trembling hand. "The examination I've carried out, with two of my colleagues, has revealed the following: Linding, Belegs, the cashier and the five employees have been literally atomized! Their blood is as dry as plaster, and we estimate that it has been subjected to a radioactive bombardment of at least 150 Roentgens."

He wiped sweat away from his forehead, darted a circular glance over his spectacles, and resumed, in a voice that was simultaneously vibrant and hollow: "As for the other one, the unidentified old man, we're absolutely certain that he's been dead for at least six months!"

He let himself fall into a chair, shook his head, and repeated, as if he were trying to persuade himself: "Six months! That's definite!"

Every eye in the office focused on the photograph of the old man with white hair.

Who was he?

Chapter II

His name was John Ferby. He had been seventy-one years old at the time of his death, following a massive cerebral hemorrhage, and he had been buried in a cemetery in Lexington, Kentucky, his home town.

Sam Forbes of the FBI was given the case, and set off for Lexington on the day after the hold-up. Sam was twenty-eight, with his feet set firmly on the ground, and the forty-page report that he was reading appeared to him to have been written by a particularly imaginative author. However, the report bore the signatures of three doctors and a district chief, and the photographs attached to it were quite authentic.

Sam lit a cigarette and turned a page.

...that it cannot have been the effect of an atomic explosion, however small, for if that had been the case, the furniture and the building would surely have suffered considerable damage. The specialists found no trace of radioactivity at the scene of the crime. On the evening following the inexplicable phenomenon, however, Detective Lowey observed that a cactus placed on a shelf in Mr. Linding's office was completely yellow. Inspector Lowey testified that during his preliminary enquiry, the plant had been bright green....

Sam turned another page, and set the picture of John Ferby down on his knee. The old man had been photographed bare-chested, and a deeply puzzling tattoo was discernible on his breast. The principal motif was the profile of a woman, Chinese or Japanese, not long out of adolescence, whose thick black hair was gathered in a chignon. To either side of the portrait were two names, reminiscent of a horrible tragedy: *Hiroshima* and *Nagasaki*; then, directly under the woman's face, the words: *Compliments of Madame Atomos.*

Sam laughed dryly. It was all so grotesque, probably lifted from the worst melodrama ever made. Someone was trying to pretend that this Madame Atomos was after vengeance, twenty years after the two atomic explosions—which seemed insane. John Ferby's cadaver had been conserved, one way or another, but Sam did not believe the road-sweeper's testimony. A guy six months dead couldn't walk....

By the end of the report, Sam Forbes was convinced that, even if the deaths were real, the presentation and the context of the pages transmitted by the Chinook authorities could only be the conclusion of the biggest hoax of the century.

He closed the file and slipped it into his briefcase, then crossed his legs and lit another cigarette. The train was making good time, and would pull into Lexington station in less than an hour....

Mrs. Ferby stood up very straight. She was only sixty, and managed a food store uptown.

"I'm quite certain that this man isn't my husband!" she affirmed, forcefully. "John died before my very eyes, and although he did have a limp, I can assure you that he didn't have any tattoo on his chest!"

Sam raised his eyes. "They're his fingerprints, Mrs. Ferby," he said, softly.

"It's a mistake!" the woman insisted. "John was buried in the south cemetery last August, and his grave is intact! I'm sure that you've made a mistake. This whole story is revolting!" She sat down abruptly and started weeping silently.

"I'm very sorry, Mrs. Ferby, but these are his prints...."

The woman sniffed and looked up at him mournfully. "But at the end of the day, Mister, John's dead! Dead! A doctor gave permission for the burial after having declared that my husband died of a cerebral hemorrhage, and I was there when he was put in his coffin. I accompanied him to his final resting-place with our family and a crowd of friends; everyone saw the coffin go down into the hole and the earth heaped on top of it...."

She fell silent, choked by her tears.

An employee darted a murderous glance at Sam Forbes and strode forward. "What Mrs. Ferby says is true, Mister," he said, aggressively. "I was there when Mr. Ferby had that attack, and I was the first to run to him. Now that I think back, I could swear that he was dead before he hit the ground."

Sam picked up his hat, excused himself and left. There was nothing left to do but obtain a warrant for the exhumation.

It took place in private, twenty-four hours after Sam Forbes' request.

A fine but penetrating drizzle was falling, and the men were skidding on the greasy earth while they maneuvered the lifting-tackle, whose chains were grating lugubriously. Same had the feeling that it really was a sacrilege that was taking place.

The coffin abruptly appeared, describing a curve at the end of the chains supporting it, and settled into the mud with a soft, repulsive splash.

Sam threw away his damp cigarette, watching the man who was plying the screwdriver, the water that was spattering the muddy coffin and the lid that was slowly coming off as the screws gave way. It was as if a hand was pushing it up from inside, and Sam sensed the malaise hanging over the little group gathered by the graveside. All the watchers had read the newspapers, and understood that the operation in progress might confirm or deny the craziest suppositions that the reporters had not hesitated to raise. There was talk of supernatural manifestations, and the nine corpses in Chinook, which retained the mystery of the death that had struck them down, leaving the door open to the most inane hypotheses.

The man slipped his screwdriver into his pocket, introduced a crowbar into the gap, and detached the lid with a dry crack. It fell to one side, and everyone leaned forward, to see that the coffin was empty.

An inscription was traced on the bottom, in white chalk:
Compliments of Madame Atomos.

Sam Forbes covered a lot of ground very rapidly in the days that followed. He went to visit the owner of the Chevrolet, learned that the car had been stolen a week before the hold-up in Chinook, and made it to the latter town in double-quick time.

He visited the bank, questioned the detectives and the doctors, and grilled Harry Diamond, the road-sweeper. He also examined the Chevrolet, but discovered nothing more than the report had already told him.

He was at the end of the trail, without a clue, privately regretting that bank robbery was a federal crime and that, by virtue of the fact, he had been put on the case. His regrets and ill-humor changed nothing, however; he had been given a job to do, and he had to see it through to the end.

"Pssh!" the Boss had said. "Sam, my lad, you can marry your Maggie after...."

After what?

That risked going too far.

To our dear child.

The crown that bore the inscription rolled a little way and settled; one of the men carrying the coffin was obliged to step over it in order not to trip. The dead woman was twenty-two years old. She had had heart trouble since infancy, and the operation that might have ameliorated her condition had put an end to her days.

The coffin went down; the hole was filled in, and while the weeping family turned way, the man who was to put the headstone in place the following day wrote in his notebook: *Mabel Wrist. Lane 60, plot 12. In perpetuity....*

Some distance away, a little yellow man inscribed almost identical words—except for the last....

It was three o'clock in the morning when the van stopped alongside the wall. The driver switched off the headlights. As one of his companions groaned, he pointed to the round pale moon, seemingly as cold as an ice-cream in its cone, but whose wan gleam illuminated the place sufficiently

The four men took a ladder out of the van, along with a flexible stretcher, a pick and a spade, and used the ladder to climb into the cemetery. They must have been experts in this sort of work, for the job was done in less than an hour. When they reappeared, nothing seemed to have been disturbed, but the body of Mavis Wrist was lying on the stretcher, and the young woman's long hair was sweeping the muddy ground.

In the dark sky, the moon seemed even colder.

On Tuesday February twelfth, a consignment of diamonds was eagerly awaited at Dubinsky Junior's store.

Junior was fifty-three years old, weighed two hundred pounds, and was no longer keeping his impatience in check. He was smoking a Havana cigar as thick as a girder, striding back and forth in the store at the pace of an Alpine hunter and squinting at the security men with the eye of a general inspecting his troops.

A million dollars....

In the back of the shop, the safe was agape, and so long as the diamonds were not secure in the shelter of the thick armor-plate, Junior knew that he would be unable to stop his feet marching, his arms waving and his cigar belching smoke like a factory chimney.

There was a mad whirl in the store. Clients were coming in and going out incessantly through the five doors opening in to Fifth Avenue—for them, everything was normal.

Junior went to the step of the first door. That was where the diamonds were to be delivered. The armored car would arrive any minute, stopping exactly in front of the door, in the spot reserved for that purpose by the police, and eight armed policemen would accompany the precious package to the safe. Good! Nothing could go wrong now! Everything was going like clockwork!"

His round eyes settled for a fraction of a second on a young woman with a pale face who passed between two display-units and headed back toward the street. Junior did not care at all about young women, pale or not; only diamonds interested him.

The young woman was a brunette, and her long hair gathered into a pony-tail, hung flexibly down over her fur wrap. She was carrying a large bag, advancing with a mechanical step, and not stopping for anything. Her gaze had an incredible fixity, her eyes slightly dilated, devoid of any gleam. An attentive observer might have thought the unblinking immobility of her eyelids abnormal.

A policeman in plain-clothes glanced at her, thought that she was probably sickening for something, and redirected his gaze to a guy with a furtive appearance. A moment went by, and then a soft purr became audible through the hubbub. Every client, every cop, and Junior himself had the sensation that a fly was buzzing in his ear—and that was all.

An order was barked outside, and an aged man, escorted by eight policemen armed with submachine-guns, made his entrance. He was carrying a black box and marching rapidly, his head sunk between his shoulders.

A young messenger-boy whistled admiringly, went out of the shop, climbed into his van and drew away at top speed. It saved his life, although he did not find that out until later.

In the meantime, inside the shop, the buzzing was amplified, and the hundred and fifty people present suddenly felt a need to stand still and shut up.

The eight policemen and the man who was carrying the diamonds stopped between two display-units; the people going out remained in the doorways, petrified in front of the people trying to get in.

Outside, gawkers gathered in front of the windows, looking in amazement at all those motionless people, while the two guards on watch beside the armored car drew their weapons and ran into Dubinsky's. Their momentum carried them forward for four yards; then they stopped in their turn, pistols in hand, neither able nor wishing to take another step.

Then the pale young woman walked calmly forward, crossing the shop floor, and reached the man who was carrying the diamonds. Slowly, she took the black box from his fingers, slid it into her bag, and headed at a modest pace toward door number five, while the buzzing sound followed her. The people who had been watching the scene though the windows tried to stop her on the threshold, but they could not get close to her. Later, those who had not died affirmed that they had run into an invisible wall.

Protected by that strange barrier, the young woman went along the sidewalk, and held out her bag horizontally. A large grey car came along, slowing down, and a yellow hand grabbed the bag. The car accelerated again, and turned the next corner.

At that moment, the young woman collapsed between two stationary vehicles, and people rushed toward her. The people who were inside the shop were seized by a great agitation.

The plain-clothes policemen tried to get out, but the maddened clients were blocking the exits. Junior uttered harrowing howls. Some people fell down between the display-units and were trampled by the terrified crowd. Women were screaming and men were shoving one another in order to get to the nearest exit, and the confusion was at its height when the ululation of police sirens burst out in the distance.

Suddenly, with frightful completeness, silence fell within the shop, and the people outside saw through the windows that dozens of corpses were strewn on the floor.

For the sake of a million dollars, there were nearly two hundred dead....

Chapter III

Sam Forbes, transformed into a carrier pigeon, disembarked at La Guardia Airport on the afternoon of February twelfth. He leapt into a waiting car and was immediately taken to Dubinsky's.

The shop was protected by a metal barrier and a police cordon, and technicians with Geiger counters were moving between the deserted display-units. An enormous crowd was standing silently outside, but the usually-noisy newspaper vendors had fallen silent, abandoning that section of Fifth Avenue.

Sam sensed that a muffled anguish was gripping the city's inhabitants. It was already common knowledge that the young woman's name was Mabel Wrist, and that she had been dead for four days. It was also common knowledge that two hundred people had been atomized and that Mabel's breast bore the terrible tattoo: *Hiroshima, Nagasaki, Compliments of Madame Atomos*. Madame Atomos' profile was on the first page of every newspaper in the USA, underlined by the caption: *Public Enemy no. 1.*

The entire FBI had been mobilized on the case, and J. Edgar Hoover, with the President's approval, had appeared on TV to make a sensational statement: a veritable declaration of war, in which he demanded the help of every American citizen. Madame Atomos had to be rendered harmless, no matter what the cost.

Hundreds of women of Chinese or Japanese origin were summoned to police stations and interrogated. Their identities and employments were checked and their fingerprints taken.

Sam Forbes got out of the car, and flashbulbs crackled. A man approached him, holding out a microphone, speaking all the while: "And this is the man the

FBI have put in charge of the Atomos affair. His name is Sam Forbes; he's five foot ten, brown-haired and twenty-eight years old. His manner is energetic. I'll try, listeners, to get a few words from him...."

Sam saw the television cameras aimed at him and took a step back, but the man with the microphone followed him, tugging on his cable. "Sam," he said, jovially, "Have you any leads? Can you tell us...."

Two policemen hauled the radio reporter away unceremoniously, and he said into his microphone. "Sam Forbes can't say anything, which is understandable, but the wink he just gave me undoubtedly signifies a great deal...."

Disconcerted, Sam went into the shop, where he immediately found himself the center of attention. The Boss was there, and beckoned his agent to approach. "Shhh!" he hissed, chewing an extinct cigar. "Sam, my lad, I have an idea that you're carrying a crushing responsibility...." He drew Sam to one side and jabbed a thumb at a group of seven people that were waiting a short distance away. "It's not like Chinook this time," he said. "We've got a hundred witnesses, but I kept those fresh for you. How much do you know?"

"Everything the press has revealed. It happened exactly as in Chinook, didn't it?"

The Boss lit his cigar and furrowed his brow. "Shhh! I'd rather be in my shoes than yours. The witnesses agree, but haven't told us anything. The dead woman came in, then stole the diamonds without anyone being able to lift a finger. She went out the same way, handed the bag to a Chink driving a grey rattle-trap, and then collapsed. Thirty seconds later there were a hundred and fifty-eight corpses inside the shop and about thirty more on the sidewalk."

"The car?"

The Boss shrugged. "It got away without any difficulty. There was panic, and none of the witnesses thought to follow it, or even of getting its plate number." He threw away his cigar, crushing it angrily underfoot. "You'll take it from here, of course. Unlimited funds. A free hand. Okay?"

"Okay."

The Boss turned on his heel, left the shop and disappeared into his car.

Sam pivoted and walked over to the group that was waiting for him. It included several FBI men familiar to Sam and a puny little man with grey hair wearing steel-rimmed spectacles, who introduced himself as soon as Sam arrived: "Dr. Alan Soblen."

Sam shook his hand. Soblen had been a member of the Atomic Energy Commission set up in 1951, and was a leader in his field.

Smith Beffort of the FBI gave Sam the necessary explanations. "Dr. Soblen will assist in the investigation. He'll be entirely concerned with the scientific aspects of the problem, but might now be able to give you his opinion as to what's happened here...."

"No," Soblen interjected, in a soft voice. "I can't tell you anything you don't already know. Nearly two hundred people have been subjected to about

351

150 Roentgens of radiation, but the extraordinary thing is that we haven't found any trace of Strontium-90 here."

Sam scratched his head. "Could you translate that, doctor?"

The scientist peered at him over his spectacles. "Strontium-90," he said, "is a radioactive isotope projected into the atmosphere by atomic explosions, which, when it falls to earth, contaminates water, soil, vegetation and crops. It is, in consequence, absorbed by living organisms and always settles in the most dangerous place—which is to say, the bones and the bone-marrow. It was, therefore, very important to find out whether that deadly isotope had been released into the atmosphere of New York." He adjusted his spectacles on his pointed nose and added: "Having found no pollution, I deduce that there has been no explosion—in which case, it's necessary to admit that this…Madame Atomos has succeeded in domesticating atoms."

A shudder ran through the group, and Smith Beffort forgot to light the cigarette that he had just raised to his lips.

"Domesticating atoms?" Sam queried. "What do you mean by that?"

Dr. Soblen took off his spectacles. "Imagine," he said, "that you possess a weapon capable of shooting a bullet at a target, which it destroys, and that the same bullet then returns to the barrel of your weapon….."

"That's insane!" groaned Beffort.

Soblen looked at him mildly. "Isn't it insane, in your view, to make dead people walk?"

Beffort grimaced, and lit his cigarette. It was beyond him.

"As for the mysterious wall with which several people collided," the doctor continued, "and which no longer offered any resistance after Mabel Wrist's second demise, I think one might classify it in the category of radiations provoked, and in some way solidified, by a revolutionary technique." He put his spectacles on again, and pointed his nose at Sam Forbes. "That," he said, in an apologetic tone, "is all I can tell you for the moment. It's not much, and rests entirely on suppositions."

Sam frowned. "You made allusion just now to a weapon capable of recovering a projectile after firing," he said. "Is it logical to assume that the weapon would have to be installed not far from its intended target."

"I don't know," Soblen replied, thoughtfully. "What are you thinking?"

Sam lit a cigarette, having offered one to Soblen, who refused. "At Chinook," he said, "a witness said that there was a car following John Ferby. When that car was found, the back seat bore the imprint of a metal object, about one foot by two, probably very heavy. Couldn't that be an apparatus—what you call a weapon—designed to control...dead people at a distance?"

Dr. Soblen squinted. "I was unaware of that detail," he said. "Your hypothesis isn't implausible, Mr. Forbes. All the more so because of the buzzing…."

"What buzzing?" Sam queried.

Smith Beffort interrupted, pointing a finger. "Over there, that young fellow on the right is the sole survivor of those who were inside the shop. I think it might be useful for you to interrogate him personally. He has a head on his shoulders and seems sure of himself."

"Let's go," Sam agreed.

They crossed the room. Beffort took out his notebook and consulted it before calling out: "Jack Urey!"

The young man got up and came toward the two men with a firm stride. He was wearing a leather jacket, and a stray curl of hair fell over his forehead. "That's me," he said, unceremoniously. "Tell me, are you going to keep me kicking my heels much longer?"

"No," Sam assured him. "Tell me what you saw, and you can be on your way."

Jack Urey put his index-finger to his nose. "To tell the truth," he said, "I didn't see anything much. I just heard that hum, and...."

"Just a minute," Beffort put in. "Tell Mr. Forbes about the girl."

"Oh, I barely noticed her. If the rags hadn't published her paper, I wouldn't have remembered...."

"Repeat what you told me," Beffort interjected again. "We're not asking for any more."

Jack Urey gave him a dirty look, then started again, ostensibly addressing himself to Sam. "Well, I was in that corner, on the second step, and I was watching the cops protecting the guy carrying the gems when the girl stuck herself in the middle...."

"In the middle of what?"

"Between them and me, of course." He turned to the door, pointing at the deserted display-units with his extended forefinger. "It was very impressive—all those cops with submachine-guns. It was like being at the flicks. In short, I think the guts were still outside when I first heard the humming in my ears."

"What was it like?"

"The noise made by one of those big flies that...."

"Yes," Beffort cut in, "We get the picture. What did you do then?"

"I went out! I had my deliveries to make." He pinched his lips and said: "I had a bit of luck, eh? A little longer, and I'd have been good for the morgue too! Can I go now?"

Sam noticed that the boy was looking round anxiously. He was afraid. "The girl," he said. "What was she like?"

"As white as her blouse and as stiff as a statue, Can I go?"

Sam agreed, and Jack Urey set off like a hare.

"He's got the wind up," Beffort observed, "and he's not alone. Look at the others...."

Sam looked at the other witnesses. There were four women and three men, all very pale, visibly intimidated. One of the women was almost lying down in her chair. She was sitting to one side and was obviously drowsy, for her chin was resting on her chest and her eyes were shut,

"They happened to be outside when the big drama unfolded," said Beffort, "and they bumped into the famous invisible wall. It's quite a trick...."

He continued talking, but Sam was no longer listening. He was looking at the sleeping woman. Her left hand was hanging down with a strange limpness, and her knees were wide apart. "Smith!" he snapped. "Fetch the doc—that woman's dead!"

Smith Beffort needed no further instruction. He headed for the exit, after having murmured a few words in Dr. Soblen's ear in passing. The latter came over to Sam, who was leaning over the young woman. "If she isn't dead," he warned, "don't touch her!"

Sam straightened up. "There's no doubt about it," he said. His gaze strayed over the other witnesses, which were still motionless. "Damn it!" he swore. "Look at that, Soblen!"

The scientist turned, and saw three men lie down on the bench they had been sitting on, while the three women collapsed limply in their chairs.

There was a commotion in the street outside, and Smith Beffort came back into the shop. A doctor and two orderlies carrying a stretcher were following him.

The doctor looked at the woman, slipped on rubber gloves, took her pulse and raised his eyes again. "Good day, Dr. Soblen," he said. "I'm sure you know what killed her, don't you?"

"Coagulation of the blood."

"Exactly. And them?"

"Same symptoms, obviously," the scientist retorted. "It's necessary to evacuate this place immediately, Mr. Forbes. Our Geiger counters aren't registering any radioactivity, but there must be something else we can't detect."

Sam made a gesture of denial. "It's not that. All these people bumped into the invisible wall—and they're dying of it six hours later...."

Smith Beffort started. "Good God!" he cried. "There are dozens in that situation—we let them go."

A profound silence fell inside the shop. It was Dr. Soblen who broke it. "At present," he said, coldly, "there must be dozens more corpses all over the city. That's frightful!"

In the hour that followed, that bad news flowed from headquarters to Sam. Eight corpses were found in the subway, ten had collapsed in the street, seven on the stairs of their buildings, and thirty-two had died at home after putting on their slippers. In spite of appearances, they had all succumbed at the same moment, and only the different paths they had travelled in going home had given the impression of a time lag. The bill for the Dubinsky operation was thus made up in the following fashion, to the account of Madame Atomos: one million dollars, 252 deaths.

Jack Urey was found and taken to hospital. He was submitted to a serious of examinations and obliged to go to bed, but the boy defied all prognoses and remained alive. With a cigarette in his mouth and his hands linked behind the nape of his neck, he scolded the doctor who was listening to his chest for the tenth time. "Come on, come on! This is getting tedious, Doc! Mother Atomos has missed me, and tomorrow night I'll be going to the ball!"

And he went—the Ureys, it seemed were hard to kill.

Chapter IV

At nine o'clock in the morning on the day after the Dubinsky affair, which was Wednesday February thirteenth, a man emerged from Penn Station and took the subway to Washington Heights in the Bronx. He stationed himself at the corner of Broadway and 193rd Street and, after waiting five minutes, was met by a woman of medium height, elegantly dressed in a brown skunk-fur coat, with very marked Oriental features.

The couple went into an expensive restaurant at 143 Dyckman Street and installed themselves in a booth in order to eat a lavish breakfast.

After a brief interval, a little yellow man wearing a soft hat drawn down over his eyes came into the restaurant and played a few records on the juke-box. He smoked a cigarette, drank a cup of coffee, and left the establishment whistling. At that moment, the companion of the woman in the fur coat got up and exited in her turn.

The two men seemed not to know one another, but they got on the same subway train and got out at 125th Street just as the doors were closing again, thus escaping any potential surveillance. They both went along 125th Street, then separated and continued on their way on different sidewalks. Ten minutes later, the man with the soft hat stopped in front of a rather shabby green Chevrolet, whose door was unlocked and which had an ignition-key in the dashboard.

His companion stopped, standing on his own sidewalk, surveying the street intently. The little man then got into the Chevrolet, started the motor, and was about to put it into first gear when a forceful hand pulled him out of the car.

"FBI! Hands up, slowly."

The Oriental saw that two other policemen in plain clothes were ready to intervene and, thinking himself lost, made a desperate move. He ducked down sharply, dived between two cars, and pulled his Colt Cobra out of its holster.

The fourth policeman, whom he had not spotted, bludgeoned him and laid him out for the count.

Thirty seconds later, still unconscious, the little man was rolling towards Sam Forbes' headquarters. An FBI agent consulted the papers that he had just extracted from the Oriental's pocket, tilted his head and read aloud: "Hisato

Keichu, thirty-five years old. Naturalized American. Born in Nagasaki, Japan...."

Mechanically, the driver stepped on the gas and switched on his siren.

Hisato Keichu's companion remained rooted to his sidewalk momentarily, and when the police car had disappeared he ran to the glass-sided telephone booth that he had perceived on the street corner. Feverishly, he dialed a number, and when the receiver was picked up he asked, gaily: "Is that you, Lou?"

"No," replied a masculine voice. "This is twelve fifty-eight thirty-four."

The man hung up, left the booth and rifled through his notebook while walking. Thirty-two signified Allison Park, thirty-three North Hudson Park and thirty-four Sound View Park.

The man hailed a taxi, had himself taken to the southern extremity of Sound View Park, settled up and continued on foot as far as the bank of the East River. A car drew up alongside him and the woman in the fur coat opened the door. The man got in swiftly and the car set off in the direction of Yankee Stadium.

"Well?" the woman asked.

"Hisato's just been arrested."

"Was it chance, or was he being followed?"

"Chance. Probably FBI men."

The woman pursed her lips. "I knew that we shouldn't use Hisato again. Madame Atomos foresaw this."

"Good. What should we do?"

The woman stopped at a red light and tuned her cold gaze on her passenger. "Sam Forbes has a fiancée," she said. "Her name is Maggie Fairbanks. Her address is in the glove compartment."

The man rummaged in the compartment and read the address. "When?" he said, simply.

"This evening."

To keep watch on all the cemeteries in the USA was too gigantic a task, and Sam Forbes had preferred to mobilize his G-men in the direction of men of Oriental extraction driving cars. At Chinook, and during the robbery of the Dubinsky jewelry store, a little yellow man had been at the steering-wheel of both vehicles, and it seemed reasonable to direct the initial search in that direction.

Sam had not, however, expected such a rapid result.

When Hisato Keichu was brought into his office, the federal agent immediately sensed that he had got his man. That intuition might have originated in the violent desire that he had to seize the first link in a chain that might be interminable, but that ambition had pushed him to help himself, and now heaven had come to his aid.

356

At first, Hisato refused to answer any questions. The bludgeon had struck him a ranging blow, and his hand often went to the nape of his neck. That was, however, his only manifestation of emotion. The fact of being accused of carrying an illicit weapon and the theft of the car left him visibly indifference.

Hisato was playing for time, waiting.

Confronted by his silence, Sam sent two men to collect three witnesses who had declared themselves able, if the opportunity arose, to recognize the driver of the grey car to which Mabel Wrist had handed the bag containing the diamonds, and waited in his turn.

The Japanese man had been standing up for two hours. His pockets had been emptied; his tie and shoelaces removed. The window was wide open in spite of the intense cold, and Sam had cut off the heating. Sam and his men went back to the office, but Hisato Keichu stayed where he was, turning white and unable to prevent his teeth from chattering.

At midday, the three witnesses were put in the presence of the Japanese man. Two of them formally identified him; the third remained hesitant. He had been poorly placed in relation to the grey car, and had only seen the man from an oblique angle, his view also being hindered by some luggage that was on the rear seat.

Sam had the room cleared, keeping only one G-man, charged with preventing the Oriental from reaching the window. Hisato's silence and his resistance to the cold demonstrated that the man had nerves of steel, and that if the situation became desperate, he probably would not hesitate to commit suicide. Sam's office was on the fifth floor.

"Admit that you were driving the grey car," said Sam, not hopeful of obtaining an answer, "and that you work for Madame Atomos,"

"Yes," said the Oriental, dryly.

Sam and the G-man exchanged a surprised glance. Hisato's sudden capitulation, which had been quite unforeseen, seemed distinctly suspicious. Sam closed the window, pushed a chair over to the Japanese man, and offered him a cigarette.

"Who is Madame Atomos?"

Hisato Keichu took a long puff and crossed his legs. He seemed less tense, and Sam had the feeling that he had been biding his time before talking.

"I don't know," Hisato replied. "I only know that she was living in Nagasaki in 1945, and that her husband and children were killed by the atomic bomb." His slanted eyes flashed briefly, and he added, without his impassive face changing expression: "I was at Nagasaki, but I was only a child when your second bomb exploded. My parents, my brothers, my sisters and my friends were transformed into ash in less than a minute. All those who assist Madame Atomos were in Nagasaki or Hiroshima. America has only known Pearl Harbor, but the territory of the USA will soon be an immense cemetery." He looked directly into Sam Forbes' eyes and said: "You can do nothing against Madame

Atomos. It has taken her twenty years to put her vengeance into execution, but now nothing can oppose her plans."

Sam restrained an impulse to lash out. "You live in a hotel," he said, in a voice vibrant with anger, "and you don't have a job. Your personal effects are limited to two worn suits, underwear, a few bathroom items and a Colt Cobra! We found fifty dollars and some small change on you. I don't believe that a man working for Madame Atomos could be in such a sorry situation."

The Japanese man smiled. "You won't get me that way," he said. "You think that men of my race are primarily concerned with not losing face, but that's a typically Occidental notion. The next few hours will show you that I'm only a pawn on a vast chessboard, and pride won't choke me to the point of trying to appear more important than I am. I drove the car in Chinook, and yesterday, and I don't know any more...."

"What about the apparatus that was on the back seat?"

"I steal a car and am contacted."

"Where?"

"At home. I'm given a rendezvous outside the city, and the apparatus is loaded into the car. I don't have to touch it. The apparatus is already working, remotely guiding a walking corpse somewhere in the city, and two dots move closer to one another on a screen. One is the corpse, the other my car."

Sam leapt to his feet. "That's a lie! In Chinook, you were following John Ferby."

Hisato Keichu shrugged his shoulders. "Hazard dictated that we were following the same route, but I didn't know that the old man was my subject. I only realized that when he went into the bank and the humming started. That sound warns me that the operation is imminent, and I get ready to act. Then I take what's held out to me and go back to the rendezvous. There I abandon the car and I get home by my own means. That's all."

Sam and his men interrogated Hisato Keichu until nightfall, but could not get any more out of him. The man was only an agent, an isolated link, and Sam anticipated that the other end of the chain would not be easy to grasp.

The doorbell rang and Mr. Fairbanks went to open it. He found himself face to face with a man armed with a pistol fitted with a silencer, and did not have time to say a single word before receiving a bullet in the head.

The man caught him as he fell, and gave a signal to two shadows, who joined him on the steps. Silently, the three men went into the house, and burst into the dining-room. Mrs. Fairbanks stood up, but a bullet between her eyes laid her out on the floor.

Maggie Fairbanks, who was watching television in the living-room, heard the faint noise of the shot and the muffled noise that her mother's body made as it fell, and got to her feet. She went through the bamboo partition that separated the two rooms, felt an atrocious pain in her skull, and plunged into a bottomless gulf.

At nine o'clock the telephone in Sam Forbes' office rang. One of the men present lifted the receiver and passed it to his chief. "It's for you," he said. "An outside line."

Sam immediately thought of Maggie. He had called her the day before, but had not seen her since the beginning of the Atomos affair. The young woman had told him in a letter how annoyed she was with him, and, with a very feminine sensibility, had concluded by saying that life apart from him was not worth living.

"Hello? Sam Forbes here."

"Have you heard from your fiancée, Mr. Forbes?" The voice was that of a woman, with a slight foreign accent that Sam could not identify.

"Who are you?" he snapped, abruptly alert.

"A colleague of Madame Atomos," the woman replied, phlegmatically. "I'm calling from a public booth, and there's no point in trying to trace the call. Here's what I have to sway: you've detained Hisato Keichu, but we've kidnapped Maggie Fairbanks. If you'd like to check, I'll call you back shortly...."

She hung up. Sam did likewise, and feverishly dialed a number, while issuing orders: "Warn the switchboard that my line will be activated shortly. Try to identify the call-booth, and have two radio-cars stay in touch with the switchboard. The usual system...."

A G-man hastily left the room and ran along the deserted corridor.

Sam listened to the telephone ringing interminably in the Fairbanks' home, and felt a horrible dread slowly increasing within him. At the fifteenth ring, he hung up and turned to his men, his features contorted. "Madame Atomos has just abducted my fiancée," he said, harshly. "In a moment, one of her acolytes will call back. It's absolutely necessary to trace the call. Warn the patrol cars to be ready to respond to any message from our offices. We have absolute priority. I'll try to keep the conversation going for as long as possible...."

Three men left the office. When the telephone rang, Smith Beffort grabbed a receiver. Sam snatched another. "Forbes," he said. "Talk."

The tense voice of the mysterious correspondent was heard: "Verification effected, Mr. Forbes?"

"Yes."

"Then here are our conditions. Free Hisato immediately—without trying to follow him, of course—and we'll release your fiancée."

"Where will the exchange take place?" the federal agent ventured.

"There won't be any exchange, Mr. Forbes. We have the advantage, and don't forget it. Free Hisato Keichu within the next ten minutes, or Maggie Fairbanks will be no more than a memory to you." There was a click.

"Hello?" shouted Sam, incredulously. "Listen to me!"

Smith Beffort gently replaced his own receiver. "Useless," he said. "She's hung up." He whistled mechanically through his teeth, and added, gravely: "You've got ten minutes to decide, old chap...."

Chapter V

It was nine-twenty. A message came from the switchboard to tell Sam Forbes that, because of the brevity of the previous communication, the place from which the mysterious correspondent had called could not be identified. The patrol cars were, however, remaining in a state of alert.

Crushed, Sam did not react.

Smith Beffort, who understood his state of mind quite well, posed the problem brutally, without attempting to minimize the consequences that an overly spontaneous decision might have. "You have full authority, but if you let Hisato return to the wild the press will shoot you down in flames tomorrow and the Boss will be obliged to fire you." He glanced at Sam and met his empty gaze. "I don't know what I'd do in your position," he went on, "but you have to act rapidly. Hisato Keichu has to be out of the building by half past, and it's nine twenty-four...."

Sam shrugged his shoulders. "I'll free the Jap, then write my letter of resignation." His hoarse voice seemed to be coming from a long way away.

Smith Beffort thumped the desk with his fist. "A nice solution! You surrender before having got into the fight. If everyone else does the same, Madame Atomos will set the country on fire without meeting any opposition!" He marched furiously across the room, looked at his watch, planted himself in front of Sam and said: "Release Hisato immediately—I'll take care of it personally."

There was a gleam in Sam's eye, but he did not budge. "The woman specified that he mustn't be followed," he said.

Beffort took the bull by the horns. "Listen," he spat, violently. "Even in broad daylight I can follow a guy while leaving my shadow in my desk drawer! Cut Hisato loose, let the patrol cars go their own way, and we'll play the game quietly. You stay here, and I'll call your hourly. I'll walk on tiptoe, of course, so long as Maggie Fairbanks hasn't been returned to you—but afterwards, the fireworks start! Go on, Sam—throw the Jap out. I'll wait for him outside."

Same gave the order to release Keichu, and Beffort left the office like a gust of wind, ran down the stairs and left the building by a door that let out into the parking lot. He climbed into his car, went around the block, found a spot fifty yards from the door through which Keichu would come, and started watching.

After thirty seconds, the Japanese man appeared, alone. He looked round, raised the collar of his overcoat and drew away from the building slowly. He came toward Beffort, and the latter crouched down in his seat, hiding in the shadows.

360

Hisato Keichu slid between two stationary cars and made a gesture. A taxi stopped beside him. The Japanese man climbed in beside the driver, and the vehicle moved off.

Surprised, Beffort began to trail him. He had expected his prey to flee like lightning, plunging into the subway, or a pick-up arranged by his accomplices, but here he was, calmly setting forth at a modest pace. It was worrying....

Sam Forbes sat in his armchair and smoked one cigarette after another. A call from the police in Tarrytown had just informed him of the death of Maggie's parents, and that news had plunged him into the deaths of depression.

At eleven o'clock the telephone rang. Sam picked it up nervously, sure that it would be Maggie, and experienced a terrible disappointment on recognizing Smith Beffort's voice.

"Hisato went back to his hotel and packed his bags," the agent told him. "We're now in Jersey City, not far from the Holland Tunnel. The Jap's in a bar; I'm in one across the road. Any news of Maggie?"

"Nothing."

There as a silence; then Smith Beffort said, in a voice he wanted to be reassuring: "That doesn't mean anything. Above all, don't torture yourself. Mother Atomos is doubtless waiting for her boy Hisato to be safe before releasing your fiancée. I'll call you as soon as possible."

He hung up, and Sam sat down again, his mind empty, completely demoralized.

At midnight the phone rang briefly, but it stopped before Sam could move. He got up, tugged on the wire, set the apparatus down on his knee, and resumed waiting.

Chilled to the bone, he woke up two hours later, with a strident ringing drilling into his ears. He grabbed the apparatus

It was Smith Beffort again. "I'm in a hurry," the agent said, rapidly. "I'm calling from Dunellen police station. Hisato was picked up by a Buick shortly after my last call and we took Route 22. The Jap's in an isolated cabin two miles from Dunellen and the Buick's gone. I'm going back. Anything new?"

"No," Sam murmured, "except that Maggie's parents have been murdered. I forgot that when I talked to you before. Don't let Hisato get away, Smith!"

"Don't worry. He's sleeping like a log in his hidey-hole, and he hasn't got a car at his disposal. I'll call again later. Bye...."

Sam hung up, and lit his last cigarette.

At four o'clock in the morning, the long wait finally produced a result. He immediately recognized the voice of the woman with the foreign accent in the receiver.

"That's perfect, Mr. Forbes—you've played it straight. Hisato's safe, and we know now that you couldn't make him talk...."

"Enough chit-chat!" Sam interjected, ferociously. "Where's my fiancée."

A ripple of laughter replied. "In our power, Mr. Forbes!"

Sam's fingers went white as he gripped the phone. "You promised to set her free!" he said, in a voice vibrant with hatred.

"We didn't say when, Mr. Forbes. First, we intend to make use of her. Madame Atomos invites you to attend the performance that will take place tomorrow morning, at nine o'clock sharp, opposite the Schwartz Bank. Goodnight, Mr. Forbes."

The click sounded lugubriously in Sam's ear, but two phrases were still vibrating in his skull: *make use of her* and *the performance.*

Sam foresaw, confusedly, that he would witness a particularly terrible scene, in which Maggie Fairbanks would doubtless play the leading role—and a murderous rage took hold of him. His mouth twisted into a mute insult and, to vent his anger, he smashed the telephone against the wall. It was childish, but it helped to make his impotence less intolerable.

The Schwartz Bank was situated in a quiet street of antiquated houses in the heart of the Bronx, and a thick mist rising from Eastchester Bay was swamping the police cars stationed under the NO PARKING notices.

In one of the vehicles, Sam Forbes and Dr. Alan Soblen kept their eyes firmly on the front of the bank.

"What's going to happen, do you think?" asked Soblen, wiping the lenses of his spectacles.

Forbes turned a face ravaged by a sleepless and anxious night toward him. "I don't know," he said, in a toneless voice. "We've been invited to a performance given by Madame Atomos, and I'm afraid that it might have a tragic ending. Ten armed men are inside the bank, and there are five more on the first floor of the building.

"If things happen the way they did at Dubinsky's," Soblen objected, "guns will be as useless as bicycle-pumps, and the men in the bank will die there."

Sam threw his cigarette-butt out of the car window. "If we find the same situation as at Dubinsky's," he said, wearily, "my men know what they have to do. Our aim is to avoid any casualties."

"How will you know that there's danger?"

"The corpses remotely controlled by Madame Atomos are easily recognizable. They can walk, doctor, but they still have a livid complexion, unblinking eyes and a mechanical gait. As soon as anyone with that appearance goes into the bank, it will be immediately evacuated via an emergency exit."

"What's your plan?"

Sam pushed his hat back over the nape of his neck and rubbed his swollen eyelids. "We'll let the corpse walk, since we have no way to stop it—but when the car comes to pick it up, or collect the loot, the road will be immediately blocked at both ends. Two trucks are ready to roll, and men hidden under the tarpaulins can open fire as soon as I give the signal. What I want, Dr. Soblen, is the remote control apparatus on the back seat of the car."

"I agree that, from our viewpoint, that's the most important thing at present," Soblen admitted. "What time is it, Forbes?"

The federal agent consulted his watch, and murmured: "Eight fifty-nine, doctor. In one minute, Mother Atomos's circus will begin its parade. Do you notice anything strange about the street?"

Soblen squinted. "Presumably you mean the fog," he said, pensively. "It's been a long time since I've seen one like it." He sniffed the air, and said: "Besides, it has an odor, doesn't it?"

Sam sniffed. "Hmm! It's coming from the docks. Sometimes, odors come out of the drains and invade the Bronx."

The radio-set crackled, and a voice emerged from the receiver. "Tom Six calling Tom One!"

Forbes flicked the switch with his thumb. "This is Tom One," he said "What is it?"

"The mist's getting thicker here," said the voice.

"So?"

"It has a funny taste, this mist. Have you taken a look at your windscreen?"

Sam saw that a thin oily sheen was spreading over the glass, but that wasn't infrequent in the city, and didn't seem unduly peculiar. "Well?" he growled. "What's bizarre about that, Tom Six? The wind's blowing northwesterly, bringing all the pestilential factory-smoke down on the Bronx."

"It's not that!" croaked Tom Six. "Try your windscreen-wipers, and we'll talk again...."

Forbes pressed the switch, and the wipers began to beat madly over the greasy surface, redistributing the oily substance in long opaque streaks.

"Tom Three here," said the speaker. "I heard Tom Six and I just tried to move my car. It's impossible. The motor's running, but the wheels are spinning as if on black ice. My partner got out, and he's now face-down on the ground. It's impossible to stay upright!"

One by one, the other cars confirmed that they were in the same situation. It was impossible to move off or to set foot on the ground. The neighborhood was suddenly impassable. The pedestrians took refuge in doorway if they were already on the sidewalk; the majority found themselves immobilized in the roadway, between vehicles that were equally becalmed, and all those people flat on the ground offered a spectacle that was both grotesque and frightful at the same time.

Dr. Soblen passed his finger over the windscreen, brought back a sample of the oily substance, sniffed it and pulled a face. "I don't know what it is," he confessed, finally.

Sam laughed. "It's nine-oh-three," he said, "and Madame Atomos has kept her word. The performance has begun." He opened the door abruptly and set his feet on the slippery ground. Before releasing his grip, he said: "At university, I wasn't bad at ice hockey...."

He let go, and immediately collapsed, departing on his back with his arms and legs spread, and slid in this fashion into the middle of the road. Immediately, he attempted to pivot, but his fingers could find no purchase, and he had the strange sensation of being separated from the asphalt by a cushion of air. He twisted his neck, and saw that Dr. Soblen was about to get out of the car. "Don't move!" he shouted. "Instead, throw me the rope that's under the seat."

Alan Soblen bent down and fetched out a tow-rope fitted with metal hooks. He fixed one end to the door-frame, uncoiled the rest and threw it to Sam, who caught the hook in mid-air, tugged gently, and pulled himself back to the car.

"Good God!" he said, when he was back behind the steering-wheel, "this is crazy. We're stuck here like flies on fly-paper."

Soblen, who had turned toward the bank, grabbed him by the arm in sudden anxiety. "Look, Forbes! The lights have just been switched off. In weather this dark, that's abnormal....."

The fog was now so thick that visibility was reduced to ten yards.

"Something's happening in the bank," Sam growled. "Did you see anyone go in while I was doing my little turn?"

"No. Besides, it's practically impossible to move around....." He interrupted himself, his eyes widening, and he pointed to the radio. "Why can't we hear anything anymore?"

Sam verified that the equipment was working and put his lips to the microphone. "Tom One calling...Tom One calling...."

The speaker remained silent, and Sam put his hand on the apparatus. "It's cold," he observed, grimly. He turned the ignition-key without any result, and turned a stony face toward the scientist. "No more juice in the battery, no more light in the bank. What does it mean, Doctor?"

Soblen blinked. His face expressed nothing but amazement. "I don't know," he whispered. His gaze fell upon Sam's wrist and looked up again immediately. "Your watch has stopped," he said. "Time has passed, but the hands are still indicating nine-oh-three!"

Sam jabbed his chin in the direction of the fog that was now extending in thick sheets, blurring the contours of the hood and pressing against the windows in large fleecy stripes. "We can't see further than three feet anymore," he said, "and we can neither move nor communicate with the other cars. In the heart of New York, we're as isolated as in a desert. If the entire city is paralyzed, Madame Atomos can kill us, set fire to the buildings, crush us or disintegrate us!"

Mechanically, Soblen took off his spectacles, and for the first time, Sam noticed that without the lenses the scientist's eyes were glaucous, empty and cold, like a serpent's.

"We're in the hands of a madwoman," Soblen said, slowly, "and we can't do anything about it." His lack of emotion was stupefying.

Chapter VI

Smith Beffort was on watch between the side road and the house, in a sunken lane furrowed by ruts that the frost had hardened, but which must be transformed into a veritable mud-bath when it rained.

In the nascent dawn, Beffort could see the house at a thirty-degree angle and a long stretch of Route 22, and beyond a curtain of bare skeletal trees he could just make out the squat mass of a large barn topped by a curious concrete tower. Apart from the barn, the region was quite deserted. During his brief round trip to Dunellen Police Station, Beffort had made a mental note of the fact that there were no other buildings on the roadside in the two miles that separated the barn from Dunellen.

The federal agent stretched himself out on the seat, lit a cigarette and, having switched on the engine, activated the heating. It was eight o'clock in the morning, but the leaden sky only gave off a parsimonious light. The cold was intense and dry, and both the ground and the leafless branches were covered by a thin layer of frost.

At eight forty-five the purr of a motor roused Beffort from his torpor. He craned his neck and saw that a Buick was drawing up outside the house. A man and a woman got out. The couple cross the narrow strip of bare ground separating the road from the house and went inside.

Beffort slid down behind the steering-wheel and stopped the engine. He was about two hundred yards from the house and it was scarcely probable that the muffled sound of the engine could be audible at that distance, but the G-man did not want to run any risk.

A few moments went by, and then the couple reappeared, accompanied by Hisato Keichu. The trio got into the Buick. Beffort reached for the ignition-key again, but the Buick turned into the lane that led to the barn and disappeared around the corner of the building.

Beffort looked hard, and after a brief lapse of time caught sight of several silhouettes at the top of the tower. Then a window opened and a strange metal object emerged slowly from the concrete block. It bore a vague resemblance to a television camera, but Beffort was too far away to make out any details. He simply noted that the object was pointing north-eastwards, and that it was exactly nine o'clock.

Time went by without anything else happening. At about nine twenty Beffort turned on his radio and happened upon a special news bulletin.

...that a thick fog has submerged an entire district in the Bronx, and the ground is covered by an oily substance that prevents all movement. In addition, the electricity and the telephone have been cut off within the perimeter. Since nine o'clock, nothing in the district has moved. We have informed you that Madame Atomos has threatened to attack the Schwartz bank, and we remind

you, without drawing any hasty conclusions, that the establishment in question is situated in the heart of the Bronx....

There was a slight commotion, and then the speaker went on: *Some last-minute information informs us that Sam Forbes and several of his men are in the affected zone, and that the FBI directorate cannot make contact with them. This last point is extremely alarming, and questions are being asked in high places as to how the radio equipment in all the G-men's cars could have broken down at the same time. Dick Slatt, our specialist in scientific questions, is going to tell you why he thinks that Madame Atomos is using an electromagnetic ray of fantastic power...*

The precise voice of Dick Slatt filled the silence, but Beffort was no longer listening. He was looking at the camera-like object whose barrel was poking out of the tower, and had abruptly realized that it was pointing directly at New York. "Good God!" he swore. "That's the explanation of the presence of the concrete tower! That barn is probably one of Madame Atomos's laboratories. The Bronx paralyzed! Shit!"

He got out of the car, took his thirty-eight from its holster and ran along the sunken lane. With a great deal of skill and a little luck, he ought to be able to reach the barn without being spotted.

Cutting through the fog, the face and then the body of Maggie Fairbanks suddenly materialized in front of the car's hood. The young woman was livid, and clad in a fur wrap that Sam did not recognize. When he met her dead gaze he felt as if his heart was going to explode. He howled and seized the door-handle, but Alan Soblen took hold of him with all his strength.

"Don't be an imbecile, Forbes! You can see perfectly well that she's been atomized!"

"In the name of God, Soblen, let me go! That's my fiancée!" He struggled savagely, but the little doctor would not let go.

"Calm down, Forbes!" he pleaded, in his cold voice. "You can't do anything, except lose your own life. Remember all those dead people at Dubinsky's...."

Maggie Fairbanks had already disappeared into the mist, and the last thing Sam noticed was the green suitcase dangling from the end of her rigid right arm.

"She's evidently just stolen the money from the Schwartz Bank," said Dr. Soblen, without any apparent emotion.

Mutely, Sam Forbes directed his hallucinated gaze straight ahead. Paralyzed by his pain, he was momentarily incapable of any reaction, and only a residue of self-respect prevented him from giving way to despair.

Soblen respected his silence, unaware of the fury that was building in his companion—which swept away his enfeeblement as a gust of wind snuffs out a candle. The doctor started when Sam exploded: "Soblen! I swear to you that from this moment on, I shall not rest until I have the hide of Madame Atomos!"

Soblen heard a crack, and saw that the steering wheel had just come apart in Sam Forbes' hands. Privately, he thought that Madame Atomos would certainly come to grief is she should ever fall into those hands....

At the southern limit of the impenetrable zone, Maggie Fairbanks emerged from the thick fog, and slid rather than walked into the middle of the roadway, where she stood still.

A murmur ran through the crowd that was gathered on the opposite sidewalk, and two cops ran forward, swinging their nightsticks. One of them had witnessed the hold-up at Dubinsky's jewelry shop, only a few yards away from Mabel Wrist, and he instantly recognized the symptoms of the terrible atomic contamination on Maggie Fairbanks' face. He caught his colleague's arm, forcing him to take a step back. "Look out, Joe!" he grated, in a voice that was suddenly hoarse. "This broad is one of Madame Atomos's corpses. Go warn headquarters—I'll keep the gawkers back."

Joe drew away in the direction of the call-box on Tremont Avenue, elbows pumping. The other cop set about herding the crowd into an adjacent side-street.

At that moment, Maggie Fairbanks came forward, leaving the part of the roadway that was covered with the oily substance, and was in an excellent position when a black Mercury hurtled up at top speed. The car braked, level with the young woman, and Maggie leapt into the back seat, with her suitcase.

The cop drew his pistol and opened fire, but the Mercury swerved into Tremont Avenue and the bullets hit the wall of a neighboring building.

For the first time, Madame Atomos had collected one of her corpses....

Smith Beffort stopped, having gone a hundred yards in the cover of the embankment, and threw himself to the ground as a bullet whined past his ear. He rolled in the ditch and raised his head. He saw a shadow move behind the barn and immediately heard the roar of an engine.

He understood that the three were about to escape, and hurriedly covered twenty yards, hugging the ground. His movement had been too rapid for the invisible shooter to have had time to adjust his aim, but Beffort knew that the other would not take his eyes off the place where he had disappeared. He crept forward in the ditch, stood up cautiously in the shadow of a tree, and darted a glance between two low branches at the barn.

He saw that the Buick was moving slowly along the pathway, and that the camera-shaped object was no longer projecting from the window in the tower. There was a whistling sound above his head. He looked up, and watched in amazement as the tree was completely consumed, already crumbling into ashes under the effect of some terrible radiation.

Breathlessly, Beffort threw himself flat in the ditch and began crawling backwards. Behind him, he heard the howl of an engine driven at full power, and a thorn-bush three feet away from him suddenly burst into flames, burning like a torch. It was reduced to ash in the blink of an eye.

With sweat on his brow, Beffort glanced back over his shoulder. He saw the Buick bearing down on him like a tornado, and the yellow face of Hisato Keichu grimacing behind the slim barrel of an unfamiliar weapon. In spite of his terror, the G-man's reflexes came into play. The thirty-eight barked three times, and Hisato swayed back in his seat as the Buick went past, groaning. Beffort followed it automatically, emptying his clip, but only had the feeble satisfaction of seeing the tail-light shatter.

A moment later, the Buick had disappeared.

Weak at the knees, the federal agent raced to his car, hit the clutch savagely while turning the radio-switch, and caught another newsflash as he moved off.

...surprising, that the Bronx has now recovered its customary animation. The mysterious fog is evaporating slowly, but the oil covering the sidewalks and the roadway is no more than an inexplicable bad memory....

Smith Beffort slid a new ammunition-clip into his thirty-eight, and cornered on two wheels. He did not expect to catch up with the Buick, only desirous of reaching Dunellen in time to launch a general alert over the radio-waves.

...if Madame Atomos has not caused a massacre this time, she has nevertheless kept her promise, and the Schwartz Bank has just lost a hundred thousand dollars. The sinister Madame Atomos used young Maggie Fairbanks to carry out the hold-up. We remind you that Maggie Fairbanks was Sam Forbes' fiancée. The latter has just resigned from the FBI....

Beffort swore dully, took a final turn and braked hard in front of Dunellen Police Station. He leapt out, climbed the steps furiously and went into the squad room like a shell. Badge in hand, Beffort identified himself and sent a message to the FBI himself, while the radio-operator beside him alerted the Highway Patrol: "A light-colored Buick carrying a woman and two men, one of whom may be wounded...."

Smith Beffort made an unprecedented effort to keep his eyes open, but slumped unconscious on the corner of the table. He had, after all, done his share of the work.

Two motorcycle cops caught sight of the Buick on Route 22, just short of Scotch Plains. They switched on their sirens and launched themselves in pursuit of the car. They caught up with it three miles beyond Scotch Plains.

The senior patrolman was named Alex Witter. He stepped on the gas and drew level with the Buick, flagging it down with his gloved hand. The driver leaned forward, revealing a woman holding a strange apparatus—similar, his colleague later said, to a short glass-fiber fishing rod—and there was a brief flash.

Alex Witter caught fire like a bale of hay, and his body fell from the motor-cycle, which went on its way alone. The other motor-cyclist cleverly avoided the fireball that Witter had become, braked and turned sideways without hesitation, giving no further thought to the Buick. He had known Alex for ten years. When his eyes came to rest on the asphalt strip again, he saw nothing but a heap of ashes, still smoking.

In his report, which he wrote that same evening, he recorded with a trembling hand that even metal objects, including the buttons of Witter's uniform, his belt buckle, pistol and helmet had been reduced to ash.

It was getting dark in the Boss's office, but no one thought of putting on the light. Sam Forbes, Alan Soblen and Smith Beffort were standing in front of the Boss.

"I understand your reasons, Sam, but they don't seem to me to be sufficient to warrant your resignation. I told you yesterday that I've given you a free hand as well as unlimited credit. What more do you want?"

Sam walked nervously to the window. "I need freedom of action," he said, looking back. "Madame Atomos merits the mobilization of every last resource I have. At the FBI, I'll be constrained by your sacrosanct regulations not to employ the illicit means that will be necessary for me to attain my objectives."

The Boss took time out to light a cigar, blinking in the fleeting light that the match gave off. "It's just," he said, finally, "that I fear you'll be very vulnerable, Sam. Besides, you're placing me in a nasty situation. Public opinion wants the hide of this damnable devil-woman as much as you do. At present, the whole world has its eyes on us—and on you, who represent the FBI. The Japanese feel involved to the extent they're sending the famous Yosho Akamatsu of the Tokkoka by plane. He'll be here tonight, and I can tell you that with a man of his stripe on the case, Mother What's-her-name is going to get her ass spanked!"

Red with fury, the Boss shot out of his armchair like a rocket and strode back and forth so energetically that the floor shook. Anger had restored the Brooklyn vocabulary of his youth, and he used it immoderately and without hindrance. "If the Jap grabs the prize before us, all the rags in the States will be on our case. I need you more than ever, and this is the moment you pick to set sail!" He spat out his cigar, ground it underfoot, and went back to slump heavily into his pivoting armchair. "Well," he said, in a tone that was suddenly soft, "I refuse your resignation, Sam Forbes. You're going to go on working for us under cover, which will allow you to strike all the low blows you need to use. Draw on FBI funds, call on my men—but rip the bandages off Mother Atomos. No need for reports—do whatever you want. Who do you want for immediate collaborators?"

Forbes thought for a moment, with his head lowered, than raised his eyes again, with his jaw set. "Smith Beffort," he said, "and Dr. Soblen. I know they'll agree."

The two men confirmed that with a gesture.

"OK, Sam," said the Boss. "Anyone else?"

Sam Forbes smiled joylessly. "Ask this Yosho Akamatsu if he wouldn't like a partner. In view of the importance of the game, that would be better than our dogging his heels."

Chapter VII

Subconsciously, they had imagined that he would be short, thin and more or less ugly, but Yosho Akamatsu was five nine, a hundred and sixty pounds, square in the shoulders and thin in the hips. He was dark-haired, and his elongated face with prominent cheek-bones had an undeniable virile charm.

The Boss made the introductions briskly, and rapidly passed on to the nub of the matter. "Sam, as you hoped, Mr. Akamatsu is in favor of a tight collaboration. Besides, before leaving Tokyo he had the same idea and hasn't arrived empty-handed. Armed with cuttings from the America press, he's ferreted through his files and discovered the true identity of the person who calls herself Madame Atomos. If you would, Mr. Akamatsu?"

The Tokkoka's special agent spoke the language of Uncle Sam with hardly any accent, and his rapid speech never stumbled over a current expression. Yosho spoke as a stream runs, with brief changes of intonation and a mobility of gesture surprising in a man of his race. Forbes sensed that he was possessed of a high-powered dynamism, a morality as straight as an arrow and a boundless enthusiasm. The man was captivating.

"First, one slight correction," Yosho Akamatsu began. "I'm not absolutely certain that Madame Atomos is really the woman in question, but let's say that I'd lay odds of ten to one. Two years ago, the Sasebo police were informed by a peasant named Masashi Shimuara that strange things were happening in the vicinity of her fields. Shimuara grows tea on the side of a hill. His house is at the bottom of the slope, and of the far side, beyond the tea-trees, there were three enormous rocks...." He paused to offer round his packet of Shinsei. "They're quite ordinary," he said, apologetically, "but I never smoke anything else...."

Sam gave him a light, and the Tokkoka agent continued: "Shimuara had tried to get rid of the three rocks cutting off his plantation himself, and then to get someone else to shift them, but their weight defied all efforts. They could have been blown up, but our peasant feared that the blast might ruin his trees, so he left them where they were. As you know, a tea-tree is a little round bush no more than three feet high, so Shimuara had a clear view of the rocks.

"One morning, the man observed that they had disappeared. He ran to the end of his field, and found nothing but an enormous heap of ash where the granite blocks had been. He thanked heaven for having accomplished this miracle, worked all day, and went to bed. The next day, two hundred tea-trees had been volatilized! Shimuara did not thank heaven for that, but went to inform the Sasebo police. They undertook an investigation, and quickly discovered an abandoned concrete building at the top of the mountain.

370

"The building had been recently constructed, and offered certain peculiarities that left the police perplexed. They informed Tokyo, and I was there that same evening. I figured out immediately that the building was a laboratory, and spotted the tracks left by a heavy truck—doubtless when the contents were removed—on the only trail leading down to the valley. Around the laboratory, within a radius of a hundred yards, there was not a single tree or pebble—nothing but earth covered with ash."

Smith Beffort scowled. "I know that tune," he said. "Out near Dunellen I was nearly burned like a matchstick! Go on, continue—I'm sure that you're on the right track."

Yosho stubbed out his cigarette-end and crossed his legs. "From the agency that sold the land, I learned that the purchaser was a woman named Kanoto Yoshimuta, and that she lived in Nagasaki. In that city, I was told that the woman had left her apartment ten year before, having resigned from the university, where she was a professor. The trail stopped there, but I found out nevertheless that Kanoto Yoshimuta was fifty years old that she had specialized in atomic research, that she had lost her family in the explosion of the second atom bomb, and that her hatred for Americans was limitless. I remind you that this took place two years ago.

"At that time, I had nothing much for which to reproach the woman, and I abandoned the case, forgetting it completely. Time passed—a year exactly—and the mystery of the *Mororan* burst forth. The *Mororan* was an old cargo ship only good for scrapping when it ran aground on a reef in the Bungo Strait. As it was sailing without a cargo at the moment of the wreck, and had little value, it was left where it was for the time being. The inhabitants of a nearby village, living entirely on the produce of their fishing, went to steal all its ropes, strip out all the woodwork and, in brief, to finish the job of making the old tub into a veritable wreck.

"One fine morning in June, however, the *Mororan* and the reef that had caused its ruin disappeared. The boat couldn't have floated away, since it lacked a bottom, and couldn't have been dragged out to sea since there hadn't been a storm. As for the reef, that was even more inexplicable! I received the information by radio, suddenly remembered the Sasebo affair, and telephoned to have all the roads giving access to the place blocked.

"We discovered a new concrete laboratory on the hill overlooking the village, and the inhabitants recognized a photograph of Kanoto Yoshimuta, but it was impossible to find any trace of her."

"Damn it!" interjected Beffort. "It seems to me, though, that you'd moved quickly enough!"

Yosho smiled amiably. "I had had the roads watched, Mr. Beffort, but not the sea! And I mention, in passing, that no point in Japan is more than six hundred miles from the coast...."

371

"What's your opinion regarding the disappearance of the Sasebo rocks and the *Mororan*?" Sam asked.

"One of my friends, Professor Omiya, thought that an extremely powerful thermal lance had been used."

"I think so too," said Dr. Soblen.

The Boss brandished his cigar. "So far as I'm concerned," he said, "there's no doubt about it: Kanoto Yoshimuta and Madame Atomos are one and the same. But how much further does that certainty get us?"

Yosho threw a file on to the desk. "This far," he murmured. "The fingerprints and photograph of Madame Atomos! The photo comes from the University of Nagasaki and is twelve years old, but fingerprints don't change, do they?"

Sam Forbes clapped the Japanese policeman on the shoulder, amicably. "Yosho," he said, "I think we're going to make a damn good team!"

"*Hai*," said the Tokkoka man. "I think so too."

Yosho Akamatsu expressed a desire to see the barn, so Sam and Beffort accompanied him, while Dr. Soblen followed them in his own car. The four men made a preliminary stop to examine the charred trees and bushes, and Yosho declared that the remains were similar in every respect to those he had seen in Japan.

In the concrete tower the Japanese policeman noticed hooks set next to the window and said: "This place has obviously never been used as a laboratory. Let's say, rather, that Madame Atomos made use of this tower to aim her electromagnetic ray at New York.

"Always inside concrete buildings," said Sam. "It's obvious that concrete plays a considerable role in the realization of our enemy's criminal projects. That might be a necessity for her, Soblen?"

The scientist pulled a face. "The material is efficacious against atomic radiations," he said, "but the thickness here doesn't seem to me to be adequate."

"It doesn't matter how it protects the operators—the important thing, so far as we're concerned, is that it's necessary. In that case, we have a radical means of preventing Madame Atomos from doing any harm."

"Yes," Yosho approved. "It's sufficient to identify all the concrete buildings in the region that aren't absolutely necessary."

"That's right."

Beffort clapped his hands. "Good idea! But we have to put it into application immediately."

They went back to the cars, and Sam's radio message triggered the biggest police operation in the history of the USA. The newspapers published special editions in the form of a tract, television and radio stations joined the dance, and within an hour of Sam's first call, all the concrete buildings in the region had been visited by the police or the civil authorities.

By midday, an impressive pile of reports had accumulated in the Boss's office, and the latter was wearing a smile that spoke volumes about his jubilation. "Fifty-three towers identical to the one in Dunellen have been identified in the vicinity of New York, Washington, Baltimore, Philadelphia and Boston. It's evident that Madame Atomos intends to attack those five cities first, and that the Chinook affair was merely a final trial, or a diversionary maneuver." Suddenly adopting a severe tone, he added: "Twenty towers surround Washington, and it's been noted that their principal windows are facing the White House. No need to draw you a picture, is there?" He opened a drawer and took out a sheet of paper. "These buildings," he said, "have been put up recently, always adjacent to farms, barns or houses rented by a certain Lydia Watanabe. The woman in question is a pretty young brunette—thirty at most, according to the witnesses She speaks our language perfectly, but he owner who've had dealings with her in declaring that, even if she isn't Chinese or Japanese, she's probably of Asiatic origin."

"A Eurasian," suggested Yosho Akamatsu

Smith Beffort started. "I know her!" he exclaimed. "She was in the Buick with Hisato Keichu!"

The Boss brandished another sheet of paper. "This report is from a motorcycle policeman. He was partnered with Alex Witter and he also mentions a pretty brunette woman. She's obviously the same one you saw, Beffort, since she was still in the Buick. This Lydia Watanabe is, I'm convinced, one of Madame Atomos's closest collaborators. In twelve hours, I'll have a picture of her circulated. Until then, I don't suppose there's much we can do, eh?"

They agreed, save for Dr. Soblen, who was sitting on his own in a corner of the office. He was reading the *New York Herald*, seemingly utterly indifferent to the progress of the conversation. The Boss, who liked to be the center of attention, spoke to him directly: "What do you think, Doctor?"

Soblen jumped and blinked. "Excuse me," he said, "but I didn't hear what you said." He looked at Sam Forbes, and said, softly. "I don't want to give you any false hope, Sam, but I'll cut off my head if Maggie Fairbanks is dead!"

Sam went pale. "What are you saying, Doc?"

"Events are unfolding too quickly for us to be able to examine everything in detail," Soblen went on, "but reading this article has made me think again, about Chinook and Dubinsky's, and the way that John Ferby and Mabel Wrist were abandoned after having done their work. In both cases, witnesses heard the famous buzzing sound, didn't they?"

"Yes," said Sam, colorlessly.

"When we saw her through the mist, Maggie Fairbanks was less than ten feet away from us. Did you hear the buzzing, Sam?"

"No, but that doesn't mean anything. Harry Diamond, the road-sweeper in Chinook, didn't hear it either."

"Because John Ferby was not yet in action—but Maggie was, since we've established that she came to our car *after* stealing the hundred thousand dollars."

Sam shook his head. "I don't believe it," he sighed.

The little man became suddenly animated. "You don't want to believe it, but it's logical to presume that Madame Atomos has kept your fiancée alive, in order to have a means of putting pressure on you at her disposal. Besides, Maggie wasn't remotely controlled by the customary car."

"How do you know?"

"The streets were impassable, remember, Sam? This newspaper has an interview with a policeman who saw the whole thing and even shot at the car. He affirms that the Mercury picked up Maggie Fairbanks outside the oily zone, and that the young woman was literally thrown into the back seat. Previously, that back seat has been occupied by the mysterious remote control apparatus...."

Uncertainly, Sam passed a trembling hand over his face. "In that case," he said, full of emotion, "how is it that Maggie obeyed Madame Atomos so passively?"

"Hypnotism," said Soblen.

At that moment, the telephone rang, and the Boss answered it. "Hello!" he said. "Yes, it's me...."

The receiver crackled for some time; then the Boss sat down slowly, and made a few notes on his blotter. "Can you repeat the time?" he asked. There was another brief crackle of sound, and then the Boss hung up and put his hands in his pockets. "Madame Atomos has just warned our central office that she intends to attack the Finnegan Bank at three thirty," he said. "She's told us not to intervene. If we make a move, she threatens to destroy the building containing the bank completely. He consulted his watch, and continued: "It's two o'clock. We've got about an hour to find a mean of preventing another hold-up. It's not much."

Sam Forbes got to his feet.

"Preventing the hold-up is nothing," he said. "For that, it's sufficient to evacuate the building and put the money in a safe place—but that's not what we're aiming for. This is what I propose: warn the directors to have the door watched, and empty the place as soon as Madame Atomos's minion appears. That way, we'll avoid a repetition of the dramas in Chinook and Dubinsky's jewelry store, and can concentrate on watching out for and following the car transporting the remote control apparatus."

Yosho Akamatsu raised his eyebrows. "Your plan is reasonable and logical, provided that Madame Atomos follows her usual procedure—but suppose she modifies her technique?"

"In that case," Sam replied, "We'll modify ours."

None of them really expected to be able to counter the action of the diabolical Madame Atomos, especially with a frontal attack, but they all thought that if an adversary telephones to advertise her next strike, she runs a considerable risk of falling prey to a poisoned arrow as she flees....

Chapter VIII

The Finnegan Bank occupied the entire ground floor of a projecting block, opening by virtue of that fact on to three very busy streets, with five doors piercing each of the three façades. At three fifteen p.m. the sidewalks were swarming and the roadway invisible beneath lines of vehicles. The intersection was a huge bottleneck, and every time a red light came on, a crowd of pedestrians invaded the void left by the cars, rushed into the large stores and created an indescribable confusion.

Shouting vendors were waving newspapers relating the discovery of the concrete towers, but the crowd remained indifferent. Madame Atomos remained a being native to an abstract realm, whose criminal acts belonged to the domain of anticipation, and the man in the street did not really believe in her. To be sure, there had been Chinook, Dubinsky and the mysterious paralysis in the Bronx, but humankind needs to see in order to believe, and only admits that reality surpasses fiction on rare occasions.

Lost among that swarming mass, Sam Forbes, Soblen, Beffort and Yosho Akamatsu anticipated that a fantastic catastrophe might leave hundreds dead in a matter of seconds.

Madame Atomos had chosen her terrain with a remarkable subtlety. That gigantic crossroads of New Yorker activity was practically indefensible; on the contrary, it presented an ill-omened vulnerability. The directors of the Finnegan Bank had refused to interrupt its activities, and the establishment's fifteen doors were allowing waves of clients in and out. If such conditions made the task of Forbes and his companions seem impossible, the density of the crowd at least established one certainty: no car, whether it were piloted by the Devil himself, could either approach or draw away faster than a man on foot.

At three twenty-eight Sam Forbes was lying in wait on the other side of the intersection opposite the main entrance of the bank. Dr. Soblen was fifty yards away, while Beffort and Akamatsu were watching the two roads along the sides of the building. Four cars equipped with radio transmitters and receivers were stationed in the adjacent streets, and it had been agreed that whoever spotted the car transporting the remote-control apparatus would follow it, then immediately establish contact with the FBI switchboard. The latter was responsible for centralizing information and disseminating it to the other three vehicles.

At three thirty exactly, as she had promised, Madame Atomos attacked. It went unnoticed by the mass, but Sam, Soblen, Beffort and Akamatsu understood immediately that hostilities had been opened, and were attentive.

Three cars came to an abrupt halt while crossing the intersection, with the result that the circulation of traffic, already slow, was decisively interrupted. A jam resulted, while people tried in vain to push the vehicles that had broken down toward the sidewalk; their tires seemed to be stuck at the ground. At first, discussion was drowned out by an infernal cacophony of horns; then, all of a sudden, the engines stopped turning and the klaxons stopped howling.

In a strange silence, some drivers dived under their hoods, while others contented themselves with stubbornly turning their mute ignition-keys. Meanwhile, on the sidewalks, sniggering groups of people accumulated—with the effect that the nascent disorder got even worse.

Suddenly, with no apparent reason, the traffic lights stopped working. Simultaneously, the lights in all the stores, the bank and the advertising displays went out. The people inside the buildings were plunged into a disagreeable gloom, and flooded toward the exits.

The intersection and the neighboring streets were quickly overflowing, and the human tide was further augmented when the people who had been on the subway platforms surged back into the open air. The subways and their moving staircases had stopped; telephones were no longer working; television and radio sets, and hairdressers' driers and helmets had also broken down. An enormous quantity of people found themselves brutally deprived of all activity, and clusters of gawkers accumulated at the windows.

With a dull tramping sound, the crowd started milling around like a furious herd of cattle, with violent reactions whenever two waves headed in directly opposite directions encountered one another. Everybody wanted to get out of the whirlpool, but as no one would let anyone pass, they all remained in place, struggling, jostling and bumping into one another violently—and very soon came to blows.

A riot broke out in the middle of the intersection. Women and children were trampled underfoot, and cars turned over. A gas tank emptied out its contents and the dangerous liquid spread out over the roadway. There was a spark, and the gasoline caught fire, drawing the flames toward other tanks, which exploded in their turn with sprays of flaming gas that fell upon the panicked crowd.

A woman transformed into a living torch ran into a shop and communicated the fire to a display-unit loaded with net curtains. Within ten seconds, the entire unit was in flames, while the shop assistants, prisoners of their enclosures, disappeared in the conflagration.

Outside, it was frightful. The intersection was literally ablaze. All the cars were being grilled on the spot, and the ground was nothing but a sheet of flame. The streets by means of which the crowd might have been able to flee were blocked by curiosity-seekers arriving from neighboring districts, and vehicles were mounting the sidewalks, trying to turn around in order to escape the disaster, crushing those who could not help getting in their way. Black stinking smoke enveloped everything, and a horrible odor of charred flesh spread through the hot air.

Sam Forbes struck out hard at someone who grabbed hold of him, and ran to the sidewalk of the bank; his clothes were in tatters and a steel shard had traced a bloody gash on his cheek. He was bundled away by a howling group and slammed against a display-window, which gave way under his weight. At the same moment, a gas tank exploded, hurling its petrol on to the sidewalk he had just been obliged to quit, and the howling group disappeared within the crackling flames.

Sam leapt inside the store, fought his way through to the back of the shop and emerged into a courtyard stuffed with cadavers. The federal agent suppressed a surge of horror and forced himself to take a closer look at the corpses, which no flame had touched.

"Get out!" howled a voice. "Get out!"

Sam raised his eyes and saw a head leaning out toward him from a fourth-floor window. "What happened?" he shouted.

The man leaned forward, his finger pointing at an archway piercing the building on the far side of the courtyard. "These people had taken refuge here," he shouted. "Then a woman carrying a suitcase came out of the service entrance...."

Sam glanced to his left and saw a little door bearing a metal plate, bearing the legend FINNEGAN BANK SERVICE ENTRANCE in black letters.

"She went across the yard," the man continued, "and the people dropped like flies as she passed. Get out! Get out! She went out that way, but she might come back...."

Forbes ran in the direction of the archway and went through it, emerging into a passageway blocked by two bodies. He leapt over them, continued straight on, and abruptly emerged into one of the streets running alongside the bank. It was the one that Yosho Akamatsu had been watching, but Sam could not see him. In any case, crazed groups were running toward the far end of the street, and Sam was hustled in that direction.

An intact corpse lying on the sidewalk showed him which way to go; he knew that the woman had crossed over when he saw the corpses lying in the roadway. In the midst of the almighty confusion Sam accelerated his pace and reached the main road. He leapt on to the roof of a car while the crowd flowed around him, and finally spotted the person he was chasing. She was walking rapidly but unhurriedly, with the mechanical gait that was peculiar to Madam Atomos's dead people; a large cardboard-pulp suitcase was dangling from the end of her rigid arm.

Sam examined the street. It was extremely crowded, and it was obvious that the remote control vehicle must be parked further away, in the avenue where the sirens of fire-trucks were blaring. The woman would take at least seven minutes to reach the avenue. That left an appreciable margin.

Sam leapt down from the roof, ran off at top speed and reached the side-street where his car was parked. As he went, he observed that Madame Atomos's electromagnetic ray had only paralyzed the intersection, and was not surprised when his engine turned over immediately.

He pulled out brutally, tearing the wing from a vehicle traveling in the opposite direction, and roared away. Twenty yards further on he was brought to a halt by the terrified crowd, and thought that his car was going o be overturned by the frantic assault, but then found himself suddenly in the clear. He floored the accelerator and the Chevrolet bounded forwards, narrowly avoiding a second human wave.

Sam turned into the avenue, rolled as far as the next intersection, and perceived Madam Atomos's dead woman moving placidly along the sidewalk at her automaton pace. A woman who had just brushed past her collapsed, thunderstruck, but no one paid any attention to her. At that moment, her life no longer counted for much, especially when there were others to think about.

Madame Atomos's instrument crossed a broad avenue, stepped up on to the sidewalk, and came to a halt. Almost immediately, a blue Chrysler stopped beside her, and the front passenger door opened. The driver grabbed the suitcase that the woman held out to him, closed the door again, and moved off.

The woman collapsed gently, rolled into the gutter and did not move again.

Sam Forbes executed a swift half-turn, spotted the Chrysler heading in the direction of Manhattan, caught up with it in less than a mile and maintained himself at a respectful distance. With his index finger he activated his radio, waited for the tone and unhooked the mike. "Tom One calling Central," he said.

The switchboard-operator was on the alert, for the response came back immediately: "Central here!"

"I'm on the track. It's a blue Chrysler and we're heading for Manhattan, presently on the point of going over the East River at Williamsburg. Over and out."

He replaced the mike, vaguely hearing the speaker repeat his position; and then, after a pause, the return call came in. Akamatsu and Beffort were already following, but there was no news of Dr. Soblen.

Level with Central Park, Sam gave his position again, and did likewise after having crossed the Hudson heading for Leonia. Via the intermediary of the switchboard, Smith Beffort let him know that he was getting closer rapidly, but Yosho Akamatsu declared that he had taken a wrong turn, and that they could not count on him in the immediate future.

Sam groaned. The Japanese man should have been able to follow the Chrysler with ease, but being alone, and not being sufficiently familiar with the city, he had become as ineffective as a new-born puppy.

Ahead of him, the Chrysler was heading west at top speed, and Sam sometimes had difficulty not losing sight of it. Once he got too close and had seen the driver's eyes looking at him through his rear-view mirror. Now he was keeping his distance, but that complicated matters.

The Chrysler took Route 56, turned on to 39 and finally turned on to 4. Sam picked up his mike. "We're on 4," he said. "Still heading west."

The speaker repeated the information, paused, then gave the position to Tom Two and Tom Three—Beffort and Akamatsu respectively. Smith Beffort was getting closer, with his foot down, having just past Leonia and joining 4 at 93. Akamatsu was a long way behind, but following nevertheless.

Dr. Soblen abruptly materialized. He had been caught up in the crowds and had only just reached Manhattan. He said that the large store had been half-destroyed, that there were hundreds dead and that it would take at least two days to clear the intersection of the burned-out cars that were blocking it.

The operator that had transmitted Soblen's message said no more, and there was silence in the car. Sam groped for a packet of cigarettes, took one out and lit it with a nervous hand, then returned his attention to the Chrysler, which had suddenly begun to slow down. Sam did likewise, leaving three cars between himself and his prey. The Chrysler suddenly swerved, passing through a side-tunnel, and Sam saw it take a dirt road that seemed to be heading toward Paramus. He turned too, went through the tunnel and grabbed his mike as he emerged in the vicinity of the dirt road.

"Tom One calling Central...."

The radio remained mute. Sam repeated himself without result. He went some way along the road before making another call, but the only response was a vague hiss. He gave his approximate position anyway, just in case, and replaced the mike because the road as gradually transforming into a sleigh-run and he required all his skill to negotiate it.

He accelerated, saw the Chrysler stopped at the bottom of the hill, and continued straight ahead, along a track that was scarcely visible but had the advantage of taking him down to a lower level, hiding him from the gaze of the Chrysler's driver.

Swiftly, the federal agent quit the Chevrolet, went back up the track at a run, and lay down behind the embankment.

A Lincoln station-wagon had just stopped in front of the Chrysler, and two men were transferring a square metal apparatus that appeared to be very heavy. The apparatus having been placed in the back seat of the station-wagon, the driver of the Chrysler took hold of the cardboard-pulp suitcase containing the money from the Finnegan Bank and climbed in beside is companion. Then the station-wagon moved off, passed in front of Sam and drew away toward 4.

Sam went back to his car, made a three-point turn, and launched the Chevrolet on the track of the Lincoln. Immediately, he tried his radio again, but he did not have time to find out whether it was still working.

Immediately after the first turn, the station-wagon had stopped, blocking the path, and one of the two men was standing in front of the car, aiming a bizarre weapon at Sam. Its slender barrel bore some resemblance to a short fiberglass fishing-rod. In a flash, the federal agent remembered the motor-cycle cop's report, thrust his door open and hurled himself into the ditch with a desperate leap.

At the same moment there was a brief crepitation, and Sam Forbes saw his Chevrolet burst into flames, melt and disintegrate. The gas tank suddenly exploded, producing a cloud of acrid black smoke, which spread spontaneously over the road, and probably saved the G-man's life.

In spite of the curtain of smoke, Sam emptied his thirty-eight in the direction of the station-wagon, firing blindly. So great was his rage that he continued pressing the trigger long after the last bullet had gone.

The roar of an engine restored the integrity of his self-composure, and he did not have time for self-criticism. For want of prudence he had nearly lost his life, but all was not yet lost.

He ran back along the road to the abandoned Chrysler, turned it around and followed the road, his jaws clenched in violent irritation, mingled with the intense fright he had experienced—but it gave way to an absolute emptiness when he passed what had once been a car. Nothing remained of it now but a miserable heap of ash, which gusts of wind were already dispersing.

Chapter IX

The Lincoln station-wagon was no longer visible when Sam reached the junction, and four routes offered themselves to his choice. The first two were formed by Route 61, and Sam eliminated them straight away. There remained the two branches of 4. One of them headed toward New York, the other continued westwards. Sam opted for the section of 4 that continued toward Paterson.

He put his foot down, passed under 62 and over the Saddle River, and continued flat out, without taking any notice of speed-limits. He was playing his last card, not unaware that if he lost track of Madame Atomos's fanatics, more crimes would be committed in the hours to come, and that the disasters would only increase in magnitude.

Sam thought momentarily about Maggie Fairbanks, but set it resolutely aside. Action alone could settle this, and any mental softness, however fleeting, could only have a deleterious effect. There are times when a man has to be able to forget the impulses of the heart, and Sam was firmly convinced that this was one of them.

He overtook twenty vehicles, went through Paterson, and continued along 504. He went past the golf courses at top speed, reached Pompton and uttered a howl of joy. Less than three hundred yards away, he had just recognized the square rear end of the Lincoln station-wagon. With immense prudence, he resumed his pursuit.

The dashboard clock indicated four-fifty, and dusk was slowly falling. In fifteen minutes the light would be inadequate and he would have to switch on the headlights.

With moist hands, Sam slid a new clip into his thirty-eight, checked the gas, and wiped away the blood that was running down his cheek with his sleeve. He did not know when the wound had opened up again, but observed in the mirror that the collar of his shirt was stained with dry blood. A downward glance reminded him that his clothes were in a lamentable state, and he reflected that the preceding hours had been singularly fortunate. He had escaped death, had just found the Lincoln again, and no cop had tried to arrest him. That was luck with a capital L!

Up ahead, the station-wagon's headlights had just come on. It left Pompton, and turned on to 202, heading for Oakland and Darlington.

Further on, the station-wagon turned on to a narrow by-road, and disappeared behind an exceedingly high wall that seemed to have no end.

With all his lights off, Sam followed cautiously, keeping watch for the Lincoln's lights. The other car slowed down and veered left, hidden once again behind the wall. Sam cut off the engine, letting the Chrysler's momentum carry it forward, and reached the angle of the wall. His eyes widened in amazement at the bare ground that he saw before him, extending all the way to the distant summit of the hill.

There was no visible breach in the wall. The razed ground was perfectly flat, but the station-wagon was no longer visible.

Sam thought about a trap, started his engine again and continued on his way, ducking down instinctively. He saw a somber mass, cut off the engine and parked the Chrysler off the road, beside a ragged hedge surrounding a low building that seemed abandoned, and went back to the road on foot.

In spite of the gloom, he could make out the long pale strip formed by the wall, and thought that if the station-wagon had stopped on the flat ground it would be darkly outlined against the wall or the horizon. There was something mysterious and incomprehensible here, and the federal agent was momentarily disconcerted. Then, as his head was set very firmly on his shoulders, he concluded that if the station-wagon had not taken off into the air, it could only be under the ground.

Slowly Sam moved over the ground, advancing step by step in the direction o the corner formed by the wall and the road, and spotted, as he had hoped, the double furrows left by the station-wagon's tires in the soft ground. He followed the tracks for about fifty yards, and then suddenly lost them on open ground, and stood there dazedly, his legs weak, incapable of taking another step and very ill at ease.

He felt a strange torpor overwhelm him, suddenly lost consciousness, and dropped like a stone.

The room was rectangular and had no windows. The concrete walls gave off a dull bluish light, and a steel door occupied one entire side of the rectangle.

The ceiling was pierced by an air-vent about three feet in diameter, terminated by a metal grille.

Sam Forbes saw that he was lying on a mat set on the ground, and that he was entirely naked. He looked for his clothes, but quickly understood, on seeing the ground and the bare walls, that the mat was the only object that had been left within his reach.

Sam did not feel anything in particular. He could not explain the origin of his unconsciousness, any more than he could estimate its duration, and no longer knew where he was.

He stood up without difficulty, stuck his ear to the door and perceived a distant hum; save for that, the silence was complete.

At a loose end, and vaguely anxious, the federal agent made a tour of his cell. Five paces by six, the ceiling within reach of an extended hand, a temperature probably somewhere between twenty and twenty-five degrees Centigrade, solid walls without any hollow resonance suggestive of an exit....

A perfect trap, from which a human being could not escape.

The grille at the mouth of the ventilation-shaft was tempting, but Sam was immediately discouraged by its rigidity. The blast of a mine would not have been sufficient to tear it away.

He sat down on the mat and examined it. It was made of braided jute, and could not serve any other purpose than the one for which it was designed.

Suddenly, the light went out and Sam was plunged into darkness. A few moments went by, and the G-man began to breathe lightly, under the impression that the air was getting heavier. He got up, felt the ceiling with his fingertips, found the grille and realized brutally that the air-supply had been cut off.

"Listen to me, Mr. Forbes," said a female vice, suddenly, "for this is the first and last time that you will have the opportunity. I am Madame Atomos. You are twenty meters underground and have absolutely no chance of escaping. You are an American, and I hate you. You will die of asphyxiation, in the same manner as your fiancée, Maggie Fairbanks, and I shall then make use of you. Goodbye, Mr. Forbes, and *bon voyage....*"

There was a faint crackle, and silence fell again. Sam started searching feverishly for the loudspeaker. He knew that the sentence could not be appealed, and only wondered how much time he might have before the lack of air did its work.

He forced himself to remain calm, but I hands were trembling as they wandered over the walls. Maggie's death was no longer in doubt now, and all Dr. Soblen's deductions had been swept away.

Slowly, Sam made a tour of his narrow cell, but the continuity of the walls was flawless. His fingers soon made contact with the grille again, and he understood that he would never discover the loudspeaker. Breathlessly, he pulled at the grille with all his might, but it did not budge. It must have been embedded in the concrete.

Sam let himself fall to the ground, exhausted. He was having difficulty breathing now, and guessed that he only had a few minutes left. He got to his feet again, painfully, and resumed the search for the loudspeaker. He hoped to be able to detach its wires and perhaps contrive a short circuit on the grille. If the current were sufficiently powerful, the metal bars might melt like sticks of wax...or break, or not budge at all.

It was problematic, but it was the only solution.

He located the loudspeaker when he had almost given up hope of doing so, in the corner of the cell to the right of the steel door. Despairingly, he felt the smooth orifice pitted with imperceptible holes. He broke his fingernails on the unassailable surface, his hands rapidly becoming bloody. Abruptly lacking oxygen, he felt his legs give way beneath him. He collapsed, coming to a rest with his back to the wall, his hands clutching at his throat, trying furiously to fill his lungs, while multicolored lights danced before his eyes, performing a frenzied saraband.

At one point, he emerged from the fantastic vortex that was dragging him down, experienced the sensation that his body was being crushed beneath tons of stone, and fell unconscious again.

His agony continued for a long time, and was extremely painful, interrupted by fugitive moments of lucidity, in the course of which he understood that he was living his final seconds, Then there was the great dive, the last sigh.

Sam Forbes died at seven twenty p.m., while Madame Atomos was in her office, carefully examining a map of Washington and pointing a neatly-filed fingernail at the White House...

The switchboard was bathed in thick smoke, and the Boss was turning round and round like a squirrel in a cage.

Sitting down wearily, Beffort, Soblen and Akamatsu were smoking cigarette after cigarette. Dr. Soblen, who was not used to it, coughed periodically, and every time, the Boss shot him a murderous glance.

The operator was at the apparatus, having just come to the end of a five-minute break.

"Get on with it!" barked the Boss.

The operator pressed his switch. "Central calling Tom One.... Central calling Tom One...." He persisted a while longer, but had addressed a negative shake of the head to the Boss.

"It's incredible!" said the Boss. "Forbes isn't a man to have us without news for such a long time. He was on 4 when he sent his last message..."

"I was about five miles behind him," Beffort said. He leaned over, stubbed out his cigarette-butt in an ash-tray that was full to the brim, and added: "I went as far as Paterson; then, as nothing came through from the switchboard, I slowly retraced my steps. My radio was working perfectly and the transmission was clear. Forbes must have got into trouble."

This was what everyone thought, but they were carefully avoiding expressing the thought.

Time passed, punctuated every five minutes by a call from the operator, but the latter's speakers remained ominously silent.

About eight o'clock, a G-Man telephoned asking for Smith Beffort, and the latter, alerted by an orderly, went back to his office. "Beffort," I said. "I'm listening."

"Davis here. I think I've got something for you. I was there when Sam Forbes started chasing the blue Chrysler...."

"Good God!" Beffort swore. "I thought the matter was top secret!"

The other laughed. "Not in the service, pal! Are you listening to me or bawling me out?"

"Go on," Beffort groaned, "but look lively."

"I know, I know! You're at the switchboard with the Boss waiting for a call from Forbes' aren't you?"

Beffort sighed. Nothing in this damned place passed unnoticed.

"Don't moan." Davis went on, "for if I hadn't been on the ball, I'd have missed the whisper with the city police chief."

"All right! Down, boy!"

"A bloke just came into see him. He'd tried to park his car in his usual spot, but it was already occupied. As the place was deserted he got his dander up and headed for the nearest police station. A beat cop went back with him to cast an eye over the car. It's a blue Chrysler, this year's model. It had been stolen this morning, but because there was blood on the seat the cop left it where it was...."

"Where is this car, Davis?" Beffort interjected, dryly. When he had that information Beffort hung up without even saying thank you and ran back to the switchboard. He brought the Boss up to date and the latter jumped.

"This might be it!" he said, delightedly. "It's the road that Sam was following. Get out there right away, Beffort. I'll give orders for no one to touch the Chrysler!"

Beffort opened the door violently, but felt a hand on his arm.

"Gently," said Yosho Akamatsu. "I'll go with you."

The Boss had acted quickly, for there were no cops prowling around when Beffort and Akamatsu reached the place.

Smith Beffort parked his service Chevrolet on the far side of the two cars that were standing on the open ground, and went to knock on the door of the small house, through which light was filtering. A tall man with a mistrustful expression opened it, and Beffort stuck his badge under his nose unhesitatingly. The other relaxed immediately and let the two men into an ill-furnished room.

"I haven't got much," he said, as if to excuse himself, "but I only come here occasionally, after work. I live in Darlington, and I'm repairing this cottage bit by bit...."

"You don't have any neighbors?"

"No, and that why I smelled a rat when I saw the Chrysler on my land. I also wondered how the guy had left again. There isn't a train station or bus-stop for miles, and the road only has the tracks of the Chrysler and my old crock."

"What's that high wall along the road?"

"Shhh! It's the Senator's estate. He only comes out in summer, and the nest is empty for the rest of the time."

Beffort asked him a few more questions; then, convinced that he knew no more, he went out with Akamatsu and went to examine the Chrysler. Traces of blood were visible on the back of the driver's seat, only noticeable because the leather was very pale. They did not give rise to any definite conclusion.

Doubt was filtering into the minds of the two men when Yosho found an empty ammunition-clip for a thirty-eight wedged between the seat and the back. They searched the vehicle more carefully, and Smith Beffort discovered a jacket-button. It was nothing special, resembling thousands of other buttons, but Beffort had a feeling that he had seen it before somewhere. It was only an impression, but Beffort added the button to the ammunition-clip and sniffed something suspicious.

"I wouldn't be surprised," he groaned, "if Sam had driven this vehicle. We'll need to lift the fingerprints from that steering wheel, and not go too far from this place...one never knows." Beffort always followed his nose.

Chapter X

It was nine thirty, and a legion of large clouds were hiding the moon behind their moving mass, so well that Beffort and Akamatsu could not see more than ten paces ahead.

Someone from the Oakland Laboratory had come out very quickly after Beffort's call. He had spent ten minutes inside the Chrysler and had set off again with a set of fresh and clear fingerprints. He would identify them and telephone the Boss; the latter would let Beffort know the result by means of the radio.

In the meantime, the inhabitant of the small house had gone home, and no vehicle or pedestrian had materialized since his disappearance. Beffort and Akamatsu were watching the Chrysler, with all their lights off, not even smoking— in consequence of which the time went by infinitely slowly.

At nine forty-five the radio crackled and the operator's voice came over the speaker: "Central calling Tom Two...."

Beffort seized the mike and reduced the volume slightly. "Tom Two here," he said.

"Sam Forbes' fingerprints were on the steering-wheel, handbrake and door of the Chrysler. There were also those of the car's owner, and a third set that can't be identified."

"Thanks," said Beffort, winking at Akamatsu.

"Don't sign off!" said the operator, swiftly. "Someone wants to talk to you."

There was a pause, and then the Boss's voice rang out: "Beffort?"

"Yes?"

"Don't do anything reckless, old man. I want you to call in every quarter of an hour. Where are you now?"

"The same place," the G-man replied, laconically.

"What for?" growled the Boss.

"I don't know what else to do! Forbes disappeared here, so I'm staying here. The guy who lives in the house claims that the road only carried traces of the Chrysler and his own car. The region is completely deserted, having no train station or bus stops. Where the Devil can Sam have gone?"

The Boss coughed—a whistling cough that sounded like a shell-burst over the radio. "Do what you want," he concluded, "but call me every fifteen minutes, okay? Until then…"

Beffort replaced the mike and turned to the Tokkoka man. "What should we do?"

Akamatsu pointed at the radio. "Our hands are tied," he said. "Calling in at intervals necessitates one of us being constantly present."

"That's what I thought, "Beffort agreed. "Listen—I'd like to take a stroll as far as the wall of the Senator's property. I'm wondering whether that uninhabited house might reveal some curiosity that would have attracted Forbes's attention." He bit his lower lip and added: "It would undoubtedly have taken something extraordinary for Sam to abandon his Chevrolet. The guy we arrested, Hisato Keichu, told us that the car carrying the remote-control apparatus—the Chrysler, in this case—went to an out-of-town rendezvous once its work was done. Forbes was following that car and must have witnessed the transfer if the apparatus into another vehicle. It's incomprehensible…."

He turned up the collar of his overcoat and put on his felt hat. Before quitting the vehicle, he removed the bulb from the ceiling-light that came on automatically when the door was opened.

"I'm going out," he murmured. "Just a little stroll. If I'm not back in thirty minutes, it's because I've run into trouble. Do you know how to use the radio?"

"Yes," Akamatsu reassured him. "Go on—I'll call the switchboard, as arranged."

Smith Beffort got out, closed the door softly, and moved away. He walked on the left-hand side of the road, placing his feet circumspectly, as silently as a cat. To the right there was an immense field bounded by the crest of a hill, the wall of the Senator's property and the narrow by-road that the G-men was following. To the left there was a barbed-wire fence protecting the land attached to the house.

Beffort had almost reached the wall when he heard the hum. It was a dull sound, like that produced by a dynamo. It was coming from the field, and the suspicious Beffort flattened himself against the wall, by the roadside.

A grating sound split the silence, and the purr of an engine replaced the hum. This time, Beffort was certain that a car was coming through the field, but could not make anything out in the darkness. It was coming forward slowly, with its lights out, but was indubitably heading for the road.

It suddenly emerged from the shadows, and Beffort threw himself to the ground.

In spite of the darkness, the federal agent recognized a Lincoln station-wagon and saw that the seats were occupied by a man and a woman. The latter was driving. As soon as the car was on the road the driver accelerated and the headlights came on. The Lincoln leapt forward and disappeared like a streak of lightning in the direction of 202. It turned toward Oakland.

Smith Beffort got up, ran back to the house and hurled himself into the Chrysler. Yosho Akamatsu was just getting ready to contact Central, and Beffort snatched the mike from him.

"Tom Two calling," he spat. "Tom Two calling."

"Go ahead," the operator replied.

"A Lincoln station-wagon is heading for Oakland right now. It's driven by a woman, with a man sitting beside her. Make the necessary arrangements for the car to be followed discreetly. Discretion above all."

"What is it?" said the voice of the Boss, abruptly.

"Perhaps lovers who were making out in a field," Beffort replied, "but that would amaze me! The Lincoln wasn't there when we arrived, and no vehicle's come along the road since. I have an idea that the Lincoln came from the Senator's property."

"Good," said the Boss. "I assume you're going to take a look at it at close range?"

"And how, Boss—with a diamond-lensed magnifying-glass!"

"Don't forget to call me, Beffort," the Boss warned. "I've blockaded the area. Our guys are piled up in Darlington, Oakland, Wanque and Midvale, waiting to take a hand. A troop of parachutists can land in your field three minutes after I give the order, and I've got six bombers standing by."

Beffort went pale. "Damn it!" he swore. "Go easy!"

The Boss sniggered ferociously. "Oh yes! Do you think the evil mother is going easy?"

"Good God!" Beffort exclaimed. "We're not sure of anything."

"I don't need certainty," the Boss growled in his turn. "Four hundred dead, a department store and two buildings burned! I'm ready to drop an H-bomb on that bitch Atomos's shadow, and if I get a sniff of where she is, I will. Understood?"

"Understood," said Beffort, in a hoarse voice.

"Listen," said the Boss, "And let's understand one another: if you're unable to call me at the agreed time, I'll be patient for another quarter of an hour, but no one will be able to get in or out of a quadrilateral of which your field is the center. If you're still mute after the second delay, lie low if you're not dead. Since Madame Atomos wants to raze the entire USA, I'll do as much myself to make sure that she comes unstuck!"

A click indicated that the Boss had just signed off, and Beffort remained standing there, mike in hand.

"He's coming on strong," Akamatsu commented, "but the game is worth the candle. If nothing stops Madame Atomos, she will indeed reduce your country to dust. Let's take a look at this wall, Beffort."

"Both of us? What about calling in?"

Akamatsu, who was in the driver's seat, started the car. "Let's take the car closer," he said. "If we go softly, we won't attract attention. The quietness of American vehicles has always had my admiration."

He moved quietly away from the open ground and went forward slowly, but, in spite of all his precautions, nothing could prevent the gravel crackling under the tires.

Akamatsu steered through the opening in the barbed-wire fence surrounding the enclosure, straightened the car up when the tires bit the earth of the narrow verge. The Chevrolet eventually reached the wall. The Japanese man maneuvered skillfully, lining up the car less than two inches from the ditch and switched off the engine. "There," he whispered. "Now we'll be spotted if Madame Atomos has her headquarters in the vicinity."

Beffort ground his teeth. "I hadn't thought of that," he admitted, "but it's obvious. A woman like her must have prodigious means of detection at her disposal."

"Let's assume the worst," Akamatsu proposed, "And that Madame Atomos will make use of her famous electromagnetic ray. We know its effects: cars and radios become useless...."

"In that case," it will be impossible for us to contact the Boss, and he'll unleash the offensive." He turned to face the Japanese man and said: "You knew that, didn't you?"

"Yes," Akamatsu replied, mildly, "but it's the only means of cutting things short. Either Madame Atomos isn't in the immediate vicinity, and nothing will happen; or she is, and the bombing will become indispensable."

"You've got some front!" said Beffort, admiringly.

The Japanese man bowed. "*Arogato gozaimas,*" he said, meaning *thank you.* "Are we going?"

"Okay. As you say, let's get moving."

They got out, went into the field and began to move along the wall. After taking a few steps, Beffort came to a halt and leaned toward his companion's ear. "I think it would be better not to put all our eggs in one basket," he said. "I'll go first. Follow me fifty paces behind. If a dog barks and I attract attention, you can intervene. Agreed?"

"Agreed."

"I'll follow the tracks of the Lincoln station-wagon. Logically, they should lead me to the place we're searching for."

The Japanese man stayed by the wall, and Beffort bent down over the ground. He could not see very much, but nevertheless made out the furrows hollowed out by the heavy vehicle. He walked in one of the furrows, so as to be sure that he would not lose it. His progress was slow, and he had the impression that the consistency of the ground had changed. The soil was firmer and, while its surface was still tormented, it was no longer giving way beneath the weight of his body.

Beffort stepped back and felt his feet sinking once again. He crouched down and touched the ground, crumbling soil beneath his fingers and sniffing it. It was good corn-growing soil and its odor was reassuring. He advanced slowly on all fours, and set his hand on the other soil. He tried to pull up a clod, but could not do it and broke a fingernail. He pressed his nose to the bizarre ground but could not detect any odor, and realized at the same moment that this was where the double furrow vanished.

Prudently, he stepped back again, and the sudden freshness of the air startled him. He sat down and loosened his tie, greedily breathing in a few pints of oxygen.

On recovering his lucidity, Beffort understood that he had just been subject to the commencement of an intoxication, without being able to determine exactly when it had begun.

Yosho Akamatsu glided to his side, and swift and silent as a serpent. "What's happening?" he enquired, in a whisper.

"I don't know," said Beffort, in a similar tone. "I nearly fell into a trap without perceiving it. There must be an area in front of us that's not authentic— an odorless soil as solid as cement.

Akamatsu leaned over, put out a hand, and straightened up again. "Or concrete," he said.

"Son of a bitch! You think…?"

"Why not? The Lincoln had to come from somewhere, didn't it?" He rested his finger on the strange material and felt an almost-imperceptible suction. Without saying a word, he rummages in his pocket, and then placed his cigarette-case on the ground.

"What are you doing?" muttered Beffort.

"Wait," said the Japanese man. "It's an experiment."

A few seconds went by, and then a faint hum rose from below ground. The cigarette-case sank very slowly, and the ground re-closed around it. Soon, it was no longer visible, and the terrain was exactly as before.

Amazed, Beffort whistled through his teeth. "Experiment successful!" he belched.

Akamatsu grabbed his arm forcefully. "Come on!" he said.

Beffort followed him at a run without asking for explanations. The Tokko-ka man reached the Chevrolet first, started the engine and set off at top speed as soon as Beffort was inside.

"Call Central," said Akamatsu, "and tell your boss to send the bombers!"

As Beffort hesitated, the Japanese man added: "Hurry up! In a very short time my suitcase will arrive down below, probably in the hands of a receptionist, and the alert will be sounded immediately."

Beffort, who had finally switched the apparatus on and grabbed the mike, and said: "Tom Two calling!"

"I'm listening," the Boss replied.

"Start the bombardment immediately, about fifty yards from the road and the property."

"Stay on the line!" the Boss said, rapidly.

The loudspeaker emitted a confused sound, and then the Boss spoke again: "The bombers are on their way," he said, coldly. "They were waiting at Lincoln Park Airport, and will be with you in a minute or two. Try to find a hole and pull in the battens!"

Lincoln Park Airport was ten miles from the objective, as the crow flies. The Boss had certainly made his preparations!

"We're on 202," said Beffort, inspecting the sky, "heading toward Oakland.

Akamatsu raced along the deserted rod, and the trees whistled like blackbirds.

"Can you see anything?" asked the Boss.

"Not yet...."

He had scarcely finished speaking when there was a blinding explosion far to the rear. Immediately, thunder was unleashed, so violent that the Boss sniggered into the radio. "You're deaf, Beffort," he joked. "I can hear the chestnuts roasting from here!" He was audibly jubilant, and his laughter filled the car.

Ten minutes later, they learned that not a single bomb had reached the ground. The six bombers and their munitions had exploded in mid-air!

Chapter XI

There was a moment of stunned amazement as the news spread. Abruptly, everyone began running around madly, like blind ants, and it required all the Boss's authority to restore calm. The police and army gave him a valuable helping hand by intervening energetically, with the result that eventually, everyone was at his post, content to remain within the limits that people ought not to cross.

Rumor had it that two FBI men were examining the interior of the quadrilateral, trying to figure out exactly what had happened.

In fact, Beffort and Akamatsu had turned back of their own accord as soon as the Boss—who had found out about it before anyone else, God knows how—had told them the news, and were heading at full throttle toward the scene of the drama.

Still far ahead of them, the last of the bombers was going up in flames, amid an immense red glow illuminating the horizon. Closer to them, the Senator's estate, reached by the flaming debris, was burning like a hayrick. The road was pitted with potholes for more than a mile; thanks to brief luminous explosions the two men were able to catch occasional glimpses of the field, which the planes and bombs had miraculously spared.

It was, however, one of Madame Atomos's miracles, and neither Beffort nor Akamatsu was impressed by it. They found themselves in a state of cold anger, which was scarcely conducive to reflection. Meanwhile, the Boss was shouting himself hoarse into his mike.

"Beffort!" he said, for the third time. "I order you to get out of the area!"

"No way! Akamatsu and I are going hotfoot to knock on Madame Atomos's door, and see whether we can poke a finger in her eye!"

"Get out of there as fast as you can! I'm sending in the paratroopers!"

"That's a good idea!" Beffort sneered. "Send them! They'll be transformed into dust before touching the ground, if their plane hasn't been wiped out beforehand. You might as well cut your losses! What do you want, a bloodbath?"

"Shut up, Beffort!" the Boss barked, ferociously. "May I remind you that it was you who called in the bombers! Can you hear me?"

"Oh yes," groaned the federal agent. "No need to twist the knife in the wound, My guilt complex is as big as a house. By the way, what's become of the Lincoln station-wagon?"

"The latest news is that it's left New York, It must be on 4 by now."

"Give the order to stop it."

"What?"

"I'm not giving you orders, Boss—but Akamatsu and me are going to try to pass ourselves off as Madame Atomos's men. No need to have them turning up immediately after us, is there?"

The Boss made a gargling sound. "Do you expect to pull it off?" he asked, incredulously.

"No." And Smith Beffort simply switched off.

"You shouldn't have done that," said Akamatsu, softly. "He'll think that we've had an accident and take measures that will risk hindering us further."

"Or helping us," Smith amended. "In a little while, this rattletrap will take the same route as your cigarette-case. How do we know what's waiting for us on the far side of that absorbent ground? If the guy in reception mistakes our Chevy for the station-wagon, we'll benefit from a significant element of surprise."

"*Hai!* I'm not denying it—but if he sees us for what we are, we risk getting fried on the spot. In that eventuality, it won't matter what measures your Boss decides to take. Hold on—we're there!"

Yosho Akamatsu swerved off the side-road, avoided the debris of the collapsed wall, and launched the Chevrolet into the field. He followed the tracks left by the station-wagon, stopped where they stopped, and switched off his engine.

Without a word, the two men checked that the windows were closed, and drew their weapons with a single movement. The Chevrolet remained motionless for a few seconds; then it began to sink into the ground as the humming sound burst forth, and rapidly disappeared.

The descent, effectuated in absolute darkness, lasted about ten minutes— but when the vehicle was immobilized again, it was still surrounded by the strange matter. Beffort tried to open the door, and then to lower a window, but his efforts were futile. Although the matter was apparently malleable in the vertical plane, it was as resistant as granite in the horizontal one.

"If we've been spotted," Beffort breathed, "they'll only have to leave us here to transform us into corpses. In a little while, we'll run out of air, and then...."

He shut up abruptly, for the wall was sliding slowly along the windows, freeing the lower sections like a rising theater curtain, revealing an oval room without any visible exit, with concrete walls pierced with thick portholes, through which a dull bluish light was filtering.

Soon, the Chevrolet was completely free of the enclosing matrix. Akamatsu lowered his window and sniffed the air. He was holding his Beretta with a flexible wrist and the barrel of the automatic was in continuous motion.

As his hand took hold of the door-handle, Beffort whispered: "Don't get out, Yosho! This room must have the same function as a submarine's airlock. I'll wager that we'll have visitors momentarily."

The portholes suddenly turned red and began to flicker frenetically, while a bizarrely modulated signal sounded stridently, with the same rhythm as the flicker.

"I have the impression," said the Japanese man, "that we're being called to order. We have to do something—but what?"

Beffort turned a taut expression toward him. "We're in this trap voluntarily, and until now no one seems to have detected our presence. Stay calm. Someone will have to come and see what's happening here."

Akamatsu made no reply. He switched on engine and the headlights, and blasted the horn. Simultaneously, the portholes returned to blue and silence fell.

The back wall of the room, which was illuminated by the headlights, pivoted slowly, unblocking the entrance to a narrow corridor. Portholes cast their pale light on its concrete walls, and the grilles of ventilation-shafts were distributed on the floor.

"Damn!" Beffort exclaimed. "You've activated the opening system."

Akamatsu smiled thinly. "That's a stroke of luck," he said. "Shall we make a move?"

Beffort got out and the Japanese man joined him after switching off the headlights and the engine. Together, the two men went into the corridor; they were in the middle of it when the concrete door closed behind them. They exchanged an anxious glance but remained silent. They were now in a place where everything was to be feared. There might be microphones hidden in the walls, and some of the portholes, duller than the others, looked like camera lenses.

Yosho Akamatsu was the first to arrive at a right-angled bend in the corridor. He examined the terrain prudently, after signaling to Beffort to remain hidden, then took a step back. "There's a staircase," he said. "We're probably on an intermediate floor of the building, for the staircase cuts across the corridor. What shall we do?"

"We'll go up." Beffort decided

"I agree," Akamatsu opined. "If our enemies have a sentry-post, it must be at ground level."

They went along the length of the corridor and began to climb the steps. The atmosphere grew sensibly heavier, and the two men began to sweat. After two floors, they emerged into a brightly-lit room and were transfixed by amazement.

Sam Forbes was standing in front of them, livid and stiff. His dilated eyes were devoid of expression, fixed on some distant point. His arms were extended beside his petrified body, as if he were standing to attention. It was a horrible sight.

"Sam!" said Beffort.

A porthole blinked. There was a crackle, and a feminine voice emerged from an invisible loudspeaker. "Your friend is dead, Mr. Beffort," it said, in an ironic tone. "He is presently under my control and will be set in motion when I direct the atom stream at him. He will take charge of killing you. I could easily do it myself, of course, but it seems much more piquant to have two FBI men murdered by one of their colleagues. When Forbes advances toward you, there will be no way to stop him, and your flight will not last very long. You will end up running into a wall, or going astray into a dead end. It will then be sufficient for Forbes to touch you for you to lose your life...."

The loudspeaker emitted a few crackles, and the vice resumed: "I shall follow your efforts on my television screen, gentlemen, but know that everything you can do will be in vain. The refuge in which you find yourselves has been empty for a couple of hours, and I am content to direct the operation from my personal shelter, some miles way. Tomorrow, the White House will be reduced to ashes, but tonight, my walking dead will spread terror throughout the United States, and nothing will be able to get in their way. Goodbye. Mr. Beffort. Goodbye, Mr. Akamatsu...."

Silence abruptly filled the room, and Forbes took his first step. Their throats tight, Beffort and Akamatsu watched him come slowly forward, with that terrible mechanical gait that nothing seemed able to stop, and the two men experienced a horrible feeling of emptiness and helplessness.

Akamatsu suddenly recovered his sense of reality. He gripped his companion's arm forcefully and dragged him toward the stairway. "We need to get away, Smith! If we let him get too close, we're finished!"

As white as a sheet, Beffort paused at the stairhead. "I can't believe it!" he murmured. Then he howled: "Sam! Wake up, old chap! Sam!"

Akamatsu slapped his face, and growled: "Don't be an idiot, Beffort! He's dead, as you know full well, and no prayer can bring him back to life!"

"I don't believe that!" cried Beffort. "Remember what Dr. Soblen said. He said that Maggie Fairbanks was acting in a hypnotic state, and Sam is surely...."

The Japanese policeman's Beretta spat fire, but Forbes did not even shudder under the impact of the bullets. A round hole appeared in the center of his forehead; others ripped through the fabric of his jacket at breast-height, but Forbes continued to advance, staring, rigid and frozen.

"Well?" Akamatsu demanded, sharply. "Are you convinced now?"

Beffort's lips began to tremble, and he recoiled toward the steps.

Forbes had crossed the room and they noticed that he was walking quite rapidly—and that the slightest error or the simplest obstacle might bring them within his reach.

"We have to get a head start," said Akamatsu, "and try to find an exit. Come on, Beffort!"

The federal agent finally emerged from his prostration and hurtled down the steps behind the Japanese man. They reached the landing from which the corridor they had already traversed departed, went down one further flight of stairs and stopped, cocking their ears.

Sam Forbes had to be in the middle of the first flight, for his footsteps were hardly audible. Akamatsu pointed at a corridor on to which several doors opened, and said: "That's exactly the kind of cul-de-sac we need to avoid. The solution of locking ourselves into one of these rooms would sign our death-warrant. Forbes is capable of waiting for us to come out again for weeks...."

"This way," said Beffort, rapidly. He had recovered his self-composure, and all of his habitual efficiency. Akamatsu followed him at a run, and they came into a long room cluttered with various materials. A corridor followed, at the end of which they found another room and larger dimensions.

Beffort stopped. "He'll get us for sure," he said, "If we can't find a means of stopping him. He's nothing in himself. He's being remotely controlled by the woman we heard. She's watching us through hidden television cameras, and that's where we have to strike."

Akamatsu nodded. "Agreed, but how? The cameras must be incorporated into the walls. To put them beyond use one after another would be a Herculean task!"

"We have to provoke a short circuit that will plunge the building into darkness!"

Akamatsu shook his head. "I thought of that," he said, "But it's no good. If Madame Atomos thinks that Forbes can't get to us, she'll kill us some other way!"

"Listen!" whispered Beffort, tautly. Forbes' footfalls were no audible in the corridor; although he was not yet visible, it could only be a matter of seconds.

Akamatsu suddenly went over to the wall and called to Beffort. "Look here!" he said, nervously. "Drums of gasoline."

The federal agent uncapped a drum, sniffed it and looked up again. "Do you think this might stop him?"

"We don't have any choice, do we?"

They emptied two drums in the corridor. The gas spread out over the concrete floor in waves, quickly forming an insurmountable pool.

Forbes appeared as Beffort was pouring out the contents of a third drum, and the federal agent leapt into the room.

"Get back!" Akamatsu ordered. He was holding a box of matches. He knelt down.

Forbes came into the danger zone without hesitation, his feet splashing in the liquid, which impregnated his shoes and the bottom of his trousers.

Akamatsu struck a match, and leapt to Beffort's side.

There was a dull explosion, and crackling flames rose up swiftly to attack Forbes, enveloping him in a red whirlwind. For an instant, the two men thought that even fire could not stop the dead man, but then the latter collapsed in a heap, without a shudder, like a steel girder crashing to the ground, while a frightful odor of charred flesh spread through the overheated air.

Akamatsu shook with silent laughter, and gripped Beffort's shoulder. "Do you know why we've succeeded, Smith?" And as the G-man interrogated him with his gaze, he explained: "Because Madame Atomos only has a limited number of cameras at her disposal! If she'd seen us preparing our life-saving operation, she would have stopped Forbes in time. It's probable that she doesn't know how her...robot came to grief, and that she has no eyes in this room. That gives us time, of which we must immediately take advantage, Come this way—we'll try to get back to the airlock...."

Chapter XII

The Boss had been calling Beffort continually for thirty minutes. Then, spitting out his cigar—reduced to a mere stub—he decided to execute the second part of his plan.

It required a further half-hour to get the heavy armaments ready to go to work, but when the artillery opened fire, the field, the Senator's house and the worker's hovel would be smashed by the shells. The watchers would see to it that Madame Atomos had no chance of getting out.

The bombardment lasted a quarter of an hour; then two hundred paratroopers were launched upon the terrain. They were armed with submachine-guns, grenades and flame-throwers and had received orders to give no quarter.

Akamatsu and Beffort were thrown to the ground by the force of the first explosions. At the same time, the lights went out, and a part of the subterranean shelter collapsed with the deafening sound of an avalanche.

A brief calm followed, then the pounding resumed, after which the rate of fire was controlled, at the rhythm of one shell per second.

The concrete crumbled in compact blocks around the two men, or disintegrated under the sustained fire, while shards as trenchant as razor blades stung the wall that had not yet given way, rebounding and whizzing away, whistling like a swarm of crazed wasps. Ten shells fell in the same place; like a nail driven into a plank, they hollowed out a giant funnel that divided Madame Atomos's lair into two shaking halves.

Stunned and covered in dust, Akamatsu and Beffort found themselves on the edge of a chaotic gulf, balanced on a narrow ledge, too astonished at being still alive to take an interest in the fall of the Chevrolet, which the explosion had hurled into the air.

Beffort perceived a glimmer light shining in front of him, and howled to draw Akamatsu's attention to the anomaly. The corridor opened in the flank of a crater. The ledge that the two men occupied led them to it, and as the bombardment was continuing, they urgently needed to find a shelter.

They ran into a tunnel under the hail of debris, getting into it just in time to escape a further collapse, and ran on while all hell was unleashed behind them. A shell struck the tunnel entrance, burying it under tons of earth; the ground shook and the light went out under the violence of the impact.

Guiding themselves along the wall, which was oozing moisture, the two men continued their blind course. Their lungs were on fire, and were obliged to pause when the ground began to slope steeply.

The explosions sounded very dull now, and when they ceased, the two men had the sensation of being buried alive.

"*Ikasa deska?*" said Akamatsu, reverting to his native language in the heat of the action. "How are you?"

"Not bad," Beffort growled, "but I'll be a lot better when I get out of this rat-hole. Strike a match, Akamatsu!"

The Japanese man took out his box, and a little dancing flame lit up the steeply-sloping corridor.

"In my opinion," said Beffort, "We've stumbled no one of Madame Atomos's evacuation tunnels. Without the bombardment, we'd never have found it. The Boss has done the trick!"

The match went out and Akamatsu slipped the box into his pocket. "We're not out of the woods yet," he said, gravely. "I'm wondering whether this corridor might take us straight to another lair."

Beffort started walking. "We can only go one way," he observed. "The tunnel's collapsed behind us, and I'm sure that the army occupying the field will fire on anything that moves. In truth, we're better off down here than up there."

They marched for some time in complete darkness, but when Beffort ran into an obstacle Akamatsu struck another match.

"A staircase!" he said. "We're getting there!"

They went up the steep steps, pushed a trapdoor, and emerged into the dining-room of an abandoned house. Looking outside, they ascertained that they were on the other side of the hill, at least two miles from the place they had just left.

The house was flanked by a large outhouse that had evidently been converted into a garage. Patches of fresh oil speckled the flattened ground, and there was a gas-can in one corner.

Beffort and Akamatsu went out on to the road, and started walking westwards, in the direction of Oakland.

At one o'clock in the morning, the Boss learned that Beffort and the Tokkoka agent had just reached Oakland. After a telephonic conversation with the G-man, he knew that Madame Atomos had escaped the bombardment and intended to launch a vast terrorist operation during the night.

The word *terror* took on its full meaning when it was employed to designate the diabolical Japanese woman's action, and the Boss did not take the warning lightly. The radio waves started humming incessantly over the entire territory, but preventative measures were concentrated on New York, Washington, Baltimore, Philadelphia and Boston.

At two o'clock, a conference in the Boss's office brought together those responsible for the security of the threatened regions, and Beffort and Akamatsu were invited to explain the situation.

Beffort spoke briefly, telling the story of how Sam Forbes had been transformed into an atomized robot, and had been neutralized by fire. Everyone present understood without further explanations that a means of destroying Madam

Atomos's walking dead had finally been discovered. There was scarcely any objection to the agreement that flamethrowers were the best weapons of destruction, but it quickly became evident that there would not be enough of them to cover a tenth part of the cities that were under threat effectively.

General Dickson started talking about incendiary grenades and Molotov cocktails, but was dryly interrupted by the Boss. "We're not fighting the battle of Normandy, general," he murmured, "and it's not a matter of blowing up the Empire State Building."

Dickson raised a head like that of a plucked parrot. "You've already used artillery, bombers and parachutists!" he yelped.

"The target was a field," Beffort reminded him, softly.

Dickson looked daggers at him, but Beffort did not flinch. He had been a sergeant in the army, and was used to generals looking daggers at him.

"If the nation is calling on the army," Dickson roared, "it's because all the usual means have been shown to be ineffective! In consequence, it seems clear that it's the army that should have the honor of taking national defense in hand!"

The Boss groaned with clenched teeth, slumped in his armchair. What he had feared was happening: the army and the civil service were coming into grotesque conflict over a question of prestige and influence, and they were going to talk for hours, uselessly, perhaps requiring the arbitration of Congress, or even the President.

At the same moment, an old woman was walking silently along a dark street in Brooklyn. Her gait was mechanical, her head was held up straight in spite of the cold, and her rigid arms were flat against her sides. She passed under a street-light, turned ninety degrees by pivoting on her heels, crossed the road without pausing or looking to see whether any cars were coming, and then resumed her progress imperturbably, amid the gusts of wind.

A man encountered her a little further on, took three more steps after having passed her, and collapsed on the sidewalk. He remained motionless for thirty seconds, as stiff and cold as a cadaver, then got up and started following the old woman, who had continued on her way.

Twenty yards apart, the woman and the man walked alongside the dark walls, then cut across another street. They had reached the middle of an intersection when a stray dog approached. The animal raised its leg against a fire-hydrant, then went up to the old woman, wagging its tail—and fell on its side. It got up again as the man drew level with it, and followed him with the strange gait of a mechanical dog.

Further on, the old woman stopped in front of a door from which a pale light filtered. The man and the dog joined her and stopped beside her. Then the woman pushed the door and went into the vestibule of a night-club, followed by the man and the dog, who were hot on her heels.

The young woman half-asleep in the cloakroom woke up and her mouth rounded in surprise. She was apparently in good health, but fell softly on to the carpet as the little group passed in front of her.

Inside the club, a hundred people were trying to forget their cares by dancing and drinking to excess. They were very fashionable people, who put on airs, and there was nothing to be seen but low-cut dresses and well-tailored suits.

On a little stage, Niles Dunkett's orchestra was playing in a subdued manner, in order not to drown out the slightly raucous voice of Suzy Trenton, who was caressing her microphone. Multicolored streamers striped the smoky space, and the laughter of enervated women punctuated the dulcet melody that Suzy was intoning as she sucked her mike.

Earlier, the ambience had been explosive, but this was what they called the soft time, although it was only a state provoked by fatigue, drunkenness and the onset of boredom. To shake up this crowd, it would have required an attraction genuinely out of the ordinary, and when the old woman, followed by the man, the dog and the cloakroom attendant appeared on the threshold, an enormous gale of laughter ran through the assembly.

Suzy's laughter vibrated in the microphone, and the orchestra stopped playing. Men threw streamers at the old woman, but she continued to advance without showing any emotion, and the laughter abruptly ceased....

The old woman, the man, the dog and the hat-check girl were stiff-limbed and had staring faces....

The group went passed the first tables, and fifty revelers collapsed on the spot, under the terrified eyes of those who were still too far away to be atomized—and then got up, advancing in their turn toward the stage....

Five minutes later, a police car patrolling the quarter braked sharply as it reached an intersection. Kearney, the driver, jogged his partner with his elbow and pointed to a strange procession that was coming in their direction.

"Take a look at that, Bill!"

The man extended his neck, whistled, and rubbed his eyes.

At two thirty in the morning, in freezing cold, a hundred people in evening dress were silently following an old woman, a dog, a man dressed in workman' clothes and a pretty blonde girl molded into a black dress."

"They must be drunk!"

"For sure," Kearney agreed. "We'll have to have a few words with them...."

The two cops got out of the car and planted themselves in the middle of the intersection, twirling their nightsticks. A taxi appeared and braked. The driver leaned out of the window, and looked at the strange procession advancing along the narrow street. His takings were down, because he had hardly picked up a fare all night. He called his company on the radio, asking them to send a few extra cabs to the location.

"Well?" shouted Kearney. "What's this circus all about?"

The old woman arrived in the middle of the intersection. The two cops and the taxi-driver were subjected to an abrupt atomization.

Augmented by the three new recruits, the macabre procession headed toward Plum Island and the Naval Air Base at Floyd Bennett Field.

Three blocks behind, a car driven by a woman in a skunk-fur wrap followed slowly. In the passenger seat was a man armed with what looked like a fiberglass fishing rod, and on the back seat a square metallic device was humming softly.

Madame Atomos's Operation Destruction was under way.

Incredulously, Lieutenant Cook watched the enormous procession that was advancing toward the entrance to the base. He saw the sentries collapse, and realized that something abnormal was happening when the latter got up again and took their places in the disparate ranks that were invading the outer courtyard of the base.

Cook sounded the alarm, leapt to the telephone, howled a brief message, and raced outside, unknowingly running to sudden death, and the most atrocious afterlife that humankind had ever known....

Naval Air Base at Floyd Bennett Field attacked by enormous silent crowd. Sentries, troops and officers have joined procession. Request orders urgently. Signed: Officer of....

Admiral Kenilworth looked as if he had been struck by a violent electrical discharge. He read the message aloud and the Boss leapt to the telephone.

At the same time, General Dickson understood that this was not a time for sterile discussions, and gave orders over another radio link for a company armed with flame-throwers to be sent to the naval air base.

Beffort and Akamatsu left the office without waiting for orders and went down to the next floor. Davis was there, deciphering messages, accompanied by about fifteen G-men. Beffort and Akamatsu learned that a thousand people had been atomized, and that the number was growing by the minute, but that the tightly-packed procession was still confined to the southern part of Brooklyn.

They feared a disintegration that would render any intervention impossible. If the atomized dispersed through the city, a fantastic catastrophe might ensue. They knew that each dead person was contagious, and that animals were not spared. Soon, rats, dogs, cats and birds would spread throughout the region, carriers of death.

Beffort and Akamatsu hurtled downstairs, climbed into a service car and headed straight for the base.

Chapter XIII

At three o'clock in the morning, the glacial temperature climbed by five degrees and the snow made its appearance. At first there were no more than a few light flakes, spiraling gracefully in the harsh glare of the street-lights, and then a terrible blizzard descended on the city.

The military convoy transporting the flamethrowers ran into difficulties in the vicinity of Newark. The snow was accumulating on the windscreens, and the wipers were impotent to clear it away. Men were positioned to either side of each vehicle to carry out that work, but the speed of the convoy was considerably reduced.

In New York, particularly in Brooklyn, panic suddenly gripped the population. Alerted by the howling of sirens, the radio and television spat out a continual stream of special bulletins, which added to the panic, and the inhabitants leapt into the cars. Within ten minutes, monstrous traffic jams had been produced at all the important intersections, preventing the police services from descending on Plum Island.

The snowstorm reduced visibility to zero, and spectacular pile-ups began to occur all over the city. Many people abandoned their cars where they were, and set off on foot through the snow, beginning an incredible game of hide-and-seek. Groups formed in order to be certain of being among living beings, but retreated automatically as they met one another, fearful that they might be dealing with Madame Atomos's atomized people.

An infernal carousel started in Brooklyn, and the night was populated by furtive silhouettes, strangely similar by reason of the snow that blanketed them.

By three twenty-five half the population was circulating through the cluttered streets, while the other half had locked the doors of their buildings in order not to be submerged. Because of that, those who wanted to return to their homes found it impossible to do so, and were condemned to wander through the tempest, fleeing from one another.

It was a demented cavalcade, and Beffort was overwhelmed. The service vehicle, blocked in the vicinity of Prospect Park, was no further use, and the messages that the radio was putting out indicated that the situation was getting much worse.

The atomized were now so numerous that the FBI switchboard spoke of a veritable human tide. The procession emerged on to Homecrest, touched Flatlands and brushed Paerdegat Basin. The air base at Floyd Bennett Field had not responded for some time, and the military convoy carrying the flame-throwers had only reached Jersey City.

The Air Force was called in. Cargo planes stuffed with GIs and flame-throwers landed at Idlewild and were immediately directed to Paerdegat Basin.

A hundred flame-throwers went into action when the procession emerged on to Canarsie, roasting the first ranks of the atomized on the spot, but quickly had to give ground.

The soldiers aimed their flame-throwers at anyone who was not wearing a uniform; a group of the living became targets and were burned to a crisp. In the whirlwinds of snow the troop became disorientated, retreating before the innumerable dead who appeared to be rising out of the ground, and whose advance was unstoppable.

At three forty the flame-throwers ran out of fuel and the soldiers opened fire with submachine-guns, rifles and pistols. It was a puerile and utterly futile reflex. The dead continued their progress, sealing the two hundred soldiers in the jaws of a mortal vice and submerging them.

Beffort and Akamatsu knew all this by courtesy of the radio, and realized that, without a miracle, Brooklyn—and then Long Island and New York—would be solely populated by the marching dead.

Around them, there was a stampede. Deprived of information, the members of the crowd were rushing in all directions, bumping into one another, knocking one another down, lashing out indiscriminately. The weak were rolling in the mud and being trampled. The wounded and the dead strewed the swarming streets, and at the windows of houses and other buildings those whom prudence had kept indoors watched the apocalyptic spectacle in terror.

Beffort and his companion got out of the car and were borne away in spite of themselves by a howling group. They struggled in concert to get free, and eventually found themselves, breathless and bruised, in the relative calm of Churchill Avenue. The roadway as cluttered with abandoned vehicles, their doors wide open, and broken suitcases were spilling heaps of clothes and various other objects in the snow.

Ten-dollar bills were swirling around a lamp-post, and a woman with a bloody nose was trying to catch them, laughing all the while. A baby started to cry in one of the cars, and Beffort took a step in that direction, but Akamatsu held him back firmly.

"This isn't the time," he said, in a calm voice. "The child might as well be there as elsewhere."

They plastered themselves against a wall to let a frenzied group of people pass by, then started running in their turn. They were no longer thinking about anything but saving their own skins—and, if possible, getting back to FBI headquarters. There was nothing else they could do.

They reached the intersection of Churchill Avenue and Coney Island, and perceived a formidable human mass heading in their direction. The crowd was advancing slowly, silently and mechanically, taking up the whole of the avenue. An old woman was marching at the head of the procession, with a workman, a dog and a young woman immediately behind her. Further away came the group in evening dress, two uniformed policemen, and then a compact mass, so tightly grouped that they seemed welded together.

Beffort and Akamatsu retraced their steps, drawing away toward MacDonald Avenue.

Suddenly, Beffort spotted the Cadillac. He threw himself on the Japanese agent and pushed him behind a small truck. "Look, Yosho!" he whispered. "In that cream Cadillac, which looks as if it's been abandoned."

The Tokkoka man leaned out. At first he thought the car was empty, but then saw the fugitive red glow of a cigarette. He looked harder, saw that a man and a woman were sitting in the front seats, and pivoted uncomprehendingly. "So what?" he said. "What about them?"

Beffort's fingers dug into his arm. "That woman," he said, "is Lydia Watanabe—the woman who was in the Buick with Hisato Keichu, and who hired the houses on which the concrete towers were built!"

Akamatsu started. "If you're not mistaken," he said, "I...."

"Remember the Boss's description!" Beffort interjected, ferociously. "A young brunette woman, pretty, thirty years old at most, Asiatic! I've only seen her once, Yosho, but I'm absolutely certain that it's her!"

Akamatsu leaned out again, and then straightened up. "The girl is probably Eurasian," he said, in a flat voice, "And I've just seen a dark object on the rear seat."

Beffort took out his thirty-eight and cocked it. "Kill the guy!" he spat. "I'll take care of the girl—we need her alive. We'll attack from behind, you to the right, me to the left. Watch out for the rear-view mirror! Ready!"

Akamatsu was already clutching his Beretta. "Whenever you like, Smith."

They ran along the sidewalk, separated, ducked down and crossed the road, keeping to the shadows. In fifteen seconds they were behind the Cadillac, and came to a halt.

Beffort raised his arm, then lowered it, and the two men rushed the doors. Akamatsu fired through the glass, killing his man with a bullet to the head. Beffort broke the other window with a mighty blow of his gun-butt and smashed it into Lydia's chin. She crumpled in a heap.

"Look!" howled Akamatsu.

He pointed with his arm at the mass of the atomized, who were emerging into Churchill Avenue, still led by the old woman.

Beffort opened the rear door, heard the hum of the apparatus placed on the rear seat and searched feverishly for a means of switching it off. In the darkness, his hands wandered over the smooth surface, finally encountering a switch.

The humming suddenly stopped, with an imperceptible hiss, and a little indicator light went out.

At the same instant, on Churchill Avenue, in Brooklyn, Plum Island, Canarsie and everywhere else they were to be found, the atomized collapsed, and the streets were covered in corpses.

Later, nine thousand of them were to be counted, but for the moment no one realized the amplitude of the disaster. A great calm descended upon the city: a profound prostration that was to last for hours, in the course of which everyone tried to recuperate. No one knew how the drama had been brought to an end, and Beffort and the Japanese agent were too busy to think of explaining it.

With the aid of their neckties, they tied up the unconscious young woman securely, and Akamatsu set about bringing her round.

Lydia Watanabe opened her eyes after the fourth slap, and looked around in profound surprise.

"Can you hear me?" Akamatsu asked, softly.

The woman looked at him and nodded her head.

"I'm an agent of the Tokkoka," the Japanese man went on, and this man belongs to the FBI. What you need to understand is that your goose is well and truly cooked, and that you needn't expect the slightest mercy from us."

The Eurasian woman spat in his face, and Akamatsu slapped her with the back of his hand, without holding back. "Where is Madame Atomos?" he demanded, in his soft voice.

"I don't know who you're talking about."

"*Ah...so deska?*" He seized Lydia's arm, took hold of the index-finger of her hand, and twisted it slowly. The young woman howled and struggled, but the finger broke cleanly and silently, like a wisp of straw.

"Now?"

Lydia bit her lips, but did not say a word.

"Your cigarette, Smith?"

Beffort obliged, and Yosho applied the incandescent end to the Eurasian woman's cheek. The hiss was confused with her howl of agony, and Lydia started weeping—but she did not open her mouth.

"Where is Madame Atomos?" Akamatsu repeated.

The Eurasian woman shut her eyes. "I don't know," she hissed. "No one knows where she's hiding."

Beffort glanced at the bodies of the atomized strewing the avenue, and turned to the young woman ferociously. "If you don't talk," he said, "you won't get out of that car alive! I don't normally hold with torture, but your crimes authorize me to cut you to ribbons with a clear conscience. For the last time, where's Madame Atomos?"

Lydia Watanabe stiffened, and her jaws contracted. The G-man's tone left no doubt as to his intentions, and Lydia had never been on the other side of the barricade. The power of Madame Atomos had always seemed so formidable to her that even at that moment, she could not believe that the American could succeed in making her talk. Before she succumbed to torture, Madame Atomos would intervene. That was obligatory, inevitable.

Akamatsu's voice brought her back to the present moment. "Let me do it, Smith. It's not a matter of killing her but of making her talk. Unfortunately, I'm

404

well used to this kind of operation. No human being can resist certain agonies. The nerve-centers are extremely sensitive, particularly in this region."

His hands gripped the young woman's hips, and she howled like an animal. Akamatsu persisted, and Smith Beffort had to exert all his strength to keep the Eurasian woman in her seat.

Finally, Lydia stopped howling, and collapsed limply in the G-man's arms.

"She's fainted," observed Akamatsu, calmly, "but that's nothing. Would you place her arms behind the seat, if you please."

When Beffort obliged, the Japanese man methodically tore off Lydia's clothes, only leaving her the skunk-fur wrap, her stockings and shoes.

"Morally," he explained, "She'll be profoundly shocked. A nude woman can't hold out for long if the...interrogation is well-crafted." He glanced sideways at Beffort and added: "I'd prefer it if you left us alone, Smith."

Without replying, Beffort got out of the car. He dragged the body of the Eurasian woman's companion on to the sidewalk, lit a cigarette and tried not to hear the cries that emerged from the Cadillac, or to see Akamatsu leaning over the nacreous body of the girl.

Lydia Watanabe lay panting in a corner of the back seat, moaning dully and continuously, but Beffort had been able to observe that she was not marked by any wound.

The car was travelling in a westward direction. Akamatsu was at the wheel, sometimes pausing to wipe away the sweat that was still running down his forehead. A rictus of disgust was still on his lips, and it was in a colorless voice that he asked Beffort to light him a cigarette.

"It's a pity that we can't alert the Boss," Beffort said, regretfully. "We'll have to be content with reinforcements from the local police."

Akamatsu grunted. "She gave in very quickly. I'm wondering whether we're really going to find Madame Atomos's lair in that place."

Beffort frowned. "Tarrytown," he said. "Tarrytown...that's odd. That name seems familiar, but I can't remember when I've heard it before."

"It's on the bank of the Hudson," Akamatsu specified.

"I know, I know...."

"The town isn't far from New York, so it's entirely natural that you've heard of it."

"There's something else," said Beffort. "Something important connected with that name. Something unusual happened in Tarrytown recently...."

Akamatsu grimaced. "Since the beginning of this affair a whole host of unusual things have happened, Smith! You'd need a memory like an elephant to conserve them all...."

The Cadillac left the New York City limits and continued along the Hudson. There was no traffic, and the snow, which was no longer falling, formed a slippery muddy carpet on the roadway, which prevented them from exceeding a modest speed.

It was while they were going through Yonkers that the G-man suddenly remembered. "Tarrytown!" he exclaimed. "That's where Maggie Fairbanks and her parents lived!"

Akamatsu flicked his cigarette-butt out into the snow. "The abandoned Fairbanks house! A dream hideout for Madame Atomos."

Lydia Watanabe groaned more loudly to hide the click of the switch that she had just depressed. With the noise of the engine, the hum of the apparatus was inaudible, and she had placed her bare leg over the green indicator light."

Chapter XIV

The atomized of New York were unaffected by the radiation of the remote control apparatus, because it was now too far away from the city, but in Tarrytown, a hobo whose seemed to be asleep under a pier east of the Hudson woke up. He abandoned his haversack, went along the quay with his mechanical gait, climbed the steps and emerged on to the docks. The man was covered in snow; his clothes were disgusting, slimed with damp, and his feet dragged along the ground.

He had not been dead long and Madame Atomos had not anticipated that the radiation would put him in motion.

The hobo walked as far as Route 19, arriving at the exact moment when the Cadillac was going past. Drawn along by the remote control apparatus, the man turned around and departed in his jerky fashion toward the town, and the Fairbanks house.

The car arrived by means of its own momentum in the narrow lane, and stopped between two trees on the snow-covered pavement. Akamatsu let the engine tick over in order to maintain the distribution of warm air, for the cold was intense, but he switched off the headlights.

It was nearly five o'clock in the morning. The night was still dark and nothing was moving in the shuttered cottages. Brief gusts of wind brought down little clumps of snow that had accumulated on the bare branches, shook television aerials and whistled past the raised windows, helping the engine to cover up the muffled hum of the remote control, apparatus.

Huddled in the corner of the back seat, Lydia was now trying to slip out of her bonds.

Beffort jabbed a thumb in the direction of the Fairbanks house, which was hidden from their gaze by a thick hedge.

"In theory," he said, "the place should have been sealed after the death of its inhabitants, and if Madame Atomos is in the house she must have taken enormous precautions not to be noticed by the neighbors. One open shutter or puff of smoke emerging from the chimney, or any noise whatsoever, and the police would have been alerted." He studied the street, where a few cars were parked, and continued in a low voice: "Even an unfamiliar vehicle would attract attention. Can you believe, Yosho, that a woman like Madame Atomos would willingly blockade herself in that house, without a possible escape route?"

Akamatsu cast a suspicious glance at the Eurasian woman and, half-turning in his seat, said: "Madame Atomos must have been surprised by your organization's riposte, Smith. The woman is guided by hatred, a passionate desire for vengeance that has survived for years. It's possible that she launched her offensive without having made sure in advanced that her rear was quite secure. Her scientific temperament has given way to an exacerbated fanaticism that has carried her off in its irresistible whirlwind. However, to answer your question, I believe, in spite of what I've just said, that Madame Atomos has anticipated every possibility."

"Okay," muttered Beffort. "That's what I think." He took his thirty-eight from its holster, opened his door, and said: "Are we going?"

Akamatsu nodded, and got out in his turn. The two men glided like shadows along the hedge, without seeing that a slender barrel in the form of a fiberglass fishing rod was pointing in their direction from the first floor of the house.

The hobo was spotted by a police car at the corner of Benedict Avenue and Route 9, and the two patrolmen stopped the vehicle.

"Hey! You there! Come here a minute!"

The man continued on his way without even turning round and crossed the avenue dragging his feet.

"What the…!" swore one of the cops.

His colleague shrugged his shoulders, rapidly turned the car around, and quickly drew level with the hobo.

"Hey, granddad, are you deaf?"

The man continued on his way. He paid no heed to the police car rolling along beside him. His stiff stance and his livid, frozen face ended up intriguing the two cops.

"He's drugged, is all!"

"He's taking the Mickey!" said the more peevish of the two. "Hey! Stop, granddad, and show us some ID!"

"You'd better catch hold of him. This guy's looking to spend the winter in chokey. The angrier you get, the more awkward he'll get!"

Furious, the driver pulled on the handbrake and got out of the car with his colleague. The two men descended upon the delinquent. When they got to within a yard of him they were atomized, and fell down in the snow. They stayed there for thirty seconds, then got up and followed the man, adopting his jerky walk.

Further on, a milkman who was beginning his round was collected by the little group; then it was the turn of two sailors on shore leave, four housewives, a postman, and a pregnant woman and her husband who were getting ready to leave for the clinic in anticipation of the imminent birth.

The thirteen atomized individuals arrived thus in the neighborhood where the Fairbanks house stood, and went into the silent lane.

Lydia Watanabe waited for the two men to draw away, and then redoubled her efforts to free herself. She knew that Madame Atomos was on her guard. It had always been strictly forbidden to switch on the remote control apparatus in the vicinity of the refuges that the terrible woman had occupied, and that transgression of the regulations could only signify an urgent warning.

In that, the Eurasian woman was not mistaken.

In the Fairbanks house, three men and two women were putting the final touches to the apparatus designed to blow up the engines of destruction, as Madame Atomos had ordered. It was impossible to take the equipment away, but it was necessary at all costs to prevent the FBI agents from taking possession of it.

At the window, the sentry had seen the Cadillac arrive; since it was behind the hedge, however, he could only see its roof. The emergence of Beffort and Akamatsu had completely escaped him, and he shuddered when a silent group approached the car.

Lydia had just freed her hands. She opened the door, and abruptly found herself face to face with thirteen atomized individuals—who, deprived of directives, were automatically tracking the apparatus that had animated them. Lydia understood in a flash that she was doomed, uttered a frightful scream, and collapsed, thunderstruck.

At the same moment, the watcher pressed the trigger of his weapon. A lightning-flash lit up the night; the hedge, the car and the atomized people were instantaneously engulfed in flames.

Beffort and Akamatsu shot the sentry, leapt over the hedge and were rushing toward the house when it exploded. The two men threw themselves to the ground, and were showered with debris. When they were able to move again, the house was blazing like a torch.

In spite of the crackling of the flames, they distinctly heard the roar of an engine, understood that Madame Atomos was fleeing, and—in spite of the heat of the conflagration—ran into the garden extended behind the house.

Beyond the garden there was a dirt track, but the car had disappeared. Nothing remained on the damp earth but the double tire-track of the vehicle that had carried the terrible Japanese woman away.

The alarm was raised fifteen minutes later, and road-blocks set up throughout the region. By six o'clock in the morning more than thirteen hundred vehicles had been stopped and searched.

Six Asiatic women who were travelling by car on Route 9 were taken to the central police station in Tarrytown, and FBI headquarters was notified of these arrests.

Beffort and Akamatsu left for New York in order to save time. It was a matter of fetching the photograph and fingerprints of Kanoto Yoshimuta, alias Madame Atomos, which the Boss had retained, in order to compare them with those of the arrested women. This decision had been taken by reason of the dispersal of police and FBI personnel, who were occupied—along with other public services—in gathering up the corpses cluttering up the streets of Brooklyn.

The Boss seemed worn out, crushed by an intolerable burden, but his face cleared when Beffort and Akamatsu came into his office. "Glad you see you've come back alive," he said, bleakly. His features were transformed again, "It's a disaster," he said, passing his hand over the back of his painful neck. The count isn't finished, but the latest news was that there were more than ten thousand dead." He lowered his eyes, moved a pencil and added, in a hollow tone of which he would never again be free: "My wife is among the victims...." He raised his head again, and said: "We've lost six men too—old hands; guys who've been working with me since the beginning: Davis, Funk, Mitchell, Martin, Bernon and Twining."

"My God!" whispered Beffort, who was hard hit. After the death of Sam Forbes, it was the worst news he had heard in years. In the course of the night he had seen hundreds of corpses, but they had always been anonymous, representing nothing more than a heap of lifeless flesh. The names the Boss had just listed had imperishable memories attached to them, and the faces of the dead men were dancing before his eyes.

Akamatsu quietly intervened. "Six women are waiting in Tarrytown. We might, perhaps, find the person responsible for this tragedy among them."

Five minutes later, Beffort and Akamatsu were on their way back to Tarrytown.

Chapter XV

Chief Inspector Rooney was waiting for the two agents on the threshold of the central police station. He welcomed them as soon as they got out of the car and immediately made them party to his anxieties.

"Something strange has happened," he said. "The six women we've detained are all Japanese. They're all fifty years old and were either born in Nagasaki or lived there before coming to the United States."

Beffort and Akamatsu remained poised on the bottom step, mute with amazement.

Rooney scratched his nose and added: "Furthermore, all these females have been victims of accidents that have necessitated operations in cosmetic surgery, and they're all missing one of the fingers on their right hands."

Akamatsu started. "The index finger?" he roared.

"The index finger," Rooney confirmed. "That's the missing one."

Beffort took the photograph of Kanoto Yoshimuta, alias Madame Atomos, out of his pocket, and waved it under Rooney's nose. "Do any of them resemble this photograph?" he demanded.

The inspector studied the print carefully, and finally pursed his lips in perplexity. "There's a similarity," he said. "I think it would be better if you took a look for yourself."

Beffort and Akamatsu started to climb the steps, but Rooney stopped them. "There's something else," he said, wearily. "Obviously, we took their names. They're all called…" He stumbled over the name, took a piece of paper from his pocket, and read: "Kanoto Yoshimuta." As his two interlocutors stood there with their mouths agape, he added, as if by way of excuse: "It seems that in Japan, it's a name as common as John Smith is here…."

They were not identical, but they all bore a family resemblance to the photograph of Madame Atomos. They lived in New York, had been in the United States for six months, but had neither relatives nor friends there. They were unemployed, were only passing through, were due to return to Japan soon, and had not met one another before being arrested by the police. Now, they were chattering away between themselves in Japanese, seemingly absolutely delighted with this unexpected little party….

Akamatsu howled an order in Japanese, and the six women fell silent, looking at him reproachfully.

"Separate them," the Tokkoka man demanded of Chief Rooney, "and make sure that they don't communicate with one another."

He pointed his finger at one of the women. "You, Madame Kanoto Yoshimuta, remain here."

The other women clucked in annoyance, and allowed themselves to be led away to other rooms.

"What were you doing on Route 9?" Akamatsu demanded.

The woman was not aggressive, but it was evident that her desire to cooperate was nevertheless very limited. She was of medium height—like the other five women—and would doubtless have passed unnoticed in a crowd. She had a black simulated leather bag in her lap, and Akamatsu observed that only the final phalanx was missing from her right index finger.

"I learned from my radio," she finally replied, "that Madame Atomos had just attacked New York. The announcer said that there were already many people dead, and that an immense procession of the atomized was threatening to overwhelm the city. I was afraid, and my one thought was to get away."

"Where were you going?"

"Anywhere."

"You don't have any baggage, do you?"

The woman smiled, with considerable irony. "If you had been in my shoes, you wouldn't have thought of anything but saving your life. It really was an every-man-for-himself situation!"

"What are your means of support, Madame Yoshimuta?"

The woman looked at her hands. "My husband had a big life insurance policy. When he was killed...."

"How was he killed?"

"He and my children were killed by the atomic bomb in 1945."

Beffort and the Tokkoka man exchanged knowing glances. This woman's past life coincided strangely with that of Madame Atomos.

"What is the reason for your presence in the United States?"

The Japanese woman hesitated; then, still looking at her hands, she said, slowly: "I was curious to see the Americans at close range. It seemed to me that the people who had destroyed Hiroshima and Nagasaki could not be like everyone else. I've realized, of course, that I was mistaken."

"Do you detest Americans, Madame Yoshimuta?"

In her native tongue, the woman replied: "You're the same race as me, sir. You know as well as I do that the Japanese detest Americans."

Akamatsu translated for Beffort's benefit, and said: "Do you approve of the actions of Madame Atomos?"

"I can't deny it. I merely regret having been arrested before my task was complete."

Exclamations burst forth, and Akamatsu had to raise his voice. "So you admit to being Madame Atomos?"

"I admit it."

A great confusion burst out in the police station. The woman was handcuffed, journalists and photographers were admitted into the room, and in less than five minutes, the population of the USA learned that Madame Atomos was in the hands of the police.

Shortly afterwards, the *coup de théâtre* became manifest. All six women claimed to bed Madame Atomos, and each of the six swore that the others were lying, proudly claiming responsibility for the crimes that had been committed.

When a confrontation was attempted, they swore at one another, and if they had not been held back, they would probably have fought savagely. Then they were locked in separate cells and attempts were made to find a solution to the inextricable confusion.

It was the Boss who ordered, by telephone, that they be subjected to the judgment of truth serum.

This is an extract from the record made of the interrogation to which the six women were subjected, having been injected with truth serum, which was published on Thursday February twenty-eighth in the New York Herald and read aloud by Sydney Barrow of the ABC television network.

(1)   What is your name?

Responses: None of the women named herself Yoshimuta; they were in reality Mrs. Kawaguchi, Tanawa, Myamoto, Ilyinskaia, Kuanru and Sudinyo.

(2)   *Where were you born?*

Responses: Nagano, Himeji, Kushiro, Gifu, Chiba, Yawata.

(3)   *Who asked you to pretend to be Madame Atomos?*

Responses: Lydia Watanabe.

(4)   *Why did you agree?*

Responses: Miss Watanabe offered me ten thousand dollars.

(5)   *How and why did you come to the United States?*

Responses: A year ago, Miss Watanabe paid me to remain at her disposal. She was the one who brought me to the United States and proved me with a residence in New York and a car.

(6)   *How did you meet Lydia Watanabe?*

Responses: She contacted me in the town where I lived and told me that she was interested in my situation. I was without resources. Miss Watanabe seemed very interested in my facial surgery and the mutilation of my index finger, and my age also seemed satisfactory to her.

(7)   *Who ordered you to travel on Route 9 this morning?*

Responses: I received a telephone call asking me to go to Tarrytown immediately. I was to drive around the town for an hour and then return to New York. If I was arrested by the police, I was to claim that I was Madame Atomos.

(8)   *Do you know Madame Atomos?*

Responses: No.

(9)   *Do you know what has become of her?*

Responses:

Mrs. Kawaguchi: She doesn't exist.

Mrs. Tanawa: She is Miss Watanabe.

Mrs. Myamoto: She's dead.

Mrs. Ilyinskaia: She's a man.

Mrs. Kuanru: She has escaped.

Mrs. Sudinyo: She's one of us.

(10) *Do you admit to having worked for Madame Atomos?*

Responses: No. I worked for Miss Watanabe.

(11) *You did, however, agree to pretend to be her?*

Responses: I thought it was a big joke and was certain that the police would never take me seriously.

(12) *Do you approve of the actions of Madame Atomos?*

Responses: Not at all! She's a criminal and merits an exemplary punishment.

(13) *Did you know that Lydia Watanabe was working for Madame Atomos?*

Responses: No. There was never any mention of Madame Atomos in the various conversations I had with Miss Watanabe.

(14) *What tasks had you previously carried out for Lydia Watanabe?*

Responses: None. She did not ask me to do anything except to remain at her disposal by my telephone, day and night.

(15) *Did you know that other women were in the same situation, and did you know who they were?*

Responses: I was completely unaware of their existence

An investigation conducted in parallel by the Tokkoka and the FBI revealed that the six women had told the truth, and after the hearing that took place six months later they were simply released. Nevertheless, they were deported to their own country, and the Tokkoka kept them under covert surveillance.

In the United States, the search for Madame Atomos continued, and the security forces remained in a state of alert for six months. As no further incident occurred during that period, it was eventually concluded that Madame Atoms had died in the fire at the Fairbanks house, and the affair was gradually forgotten.

Smith Beffort accompanied Yosho Akamatsu to La Guardia airport to see him off.

"Forget all this," the Japanese man advised him. "It's obvious that Madame Atomos is dead."

Beffort remained serious. "I don't believe so, Yosho. "That woman has slipped through our fingers, and when we've forgotten her, she'll be back!"

Akamatsu's laughter was forced. "Don't be so pessimistic, Smith...."

The flight was called, and the two men parted.

Beffort remained standing there for some time after the aircraft had vanished in the sky, thinking about Sam Forbes, his dead colleagues and the thousands of victims of the Brooklyn tragedy. Finally, he drew away with his head bowed, and lit a cigarette.

Perhaps it was only his nerves, but he was convinced that Madame Atomos, concealed in the crowd, was watching him....

Forthcoming

FRENCH TALES OF MAD SCIENCE 2
Jules Janin: *The Magnetized Corpse* (1845)
Edward Rod: *Dr. Z's Autopsy* (1884)
Michel Corday: *The Mysterious Dajan-Phinn* (1908)
Maurice Renard: *Doctor Lerne, Subgod* (1908)
André Couvreur: *An Invasion of Macrobes* (1909)
Jacques Spitz: *Dr. Mops' Experiment* (1939)

FRENCH TALES OF MAD SCIENCE 3
Georges Eekhoud: *Tony Wandel's Heart* (1884)
Jules Lermina: *The Elixir of Life* (1905)
Edmond Haraucourt: *Dr. Auguerrand's Discovery* (1910)
Gaston de Wailly: *The Murderer of the World* (1925)
Eugène Thibault: *Radio-Terror* (1929)

www.ingramcontent.com/pod-product-compliance
Lightning Source LLC
Chambersburg PA
CBHW020252030726
47499CB00001B/169